THE *Captive* BRIDES COLLECTION

9 Stories of Great Challenges Overcome through Great Love

THE *Captive* BRIDES COLLECTION

Susan Page Davis, Cynthia Hickey,
Jennifer AlLee, Angela Breidenbach,
Darlene Franklin, Patty Smith Hall,
Carrie Fancett Pagels, Lucy Thompson, Gina Welborn

BARBOUR BOOKS
An Imprint of Barbour Publishing, Inc.

Contents

Love's Labours Found

by Jennifer AlLee

Chapter 1

Montserrat, West Indies
1655

The immovable wooden planks of the dock felt strange beneath Temperance's feet. She had endured the voyage, with one day blurring into the next until time itself seemed to stop. Two weeks, two months, two years? How long the nightmare had lasted she could not say, but one thing that had never stopped was the constant swell, rise, and fall of the ship. It had become her constant, the only thing she could depend on from moment to long moment. Now, the disorienting lack of movement sent her stomach lurching in protest. If not for the fact that her stomach was empty, she surely would have been sick right there.

"Move along!"

The chain attached to the shackles that circled her wrists rattled then jerked. She stumbled forward, barely avoiding a collision with the woman in front of her. Maud? In a futile attempt to pass time and remind herself that she was indeed a human being and not an animal, Temperance had done her best to learn the names of the others in the dank hold of the ship. At first, there had been so many of them, it was hard to remember who was who. But by the end, the weak and sick had succumbed. Now, Temperance was fairly certain she could call the ones left by name.

They shuffled along the edge of the dock, a single-file row of chained women, too humiliated or too weak to raise their heads. Temperance noted the shoes of the people that hurried past, men and women no doubt going to meet one of the merchant ships. And she listened to their derisive comments.

"Irish filth."

"Sewer rats."

"Diseased vermin."

"I find them comical," said a male voice. Then a walking stick shot out and cracked Temperance on the ankle. She yelped, and the man laughed. "You see? These creatures make the most entertaining sounds."

Temperance blinked against the tears that clouded her vision. Creatures. That was all they were now. Merely creatures.

From the sounds behind her, she knew the man was continuing to poke and antagonize the other women. He would have his fun and then, as long as none of the women spoke back, he'd go on his way as if nothing had happened. Temperance just hoped that—

"Get on then with ya!"

Her heart sank. *Irene.*

"I'm a human, same as you!"

If anyone was going to speak up, it would be Irene. The chain jerked Temperance back and the entire line stopped moving. Daring to look behind her, she saw the man, cheeks red as bog berries, pointing the tip of his walking stick at Irene's chest.

"You are nothing like me," he spat out. "You are a worthless gutter rat. Go back to the drink where you belong."

Irene grunted as he jabbed her hard. She lost her balance and stumbled sideways. Had her arms been free, she might have righted herself, but in her current state it was no use.

Even before Irene hit the water, Temperance anticipated the danger. She tried to move away from the side of the dock, but as one captive after another was pulled into the harbor, the chain jerked her closer to her demise.

This was it, then? This was how her life would end? "No!" she screamed in defiance. "Father in heaven, no! Help me!"

She was still screaming as she flew backward and splashed into the water. She tried to kick her feet and go upward, but her skirts tangled around her legs and the heavy chains pulled her down along with the others. Looking up toward the surface, she saw light, then a shadow blotted it out. Her lungs burned as she fought to hold her breath. She could do it no longer. This was the end.

Something grabbed the shoulder of her dress and pulled. As her head broke through the water, she spat and sputtered then focused on the face of her rescuer. The sharp angle of his jaw, his hair falling forward in brown waves as he pulled her shackled wrists up onto the dock.

Still holding her so she wouldn't slip back down, he yelled over his shoulder at the onlookers. "Help me!" When no one moved, he yelled again. "Would you let your property sink to the bottom of the harbor?"

Property. Temperance's stomach clenched at the word, but at least it had the desired effect. Reminded that the women had monetary value, the men rushed forward, grabbed at the chains, and pulled the others up from the water.

A strong arm went around her waist as her rescuer pulled her the rest of the way onto the dock. He let go and turned to help those still in the water, but because of the chain, she was almost pulled back in.

"I have you," he said, holding her firmly. "You are safe."

His words were kind, but he was so very wrong. She would never be safe again. He was a stranger, but he had saved her life and, perhaps an even greater gift, had treated her like a human being. She needed him to know the truth.

"This is a mistake." Her fingers dug into the fabric of his sleeve, and she dared look him in the eye. "I committed no crime."

He held her gaze, brow furrowed. "What is your name?"

"Temperance."

A blink, then a nod. "I am sorry, Temperance." And he looked away.

Of course, he had no reason to believe her. She hung her head, focusing on the rough wood below her, how the water had stained patches of it a dark brown. All around her, voices shouted, chains rattled, women cried and coughed. Temperance strained to identify each sound, determined not to think about the feeling of the arm that still held her, or the look of doubt in the eyes of the man who had saved her.

The woman began to shake, shivering from cold, or from fear, or both. Edward removed his jacket, carefully, one arm at a time, to retain his hold on her and ensure she did not fall from the dock, then put it over her back. A sob escaped her lips, but instead of looking at him, she hung her head lower, shoulders hunched.

Edward's brows drew together in concern. *Could she be telling the truth? Was she innocent of whatever crime had brought her here?* If so, surely those in charge would want to know. Perhaps he could help—

"Edward!"

At the sound of his name being called, he looked up but saw only a crush of men securing their prisoners. Then a young man broke through, and Edward expelled a relieved breath.

"Jonathan. As you can see, my attention was needed elsewhere." He glanced down at the shivering woman huddled on the dock.

"When I failed to find you, I asked myself, 'Where might Edward have gone?' When I heard the commotion, the question was answered."

Edward frowned. "There was no choice to make. She would have died."

"She is a prisoner," Jonathan said bluntly. "Drowning today may have been more merciful than whatever fate awaits her."

No matter how he wished to argue the point, Edward remained silent, knowing his brother was right. He'd saved her, but to what end? A brusque voice caught his attention and he saw that the overseer was making his way down the row of chained women, moving in their direction.

"Here now." Edward touched the woman's chin with the tip of his finger, and she lifted her head. Even in her bedraggled state, there was something graceful in the curve of her neck, the pale white skin reminding him of a swan. Banishing the thought, he fastened the top button of his jacket to stop it from sliding off her shoulders. "Keep this as long as you can."

She looked at him, gray eyes wide and stormy, and nodded. Edward helped her to her feet just as the overseer stepped up.

"What's this then?" The rough man flicked the empty sleeve of Edward's jacket with one finger.

"I put it on her," Edward said. "You'd do well to let her keep it."

The man frowned and pushed a lump of tobacco from under his lip to his cheek with his tongue. "Why is that?"

"Because I have a very long memory, and should I find myself in need of more servants at the Aldridge Plantation, I will naturally deal with the man to whom I owe a favor."

Jonathan snickered, but Edward ignored him, focusing instead on the overseer, who now appeared more than happy to comply.

"Yes, sir, that does make right good sense." He spat a stream of tobacco juice on the dock then wiped his sleeve across his mouth and moved on to the next woman in line.

Temperance's shoulders fell as a relieved sigh escaped her lips. "Thank you."

Edward nodded. There was no more reason for him to stay there, but he did not want to leave. Her plea of innocence rang in his ears, but with nothing more than her word, he was helpless to do anything of consequence.

He put his hand on her shoulder and squeezed it through his jacket. "God be with you, Temperance."

As he turned and walked away, he was sure he heard a sob. It took all his self-control not to look back.

"Few things in life are constant," Jonathan said, keeping pace beside him. "But one thing I can always depend on is Edward Aldridge coming to the aid of a distressed damsel."

"Act coarse if you like, brother. But I do not believe even you would have left her in the water to die."

Jonathan shrugged as if it made no difference. Five years younger than his brother, Jonathan could be unreliable and self-indulgent, but he had a quick mind and a good heart.

"Be that as it may, I would like to get to the tea shop before the breakfast blend is gone."

Edward eyed his brother with a smirk. "You mean you want to get there before Miss Pratchett leaves for the day."

"Perhaps." Jonathan looked away, but not before Edward saw the blush staining his cheeks.

"Go on ahead," Edward said with a wave of his hand. "I will meet you at the wagon when I finish here."

Jonathan looked back at him, an eyebrow cocked. "What other business do you have on the dock? Hoping to find more women in need of rescuing?"

"My business is my own." Edward crossed his arms, drawing himself up to his full height, and looked down at his brother. "You had best see about yours."

Joking and teasing was all well and good, but Jonathan knew when Edward had had enough. After a quick nod, he turned on his heel and hurried in the direction of the tea shop. Once he disappeared around a corner, Edward relaxed and huffed out a sharp laugh. They lived on an island that grew and processed the finest coffee anyone could want, yet Jonathan sought out that weak English tea. Only a woman could explain that.

Edward turned his attention back to the line of prisoners on the dock. The woman—Temperance—was looking at him. As soon as he caught her eye, she jerked her head, breaking their gaze. Several wagons had stopped close by, no doubt driven by representatives from the plantations that had reserved new workers. Most were strangers to him, but there were three he knew. Two were the overseers from the Dalton and Rawlings plantations, places where a servant, if they followed orders and caused no trouble, could live to see the end of their indenture. But Edward's brows lowered in a deep *V* when he saw the overseer from the Exley Plantation had not come alone. Sitting beside him was Simon Exley himself. It was his custom to come to the dock and handpick the servants to be indentured to him, often replacing some of the more sickly ones with those already designated for other plantations. Edward liked to think he could find something good and admirable in any person. To date, he'd found no such qualities in Exley.

The dour man moved along the line of women, flicking his finger to indicate which ones he wanted. Edward held his breath when Exley stopped in front of Temperance and growled some direction. She lifted her head, keeping her eyes averted until Exley grabbed her chin and forced her mouth open. He looked at her teeth as though inspecting a horse. Bristling at such brutish behavior, Edward moved closer. Not only did he want to hear what was being said, he wanted to be close in case Exley's treatment of her became any worse.

Exley glanced at the foreman standing beside him. "Quite a bunch of half-drowned rats today. I've a mind to refuse them all."

The foreman nodded and wrung his hands, showing none of the bravado he'd expressed earlier to Edward. "There was an accident, sir. One of the clumsy curs fell into the drink. But we got them out. Did not lose one of 'em."

Edward looked down at his shoes, still soaked and oozing water, and shook his head. If it had been up to that man, a good many of the ship's ill-fated passengers would have drowned.

Exley did not commend the foreman for his quick action. Instead, he turned his attention back to Temperance. "Not much to this one." His voice rumbled like carriage wheels across cobblestones. Scratching a red, scaly patch of skin on his cheek, he looked her up and down. "I suppose she'll do."

"Aye, sir, she'll do whatever you like her to do." The foreman grinned and was rewarded with a lecherous laugh of agreement from Exley before they moved down the line.

It took all of Edward's self-control to stay where he was and not confront the man. Instead, he focused on Temperance. There was no doubt she was scared. The encounter with Exley should have broken her further, but it hadn't. She kept her head up, shoulders pulled back, and took in a long, slow breath. It was as if she prepared for battle.

An odd, completely illogical sense of pride expanded Edward's chest. She was a fighter, which was good. It would take every ounce of strength and courage she possessed to survive the life awaiting her. If Edward believed in divine intervention, he would pray for her. But, as he had begun to doubt whether God cared, he'd simply have to hope for the best.

Chapter 2

The wagon bounced over the crude road, jarring every bone in Temperance's body and clacking her teeth together with such force she feared they might break. The dozen or so other men and women around her were silent, save for the occasional grunt when a wheel met a deep rut.

There had been a moment back at the dock, when the shackles were removed from her wrists, that Temperance believed she was free. Somehow, they'd realized she wasn't a criminal and were letting her go. Then she had been grabbed by the arm and forced to get into a wagon where she was once again shackled, this time around her ankles. At that moment, the last faint glimmer of hope died and she faced the truth. She was to be an indentured servant, even though she had willingly boarded the ship that brought her to the West Indies.

How had her good intentions gone so horribly wrong? She pulled the jacket more tightly around her, even though she was now thoroughly dry and the weather too warm for the additional layer. She buried her face in the wool, relishing the musky, male smell. It was a relief after the stench of the ship's hold and a brief respite from the odor of herself and those now around her.

"Ye cannot keep et."

Without loosening her hold on the jacket, Temperance looked in the direction of the rough voice. A man sat almost directly across from her. His hair and beard were long and matted, his clothes little more than rags held together by tenacious threads, and pale pink scars marred his dark skin.

"Why?" Her voice was weak, barely a thin whisper.

"Ye're property now. Only things ye get are what they give ye." He snorted in disgust. "An' most of that is nothing ye want."

"Quiet!" the man driving the wagon yelled then flicked a whip behind him, not appearing to be aiming for anyone in particular.

Nearly everyone in the back of the wagon flinched and ducked their heads. Still, the tip of the whip caught one woman on the neck. She screamed then clasped her hand over her mouth as a thin trickle of blood flowed from under her ear.

"Enough." The man sitting beside the driver scowled over his shoulder. "Another sound and you'll wish you'd drowned in the harbor like the vermin you are."

It was the same man who had examined her teeth back on the dock. If she understood what was happening, he was also the man who had purchased her and the others in the wagon. He held their lives in his rough, dirty hands.

Temperance's fingers dug deeper into the wool of the jacket as she fought back her sobs. She inhaled deeply, focusing on the smell, remembering the man who had been so kind. *What had his friend called him? Edward.* He'd saved her life. Had she even thought to thank him? If she saw him again. . . Temperance squeezed her eyes shut and shook her head. What a fool she was. She was now a servant and no better than a common criminal. She would never see him, or anyone she cared about, ever again.

"Home at last," one of the men up front grumbled, although Temperance had no idea which.

Barely raising her head, she opened her eyes and looked at their destination. The wagon drove through two huge open gates. Made of thick black metal and designed with swirls and elaborate patterns, they were more intricate than any Temperance had seen back home. The wagon continued down the dirt road, hurrying past a house so grand, it had to be where the owner of the plantation lived. The road twisted, going around a long row of palm trees, and the rest of the grounds came into sight.

Fields of strange tall plants stretched to the horizon. Although she had never seen sugar in its raw form, Temperance thought that must be the crop. The plants quivered as though alive, but it was only from the workers who moved among the rows, some coming out loaded down with overflowing baskets and burlap slings, which they dumped into a waiting wagon. They were mostly dark-skinned men and women, but here and there she saw others who reminded her of home. Either Irish criminals or innocent souls who'd fallen into the same trap she had.

They passed the fields and came to the edge of a cluster of trash mounds. But then a person walked out of one and Temperance was shocked to see they were, in fact, makeshift huts.

The wagon jerked to a stop, and the driver jumped down and moved around to unshackle their ankles.

"This is your home now." He spoke in a flat, uninterested tone, as though he'd said the words a hundred times and never believed them to begin with. "Work hard, obey orders, and we'll have no issue."

Several slaves approached the wagon and waited for the new arrivals to get down, then separated the men from the women and led them away.

"This one." The master blocked her path. "Scrub this one down and bring her to the main house. I do believe she could be of use."

He grabbed her chin, and for a moment, Temperance thought he was going to check her teeth again. Instead, he tilted her head up, forcing her to look into his eyes. It was a move meant to intimidate her, but instead, something inside her flared to life. *How dare this man presume to call himself master?* She knew no master other than the Lord God Almighty. She was a human being, not a tool to be used until it rusted and broke, only to be discarded and replaced by another. Her eyes narrowed as she tried to convey all she was feeling in one look. There was fight left in her after all, and fight she would until she could fight no more.

The master. . .no, she would not think of him that way. She would not give him the power behind the title. He was cruel, an ogre. Yes, that was it exactly. He was a monster.

The monster sneered and released her. "That attitude will not last long." Then he and the driver climbed back into the wagon and rode away.

Temperance began to shake. Her head dropped, shoulders curved forward, spine bowed. It was as though her body was folding in on itself. A hand, strong but not rough, curled around her upper arm, keeping her upright. She turned her head to see a stout Negro woman. The woman did not smile, but there was an unmistakable kindness in her eyes.

"Another Irish, yes?" She did not wait for Temperance to answer. Just shook her head and clucked her tongue.

"Can you help me?" Temperance begged through lips so dry she feared they would crumble into dust if she said much more.

The woman ignored the question. "I am Ruth. Come along, child." She pulled Temperance forward, taking her slowly to a clump of palm trees.

They walked between the trees and came to a small cleared spot. A huge metal pot sat atop an open fire. Inside the pot, steam rose from the bubbling liquid. Temperance wrinkled her nose. The air smelled foul, like charred meat left too long on a spit. Looking around, she saw another fire, this one simply a mound of kindling and flame. Temperance pulled back, afraid of what it all meant for her.

Ruth patted her shoulder. "No need to fear. You must be cleaned."

"Truer words have never been spoken." A woman came through the trees. From her clothes and the way she kept herself, Temperance was sure she was a slave, too. But her heart leaped at the familiar lilt and cadence of the woman's voice.

"This is Lily." Ruth inclined her head toward the other woman. "Another Irish."

"I'm Temperance." She extended her hand in a weak attempt at courtesy, but Lily took a step backward.

"No need for that here. And certainly not before you're deloused." Lily pointed at the bubbling pot.

"But that water is scalding."

Lily snorted out a laugh. "That is only to clean the brushes. Hot water is too good for the likes of us, isn't it, Ruth?"

Ruth frowned in reply.

Lily shook her head. "The sooner you accept your new station, the better. Now take off those filthy clothes."

"What? Here?" Temperance looked to Ruth, hoping she would contradict Lily.

"You need a scrubbing," Ruth said. "It is easier if you do it quick."

"Where did you get that?" Lily asked as Temperance undid the top button of the jacket.

"A man at the dock. He saved my life."

Lily clucked her tongue. "Shame to toss it in the fire."

As badly as she wanted to argue, Temperance knew better. She took off the jacket and held it to her face one last time, committing the scent and feel of it to memory, before dropping it to the ground. Humiliation burned her cheeks as she removed the rest of her clothes. Thankfully, Lily kept up a steady stream of chatter, giving her something else to focus on.

"A man saving your life. That was a miracle right there. And he gave you a gift. Count it as the last kindness you'll have for a while. Here, you will not have anything the master doesn't let you have, and that is not much. Not even your name."

Standing in only the skin God gave her, Temperance crossed her arms over her chest and shivered. "They change your name?"

Ruth came forward with a long-handled brush in one hand and a pail of water in the other. "I am from Africa. No one in Africa is called Ruth."

She took a lump of soap out of the water and began the scrubbing. The water was cold, and the lye in the soap burned as the hard brush bristles scraped across Temperance's skin.

Desperate to distract herself, Temperance looked at Lily. "You too?"

"Oh, yes. I was born Siobhan Sullivan. You can expect a new name as well." Lily tapped her fingertip against her bottom lip. "Perhaps Daisy. Or Gladiola. Exley names the new white women after flowers, although I couldn't tell you why. What do you think, Ruth? Is she a Pansy? Or perhaps Rose?"

"Three Roses have come and gone. Bad things come with that name." Ruth spoke as she scrubbed.

Temperance did not ask where the women named Rose had gone or what bad things had happened to them. Instead, she squeezed her eyes shut and prayed to awake from the nightmare she was surely having. As if walking in her sleep, she allowed herself to be scrubbed not once but twice, from top to bottom. She kept quiet as Ruth proclaimed her hair was too matted to save and hacked it off just above her shoulders before washing it with such enthusiasm Temperance expected to find holes in her scalp. When Ruth handed her a pile of undergarments and a shift, Temperance obediently put them on, even though the rough muslin reminded her of potato sacks. Lily continued to talk, but her words had become a mosquito-like drone. What difference did it make what she said? It hadn't taken Temperance long to understand that surviving in this place meant doing as she was told.

As the world around her began to spin and the earth beneath her feet tilted, the thought flitted through her mind that no one had told her to faint, but she was doing so anyway.

For a brief, blessed moment, in the fog between sleep and consciousness, Temperance forgot where she was. With her eyes still closed, she felt her bed beneath her, the lumps in the straw tick familiar and comforting. But with her next breath, the pungent smells of sweat and dirt and waste made her stomach lurch and there was no doubt of the reality of her situation.

"Welcome back." The voice was Lily's. "When you can, sit up and drink this."

Temperance pushed herself up slowly on the dirt floor then took the cup Lily offered. It was rough, carved from some kind of light wood. She took a careful sip but nearly choked on the liquid.

"It is vile," she said between coughs. "What is it?"

"An herbal remedy. It tastes like poison, I know, but it will help you regain your strength." Lily put a plate, just as crudely hewn as the cup, beside Temperance. "And eat this. Before you say it looks like scraps, that's because it is. We forage and use whatever we can."

Taking a gulp of air, Temperance held her breath and forced herself to swallow the brew. Then, thanks to her gnawing hunger and the small amount on the plate, she finished the food just as quickly.

"Thank you."

Before either of them could say anything else, they were approached by a man. He was imposing, nearly as broad as he was tall, with a head as devoid of hair as his upper lip and chin were covered by it.

"What be going on here?" He stopped and looked down at them with his legs planted wide and his beefy hands curled into fists at his sides.

"New stock today." Lily got to her feet and motioned to Temperance to do the same. "The master wanted her clean and taken to him. I was helping."

Temperance tasted the bitter herbs at the back of her throat, threatening to bring up everything she had just eaten. Was Lily on her side, or the side of the monster?

The man shook his head. "He will not be seeing anyone today. Get to work. Both of you."

"Yes, sir." Lily bowed her head then poked Temperance in the side.

"Yes, sir." Temperance imitated Lily, keeping her head down until Lily grabbed her by the arm and propelled them both out of the clearing.

The man called after them. "If I find you lazing about again, you'll suffer more than my displeasure."

When they'd gone far enough not to be heard, Temperance asked, "Who was that?"

"Jonas. He is the overseer. Better than most, which doesn't mean much. But he'll let you say a word before resorting to the lash."

Temperance pulled her arm away from Lily. "I do not appreciate being called stock."

"I do not like it, either. But that is what we are now." Lily sighed, slowing her pace. "We are slaves. It goes easier for us if we act as if we know our place, even though we do not believe it ourselves. Today, our place is in the mill."

"What do I do?"

Lily glanced over, her eyes sad. "Whatever you're told to do."

Chapter 3

By the time they returned home, Edward's clothes had dried, although his shoes were still waterlogged. With every step he took—following Jonathan from the wagon, across the yard, up the stairs, into the foyer—not only did he experience the undesirable feeling of wet wool against leather, his mind unavoidably flashed back to Temperance.

"This is a mistake. I committed no crime."

It wasn't the first time he'd heard such proclamations from the indentured. But it was the first time he'd believed the person claiming it.

He'd barely had time to shut the door when a servant ran up to him, a pair of slippers in hand. "Welcome home, Mr. Aldridge. Let me take those wet shoes before you catch your death."

Edward stepped out of the shoes, peeled off his socks, and slid his feet into the slippers. "Thank you, Ami."

The woman gave a quick bow then hustled away.

Jonathan chuckled. "She must have been sitting by the window, waiting for you to get home. What is the secret behind such well-behaved slaves?"

"I prefer to call them servants," Edward said easily. "And I simply treat them like human beings."

Edward went into the study with Jonathan close behind. "Such a radical assertion, brother. There are those who would go so far as to call it heresy."

With a grunt, Edward dropped into a wing-backed chair and extended his feet toward the waiting fire blazing in the hearth. "What heresy can there be in kindness toward our fellow man?"

"Ah, yes, but are they men, or are they beasts?" At the sideboard, Jonathan took the stopper from a cut-glass decanter and poured amber liquid into a glass. "If they are beasts, as many claim, then do not we, in fact, have dominion over them?"

Jonathan held up the decanter, offering to pour another, but Edward declined with a shake of his head.

"They breathe the same air, they laugh and cry and speak as we do." Edward leaned forward as Jonathan sat in the chair across from him. "How can you look at them and call them beasts?"

"I do not," he said with an innocent smile. "I am merely repeating what I've heard others say."

"And what do others say about the Irish indentured? They are treated with the same callousness as the African slaves. Do people also claim the Irish are not human?"

"Ah, this explains the darkness of your mood. Cannot get the Irish lass off your mind, eh?"

Edward leaned back and sighed. "She said she was innocent."

"And you believe her?"

He'd pulled her from the water and saved her life. He'd looked into her eyes and it was as if he could see her soul. Did he believe her? "Yes. I do. And now she is with Exley."

It was all he needed to say to convey his concern. Exley was widely known as one of the cruelest slave owners in Montserrat. Had he saved Temperance simply to deliver her to a fate worse than death? After that brief moment on the docks, he felt responsible, not only for her current situation but for her future welfare.

"Oh dear. I know that look." Jonathan drained his glass and set it on the table beside him.

"I do not know what you mean."

"You're trying to think of a way to liberate her."

"You, little brother, are too smart for your own good." Edward leveled a finger at him. "But you're wrong. Whatever thoughts I have on the subject are just that. Thoughts and imaginings that will amount to nothing. According to the law, she is the property of Exley until her indenture is completed."

A wail cut their conversation short. Edward glanced up at the ceiling but otherwise did not move.

As the crying continued, Jonathan shifted uncomfortably. "Perhaps you should check on your son."

"Ami will take care of it." As if summoned by his words, the servant ran through the hall and up the stairs. A few minutes later, the crying turned into a snuffle and then stopped.

"Have you thought of procuring a nurse just for. . .what name did you settle on?"

"I did not."

"The boy still has no name? It has been over a month. Do you not think—"

"I think I know how to run my house." Edward stood abruptly. "It is getting late and I have work."

Jonathan rose in response. "In that case, I shall take my leave." He strode to the study door then stopped and turned back. "What happened to Madeline wasn't your fault, nor was it the fault of your son. Grief is expected, but punishing yourself won't bring her back."

He let Jonathan leave without challenge. How could he deny his brother's words when he knew they were right?

Lily walked slowly from the mill. Behind her, Temperance moved slower still. The moon above was huge, casting its pale light on the palm trees, creating shadows more menacing than they should be due to the squawks and yips and squeals of animals she couldn't identify. From somewhere in the distance came the sound of the ocean as it swept onto shore then whisked away. It was a steady reminder of how she got here, and the only way she could possibly leave.

"If you cannot keep up, you'll be left behind," Lily called back over her shoulder.

"I'm trying."

Each step took an inordinate amount of effort. Every piece of her ached, from her cut and bleeding fingertips clean through to her bones. She stared down at the ground as she walked, certain the dark concealed a great pit waiting to swallow her up. But instead of a pit, she stumbled over a stick or a root and fell to the ground. Pain shot through her knees as she landed on them. She put out her hands as she fell forward, scraping her palms. Jarred from the impact, her head pounded and the pain in her body, which she had been sure was the most pain she could possibly endure, increased.

This was it, then. Her breath came in short, hard gasps as hot tears spilled from her eyes. This was where she would die, alone in the dirt, with no one to mourn her.

She was on her hands and knees when Lily knelt beside her. "Are you giving up, then?"

The weight of the question pushed Temperance down, first to her elbows then to her side. Dirt and leaves scratched her cheek. She looked up at Lily, silhouetted by the moon. Or was it the angel of death, come to take her home?

"What's the point in fighting?"

Lily put a gentle hand on Temperance's shoulder. "The point is to live. When we live, we show them they cannot break us."

Images filled Temperance's mind. She saw the faces of all those who had lied to her, abused her, lorded over her. She saw the monster, his eyes cold and cruel, so sure he was better than she. Twice now she had stared right back, refusing to let him see her fear. If she gave up, it would all be for naught. If she gave up, he would be victorious.

She struggled to push herself up. With Lily's help, she was able to sit upright. Swiping her tears away with the back of one grubby hand, Temperance made her decision.

Supported by Lily, she stood and walked to the hut Lily called her own. The roof—what there was of it—was so low they had to bend nearly in half to get inside. The space itself was barely large enough for two of them to sit. Yet Temperance found the relative privacy of the space comforting.

" 'Tisn't much," Lily said, "but we make do." Without explaining why, she turned back around and left the shelter.

The minutes stretched, and Temperance began to wonder if Lily was coming back. She wanted to lie down, but doing so would take up all the available space, so she waited. Finally, she heard footsteps outside, quickly followed by Lily ducking back into the shelter.

"Here." She handed Temperance a bowl of what looked like soup. "I begged Ruth for it. If you want to know where the meat came from, do not ask. I do not know myself and I prefer it that way."

After taking a careful smell and deciding it was worth trying, Temperance lifted the bowl to her lips and sipped. As she ate, Lily sat quietly, her back leaned against a tree trunk that made up half of one of the shelter's walls.

"Here." Temperance handed the bowl back to her. "I left a bit for you."

Lily began to smile, but her expression quickly changed to a sardonic grin. "If someone gives you food, you eat it. All of it. You should have kept this for yourself." Then she gulped down the last bit from the bowl.

"How did you get here?" Temperance asked.

Lily shrugged. "The same way you did, I expect. What did they promise you? Let me guess. . .food, lodging, and a position as a house servant?"

Temperance looked away, ashamed she had been so gullible. "A governess."

"Even better." Lily cackled out her response. "They did make it sound lovely. As for me, well, I would have taken just about anything to get off my back."

Temperance jerked her head toward Lily. "You were a. . .you–"

Lily cut her off with a look as sharp as a scythe. "I did what was needed to survive and to feed my family." She sighed, the toll of her struggles bending her back and dragging down her shoulders. "Not that it was much good. It only delayed the inevitable end. When I buried the last of them, my son, all I wanted to do was leave that cursed place."

"My family is gone, too. My parents and my brothers." Grief clenched Temperance's heart, nearly as strong as the day her dear Johnny left the earth. "I was desperate for a better life. A fresh start. What a foolish child I am."

Lily reached out and patted her leg sharply. "Now then, do not be thinking such things. Smarter women than you and me have been fooled, no doubt." She yawned and stretched her arms above her head. "Morning comes too soon, and with it another day of labor. 'Tis time to sleep."

"Where should I go?"

"Nowhere. You shall stay with me." She stretched out on the ground, back pressed against a wall of palm fronds, her legs sticking outside the entrance. "The quarters are tight, but not nearly as close as the hold of a slave ship, eh?"

"That is very kind. Thank you."

Lily groaned. "Kindness has nothing to do with it. We're stronger and safer if we look out for each other. I help you, and when you are stronger, you help me. Are we agreed?"

A spark of hope lit within Temperance. She would never be happy in this place, but just maybe, with Lily's help, she could survive it.

"We are agreed."

Chapter 4

Time did not move normally on the Exley Plantation. The days dragged by, hour after hour of back-breaking, soul-numbing labor that felt like it would never end. Yet the nights flew by, as if no more than mere seconds had passed between closing her eyes and waking for another day of misery. Temperance lost track of how many days had passed. Only by observing the changes in the moon did she have an idea of the actual passing of time.

She was in the mill, perspiring from the heat of the boiling fires as she fed cane into the presser, when Jonas walked up.

"Come with me," he said.

After a quick look at Lily, Temperance hurried after the overseer. Outside the building, the breeze off the water cooled the fire in her cheeks, chilling the sweat that clung to her skin. She did her best to focus on that, rather than the unease in her spirit. It wasn't right. The overseer would have no reason to talk to a slave who had done as she was told. The only reason Temperance had seen any slaves going with Jonas was when he took one for punishment. Had she done something wrong without realizing?

When they went past the slave quarters and continued in the direction of the house, Temperance knew it was worse than she had thought. She had hoped the monster had forgotten about her, but apparently, he hadn't.

"Go to the back," Jonas said, pointing. "Someone will get you when he is ready."

He walked away, leaving Temperance there. From where she stood, she could see the huge iron front gates. All she had to do was run, push her way through, and she would be free. At least until someone found her, brought her back, and whipped her within an inch of her life. She had already been told stories about the harsh punishment received by runaway slaves. They were meant to discourage escape attempts, and they worked.

Temperance did as she was told, going to the entrance used by the house servants. The door opened and a large African woman came out holding a large pot of water with both hands. She looked Temperance up and down, quirking an eyebrow in question.

"I was told to wait here," Temperance said.

"You'd best wait, then." The woman emptied the pot in the dirt then went back into the house.

It wasn't long before the door opened again. This time, Simon Exley stepped outside. Temperance crossed her arms, wishing for a more effective way to shield herself from his leering looks.

"Hello, Ivy."

The timber of his voice sent a chill through her. "My name is Temperance."

"Not anymore. Do you know why I take on indentured servants?"

She did not answer, but she did not look away. She looked him in the eye as he continued to speak.

"Because I believe in redemption. You were borne across the ocean to start a new life. Before that can happen, you must shed your old self and atone for your sins. I offer you a means to that atonement."

Temperance hugged herself more tightly. She wanted to pray to God for help, but the monster claimed to be a servant of God. Was it a way to manipulate her and get what he wanted, or did he truly believe it? Either way, she now saw how truly dangerous he was.

He stepped closer and wrapped his meaty fingers around her upper arm. "Are you ready to atone for your sins?"

Temperance pulled back, but he yanked her closer. She pressed her palms against his chest, trying to push him away.

The monster laughed. "It will be my pleasure to purge your soul of the sin that blackens it."

She could feel the heat of his breath on her cheek, smell the mingled scents of rum and at least one rotted tooth. Panic rose from the center of her being and escaped in a shout.

"No! Unhand me!"

The slap across her face came quickly. "A slave should know better than to deny her master."

He advanced, and Temperance steeled herself. At the same moment, the kitchen door opened again and the large woman came back out.

"Excuse me, sir. Sorry to bother. Your wife needs you."

The monster let go of Temperance and backed away, his face a contortion of anger and frustration. "Tell her I am on my way." The servant nodded and went back inside. The monster called out behind him. "Toby!"

An older male slave, with a limp that made him appear to be hopping, hurried over. "Yes, Master Exley?"

"Take this slave to Jonas. She needs to learn her place." He stalked away but spat out before going into the house, "Next time, you will obey me."

Toby shook his head. "Missy, I shore am sorry I have to do this. Shore am sorry."

"You do not have to go with me," Temperance said softly.

" 'Fraid I do. Hafta do as the master says. And if you do not do as told, then it is my skin to lose."

"I understand." As they walked back the way she had come, Temperance once more looked at the gate.

"Toby, has anyone ever left here?"

"Of course. Lotsa ways to leave a place."

"You know the way I'm talking about."

Toby looked at her, his brows drawn into a deep frown. "Some have tried. Some always try."

"Have any succeeded? Please, I just want to know."

He was silent for so long, Temperance was sure he'd decided not to say anything else. But then he sighed. "Two."

Her heart leaped. Two slaves had escaped. "How did they succeed?"

"Oh, no," he said with a humorless laugh. "I've said too much as it is."

"I give you my word, on the graves of my mother, father, and two brothers, I will never tell anyone about this conversation. Please."

Toby wagged his head. "I shore must be going soft in my old age. Shore must be."

The details he had were sparse, but Temperance listened intently, repeating the facts over and over in her head, committing them to memory. If she lived through the overseer's lesson in obedience, she would do more than just survive.

She would escape.

"I was afraid of this."

From somewhere far away, Lily's voice penetrated the thick fog that surrounded Temperance. She tried to answer, but her mouth was so dry words refused to form. All she could manage was a low moan.

"Do not move."

The fact that she was told not to move made Temperance try to move, an action she immediately regretted. Intense pain radiated across her back and through her limbs. *No*, Temperance thought before she lost consciousness, moving was a bad idea. Lily had been absolutely right.

There was a cold cloth on the back of her neck. There was less fog now, more pain. Temperance groaned. The cloth left her neck and was pressed against her dry lips.

"I know you want to sleep," Lily's voice called to her. "But I need you to open your eyes. Just for a little while."

Such a simple request, yet Temperance found it nearly impossible. It felt as though her eyelids were pasted shut. Dried tears, no doubt. She remembered crying, sobbing, hating that she showed weakness, but unable to stop herself from doing so. Since she couldn't open her eyes, she tried to speak. The sounds she made were more like words than before, but still unintelligible. The cloth, wetter this time, was again pressed to her lips.

"Did I not tell you? Do as you are told." Lily kept up a steady stream of chatter. "But I knew. I knew this would happen. Couldn't you listen?"

Finally, Temperance was able to get out a word that made sense. "No."

Lily sighed. Temperance forced her eyes open. Her vision was fuzzy, but she saw her friend, shoulders sagging and face streaked with tear tracks, kneeling beside her. Gritting her teeth against the pain, Temperance slowly moved her arm across the ground until she could touch Lily's knee.

"Thank you."

Lily put her hand gently on Temperance's head. They stayed that way, quietly connected, while Temperance replayed the last day in her mind. There was something she wanted to remember, needed to remember, but what?

"Ivy."

Lily tilted her head. "What did you say?"

"Ivy. That was the name he chose for me." The recollection brought on a cascade of memories, one after another, each one triggering intense emotions. Temperance was tired. So tired of being afraid and helpless. So tired of letting others decide her fate. Yes, the choices she had made had gotten her into this mess, but the choices she had yet to make would get her out of it, or she would die trying. "Help me sit up."

"You shouldn't move too much. The wounds—"

"Please. Just help me."

"You are a stubborn one, I'll say that," Lily grumbled. "At least move slowly."

"I believe that is the only way I can move."

With some difficulty, and a great deal of pain, Temperance sat upright. Pinpoints of light danced in the air and a thudding beat pulsed within her ears.

"Here." Lily gave her a cup of water.

After swallowing the last drop, Temperance put the cup on the ground and looked at Lily. "He told me he would purge my blackened soul of its sin. That he was the vessel through which I would find atonement."

The revelation did not seem to surprise Lily. "He has created the perfect excuse. It absolves him of his own sin by virtue of the aid he offers to others."

"You've been called to the main house before, haven't you?" When Lily nodded, Temperance continued. "What did you do?"

"Exactly what I told you to do. I obeyed." Lily shrugged. "And yet, here I am, still a slave, no better off or worse than you. So who made the right choice?"

"You weren't whipped."

"Not that day, no. But when the master tired of my. . .company, he ordered me whipped to remind me of my place and sent me straight back here." Lily exhaled a ragged breath. "I gave up a piece of my soul for a few days away from the fields. Today, you lost some flesh but held on to your dignity. I misjudged you, Temperance. You are a much stronger woman than I."

Lily's admission gave her the courage to continue on. "Have you ever thought of leaving this place?"

Lily laughed. "Every day. Wait. . .do you mean seriously considered running away?" She shook her head hard. "No. Never. What happened to you today is nothing compared to what they do to a runaway slave."

"Only if they catch you."

"Have you taken leave of your senses? Of course they would catch you. And even if they did not, where would you go? There isn't a freeman on this island who would help you."

Temperance attempted a smile, but even that caused pain. "I believe there is at least one man who would."

"Who?" It only took a minute for Lily to make the connection. "The man who saved you at the docks?" She threw her hands up in frustration. "It is far more likely that he was concerned about losing merchandise than about you losing your life. How many slaves did he buy that day?"

"I do not believe he took any." Thinking back, Temperance remembered his look of genuine sadness before walking away.

"That proves nothing."

"He looked me in the eye and called me by name."

Lily's eye narrowed. "He did?"

"God be with you, Temperance." She could still hear his voice, speaking a blessing to her in a place many would say God had abandoned.

"His name is Edward. He told someone else the name of his plantation." She thought back. "Aldridge. The Aldridge Plantation."

"Well, gal, you may very well have run across the one man who would help you."

"Help *us*." She grabbed Lily's hand. "We can both be free of this place."

Conflicting emotions warred with Lily's countenance. Hope, trepidation, fear. . . everything that Temperance felt when she thought about running away.

"Now it is I who has thrown common sense to the wind." Lily nodded. "All right. But we have to wait until you've had a few days to heal. Until that time, we will make plans and prepare, but you must not speak of this to anyone. Most here would trade their closest friend's secrets if it meant receiving a kind word and a cup of rice from the overseer. Do you understand?"

"I do."

"Good. Now you must sleep." Lily shifted and motioned for Temperance to lay her head in her lap.

As Lily stroked her hair, Temperance felt some of the tension leave her body. She quickly fell asleep with the rich, soothing voice of Edward Aldridge in her head.

"God be with you, Temperance."

Chapter 5

The days took on a new dimension for Temperance. She had been moved from the mill out to the field. It had probably been intended as an additional punishment, but Temperance was glad for it. In the mill, a distracted slave working at the cane presser could easily lose an arm—or worse—and Temperance was most undoubtedly distracted.

She dragged long pieces of cane from the fields after the men had hacked through the woody stalks with machetes, all the while thinking about the plan she and Lily were devising. It was good to be outside, able to observe the comings and goings of others on the plantation. She saw storage buildings for tools, supplies, and various other things. She also found where the horses were kept when not pulling the wagons back and forth. Not surprisingly, the animals had better shelter than the slaves did. Rather than breaking her spirit, the fact fueled her desire to escape.

One early morning, as the sun had just begun to peak over the horizon, Temperance went to the spot she had been brought to the first day. The boiling pot was still there, no doubt waiting for the next time it was needed, but the space was otherwise empty. She scanned the ground until she found what she was looking for. Charred wood and scarred earth marked the place where the clothes had been burned. She crouched down and began digging through the cold, damp pile of scraps and ash. She sifted through it until finally uncovering the reason for her mission.

The rest must have been scavenged by other slaves. There was only one left, but one was enough. She rubbed the metal button between her fingertips, removing most of the soot. Embossed on it was an eagle, which she hadn't noticed before. Its wings were open, not in preparation for flight, but more in an expression of protection.

Temperance stood and slipped the button into her dress pocket. It was a tangible symbol of her goal, and a reminder that there were still good people in the world.

She left the clearing and went to the field to endure another day of labor.

Half a moon hung in the sky like a perfect half of a white porcelain plate. Temperance returned to the shelter, wanting nothing more than to collapse into the brief relief of sleep. Instead, she found Lily waiting for her.

"There you are." Lily jumped to her feet and grabbed her wrist, pulling her forward. "Come on."

Temperance tugged in the opposite direction. "Wait. Where are we going?"

"They butchered a cow today. If we hurry, there may still be some bones left."

With bones to boil, they could at least make a weak broth. As much as Temperance wanted to refuse, she knew better than to ignore the opportunity.

"All right."

They left the slave huts and went in the direction of the animal enclosures. Temperance wondered if this was the first time a cow had been butchered since she arrived, or if it was simply the first time the remains were available to the slaves. The more she thought about it, the less sense it made.

"How often does this happen?"

"From time to time." Despite Lily's usual proclivity to chatter on, she did not expound on her answer.

"I find it surprising the monster would leave anything behind for our benefit."

Lily looked at her. "The monster?"

"It is how I think of Exley. The title of master implies respect, something I cannot give him."

"Be careful." Lily looked in the direction they'd just come from then back at Temperance. "If he heard you say that, he would be very angry."

Lily sounded as if she was afraid. A shiver crawled up Temperance's spine and she stopped in her tracks. "What's going on?"

"Oh, Temperance." Her friend's voice shook as she tried to hold back a sob. "I'm sorry. I'm so sorry."

Temperance's heart sank. "What did you do?"

"I did not mean to, but the more we talked, the more real it became. I was so scared that we'd be caught. And I thought, if it wasn't going to work anyway, something positive should come out of it."

It all fell into place. "You did not bring me here to collect cow bones, did you?" Sobs were the only answer. Temperance should be furious, but instead, a strange calm washed over her. She had always known betrayal was a possibility, and she had planned for it.

"Listen to me." She took Lily by the shoulders and shook her. "Listen. Tell him I fought you and got away."

Before Lily could answer, Temperance shoved her hard, sending her to the ground. Lily screamed. Then Temperance ran.

The plan she had made with Lily had been to go east, but now, Temperance went west. There was a better way, one she had kept to herself. No longer did the thought of falling in a pit frighten her. When she stumbled, she regained her balance and kept going. Twice she fell, but she wasted no time, getting up and moving again. She ran with all her might, knowing that her life depended on it. All those hours of thinking and plotting while she toiled in the fields hadn't been for nothing. Even with only half the moon lighting her way, she knew exactly where she was going.

Wherever we are, it is always the same moon.

Edward gazed up. Only half of the old man's face showed, exactly as it had been the night he and Madeline agreed to marry.

THE *Captive* BRIDES COLLECTION

He walked on, propelled by the turmoil that had long been his soul's constant companion. As always, he questioned his decisions. Around and around he went, working out various scenarios in his mind, imagining how different things would have been if he'd done this or done that. By the time he reached the edge of his property he saw, as always, that the blame rested squarely on his shoulders. He was at fault, with no way to right the wrong.

The mournful howl of hounds in the distance drew Edward's attention. That sound meant only one thing: a slave had escaped and now was being hunted. With a sigh, Edward turned and walked toward the house. He had no intention of being drawn into such grisly business.

As he went, another sound caught his ear. This wasn't a dog or a wild animal. It was a muffled gasp, definitely human.

"Who's there?" He looked around for any shadows or shapes that seemed out of place. "Make yourself known."

Another gasp, not at all muffled this time. An arm extended from behind a tree. "Sir. Here."

Edward hurried over. A woman leaned against the palm's trunk, grasping it as though it was the only thing keeping her upright. Although he could barely see her face, he knew immediately who it was.

"Temperance. You're the one they're looking for."

She nodded. "Please. Help me."

She had asked for his help once before and he hadn't given it, adding one more regret to a lifetime of them. For once, he was given a chance to make a different choice. To change her life and, by extension, his.

"Be very quiet and do not move from this spot, no matter what you hear."

She pressed her forehead against the tree trunk. "Thank you."

The braying of the hounds increased as they came closer. Edward walked back to the edge of his property, his stride measured to reflect an air of calm assurance. The glow of torches bobbed between the trees. When at last he could make out the men's faces, he raised his hand in greeting.

"Good evening."

The man in front eyed him suspiciously. "Who might you be?"

"Edward Aldridge, owner of this plantation. And you?"

Looking embarrassed, the man pulled back his torch. "Forgive me, Mr. Aldridge. I did not recognize you."

"The evening shadows can fool the eye." Edward motioned to the other men. "What concerns me is that you've brought a search party to my property in the wee hours. What is all this about?"

"A runaway slave, sir."

"You saw this slave here?"

"No," the man said hesitantly. "But the dogs followed the scent, brought us here."

Edward laughed. "The evening air must be fooling the dogs. I assure you, gentlemen, the person you seek is not here."

"How can you be sure?"

"Because I've been on my nightly constitutional. If a stranger had come through here, I would know." Before the man could push the issue, Edward continued. "If you'd be so kind as to leave my property, it is late and I do need to get some rest."

During the exchange, the dogs hadn't stopped sniffing the ground. Now, one of them jerked up his head, howled, and strained at the leash. Edward definitely needed to make them all go away.

"A runaway slave will be easy to spot. I give you my word that if I see one, I will have him apprehended and will contact you. Who is your master?"

"We are freemen, sir, under the employ of Simon Exley. And the slave we're tracking is a woman."

"A woman. I see." Edward laughed. "Well, I'm sure you do not want to explain to Mr. Exley how a slave, and a mere woman at that, eluded your capture. You'd best be on your way."

The leader of the group frowned, and the ones behind him began to grumble. It was the reaction he'd hoped for. With their pride wounded, he doubted they'd choose to stay and risk further insult.

The leader gave a curt nod. "Good evening to you, then, sir."

Edward watched them leave, waiting until the torchlight faded and the dogs could no longer be heard. Then, on the slight chance that someone might still be watching, he walked slowly back to the tree.

She was exactly as he had left her, one arm around the trunk and her forehead pressed against it. From this new angle, he could see that the back of her dress—if you could call what was left of it a dress—was soaked through with blood. What had Exley done to her?

He put his hand gently on her shoulder and her head jerked up.

"It is safe now," Edward said. "They're gone."

"Thank you." She let go of the tree, took one step toward Edward, and immediately fainted into his arms.

She dreamed she was back in Ireland. A crisp breeze fluttered the sheer window coverings, carrying with it the scents of ocean salt and clover. Her mother sat beside her on the bed, stroking her forehead and singing.

"Mother?"

"Shh, my daughter. No one will hurt you now."

Temperance was confused. Had all that came before been a nightmare? Was she now in the land of the waking?

"Your trials are not yet over," Mother said. "But know that God has His hand on you."

The edges of Temperance's vision began to go dark and the image of her mother faded. Temperance struggled to sit up, reaching for her, begging her not to leave.

"There now. If you're not careful you'll hurt yourself again." This was a new voice, female and without the brogue.

When Temperance opened her eyes, she expected to find herself on the ground, in some kind of slave holding pen, most likely shackled to prevent another escape attempt.

But she was in a simple room with wooden walls and a real, complete roof. She wore a nightdress, the fabric soft and clean, and beneath her was an actual mattress on a metal frame. A woman sat on the bed beside her, but it was not her mother.

The woman's skin was dark, her cheeks full and rosy as she smiled. "Good to see you awake, child. Do you know where you are?"

Temperance tried to think, to remember how she had gotten to this place, but the edges of her memory were draped in a fog. "No."

"You're at the Aldridge Plantation." The woman dipped a washcloth in a basin on a small table by the bed, wrung out the excess water, then used it to dab at Temperance's face.

It all rushed back: running, the determination to get away, the fear of being caught. "I ran away. And Mr. Aldridge found me."

The servant beamed as if proud that Temperance remembered so much. "That is right. Mr. Aldridge has been worried about you."

"He has?"

"Oh, yes. 'Chinaza,' he said to me, 'you stay with her until she wakes up. You take good care of her.'"

Edward. . .Mr. Aldridge. . .was worried about her? Temperance tried not to think about it. "Chinaza? Is that your name?"

"Since the day I was born."

So Mr. Aldridge did not change the names of his African slaves. The more she learned, the more she was convinced she had been right about him.

"May I try to sit up now?"

"Yes, but be very careful. The wounds on your back must've broken open when you ran. I bandaged them, but they could open again."

Chinaza put an arm around her shoulders and helped her move forward. There was pain, but then pain had become a constant part of her life so she clenched her jaws against it. When she was upright, Chinaza put a pillow behind her back and helped her lean against the wall.

Temperance exhaled the breath she had been holding. "That is better. Thank you."

"Now you need to eat something. I'll fetch a tray and be right back." Chinaza left the room and shut the door behind her.

For the first time in a very long time, Temperance was alone and safe. It was an overwhelming feeling and one she was afraid to embrace. There was no way to tell how long it would last. What would happen after she was strong enough to work? Would she be turned back over to the monster? Even if she was allowed to stay, what if the monster found out she was here? She had to be a fool to relax and drop her guard now.

Her mother's words from the dream came back to her. *"But know that God has His hand on you."* It would be easy to believe God had abandoned her, left her to fend for herself in an unthinkable situation. Yet, whenever her life had been threatened, He'd given her a way out. She wasn't ready to feel safe, but she certainly could admit to being thankful.

Closing her eyes, Temperance said a brief prayer as tears flowed freely down her cheeks.

Chapter 6

Edward paced the floor of the study as he waited for Temperance to be brought to him. He'd spent the better part of the night wrestling with the situation at hand, but he was no closer to a solution than when he started. The only thing he knew for certain was that he must speak with Temperance to discover all the facts.

"Excuse me."

The voice that called to him was faint. He turned and found Temperance standing in the doorway, eyes downcast and hands clasped together in front of her.

"Come in." Her movements were stiff as she walked toward him. No doubt she was in great pain. "I hope you are feeling better today."

"I am. Thank you, sir. And thank you for the food. And the dress." She pressed her palms against her skirt and finally looked up. "You've shown me great kindness. More than I can possibly repay."

The sudden burst of thankfulness made Edward uneasy. "I'm glad you are well. I want to know more about how you came to be in Montserrat." He motioned to a chair. "Please, sit down."

She looked at him questioningly, as though his request might be a trap. He sat, and again motioned to the chair. This time, she followed suit.

"You claim to be innocent of a crime. If that is true, why are you here?"

She hesitated then launched into her story. She told him of losing her family in Ireland. How she wanted a better life and believed one waited for her in the West Indies. "It wasn't until the ship was at sea that I realized something was wrong. Several other women and I were taken below. The hold was filled with so many people. Some were prisoners, some said they were taken against their will." The memory of what she had been through made her shudder. "The conditions were beyond imagining."

"Is there any way to prove your story is true?" Edward asked.

Temperance shook her head. "I do not know how I could. All I have is my word."

Which was a problem. If Temperance was innocent of wrongdoing as she claimed, that made her indenture invalid. But the only proof was her word, and the word of a slave was worth nothing to a judge or constable. There was also the matter of Simon Exley.

"Why did you run?"

It took no coaxing to answer this particular question. "Simon Exley is an evil man. He speaks of redemption and atonement, but he wants only to take advantage of those below him to satisfy his base desires."

It was no secret that, in a system where people were treated like chattel, their owners sometimes did things that should be condemned. The practice sickened him, but hearing about it firsthand from a woman who had endured it stirred up an anger the likes of which he hadn't felt before.

He wanted to help her, but how? It was a crime to harbor a fugitive slave. If he let her stay and the authorities found out, he would be taken to prison. The alternative was to return her to Exley, which was out of the question.

The crying began upstairs. A moment later it stopped, but then it began again. Edward squeezed his hands closed and shut his eyes. It was so hard to concentrate when the boy cried. It was one more reminder of how miserably he'd failed his family.

"You have a baby?" Temperance's eyes lit up.

Before he could respond, Ami walked into the study holding the crying baby and a blanket in her arms.

"Beggin' your pardon, sir. I hate to bother, but I'm worried about the young sir. I've changed him and fed him, but he just keeps crying." Ami bounced the child as she talked, turning his wail into a staccato shriek.

"Have Byron ride into town and fetch the doctor." It was the only thing Edward knew to do.

Temperance stood up. "Excuse me. Might I have a try?"

Ami looked to Edward for permission.

"Do you have experience with babies?" Edward asked Temperance.

"I do, sir. Quite a bit. My mother was a midwife, and I often helped her."

That was all he needed to hear. He gave an affirmative nod, after which Ami handed the baby to Temperance.

"There now, handsome boy. Whatever is all this crying for?" She spoke to the baby as if he could understand. Her tone was low and melodic, as if she were preparing to sing. The baby still cried, but he was looking at her, waving his tiny fists in the air.

Temperance knelt on the floor. While holding the baby in one arm, she spread the blanket on the floor. Gently, she laid the baby on the blanket. As she wrapped the blanket tightly around him, she did in fact sing.

"Hush little baby, don't say a word,
Daddy's going to buy you a mockingbird."

Temperance stood up when she was done, holding the baby close to her chest. The only part of the boy that wasn't wrapped was his head. He couldn't move his arms or legs, and he appeared to be perfectly content. Even better than that, he had stopped crying.

Ami's mouth dropped open in amazement. "How did you do that?"

"It is called swaddling. My mother taught me." She swayed gently from side to side, smiling down at the baby as she spoke. "It helps the babe feel secure and safe."

The boy cooed in response and Temperance laughed. "That is better, isn't it? Such a wee, bonnie lad. What is your name?"

"He doesn't have one," Ami said.

At last, Temperance took her eyes off the boy. "No name? Why ever not?"

"That is a family matter," Edward said brusquely.

Realizing that she had spoken out of turn, Temperance demurred. "Of course. Forgive me for being so bold."

He nodded then turned to Ami. "Please take the boy back to the nursery."

It was clear that Temperance did not want to relinquish the baby, but she did, transferring him to Ami. When the servant had left the room, Edward turned his attention back to the crisis at hand.

"Why did you come here?"

Temperance appeared confused by the question. "Sir?"

"It is a crime to harbor a runaway slave. Simply having you in my home is breaking the law. So it behooves me to know why you chose to run from one plantation only to go to another."

She crossed her arms over her chest, as though protecting herself from the inevitable. "You showed me kindness, sir. I believed that you would look on me as a human being and help me. Which you have. But I did not think about the danger it would bring upon you and your house." She took in a deep, ragged breath. "If you let me leave, I will face my punishment and will not tell anyone I was here."

He needed to think. "Sit," he said with a harsh motion back to the chair.

She sat on the edge, looking frightened and alone. Hands clasped behind his back, Edward began to pace the floor.

What was he to do? There was no good answer. The right thing, the godly thing, would be to take the woman in and protect her from those who sought to do her harm. But in the eyes of the law, not only was that not the right thing, it was illegal. He hated the system that allowed men to lord over others, simply because they were born of a certain status or a certain location. But it was the system within which he lived. The question was, would God have him do that which was morally right or that which was legally right?

A new thought occurred to him. What would he do if he were not at odds with the law? Temperance had come to Montserrat believing a governess position awaited. After seeing her with the baby, he would not hesitate to appoint her as his caretaker. In that way, she could be the answer to a prayer. But there was still the problem of Exley. As distasteful as it was to Edward, she was still Exley's property. There was only one way to keep her at the Aldridge Plantation.

Edward had to purchase her indenture.

The wagon jerked as the wheel hit a rut, bringing back the awful memory of her first day on the island. Sitting on the rough wood, with shackles on her wrists and ankles, was almost too much to bear. But as Edward had explained, it was necessary.

"Exley will never give you up if he knows the truth," he had told her. "The man is ruled by greed and power. We must make him believe the transaction is his idea and is in his best interest."

It was the reason Temperance was chained, wearing the stained and bloody dress she had been found in, and being taken back to the Exley Plantation. Edward sat in the front of the wagon. Driving was his brother, Jonathan, who'd been made aware of the deception and had agreed quite enthusiastically to help.

"Do you remember the plan, Temperance?" Edward said, glancing over his shoulder.

"Yes." One small word, but it quivered with fear and trepidation.

Edward, however, spoke with quiet, calming assurance. "Whatever happens, no matter how angry I seem or how harshly I speak, hold tight to the goal."

"I will."

"You two had better stop talking," Jonathan said. "I can see the gates from here."

Her stomach clenched and Temperance was afraid she would be sick. Squeezing her eyes closed, she repeated one phrase over and over in her mind.

God has His hand on you.

It wasn't long before Jonathan brought the wagon to a stop and Temperance opened her eyes to her worst fear.

A slave approached the wagon, but before he could speak, Edward jumped down and began to bark orders.

"Tell your master I want to talk to him. Now." When the slave did not move fast enough, Edward walked past him. "If you refuse, I will get him myself. Exley!" he yelled in the direction of the main house. "Exley! We have business, you and I!"

Temperance cowered in the back of the wagon as the front door opened and the monster came onto the porch. He had a napkin in one hand, as if to make the point that his dinner had been disturbed.

"Aldridge," he said dryly. "What an unexpected pleasure. What brings you to my door this evening?"

"A trespasser was found on my property. I believe it is one of yours."

The monster's eyes narrowed and he walked around the wagon. When he saw Temperance, his lip curled into a lecherous sneer. "Ah, my little poison Ivy. I knew you'd pop up again."

As he spoke, Jonathan came around the back of the wagon and grasped the chain of the wrist shackles. "Come along, then."

Once she was standing on the ground, Exley approached. "I'll take that." He grabbed the chain from Jonathan and jerked her forward. "You are in a world of trouble," he growled.

This time, Temperance knew the slap was coming. Even so, he hit her with such force it sent her reeling and she fell to the ground. When she looked up she saw Edward, standing behind Exley, hands clenched into fists and eyes staring daggers. Their eyes met, and Edward relaxed. He wanted to protect her, she knew that, but they couldn't give the monster a hint of their plan.

Exley turned back to Edward. "Thank you for returning my property, Aldridge."

"You do not seem to understand why I came. The wench deserves to be punished."

"I assure you, she will be."

"Not good enough." Edward shook his head. "She trespassed on my land. She stole from my storehouse. I am the one who has the right to inflict punishment."

Temperance held her breath. If the monster agreed, the plan would fall apart. But Edward had been sure that Exley would never let another man come onto his property and be seen by the slaves as stronger than himself.

"Out of the question," Exley growled. "No one punishes my slaves but me or my overseer."

"I demand you make an exception."

Exley tilted his head, as if examining Edward. "You've changed your tune, Aldridge. You've never been known as one to relish the infliction of pain."

"Years of dealing with slaves and their ways have re-informed my opinions. This filthy gutter rat stole from me. If she belonged to me, I would have dealt with the problem already."

He looked down at Temperance with such contempt that she felt like trash. She told herself it was a necessary part of the deception, but that knowledge did not make it sting any less.

"Well, Aldridge, you may have stumbled onto a solution. Buy this one from me and you will be within your right to dole out any punishment you wish."

Edward wrinkled his nose in disgust. "I have no use for a scrawny, disobedient thing like that. Why should I waste good money?"

Exley's lips pulled back into what some might call a smile. To Temperance, he looked more like a predatory animal about to pounce.

"You want satisfaction," he said. "The only way you can have it is to make this purchase. How much is the ability to exact your pound of flesh worth to you?"

Edward looked from Exley to Temperance, who still cowered on the ground. After a moment of consideration, he looked back to Exley. "What is your price?"

Exley stated his amount. Jonathan barked out an incredulous laugh.

"You cannot be serious," Edward said. "I could purchase two fine horses and a pig for that amount."

"You could indeed." Exley shrugged, as if none of it mattered to him. "The choice is yours."

Temperance bowed her head under the weight of those words. The price was too high. No matter how noble Edward's intentions, she would never expect anyone to part with so much money to save someone he barely knew. Edward would leave her there, and by nightfall she would either be dead or wishing she were.

"I will pay your price."

Her head shot up and she was barely able to stop herself from smiling. Edward looked grim, reminding her that the deception was not over yet.

The monster, looking quite pleased with himself, extended his hand. "We have made a deal, then." The two men shook hands. "Come into my study and I will sign over the contract of indenture."

Edward followed, but turning before going into the house, he addressed Jonathan: "Put the thief back into the wagon." Then, after a wink that only Temperance and his brother could see, he went inside.

Grasping her shoulders in a way that was much gentler than it seemed, Jonathan helped her to stand. As she was getting in the back of the wagon, he whispered in her ear: "After today, I believe we should return to England and seek employment at the Old Globe."

She smiled to herself then stretched out on her side. With Jonathan standing watch and Edward inside arranging her liberation, Temperance allowed herself to relax and to sleep. Perchance even to dream.

Chapter 7

It was immediately apparent that life on the Aldridge Plantation bore no resemblance to what passed for living at the Exley place. The fieldworkers had bunkhouses to stay in. They were rough and plain, but the walls were made of wood and the roofs did not leak. House servants had nicer living quarters near the house. As for Temperance, her position as governess required her to see to all the baby's needs, so she was given a small room connected to the nursery.

Temperance opened the double doors at the end of the nursery and stepped out onto a small balcony. It was just big enough for a chair and small table and had become one of her favorite spots. From there, she could look across the fields of swaying tobacco, or at cottony clouds floating in a robin's-egg-blue sky. In the distance, she could make out the shoreline and imagine the waves crashing upon the rocks just as they did in Ireland. When she left her home, she had believed it was to start a new life as a governess. Now, that was exactly what she was doing.

With a smile, Temperance went to the crib and looked down at her young charge. Over the last few weeks, she had become accustomed to his sleeping patterns and had developed something of a routine. This was the time of day she usually sat on the balcony and read, but she had finished her book yesterday. There was only one thing to do.

Leaving the nursery door cracked just a bit in order to hear the baby if he woke, she slipped down the stairs and into the study. What a rare gift it was to be able to access a treasure trove of literature on a whim. She returned the book she had read to the shelf from which it came and scanned the spines for her next choice. She could spend many happy hours doing nothing but exploring this single room. Besides the books, it was full of so many beautiful things.

A globe, inlaid with gold leaf and able to spin, stood in one corner. A lovely sideboard was covered with crystal decanters and glasses that threw rainbows on the wall when the sun hit them in just the right way. But her favorite item was the chess set with intricately carved pieces of ebony and ivory. She picked up the white knight, which was an actual knight on the back of a rearing steed, and rubbed her thumb across it.

"I do not have to worry about you stealing chess pieces, do I?"

She let out a little yelp, turning in the direction of the voice. The piece fell from her hand and bounced on the rug.

"What? No, of course not. I came to borrow a book and saw the board. I'm sorry. I shouldn't have touched it."

Edward held his hands up as he came into the room. "I did not mean to scare you. And I never for a moment thought you were stealing. It was a joke. Quite a bad one, I'm afraid."

He picked up the knight and placed it back on the board. "Do you play?"

"Yes, but not for a long time. My father had a set. After he died. . .we sold it to buy food."

"I'm sorry."

"One does what one must." She clasped her hands together and took a step back. "I should go. I must check the baby."

Edward glanced at the ceiling. "It sounds as though everything is fine upstairs. Would you like to play a game?"

Her eyes grew wide. "With you?"

"Yes, with me." He laughed. "I haven't played in a very long time, either, so it will be an equal match."

"All right," she said with a dip of her lashes. "I would enjoy that."

As he set up the board and the playing area, Temperance couldn't help but think how strange it all was. As far as the law was concerned, she was still a slave by way of indenture. But with Edward, she did not feel like a slave. She was a servant, a position that held no shame.

He turned the board so the white pieces were hers and told her to go first. After moving a pawn, she dared to ask the question that had been bothering her.

"Sir, why have you not given your son a name?"

His hand stopped in midair, his rook hovering over the board. He placed it a bit too firmly, making all the pieces shake. "I cannot."

His answer made no sense, but she knew that repeating the question would only make him stop talking. So she tried another approach. "A child needs a name. We cannot continue calling him *the boy* his entire life."

"It has worked this long." Edward sighed. "If you think it is so important, perhaps you should decide on a name."

"Me?"

"Yes. You spend more time with him than I do. I cannot think of a better person for the task."

Temperance could. His father. But it wasn't fair for the child to be nameless.

"All right," she said. "I will."

"It is good to have that settled." He motioned at the board. "It is your turn."

She stared at the board but was still thinking about the baby. Maybe, after he had a real name, his father would see him for the beautiful person he was. At least it was a step in the right direction.

The moon was full, and Edward stared up at it, trying to make sense of what his life had become. He was a widower, with a nameless child and an indentured Irish servant who moved him more than any woman he'd ever known. If he felt guilty for not loving

Madeline enough, he felt even more guilty for the pleasure he found spending time with Temperance.

For several years, Edward had wished he'd never come to Montserrat. He should have stayed in England, refusing to take part in the marriage arranged by his parents. But his sense of duty would have none of it. Madeline's parents were well off but of unproven stature. The Aldridge name was old and respected, even though poor business choices and all-around bad luck had reduced the family fortune to almost nothing. A union between the two had made sense, even though it meant Edward and Madeline had to sail to the West Indies to run the tobacco plantation.

Edward had tried to make Madeline happy, but no matter what, melancholy was her constant companion. Even during her pregnancy, she worried about everything that could go wrong. The one thing neither of them had considered was that she would die in childbirth. As it turned out, they should have.

It was impossible to look at his son without thinking about Madeline. And even though it made no rational sense, he placed a portion of the blame for her death on the child.

As he walked, the usual sounds of surf and nature combined, resembling a song from his childhood. How had it gone?

A moment later he realized he wasn't remembering the words, he was hearing them. When he turned back to the house, he saw Temperance, the baby in her arms, standing on the nursery balcony. The light from inside surrounded them in a way that was almost angelic.

Temperance looked down and saw him. She appeared surprised, but then she waved and motioned for him to come upstairs.

That was odd. Temperance was a devoted, hardworking servant, but she never initiated contact with him. Come to think of it, it was curious she was up so late with the baby.

He hurried into the house, his steps coming faster and faster until he bounded up the stairs two at a time.

Something was wrong.

The door burst open and Edward darted into the nursery. "What's the matter?"

Temperance continued swaying and patting the baby's back. "I do not know. He is a little warmer than usual. I think it is a fever, but I'm not positive. It could be nothing, but I thought you should know."

"Yes, of course." He reached out, as if he was going to touch the boy's head but then pulled back. "When will you know if it is cause for worry?"

"By morning. If the fever worsens, you should call for the doctor." She leaned her cheek against the baby's head. "Try not to worry. I will be with him all night."

Edward nodded, his brow furrowed. He was almost out the door when Temperance called out. "Sir? You should also know, I've chosen a name for him. Liam."

"A fine name. Thank you." He left, closing the door gently behind him.

Temperance pressed her lips against the baby's forehead. "Sweet Liam, your father does love you. He just has no idea how much yet."

For the next few hours, Temperance did not leave Liam's side. She put him down a few times, hoping he would be able to sleep, but each time he began fussing as soon as she walked away. And each time she picked him back up, she was sure he was warmer than the last time she had held him.

It was well after one o'clock a.m. when Edward came back to the nursery.

"I couldn't sleep," he said. "How is he?"

"He feels warmer."

This time, when Edward reached out, he touched the silky hair on his son's head and frowned. "I'll get the doctor."

"Not yet. Sir, I would like to try something. A remedy my mother used. I expect you have the necessary ingredients in the kitchen."

"Tell me what to get."

She shook her head. "There are certain measurements, and then it must be boiled. It is better if I do it."

"Are you making a tea?"

"No, a poultice. Here." Before he could refuse, Temperance held out the baby. "You stay here with Liam."

She could see he was uncomfortable as he shifted his son awkwardly in his arms, but he was also a bit awestruck. Temperance smiled and wiped a bit of drool from Liam's chin. "Mother always said your life changes in the moment you first hold your child. You two get acquainted. I'll be back as soon as possible."

Holding her skirts up out of the way, Temperance scurried down the stairs and to the kitchen. Despite her worry for Liam's safety, she couldn't help but wonder if this was another one of those times when God's will would be accomplished in a quite unexpected way.

There was a miracle in his arms.

Edward gazed down at the little boy, his son, and felt as though his heart might burst from his chest. Suddenly, all his reasons for keeping his distance were meaningless.

"I am so sorry." He looked down at the little red face and spoke his heart. "I wasted so much time. I was hurt, and I blamed you. But none of it was your fault. None of it."

He walked from one end of the room to the other, trying to imitate the gentle bouncing motion he'd seen Temperance using. Liam was still fussing, but he was also looking up into his father's face. Edward wanted to think he recognized him, although it was unlikely. It made no difference. What mattered was that his son get better.

"I promise to be a good father to you. No matter what."

Feet pounded on the stairs and Temperance burst into the nursery in a most unladylike way. "I have it."

As she drew closer, Edward noticed an unpleasant odor. "Is that the poultice I smell?"

"Yes."

"It is offensive."

Temperance smiled. "Good! That means I made it correctly."

Edward was not at all sure he wanted it going anywhere near his son, but he'd trusted Temperance this far. She wanted to help Liam as much as he did.

While Edward held the boy, she peeled back the blanket and put the poultice on his chest, beneath his nightdress. Then she made sure the blanket was tightly rewrapped to hold it in place.

"What do we do now?" Edward asked.

"We wait."

They took turns holding the baby. To pass the time, they shared stories of their families. She told him about her parents and two brothers. He told her about jokes he played on his brother while they were young. And then he surprised himself by telling her about Madeline.

Eventually, they both fell silent. Temperance was holding Liam. As she had many times over the hours, she put her lips against his forehead.

"Edward," she said, her tone excited, "I believe his fever has broken."

He stroked Liam's head. It was covered in a fine sheen of sweat and was noticeably cooler. "Thank the Lord in heaven."

Temperance sighed with relief. "He holds us in His hands."

He did indeed. It had been a long, sleepless, nerve-wracking night, but Edward felt more blessed than ever.

Chapter 8

After the fear of losing his son to illness, Edward felt as if he were a new man, embracing life to the fullest. He no longer kept to himself, going for solitary walks at night. Instead, he chose to stroll during the day with Liam and Temperance. In the evenings after supper, Edward and Temperance had taken to playing chess. On their walks and during their games they learned more about each other, laughing or crying, depending on the story being shared. At the end of two months, Edward could avoid the truth no longer: he had fallen in love with Temperance Simms. The question remained, what was to be done about it?

"What do you want to do about it?" Jonathan asked one day.

They were walking through the tobacco-processing building, checking on equipment and making sure the workers were keeping up with production.

"I want to marry her," Edward said.

"Then that is what you should do."

"That is an easy thing to say, little brother. But it is more complicated than that. She is a slave."

"Yes, and you own her." Jonathan chucked him in the ribs with his elbow. "It seems that would make the whole thing even easier."

Perhaps Jonathan had a point. But there was the matter of what people would say and how gossip would spread.

"I know what you're thinking," Jonathan said. "You're worried about social propriety, aren't you?"

Edward did not answer, which was all the answer his brother needed.

"Exactly as I thought. You know how I feel about social propriety."

"I know how you feel about almost everything," Edward said.

"Then I do not need to say it. But let me say this. You did the socially accepted thing when you married Madeline, and you were miserable. Taking Temperance as your wife might be scandalous, but if the last few months are any indication, it will make you happy."

Jonathan was right. Edward decided then not to make any more excuses. He would talk to Temperance that very night and share his intentions. If all went well, they could be visiting the town preacher before the week was over.

That night, Temperance went to the kitchen to take her evening meal with the other servants, just as she always did. But before she could sit down, Ami waved her away.

"Mr. Aldridge told us to send you to the big dining room."

Temperance did not understand. "Whatever for?"

"I expect he wants to share a meal with you," Chinaza said, batting her eyelashes flirtatiously.

The others at the table began to giggle. "You're all so funny," Temperance said. "He most likely wants to discuss Liam."

On her way to the dining room, she took slow, deep breaths. Her idea would have been a good one, except they always talked about Liam. They'd spoken of him earlier that day. Then what was this about? Had she done something wrong? Had he changed his mind about keeping her? She would find out soon enough.

He was sitting at the table when she arrived, but he jumped up as soon as he saw her. "Temperance. Hello."

"Hello, sir."

"You do not need to call me sir anymore."

"All right," she said slowly. "Mr. Aldridge, I—"

"Edward," he interrupted. "Please, call me Edward."

She had thought of him as Edward since the day he saved her, but she had never used his name to his face. Rather than give it a try, she just nodded.

He pulled out a chair at the table. "Have a seat."

An uneasy feeling went through her. None of this made sense. "Sir. . .Edward. I do not understand. What is this about?"

His smile fell away. "Dinner. I want to have dinner with you."

He ate dinner alone every night, so it was no surprise he would be lonely. Still. . . "Is that all?"

"I want to talk. About my feelings." He looked away as if weighing his next words carefully. "I want to talk about my feelings for you."

Temperance opened her mouth, but no words came out. He had feelings. For her. The idea was both thrilling and terrifying.

Edward stepped up to her and took one of her hands in both of his. "You have changed my life, Temperance. You reunited me with my son and brought joy back to this house."

"You saved my life. Twice." She looked into his eyes, searching for any possible deception but found none.

"I know it may seem sudden, but I love you, Temperance."

A shocked sob tore from her lungs. "But I'm a slave."

Edward shook his head sharply. "No. You're a woman. A beautiful woman who has opened her heart to my son. And, I hope, to me."

There was no stopping the tears that spilled from her eyes. For the first time she reached out and touched him of her own volition, cupping his cheek with her palm. The simple act made her cry even more.

"Edward," she said between sobs, "I love you."

He put his hand behind her neck, his fingers weaving into her hair, and bent down to kiss her. When their lips parted, he looked into her eyes, their faces just inches apart.

"Will you be my wife?"

Temperance laughed. She cried. And then she answered him in the only way she could.

With another kiss.

It was one week later when they took a family trip to see the pastor. With Jonathan as their witness and Liam the only guest, Temperance and Edward were joined in holy matrimony. The bride wore a dress of pale green silk that she had found while poking around the house. Edward said it wasn't right that she should wear not just a hand-me-down as a wedding dress but one that had belonged to the groom's late first wife. Temperance had waved away his concerns, saying there was no reason to waste perfectly good clothing and, in any case, they were new to her.

"Would it be all right if we walk through town?" she asked.

"Of course." Edward held Liam in one arm and crooked his other for Temperance to hold on to. "Is there something in particular you hope to find?"

"A dry goods store. I would like to purchase fabric."

Edward nodded. "Ah, for that new dress I promised you."

"No," Temperance said with a laugh. "To make clothes for Liam. And perhaps a matching shirt for you."

Jonathan snorted. Edward shot a cross look at him but couldn't keep from laughing. "Not even your barbs can dull my spirits today."

They had almost reached their destination when a familiar voice stopped them in their tracks.

"If it isn't the venerable Mr. Aldridge." Simon Exley crossed the street in their direction.

Temperance's legs began to shake and she feared they might give way from under her. Edward and Jonathan closed ranks so that she was almost completely blocked.

"Who might that be cowering behind you?" The monster's gaze was locked onto her. Then his head tilted and his eyes narrowed in recognition. "Poison Ivy. You certainly have changed."

"She is my wife," Edward said evenly, "and you will address her as Mrs. Aldridge and give her the respect she deserves."

At the mention of the word *wife*, Exley ceased to find humor in the situation. Anger rearranged his features and his eyes reflected nothing but darkness.

"You deceived me," he spat at Edward.

"He did nothing of the kind," Jonathan spoke up. "She really is his wife. And if you do not show her respect, I may introduce you to my fists."

Jonathan may as well have been a fly for all the attention Exley paid him. His eyes never left Edward.

"You misrepresented your intentions."

"Did I?" Edward paused as if thinking then continued. "It occurred to me that to beat a person into a bloody pulp by way of discipline is ignorant and barbaric. Neither of which are traits I prefer to be associated with."

"You are weak." Exley stabbed his finger in Edward's chest. "If I had known, I would never have sold her to you."

Edward stepped forward, blocking Temperance so much that she had to lean to one side to see between him and Jonathan. "That is precisely why you did not know. You are so driven by your need to control others, you could not recognize that we were controlling you. Now tell me. Which one of us is weak?"

By that time, a crowd had gathered, collecting news to share with whomever they came in contact with, and no doubt hoping to see a fight.

"This is not over." Exley lowered his voice to keep the spectators from overhearing. "I'll show you just who's weak. And Poison Ivy will learn the power of a real man."

Exley stalked away and the crowd dispersed.

Temperance put her hand on Edward's back. "He said that it's not over. What does that mean?"

"There is nothing to worry about. You are safe with me. Always."

More than anything, Temperance wanted to do as he said, but how could she keep herself from worrying? She knew that her husband would protect his family, with his life if necessary. But Temperance was not willing to let it go that far.

After the unexpected run-in with Exley, none of them had the desire to shop, so they went straight home. Edward and Jonathan did their best to raise her spirits, but Temperance was beyond cheering up. It wasn't until they were back home that she felt truly safe. It was made even better when Liam attempted to kiss her. Anyone else would say it was simply his open mouth making drooly, toothless contact with her chin, but Temperance was positive he meant it to be a kiss.

She had put Liam down in his crib and was standing on the nursery balcony when an arm slipped around her waist. Temperance let her head fall back against his chest and sighed. "Hello, husband."

"Hello, Ivy."

Her blood turned to ice in her veins. She tried to struggle, but Exley was too strong.

"I suggest you calm down before you wake the brat." His voice rasped in her ear as the point of a blade pressed against the side of her throat.

She stopped fighting. "I will do whatever you say as long as you don't hurt my baby."

He forced her from the room and down the stairs.

The house was oddly quiet. "Where is my husband?"

Exley laughed as he pushed her ahead of him. "It is quite a fantasy world you have here. Your husband, your baby, your dress, your house. It all belonged to another woman. If not for her untimely demise, your devoted husband would never have looked at you twice."

Temperance pushed down the urge to shout, to cry, to run. It was important that she stay calm. "What do you want?"

"You truly are dim." They had come to the study, and Exley pushed her roughly inside. "I want what is rightfully mine. I intend to take what you refused to give me and then dispose of you. Just as I disposed of your husband."

The room spun and Temperance fought to keep control. "You're lying. Edward is not dead."

"Perhaps he is. Perhaps he is not. Either way, he will not be coming to your rescue."

As Exley forced her farther into the room, Temperance carefully took control with a little side step here and there, until she was just in front of the sideboard. Exley had let go of her, but he was still raving, waving the knife in her direction, slashing through the air to emphasize his words. Temperance thought back to their earlier run-in with Exley. She needed to throw him off the way Edward had.

When he paused to take a breath, Temperance seized the opportunity.

"You never really owned me, you know."

He stopped moving and glared at her. "I bought you. In the same way I would buy a cow or a mule. You are property. Nothing more."

Temperance shook her head. "I never called you master. Not once. Because you didn't deserve the respect of that title. Do you want to know what I did call you?"

"No. I don't care."

"I will tell you anyway." As she spoke, she slowly reached behind her with one hand, feeling for one of the tall-necked decanters. "I called you 'the monster.' Because that's what you are. A small, weak, monster of a man."

With an angry bellow, he threw the knife across the room and rushed at Temperance, his hands reaching for her throat.

With all her might she swung the decanter around and crashed it soundly against his head. The impact knocked them both down. Exley landed on his back, rolling and moaning with one hand pressed against the side of his head. Temperance landed face-down on the floor. As she pushed herself up, she saw the knife only a few feet away. She reached for it, but Exley managed to grab her ankle and pull her away. She kicked out with her free foot and caught something with the heel of her shoe. The globe teetered on its stand and the whole thing fell on top of Exley. As he scrambled to get out from under it, he knocked over the table with the chess set, sending pieces bouncing and rolling across the floor. The heavy board barely missed falling on Temperance's head. She once more tried to get to her feet, but Exley grabbed a fire poker from the hearth and ran at her with it high over his head. Temperance grabbed the chess board and held it up like a shield. As she steeled herself for the impact, Exley's foot hit one of the pawns, knocking him off balance. He tried to stay upright but instead fell forward, his head making direct contact with the block of marble Temperance was holding, knocking her on her back.

Temperance raised her head and looked down. The chess board was flat against her stomach, and Exley—who appeared to be unconscious—was lying with his head on top of the board.

A noise came from the doorway. Edward stood, his clothes torn and dirty, blood matting the hair on one side of his head, looking at his wife as if seeing her for the first time.

"Well," he said slowly, "I would call that checkmate."

Temperance pulled herself out from under Exley's head and hurried over to Edward. "Never underestimate the power of a pawn." She threw her arms around his neck and kissed him. "He told me you were dead."

"You didn't believe him, did you?"

"Not for a second."

Edward touched his bloody hair. "I do have an enormous headache." He looked around the study. "We will tend to this mess tomorrow."

Temperance pointed at Exley. "What about him?"

"I shall bind him securely until the constable arrives."

"Good idea."

Edward tightened his hold on Temperance. "I promise you, my dear wife, you are safe."

Temperance melted against him as waves of gratitude washed over her. She'd prayed for a new life and now, held in the hand of God and the embrace of her husband, she had one.

She was safe. She was free. She was loved.

Jennifer AlLee believes the most important thing a woman can do is discover her identity in God—a theme that carries throughout her stories. She's a member of American Christian Fiction Writers and RWA's Faith, Hope and Love Chapter. When she's not spinning tales, she enjoys board games with friends, movies, and breaking into song for no particular reason. Jennifer lives with her family in the grace-filled city of Las Vegas, Nevada. Please visit her at www.jenniferallee.com.

His Indentured Bride

by Angela Breidenbach

Acknowledgments:

In huge appreciation to Jason Sherman, filmmaker of *The King's Highway*, for allowing me access to screen his film about the history of the King's Highway and Philadelphia history prior to its distribution and release. His painstaking research added beautiful setting details and historic moments. For more behind-the-scenes to the making of this story and to view *The King's Highway*, I strongly suggest getting a copy of the DVD and watching it with your family before much of our country's history is lost.

Reader tip: Maire is pronounced MY-ree, with a slight trill on the *r* for authenticity.

Chapter 1

Ayr, Scotland
May 1773

Maire, I'll send for ye as soon as I can." The noise of the market, the braying donkey, the fishmonger chasing away skinny, howling cats, faded into nonexistence under the waterfall of silent tears he'd cost her.

"No! No, ye cannae go and leave me! We were to go to America together after the weddin'."

"John McGowan cannae afford two of us at once. But he will bring ye next, and I'll be there to help him." Kirk curled his sweetheart into his arms. One week more and they'd have married. The banns read and only the ceremony left. But he couldn't stay with no means of support from already overtaxed, over-divided family lands stretched to feed too many. He had to take this opportunity. The vessel wouldn't wait to sail for a poor man's wedding any more than the sea would agree to hold the storms at bay.

"Da will ne'er allow me to come to ye alone." Tears coursed down her face as she grasped his collar, tightening her knuckles into the tweed. "No' like this. There's yet another way."

"There's nothin' for our future here, love. Nothin'." He pressed her head to his heart. "I dinnae want this, but there's no way 'round it, Maire, and ye know it well."

"But as a slave!"

"Indenture." He corrected her. "Only two years, and John 'tis a good man from Ayr. When I leave John's service, he'll fit me with two new suits of clothes, a year's rations, and I'll have learned a new trade." How could he convince her his childhood friend's offer opened a prospect they couldn't pass up? "All I ken is farmin' in a place I cannae farm. There's no land left. Should I feed my family weeds pulled from the unkempt roads?" Many already supplemented the little they had this way to fill their bairns' bellies. Kirk held back a grimace. Within the next few years they'd all be down to mud in their stew pots. "I'll learn to farm more than potatoes and oats and be able to run all the aspects of a gristmill. Maire, what would ye have me do?"

Her tears still wet on her face, she brushed them off and stepped back with a flash in her eyes. "We're all but married and ye cannae wait to leave me, Kirk Lachlan." She dropped her chin a moment, breaking eye contact. As she lifted it, she pointed at the dock where the small boat waited in the distance to take him to the larger port. "Then go. I'll ne'er beg a man again. I have me pride." She turned her face away from him, tightening her lips, her arm straight as the wooden road sign they'd passed pointing toward town. People teeming all around them, gawking at the lovers' quarrel, yet she seemed alone and small in the chaos with her dark, beribboned hair dancing in the spring breeze.

"Maire—" He moved to touch her ivory face.

She jerked out of his reach, stiff as the cliffs along the coast. "Ye've made yer decision. 'Tis yer right as head of the family. Ye'll have a full belly. Won't it be a lonely, cold bed ye lie in without a wife to warm ye as what food ye swallow curdles?" Her lips and cheeks, normally rosy, paled. "Go, then, ye've made me a hollow existence. Betrothed, but no' married." She closed her eyes to him, to their lost future.

He caught her hand. "Maire, me lovely lass." He tugged her close but not for so long as to raise gossip against her virtue. Forehead to forehead, he spoke of the future he saw. "I'll send for ye as soon as I can find a safe passage. Ye have me word. I'll not leave ye bound, but ne'er touched." He tipped her chin up with the tips of his fingers, urging her to meet his gaze with her gray-green eyes. "Maire, look on me, lass. It takes all me strength to do this as it tis." He said her name with all the longing of a man already heartsick for home. "Maire."

She raised her face, steeped in misery, to his. Tears slid slowly past lips he longed to kiss.

"Ye have me heart as I have yers. Trust me now to do what is best and right as God means a man to do for his family." He cupped her face, using his thumbs to whisk away her tears. "I've taken me betrothal oath, and none other shall have ye. But I would have a life for us and our future bairns. Would that I could do so here."

Kirk guided her attention to the raggedly dressed crowd, the skinny children, and the scant or vacant food stalls. "How, love, do you see our bairns? Starvin' and barefooted as the likes of these? Or full-bellied and growin' like the tall trees they say build strong cabins on land a man can own himself?"

Slowly, she nodded. "I hear ye. I do. But me heart is breakin' hard like the last egg on a cold winter night. What if you—"

He hushed the words before they spilled from her lips. He drew her to the side of a stall, out of view, and held his betrothed as close as he dared. A moment to last a year. "I will send for ye as soon as I can provide an indenture for ye. I made a promise in front of our families and the church. Ye'll be with me within the year." He kissed her soundly, breathing in the scent of her, the feel of her in his arms, the hope of what would come. "Do ye know I'll do it?"

She studied his face and gave him a small nod. "I know ye will, Kirk Lachlan. But I dinnae know if me father will let me come to ye in such a manner—or if ye'll survive."

"I'll survive, bonnie lass, for I have ye to love."

June 1774

Seamus Greer held a couple of letters tied with twine, his head bent as he removed his coat and then hung it on a peg by the door. "More ramblin' from the lad for ye, daughter." As he plunked them on the worn wooden table, he said, "I've had a wee visit this morn with the reverend."

Maire set aside the straw broom. "What could ye be needin' that for, Da?" She angled her head and tucked errant strands back under her white ruffled dust cap. With an impish grin she asked, "Have ye been secretly sinnin', then?"

"Aye, ye've uncovered the truth of it." He grinned back at her. "I spend me nights raisin' the pints instead o' the prayers." He chuckled at his own jest. He hadn't missed a day of worship in decades except for the day Maire entered the world squalling for her place in it, he said. A moment less than the twinkle of a star, then her father sobered. "The year is up." His voice gentled. "It's best ye dinnae waste yourself any longer waitin' on that boy." He tapped the packet. "He's no' found a way for ye to go or comin' home. 'Tis time to free ye to get on with life, become a real wife and mum. This is no' the life I want for ye, a spinster in a crofter's hut."

The breath caught in her chest, her heart slamming against lungs and ribs. "No! I'm able to make up me own mind." She focused on controlled breathing. "I will stand by me promise." Would she have to defy her father for her husband's sake? "Da, the banns were read, we vowed to be wed, regardless of the day. Would ye have me break that vow and be disgraced in front of God and country?"

"Maire, ye've been abandoned before the marriage was sanctified. Ye'll no' be held to—"

She stepped backward as if he'd taken the horsewhip to her. "Da, no!"

His wrinkled face softened, but he offered calm consolation that smacked the truth the way she whacked dirt out of the small rug in the yard. "There's no disgrace on your part, and ye could find a man who willnae abandon his bride for siftin' chaff in the wind."

Emotion wouldn't phase him. She'd watched many a woman dissolve into tears to get their way. Manipulation wasn't her manner, though. His announcement may have drawn a shocked reaction, but Maire studied people. She studied the most successful in the community. They reasoned through a problem and stood by their convictions. The question wasn't whether she could break the betrothal. The question was deeper, at soul level. Would she keep her word? Da needed to know she loved Kirk and her promise to be his wife came from profound conviction. If she gave up that promise, to the man she loved, how would any vow she made to another man have value? How would she?

"Twenty is young yet. Young enough, and beautiful like your mother, to still marry well. Ye have her sparklin' eyes like the moss in summer."

"I'll no' marry another. Leave it alone, will ye?" Maire picked up the packet, untied the string, and opened an unusually fat envelope. "Da, do ye see this?" She held out the paperwork. "He made good on his word. I told ye he would."

Her father took the documents and painstakingly read the indenture agreement, stopping near the end of the page. "How does this mean he's takin' ye to wife?" He pointed to the last few lines and watched her face closely. "What if John McGowan sells your contract?"

She craned to see the terms. Then looked at the note included in the envelope. "Ah, see?" She reached over his shoulder to point at the flowery script. "This is a standard covenant for three years, no' the four we'd expected I'd have to sign. This is good, Da! John McGowan has said he means for Kirk to buy out my contract as soon as he's able. His service will be done a year after my arrival. Then what earnings he makes will go toward repaying this agreement." Maire went to the cupboard and withdrew a quill pen and ink pot. " 'Tis but a loan in exchange for work." She sat at the table, poised to sign.

"That's three more years ye'll be waitin'. There are good men here yet." Her father placed a hand on her shoulder. "Maire, lassie, sleep on it. Payin' back a man is no easy road. For a woman—" He wiped a hand across his face as if the strain would disappear like mud on a cloth.

"Ye've managed it yourself, Da. Why would ye think the less of me to be able to do the same?"

"I don't think less of ye, Maire. I'm your father. How am I to protect ye as an unmarried woman across the ocean? All that time plus the journey. It's a long road to give yourself."

"Less if Kirk pays it ahead as he means to, Da." She looked up. "But given that John McGowan is his friend, wouldnae it be possible to wed when I arrive? Then ye've naught to fash about."

"Aye, anythin' is possible, but ye fail to see this is a business transaction. Business will come first, as it tends to do." He sighed. "Think careful, lass, afore ye regret a rash decision. The future tends toward the unexpected."

"Unexpected can also mean blessings, Da." Maire covered his hand with hers. She gave her father a reassuring smile. " 'Twas me da who taught me to honor me word. I willnae fail him or the man I mean to marry."

He nodded. "The Good Lord says let your yes be yes and your no be no." He dropped his hand and sank into the creaky wooden chair near her. "Some days that's harder than others."

"Da, I love ye. But me yes is yes."

"If 'tis your wish, I'll see ye through it. Ye'll have a home here as long as I draw breath, child." He patted her hand and then held it with a gentle squeeze. "But I wish for ye a family of your own."

Maire leaned in and hugged her father and then signed the document with him as her witness. He blinked hard, but made his mark. Oh, the pain it must cost him! Her mother and two brothers long gone and buried. Her sister's family moved to Glasgow for work since there was no more land to divide. Her own departure would leave him with only one of her brothers, who would inherit the last of the small parcel they worked together. What would happen when Sean's sons grew into men?

Maire couldn't look her father in the eyes just yet. She couldn't see his strength falter and still go through with this terrifying plan. But she couldn't give up hope that her betrothal would become a real marriage to the man she loved. A marriage the likes of her parents' deep, satisfying partnership.

She whispered, "Da, I want what ye had with Ma." But would she see him again this side of heaven?

He nodded, pressing his lips together until his beard and moustache closed and appeared as one. After a long gaze, he went outside.

Her heart squeezed so tight she could barely breathe. She never wanted to make as painful a choice again. Maire pressed Kirk's letters to her and then tucked them in a box with the stack she'd kept, one for almost all the weeks Kirk had been gone. Those he'd written aboard ship describing the terrible conditions, to those written on his half day off each week proclaiming the beauty of Pennsylvania and opportunity to come. But this last missive, with prearranged second-class passage to be paid on healthy arrival in Philadelphia and the indenture covenant, assured her of better accommodations than he had endured in steerage. She'd follow Kirk's directions and be in his arms as fast as the ship could sail. She read the last lines again.

I'll work alongside ye, truly a companion, until we wed and then thereafter until the Good Lord calls me to eternity. Come to me quickly!

All my love, Kirk

If only she could engrave those words across her heart. Her stomach flipped in circles. She'd be on a ship in a fortnight. How long after she arrived in Philadelphia until she'd be a bride? Kirk hadn't written details. Long letters, ink, and postage would be too costly as he saved to purchase her contract.

Chapter 2

Maire followed Kirk's preparation list, checking it constantly, for her journey to America. Her satchel held two full outfits, pockets that tied closed under her skirts for the coins she'd need during passage to purchase what little supplies she could, an extra-large hooded cloak to double as a blanket, eating utensils, canned lemons to ward off the rickets, and a large wheel of cheese wrapped well. She carried a small pillow fashioned by cutting a larger one down, wrapped it in another blanket, and tied it off with a knotted sheet. She'd have little space, but a cot.

Though her arms would be full, she left so much behind. Maire ran a hand over the tables and chairs, the dishes she'd stacked on the sideboard, and then folded back the quilt that lay at the foot of her father's bed. She wanted to take the feel and scent with her. How could she keep these precious moments and all those that had gone before safe in her heart? Would she forget the way her father read the Bible at night? The sound of his voice? Would she remember the color and scent of heather in bloom or the sound of the rain trickling down the thatched roof?

She had to go now before she changed her mind. "Da, I've a bit of food to pack and then off with us." She rushed to distribute what she could carry between the satchel and the bedroll so as not to delay their departure.

"No need to shout down the county, daughter, I know 'tis time." He moved to the door. "I'll be gettin' the horse and cart, then."

Her hands froze at the gruffness in his voice. "Thank ye kindly," she whispered and then continued her work wrapping up the oat cakes that would travel light though the pickled eggs would weigh her down a bit until she ate them. But Kirk had said rations were scarce on board. She left the kitchen area clean and set a plate of oat cakes on the table from the batch she made this morning. The last breakfast she'd ever make for Da. She'd added a bit of extra sugar on top to sweeten them so he'd remember the best batch she'd ever made.

Tears stung her eyes remembering her mother's admonition to always leave a sweet taste when departing. One never knew how long t'would be till ye met again. She'd meant word and deed. In this case, Maire's choice left a bitter taste. Her oat cakes a pittance offering. Maire set a small pot of honey beside the plate as her mother had done her last night on earth. It'd cost Maire dearly, but Da would know it meant she wanted no bitter words between them. *Lord, grant that we meet again afore that great day.*

The door creaked open, letting in the cool spring air. "Well, then." Da stood there with the morning sun at his back, a dark outline.

Would her children never meet him? "Couldnae ye come wi' me?" Maire clutched the back of the chair her father had made as a wedding gift for her mother.

He moved with heavy steps. Enfolding her in his arms, he said, "When a body gets so auld, he gets set in his ways." He stroked her hair. "I hate to see ye go, lass, but I ken ye must. E'en from the first, the midwife said ye'd make sure the whole world knew of ye." His breathing deepened and controlled as his embrace tightened. "There's no way of it for ye here. The Clearin' showed us that." His eyes dimmed. Their people had come from the Highlands a few generations back. Driven down in search of safety and peace. That the Clearings happened so recently, all Scots knew there'd be no going back to the old ways now. "Your man is speakin' true. The future is forward, not back." He looked her in the eye. "Ye ken ye're loved, dinnae ye?"

"Aye, Da." She turned her wet face up to kiss his cheek. "I do."

He touched the honey pot with a nod then went to the sideboard. With a hand on the family Bible, he said, "Tell your bairns of your people. I've written them all in over the years as me father and his father did." He gestured her over and put the book in her hands, covering them with his. "Write all the new ones. Tell of those gone afore. All the stories ye've heard since birth." He looked deeply into her eyes. "They'll ken who they be if they ken whence they come."

She hugged him all the tighter and muffled against his shoulder. "I promise."

He pushed her away but held her upper arms as he looked her over. "Me beauty of a daughter, your mother would be proud. Ye look just like her. I'll miss the reminder." His eyes misted and took on a distant glaze as if he communed with his wife and forefathers already.

"Da?"

He went to the chest at the foot of the bed and lifted out the Greer tartan finely woven with a background of blue, striped and crossed with red, white, and yellow. The *arisaid* her mother wore as a wedding cloak and would have worn over her dresses daily had the tartan not been outlawed.

"Go wi' me blessin', but ken ye cannae wear this until ye've left Scotland far behind." He rolled the woolen garment tightly and stuffed it deep into her bag. "Dinnae let them see it or they'll arrest ye. Keep to your plain clothes until ye ken 'tis safe."

"I dinnae ken what to say." The Greer tartan had long been hidden since the king had outlawed any clan colors and weapons. She'd only seen it late at night when her family gathered for stories around the fire. Stories of the heroes and stories of the old ways high up in the hills. "I'll be blessed to wear it on my wedding day." She smiled at her father. What had he been like as a dashing young man awaiting his bride nearly thirty years before? Would Kirk be so steady a husband?

"Wouldnae that be grand, lass? Wouldnae that be grand?" He tucked in the matching sash and pushed it deep down. "Gi' me ye other things and let's be off." He lifted the satchel and the bedroll, going quickly to the cart. His sadness weighing him down more than a heavy bag ever could.

Lord, please, I want me da to see me weddin' day. Consider Thy servant's request.

Chapter 3

Philadelphia, Pennsylvania,
July 1774

The vessel sailed into a calm harbor in the early morning hours, a full day after her expected arrival. After the first-class passengers disembarked, the crewmen hustled, nearly shoving Maire down to the landing into a crowded waiting area with the other indentured Scots, Europeans, and slaves for sale. Her feet judged each step wrong, as if the sea still rolled beneath her or the pier was built on floating barrels. Either way, Maire crept forward, carrying her belongings.

The Port of Philadelphia teemed with people, baggage, animals, and the awful smell of fish mixed with city life and unwashed passengers. She approached two men, one that managed her passage from Scotland. "Sir, where do I meet—"

"Over there, girl." The quartermaster pointed to a huddled line of men, women, and children who'd been aboard her ship. Nearly a hundred people, many ill from poor conditions below deck during the crossing, waited to be redeemed.

"But, sir, those people have no indenture or family to pay their debt. I have a redemptor." She showed her contract as she had on departure. "The good John McGowan from Ayr and now of Pennsylvania has promised to pay on my safe arrival. He's a millwright."

He squinted at the paper without looking at Maire and shoved it aside. "This is contingent on both your arrival and the redemptor's. If he isn't here to settle your passage by the time the last of these are gone, the company reserves the right to settle your debt. I'll have no other option but to find you another purchaser." He checked a name off his list against the payment receipt a wealthy merchant in a white wig and an intricately embroidered coat handed over. "That'll do, Mr. Pearson. Choose your servants from the group yonder. There are several healthy enough once you clean them up." He waved toward a group of ladies. "Those came with no redemptor assigned. Most are in the age range you like for your weavers. Perhaps one will make a good wife."

"What would this girl cost?" Mr. Pearson let his curious gaze grow too familiar. "She appears quite healthy, if a little underweight. Possibly quite beautiful once she's recovered from the travel and dressed appropriately."

Maire tugged the arisaid further forward, concealing more of her face. She ignored the man and locked her gaze on the warehouses that ran the length of the port. It seemed to go on forever into the city. There had to be an easier way than this to find travelers.

The quartermaster thumbed a gesture. "This one came second class. She has the airs to go with it, as well as the higher fees." He glowered at Maire. "I doubt you want a servant that can't listen in your service, sir. Perhaps she's addled." He pointed her again to the mishmash of bedraggled Europeans who, like her, sold themselves with the hopes of a short-term service in exchange for a better future. "Go to where I tell ya, girl!"

"She must be of high value to the person who arranged her passage." Pearson's blue eyes pierced Maire like he expected an answer. "Tell me, are you a courtesan, that you'd be given better accommodations?"

Maire colored and shook her head. "No." She swallowed her pride as panic ratcheted up the beat of her heart. The richly dressed man had not taken his eyes off her regardless of how bedraggled she appeared. She and the others had little bathing options since home but a rare bowl of seawater and the sliver of soap she'd brought. Did she appear wanton? She'd be better off waiting for Kirk and John McGowan away from rudeness the likes as that display. She found an uncomfortable perch on a rough bench. Her stomach grumbled. Her rations were long gone, and though she'd traveled in a cramped cabin with four others, there'd been no food provided as they slid into the harbor that day. The rolling motion hadn't stopped yet, either. But her empty belly sloshed as if still rocking on the waves.

Mr. Pearson walked all the way past the long, haphazard line of hopeful servants. He stopped in front of Maire. "Who is it you expect, girl?"

"Sir?" She held up a hand to block the glaring sun she couldn't escape. It flashed and winked off the water as much as it flaunted itself in the beauty of the blue summer sky. Though she'd been on deck a little each day, Maire and most of the travelers spent their time below deck. Her eyes had yet to adjust fully to the constancy of bright sunshine and the steamy humidity on the wharf.

"Who do you expect to claim your contract?"

"My betrothed and his friend."

"I see, a tale I've heard before. Tell me, what are your skills?" He lifted a brow as if he watched a curious beetle.

What business was it of his? "I'm of no concern to you, sir." She turned, adjusting on her perch to face away from him.

"As a potential purchaser, I beg to differ." His expression changed from curious to hard. "I asked for a list of your skills."

She stood, putting a hand on her hip. This boorish man would not intimidate her. "What business have ye with me, sir, that ye should be so liberal?"

He cracked a sardonic smile that held a hint of warning. "Are you unaware that if property is unclaimed it goes to auction?"

She folded her arms. "That's no' to do with me. I have me bags right here."

He threw back his head and laughed. The seagulls flew up, swirling in a cacophony. "You, young lady, are the unclaimed property."

"I am no' unclaimed and no' any man's property. Ye'll be best to hire ye servants and leave me be." The satisfaction on his face irked her.

"How unfortunate it appears you may be in a much more precarious situation than you realize. Indentured servants may not marry until their contracts are complete without their master's permission. Of course, some exceptions may occur." He shrugged as if talking to a halfwit. "But then, a child born while the mother is in the state of indenture adds to her service. Do you suppose the law means from birth, or when the child is weaned?"

"I'm sure ye're only trying to alarm me." She turned her shoulder to him further. "There's no such law."

"Ah, but there is. As a merchant in fine cloth, the law and how it affects those I employ matters dearly to me." His concerned expression was less than authentic. "Then, there could be any number of hazards delaying your true love, from a cart overturned to savages."

The woman next to Maire gasped.

"Unless they're somewhere in Philadelphia. I'm sure it's only a minor delay. Outside the township, well. . ." He added a *tsk, tsk, tsk* as if savagery were an everyday occurrence. "One never knows."

Kirk had not written of savages and such things. He also had not told her in his limited access to paper exactly where John McGowan's small holdings stood. Could they have been set upon by savages? She tried to hide the shiver, looked away from him, and scanned the masses scurrying to and fro, travelers arriving and departing in a constant stream. "They'll be here. I have faith."

He flipped open a fancy pocket watch. "And I have time. I believe I'll wait." He tipped his tricorn hat, a glint in his eye. "I've chosen the two I came for, but a servant such as yourself would be most beneficial in my business."

"Sir." The other woman tugged on his silk coat. "Sir, I'd be happy to work for ye to avoid those savages. I ain't got no redemptor yet."

He barely acknowledged her. "You do not have the qualifications my establishment requires."

"I may not be much to look at, but I work hard," she pled.

"A shame you're not much to look at, as you say. That is a requirement."

The woman looked stricken and pushed herself as far away from him as possible on the crowded dock and curled around her knees.

Maire's stomach stopped rolling, reared up, and smashed her insides as if the sea pounded surf against the sand. What could she say to soothe the poor woman's humiliation? "Sir, I'm already indentured. I've no need of what ye offer."

"Only if you're redeemed. Maire Greer, is it?"

That he knew her name without a proper greeting set her knees to shivering. " 'Tis so." She looked away again, watching for Kirk.

"Should you find yourself with a choice of being sent back across the sea—" He spread his hands as if offering the world at her feet. "It would be better to stay than starve during the crossing or in Scotland. Ayr, is it? I can offer you the ability to stay under my protection."

Her eyes widened. He knew her name and where she came from? Did being an indenture mean no privacy? She eyed the quartermaster with annoyance and then the sun as it dipped lower. "They'll be along." She put as much bravado into her words as she could. *Lord?*

"I'll go add my name to bid for unclaimed property, in case you need my help." He tipped his hat again, but his eyes roamed freely, inspecting her potential for an unnamed position.

The line of waiting servants diminished quickly while she still sat alone. Thankfully, the plain woman was sold to a family for help with their children and not to a questionable business. Her words looked to be prophetic, though. She'd work hard caring for that unruly passel. Maire sent a prayer heavenward for the woman as the sun slunk toward the horizon, hiding its brazen blaze behind a few cooling clouds.

What if the delay stretched past the day? Surely the authorities would give her a little time before deporting her? Or if something terrible happened to Kirk while she came across the ocean? Surely, they'd give her the choice of going home rather than selling her work to the highest bidder. This strange man, who seemed to have ulterior motives, might also twist a tale his direction. She glanced at the quartermaster. How did the law work here? Maire strained to see past the ships, conjuring the shores of Scotland, her father stoic and somber, holding his hat over his heart.

All too soon, only the exhausted servants waiting to leave with the merchant remained miserably hunkered against the warehouse wall behind her. He lounged on a nearby bench, watching.

The quartermaster signaled. "Come, Mr. Pearson. We'll finish this business so we can all be on our way." Though commotion went on all around, her ship's cargo and commerce reached completion.

Mr. Pearson rose, covered the short distance between them, and took Maire's elbow, raising her to her feet. "It appears I have won the bid." He called to the other girls. "Get her things with yours."

"Sir!" She tried to pull away from his manhandling, but he squeezed his fingers into her forearm, palm cupping her elbow, preventing escape and forcing her forward.

He smiled at her as if he'd won a card game. "An indenture here means you have no rights until you've earned out."

"I dinnae believe ye." Maire locked on the stranger's strong grip cutting off her circulation. "Let go!" She looked up into his hard face and planted her heels. "I'm no' goin' with ye. Let go!"

He jerked to a stop, leaned in, and growled, "What that means, girl, is that if you continue to struggle, I will show you how to obey." He twisted her wrist tighter. "Do we understand each other?"

"We do not!" People of all sorts scurried in all directions. Why didn't anyone come to her aid? Was America so rough that women could be dragged off without a thought? Was she considered so worthless?

"Maire!"

Kirk? Where had he called from on the busy dock? Then she saw him clamp on to Mr. Pearson's hand, yanking his fingers away. Maire stumbled at the sudden release, thudding to the ground. The welts from his fingerprints would bruise. She cradled her arm.

"Ye'll keep yourself from touchin' me woman, sir." Kirk moved in between the offender and Maire. He leaned down, slipped a hand around her waist, and helped her up. Moving his arm around her waist, he snapped, "Be on your way."

The man's face reddened, anger stiffening his shoulders. "I've already started the proceedings to purchase this woman." He pointed at Kirk's chest. "It is you that are in my way. Step aside, wretch."

Another man strode across the distance from the wooden landing, leaving the quartermaster shaking his head at the fuss as if it spoiled his day.

"I've already completed my transaction for Miss Greer's indenture as promised to the ship's captain, sir. John McGowan." He held out a hand. "The lady's contract is not available for auction."

Mr. Pearson pointedly ignored the offered handshake. "We shall see." He turned on a heel and made for an unlucky man watching from a distance.

Though her body ached from the long voyage and hours seated on hard wood waiting, relief surged through her veins. Her beloved held her close, with his childhood ally John McGowan beside him, protecting her. All would be well now.

Mr. Pearson collected his two servants, but as he walked past them, his eyes did not leave Maire's except to shoot a challenging glare at Kirk. The ugliness of revenge marred his otherwise striking appearance. A man so tall and well formed belied the innocence his handsome countenance portrayed. So different from Kirk's russet-haired, earthy masculinity.

Had any of his words held truth? "What can he do to us, Mr. McGowan?" She watched him stalk away.

"Nothing, Maire. By law ye both belong to me. Once ye've paid me back the passage, then ye'll belong to no one except yourselves." He bent to pick up her scattered belongings from where the girls had dropped them. "Kirk, help her along. She must be exhausted." He led them from the wharf to the waiting buggy, apologizing for her wait. "The mill's waterwheel cracked a bucket. We'd been repairing it when word came the ship finally arrived a day late."

"We had a day of no wind in the crossing," Maire explained. "I thank ye for me safety today and for bringin' me to Kirk."

"We're glad you arrived safely." He added, "My wife, Abigail, is anxious for a woman's company. She's also delighted to have help with our bairn due in a few months' time." He slid her bags onto the carriage boot. "Let's get on our way. We have to fix that broken waterwheel or lose another day's income. The tax man comes calling either way."

The men shared a hamper of bread, cheese, and cider. To her delight, Kirk lifted out a cloth filled with strawberries. "John's wife thought you'd like a few after the journey. We have a small garden in the back of the house."

"Tell me about it, please, everything." She bit into a sweet, juicy berry. The men laughed at her sigh of pleasure.

"Abigail won a prize last year at the fair with her strawberries." John's chest puffed out a tad. "With your beau here, we've added on to the mill, making it able to take larger orders. He's good with the mechanics."

Kirk described their new home as expansive land covered in trees as far as the eye could see, except fields. Each year they cleared more acreage for planting. "You'll have a room, as the house has two stories. No thatching, Maire, but a wood shingle roof with a large courtyard between the house and barn. And John and Abigail have their own well. No waiting in line for a bucket of water. The mill we finished updating not long after I arrived." He and John had a companionable manner.

Maire loved the sense of accomplishment written all over Kirk's body. The confidence impressed her. No more a strapping lad, but a strong man nearing twenty and one who had done great things since she'd last seen him. His shoulders and arms had filled out as well. "It's already working! How wonderful."

"John set the mill back a distance from the house so the noise wouldn't be bothersome." Kirk described the winding Pennypack Creek and the various grains the neighbors brought to grind. "They're a hardworking lot, mostly Scots and Germans who've emigrated as we did."

Maire ate a little at a time, allowing her food to settle, while staring at all the new sites of Philadelphia from the beautiful cobblestone to the fine shops they passed. The buildings all so finely carved they looked more like a palace should to her.

Kirk pointed out the church they'd attend on Sunday and Pennypack Park where they could stroll on their half day after services. The elegance of each building so grand compared to the thatched roof homes of Scotland's countryside. How were they so rich here if the king was so demanding? Women wore gowns the likes of which Maire had never seen in her village. What would it be like to have such fancy skirts?

Still, the malevolence in that man's eyes haunted Maire and sent a spasm through her. Would they really be safe under John's protection?

Chapter 4

September 1774

John and Abigail treated her kindly through the summer. As Abigail grew closer to her lying in, Maire worked to prepare the tiny layette and pack the clothing the new mother would need. She also prepared meals with her mistress, taking over more duties as the babe grew large. The time spent in gardening and kitchen duties with companionable chats built a strong friendship and pleasant living arrangements. The day before they'd loaded the trunk into the wagon. Mistress Abigail would spend her confinement with her womenfolk for her first birthing.

"Ye must be starved." Maire set a wooden trencher filled with last night's soup before Kirk. Then she set about peeling a pile of potatoes while Kirk ate the dinner he'd missed. Though they'd have a tasty shepherd's pie for supper, she needed to ferment yeast for several rounds of potato bread for the week. She'd send some with John when he went to visit his wife.

"Did Abigail settle in well at her mother's?"

Kirk smiled. "The woman is entirely enthused about her first grandchild. I think poor Abigail was missin' home for the peace and quiet afore the night 'twas done. Ye'd think her mother was a hummingbird the way the woman flits around."

Maire giggled. "I'd flutter around her meself in the same spot." She worked quickly, dicing vegetables while Kirk regaled her of the latest news he'd heard at the inn. "Will-nae John allow you to his table to keep himself company while Abigail is confined? Especially now ye're a freeman?"

Kirk winked at her. "Aye, he would. But then I'd miss me pretty lass. Friends or no', I work for the man, but I'm longin' for ye."

Maire gave him a quick smile. "'Tis good he could take you on as a hand."

"Once the crops are in and the grains are milled, I'll have more work come winter at the mill. John has sent for a new indenture to help with the fields."

She nodded. "'Tis a grand improvement. I'm proud of ye." They'd grind corn, wheat, rye, and oats as the community needed. With only a handful of mills, each stayed busy.

"I'll be able to remain in me room in the barn in exchange for other chores as we build up the mill. We'll save what we can together. 'Twill be a few months till the new indenture takes over work I do now."

"Such a blessin' we have in his friendship. I've ne'er heard of a better way to help one another as he's been able to do." Kind and just in his supervision, John McGowan had brought several others from Scotland. All worked to pay him back, helped him clear trees and then plant the fields, build the small gristmill, and then went on to build their own lives. None had been ill-treated. "Mayhap one day we could do the same for our people."

"What if that were possible sooner than later?" Kirk kept his eyes on his plate. "There's been news of further men enlisting in the cause for freedom." He glanced at her. "We'll need to choose, ye ken."

"Choose? Choose what?" Maire paused her work, hands over the bowl. "I dinnae ken what ye're sayin', Kirk."

"Look at this." He produced a newspaper. "At the Red Lyon today, I overheard some men speakin'. There's a group called the Continental Congress plannin' the coming independence, Maire." He chewed on the bread as she glanced through the news piece. "A little more than a year and I'll have your covenant pledge to me through marriage and no more through contract to another man, good or no'. A life of our own with little but love. If we stay in Pennsylvania, we must choose to which country to pledge our allegiance. They'll no' let us remain neutral in the comin' war."

"War?" The knife clattered to the table. She'd been to market and heard rumors. She'd eaten in the tavern as the news passed table to table while travelers took refreshments and waited for stagecoaches. The Intolerable Acts had the colonies squirming under the heel of the king's punishments, first closing Boston Harbor and then putting a British governor to rule who sent the accused across to England for trial. No one could attend to plead their cases, and so they were dropped without prosecution. But the king had always done as he pleased. Why should that change their plans?

"Kirk, ye're shakin' me to the bone. The king is the king. What have we to do with the machinations of politics and war?" Maire threw the potato chunks into the pot boiling over the fire, starchy water splashing over the sides. Steam hissed from the coals. "I dinnae come across the ocean to—"

"Ye must listen. Things are changin' and the colonies cannae continue unrepresented. Look at what happened in Scotland. They came in and changed our way of life." He gentled his voice at the thunder in her expression. "Where would ye have us run then? We've done that already and look where we are. Give me the chance to start our life." He moved to take her in his arms when a rapid thumping on the door jolted him away from Maire.

She brandished a wooden spoon and lowered her voice as she went to answer the unexpected guest. "Ye're no joinin' an army to fight for naught, I'm tellin' ye."

This late in the day, she'd be adding another mouth to the meal with precious little prepared to stretch. They all worked together to minimize expenses. John had extended himself to bring Maire over and buy seed for his fields. The same as he'd done for Kirk and three others before him. Each time he'd come out the better for it. After all, he had first come as an indentured servant himself. He understood the hardship. He was far from rich, but each man had more than earned their cost and lent to the greater growth of the farm and gristmill. Kirk and John planned to build a partnership farming and milling, maybe adding a second mill farther up the creek. With Kirk's training in the mill, both men were good at it and confident of the future.

They'd managed the first phase of the plan now that Kirk's indenture had been completed. The next phase came from bringing more Scottish indentures by pooling sweat, funds, and lands. More friends would come. Eventually they'd be able to rebuild their village, one person at a time. Perhaps her children would meet their grandda one day and their cousins.

Maire's heart pitter-pattered at the thought of seeing Da. They could manage it, if they all kept working together as well as they had through the summer. She had a dreamy smile on her face as she pulled the heavy door open.

Maire froze. Heat from the kitchen fire coupled with the sunny fall afternoon didn't stop the chill that raced up her back and down her arms raising tiny hairs like soldiers on guard duty at Fort Mifflin.

"Maire." Mr. Pearson gave a curt nod. "I've come to speak with your master."

Kirk moved to the door and pushed Maire behind him, blocking her body with his. "Ye'll no' be needin' to do that."

"What I'll not be needing is an ignorant servant's interference." He stood his ground.

"I'm no servant, sir. I am a freeman like yourself." Kirk stood his ground as well.

"I highly doubt that, freeman or not." Mr. Pearson smirked. "Maire, I'm quite sure it's your duty to announce visitors to the master of the house, regardless of this loitering freeman." He never took his eyes off Kirk's face. "Shall we see what happens if you don't fulfill your duties?"

Kirk's expression darkened, but he didn't move aside. "Maire, fetch John, if you please." He crossed his arms, blocking the entrance. "Go on now." He motioned with his head. "He'll be no' bent by the likes o' this man."

Maire's skirt flared as she spun and marched from the kitchen muttering a prayer. "Lord, what have I done to gain such attention? Consider your servant kindly."

Kirk returned from assisting John in the mill after what seemed like hours. They went on working while Pearson discussed the temptations of independence. But it'd given Kirk the chance to listen to the man make his case while weaving in the glories and spoils of war and the future promises of the fledgling nation that would default and crawl back to the king. Pearson seemed focused on enticing John with the riches the British would pay for his service while hammering at the fact he knew of his debt. Had he hired someone or done the inquiring himself?

Kirk didn't like what he heard one bit. Every now and then he locked eyes with John to show his disapproval. But the temptation existed. Should the finances teeter, he had every reason to expect Pearson would swoop in and snatch up Maire. Of that he was certain. In the space of that hour, while Kirk fed the hopper wheat from a customer, Mr. Pearson had offered to purchase Maire at least three times to "ease the McGowan family burden." His tone had wavered on the edge of polite as he made his case. The McGowans still owed a loan on seed. All too vulnerable a spot with a vulture hovering on the fence post watching a new calf fatten for the feast.

"Mr. Pearson says he was asked to approach John for the British supply line." Kirk entered the kitchen in a nasty mood. "We need to watch that man. He's conniving, but I cannae see what he's plannin'."

"He's no' a good sort." Maire set the rolling pin aside. "What did John say?"

"That ye're stayin' right put. He said he needs ye to help his wife when she returns from her mother's with the wee laddie." Kirk hugged Maire. "I cannae wait to one day have a wee laddie of our own."

"I cannae wait to see their new babe. His da is so proud." She grinned, a bit of dreamy hope in her eyes. "I'm relieved he dinnae sell me. That Pearson man scares the devil out of me."

"I told ye John 'tis a good friend. He's no' lettin' a cur such as that take ye away from me." Unless there wasn't enough harvest to pay off the spring debt. Kirk knew there'd be enough. He visited the fields daily. There'd be nothing to worry about.

But to gain Maire's freedom sooner, he'd work longer hours and make sure the oats and barley came in on time. He'd forgo his half-day rest to supervise the milling and get the product to market ahead of the competition—for the highest prices before other farmers brought in their goods. Quite possibly his extra efforts would help him avoid the need to enlist on the American side for the promised enticements he'd learned of in the last hour. Five dollars a day sounded good after pennies in a week. He and Maire would make the very best of the situation, marry, and support the bid for independence together, another way. Possibly providing food and supplies to the troops. But so much depended on elements not all in his control—like locusts, or a glut of grain on the market, or if the waterwheel broke down again and customers moved their business to the mill downstream. All of which had happened at one point or another the last few years.

"Why such a worry on your brow, then?" She smoothed the furrows in his forehead until he relaxed his expression. Her luminous eyes seeking answers and offering encouragement. Eyes that shimmered with trust, enough trust she'd followed him halfway across the world.

He had to protect her. He alone had put her in this precarious situation. Kirk took hold of her fingers, bringing them to his lips, and kissed the tips lightly. "There's no worry, lass. A bit o' hardworkin' days ahead." He grinned at her. "I'll be needin' that good Scottish sustenance from your hands to keep my strength these next few weeks."

"Aye, love, I'll feed ye well." She patted his flat stomach. "Ye'll be fatter than the hog." She twirled away, chuckling over her shoulder.

He followed her and caught her hand again. "Maire, I've been thinkin' hard."

"And when are ye no' thinkin'?" She handed him a bowl of berries.

"They dinnae just speak of the crops and contracts." He watched her face and measured his words. "There's war comin' and soon. I heard them say men who serve will be paid a daily wage and awarded land, much land to start a homestead. Some along excellent creeks with good water flow for a mill."

"That's no' to do with us." She swept the back of her wrist against her forehead.

"I ken the Pearson man's intent with John." He laced his fingers with hers. "He meant to goad John to greed. Then if he joined, he'd be gone from the farm and his business while they faltered." He left the inference hanging.

"A wily snake, that awful man." Maire crinkled her nose. "John saw through the poison? He has a family now. This is no time to traipse off to play soldier."

Kirk inclined his head. "He did." He lifted his gaze, head still bowed. "I've been thinkin' I could join the campaign for freedom if the crops don't pay out enough." The silence stretched a moment while his blood beat in his ears.

"Ye say there's nothin' to worry about?" She tugged her hand back, wrapping her arms around her waist. "How can there no' be worry when you're willin' to risk yer life for another man's war?"

"Maire, lass, this is no' another man's war. This is the same king what took all we had in Scotland. The same king who taxes so deeply our own master bows under the weight of it, and it's no' a bow of fealty. 'Tis a forced bow of burden. Should we stay or should we go, we bow low with broken backs." He let her have the space she needed to process his words. He watched the expression on her face shift from thunderous to helpless. "The news the Pearson man brought with him changes our plans."

"Why?"

"We need to marry now to protect you."

"How cruel of you to dangle our weddin' in front of me. What happens should I bear a child? My indenture gets extended for the lost time and the money it takes to care for me. That's another mouth to feed for John at a time things are so tight." She stomped to the table. "I came across the sea to build a life and a family with you. When I do that, I dinnae want me days split between loyalties as ye say the colonies are doin'." Maire plopped a hand on her hip. "You're a freeman. Go fetch work, then. One more year and we've done what we set out to do. Why risk that when we're so close? Why risk our future? One child leads to another and another. Would you have me indentured for so long?"

"No, Maire. No. I hadnae thought of it that way." He'd work himself to the bone to claim the woman he loved. "I only want to be sure no man can take ye from me." He'd free her or die trying.

"Aye, I ken we cannae wed till we're free. I can no put a child willingly into servitude and I cannae serve another and be your wife." She rolled the pie dough across her hand then slapped it into the clay dish. "But we cannae wed if you're dead!"

"Heed me, lass. I would have you with me, and have a home and land for our bairns. Without that, how am I to provide?" Without her, how would it matter?

"We'll find a way." She lifted flour-covered hands, gesturing around the room. "I'm here in America. We found a way to get this far. Ye'll surely find a better choice."

"This is the most sure choice next to the powers solving it peacefully." He caught her around the waist, settling her busy, irritated movements. "This is the way, Maire, should the crops fail."

"Sure? No, 'tis only sure ye'll lose your life and then what?" She turned her back on him. "Da was right. I should not have come." She held a hand to her face.

"Maire." With a quiet whisper, he said, "Maire, me love, trust that I'll be safe and come for ye. God will watch over us while we're apart."

"I'll pray ye're safe, but trust is no' so easy to gain, Kirk Lachlan."

He gently turned her around by the shoulders and caught her sad, frightened gaze. "I'm comin' back for ye, if I go. We've a long life to live." He pressed her palm against his heart.

"I'm in a strange land with no family to go to and ye decide such." She hung her head. "What's to become of us?"

"I'd be doin' this for us, Maire. For us."

"I don't need a grand house or it filled with pretty baubles. Just bairns. Our people have survived against all odds for centuries. Centuries!" Her face had drained of all color as she lost the heady steam in her words. "I only need my husband at the end of this contract, ye ken? Only you."

"To look at ye so beautiful and so close and no' be able to take ye to wife has been more than I can bear. To have another man own your body, commanding your days, even be he kind and generous. . ." He shook his head. "No more can I wait living separate."

"Then let go of this foolishness, Kirk. We'll be together soon."

Kirk looked around to be sure they weren't heard. "Whatever we do, the English are comin'. They've made a law the troops can take any house, barn, everything. There's no home protected now, Maire. Should we marry and build a home even on a wee spot o' grass, John says what Pearson passed on is true. They can take it all. The house down to the last blade o' grass to feed their horses and house their men." He leaned his forehead against hers. "But worse, my love, is that unless I free ye, they can claim ye in the name of the king to serve the troops or ye can be auctioned off should John fail his taxes or his debts."

All the color drained from her face. "He's no' goin' to do that." Maire whispered back. "Ye said that won't be happenin', did ye no'?"

"Aye. This time. But what happens the next year? The king adds more odious laws. He raises the taxes or adds a new one? People's homes and slaves are already bein' commandeered. Mothers and babes turned out in the street so troops have a roof. Slaves and indentures taken in the name of the king." He rubbed the back of his neck. "They're comin' this way, Maire. There's nothin' to stop the Crown except the people rise up and declare independence. Ye see that now, dinnae ye?"

"Aye, I see we can be tried for treason just speakin' it." She whispered, red fanning across her cheeks. "Either way, it's in your head to get killed."

"I cannae allow what's comin' to take ye from me. I cannae allow me fear to get in the way of keepin' me promise to ye or our future bairns. I'll be goin' to join up and stop those redcoats afore they conscript me and steal ye away, if I must."

"Can we no' wait till harvest is in? Mayhap it is large, and earnings would solve the dilemma."

"Aye, love. We'll wait and see."

Chapter 5

Maire stared out the tiny window at the stars until the wee hours, unable to slow her thoughts or dampen her angry heart. With Abigail gone, she had no other woman to share her fears and feelings. When happiness came the closest, it took off like a doe spooked by a dog. Finally, she nodded off and dreamed of home. Of tending a bubbly pot of stew over a smoky peat fire. She sighed in her sleep, burrowing into the small feather pillow with the scents of home she'd brought from Scotland so many months before.

The aroma puzzled her, not quite right for lamb stew. She ran to stop the stew from scalding, but the pot toddled away, leaving flaming footprints where it had been. She found herself outside, chasing the pot as it exploded into a field of homeless waifs, trailing sparks over the thatched roof. Maire watched, helpless, as the flames licked up the walls and engulfed the cottage. Gone. Scotland, her home, her hope, all gone.

Coughing woke her. Smoke! Had the chimney stopped up? Curls of shadowy fingers grasped at the windowsill. Orange light flickered through the tiny attic windowpane near her bed. A dark figure looked up and then darted away from the fields, outlined against the flames, toward the mill. Kirk or John? She couldn't see well enough as the wind kicked up the smoke, blowing through the grain with a frenzy. The fields glowed already, encroaching on the stand of trees curling around the back of the property that led to the mill.

No time for a full dressing, she ran for the stairs, grabbing her mother's arisaid for modesty. "Kirk! John, fire!" As she flung the tartan around her, Maire skidded to a halt at the top of the narrow landing. No, no, no! Fire already covered the bottom of the stairs. "Kirk! John!" Frantic, she tried to scream but inhaled so much rising smoke it choked her, searing her throat. She covered her mouth and nose with the edge of her plaid, moving down a few steps to poke her head around the railing. The fire hadn't yet made it to the center of the kitchen. It hadn't started in the fireplace? Coughing racked her ribs with spasms so hard she could barely draw another breath.

She could escape if she jumped from halfway down. The garden door stood wide open to fresh air. A quick glance over her shoulder, the flames claimed the bottom stair emboldened to cover the next—she had no choice. Hiking up her nightgown, Maire clambered over the railing, clinging to the stair edge. The breeze from the door whipped at her cape and fanned the flames into a fury. They raced up the narrow staircase. She flung herself as far into the kitchen as possible.

She heard the pop even as she felt her ankle give way. She screamed in pain, sucking more hot smoke deep into her lungs. The fire ate up the floorboards like piglets gobbled slop. Her bare feet reddened against the heat. Maire pulled herself toward the door, hacking and wheezing, elbow over elbow until all went black.

Kirk saw the flames shoot above the trees from the road. Maire! He urged the horse faster, until it ran full out down the path that followed the creek along John's property. He cut away from the mill path, heading straight to the house, ducking branches. Engulfed in flames, the field lit up the property as bright as the noonday sun. He didn't see Maire anywhere. She'd be sleeping in the house. He grabbed a bucket from the well, doused himself, and dove inside. The heat around him sucked his shirt dry.

He spotted Maire on the kitchen floor, almost to the door, with the fire playing gleefully at her feet. Her feet and ankles red and blistering, and her tartan cape, already smoking at the hem, suddenly lit up.

Kirk stomped out the flickering flames and then lifted Maire's still form into his arms. He bowed his head over her, shielding her from falling embers, and ran from the house. "Lord, grant your mercy." A moment later the house collapsed in on itself, scattering beams and sparks in the hot wind.

Kirk cradled Maire in her cloak, cautious of the burns on her feet as he carried her into the courtyard, near the well. Setting her down, he drew out water to cool her burns. He lifted the ladle and bathed her feet, scooping water up her legs. The firelight revealed a heavy bruise near her ankle. No wonder she couldn't get out. "Lass, open your eyes. Please." He checked her arms, hands, and leaned her forward to check her back. Her breathing seemed ragged but easing in the fresh air.

The fire began to blow itself out now the fuel in the field had burned up. A neighbor from the next farm drew as close as he could in his wagon, the mule team protesting. He'd brought several other men with him. "She alive?"

"I need to get her to a doctor." At Kirk's nod, the farmer helped Kirk lift and gently settle Maire in a makeshift bed of straw. He straightened her tattered cloak to protect her as best he could from further scratching.

"I'll have one of my men take you to Benjamin Rush. He'll know what to do."

Kirk edged in beside her, laying her head and shoulders across his lap, to steady the ride into town. He folded the tartan edges around her arms and covered her with a blanket the neighbor found under the wagon's bench seat. He left her feet open to the cool air, free of irritation.

"Maire, let me see the spark in ye." She didn't stir, breathing so shallow he feared she scarcely lived. "Please, wake up." Would they be able to save her? He smoothed the tangled hair from her beautiful face. He winced at the pain she'd feel for weeks from the burns and the break.

"It may be kinder to let her rest, son. Her injuries and the conditions of the road..." The neighbor looked away toward the fields and then the house and back at Maire, pressing his lips together. "Where is John McGowan and his wife?"

"The babe." Kirk said. "John took his wife for her lyin' in to her mother. He left to bring Miss Abigail home after the christening later this week."

The man nodded. "It's a blessing to have good news. We'll do what we can."

"He'll be most grateful, as am I."

The neighbor led John's gelding over and tied him to the back of the cart. Then he called one of his field hands off the bucket brigade working on the barn. "Drive them to 930 Adams Avenue. Bring back Mr. McGowan from his in-laws. He'll be needed more here at the moment than with his wife. Perhaps he'll make it back in time for the christening."

"I cannae thank ye enough."

"May God be with ye both." He gave one sad sigh. "And with the McGowans."

The driver snapped the reins and clucked his tongue. "We'll git you there, suh. You leave it to ole Jesse."

"Easy goes the way." The neighbor called last instructions. "That girl is sorely wounded."

They crossed Pennypack Creek as the sun rose. Shadows from the Frankford Avenue Bridge laid dark circles from the three stone arches. The city began to wake, pouring out into the streets in the early morning hours. Jesse wove in and out of the roads, calling to clear the way. "We's got us an injured woman here! Let us through—clear the way!"

Maire moaned, and that weak sound caused a spate of spasmodic coughing. Kirk steadied her as best he could, but his heart clenched at the pain each bump in the road inflicted on her.

Once at the doctor's residence, the driver dashed to the door. A pause and then a younger man than Kirk expected came out a few moments later in his banyan and nightcap. As Dr. Rush looked at Maire's blistered feet and watched her endure another coughing episode, he said, "She needs pounded ice to draw out the fire and we must watch for pneumonia. Get right to the hospital. I'll change and meet you." Already halfway to his door, he waved them off. "Don't wait for me. My horse will be much faster."

The roan whinnied and pulled to rear up at the burnt odors floating toward him. Kirk clamped down on the reins, holding the horse's head in place. "Whoa, now. All's well, boy." He urged the horse forward toward the barn. The smell of smoke still in the air.

John met him at the well in the courtyard. "How's Maire?"

Kirk dismounted and gave his friend a somber look. "Doctor Rush says she'll recover, but 'twill be a bit. She's no' to speak or she may ruin her vocal chords. She cannae walk—" His voice cracked. "John, I dinnae know what I'd do if I lost her."

"Ye haven't, lad." He put a hand on Kirk's shoulder. "We've been prayin' all day. She's goin' to be good as a shorn sheep what's got to regrow its wool. It just takes the time. Ye have to let the Lord do the healin'."

Neighbors from around the area joined them, looking worn from the night and the morning's efforts. One woman brought two plates of food. "We haven't much at the moment, but you're sure needing some nourishment from the looks of you. Some milk fresh from the cow this morning and johnnycakes. I've nothing to put on them, but they'll fill your stomach and build your strength. You're welcome to come to supper tonight."

"Thank ye, ma'am." John said. "I hope if ye need us, we'll be as good a neighbor in return."

"I'll send some of my canned goods when your lady is ready to come home with the baby. God's grace it was her time. Probably saved all of you." She smiled and moved back to the makeshift kitchen with a fire pit.

Kirk didn't know if he'd rather laugh at the irony of the outdoor cooking fire where the fire had demolished so much of their livelihood or be amazed at the good it could do after such destruction. "The mill, then?"

John rubbed his soot-covered hand across his ashen face. "No. 'Tis collapsed on itself, same as the house." He pointed at the blackened trees that stood a sorry sentinel at the bend in the creek. Two trunks tipped onto each other, the rest devoid of fruit and branches. "The field led it right there to the apple trees and beyond. All gone—save the barn, thanks to our friends."

The remaining men loaded buckets and shovels to head back to their farms. John and Kirk shook hands around the group, thanking them for their efforts. Everyone had worked through the night, breeches and waistcoats near as black as their surroundings.

"Without these willing men, I'd surely have lost the rest. I have a few barrels of flour and corn in the storeroom and some of the garden survived, though I dinnae ken how. Mayhap the cellar has a bit in it. We can eat for now and have a roof over our heads." John waved a hand toward the fields and then the stream. "I dinnae ken where to start with winter not far off or how we'll make it through to the next harvest."

Kirk surveyed the burned-out landscape. "It appears we start where there's the most need. Ye'll need income. Let's start at the mill since we have a roof."

"Aye, 'tis a good plan for now." They sat down at the well, backs against it to eat and rest. "We'll see how the king treats a tragedy." He shook his head. "I doubt so kindly when taxes are due."

"Kirk, I've something to show ye." John led him around the tangled mess that had been the house. He pointed to a line of footprints leading toward the creek that had dried into the garden mud. "Did ye come home this way or see anyone?"

"No. I spied the smoke and rode the gelding along the creek to the path that cuts through the woods. It's faster." They walked farther along, following the swath of green. "How a fire could set on a field and skip round to the mill—" Kirk stopped at the line of blackened trees and turned around. From the slight rise in the land, he could see that the walk he'd just made with John and the path to the road were untouched. "Someone set the fields ablaze, used this path to torch the mill, and then had to have escaped behind me."

" 'Tis my thoughts as well, and I dinnae ken how to unravel the who or the why of it." John gestured at the scene below them. "I'm ruined."

"Ye still own the land and the access to the stream. And, we have a roof over our heads better than the crofts back home. It may be a barn, but 'twill keep us warm enough. Have ye determined the salvage at the mill?"

They walked the last quarter mile around the bend in silence, the only sound being from their feet traipsing over the rocky ridge. The birdsong, so normal, dismally absent. The wood frame of the building and roof were charred rubble. The remaining half of the waterwheel created a decorous waterfall.

"The foundation is still sound."

"Aye, we'll rebuild. But I'll have to first buy tools and fodder for the animals. I've got nothin' left but what's in the barn."

Kirk helped John lift the debris off the grinding stones. "A bit of cleanup and they'll work."

Nodding, John said, " 'Tis no small feat, though. I've no more credit for the tools and supplies. The crops and milling were to pay that and me taxes. The only thing left worth anything is the new workman, who isn't here yet, and Maire's indenture." He added, "I hope 'twill not come to that, my friend."

"What can I do?"

John shook his head and ran a hand through his unkempt hair. "I dinnae ken right now. I dinnae ken."

Chapter 6

The nurse helped Maire into a soft worsted wool in apple green with a soft lace kerchief overlay. The gown arrived with a matching cloak that morning. She had no idea who'd sent it, but proper clothing rather than the required bedclothes meant she'd be allowed out of bed. The Pennsylvania Hospital had saved her singed arisaid, but the smell of smoke made it impossible to wear, even if it hadn't been improper dress. Once able, Maire desperately wanted to care for her mother's plaid. How much of it would she lose? And then it struck her. She'd lost Da's Bible. Her last memory was of it on the little shelf that acted as her toilette. Her heart ached, her feet still stung, and she couldn't manage on her own with the bone in her ankle broken. *Lord, can there be any more done to me? Grant mercy in Your kindness.*

Maire marveled at the magnificent architecture, the double curling grand staircases, and stonework in the central hall. The hospital resembled a palace more than a place to administer healing if this were all to see.

Three men crowded around Doctor Rush, making decisions about Maire without her input. The nurse had better things to do than keep her company in the great hall of the Pennsylvania Hospital. But the men seemed to have forgotten both women in their heated discussion that rang off the cold marble walls and up into the domed ceiling.

"You're all here to see to Maire Greer's care?" The doctor stepped backward as the three men launched again into explanations with raised voices. John asking about accommodations for an invalid, Kirk for the right to assume care as her betrothed, and the new arrival, Mr. Pearson, badgering John for her indenture. None of them wanted to listen to the patient.

"She'll need complete rest the next few weeks, and then I'll evaluate her vocal chords and burns once again, bleed her if necessary to rid her of any lingering infections." The doctor instructed all of them. "I'll have no argument about it. It seems impossible to determine where she should go and with whom. If there isn't a proper place for this young lady to rest, then she will not leave."

"Is it possible to make payments, sir?" Truth be told, Kirk's newly gained freedom gave him no higher status in the outcome of his betrothed's fate. He didn't own the indenture and he had very little money.

"Of course. There are ways to manage the payments or to apply for charity." Doctor Rush signaled to the nurse holding paperwork who appeared as stymied by the ruckus as Maire. "We do not discriminate here on—"

"I cannot see what the difficulty is. I've paid the monies due for the girl. Since I managed the full payment with no charity needed, we should simply finalize the agreement as to her continued care." How Mr. Pearson learned of the billing situation was a mystery to Maire. He turned up at the least expected moments like a spider dropping onto a teapot. With a creature like that on the handle, one simply refused the tea.

Listening to them not listening to one another gave her a headache. She had to try to speak. John and his family were near destitute. If Kirk took on the extensive costs, his only option would be the military. She couldn't stomach his loss with so much else in ruins.

"Kirk—" Maire croaked his name and waved her hand to gain his attention from the wooden wheelchair. The nurse attempted to calm her as if she would hysterically leap from the seat. The hospital agreed to loan the chair on the word of Doctor Rush until the blisters on her feet and the break healed, though she might need it a few weeks longer until the tenderness subsided. The lesser burns up her ankles had only taken a matter of days. But her toes and the balls of her feet hadn't fared so well. They'd taken careful dedication against infection and many painful dressing changes over the last two weeks. The burning turned to intense itching as her feet healed. Walking, even standing, would be out of the question until the bone righted itself and the tenderness subsided.

Kirk put a finger to his lips. "Ye cannae speak, me bonnie lass, or ye'll ne'er speak again. The doctor said ye're vocal chords must mend fully." Tension and deeply grooved worry carved through his face as the other men discussed Maire's fate.

She kept silent as everyone spoke around her and for her. John's crops, mill, and most of the garden had gone up in smoke. The desperation in his voice pierced Maire's heart. "Kirk, to pay her medical bills I would have to sell my land. What else have I to care for my own family? Anything I sell must out of necessity go to sustenance, tools, and rebuilding."

"I hear ye, I do. But cannae we do this together? I'd be there with ye all the way. I won't leave without helpin' ye to rebuild."

"Gentlemen, the solution has been provided." Pearson turned to John. "With the financial difficulty in the loss of your property, might I suggest you sell Maire's indenture to me."

Kirk held up a hand. "Ye'll no' consider other ways?"

"The gown she wears I've also given. Will you be able to clothe your family and Maire? I think not."

Maire plucked at the pretty floral petticoat between the panels of her Brunswick to avoid Kirk's surprised stare. *How was she to know?*

"No!" Kirk bit out at Mr. Pearson's assumptive tone.

John's shoulders slouched. "My friend, I cannae keep an indenture with no funds to pay out. I cannae support Maire in the state of my affairs. Where would she be able to rest that willnae cause her more difficulty, in a horse's trough? And I cannae let her starve, as she's my responsibility under the law. I see no other way." John scrunched his face as if he'd felt a knife twist in his gut. "Ye ken the problem. I have a wife and bairn first and a duty to see Maire safe even though I cannae do it meself."

"Then I can do nothin' to stop ye?" Kirk's fist closed at his side and his jaw clenched.

"Would that it could be different. Ye haven't enough funds to pay for one of the months let alone the remainder plus the hospital, have ye?" At Kirk's miserable shake of his head, John said, "I have none, either." He turned to Mr. Pearson. "Ye'll pay all her bills and provide a safe haven till her contract is fulfilled?"

Pearson wore the expression of a conqueror. "With expediency. You'll have the funds for her indenture immediately also." Mr. Pearson shook hands first with John, sealing the deal, and then with the doctor. "Dr. Rush, I'll have a payment to you this afternoon." He pushed through Kirk to take hold of Maire's chair. "With your permission, Doctor, I'll see to her home care."

"You're quite a brave young woman." The doctor took Maire's hand. "I wish you a speedy recovery. I'll see you in two weeks."

Her new owner wheeled her to the hospital entrance. What would happen to her if she ran? Would she make it even a few steps? She bowed her head and prayed, a tear landing on her folded hands. What else could she do? She had no voice and no choice. Maire kept her face averted from everyone as her new owner wheeled her away. What good would come from Kirk seeing her humiliation or she his? She wished no further harm on John and his family. They'd suffered beyond and had done all they could with the little that remained. *They have no choice, either. Aye, I ken. Lord, grant me peace in this pain. It's deeper than the burns. I cannae do this alone.*

Mr. Pearson lifted her from the chair, holding her body too tightly to him for Maire's comfort while the others looked on. He took her down the sidewalk to his handsomely outfitted phaeton. "You're lighter than I expected."

She couldn't stop the words, but her throat hurt for the effort of producing the rough sound. "I'm no' a sow."

He halted in place a moment and looked at her with an amused expression. "Far from my thoughts, though you'd best remain silent or you will sound like one. Rather, I meant to pay you a compliment, that you're quite pleasingly formed."

She dropped her gaze as her cheeks warmed. No man but her father and her betrothed had put his arms so intimately around her. No man had ever said words such as that before!

"Maire, I've the perfect room for you as you recover," he said close to her ear, sending a convulsive shiver down her neck. Then he put her down on the gleaming leather seat of the black phaeton.

His driver, a slave by the looks of him, lowered the top and managed to get the rolling chair into the second seating area. "I'll drive. You may walk home, Bartholomew."

Stunned, Maire watched the black man move out of the way. How far did they have to go? The man gave her an encouraging nod. No words passed, but they each knew what the other left unsaid. Maybe she'd found an ally in this new place. As she turned forward, she caught sight of Kirk, and she knew by the set of his jaw and thunderous glare—there'd be no holding him back from war now.

Her room in the large manor, though small and with its own dressing area, stretched larger than the entire cottage in Ayr. Etta, a sweet young girl with lovely caramel-colored skin, helped her get around and cared for her needs, but the lack of privacy to see to herself wore on Maire's nerves. Etta couldn't read or write and Maire couldn't speak. They devised the most rudimentary hand signals to communicate. Each time Maire tried to send the girl away, she'd become emphatic that she stay. "No, miss, the master, he say I tend you."

Mornings, Mr. Pearson came to carry her down to the breakfast room while his slave, Bartholomew, carried her chair. In the evening, after he returned from work, they dined and he carried her back up with Bartholomew trailing. Etta chatted to pass the time as she helped Maire dress or undress but oddly spoke not at all when her master was present.

After a fortnight, Dr. Rush made a house call.

"Open and let me see you try to say a-a-h." He stuck an ivory tongue depressor in her mouth.

"A-a-h," she managed with no coughing while he examined her.

"Her throat appears to be returning to normal, though it may be some time yet before we know how her voice is fully affected." He withdrew the depressor, directing his comments to Mr. Pearson. "But with trauma such as this young lady's, we treat it cautiously. I'll approve short sentences, only those most necessary, for another week or two. We wouldn't want to tax those vocal chords." The doctor placed his ear to her back. "Her lungs seem clear as well, light handiwork such as needlework and reading shouldn't fatigue her. I think she can progress from soft foods to normal meals as well."

"Thank ye, sir!" She sounded like she'd swallowed sand. But relief sang through her veins. The first few days had been less difficult, as she needed a lot of sleep. Gradually, as she convalesced, Maire dissolved into absolute boredom with both her idleness and her diet. Finally, she had something to keep herself from going mad. Once the doctor completed his exam of her feet, he departed with the last instructions to continue use of the chair until she could comfortably wear shoes and walk without pain.

After a supper of roasted chicken, carrots, and apple cobbler, Maire was ready to retire.

"I'll crawl. I'm tired o' bein' carried like a wee bairn." Tired of the wrong man's arms around her. Tired of the enforced rest.

Mr. Pearson lifted an eyebrow. "Crawling up the stairs may prove difficult, Maire. Certainly, not in your new gowns."

"I dinnae ask for these fancy clothes." She wore a light-blue striped gown with a white stomacher and petticoat. Not a uniform, but quite a bit finer compared to any of her homespun. From owning no more than three all her life, seven gowns now hung in her wardrobe.

"My business is fabrics. You'll wear them as I see fit." His tone gave her no room to contest as he chastised her. "No more of that gutter talk, either, Maire. From now on you'll speak properly or not at all. I rather preferred your silence to this rubbish. It doesn't uphold the social conventions of my home."

How? "Aye, sir."

He narrowed his eyes. "Yes, sir. Repeat it."

"Yes, sir." *Ye may speak properly, but that no' makes a hog naught but a tasty ham.*

She swallowed back the words. Now she understood Etta's hesitancy to speak in his presence.

"In private, you're to call me Julius. Moreover, Maire, it grieves me to tell you I've had to add the physician's bill and your lost time to your contract. Quite sad the circumstances." He handed over the revision granted by the court. "But rest assured, you'll be comfortably cared for while you pay off your debt for the additional two years. We may come to some kind of agreeable arrangement."

She looked at the judge's signature and seal. "But I had no chance to speak?"

"Your testimony was not needed in this situation."

"I cannae—"

"Enough." He held up a hand, the ruffles of his sleeve dangling above the empty platter. "Speak when you're spoken to until such a time as you're able to properly. That will ensure healing as well."

Maire clamped her mouth shut, seething. She still couldn't walk well, though her lungs and throat had healed enough for comfortable conversation. Would she always sound so gravelly? The doctor warned her to be a woman of few words. That might be a blessing since her words tended to cause trouble! *Yes, sir. No, sir.* She bit the inside of her bottom lip before the sass in her mind came out of her mouth. The less she antagonized him, the less difficult her enforced position would be to tolerate. But two more years? She'd recovered enough energy to use her hands in two weeks. Maire let her gaze drop to her feet. It'd be another few weeks, though, before she'd comfortably walk short distances. Maybe longer. How had the courts determined weeks equaled years? She hadn't started the fire. Why did she have to be punished like a criminal? Lost time, that made sense when time equaled money. The cost to pay back her medical bills also made sense. But that her labor, compared to the actual time and cost, was considered so lowly, thwarted logic. How could they assign such a ridiculous wage as to make it nearly worthless?

"I have engaged a tutor to teach you the skill needed to spin and work with fine fabrics. With the difficulty in acquiring goods, my shelves are already thinning. You will be required to learn the elegance of embroidery and eventually, when you're fully healed, all the aspects of spinning fine threads into saleable materials."

She'd spun from wool. Her skirts had been homemade and not badly. "But, sir—"

"Eh, eh, eh." He waggled a finger and then looked down his nose at her bandaged feet. "Since you aren't able to do much else, the only other option would be to sell your contract where no walking is required. I'm sure many taverns have upstairs lodgings for an enterprising, attractive young woman." His open stare spoke volumes. "Speaking properly will also assure I have no misgivings about such a merciful decision."

Maire fully understood the "merciful decision." How could he consider that kind of threat? There had to be some law that would protect her if Julius tried to enact such a cruel transaction. She couldn't take a chance. Would that this man had a wife or daughters to soften his black soul!

With no one to defend her, Maire lowered her eyes. He had no need to see her true feelings. "Aye—I mean, yes, sir."

"You will have a quota. Fail that and we shall see what means of correction produce the proper results."

She swallowed. "Yes, sir."

"You shall speak properly or be kept in the barn."

The barn? That might be an opportunity. She'd lived in far less gracious surroundings.

He sipped a cup of tea. "To that end, you shall have regular lessons in etiquette as well."

"Yes, sir." Why would he invest so much in her unless he planned to keep her indefinitely? She forced herself to breathe evenly. Once the terms of the indenture were met, extension included, he'd have no grounds.

"Once you've gained proper language skills and manners, I'll evaluate you for a higher position."

Her eyes went wide. "Higher position?" A skilled position in any other circumstance would be a coveted opportunity. Her eyes narrowed. What snare had Julius just set?

He merely smiled. "One must have decorum and know one's place. If you apply yourself, then I will decide your reward. One that is mutually beneficial, I think." He stood, coming around the table, and held out his arms. "Come now."

She lifted her arms and wound them around his neck, as he liked. "Bartholomew?" He called for the man to carry the chair.

Chapter 7

By the next week, Maire's toes and the balls of her feet no longer needed dressings. As the prickly tenderness subsided, Etta helped her into stockings and loose slippers. Later that morning, Maire stood for the first time in over a month. "I did it!"

"You shore 'nuf did, miss." Etta grinned and helped her settle back into the chair. "We's best be careful wit' you now."

"Etta, would you like to learn to read or learn all that I'm learning?"

"Oh, yes, miss. An' I could show Bartholomew?"

"Bartholomew." The two shared a conspiratorial smile. "I thought there might be something between you."

"He a good man, miss."

"Yes, he is."

Etta leaned in. "I hears a young man been tryin' to see you. My Bartholomew might could fix somethin' up."

"Kirk!" Maire's heart somersaulted. "I'd be grateful. But how?"

"This mornin', after the master leave, you stay in the breakfast room nearest the kitchen. The cook will be out to weekly market by then. Mebbe a delivery boy shows up? I hear a strappin' fine Scotsman has been takin' odd jobs like that." She lifted her hands. "I dunno, mebbe I'll be doin' a chore and don't hear no door knock." Etta cocked her head at the knock on Maire's bedroom door. With a finger to her lips, she crossed and opened the door. "Mr. Julius, sir, she's ready."

Mrs. Caroline Smythe-Worthington, a youngish widow with heavily powdered and styled hair in the height of fashion, arrived each Monday through Friday at ten and left by two, assuring a mealtime or tea for training. The lady seemed to enjoy being engaged to teach etiquette and embroidery and the finer points of conversation. "One does what one can for the less fortunate."

Since there were no other indentures under tutelage, the only thing Maire could think was that Julius planned to engage her in assisting with the sale of fabric in his shops.

If it weren't for the distraction Maire had with the education, and the company, she'd be quite annoyed at the cloistered schedule. The lessons included proper English, recognition of fabrics and designs, and etiquette at the dining table and with guests.

Caroline leaned in to check Maire's stitch pattern and pointed with her needle at the design. "A little tighter there. Evenly distanced stitching is imperative." She sat back against the velvet settee. "A lady's embroidery skills should be exemplary."

Maire asked questions about current events, hungry for the outside world and deeply homesick for her friends.

Caroline only too happily regaled her with the most recent gossip and news about the colonial bid for self-rule. "Anyone knows loyalty to the king is the way to go. Why, my husband would never have picked up arms against our sovereign. You Scots know the foolishness of that already, don't you?"

Maire ducked her head to hide the flare of anger and chose to overlook the woman's offense. After a moment, she affected an interest in the introduced conversation topic as she'd been taught. "Do you entertain these soldiers?"

"I haven't, as yet, but I've been to soirees, and they're the most delightful dancers."

The image of Caroline dancing around the room with soldiers in clunky boots and clattering swords made Maire giggle. "I have nae danced—"

"Have not."

"Have not." Maire repeated, closing the consonants on each word with exaggeration to get them right. "I have not danced with a man afore."

"Before," Caroline corrected without raising her eyes from her own embroidery work.

Dutifully, Maire repeated, "Before." She crossed her eyes at Etta, who watched from across the room.

Etta plopped a hand over her mouth to stifle a giggle.

"When you're able, possibly we can add that to your education." Caroline rose. "I'll speak to Mr. Pearson when next I see him. Etta, do find my cloak and call Bartholomew to drive me home."

Maire had Etta push her through to the entry and wished Caroline a good day. Then she directed Etta to leave her in the breakfast room with tea. "I'm sure you have other chores I'm keeping you from, yes?"

Etta tapped a forefinger against her chin. "Why, I'll be. I done forgot to make your bed, Miss Maire."

"Oh my, you best be quick, then." They giggled together. Each doing their best to ease the other's situation.

Maire tested her leather slippers and walked slowly to the delivery entrance. Not a moment later, Kirk knocked and she threw the door open. "You're here! I've missed ye so!"

He hugged her tight. " 'Tis good to hear your voice again."

"Well, it's no' the same. I cannae sing much, but I'm free to speak as I will now."

" 'Tis a bit of a come-hither to it," he teased. "Ye have the song of a siren to me."

She blushed. "How's Abigail and the babe?"

"They're well and send their prayers. The laddie is growin' strong. We're all still in the barn, but 'tis a warm space. The wee one seems the stronger for it."

"I'm glad." She squeezed his arms. "Are ye gettin' enough to eat?"

"Aye, lass. We're makin' do." He looked her up and down. "How is it ye're standin'?"

"Are ye surprised? I cannae walk more than the few steps from the table, but I'm healin' a bit more each day. The faster I do, the faster I can work off me time." She laid a hand on his chest. "I just want to feel you're real and no' a dream."

"I'm real." Kirk covered her hand with his warm one. "Should ye rest?"

She shook her head. "I've been sittin' for weeks now. Just tell me news, anything, I want to hear it all."

"We know the fire was set and no accident, Maire."

"I saw a man from my window. But I thought 'twas you or John."

"Ye saw a man?" He looked over her shoulder at the sounds from the hall. Lowering his voice, he asked, "Could ye describe him?"

"No, he was too far away." She heard the *click-clack* of heels on the wood floor. "Quick, off with ye," she whispered, and pushed Kirk out the servants' entrance. A new cravat for Julius sat on the table nestled inside the tailor's box.

"Maire—" Caroline had nearly caught Maire and Kirk. "Are you having tea in the kitchen?" She walked in, curiosity in her wide-set brown eyes.

"The tailor's boy came," Maire answered as she picked up the box and, as gingerly as she could, made her way back to her chair. "Don't you think this silk cravat will be dashing on Julius? I thought I could add some lace with those new stitches you taught me." She made a mental note to do exactly that to avoid suspicion.

"You're walking!" Caroline's brow wrinkled. "You shouldn't be putting such strain on yourself. Where's Etta?"

"I'd just sent Etta to finish her chores when I heard the knock." She smiled as if she'd been keeping a special secret. "I've been trying a step or two in private, as a surprise." She eased herself back into the chair. "Promise not to tell? I'd be terribly mortified if anyone saw how unstable I am still."

"You're going to be such an asset to Mr. Pearson. He'll be so pleased with your progress, dear, taking on household needs by directing the help, and such a wonderful surprise to see you up and about."

The lady held a fan. "Halfway home I realized I'd meant to give you this to practice. I hope you don't mind I came back?" She flicked her wrist, and the fanciful piece spread out like a rooster's tail. "Do you see how that works?"

"I do, but what would I need that for to make and sell a bolt of silk?"

"Make and sell?" The lady tipped her head to the side and giggled nervously. "Ladies simply don't do that."

"But what good would I be with all this education otherwise?"

"I'm sure Mr. Pearson means to give you the proper societal necessities. You'll need to understand his business in order to sympathize with him at the end of a day as any wife should."

Wife? Surely, Caroline misunderstood the arrangement. "I don't—"

"Do you expect to help your husband in his warehouse?" She brushed off her own ridiculous suggestion. "Of course not."

"Husband?" Is that what he'd meant by higher position? "Caroline, I'm betrothed to—"

"Yes, I know it's a bit awkward, but the cook and housekeeper have assured the church propriety has been observed. It's a shame you've had to delay your wedding to heal from the fire. What woman wishes to be ill on her wedding night? Mr. Pearson, the dear man, wants you to be able to walk down the aisle of your own volition. And now you can!" Caroline hugged Maire. The scent of roses clung to her. "He'll be overjoyed."

Maire masked her shock. "Not a word, Caroline, please."

"Not a peep, but it will be so hard!"

The roaring in between Maire's ears sounded as loud as the mill at full capacity. The "dear man" hadn't asked this Scottish woman whether she wanted to walk down the aisle. Her own volition? She'd be tarred and feathered first!

How could she get word to Kirk before it was too late?

Chapter 8

B artholomew rolled Maire out onto the porch and leaned down, whispering in her ear. "He's in the carriage house." Because of his strength, Julius had set him to the task of carrying Maire and her chair up and down the stairs when he was away seeing to business.

"Such a risk after the last time," she whispered back, leaning into her friend as he helped her to her feet. The effort was easier than it had been in the beginning of her recovery, the sensitivity less but still noticeable.

"He knows it, Miss Maire. But he out there in the third stall and say he hopes you'll come." Bartholomew held out his arms. "I'll carry you, ma'am. I knows those feet still hurtin' you."

"The shoes don't hurt nearly as bad as they did last week." Maire worried about what Julius would do if he caught them. Bartholomew would get the whip. She couldn't allow that to happen for her sake. "I dinnae—don't want to get you in trouble." She could tolerate a little more time on her feet for the sake of a walk outdoors—and a moment in Kirk's company—without risking others. Bartholomew didn't need any of the other slaves caving under pressure and tattling. "You just leave me here as if I'm getting a breath of air."

"Yes, ma'am. If'n you hurry before Master Pearson come home from the warehouse you might can see your fella for a few minutes." Bartholomew smiled, something rare except in Maire's presence or his sweetheart's. "He sure loves you fierce like."

"I hope it doesn't get him killed, my friend."

"He gonna be all right. Jes' go on an' see him quick." He scanned the lane coming toward the house. "I'll try to come git you if I sees the master comin'."

"Thank you." Maire gingerly tested her weight as she took each porch stair at a measured pace. She tentatively made her way across the cobblestones, wary of her balance. The rounded toe on the shoes and the lower heel helped immensely.

Kirk came to her side from the shadows. "You're walkin'." He touched her lips in a sweet kiss. " 'Tis good to see ye on the mend."

"Aye." Still, she sank onto the hay bale outside the empty stall. " 'Tis taken a bit of work, but I'm able to move about slowly."

"Are ye well, aside from the burns? Your message worried me greatly, comin' so fast from whence we last met."

She nodded. "I had to see you."

"I'll come anytime ye send for me, Maire, if 'tis within me ability." He kissed her knuckles. "But there's somethin' I have to tell ye." He reached into his coat pocket and pressed a folded pamphlet into her hands. "At the tavern, I heard a man read this aloud. They said his name was Paine. But Dr. Rush was there agreein' with him. The verra doctor what cured ye, me love."

She held it close to cipher in the dim light. "Common Sense, addressed to the Inhabitants of America. Who wrote it?"

"No one knows. But he's a fine logician, he is. And that man, Paine, read it with as much oratory passion as if he wrote it himself."

Raising her eyes to his, she asked, "What's it about, then?"

"A man's no' got a right to rule another just by heredity. He goes on about designing a new government using, of all ideas, a lottery between the colonies."

"A lottery? How would one run a government with gambling, then?" She shook her head in disbelief. "I think ye're funnin' with me."

"No, Maire, 'tis true. What it says is the colonies would have districts with delegates. Those delegates would meet in a congress and annually elect a president. A man of the people, Maire, no king to mete out laws like a whim for a sweet. The lottery would ensure each colony the opportunity to proffer a president once every thirteen years."

"How could such a thing be?"

"Three-fifths of the congress would have to agree for a law to pass. No' one man forcin' his will to fill his coffers at the expense of the people. A government for the people."

" 'Tis goin' to get the man killed if they find him. My tutor says there are loyalists and soldiers everywhere." A little shiver shook her and set her teeth to rattling. "Dinnae get mixed up in this."

He wrapped an arm about her shoulders and circled her with the other, adding his warmth in the crisp cold of early winter. "I've enlisted, Maire."

She leaned into him, resting her head on his chest, feeling the beat of his heart under her cheek. "What happens if ye dinnae come home, Kirk?"

"We cannae think so, love. We cannae." He tightened his arms, confidence pouring into her. "Maire, me beauty, there's nothin' else I want to do but be with you. This is no' a wee passin' fancy. The war has started and Philadelphia is the heart of it. This day we choose to live free. We cannae allow the king to tax and take and torment with such unjust abandon as he did to us in Scotland. We cannae leave the battle to our children or their children."

She hadn't yet told him of Caroline's unintentional slip of the tongue. Of the plans Julius would carry out if he knew she could walk. "We have enough trouble. Can't ye stay and mill the grain for the men who fight? Who will do so if all the men go? Tell me that, Kirk."

"What kind of man would I be to turn over me duty to others? If any of us are to have dignity and pass that on, then 'tis up to us to make that happen. Heed me, woman, this is no' about two people any longer, ye ken? 'Tis much bigger than us."

"Then tell me, man, how will ye care for yourself?"

"As a freeman, 'tis up to me to prepare. I've a rifle already. We've nearly got the mill rebuilt. John has granted me rations as per our agreement, as much as I can carry. When I come through, he'll resupply me as he can, and I'll hunt as I can."

"Corn and oats? How will you eat that marching into battle in the dead of winter?"

"Maire, I dinnae come to talk strategies." Kirk motioned for her to move over. "I come to tell ye I'm goin'. It's all the faster we'll be together in a holy matrimony and no man can tear us apart."

"When do ye go?" Her mind spun at the long list of things he'd need to survive—if he survived. Could she use her new skills to at least get him warm clothing?

"In a few weeks."

In the little time left, with all her time scheduled, she'd do what she could. "Will ye see me afore ye go?"

"Aye." He pulled her to him. "They're goin' to reward freemen that serve even short term in acreage, Maire. A lot of land in the west of Pennsylvania. With that, I'll be able to sell off enough to buy yer indenture. Then we can farm the rest. God willin', we'll have a creek to build a mill of our own."

"If I'm still—"

The sunlight suddenly broke into the shadows as Julius flung open the door.

Kirk and Maire jumped apart.

Julius wore a greatcoat, adding a menacing dimension to his size. "You!" He grabbed the horsewhip and cracked it, barely missing Kirk. "Get away from my woman and off my property!"

"Your what now?" Kirk challenged.

Fearing for Kirk's life if he was found with the pamphlet, Maire stuffed it into her sleeve, the long linen ruffles concealing the ends. "No, Julius, please. He's going. He only came to say good-bye."

"I don't care why he came, Maire. Stay out of it." Julius cracked the whip again, backing Kirk into the wall. "If I catch you sniffing around my property or my woman again I'll have you arrested."

"Julius." Maire stood and stepped in between the men.

His eyes went wide. "You're—"

"Let him go." She moved slowly, keeping her eyes locked on Julius. "He's said what he came to say. Kirk is leaving now."

"Maire, you came out here on your own?" He looked from her feet to her face.

"Yes, sir, I did." She kept putting one foot in front of the other. "I wanted news from home. That's all." But he kept the whip. He'd use it again if she didn't do something. "I'm sorry, I—" The next step she cried out and stumbled, pitching forward.

Julius snatched her up, lifting her close to his chest. "I have you." The timbre of his voice hard as iron. Julius's eyes narrowed as he looked again at Kirk. "Get out." He turned and carried Maire back to the house as a light snow began to dust the ground. "Don't disrespect me, Maire. You've done so well up to now."

"I understand, Julius." But she didn't regret seeing Kirk. She'd risk it one more time, if she had half a chance.

"Etta!" He set Maire on the sofa nearest the fire rather than in her wheelchair. "Take our things and bring tea in here. Be quick. Miss Maire is shivering."

"Thank you." Maire watched him pace the floor. She retreated into her silence, afraid to open a conversation she didn't want to have or assume the direction he would take it.

"Tell me how long you've been hiding this"—he waved a hand at her—"this development from me."

"I haven't—"

He raised a brow.

She dropped her gaze to her clasped hands. "I've been practicing for a week privately."

"A week."

"I'd thought to surprise you." She thought of Caroline. "You can check with my tutor, if you please."

"After all I've done for you." He leaned his hands against the mantel and stared into the fire. "I'm to believe I didn't interrupt a tryst with another man and you weren't planning to run away?"

It was her turn to be surprised. "Run away?" She heard a slight gasp from the hall. Etta.

"What am I to assume when you're fully dressed, wearing a heavy cloak, and can walk?"

"No, sir. I wasnae—" At his icy glare Maire corrected and slowed her words. "I was not planning and do not have plans to run away."

Etta brought in the tea tray with nutmeats, cheese, and small slices of bread along with a hot pot of black tea.

"That will be all, Etta. There'll be no interruptions."

Etta nodded and glanced at Maire with compassionate eyes.

"Show me what you've learned about serving tea." He took the wing-backed chair adjacent to Maire. "We've matters to discuss now that you're able to walk."

"Yes, Julius." She lifted the teapot. "Would you have me work in the shop now?" She poured a cup. "I think I could do it if I rest my feet now and then. They're tender if I'm on them too long, as is my ankle."

"What gave you such an idea?"

"You've mentioned a higher position." The pot dangled in the air over the second cup as she glanced up at him.

"Maire, it's time I take a wife."

"I see." *Please, no, Lord, let Caroline be wrong.* She set the silver pot on the trivet before she dropped it on the beautifully woven rug.

"The reason I've spent so much in education for you is not that you're an indentured servant, but that I have an offer for you to end that arrangement."

Lord, where are You? Help me! Could he see her panic?

"I'm prepared to absorb the costs of your medical, educational, and physical care over these last few months if you will agree to become my wife."

Maire sat staring at him.

"Maire?"

Kirk's company had marched in formation, practiced shooting and every other form of military exercise known to the commanding officers, for weeks. They'd march from Philadelphia en route to Canada to join Colonel Benedict Arnold in Quebec tomorrow in hopes of shoring up his defense after the disastrous attack of December 31. They'd have a short time to report in for supplies, mail call, and official orders before moving out. Kirk had procured a few hours' leave for personal business. He'd sent a young messenger to find Bartholomew. If his message made it to Maire, the information he had to pass on would make all the difference for them.

As he neared the Frankford Bridge, he spotted Bartholomew doing his best to block the winter wind for Maire. He jogged to meet them.

Her smile warmed his heart on this cold, blustery day. "Come inside the carriage. I haven't long, but I can offer you a moment's respite."

"I have good news for ye, love." Kirk unrolled the paper. "This is from the man who started the fire at John's. He'd been deep in his cups when he confessed being paid to set fire to a field and mill. The man was beside himself, eaten up thinkin' he'd killed a woman he saw at the window. He never meant to set the house ablaze. The fire got out of control."

"You found him?" The wind died down a bit.

"I stumbled on the man at the Red Lyon the night I went to join. I'd just finished signing me name when the man cried out to save him from the banshee. In his stupor, he thought the woman became a banshee and hunted him day and night. He couldn't rid himself of the face tormenting his dreams so he spent himself into a lush."

"A banshee." She looked to heaven. " 'Tis heavy guilt to think a demon is after ye."

"After sobering the sot up, I got him to write a confession. There'd been so many witnesses to the confession, the man went to the jail. But Julius Pearson will stand trial for hiring the vagrant and nearly costing your life."

"I cannae believe ye've done it!"

"Maire, how did you get away?"

"I'm to do the household shopping, Kirk." She kissed him. " 'Tis enough to be here with ye and tell ye I'll always love ye." Her tone seemed odd to him.

"Maire, will ye be safe returnin'?"

"Ye have no fear to go to battle, yet ye worry when it comes to me." She lifted a valise. "I've made these for ye to wear. I hope they'll keep ye warmer."

He opened the top and pulled out thick wool stockings in a red, blue, and yellow tartan with a white garter made of linen. Then knit mitts lined with the same pattern, and a heavy plaid cravat to keep his chest warm. He recognized the weave. "Maire, this was your clan plaid, and ye made these things for me? I cannae tell ye how much it means to me."

"There's a waistcoat, too, but then I ran out of material. I couldn't make any breeches. There's only a strip of it left." She kissed him again, sweet and long. "I must go now. God go with ye. I pray we meet again this side of heaven."

Epilogue

Maire stood in front of the justice with Kirk by her side. Julius glared as he was led away to be deported. His business and home confiscated for the use of the new American government. All his slaves sold, including Maire's contract. "You have the funds to purchase this woman's indenture from the court?"

"I do, Your Honor. I've sold some land awarded me for my service to the country."

"Very well, then, I see no reason to delay." His gavel banged. "Pay the clerk and you may go about your business."

"If it please the court, sir, I'd also be interested in the slaves Bartholomew and Etta."

"For what purpose is this request?"

"Your Honor, I am building a gristmill to help the cause. I could use the help."

"You also have enough funds to purchase said slaves?"

"Yes, sir, I do."

"Pay the clerk." He waved them aside before Kirk had a chance to say anything else.

The trees gave way to a small meadow filled with spring flowers. Maire couldn't have asked for a more beautiful spot to build a home, raise children, and spend the rest of her days. "When can we move in?" She looked at Kirk with glowing eyes.

"Today, as soon as the preacher and our witnesses arrive." He tied the horses loosely to a fence post on the edge of the woods where they could easily wander to the creek bank. "I've sent for others to help us finish the barnyard, cut timber for our gristmill, and plant fields. With the new apprentice, we'll have the mill running in time for harvest."

"All our dreams are comin' true." Maire marveled at the sunshine spilling across the green grasses, how the flowers stretched their petals heavenward, and that deep in the Pennsylvania woods a small log cabin held the future. "If only Da were here to see this. I don't think the message reached him, or I'd have heard by now."

"Did I forget to give you this?" Kirk searched his pockets. "It's here somewhere."

"A letter? Ye have a letter from Da and ye—"

He grinned. "I didnae forget." He lifted his fingers to his lips and whistled. "Someone else is delivering the message."

The cabin door opened. Seamus Greer, followed by Sean and his family, filed out onto the porch. "We havin' a weddin' finally?" her father called out to them.

"Da! Sean!" She picked up her skirts and ran into their arms, reaching out to scoop her sister-in-law and little nephews into the family circle. "I cannae believe it!"

She looked at Kirk, shaking her head, joy emanating from her in the exuberant, noisy reunion. "I cannae believe it!"

Her father laughed and left the group to meet Kirk with a handshake. "I've ne'er seen me girl so happy."

"Da, how could ye no' tell me ye were all coming?"

"I thought I'd bring the message meself. The letter would travel on the same ship, I says to meself, why not say it in person?" He laughed and hugged her again.

"How?"

"The lad sent over an apprentice position for Sean here. Without him to work the land, me auld bones couldnae manage. I sold the farm. Should your sister's family choose to come, the lot o' us will work together. So Kirk Lachlan says."

Kirk nodded and wrapped an arm around Maire's waist. "Will ye wed me now?"

"Aye." She took the strip of cloth, checkered in red, blue, and yellow and slipped it across her shoulder. She may not wear the full arisaid, but a bit of her history would walk this day with her.

The circuit-riding preacher jotted a note into his journal:

May 1, 1776, does this day come the bride, Maire Greer, to wed of her own volition the groom, Kirk Lachlan. . . . Bride's occupation—homemaker and weaver. Groom's occupation—millwright.

Angela Breidenbach is a bestselling author, host of *Lit Up!* with Angela Breidenbach, and the Christian Author Network's president. And, yes, she's half of the fun fe-lion comedy duo, Muse and Writer, on social media.

Note from Angela: "I love hearing from readers and enjoy book club chats. To drop me a note or set up a book club chat, contact me at angie.breidenbach@gmail.com. Let me know if you'd like me to post a quote from your review of this story. If you send me the link and your social media handle, I'll post it to my social media with a word of gratitude including your name and/or social media handle, too!"

For more about Angela's books (especially more Montana-inspired romances) and podcast, or to set up a book club chat, please visit her website: http://www.Angela-Breidenbach.com Facebook/Instagram/Pinterest/Twitter: @AngBreidenbach

The Suspect Bride

by Susan Page Davis

Chapter 1

Oregon,
1890

Verity Ames carried two plates of the roast beef dinner special out into the White Pine's dining room and set them before two ranchers seated at the long table.

"Now, don't that look fine?" said a cowboy from the Flying J Ranch with a wide grin. "Did you make that yourself?"

"I surely did," Verity said.

His companion, also of the Flying J, nodded. "Smells good, too. Thank you, darlin'."

Verity waved away his sweet talk. "Enjoy your dinner, boys."

She strode back to the kitchen for a fresh pot of coffee. Usually the owner's wife, Bertha, handled the serving while Verity kept on cooking and dishing up bowls of stew and plates of roast beef or chicken dinners, but today Bertha had pleaded illness, so Verity was alone. The boss, Obie Cogswell, could have helped if he wanted to, but he insisted his job as owner was to greet the customers and make sure they felt welcome. In other words, he sat through most dinner hours chewing the fat with the ranchmen and merchants who came in to eat.

She grabbed the steaming coffeepot and pushed the second pot over to the hottest part of the stovetop. In the dining room she made the rounds, topping off cups and offering coffee to those who hadn't yet claimed a serving.

She looked up as more diners entered the restaurant. Mr. Hermon, the banker, came in, and the entire Leare family, no doubt in town for shopping. Behind them came a well-built young man wearing a suit and carrying his bowler hat. Verity nodded and smiled. He nodded back and headed for his usual seat, as far from the door as he could get.

She could set her watch by Jack Whitwell, if she carried a watch. He came in every day at ten past noon. Verity took Sunday off, but the restaurant stayed open, and she would almost bet he came in Sundays, too—if she were a betting woman.

A lot of bachelors ate at the White Pine if they could afford to because the food was so good. It wasn't the finest restaurant in town. It didn't have a glittery chandelier and linen tablecloths like the Willamette Hotel's dining room, or piano music and candles like the Sunset. But if you wanted tasty, hearty food at noontime, everyone in town knew the White Pine was the place to go.

She quickly set a cup and saucer at Mr. Hermon's elbow.

"Good day, Mr. Hermon."

The banker smiled up at her. "Hello, Miss Ames. Where's Bertha today?"

"Feeling poorly." Verity poured strong, hot coffee into his cup. "You take sweetening, is that right?"

He nodded, and she moved up the table to grab a sugar bowl and set it within easy reach for him.

"I'll have the stew and biscuits, please," Mr. Hermon said.

"Coming right up."

Another cowboy wandered in and found a seat down near Jack Whitwell. Verity threw a pleading glance at Obie, but the restaurant owner ignored her, expanding on a story he was telling the barber and the stagecoach station agent. He waved his hands about as he spun the yarn, and the other men guffawed. Verity puffed out a breath. She was on her own.

She poured coffee for Mr. and Mrs. Leare and took the family's dinner order, glad she'd fried extra chicken this morning since three of the four Leares wanted it. She grabbed two more mugs from the sideboard and at last reached Jack and the cowboy.

"Hello, Mr. Whitwell. Here's your coffee." She set a mug down and slid the other across the table toward the cowboy.

"Thanks," Jack said. "You're busy today. Where's Mrs. Cogswell?"

"Sick. What'll you have?"

"I'll take the roast beef, if you've got plenty."

"I think there's just about one serving left," Verity said. She smiled at the new cowboy. "You weren't hankering for roast beef, were you?"

"Not if you've got fried chicken today," he said.

"I do. It'll be here in just a minute. I have to serve the Leare family and Mr. Hermon first."

"No rush," Jack said, and she knew he meant it. Jack usually lingered over his meal. Sometimes she was able to go out and help Bertha clear off the tables when most of the other customers were gone, and then she might get in a word or two with the quiet lawyer. She looked forward to those snippets of conversation. Anything Jack Whitwell said interested her.

She slid her last pan of biscuits into the oven and took Mr. Hermon's bowl of stew out to the dining room. He got a plate of biscuits and a fresh butter dish with it. It didn't hurt to treat the banker a tad special and not make him get his butter from the greasy, messy dish twenty other people had dipped from. She made sure salt and pepper shakers sat near his place.

The Leares were next: three chicken dinners and one roast beef. She hurried, but one of the girls complained that the biscuits were cold.

"I'm sorry," Verity said. "I've got a new batch in the oven, and as soon as they're ready, I'll bring you some piping hot."

That seemed to mollify them. She didn't tell them it would be ten minutes or so before they were done. To her relief, no new diners had come in while she was in the kitchen, and three or four had vacated their places. She went to get Jack's and the cowboy's dinners.

"I'm sorry the biscuits aren't hot," she said as she set down their plates. "I have more in the oven, and I'll get you some hot ones when they're done."

The cowboy picked one up and held it between his hands. "Not stone cold. I'd say that's purty good, Miss Verity."

"Thanks. Buck, isn't it?"

"Yup. I'm at the Broken Wheel Ranch."

"Nice to see you." She turned her attention to Jack.

"This looks fine, Miss Verity."

She smiled. "Thank you. Can I get you anything else, Mr. Whitwell?"

"No, ma'am. I might have some pie later."

She nodded. She'd come in at dawn to bake a dozen pies. "We've got apple, custard, and mincemeat. Want me to save any of those with your name on it?"

"I like your custard real well." Jack had a way of looking deep into her eyes when he complimented her cooking that made Verity want to swoon. Those rich brown eyes of his always made her heart jump up and hover then flip-flop down again.

"I'll save you a nice, big piece." She glanced at Buck. "How about you?"

"Apple." He took a big bite from a chicken leg and smacked his lips.

Verity nodded. "I'll be back."

Funny how the highlight of her day was exchanging a few words with a shy legal man. At least she figured Jack was shy. He'd been away at law school when she started working at the White Pine, but he'd returned last fall, after he passed the bar exam. He'd set up his office in a tiny room off the haberdasher's shop. Clients had to go through the shop to get to Jack's office.

He had come into the White Pine nearly every day since. It had taken him three months to speak to her, other than giving a terse order on the occasions when she waited on him.

Then one day Bertha had come into the kitchen with a tray of dirty dishes and told her, "That lawyer fellow, Whitwell, said to tell you the gravy was extra good today."

Verity smiled every time she thought about it. From that day onward, she'd made a point of looking into the dining room during the dinner hour, and when Jack Whitwell was there, she tried to find a chance to offer Bertha a hand clearing off tables. Jack always smiled when she worked in his vicinity, and sometimes he said hello or remarked on the quality of his dinner—always with approval. She was sure Jack liked her, but of course he had never said anything like that.

Jack ate his roast beef dinner slowly. It was tasty, and he wanted it to last. Buck Fuller, across the table, was nearly done with his fried chicken feast, but Jack liked to savor each bite, especially when Verity Ames was within view.

She bent over the far end of the long table, gathering in dirty plates, half-empty cups, and soiled cotton napkins. She was working all alone today, and she'd had a hard time keeping up with the orders. He'd heard her tell two men the roast beef was all gone, but they still had stew left. He tried not to feel guilty for claiming the last serving of roast beef.

He also tried not to stare at Verity. Instead, he shot a glance her way now and then. Even so, it was hard not to pause when he watched her. A chuckle from Buck told him he'd been caught at it.

"She's easy on the eyes," Buck said softly.

Jack cleared his throat and reached for his coffee mug, studiously looking past Buck, toward the window.

"More coffee, gentlemen?"

He jumped when she spoke. How had she sneaked up so close in such a short time? And she had Buck's apple pie on a thick ironstone plate in one hand, with the big enameled coffeepot, blue with white spatters, in the other.

"Yes, ma'am," Buck said jovially, holding up his mug.

Jack set his carefully on the table closer to Verity and nodded. She poured it nearly full and caught his eye as she moved the pot away.

"I'll bring your pie out whenever you're ready, Mr. Whitwell."

He wanted to say, "Call me Jack," but he could already feel his cheeks warming. He managed a low, "Thank you."

When she moved away, Buck shook his head, chewing. He swallowed and grinned at Jack. "She sure can cook. If I had my own place, I'd pop the question on that one."

Jack tried to laugh, but he couldn't. He had the feeling Buck knew just how uncomfortable the light remark made him.

The cowboy eyed him keenly. "You got your own place?"

"Not yet."

"Hmm." Buck took a swallow of his coffee. "I ain't one to settle down. Most cowboys just ain't. But a lawyer, now. . ."

Jack wished he had the nerve to get up and move to another spot.

Finally, Buck finished his pie and his coffee, coming out even at the end. He pushed his chair back as Verity came from the kitchen to take a tardy diner's order.

"You got any more apple pie?" Buck asked.

"I might," Verity said. "You buying?"

"Sure, I'll take a piece with me, if you can wrap it up."

"I'll be right with you. Just let me take this gentleman's order."

Jack poked at the last bite of baked potato and swirled it in the smear of gravy left on his plate. Maybe when Buck finally cleared out, Verity would bring his custard pie. There were only three customers left, besides the newcomer. Obie Cogswell had wandered outside when a couple of the merchants left. Maybe he would have a chance to speak to Verity again. Maybe, if he dared, he could ask her if she was planning to attend the church social on Saturday. Jack's heart tripped faster, just thinking about asking her. Would he be able to get out an invitation? He'd wanted to ask her out last week, when a traveling magician was in town, but she'd mostly stayed in the kitchen that day, and he hadn't had a chance.

She chatted only a moment with the new diner and then headed for the kitchen. She emerged a minute later with a tray and handed Buck a small parcel wrapped in brown paper.

"That'll be an extra dime, and thank you very much."

Buck handed her the dime and took the package. "'Bye, Miss Verity. See ya."

" 'Bye now." She walked to the new customer and set his plate and a glass of water off the tray. She exchanged pleasantries with the man, and finally she picked up the tray again—a tray that held only a generous slice of custard pie—and headed Jack's way.

"Sorry to keep you waiting, Mr. Whitwell."

Jack cleared his throat. "It's Jack." There! He'd said it. "And it's all right."

Her smile just about did him in.

"Would you like more coffee, Jack?"

"Maybe half a cup?" He wondered just how red his face was. Hers looked all smooth and pink, with a sheen of perspiration on her forehead, but that was understandable. She'd been working in the kitchen for hours.

He watched her as she topped off his coffee, trying to work up his nerve for the next step. If she said yes, maybe he could escort her to the social. And if she agreed to that, maybe he could ask her that night if he could court her. She lived with her sister and brother-in-law on Spruce Street. He knew just where the snug two-story house sat, and what route her brother-in-law, Sherman Baker, took every morning to his jewelry store on Main Street.

She glanced at him, still smiling. "Anything else, Jack?"

"Well, yes. Uh. . ." He cleared his throat again.

The front door flew open, and Sheriff Midland strode in. He paused and looked around, and his gaze focused on Verity. He walked toward them.

"Miss Ames."

"Yes, Sheriff? Can I get you some dinner?"

"No, I've had my dinner, thank you. You're under arrest."

The metal coffeepot clattered to the floor, splashing coffee on Verity's hem and the pine floorboards.

Chapter 2

Whatever for?" Verity took a step backward and stood wringing her hands and staring at the sheriff.

Midland stopped in front of her and pulled in a deep breath. In his most official voice, he intoned, "Hold out your hands, please. You'll have to come with me."

"But what—? I—" She looked helplessly toward Jack.

He caught the pleading in her blue eyes and pushed back his chair.

"Sheriff, what's the meaning of this? Miss Ames has been here all morning, working hard."

"Can't help it." Midland stepped forward and snapped his handcuffs onto Verity's trembling wrists. The few remaining customers stared unabashed at the drama.

"Come along," the sheriff said.

"Wait," Jack cried.

Midland froze and looked at him, and Verity caught a deep breath.

"I'm Miss Ames's attorney," Jack said firmly. "I'd like to be there when you question her. With her permission, of course."

She nodded, her face a stricken mask. "Please," she whispered.

Midland scowled. "I suppose. After I get her settled in the jailhouse. Come on, Miss Ames." He took her by the arm and steered her toward the door of the restaurant. Jack grabbed his hat off the bench and hurried after them, regretting that he'd delayed eating his pie. But Verity's defense was much more important.

Mr. Cogswell almost ran into Verity and the sheriff as they went out the door. He pulled up short and stared at the handcuffs on Verity's slender wrists. "What's the meaning of this, Bob?"

Sheriff Midland didn't stop walking, forcing Cogswell to step out of the way. "It's a matter of business, Obie."

"But—but she's my employee!"

"Can't help it." Midland kept walking, propelling Verity toward his office.

Jack stepped out the doorway and down the front steps.

"What about the day's receipts?" Cogswell screamed.

"It's in the tin," Verity replied, turning in Midland's grasp and looking over her shoulder. "It's all where we usually keep it."

"I'm Miss Ames's lawyer," Jack said quickly to Cogswell. "I'm going over to the sheriff's office to see what this is all about."

"Good, good." Mr. Cogswell stood there, staring after them.

Jack hurried down the boardwalk. Bob Midland might be a force to reckon with, but he couldn't go around arresting people and not telling them what for. When he got to the sheriff's office, Midland already had Verity in the first of the two cells and was locking the door. At least the handcuffs were off now.

"I need to send word to my sister." Verity's voice cracked.

"Your lawyer's here. He can tell your sister," Midland grumbled.

Jack stepped inside the office and closed the door. "Sheriff, what exactly is Miss Ames accused of?"

Midland whirled toward him. "Just hold your horses, Whitwell. I've got to do a little paperwork. The county attorney gets testy if I don't do it right away."

Midland crossed to his desk and sat down in the creaky oak chair. He took up a fountain pen and began carefully filling in some information on a sheet of paper. Jack looked toward the barred wall of the cells. Verity clung to the bars on the near one's door, her eyes beseeching him. Jack couldn't ignore her silent plea. He took two steps toward her.

"Hold it, Whitwell."

Jack whirled toward the sheriff. "I need to talk to my client."

"Don't be in such an all-fired hurry."

"Then talk to me." Jack's heart hammered. Bob Midland scared him a little. He was three inches taller than Jack, and he probably weighed fifty pounds more. He'd been known to pound the stuffing out of a drunk, and he'd shot down two bank robbers without a moment's hesitation, or so the stories went around town. But if he was going to help Verity, Jack would have to stand up to him and demand that her rights were observed.

Midland sighed and threw down his pen, splashing a bit of ink on his desktop. "It seems Miss Ames's brother-in-law is missing."

Jack tried to digest that. He looked at Verity, behind the bars. She looked back, her mouth open in surprise.

"And how does that make it your business to arrest Miss Ames?" Jack said.

"Well, Mrs. Baker summoned me to her house about an hour ago. When I got there, I found her husband's study in disarray. There was blood on the floor."

Jack frowned. "Go on."

Midland shrugged. "After investigating, I concluded that Miss Ames is a likely suspect."

Jack stepped closer. "Suspect for what? Messing up her brother-in-law's study? Dripping blood on the floor? I don't see any cuts on Miss Ames. What's the charge? And what evidence do you have that says she was even there?"

The sheriff frowned and glanced toward Verity. "That's for me to know for now, Whitwell. I need to do some more investigating. When I have all the facts in hand, we can talk."

"Then you can't keep her here," Jack said. "If you're not charging her, you can't lock her up."

"Then I'll make the charges formal right now. I wanted to wait a bit—"

"In that case, you should have waited a bit to take her into custody." Jack was gaining steam, feeling more confident as the sheriff's shaky grounds for the arrest became clearer.

"I don't know but she'd run away," Midland said with a stubborn edge.

"Run away? She went to work this morning and was there all day, toiling hard, until you came in and stopped her. She's not going to run away, or she'd have done it."

Midland scowled. "She's staying here unless I find out she's innocent."

"No," Jack said. "She's not staying here unless you charge her with a crime."

"All right, then." Midland picked up his pen and sorted through the papers. "Miss Ames, you are charged with murder."

Jack gulped. "Murder?"

Verity looked as though she'd have collapsed if she weren't hanging on to the bars.

Midland nodded. "That's the charge."

"You said Sherman Baker was missing," Jack noted. "You didn't say he was dead."

"It's still the charge." Midland started writing.

"Based on what evidence?"

"All in good time, sonny."

Jack watched him for a moment, fuming inwardly. He tried to get hold of his swirling thoughts. This was no time to get angry.

What could possibly make Midland think Verity Ames had killed her brother-in-law? There had to be something that made him believe it. Or was he just settling an old score with her? Uneasily, Jack glanced at Verity. Her shoulders had slumped, but she still stood at the cell door. He'd heard things in town not long after he'd come back and set up his practice. Whether they were true or not, he didn't know, but if there was anything to the rumors, Sheriff Midland might have reason to hold a grudge against Verity. Had he arrested her out of spite?

He cleared his throat. "I need to speak privately to my client, and then I'll be on my way."

Midland didn't look up but waved a languid hand toward the cells. "Be my guest."

"I said privately."

"This is as private as it gets, sonny."

Jack stood his ground for a moment. It probably wouldn't do any good to push the matter now. He would choose his battles with Midland. And he had a feeling there would be plenty ahead.

He walked over and stood facing Verity, with the barred door between them.

"Are you all right?"

She nodded, her eyes glistening with unshed tears. "I don't understand this at all. Did you mean it when you said you'd act as my lawyer?"

"Of course."

She sighed and closed her eyelids for a moment. "Thank you. If you won't mind telling Prudence I'm here. . ." She looked up at him.

Jack nodded. "I'll go over right away. But I'll come back later this afternoon, after I have a chance to find out a little more."

Verity looked up at him. "He said Sherman is missing."

"Yes, but he's tossing a murder charge about. He knows something he's not telling."

"I can't imagine what." She let out a little sob. "Prudence must be distraught. I should be with her."

"I'll express your condolences. How long have you lived with her and Mr. Baker?"

"Since they were married," Verity said. "Prudence was made my guardian after our parents died."

"I see. Was everything all right between you and the Bakers?"

"Everything was fine. Normal."

Jack took what she said at face value, but still, the troubled cast to her blue eyes made him wonder if there was more to the situation.

"Did you see Mr. Sherman this morning?" he asked.

"No, he wasn't up when I left for work. I have to be at the restaurant early, to start breakfast. I usually leave the house by five, and Sherman and Prudence haven't usually risen by then."

"I see." Jack's mind raced. He wished Bob Midland wasn't sitting at his desk ten feet away. Jack had no doubt he could hear every word they uttered. "What about the study? Did you happen to look in there?"

"No, I rarely go into that room. Sherman has all his papers from the business in there."

"Not at the store?"

"He brings his paperwork home. They have a back room at the store, but that's mostly where they work on people's jewelry—repairs and such. I suppose they have some records there, but he does most of the ordering and correspondence at home."

Jack nodded. "All right."

"What will happen to me, Mr. Whitwell?" She stood on tiptoe and peered anxiously over his shoulder.

Jack turned around enough so he could see Midland, still sitting behind the desk, ostensibly engrossed in the papers before him. He leaned close and whispered, "I hope to have you out of here soon. If I can't manage that, I'll ask your sister to bring you some things."

She nodded, her face white. "I can't believe—" She broke off and looked into his eyes. "This is so ghastly. I would never hurt Sherman."

"Don't despair. As far as I can tell, the sheriff doesn't have a body or a murder weapon or even a motive." He watched her closely but could tell nothing from her reaction, but he wondered if there was more he didn't know. He would have to arrange more privacy if Midland continued to hold her, that was certain.

Jack left the sheriff's office with a curt nod to Midland and headed for Spruce Street. The Baker home was set back from the street on a large lot, with two large oaks shading the front yard. The house looked well cared for, and it was larger than average for the town. The house of a prosperous man but not a mansion.

He walked up to the front door and knocked. He knew Mrs. Baker by sight from observing the family from a distance at Sunday services. When the door opened, he was surprised to find himself facing a middle-aged woman with a dour face, wearing a plain gray dress and an apron.

"Hello," Jack said. "I'm Jack Whitwell, here to see Mrs. Baker."

The woman raised her chin and eyed him with misgiving. "She's had a shock, poor thing."

"Yes. I'm sorry, but I must speak to her."

"She's in the parlor." She led Jack to the parlor doorway. "Mrs. Baker, that smart young lawyer is here to see you." She stepped aside.

Jack entered to find Prudence Baker rising from her upholstered chair. She wore a stylish blue morning dress, and her golden hair, the same shade as Verity's, was caught up in a cascade of curls. Her complexion looked blotchy, however, as though she hadn't powdered her face that day, or had scrubbed all the powder off in a fit of weeping. Her eyes were red, and the skin around them puffy. She came to meet him, extending her hand.

"Mr. Whitwell, isn't it?"

"Yes, ma'am. I'm so sorry to bother you during this difficult time, but I'm here on behalf of your sister."

Mrs. Baker's blue eyes snapped. "Verity? What has she to do with this?"

"Nothing, that I know of. However, some folks think otherwise." Jack glanced at the woman who had ushered him in. "May I speak to you in private, ma'am?"

"Of course. Martha, would you mind fixing us some tea?" Her gaze shot to Jack. "Unless, of course, you'd prefer something else, Mr. Whitwell."

"No, tea is fine, thank you."

The other woman nodded and left the room. *A hired woman*, Jack thought. A cook-housekeeper perhaps. But if the Bakers were so well off, why did Verity need to work so hard at the restaurant?

"Won't you sit down?" Prudence gestured toward the settee near her chair, and Jack seated himself.

"I think it best to come to the point," Jack said. "I've just left the jail. Sheriff Midland has your sister there, under lock and key. Miss Ames asked me to inform you of her whereabouts."

The shock on Prudence's face was unmistakable. Jack didn't think she was feigning.

"What—why? I don't understand."

"He is charging her with your husband's murder," Jack said gently.

"My husband's— Oh!" she covered her face with her hands. "Then Sherman is dead?"

"I don't know, ma'am. The sheriff said at first that he was missing, but then he declared he was charging Miss Ames with murder. Your sister claims to know nothing of the matter. She says she didn't see you or your husband before she left this morning for her job at the restaurant, and there are plenty of people in town who can vouch for her being there all morning. So I'm as much at a loss as you are."

Prudence lowered her hands and stared at him, breathing rapidly.

"He thinks she had something to do with Sherman's disappearance?"

"Apparently," Jack said. "Perhaps you could tell me what took place here this morning and what passed between you and Sheriff Midland when he came here."

She drew in a deep, shaky breath. "All right, if you think it will help."

"Just to be clear, your sister has agreed to let me represent her. My first object is to have her released from jail, but I need to know the circumstances. She is totally in the dark."

"Of course. I confess, I'm as baffled as she is. I went out this morning to attend a Ladies' Aid meeting, and when I came home—" She sobbed and pulled a handkerchief from her cuff. "Oh, dear, it was terrible."

"What was terrible?" Jack asked.

She swallowed hard and dabbed at her eyes with the hankie. "The door to my husband's study was open. He usually leaves it closed, so I thought perhaps he had come home from the store early for dinner. I walked down the hallway and looked in, expecting to find him at his desk. Instead, I found a horrible disarray. My first thought was that someone had broken in and robbed us."

"But you don't think that now?"

"I don't know what to think." Prudence shook her head. "I went immediately to the kitchen. Our cook, Martha Ives, was there. I asked her if Mr. Baker had been home. Martha said she didn't know. She'd only come in a few minutes before me, and she went in through the back door. She hadn't been out into the front hall."

"What did you do next?"

"I ran upstairs to see if by any chance Sherman was in our chamber, but he wasn't. I went back down and asked Martha to run to the store. I told her I feared we'd been burgled while I was at the Ladies' Aid, and I wanted Sherman to come home at once." Fresh tears flowed down her cheeks. "But it was so much worse than I'd feared. Martha came in a few minutes later with Sherman's partner. He said my husband hadn't been to the store this morning."

"Not at all?"

"No. And when I showed him the mess in Sherman's study, he went at once to fetch the sheriff."

Jack thought about that. "Did you think anything was missing?"

She spread her hands, and her diamond ring caught a ray of light and sparkled. "Who could tell? His papers were strewn about—here, let me show you."

She rose, and Jack jumped to his feet. He followed her out into the hall and a few yards along it to another door.

"In there."

He opened the door and peered inside. The room was indeed in disorder, with books and papers thrown carelessly about, drawers open on the large mahogany desk, and shelves cleared with abandon, the contents lying on the floor.

"I see." He looked at Mrs. Baker, who stood in the doorway frowning. "What about the rest of the house?"

"I didn't find anything else disturbed. My jewelry box, for instance. It was untouched. As I asked the sheriff, don't you think a burglar would help himself to that?"

Yes, Jack thought, *unless he was interrupted.* "Perhaps he heard your cook come in and ran off."

"I suppose that's possible. But then the sheriff spotted the blood." She shuddered.

Jack arched his eyebrows.

"Over there, where he sits." She pointed toward the desk, and Jack walked cautiously around it. Sure enough, a large patch of drying blood marred the hardwood floor, and the arm of the desk chair was also smeared with it.

Mrs. Baker sobbed. "It looks as if he was attacked."

"Easy, now. We don't know that it's Mr. Baker's blood."

She stared at him and sniffed. "Then whose? If the burglar injured himself that badly, surely he'd be lying here on the floor, and Sherman would have been at the store."

"I'm not sure what it all means," Jack said, "but I don't see how it implicates Miss Ames."

"Neither do I." Prudence turned toward the hall and said, "Oh, thank you, Martha. Just put it in the parlor." She turned back to face the room. "Our tea is ready."

"Let's go and sit down, then." Jack couldn't see how further examination of the study would help him, since he had no idea what had been in the room this morning or what might be missing.

He followed Mrs. Baker back to the parlor, where Martha had set the tea tray on a small side table. Mrs. Baker sat down, and he was about to seat himself when a firm knocking sounded on the front door.

Chapter 3

A large man of about thirty years, dressed in a good quality black suit, brushed past Martha and strode into the room.

"Prudence! I've just seen the sheriff again, and he's arrested your sister."

Mrs. Baker stood shakily, and Jack leaped up, watching to see if he needed to catch her on short notice.

"So I have heard," Prudence said. "I can't think why he would do that."

The man advanced toward her but paused when he glanced at Jack.

"Do I know you?"

"I'm Jack Whitwell, Miss Ames's attorney."

"Oh, of course. I've seen you around." He extended his large hand, and Jack took it. "Thomas Phillips. I'm Sherman Baker's partner."

"There's no word of Sherman at the store, then?" Prudence quavered.

"I'm afraid not." Phillips went to her side and guided her down onto the settee, taking a seat beside her. "We haven't heard a word from him all day. Most unusual."

"But why has the sheriff detained Verity?" Prudence scanned Phillips's face anxiously. "She can't have anything to do with this.

Phillips looked a bit sheepish. "I'm afraid that might be my fault. After we left here this morning, the sheriff asked me if I know of any conflicts Sherman had recently. I told him about the argument he had with Verity a few days ago, and the sheriff seemed to find it very interesting." He glanced at Jack. "I'm glad to hear she has legal representation. This is probably all a to-do over nothing."

"You think Sherman is all right, then?" Prudence asked. "Because the sheriff seems to think he's d–dead."

"I don't know what's happened," Phillips admitted, "but I expect we'll find out."

Jack sat forward. "Could you tell me about the argument you referred to?"

"Oh. Well. . ." Phillips looked at Mrs. Baker.

"I didn't know they argued," she said fretfully. "They've wrangled a bit over the dinner table about Verity's inheritance. You say she went to the store and spoke to Sherman about it?"

"Yes, one day last week she came into the store and asked to speak to Sherman. He took her in the back, and I heard their voices raised, so I closed the door. I only caught a few words, but I think it was as you say, Prudence—concerning the money she inherited from your parents."

Prudence sighed.

"Can you tell me about that?" Jack asked gently.

"It's a sensitive topic in this house, I'm afraid," she replied.

"It's a family matter, for sure," Phillips said. "I should get back to the store anyway. I'll leave you to discuss it in private."

"Thank you."

Jack stood, and Mrs. Baker got up and accompanied Phillips to the front door, thanking him for coming and extracting a promise to notify her if he heard anything at all about her husband. She returned a moment later and resumed her seat with an exasperated air.

"I really don't think this matter is serious enough to make the sheriff think Verity would do Sherman harm," she said. "Oh, look, our tea is getting cold."

"That's all right," Jack said. "I would like very much to hear about Miss Ames's inheritance. If there's nothing in it, I can make that case to the sheriff. But if there is something there, I need to know the details."

While he spoke, Prudence had poured out two cups of tea. "I should have offered some to Thomas." She held a cup and saucer out to Jack.

It was still warm, and he took a gulp.

"Sugar?" she asked. "Cream?"

"No, thank you. But perhaps you could ask your housekeeper to put together a bag for Miss Ames. I don't know how long she will be detained, but I'm sure she could use a few personal items."

Of course. Prudence left the room for a moment and then returned.

"Martha is seeing to it." She sat down, sipped from her cup, and set it down. "Verity was only thirteen when our parents died. It was a carriage accident, and they both passed away the same hour."

"I'm very sorry. That must have been difficult for both of you."

"It was." She sat still for a moment as though letting the memories wash over her. Her lips twitched. "Sherman and I had been married only a few months. As her closest living relative, I was made Verity's guardian."

Jack nodded. No problem so far. "And your husband?"

"Sherman was made a trustee of her money. Verity and I each inherited a substantial sum. Our parents' home was sold and the proceeds divided."

"And you received your share immediately?" Jack asked.

"Yes. Verity's was put in trust pending her twenty-first birthday, which came around last February."

"Eight years." Jack peered at her. "Did she receive her share then?"

Prudence hesitated. "Sherman thought it best that she not receive it all until she married. Verity was quite upset about that and said the money was legally hers."

Jack nodded and kept silent. Unless there were terms to the trust that she hadn't revealed, Verity was right. Her trustees should have planned in advance to turn it over to her on the day she reached her majority.

"Sherman had invested the principal for her, and he explained that she would suffer fines if she liquidated it too soon. But he promised to do it as soon as was practical. He didn't want her to lose money because she was too eager."

Jack tried to keep his voice even, but it sounded to him as though Verity might have had a reason to be peeved with her brother-in-law. "Surely that was up to Miss Ames."

Prudence lowered her eyelashes. "Sherman knows so much more about these things, Mr. Whitwell. I'm afraid Verity just doesn't understand finance or how long these things take. I don't claim to understand it myself."

Jack eyed her closely. Was she really that naive? "Do you think your sister harmed Mr. Baker, then?"

"I don't like to think that, but, to be honest, I don't know what to think. It's all such a muddle."

Jack rose. "I should be on my way. Is there any message you would like me to convey to your sister?"

Prudence hesitated. "It's so distressing."

Jack nodded. "Right, then. Good day, Mrs. Baker. I can let myself out." He strode for the door.

Once out in the bright daylight, Jack set his course toward the jail. Verity obviously couldn't count on her sister's support. His path led him past Baker and Phillips Fine Jewelry. He slowed his steps and gazed at the items displayed in the front window—a tray of pocket watches, and a gold pendant set with a purple stone that might be an amethyst, hung on a board lined with black velvet. He couldn't see any prices showing.

He went in and spoke to the clerk at the counter, but the conversation yielded nothing helpful. Back out on the sidewalk, he squared his shoulders and headed for the nearest saloon. Ordinarily, he would steer clear of such establishments, but when it came to finding evidence, he would leave no stone unturned. He'd heard whispers when he first came back from law school, and he couldn't think of a better person to ask about them than a bartender.

Verity sat on the edge of the iron cot, thankful that her cell's twin was unoccupied. It was bad enough being thrown in here falsely accused, but she wasn't sure how she would stand it if some miscreant was locked in the other cell.

Weeping would do no good, she decided early on. Instead, she tried to work out what had happened at Sherman and Prudence's house this morning, and how anyone could possibly imagine that she was involved.

The sheriff came in and sat down at his desk, the chair creaking in protest. Verity had been pondering her situation for an hour when the front door was flung open. She couldn't see the newcomer unless she stood and went to the front of the cell, but she didn't need to. Obie Cogswell's voice was unmistakable.

"Sheriff, I demand that you let Miss Ames loose."

"Why would I do that, Obie?" Midland asked mildly. Verity could almost see him leaning back in his chair and gazing up at her employer.

"I need her over at the restaurant. Bertha's sick, and I got nobody to start cooking dinner."

"That's not my problem." Midland's chair creaked.

Obie swore and stomped out, slamming the door behind him.

Verity let out a long, shaky breath. How long would Sheriff Midland keep her here? And could Jack Whitwell do anything to help her?

Jack. She had thought a mere two hours ago that he might ask her to go to the church social with him, and wondered if the handsome young lawyer could possibly view her as wife material. She'd felt an attraction to him from the moment she first saw him six months ago, and everything she heard about him in the restaurant and about town confirmed her first impression. He was an honest, diligent, God-fearing man. Verity had dared to think he might notice her, and when he did, that he might favor her with his attentions. A home, a life together, a family—all of that was wound up in her longings and her thoughts of Jack Whitwell.

Now her dreams were shattered. How could he ever look at her that way when she had been imprisoned? Her only reason for hope was that they lived in the West. If this had happened in the East, her reputation would be ruined, beyond redemption. No decent woman could overcome the scandal of having been to jail. Out here, people were not so fussy about one another's past. She could go to another town and find work and start over. Someplace where no one knew her—maybe Texas or Kansas or Montana. But she would have to leave Oregon, and she would have to tear up her dreams of a life with Jack Whitwell. That's if she got out of jail. She dared not think of the future if she was convicted of a serious crime.

The door of the jail opened again, and a deep, mellow voice spoke.

"Sheriff Midland, may I speak to you outside?"

Verity's heart leaped. She would know Jack's voice anywhere. Usually he spoke in soft, gentle tones in the restaurant, but her brother-in-law had told her that in court, Jack spoke up with confidence and authority. He knew the law, and he knew how to present it. She had hoped that one day she might get to hear Jack try a case.

And now she would. The irony squeezed her heart into a tight little wad. Her only handkerchief had passed its usefulness, and she caught fresh tears on her apron, glad she'd been wearing it when the sheriff arrested her.

Heavy footsteps on the plank floor, and then the door closed again. She realized she had held her breath and let it out slowly. Why had Jack asked to speak to the sheriff outside? Only one reason came to mind: he didn't want her to hear what he said. That didn't bode well for her case.

He was there suddenly, before the barred door, and she gasped.

"Jack!" She lowered her gaze, knowing her face was scarlet. "Mr. Whitwell."

"May I speak with you?" Jack asked. "I brought over a book to show the sheriff that a client has the right to private counsel from her attorney." He held up the law book for a moment.

"If you think it would help."

"He wouldn't let me come in the cell or let you come out, but I think that if you come closer and we speak in low tones, not even someone listening beneath the cell window would hear us."

She rose hesitantly and approached the door.

"That's better," Jack said with a smile.

"Did you see my sister?" she whispered.

"Yes. She sent you a few things." He raised his other hand, which held a small satchel containing the items the cook had packed for him. Jack frowned, wishing he could put a better face on things for her. "Mrs. Baker is confused and distressed. She doesn't know what happened. She said she came home from the Ladies' Aid and found Mr. Baker's study in disarray and blood on the floor. I saw it, and I couldn't make much of it, either."

"Do you think Sherman was injured?"

"Possibly. Or perhaps a burglar entered the house while it was empty."

"Or maybe a burglar entered and came upon Sherman and injured him," she said.

"Yes." The same thought had crossed Jack's mind, but he hadn't wanted to say it.

"That would account for Sherman's absence," Verity said.

"Not really." Jack couldn't let that go by without comment. His analytical mind told him there was more to the tale. "If a burglar injured him, wouldn't the thief then run away and leave Mr. Baker there on the floor? Or if he was conscious, would not Mr. Baker seek immediate help? But he's been missing for four hours now, perhaps more. Mr. Phillips said he never arrived at the jewelry store today, and it is his custom to be there before nine in the morning."

"You've spoken to Thomas Phillips, then?"

"Yes, and a shop assistant at the store, as well as you sister's cook, Martha Ives. None of them was very helpful."

"They think I did something to Sherman?"

"Nobody's saying that, in so many words, but they wonder why the sheriff fixed on you."

"I'd like to know that myself," she admitted. "I was at the White Pine all morning."

"Yes, but no one admits seeing him after you began serving customers this morning. Since no one really knows when he went missing, it's difficult to prove you were otherwise occupied at the time."

The hope drained from her features. Jack sighed. He hadn't wanted to get into this, but he guessed he had to.

"There's something else, and it may be in your favor."

"What?"

"Some folks think maybe the sheriff holds things against you."

Her red-rimmed eyes snapped. "What do you mean?"

Jack swallowed. "Well, I heard a few things. It seems last year—before I came back from law school—that Sheriff Midland—well, that he had his eye on you."

"I'd rather not discuss it." She turned away and walked a few paces from him.

"I'm sorry, Miss Ames," Jack said. "I don't really want to talk about it, either, but some folks seem to think the only reason Midland arrested you is that you gave him the brush-off."

She sighed and turned with agonizing slowness then inched forward until she stood about two feet from him.

"It's true. He came around the house a couple of times. Sherman thought he was a great catch, but—" She shivered.

"Not to your taste?"

"No. He—" She stopped and eyed him warily. "I don't suppose I need to catalog his faults for you."

"Indeed you do not." Jack knew that Midland could drink hard and fight with the rowdiest of them. If he brawled in the line of duty, to bring roughnecks under control, that was one thing, but he seemed to enjoy it. Off duty, he came very close to breaking the laws he enforced most of the time. He could swear like a stevedore, too—or Jack assumed so. He'd never been around docks to hear stevedores swear.

Firsthand, Jack could testify that Midland never attended church and that he bullied minor offenders. In court he exhibited a boastful, superior attitude. Though it probably wasn't proper, Jack found his spirits were lighter knowing Verity had rejected such a man.

"Has he mistreated you since then?"

She shrugged. After a few seconds she said, "He's not been courteous."

"Ah." Jack suspected that was an understatement.

"Surely you don't think he would arrest someone for so petty a reason?"

"I don't know," Jack said. "Perhaps he saw an opportunity to give you some grief. Or perhaps he knows something we don't—something that implicates you more strongly than the bits I've turned up."

She raised her gaze to meet his. "And what have you turned up, Mr. Whitwell, if I may ask?"

"You may." It went against his nature to discuss such unpleasant things with a lady, but she was, after all, his client, and she had no husband or father to shield her from the distasteful details. "I'm told you argued last week with Mr. Baker. Over money."

She froze for a moment then exhaled. "It's true. He's in charge of my trust fund, and he says I can't have it right away, though my father's will said I could have it on my birthday."

"Did you think Mr. Baker was deliberately withholding the money from you?"

"It occurred to me, but I don't know why he would do that. My sister inherited an equal amount, and his business seems profitable. They live well."

"Appearances can be deceiving," Jack said softly.

She glanced sharply at him. "You don't think I'm impertinent to wonder?"

"Not at all. Anyone with any common sense would wonder."

"My sister hasn't much common sense. I'm afraid Sherman thinks I haven't, either."

"He's wrong about that, isn't he?" Jack asked.

She blinked twice. "I'd like to think so, but it's not always prudent to let people know."

He smiled. More and more, he liked her. She had surely been crying before he came, and who could blame her? He must find a way to help her out of this mess. He couldn't imagine otherwise.

"Is there anything else you can tell me?" he asked.

"I can't think of anything. Sherman said he would get the money for me as soon as he could. It involved selling some shares and having it transferred."

Jack nodded. "You must tell me everything you know, even if it seems unimportant. If you think of something tonight, tell me in the morning. I'll come back then."

"I will."

Jack believed she would. "I'll keep digging and see what I come up with. The sheriff says he'll probably hold you over the weekend."

"What?" Startled, she stared at him. It was Friday, and that would mean at least two nights at the jail.

"I'll ask him to let you have your things when I go out," Jack said. "He'll probably have to go through them as a matter of routine, to make sure there's no contraband in the bag."

"My sister wouldn't do such a thing."

"I'm sure she wouldn't. As I said, it's a matter of routine."

"What happens on Monday?" she asked.

"He plans to have you transferred to the capital for a court appearance."

Verity's face paled. "Must I?"

"I'll be there," Jack said. It would mean going to Salem and staying overnight in a hotel there, but he couldn't let her go into the courtroom alone. "I'll make sure the sheriff tells me when you'll appear, and I'll be at your side."

Her breath came in quiet little gasps. "Thank you, Mr. Whitwell."

"You're welcome."

"Do you need for me to pay you in advance? You'll have expenses."

"Let's worry about that later."

"I have some money saved. From my job. Even if I don't get the trust fund, I shall make sure you're paid."

"Please, don't distress yourself over it. Just rest." He smiled. "Is there anything I can get for you that will make you more comfortable? A newspaper perhaps, or a book?"

"N—no, thank you."

"Miss Ames," Jack said, "if it is any solace, I can't believe you are capable of killing anyone."

"I'm not!" She gave a sob and turned her face away.

Jack took out his clean handkerchief and extended it through the bars. "Perhaps this would be useful?"

She took it with shaking fingers. "Thank you. I suppose that's something you could get for me—a dozen clean handkerchiefs."

"I'd be happy to."

She lifted her chin. "On second thought, don't. I shan't give the sheriff the satisfaction of hearing me weep all night."

THE *Captive* BRIDES COLLECTION

Jack left the jail after watching Midland give the bag a cursory examination and deliver it to Verity. He had actually talked to her without tripping over his tongue. They'd had a somewhat lengthy, sensible conversation, and he came away feeling that she trusted him and perhaps even liked him. He tamped down his elation. If he wanted any chance at all of a future with Verity Ames, he had to find the evidence Sheriff Midland apparently didn't care to bother about—the evidence that would keep her from the hangman's noose.

Chapter 4

Prudence came to the jail the next morning, before full daylight. Verity wondered if she'd chosen this time so that none of her friends would see her enter the jail.

"Verity." She stood before the barred door, staring in at her.

Verity rose from the lumpy mattress on the cot and walked over to face her.

"Prudence, what is going on? Why am I in here?"

"I don't know, dear. I couldn't sleep."

"Is there any word of Sherman?"

"No, he's. . .he's not been found."

Verity eyed her cautiously. Her sister spoke as if she expected the next news of her husband to be the discovery of his bloody corpse.

"I had nothing to do with him going," Verity said fiercely. "You can't believe otherwise."

Prudence would not meet her gaze. "I don't know what to think. You were angry with him about the trust."

"Yes, but I didn't bludgeon him because of it. I kept at my work and my usual daily pursuits. Sherman said he would take care of it."

"He did." Prudence let out a tremulous sigh. "This lawyer who came to the house. . ."

"Jack Whitwell?" Verity asked.

"Yes. He's defending you?"

"He is. But the sheriff won't tell us why he arrested me. Surely the words I exchanged with Sherman a week ago aren't strong evidence."

"No, there was more," Prudence said. "I should have told Mr. Whitwell yesterday, perhaps, but I wasn't sure what was what, or. . .or if we could trust him."

Verity pulled back a bit and studied her. "Of course you can trust him, Prudence. He's an honest man, and my life is in his hands."

"I didn't mean. . ." Prudence held out her hands, palms up, in a futile gesture. "I just don't know what to think, what to feel. Am I widowed? Should I grieve? I feel as though I'm turned to stone, and I can't move until Sherman is found."

"Until he comes home, you mean," Verity said gently.

"I daren't say that. What if he's dead? If he were alive, surely he would get a message to me."

"You said the sheriff has evidence against me. Tell me what it is, so that Mr. Whitwell can discredit it."

Prudence's eyes narrowed. "I'm not sure I should."

"But. . .Prudy, I'm your sister. Surely you know me well enough to be certain I didn't harm Sherman."

"The sheriff thinks you might have."

"Why? Why does he think that?"

Prudence glanced over her shoulder, toward the closed door of the office. The sheriff had withdrawn to give them privacy. He had said he would go for breakfast and come back in half an hour.

"He found something," Prudence whispered. "In your room."

"In my room?" Verity recoiled at the thought. "Bob Midland was in my room?"

"He searched it yesterday. Before he arrested you."

Verity's jaw dropped. She tried to take that in. "You've known something all this time and didn't tell me or my attorney?"

"Shh." Prudence looked around again then stepped close to the bars. "It was a necklace. A diamond necklace. It was in your dresser. I didn't know you had such a thing, and I told him so."

Verity caught her breath. She swallowed hard. "Prudence, could you please find Mr. Whitwell and ask him to come here?"

Jack dashed along the sidewalk dodging early shoppers. Had the sheriff planted evidence in Verity's bedroom? Had someone else? He couldn't bring himself to believe that she would withhold something that important from him.

To his relief, Sheriff Midland was not at the jail. Instead, a deputy Jack knew fairly well sat in the sheriff's chair with his feet propped up on the desk. He swung them down to the floor with a thud when Jack entered the office.

"Mr. Whitwell. Can I help you?"

"I'm here to see my client, Zeke."

"Oh. I'm s'posed to keep an eye on things while the sheriff's out."

"That's fine," Jack said. "You can step outside and keep an eye on the door from across the street, can't you?"

Zeke scratched his chin through his short beard. "I s'pose I can."

"Thank you," Jack said.

He watched Zeke until he'd gone out the front door and closed it, then he turned toward the cell. Verity was already at the door, eyeing him anxiously through the bars. Jack walked over and took a deep breath.

"Good morning, Miss Ames."

"Did Prudence tell you?" she asked.

"Yes, she came to my office. This necklace is, I suppose, the evidence the sheriff thinks he has against you. Did you know about it? Is it yours?"

"I knew about it—that it was there, not that the sheriff had seen it."

Jack's heart sank. He had hoped she was unaware of it. "Apparently he thinks it links you to Mr. Baker."

"Well, Sherman gave it to me," she said, frowning.

"Really? Because his wife seemed to know nothing about it."

Verity sighed and shook her head. "I gathered as much. I suppose I ought to have told her, but I assumed Sherman would. I didn't want to take it at first."

"Why did you? And why did he give you a costly piece of jewelry like that?"

"It was after our argument." She spoke in such low tones, Jack could barely hear her. He leaned closer to the bars to catch each word. "He offered it to me as surety that he would get my trust money for me. I felt it was to pacify me and make me stop clamoring about the money. I didn't want to take it, because I was afraid that it would give him an excuse to delay paying me."

"But you did take it." Jack watched her closely, and she nodded.

"I felt I owed him a show of trust. When I took it home, I got to thinking that if Sherman didn't come through with my inheritance, then I would at least have something of value. If necessary, I could sell it and use the proceeds to go away and get a new start somewhere else, away from Prudence and Sherman."

"You haven't liked living with them?"

"It's been all right, but. . ." She looked up into his eyes. "This money thing has put a strain on us all, I'm afraid."

"You didn't entirely trust your brother-in-law."

"I wanted to." She pushed back a wisp of hair. "I was going to give it back to him, Mr. Whitwell. I thought that when he paid me the trust money, I would return the necklace to him, and he could replace it in the store's inventory."

"So, he took the necklace from the store and gave it to you that same day?"

"Yes. I saw him take it from one of the display cases in the shop."

"Did his partner know about this?"

"I'm not sure. I should have spoken to Prudence about it—I see that now. But I'll admit I was put out with Sherman, and I didn't see why I should have to straighten things out, when it was his job."

"Yes." Jack stared across the cell behind her without seeing the dreary chamber. If only Sherman Baker were around to answer a few questions. "Do you know the value of the necklace? Is it worth as much as your trust fund?"

"Not nearly. My understanding is that the investments of the trust have grown. Prudence has told me more than once that I won't need to work anymore after I get it. That necklace is quite dear, as necklaces go, but my inheritance should be twenty times its worth."

Jack pulled in a careful breath. He would check with Thomas Phillips to see how much the piece had cost, but he didn't need to do that in order to be certain Verity Ames would be a wealthy woman once she received her trust fund. "I'll make some more inquiries," he said.

"Fine." Verity raised her chin. "Do what you must."

Still Jack stood there. How had he ever thought he could have a social relationship with this lady? The image of her in her apron at the restaurant, smiling as she served the diners, came to mind. Verity was a much more complex young woman that he had thought.

After a long moment, he asked the question that burned between them. "Why didn't you tell me about this yesterday?"

"I wasn't thinking about the necklace. And after you'd left, when it did cross my mind, I only hoped it wouldn't come up. It doesn't look well, I'm afraid. Ladies don't accept expensive trinkets from their brothers-in-law. But I assure you, Mr. Whitwell, there was nothing. . .improper between me and Sherman." Her chin was set at a stubborn cant, and tears glistened in her eyes.

"Of course not," he said quickly. "I wouldn't think so."

"Oh, wouldn't you? Some people would."

"I suppose so." The sheriff crossed his mind.

She choked on what might have been a sob. "I only wanted what my parents left me, and if that caused a rift in the family, I was sorry, but I didn't think it meant Sherman should cheat me."

Verity spent a gloomy Saturday in the jail. Bertha Cogswell, having recovered her health, came around midmorning, bringing Verity a well-cooked early lunch. Dressed in her faded blue calico, a generous apron, and a rather silly hat, she bribed her way in by presenting Bob Midland with a plate of raised doughnuts, well sugared.

"My dear, I'm appalled," she informed Verity as the sheriff unlocked the cell door.

"I'm sorry," Verity said meekly.

"I'm sure I'd have made a quicker recovery if I hadn't been so distressed over you. When Obie told me you were in jail, I could scarcely believe it, and that made it harder to breathe, which was bad enough with the cold I was nursing."

"I'm so sorry."

Sheriff Midland took the heavy basket from Mrs. Cogswell and shoved it through the open cell door, into Verity's hands.

"I'll see that your dishes get back to you," he told Bertha, shutting the door again and locking it with a flourish.

"Please do," Bertha said. "Now, give us a few minutes to talk."

The sheriff shuffled over to his desk, where he sat down heavily and began wolfing the doughnuts.

"I know they feed the prisoners with the plainest, cheapest food they can get, and I thought it was time you had a decent meal." Bertha didn't bother to lower her voice. Of course, Midland heard, but he merely scowled while chewing his doughnuts.

"I do appreciate it so much," Verity said.

Bertha turned around and fixed Midland with a malevolent gaze. "When can she come back to work, Bob? We need her at the restaurant. I can't run it by myself."

Midland swallowed. "Might be awhile. She'll be going to Salem Monday, to stand before a judge."

"Good heavens." Bertha rolled her eyes skyward and turned back to Verity. "Whatever did you do, child?"

"Nothing, I assure you," Verity choked out. "Believe me, I would much rather be in the kitchen at the White Pine than here." The basket weighed on her arm, so she set it down on the plank floor.

"I shall leave you," Bertha said. "Obie has hired Penny Jones to come in and help with the serving, but I do miss you, girl. Come back as soon as you can."

"Thank you," Verity said, but she didn't dare promise to return to work. How could she, with everything so uncertain?

Bertha paused at Bob Midland's desk. His mouth was once more full of sugary doughnut, giving her ample opportunity to upbraid him again.

"I don't know what's wrong with you, that you would think that girl capable of a crime. She's a sweet, hardworking young thing, and there's not a devious bone in her body. I certainly won't be voting for you next election day."

The sheriff chewed furiously, but he wasn't able to swallow quickly enough to retort before Bertha stormed out and slammed the door behind her, giving window-rattling emphasis to her tirade.

Verity carried the basket to her cot and sat down on the edge. She couldn't eat, even though the smell of Bertha's cooking was much more appetizing than what Midland had brought her for supper last night and breakfast this morning. She could be hanged for murder or forced to spend the rest of her life in the state prison. She wasn't sure which would be worse.

She took small comfort knowing Jack Whitwell was out there trying to get her released. But what could he do, when it came right down to it? Bob Midland had the advantage in this case. He had the power to hold her, and he held the key to the cell door.

She should have told Jack about the necklace first thing. The fact that she'd taken it from Sherman embarrassed her now. What would people in town think of her when they found out? Jack had only his faith in the law and a client who had held back information from him.

Yesterday he'd believed her innocent. Did he still believe in her? Bertha was on her side, but she didn't know about the necklace or the tension between her and Sherman. Prudence, her own sister, had doubts. Was Jack revising his thinking, too? Verity pulled out the handkerchief he had given her and caught the tears rolling down her cheeks. It was Jack's job to see that she got a fair trial, but he didn't have to believe in her innocence.

Chapter 5

Normally, Jack took it easy on Sunday, but time was running out. He had only this one day to find evidence that would help Verity. After church, he had dinner at the White Pine, as usual, and as was his custom he lingered over his coffee and pie. This time his motive wasn't to speak to Verity. Obie was actually serving today, along with a thin, pinch-faced woman Jack didn't recognize.

He waited for the dinner crowd to thin out and then approached Obie.

"Mr. Cogswell, I wondered if I could have a word with you and your wife."

"Bertha's in the kitchen."

"I know. I had a piece of her apple pie, and it's the best in Oregon, for certain. I'd like to speak to the both of you."

"Well. . .what about?" Obie asked.

"About Miss Ames."

"We'd sure like to see her out of jail and back in here. My wife needs her in the kitchen. Today it was a madhouse in here." Obie leaned toward Jack, his florid face somber. "We've hired on Mrs. Jones, but she's not very quick, if you know what I mean. I've had to run back and forth myself for the last hour and a half with plates and coffee and—yeah, we need Verity, that's for sure."

"I'd love to see her released, sir, and that's why I'd like to talk to you and your wife."

"Hmpf. All right." Obie glanced toward the door as a couple who had finished their dinner opened it to leave. "But not very long."

Jack followed him into the kitchen. Mrs. Cogswell was cutting a blackberry pie and setting the individual pieces on small plates. Meanwhile, Mrs. Jones poured hot water from an enormous teakettle into a dishpan.

"Easy now," Bertha said, eyeing the other woman sharply. "That other kettle won't be hot for twenty minutes, and you'll need some of that to rinse with." She looked up at Obie and Jack. "Well, Mr. Whitwell. What's the occasion? Obie, are there any new customers out there?"

"Just one. Roast beef."

Bertha took a thick ironstone plate and filled it with slices of tender roast beef, a dollop of mashed potatoes, gravy, sliced carrots, and a biscuit. She walked over to Mrs. Jones.

"Take this out and then come back and do those dishes if there ain't any new customers."

Mrs. Jones dried her hands on her apron, took the plate, and left the kitchen without a word.

"Now, then," Bertha said to Jack, "we'll do anything we can to help Verity, but I don't see what that would be, Mr. Whitwell."

"Are you willing to be a character witness for her, ma'am?"

"Why, sure, if it's right here in town."

"It might mean a trip to Salem."

Bertha shook her head. "I'm slowing down, I'll tell you, and Verity had taken over as main cook here during the day. I usually come in before lunchtime and help out, then I prepare supper. Verity is in charge here from 5:00 a.m. to noon, and she usually doesn't leave until two o'clock or later. She's my right hand."

Obie nodded. "It's the truth. Bertha and I started this place doing everything ourselves, and then we started hiring waitresses. But over the years, it's gotten so we depend more on the employees. Verity's the best cook we've found, and if we lose her, we'll be in a fix."

"We're in a fix now," Bertha added. "I'm downright exhausted. I've got a woman coming in to help me cook supper, but I can't take this all day on my feet business anymore."

"And we haven't found anyone who cooks as well as Verity, or who's as dependable." Obie shook his head. "She comes in at five and lights the stove. I never have to worry about whether she'll be on time or not. If I decide not to come in until six, why, there she is, serving up flapjacks and eggs to all the cowboys and miners. And she never complains."

"That's true," Bertha said. "If I'm out of sorts and can't help her, and she has to cook and serve with no one but Obie to help, she's just as cheerful as ever."

Obie nodded emphatically. "I suppose we'll have to look for a new cook now. Best hire a couple more waitresses, too." His face drooped in glum lines.

"Not so fast," Bertha said. "It's true, we need more help, but let's not give up on Verity yet. You're going to get her off, aren't you, Mr. Whitwell?"

"I certainly hope so," Jack said.

Bertha shook her head. "There's no way that sweet girl shot her brother-in-law."

"Shot him?" Jack said. "I wasn't aware that he'd been shot."

"Well, killed him. They're saying she killed him somehow."

Obie scowled at his wife. "If she'd shot him, someone would have heard it."

"Then how do they think she killed him, that little bit of a thing?" Bertha asked.

Indeed, Jack thought. What means had the killer used? What weapon? And what motive drove him? Because he still couldn't swallow the idea that the killer was Verity Ames.

Mrs. Jones came in from the dining room carrying a tray piled with dirty dishes. "Two prospectors just blew in. They want the chicken."

"Well, I'll leave you folks to it," Jack said. "If you think of anything else, drop by my office."

"I expect we'll see you here for supper," Obie said with a chuckle.

Jack put his hat on and nodded. "I expect you will."

He made the rounds of the little town, talking to anyone who would listen to him. The minister allowed he'd always found Miss Ames to be devout and honest. "But people are capable of evil we wouldn't suspect if they're backed into a corner," he added. "I'm not sure you should be pursuing this line of inquiry on the Lord's Day, Mr. Whitwell."

"Well, sir, ordinarily I wouldn't, but I think our heavenly Father will forgive me trying to save a life on Sunday."

"Do you think it comes down to that?" the pastor asked.

"I don't know, sir. I won't know until I hear what's said in court."

A visit to Sherman Baker's partner seemed in order, so he went to the jeweler's house. Thomas Phillips admitted him to his den and offered him a glass of whiskey.

"No, thanks," Jack said. "I'm here to ask you about a certain diamond necklace that Mr. Baker apparently took out of the store's stock."

Phillips nodded, frowning. "Prudence told me yesterday. I wasn't aware of it, at least not as anything of importance. I didn't recall the incident, so I went and checked our store's ledgers. The item was marked down as sold at a discount. That's what we do if we buy something from the store for personal use or a gift. We buy it at cost and mark it down as discounted."

"I see. So there was nothing underhanded about the way Mr. Baker got the necklace?"

"We do it all the time for our wives' birthdays and other gift-giving occasions. I let my son buy his fiancée's engagement ring on discount last fall. Nothing shady about it."

Jack thanked him and went to the railroad depot but wasn't able to learn anything of use there or at the telegraph office. As he walked wearily back toward this boarding-house, he saw Richard Hermon, the president of the bank, driving out of his dooryard in his buggy. On impulse, Jack held up a hand.

"Mr. Hermon, are you in a hurry? I'd like a word with you."

The banker stopped his horse and eyed Jack curiously. "What is it, Whitwell?"

"I'm representing Miss Verity Ames. You've probably heard that she's charged with her brother-in-law's murder."

He nodded. "Shocking. But what does that have to do with me?"

"Well, sir, the sheriff's pretty close-lipped as to why he thinks she might have done this dastardly deed, but the truth is, I haven't seen one shred of evidence yet that says Mr. Baker is actually dead. And Miss Ames was at the restaurant where she works from five that morning to noon. There are dozens of witnesses who will verify that."

Hermon frowned. "I still don't see. . ."

"It's the supposed motive, sir. Mr. Baker was a trustee of Miss Ames's inheritance from her parents."

"I can't really discuss that, Whitwell. Unethical, you know."

"I understand, sir. But an innocent young woman is accused of a capital crime on pretty flimsy evidence. I don't want to see her hanged on trumped-up charges."

The banker sat for a moment scowling. His horse twitched and turned its head around, trying to reach a fly that had settled on its neck.

"I'm on my way to the cemetery," he said at last. "I visit my wife's grave every Sunday."

Jack swallowed hard. "I'm sorry, sir."

"I expect it will be quiet there, and we can talk." Hermon jerked his head. "Climb up."

Jack got into the buggy, and Mr. Hermon drove in silence out a side street to the town's cemetery. It lay half a mile from the bustle of Main Street, in an open field holding only a couple of dozen markers but with plenty of room for more. They drove up close to a stone marker with the family name HERMON engraved on it, and JOSEPHINE, BELOVED WIFE, 1841–1885 beneath.

Jack got down and stood by while the bereaved husband laid an armful of cut flowers on his wife's gave. They stood in silence for a minute, Jack by the buggy and Mr. Hermon next to the burial plot. When the banker returned and got into the buggy, Jack followed suit, but Mr. Hermon did not take up the reins.

"I've been Sherman Baker's banker for more than ten years," he said. "Everything that happens in that bank has to be confidential."

"I understand, sir." Jack's hopes of gaining some useful information sagged.

"Up until now, if you'd have asked me about Baker's character, I'd have said he was a sterling member of the community."

Jack's spirits took a quick reversal. "Up until now, sir?"

Hermon looked over at him. "When the Ames girls' parents died, Sherman was put in charge of their trust fund. He was young, but I thought he was a good choice. He was married to the older girl, and he seemed to me a solid, honest man."

"Was he the only trustee?" Jack asked.

"No, there was another man, a friend of their father's. He passed away last year."

"I'm sorry to hear that."

"Yes. So was I. Usually when that happens, another trustee is appointed. But Verity was so close to her twenty-first birthday that it was neglected. Sherman came to me and explained the situation and said he felt it was too much trouble to put another person in for eight months or so."

"And you agreed?"

"No." Mr. Hermon looked away, toward his wife's grave. "I did not agree, but it wasn't up to me. I didn't like it, but it was true that it would be settled and done within a few months. Or so I thought."

"Miss Ames has not received her inheritance," Jack said.

"That's right." Hermon sighed. "Baker had put most of the money in bonds. When they were due to mature, I expected him to redeem them and put the money in a holding account, until Miss Ames was eligible to receive it."

"He didn't do that?"

"He did cash them in, but he only left part of the money in the bank. The rest of it, he said he was going to put into a short-term investment. That seemed a bit risky to me, but he evaded my questions as to what the investment was."

"You think he took the money for himself?" Jack asked.

Hermon held up a hand. "I don't know what he did. He might have put it into something he thought was a sure thing and lost it all. Don't ever invest in a sure thing, Mr. Whitwell."

Jack's smile was short-lived. "So, he never returned that money to the account?"

"No, but that's not illegal. Not all of the money in a trust fund has to be kept in the same account. Sherman could have bought shares in a business—a mine, for instance, or a railroad—or even stashed the money in another bank."

"Did he withdraw the money left in your bank on Miss Ames's birthday?"

Hermon's face darkened. "A month before."

Jack sat still, considering that. "Miss Ames says she hasn't received any of the inheritance."

"I believe it, in light of the irregularity with which Sherman Baker handled her funds."

"He gave her a diamond necklace, out of his jewelry store's inventory, as a sort of earnest of the money she would be getting."

"I don't know anything about that. All I know is that all of the money in that trust fund was removed from our bank, about two-thirds of it when the bonds matured last summer, and the rest last winter, about a month before the young lady's birthday."

"Has Miss Ames ever come in and talked to you in person about it?" Jack asked.

"No. I assumed she was letting Mr. Baker handle it. Perhaps I should have contacted her, but that's not the usual way."

"I suppose not." Jack frowned. Women were usually left out of these things. Let the man of the family handle it. But what if the man of the family was incapable—or dishonest? "The sheriff thinks Mr. Baker is dead."

"So I've heard." Mr. Hermon gathered the reins and clucked to the horse. They made a circle around the far end of the cemetery and trotted back out to the road.

When they got into town, Jack said, "You can let me out in front of my office, sir. I have some work to do."

"As you wish." Mr. Hermon halted the horse in front of the haberdashery, which was closed for the day. Jack took out his key.

"Thank you very much, sir."

Hermon leaned toward him. "Every word I've said is in strictest confidence, young man. Of course, if it becomes a court matter..."

"I'll apply first thing tomorrow for a warrant," Jack assured him.

"Yes. For all of Baker's banking records with our institution."

Jack arched his eyebrows. Was there more that Mr. Hermon wasn't telling him? They had only discussed Verity's trust fund, but Baker must have personal accounts with the bank as well. And business accounts, for the store.

"I'll be sure to do that." He tipped his hat to the banker

Chapter 6

On Monday morning, Verity had reached despair. The sheriff had brought in her breakfast of flapjacks and coffee and told her that she would leave at nine o'clock on the stagecoach for Salem. The deputy had brought her a basin of warm water and a towel, so that she could wash up, and they left her in solitude while she performed her ablutions and put on the plain brown dress Prudence had sent over.

She still felt grimy as she pulled the dress on over her head, and her hair was a mess. She'd had no chance to wash it. She combed out the tangles as best she could and tied the locks behind her, so that her hair fell down the back of her dress. She didn't have a mirror or enough hairpins to manage a respectable hairdo. She expected that she looked the part of a female convict. She sat down on the cot to wait.

No one but Bertha had come around to visit her on Sunday. It was kind of Bertha, but Verity would much rather have seen her sister or her lawyer.

Prudence's absence told her that her sister truly believed she had done something awful. This grieved her. They were separated by eight years, but they had always been close. Since their parents' deaths, Prudence was the only relative she had, except for some unknown cousins back East. Verity loved her sister and had always looked up to her. She had liked Sherman well enough, too. At least, up until the question of her trust fund caused friction. But he had put up with her and humbly accepted a small quarterly stipend for her care and generally treated her like a younger sister.

Jack Whitwell was another story.

He hadn't come to the jail at all on Sunday. Did that mean he'd lost faith in his ability to free her? Maybe he was a strict Sabbath observer. Some people were vehemently opposed to any kind of work on Sunday. But hadn't Jesus said it was all right to pull your ox out of a ditch on the Sabbath, or something like that? She was in a ditch. A deep, muddy one.

From beneath her thin, lumpy pillow, she pulled out Jack's crumpled handkerchief. She ought to ask Bertha to wash it and return it to him, now that she had the clean set he'd brought her from the general store on Saturday. But somehow she didn't want to let go of the man's plain white square of cotton he'd given her straight from his pocket.

At the moment he'd given it to her, Verity had hoped. She had expectations of Jack. He would help her. He would find evidence to exonerate her. He would make Sheriff Midland unlock the cell door and set her free.

Now she was being shipped off to Salem, without a word from Jack. He had sounded confident on Friday. She had imagined him beside her in the courtroom. But what if he wasn't there? What if she had to face the judge alone? What would she say?

The sheriff came in and unlocked the door to her cell.

"All right, Miss Ames, let's get over to the stage stop."

Verity already had two of the dainty new handkerchiefs in her pocket, but she stuffed Jack's up her sleeve. She stood and walked woodenly to the door.

"Hold out your hands." He quickly put the handcuffs on her wrists. At least he didn't cuff her to himself. That would have been an indignity she couldn't bear.

"Why are you doing this to me, Bob?"

His gray eyes widened. "I'm not doing anything to you, Verity. You brought this on yourself."

"You know that's a lie. Is it because I turned you down?"

"It's because of Sherman Baker's going missing. You know that."

"You've charged me with murder. Why not kidnapping?"

He smiled grimly. "Come on, Verity. You're not big enough to kidnap a man and hide him someplace."

"Oh, but I'm big enough to kill one and dispose of the body in some secluded place where you haven't been able to find it?"

His gaze wavered, and Verity pulled her shoulders back.

"You haven't been looking very hard for a body, have you, Bob? You're satisfied with having me humiliated and perhaps even executed."

"I didn't want that."

"So you say. Why haven't you been out there looking for an unmarked grave if you believe in this folderol?"

He took her elbow and propelled her out of the cell. "Come on. The stage will be leaving in a few minutes."

It had felt good to confront him with the injustice of it. The whole thing was absurd. And yet, it was real.

She walked stiffly beside him the block and a half to the stage depot. Pedestrians stopped and stared at them. People she knew, people she had served meals to, people she had sat beside in church gaped at her and the sheriff.

They were nearly to the stage stop when Bertha Cogswell rushed across the street, panting.

"Verity, child, take this." She held out a gray knitted shawl.

"That's kind of you." Verity started to reach for it, but the handcuffs restricted her movement.

"Here." Bertha shoved Midland aside and wrapped the shawl closely about Verity's shoulders. "There, now."

Tears sprang into Verity's eyes. "Have you seen Jack Whitwell?"

"He didn't come in for breakfast this morning." Bertha's eyes were troubled. "He's usually very punctual."

Verity's heart sank. So, Jack hadn't wanted to be seen in town this morning, or give her few supporters a chance to question him.

The stagecoach sat in front of the depot, and the driver climbed up to the box.

"Let's go," Midland said and tugged her toward the coach.

The station agent held the door for them and closed it after she and the sheriff were seated side by side on the backless middle seat. The passengers on the front and back seats nodded and stared but didn't offer greetings. Verity pulled Bertha's shawl close around her and held the leather strap overhead. The stagecoach started with a lurch.

Jack tied his bag of clothing behind the saddle of his rented horse and slid some documents into the saddlebag. He had planned to take the stage to Albany this morning but decided riding a horse would give him more flexibility in the errands he wanted to run. He could take the train from there to the capital.

Would he ride the same car as Verity and Midland? That could be good, or it could be very uncomfortable. Midland probably wouldn't let him sit with Verity, and it would be impossible to have a private conversation with her. Too bad. He had a lot to discuss with her.

He led the placid horse to the door of the livery stable. Thomas Phillips hurried toward him from the street.

"Mr. Whitwell! I'm glad I caught you. They told me at the haberdashery that you were leaving for Salem."

"Yes, I was just about to set out."

"I went to the sheriff's office first," Phillips said, panting a little, "but he'd already left. Taking Miss Ames to court, I guess."

"Her hearing is tomorrow," Jack said.

Phillips nodded. "I probably should have told the deputy, but I didn't like to. He's not the brightest man I know."

"What is it?" Jack asked. "Something to do with Miss Ames's case?"

"Maybe. I'm not sure. But after all the to-do about that necklace, I decided to take inventory."

"And?"

"We had a cache of gems in the safe at the store. It's gone."

Jack caught his breath. "Since when?"

Phillips shook his head slightly. "I haven't personally noticed it was there since last Monday, when one of our suppliers was here from Portland."

"And who has access to the safe?"

"Me and Sherman." Phillips eyed him anxiously. "Do you think whoever killed him made him open the safe first?"

"I don't know," Jack said. "Can you give me a list of the missing jewels? Or at least an estimate of their worth?"

This would slow him down, but he had a feeling it was worthwhile.

They boarded the train in Albany. Verity tried to keep the shawl over the handcuffs and chain, so that other passengers couldn't see them. The sheriff took care of her ticket and seated her in a window seat, with him on the aisle.

She watched other passengers board, hoping no one she knew would see her, and yet wishing desperately that Jack Whitwell would appear in the aisle. Her lawyer had to be with her at the hearing, didn't he? Where was he? Would Prudence come? She had little hope of that. Her sister thought her guilty.

"What will happen to me after the hearing?" she asked the sheriff.

He took his hat off and settled it on his knee. "If the judge says you should be held over for trial, you'll probably stay at the county jail. If not, then I expect you'll go free, at least for now. If more evidence turns up later, they can try you then."

"So, even if I'm set free, I could be arrested again at any moment?"

"That's about the size of it."

She sighed. "Mr. Midland, do you despise me so much as that?"

"Just doing my job."

"You should be out looking for the real guilty party. You know I didn't do anything to Sherman."

"I know no such thing."

It was hopeless trying to reason with him. She leaned back and closed her eyes. Her silent prayer was that this would end. Either she would be sentenced for execution, or she would go back home—to Prudence and Sherman's home. But how could she? Her sister would look at her every day with accusation. How could they ever live in harmony again? Verity wasn't sure which possible outcome would be worse.

Jack turned away from the telegraph window and paced the lobby of the hotel in Albany, where the office was situated. This was the nearest place anyone from his little town could get a train. If Sheriff Midland took Verity on the morning stage to Albany, they would arrive here shortly after noon and in Salem around three o'clock. He hoped she wouldn't appear in court until the next morning, because his investigation would take longer than he'd expected. But he had to be sure of the facts. He had more questions to ask in this town, and he had cast his net farther afield via telegraph. He needed time.

He went over to the grilled window again. The operator looked up.

"I'm going over to the railroad station, but I'll be back. I figure it will take them time to deliver my message and get an answer."

The operator nodded. "That's right, sir. Probably a half hour, at least."

Jack had already questioned the station workers as to whether Sherman Baker might have traveled that way recently, with no results.

"Has the train for Salem left yet?" he asked the stationmaster.

"Fifteen minutes ago."

"Is there another today?"

"Not until five fifteen." Jack turned away with a deep sigh. He had hoped to catch Verity there, to reassure her that he was working hard on some new leads. But he'd gotten caught up in following the trail and missed her.

The stationmaster couldn't say for sure whether Sheriff Midland had taken the train. Jack went to the stagecoach depot, where deft questioning and two bits placed in one of the tenders' hands confirmed that a lawman had disembarked from the stagecoach and headed for the train station with his female prisoner.

Jack berated himself. He should have left word for Verity, but it was too late now. He couldn't very well send her a telegram at the Salem jail. Besides, his funds were running low, and he had to reserve plenty to get him to the capital. He hoped his friend at the law firm there would put him up for a few nights.

He had nothing to do but go back to the telegraph office.

A terse reply from the sheriff in Corvallis awaited him. Jack read it twice and smiled. He had feared the sheriff would refuse to give out the information he'd sought, but apparently the fact that it concerned a murder case was enough.

"Here's your other reply coming in," the operator said.

"Great." Jack waited and took the paper from his hand a minute later. He read it and smiled.

The Salem train station was a mile from the center of town, and they had to take an electric trolley car from the depot to the vicinity of the marshal's office. Verity kept her gaze lowered, but her cheeks were on fire. She knew all the other passengers stared at her.

They disembarked from the trolley and walked toward the imposing courthouse. Under other circumstances, Verity would have paused to admire the wedding cake architecture and the tall clock tower that loomed above them.

"County jail's in the basement," Midland said.

Her chest tightened and her heart beat wildly. Pulling in each breath took concentration as they entered the building and descended the stairs to the dim recesses of the jail.

"Have you heard from Mr. Whitwell?" she asked.

"Nary a word," the sheriff said, a bit smugly.

She hated that she'd asked. Midland turned her small bag of personal items over to the jailer and faced her somberly. "I'll see you in court tomorrow, Miss Ames."

This cell was smaller and darker than the one back home but better furnished. It was one of a line of cells, and shouting came from those farther down. Verity shivered and looked up at the deputy escorting her.

"You won't be here long, miss," he said, as if that made everything all right. He closed the door on her and locked it. Verity took a moment to let her eyes adjust. The cell had no window but was dimly lit by lamps out in the hallway.

She edged slowly to the cot and felt it. It had a linen sheet over a straw tick, and two folded woolen blankets. At the end farthest from the door was a pillow covered in linen. It felt less lumpy than the last one, but she shuddered at the thought of how many heads had lain on it before hers. She sat stiffly on the edge of the cot for an hour, hearing only distant murmurs, footsteps, and thumps.

Finally someone entered the hallway outside the cell doors, and she heard wheels turning on the stone floor as something was pushed along. A deputy came into sight, pushing a cart. He stopped at her door.

"Dinner, miss."

"Oh." She was surprised that her food was delivered to her cell here.

"The others will be going to the dining room to eat," the man said, "but seeing you're the only woman in here right now, the jailer said to bring yours down."

She swallowed hard. "That's very kind."

"Practical is what it is." He opened the cell door and carried in a tray, which he set on top of her washbasin. "I'll come back for that later."

"Thank you." Before he could leave, she asked quickly, "What happens to me? Do I go to court tomorrow?"

"I understand you'll have a hearing, yes, ma'am."

"A hearing? Not a trial?"

"Not yet," the deputy said. "That takes a while. My understanding is, they have to decide whether to hold you over for trial or not."

"I see." Jack had said something like that the day she was arrested, but she'd been so terrified she'd forgotten most of it.

The deputy paused and lowered his voice. "Best if you keep back, away from the door, when the men pass."

She gulped. "They'll go past here?"

"Yes, and when they return."

"All right. Thank you."

She heard him unlocking the other doors. Apparently a second man was with him as guard. The other prisoners talked loudly, and some coarse jokes reached her ears. Verity wrapped the shawl around her and huddled in the corner behind the washstand. When the men shuffled by, she kept her eyes lowered, but she estimated there were less than a dozen of them. The guard wouldn't let them linger near her cell, and they were soon gone.

Verity carried her tray to the front wall, where she examined its contents in the poor lighting. The main offering appeared to be a stew heavy on beans. She had also received a bread roll, a sour pickle, and a flat slice of cake. It could be worse. She took the tray to her cot and ate quickly. She had barely finished when the deputy returned and paused outside her door.

"Got a message for you, miss."

"What?" She stood, brushing crumbs from her bodice.

"Got a message here. You done with your tray already?"

"Yes."

He unlocked the door and came in, holding out a slip of paper. Verity handed him the tray of dirty dishes and squinted down at the message. As the deputy left, she followed him closer to the door, where she could see better. On the paper were the words, "Take hope. J. W."

She gasped. "Where did this come from?"

"A fellow brought it in. He said he was your lawyer, but the jailer told him he couldn't come down here this late in the day."

"Thank you."

He left, and soon the other prisoners tramped past, returning to their cells. Some of them sneered at her and hooted as they passed, and the guard barked at them to quiet down.

Verity didn't care. She sat curled up on the cot, leaning against the wall, and clutching the message in her hand. Jack was here! He had tried to see her.

Take hope.

Did she dare?

Chapter 7

Jack waited in the courtroom the next morning, restless and on edge. He wanted to see her, to know she was all right. He'd heard horror stories about the treatment of women prisoners. He should have cut short his time in Albany yesterday and come up here earlier. But then he wouldn't have gotten all the information he planned to present to the judge this morning.

The prosecutor came in, carrying a leather briefcase. Someday, Jack would have to get one of those. In the meantime, he carried his papers in a pasteboard folder. He had met the prosecuting attorney on a couple of other occasions, and he stepped over to the opposition's desk to greet him.

"Whitwell. Good to see you again." Gilbert Sutherland shook his hand with a rueful smile. "I hope I don't get trimmed as badly as I did last time I went up against you."

"My client is innocent," Jack said.

Sutherland's smile broadened. "Of course. I read the plea."

"No, I mean it," Jack said soberly. "You have no case."

"We'll see what the court thinks."

"Yes, we will." Jack went back to the defense table and sat behind it, but he couldn't stay down long. He rose and went out into the hallway. Was she here in the cellar of the building? Or had they brought her up to an anteroom? He wasn't sure where they would keep her until the hearing began. He paced the length of the main hallway twice and went back to the courtroom.

At last she came in, accompanied by a sheriff's deputy. She looked pale. Her hair was pulled back in a knot at the back of her head, and her dress had not seen an iron for a long time. As they came down the aisle, her gaze locked on Jack, and she inhaled sharply. Two spots of color formed on her cheekbones. He stepped forward to greet her.

"Miss Ames."

"Mr. Whitwell. I feared you wouldn't come."

"Did you get my note?"

"Yes, last night." She looked down as the deputy fumbled with the keys to remove her handcuffs. When she was free, Jack took her elbow and guided her to the chair next to his.

"I would have come sooner, but I was detained, gathering evidence."

"I should have trusted you," she said softly. "I'm sorry."

"Don't be." Jack dared to reach over and give her wrist a gentle squeeze. "I'm sorry I didn't communicate with you more. Did they take care of you?"

"I suppose so. But do you really think I have cause for hope?"

Her brown eyes were so full of pathos that Jack's heart wrenched. "I do," he said quietly.

"But before we left to come here, I heard Sheriff Midland tell one of his deputies that he was going to meet with the state prosecutor before the hearing. He said terrible things about me, Mr. Whitwell. Falsehoods."

"Like what?" Jack asked.

"He said I screamed at my brother-in-law the day I went to see him at the store. That's not true. We did have words, and I was not happy with the outcome, but I assure you, there was no screaming."

At that moment, the judge entered and took his place at the bench. Jack stood automatically. Verity rose more slowly at the bailiff's call of "All rise."

When they sat down again, Jack leaned toward her and whispered, "I'm sorry we didn't get a chance to talk over my presentation."

After the preliminaries for the hearing, Sutherland rose to give an opening statement, saying that evidence pointed to Miss Ames's guilt in the murder of Sherman Baker.

When it was Jack's turn, he stood and pulled in a deep breath. "Your Honor, we shouldn't be here. The state has no case against Miss Ames. In fact, it hasn't even got any evidence that a murder took place."

A gasp went up throughout the room, which Jack found very satisfying.

"Your Honor, the state is going to claim that Miss Ames was angry with Mr. Baker for withholding her inheritance, of which he was a trustee. They are asking for several months to collect evidence. That's because they have nothing. But I have with me proof that can settle this matter today. Mr. Baker shunned his duty as a trustee. He cashed out the bonds in Miss Ames's trust before her birthday, and yet he did not turn the money over to her, stalling with excuses. Instead, he took a diamond necklace worth about four hundred dollars from his store's stock and gave it to her, saying it was a surety that he would deliver her much larger inheritance in good time."

Jack walked up close to the bench and looked the judge in the eye. "Instead, I can show the court papers from the president of the bank that tell when the bonds were cashed. I also have a statement from Mr. Baker's business partner saying several valuable gems are missing from the store's safe. And I have evidence that Mr. Baker took a train from Corvallis the day he disappeared. That man is alive, Your Honor, and I submit that Miss Ames's trust fund and the gems went with him to San Francisco."

"I'd like to see it," the judge said.

Jack stepped up and laid papers on the bench before the judge. "We have here a letter from the station agent in Corvallis and a telegram from the marshal in San Francisco. As you can see, it tells the hotel in which Mr. Baker registered last week. The marshal is keeping an eye on him, sir. If you issue a warrant, the marshal will take Mr. Baker into custody and have him sent back here to answer to the State of Oregon."

The judge examined the papers and then eyed him closely. "Mr. Sutherland mentioned blood found in Mr. Baker's home."

Jack nodded. "I saw it, and I have no explanation for that, Your Honor, unless Baker deliberately placed it there to mislead his wife and the law officers she summoned. If you would like more evidence, I have signed statements from Miss Ames's employers saying she was at her place of employment all morning the day of the alleged crime."

The judge looked at Sutherland. "Do you have anything to add, Mr. Sutherland?"

The prosecutor rose slowly. "No, Your Honor, except that I was unaware of any of this."

"I apologize," Jack said. "I only got most of it yesterday, and when I arrived in town last night, your office was closed."

The judged looked down at the papers again and was silent for about a minute as he scanned each one. He lifted his chin and gazed at Jack. "At this time, the court will not pursue charges against your client, Mr. Whitwell." He looked over at Verity, where she sat wide-eyed behind the defense table. "Miss Ames, you are free to go."

"Thank you, Your Honor," Verity whispered.

The judge nodded. "And Mr. Sutherland, I will issue a warrant for Mr. Sherman Baker. You'll concentrate your efforts in that direction now."

Sutherland stood. "Yes, Your Honor."

As Jack turned around, he glimpsed Bob Midland slipping out the courtroom door. He hurried to Verity's side, and she rose uncertainly.

"Congratulations," Jack said, smiling broadly. "You're free, as the judge said."

"Thank you. What now?"

"Now we go find some dinner, I think. The next train to Albany won't go until half past two."

Verity smiled but then sobered. "Are you sure you want to be seen in public with me?"

"Of course. Not just today, but every day, if you'll let me."

She blinked and gazed into his eyes for a long moment, uncertainty hovering there. Jack crooked his arm, and she took his elbow. He grabbed his pasteboard folder from the table and headed for the door with her.

Verity could scarcely believe she was free. Jack insisted on taking her to a fine restaurant near the capitol building.

"I'm not sure I can eat," she said when they were seated.

"The food is very good here, I'm told." He set his hat and folder on an empty chair and picked up the menu card.

Verity read down through the entrees. Salad. Baked salmon. Pork loin. They offered eight main dishes at noontime! And the meals sounded much fancier than those they prepared at the White Pine.

A waitress passed them carrying a laden tray, and Verity smelled fresh bread and gravy. Her stomach growled. Maybe she was hungry, after all. Her bowl of porridge at the jail was a distant memory.

"The pork sounds good." Jack eyed her hopefully.

"I think perhaps I could eat after all," Verity said. "I'll try the chicken."

Jack smiled. "Good. It's just nerves, I expect, that make us feel that way. I couldn't eat much myself this morning, knowing I was going into court."

She nodded. "I can't begin to thank you. You believed in me when no one else did."

"It was my pleasure. My distinct pleasure."

"I'll pay you as soon as we get home."

Jack shook his head. "Wait until you get that trust money." He picked up his glass of water and took a sip.

Verity realized he was embarrassed that she had mentioned his fee. "It's all right," she said. "I have money from my job."

He fiddled with his cutlery, lining up the bottom of the knife and spoon precisely. "I don't feel as though I should charge you."

"Of course you should." She cocked her head to one side and studied him. "This is your job, Jack. You earned your fee and perhaps a great deal more. I ought to pay you extra."

He waved a hand and shook his head. "Please."

"All right, we'll discuss it later, but I *am* going to pay you, and I want you to charge me your usual rate. I know you put in a lot of hours getting all of that information."

He didn't look at her but was seemingly still intrigued by the silverware.

"Jack."

He looked up at last, his eyes bright. "All right. I'll. . .send you a bill."

"Perfect. Just don't forget."

The waitress returned, and she sat back while he gave their order. Over the next half hour, to Verity's delight, they talked about a wide range of subjects, mostly unrelated to her case. When Jack insisted on paying for their meals, she started to protest, but he gave her a meaningful look, and Verity swallowed her words. For some reason, it was important to Jack to pay for it. Not that she had any money with her. She had come to Salem with only the clothes on her back and Bertha's shawl.

As they walked to the train station, she thought how very normal this was, walking along in the sunshine with a dashing young man. But it wasn't normal at all, not for her. On an average day, she would be at the White Pine at this time, washing up after the lunch crowd, having been on her feet nine hours or more.

They stepped up to the ticket window, and Jack purchased two tickets for Albany. Verity didn't protest. She would have to think of something nice to do for Jack tomorrow or the next day.

"I wonder if Prudence knows," she said as they turned toward the platform.

"Probably not yet," Jack said. "I'll see you home, and if you need help breaking it to her, I'll be there."

Bob Midland stood on the platform, also waiting for the Albany train. Verity stopped walking when she saw him, and Jack stopped, too.

"I don't wish to see him," she whispered.

They hung back at the edge of the waiting crowd. The train came in, and they were among the last to board. Jack led her to the door of a car ahead of the one Bob Midland had entered. Even so, when they started down the aisle, there he was, seated and arranging his hat on the vacant cushion next to him.

He glanced up and locked eyes with Jack.

"Well, heading home?" he asked, but his voice lacked the confident tone he had used when speaking to Verity or Jack over the last few days.

Jack paused next to his seat. "I wouldn't get too comfortable if I were you, Sheriff."

They went on down the aisle and found seats together toward the back of the car. Verity settled by the window and looked over at Jack.

"Do you think he'll try to bother me again?"

"He'd better not," Jack said. "I hope to see that he can never harass you again in an official capacity."

"How will you do that?"

"I intend to start a campaign against him as soon as we get home. I'll convince the people not to vote for him again, ever."

Verity smiled. What a splendid idea.

Darkness was falling when the stagecoach reached the little town, and Jack helped Verity down. The sheriff had left them at Albany, and Jack supposed he preferred to rent a horse than to ride with them in the coach. They claimed their few possessions and walked away from the stage station.

"You're tired," Jack said. "Shall I get a buggy at the livery?"

"It's only a few blocks," Verity said, almost scandalized at the idea of wasting money like that.

When they reached the Baker house, Prudence was sitting alone in the dim parlor. Verity rushed to her. Jack paused in the doorway.

"Prudence, I'm here. I'm free." Verity knelt by her chair.

Her sister turned her head and looked bleakly at her. "I'm so sorry."

"What do you mean?"

"I doubted you. I shouldn't have." Tears trickled down Prudence's cheeks. "Oh, Verity, what shall I do?"

Verity pulled her sister into her arms. Prudence dissolved into racking sobs. When she quieted a bit, Jack stepped forward and offered Verity his clean handkerchief, as he had on another day.

"Thank you." Verity took it and gave it to Prudence.

Her sister applied it to her tears. Her breath still came in sharp gasps, but she glanced up at Jack and then back at Verity.

"Sherman is being arrested in California. How can this be?"

"Someone told you," Verity said, sending Jack a fierce look of appeal.

"Sheriff Midland was here."

So, he'd not only beaten them home, he'd scuttled to Prudence to give her the news.

"I'm sorry," Verity hugged her again.

"Why did he do it?" Prudence asked.

"I don't know."

They sat with her for an hour, during which Verity told her about the hearing and Jack slowly laid out the probable events that would unfold where Sherman was concerned. Prudence seemed still to be shocked, and she implored Verity not to leave her.

"I'll stay with you," Verity said. "Have you had dinner?"

"No. I sent Martha home. She said there's food in the kitchen."

"Then I think we should eat something," Verity declared. "Jack, will you join us?"

"I should stop by my office, in case anyone has left messages for me. But I would like to call on you ladies tomorrow, if I may."

"Please do."

Verity walked with him to the front door. "What shall I do, Jack? Should I call a doctor for her?"

"Try to get her to sleep tonight," Jack advised. "She'll feel better in time."

"Yes. We'll all need time to sort this out." She shook her head. "I can't imagine why Sherman would go off like that with my money and leave Prudence behind distraught."

Jack took her hand. "If there's anything I can do, please let me know. And, Verity, I meant what I said in Salem. I'd like to keep company with you. There's nobody else to ask, so I'll ask you. May I court you?"

Verity drew in a deep breath. "I would like that very much, Jack."

The following Friday evening, Jack approached the Baker house carrying a small bouquet of flowers from his landlady's garden. He had never taken flowers to a woman before, and he felt very self-conscious as he walked along Spruce Street.

He'd been very busy since Verity's hearing. More people had found their way to his little office off the haberdashery in the last ten days than in the entire previous six months. If business kept up like this, he'd be able to move to a bigger office soon and think about someday buying a house.

Verity came to the door, and he smiled. She looked lovely in a stylish powder-blue dress. Her hair was clean and shiny and her eyes bright.

"Good evening, Jack," she said.

"Good evening." He held out the flowers.

She looked at them, and her face went all soft and happy. "How sweet. Thank you. Come right into the parlor, won't you?"

He waited while she fetched a vase from the kitchen. When she came back, she set the bouquet on a side table.

"They're beautiful."

"So are you," he dared to say.

She flushed and took a seat in a wing chair. Since that precluded him from sitting too close to her, he took a seat on the settee.

"How's your sister?"

Verity sobered. "As well as can be expected, which really isn't very well."

Jack nodded. He'd heard from Verity on Sunday about the marshal's visit. When Sherman was arrested in California, he had not been alone but had been traveling with a female companion, who was also arrested. Mrs. Baker secluded herself at home since the news broke.

"I hope she'll be able to carry on." Jack didn't really know what to say.

Verity shrugged. "They've recovered the money Sherman took, but it seems he met a buyer almost as soon as he arrived in San Francisco and sold the gems. Mr. Phillips hopes to be compensated, but I'm not clear yet on that end of it."

"He came by my office yesterday and asked me to represent him in the matter," Jack said. "It's likely most of the price Mr. Baker received for the gems will go to him eventually."

"I hope so." Verity sighed. "Prudence is talking about moving back East, Jack."

"Oh?" He wasn't sure he liked the sound of that.

"She wants to get away from all the gossip and the memories."

"I see. Would you. . .go with her?"

"No," Verity said firmly. "I'll stay with her here as long as she wants me, but when she's feeling better, or when she decides to move away, I look forward to having my own life."

That sounded better, and Jack couldn't help smiling, although he felt bad for Mrs. Baker. "I'm glad to hear it."

"I almost forgot." She stood, and Jack jumped up. "Oh, no, sit down. I have a gift for you, and I left it in the dining room."

"A gift?"

"Mm-hmm." She left the room, and he waited, mystified. She returned a moment later with a handsome leather briefcase. She put it in his hands. "I noticed in the courtroom in Salem that you didn't have a satchel for your papers. I think this is the kind successful lawyers use."

Jack felt his face heat. "Any lawyer would be overjoyed to have something like this." He looked sharply at her. Was giving him such a personal and expensive gift a signal?

"I know I paid you for the work you did for me," she said, taking a seat beside him on the settee, "though I don't think you charged me enough. But I wanted to give you something to show you my great gratitude, and beyond that, my esteem."

Jack's chest tightened. He laid the briefcase carefully on the table.

"May I?" he reached for her hand.

Verity smiled. "Yes. You may."

Jack's heart soared.

Six months later

Verity and Jack stood before the minister in their little church, with half the town squeezed into the pews behind them.

"Do you, Verity, take this man to be your lawfully wedded husband?"

"I do," Verity said, looking up into Jack's shining brown eyes.

"And do you, Jack. . ."

Verity pulled in a deep breath. She was so thankful for all the blessings God had showered upon her. Jack had waited patiently for her, while Prudence adjusted to her new situation and sold the big house to repay some of Sherman's debts. She was now settled with a cousin, back in New Jersey, and Verity was free. Not just free of the ridiculous charges Sheriff Midland had lodged against her, but free to begin a new life with the man she loved.

Verity had continued to cook at the restaurant while Jack worked on her case for weeks, and she had received her trust fund at last. They had pooled their resources and bought a small house on the outskirts of town. They would move in this afternoon, and she knew they would be happy there.

"I now pronounce you man and wife," the minister said.

Verity smiled up at her husband, and Jack leaned down to kiss her. Then he took her hand, and they turned to face the congregation together. They walked out of the church and over to the restaurant, where the four-tier cake Verity had baked herself took pride of place in the dining room.

Bertha Cogswell hurried in after them. "There, my dear, sit down over here. You'll not be serving the guests today."

She bustled toward the kitchen, and Jack had just time to steal another kiss before the townspeople flooded in to congratulate them.

The front door opened, and Zeke Small, the new sheriff, came in. He focused on Verity as he strode toward them. Her lungs squeezed, and Verity couldn't breathe. She stared at the shiny star on Zeke's chest.

"Mr. and Mrs. Whitwell," Zeke said in a solemn voice.

Verity clutched Jack's arm. *No! Not again.*

"Can we help you, Sheriff Small?" Jack asked.

"I want to offer best wishes to the bride, and congratulations to you, sir."

Jack grinned and shook his hand. "Well, thank you, Sheriff."

Verity pulled in a slow, deep breath and managed to smile as she clasped Zeke's hand. "That's very kind of you, Sheriff. Be sure you have some cake."

Susan Page Davis is the author of more than seventy Christian novels and novellas, which have sold more than 1.5 million copies. Her historical novels have won numerous awards, including the Carol Award, the Will Rogers Medallion for Western Fiction, and the Inspirational Readers' Choice Contest. She has also been a finalist in the More than Magic Contest and Willa Literary Awards. She lives in western Kentucky with her husband. She's the mother of six and grandmother of ten. Visit her website at: www.susanpagedavis.com.

His Golden Treasure

by Darlene Franklin

He upholds the cause of the oppressed and gives food to the hungry.
The LORD sets prisoners free.
—PSALM 146:7 NIV

Chapter 1

Goldie Hatfield scurried down Morton Street, hurrying past the cribs as fast as she could. None of the half-naked women hanging out windows paid attention to her passing. They'd known her all her life.

Work had kept her at Porter's longer than usual, and she wanted to get home before night fell. Her daytime job supplemented her income as a server at Madame Amelia's House of Pleasure. She continued her rapid progress past the multistory cow yards, glad she lived in better surroundings.

In her rush, she didn't see the well-cut trousers until she stepped into the street and crashed into a masculine chest.

She stepped back, ready to run, but a strong arm clamped on hers. "Miss, you shouldn't be here." His voice betrayed his New England roots. "No lady belongs on this street."

He wasn't a customer. If she had to guess, she'd say he was a preacher from one of the churches on Union Square. They occasionally wandered into its bawdy neighboring street.

"I live here. Not that it's any of your business." Where were the do-gooders like this man when Goldie's mother needed help, back before Goldie was born? "Now let me go, so I can reach my home before the sun goes down."

He stepped back. "I apologize." His gaze didn't waver as he reached into a pocket and handed her a pamphlet. "If you ever change your mind. . .you can find help at Church of the Good Shepherd."

"You looking for a piece?" Big Jim, the guard at one of the houses, asked the stranger. The preacher took another step back, avoiding a confrontation. As he walked away, he formed an okay sign with his forefinger and thumb, the signal unseen by the guard who repeated his offer of help.

The man showed common sense. That was a rarity among preachers in this part of the city. She wanted to watch where he went but didn't. If she decided to look for him, she had the information. Now she had to skedaddle home or suffer a scolding from Madame Amelia without supper before her evening shift began.

The cook met her at the side door. Li Min's past remained a mystery, but she treated Goldie like a daughter. She held out a bowl of savory beef and rice. "You late tonight. Eat, quick, change. Missy Amelia not like it when you not here."

The savory meal deserved more attention than the handful of swallows it took to consume it. Maybe that's why she enjoyed breakfast. If she woke early enough, she could take her time with it. "Thanks. I'll be down as quick as I can."

Goldie sped up the stairs to the small room she used to share with her mother. A large sign posted on her mirror read DRESS FITTING MONDAY 3 P.M.

Most girls would love to have new dresses lavished on them as their seventeenth birthday approached. Not Goldie, not with the implications they carried. The dress in question was gorgeous, lifted straight from the pages of *Godey Lady's Book*, the material a foamy green silk with a bow as big as the bodice attached to the right side. It was so wide Madame Amelia might have to widen the door frame to accommodate it. Goldie choked back a laugh.

She changed quickly and tripped down the stairs faster than the cat she kept hidden in their room and made it to the front parlor as the clock rang seven bells. When the last gong sounded on the clock, the doors swung open. Madame Amelia called to the waiting customers, "Welcome, welcome to Madame Amelia's House of Pleasure."

About two dozen men entered, a disappointing number. The madame would be upset if the traffic didn't pick up. She waved Goldie forward to start singing. Her contralto drew men like a siren.

Not that Goldie took pleasure in her voice. She'd rather serve tables and clean spittoons than woo fathers and husbands to the house of pleasure. But Amelia had recognized her potential from the time her mother had taught her simple children's songs. At first Goldie had refused to sing, holding the music inside her.

Li Min had counseled her—for Mother had died by then—"Sing, my songbird. You must sing, or die. Your voice will be all the stronger when at last you escape your cage." With the cook's encouragement, Goldie sang. Tonight, like many nights before, she talked with men who had known her since childhood and treated her like a daughter.

Hours later, well past midnight, she made it to bed. The reminder about the dress fitting taunted her. If only she could cancel it. She didn't want Amelia spending so much on her.

Goldie crossed her fingers behind her back. Just one more week, two weeks at the most. Before long she would have the money she needed to leave Morton Street behind forever. Where would she go? If she knew she had a place to go without ending up in a position worse than the one she left behind, she would leave in a heartbeat.

If God was loving and didn't judge for her birth, which she didn't control, if He was real—then He would make a way.

Joshua Kerr walked slowly from Maiden Street to the Church of the Good Shepherd, a storefront property backed up to the churches on Union Square. Calling the space a church was almost laughable, if God wasn't doing such miraculous things through them.

He looked up at the sky. "I knew You had a sense of humor the first time I saw an elephant. But calling the single son of one of Barbary Coast's most notorious businessmen to reach out to soiled doves—what did You think You were doing?"

Pealing church bells greeted his prayer, and Joshua nodded. God was laughing with him. He headed home. Inside the church, the aroma of his sister Jane's ham and beans drew him to the kitchen. His stomach rumbled. Wordlessly she handed him a bowl.

He stood by the stove and ate slowly, savoring the taste. As usual, Jane had coaxed the last measure of flavor out of the dish. His brother-in-law, Matt Benson, was absent. Silence settled over them as Joshua ate and Jane cleaned. If she continued scrubbing, there wouldn't be any more wood left in the room. He finished off the beans with half a glass of milk and washed his dishes while his sister worked on the stove. Either she was afraid the place would fall back on its previous filthy state—or she was upset about his recent visit to Morton Street.

"We need to talk," Joshua said. Whatever their differences, they'd managed to remain a united front in sight of their congregation.

"We do indeed." Matt Benson, Jane's husband, made his appearance. "But later. The kids have shown up for their lesson."

"I didn't see them come in." Jane rushed past Joshua into the main room.

Discussions were postponed too many times, but Matt was right. The needs of their congregation came first, and the children were a priority.

Watching Jane work with the women and children was a joy to behold. So far God hadn't blessed his sister and brother-in-law with offspring. Jane poured all her pent-up maternal longings into the children God had led their way, many of them by-blows of the ladies of Morton Street.

Abandoned, orphaned, homeless, or just plain neglected—helping two dozen children at a time took twice the money they had budgeted. Jane eked every penny out of the dollar of their sizeable inheritance. Enough remained to fund them for years to come.

The three of them agreed on one thing: to invest their inheritance into the Good Shepherd mission. Nothing could undo the havoc their father had caused two decades earlier, but they were determined to give back wherever possible. That included teaching children and adults how to read.

Jane had prepared the lesson earlier that day, copying Bible verses of varying lengths onto the blackboard. The youngest read three words: "Jesus loves me." The most advanced took turns reading the daily Bible passage. A few adults learned alongside the children.

They used a common reading plan so anyone who wanted could prepare ahead of time. Every night they read from both the Old and New Testaments. Matt had designed the schedule for 1873, which allowed them to read about Passion Week during Lent and Christmas during Advent.

The men took turns sharing a short sermon each night. On the days Joshua didn't teach, like today, he spent his days on the streets. Jane accused him of going out even when he was scheduled to preach. Truth be told, he did sometimes. The real-life struggles of the people of the Barbary Coast inspired his passion to share God's love with them.

Matt maintained the building. He helped their members, men and women, learn a trade. Joshua oversaw outreach. Every day brought more people to help. Jesus had said the fields were ready for harvest, hadn't He? That was Joshua's calling.

Jane and Matt agreed. They just wished he didn't spend so much time on Morton Street.

He didn't blame them. He couldn't shake the young blond he had met today from his mind. Her dress suggested an ordinary, safe job like a salesclerk, but she walked down Morton Street as if she belonged there.

The kind of woman his father would have pursued for his own pleasure. Joshua planned to pursue her with an equal passion—to woo her to the Lord.

He prayed God would cause their paths to cross again. Maybe she would even come to one of their services.

Maybe she should go somewhere, anywhere, else, because she also stirred something hidden deep in Joshua's heart.

Because she also looked like the woman he would like to marry one day. Someday.

Chapter 2

The sun woke Goldie as it did almost every day of the year. Some days, especially during the summer, she allowed herself to sleep again. But throughout the rest of the year, she arose with the sun.

Mother used to say, "You're my Goldie, my ray of sunshine." Five years had passed since her mother's death, five lonely years. She was blessed to have a roof over her head and food to eat, but no one could take her mother's place.

Savory aromas told her Li Min was poking around the kitchen. Goldie reached for the dress she had worn at the store yesterday. She hadn't hung it up properly in her rush to appear on time downstairs. She shook it out, decided it could go another day without ironing, with Monday, wash day, approaching.

When she shook the dress, a piece of paper fluttered to the floor. She read the pamphlet the preacher had given her yesterday. The Church of the Good Shepherd was located on a side street, not on Union Square. She wadded the paper up and dangled it over a trash can.

Hadn't she just asked God, if there was a God, to reveal Himself? Perhaps she shouldn't ignore the invitation thrust into her hand. Perhaps she should attend. Her work dress should make suitable attire for church.

She buried the pamphlet in her pocket and made her way down the stairs. Li Min dropped an egg into the frying pan when she walked through the door. "One egg sunny side up."

"You don't have to do that for me," Goldie said. "You don't fry eggs for the others."

"The others don't get up early. No time to fry egg." Li Min put together Goldie's favorite breakfast foods: two slices of perfectly toasted bread with butter and jam, a cup of coffee, black. Fresh-squeezed orange juice when it was available, but not today. Goldie watched the magic until Li Min slid the plate in front of her. Goldie took her time with the food, from spilling the yoke with the tines of her fork to chasing the last of the gooey yellow goodness around the plate with a corner of her toast.

"Have you ever heard of a church called the Good Shepherd?" Goldie hoped to slip the question by her friend.

Li Min's head jerked up, her eyes sparkling with interest. "They do good things. Help widows and orphans, like God say."

"They invited me to come by. The service starts at nine."

"Leave now. You get there on time."

Why not? That brief visit with the unnamed preacher had awakened a curiosity in

Goldie, both about the man and the God he claimed to represent. As soon as she finished eating, she headed out.

At this early hour, Morton Street was the quietest street in all of San Francisco. Some days Goldie indulged her passion for walking, wearing out the soles of her shoes as she trudged up and down the tall hills dotting the city. She'd walk and imagine a story about her parents. Sometimes her father was trapped in a loveless marriage. Sometimes he died before he knew her mother was pregnant. Any of the stories was better than the truth, that her mother hadn't known who her father was. She told Goldie they were lucky to be with Madame Amelia who treated her girls well and allowed mothers to keep their children.

Compared to orphans living on the street, Goldie had it good, but she refused to repeat her mother's mistakes. As soon as she had enough money to rent a place of her own and support herself, she would leave.

The man had promised the Good Shepherd Church would help, if she could find the building. She wandered around the backstreets of Union Square, keeping out of sight of the stuffy churchgoing population. Despite her modest dress, her outfit, from her shoes to her morning coat to her jaunty hat, betrayed her origins.

When she hadn't found the church after one turn around the block, she closed her eyes to picture the streets in her head. That was the problem. She was on the wrong side of the square. The church must be on the south.

Her pause had drawn the attention of a couple headed for the back door of one of the churches on Union Square. They stopped for a moment's chatter before the wife marched in Goldie's direction. "You don't have to live like this, you know." The lady's voice was kind, but Goldie had heard the sermon too many times before.

Goldie lifted her chin. "I have no idea what you're talking about. I'm on my way to church." She took off at a quick pace, thankful she had figured out the route to the church—one taking her away from the couple's church.

She passed by the Good Shepherd twice before she recognized it. It looked more like a store than a church, but someone had painted the name of the church as well as a shepherd with his flock on the show window. A church with painted windows instead of stained glass. She had never heard such a thing.

Inside, two dozen children sat on the floor, listening to a young woman. The teacher looked up when the door closed and she hurried to welcome Goldie. She was attractive, with her pleasant features and soft brown hair. With some of Madame Amelia's special treatments, she would be quite handsome.

"Welcome to Church of the Good Shepherd. We're so glad you joined us today. I'm Jane Benson. It's almost time to begin. Here, come sit with me."

She led Goldie to a seat at the front, defeating her plan to slip out if she became uneasy.

Jane made small talk with Goldie, not asking a single question about her home. Goldie started to relax—until *he* came in.

Dressed as informally now as the first time they met, a Bible in his hand and a smile on his face, the man she had met yesterday entered the room from the back. If he had seen her, he didn't show any sign of it. He was talking with the children.

"That's my brother, Joshua Kerr. He preaches here with my husband," Jane said proudly.

Voices stampeded through Goldie's head. She'd guessed he was a preacher but hoped he wasn't. The preachers who made their way to Morton Street didn't boast about it. It was whispered about in the corners, with pity for their wives.

But this—Joshua—seemed different. Even his name was different, a good, strong name. She shushed the voices in her head, determined to focus on this stranger's words. To see if God had something to say to her after all.

The children fidgeted the way they always did before the service began. Participation in the Sunday service was a right won throughout the week, by those who worked the hardest and progressed the furthest. Jane's idea honored those who worked twice as hard as well as those who learned easily. Jane usually sat with them, but she had taken a seat on the front row, alongside a visitor.

When she leaned back, revealing a glimpse of their guest, Joshua swallowed his gasp. The girl he had met in Morton Street had come to church. *Forgive my doubt, Lord.*

The girl looked as uncomfortable in her chair as did Mrs. Johnson, the oldest member of their congregation who struggled to get to church but refused to give in to her age.

Jane's glance pled with Joshua to give her a few more minutes. He obliged, taking a seat at the back. His sister leaned toward their guest, pointing to her open Bible. She ran her finger across the page, her lips forming the words.

The men's class ended, and Matt walked among the congregation, distributing hymn sheets. The people sang every verse of every song. Joshua could name two dozen hymns they knew by heart. "Amazing Grace," popular ever since John Newton first penned the words, was on every Sunday's order of worship. "All Hail the Power of Jesus' Name," with the fun up-and-down notes of *dia-a-dem*, was also popular, as well as several Wesleyan hymns.

When the rows filled with people and the song service started, Joshua allowed himself to study their guest. From the first syllable of "Amazing Grace," he heard her voice, a deep, rich contralto made to sing in a heavenly choir. Her right foot tapped in time with the music. With the less familiar hymns, she listened for a few measures before sounding out the melody.

He could have listened to her for an hour, but after the last verse of "O for a Thousand Tongues," Jane rose to begin the Bible reading. "Five people will read from the fourteenth chapter of John, verses one to nine."

The children rubbed their hands together. *Five* readers were an unusual treat. Jane had listed four children. They had all memorized the sixth verse, "Jesus saith unto him, I am the way, the truth, and the life: no man cometh unto the Father, but by me." Jane assigned the first seven verses and then looked around. "For verses 8 and 9, we are having a special treat. Our guest today, Miss Goldie Hatfield, will read them for us." Applause greeted her announcement.

The girl's name was Goldie—appropriate, with her hair of spun gold. And she could read—many first-time visitors couldn't.

Joshua sat forward, eager to hear her read. The verses, so familiar to him, might come with difficulty to someone unused to Shakespeare's English. Unless she read the Bible regularly? Hmm, that would be an unexpected development.

Jane invited their guest to stand and face the congregation. High color stained her cheeks. Goldie cleared her throat and began reading. " 'Philip saith unto him, Lord, show us the Father, and it sufficeth us.' " She sounded out *sufficeth* but quickly continued when Jane nodded her approval. " 'Jesus saith unto him, Have I been so long time with you, and yet hast thou not known me, Philip? he that hath seen me hath seen the Father; and how sayest thou then, Show us the Father?' "

Goldie read the scriptures with the cadence, the theatricality, of an actress. "Hast thou not known me, Philip?" She read it as if acquainted with the passage and its importance, but the way she followed every word in the Bible suggested she wasn't at all acquainted with the words.

Joshua came to the front for his part in the service. "Thanks to everyone reading today. Congratulations are in order. . ." he listed the children. "And a special thanks to our guest, Miss Hatfield"—he had written down her name, a habit he had gotten into to be sure he didn't forget and embarrass himself—"for your beautiful reading of Philip's important question and Jesus' answer."

The color in their guest's cheeks had gone down, as if she was more comfortable with this kind of praise than their earlier welcome. Perhaps she was a performer of some kind.

One of the mothers in the group stood to her feet. "I'd like to hear more from Miss Hatfield. Are you new to the area? I can tell you, you won't find a better group of people than here at Good Shepherd Church, or better preachers, neither."

Panic came into Goldie's eyes. They never asked their guests to introduce themselves for that very reason. They didn't want to frighten away people. If anyone was in Christ, they were a new creation. Period. Their past no longer mattered.

He cleared his throat. "I invited Miss Hatfield myself, although I was unaware of her hidden talents. We are blessed by your presence." Some in the congregation knew of his haunts, which was enough of a warning not to probe further.

She relaxed.

The way she had read Philip's questions made it feel like they were her questions as well. *Show me the way.*

In the verses they read, Jesus had said "I am the way," but Philip didn't understand what He meant. Goldie must not, either.

Joshua led in prayer: "Use this service as Your instrument to shed light on Your way today. You are the way. Help us to show *You*. Because once we have seen *You*, we have seen the Father as well."

Most of their congregation had heard the sermons starting with the first chapter of John, following the great "I am" statements repeated throughout the Gospel. "I am the

Light." "I am that water." "I am the resurrection, and the life." "I am the good shepherd."

Goldie hadn't heard one of those sermons. Joshua prayed God would fill in the gaps in her mind with His love in her heart.

Matt started his sermon with a reminder that Jesus was the Word of God, God Himself in the flesh. He explained what being the life, way, and truth meant. Jesus was the only road for man to get to God. He ended with inviting the congregation to quote John 3:16 with him.

Everyone in the room chimed in with the first words: " 'For God so loved. . .' " Everyone except Goldie, who frantically turned the pages of the Bible. She located the verse in time to finish with everyone else: " '. . .have everlasting life.' "

If Goldie didn't know John 3:16, she didn't know the Gospel. Passion stirred Joshua's heart. His mind knew there were people who hadn't heard the Christian message, but he hadn't thought about that person living within a mile from his front door. . . .

Matt continued with the sermon. "Let's repeat that verse. Instead of reading, 'For God so loved the world,' put your name in there. I'll say 'For God so loved Matt.' And 'that Matt believeth in him.' Make it personal. I stand at the crossroads of Matt's way and the Way of Jesus. If I choose to go Jesus' way, I'll have eternal life. But like verse eighteen says, if I choose to keep going my way, I'll be condemned."

They read three verses that way. Some people struggled with substituting their names but not their guest. Her lips formed "Goldie" each time, and her face grew sadder with each repetition. Joshua imagined her jumping to her feet like the Philippian jailer, asking, "What must I do to be saved?"

During the invitation, he prayed harder than ever. She didn't stir, and no one else came forward, either.

As soon as the service ended, Goldie disappeared. By the time they said good-bye to all the morning congregants, discouragement had squeezed out the excitement Joshua had felt earlier. Matt had preached the Gospel, and not a single person had responded.

Goldie wasn't the only person who had said no, who continued to refuse God's gift of salvation. Many of the children had been saved but not many of the adults. They were changing people's lives but not their hearts.

Gloom settled over Joshua, although he knew the feeling would pass. At that moment, though, disappointment clung to him like the odor of yesterday's fish.

Maybe he was like Jeremiah, called to preach to people who would never listen.

Chapter 3

As soon as the final prayer ended, Goldie headed for the exit. Li Min would be preparing lunch, but the thought of food made Goldie sick.

Instead, she walked, turning here and there. The preacher's sermon kept running through her mind. He'd made the Bible come alive, putting her name right there in writing, in case she hadn't already heard the words pounding in her heart. "For God so loved the world, that he gave his only begotten Son." She didn't know exactly what *begotten* meant, but she'd bet it was something special, something holy.

Goldie had heard somewhere that Jesus' mother wasn't married when she got pregnant. An unwanted baby drove some women to places like Morton Street. And if that girl claimed God was the baby's father—she would be pitied as crazy at best or punished for saying such an awful thing.

But the Bible said it was true. If anyone had seen Jesus, they had seen God Himself. Like Jesus was the spitting image of God.

Goldie turned around another corner and found herself at Union Square, standing in front of the church she had avoided that morning. If she continued around the corner, she'd find her way back to the Good Shepherd Church.

Jesus said He was the Way. Maybe she should ask Him to give her a better sense of direction. Would Joshua find that funny—or heretical? She turned another corner and found herself where she had started: standing in front of the building with the picture of the flock of sheep. Jane was standing at the front window, cleaning the glass.

Jane glanced up and spotted Goldie. Jane was through the door and by her side before Goldie could move. "I hoped to see you again, although I didn't know it would be so soon."

"I must have walked in a circle." Goldie often wandered when she was lost in thought.

"Please join us for dinner." Jane waited for her answer.

Goldie's stomach chose that moment to grumble. Why it should complain when she'd had a perfectly fine breakfast, she didn't know.

"That settles it. You're coming with me." Jane took a step toward the church.

Goldie debated for a few seconds. "I'm not hungry."

"We're not having anything fancy, just sandwiches and warmed-over soup. Join us for tea and a bite to eat. I'd love to get to know you better."

Goldie didn't protest again as Jane led her inside the church. Joshua was sweeping the floor as if he were chasing away the dirt from his soul. The thought made Goldie want to giggle.

"Matt, Joshua, we have company for lunch," Jane announced.

The tall man who had preached came to the kitchen door. "Good to see you again, Miss Hatfield."

"That's my husband, Matt Benson. And I believe you've already met my brother."

Goldie couldn't bring herself to meet his eyes. He must know she lived on Morton Street, and what that implied. Had he told his family about her?

"Goldie was passing by our doorstep once again. God reminded me I was remiss for not inviting her to join us earlier." Jane's voice ran a little high, her words close together.

"We weren't properly introduced. My name is Joshua Kerr." Joshua came forward with his right hand extended. "I'm glad you accepted my sister's invitation. I enjoyed listening to you read from John 14. Some people read the Bible out loud as if it's the most boring story in the world."

Boring? It was a good story, and Philip had asked an obvious question. The same one she had asked that morning, in fact. *If You are God, show me the way.*

She bet Joshua could quote the verses as if he knew every punctuation mark between the words. His passion reminded her of the cries she heard through the walls at night. Coming from the throat of a preacher, about God—she didn't know people felt that way.

Joshua was handsome but didn't seem to realize it. His clothes were well cut but worn, as if he had fallen on hard times. As if his mind was too occupied on other things to bother about his appearance. Or maybe he needed a wife to take care of him.

Shame washed over Goldie. The ladies at Madame Amelia's learned how to discern a man's character, his interests, needs, and weaknesses, to make up for things missing at home. They'd make a meal of an unmarried preacher like Joshua. Or maybe not. She hoped he was different.

They all looked at her, as if waiting for some response to Joshua's compliment. "I love to read. Sometimes I read aloud, pretending to take the part of different characters in a scene."

"How fun." Jane clapped her hands together. "Our children's class would love to hear you read."

"And sing." Joshua nodded. "You could lead children to our door like the Pied Piper."

Goldie drew back, afraid they would demand a commitment at that very moment. "I'm surprised you'd want someone like me singing God's songs."

Jane tilted her head back and laughed. "Honey, praise from an honest heart honors God. And music draws me closer to God. Why, you might be helping yourself as much as you're blessing the rest of us. If you ever want to sing, just say so."

Joshua realized his mistake as soon as the words left his mouth. "But that's a topic for another time. We do indeed hope you will grace us with your company again. We have an informal gathering every evening, if you're interested."

He wanted to ask if she felt any inclination to exchange Goldie's way for Jesus' way, but he didn't. If he asked right this minute, she'd run down her hole quicker than a jackrabbit, and he wouldn't know how to reach her. He doubted she'd give them her address.

He wanted to open her eyes to the truth of her situation, but only God could do that. "I'm selfish enough to hope you enjoyed the service and that you'll want to come back."

"Come now, Joshua. She doesn't need to hear the sermon all over again." Matt poked his head out from the kitchen. "Lunch is waiting."

After Joshua returned thanks for their food, he speared his sister with a look. *Please talk with our guest.* He had been told that his conversational style resembled a priest taking a confession. He struggled with making small talk.

"Are you from San Francisco, Miss Hatfield?" Jane asked.

Goldie nodded. So, she was *born* here in the fifties, when women were still rarer than the gold that drew men from all parts of the globe. "We aren't so lucky. Our father lived here during the height of the gold rush, but we grew up in New York. After he died, my sister and I came to San Francisco for the harm he caused when he lived here."

Goldie looked at him with interest. "What was he involved in?"

Joshua blew the air out of his cheeks. "That's a fair question, but I don't know the complete answer. I'm not sure if he was part of the vigilante committees who acted in the place of the law or a prospector who struck it rich or a speculator."

"Most likely he dabbled in all of that, and even more we don't know about," Jane said. "After he returned east, he poured his fortune into legitimate enterprises and increased his fortune."

Matt jumped in. "This is such an amazing city. Jesus told His disciples to go into all the world to make disciples. Here in San Francisco, the world comes to us." They freely told the story that had turned their worlds upside down and brought them to the city by the bay.

Goldie chuckled. "It's the only home I've ever known. I'd like to see more of the country. But a body has to come from someplace, and San Francisco is a grand city."

The longer Goldie talked, the more she entranced Joshua. She dressed modestly, as if to cover up her natural beauty. Well spoken, educated, cultured, a good conversationalist, a talented performer—she could easily be the wife overseeing one of San Francisco's elite families.

Instead she was—probably was—a woman trained to use those arts to beguile men into sin. He liked her, prayed for her salvation—and knew he should limit any contact with her. God help him, his heart rejected the thought. She drew him as surely as honey lured bears into a trap.

If he asked for her help, maybe she'd relax. "Maybe you could show us some of your favorite places."

Goldie's face fell flat. "I don't know about that."

Jane returned Joshua's earlier look. *Say something.*

"As you said, it's a grand city. Maybe we can go exploring another time. Have you seen Colton mansion?"

"Not yet." She shook her head and redirected their conversation. She listened and asked questions, drawing information from the three without revealing much about herself. The meal ended, conversation petered out to a trickle, and she made getting-ready-to-leave noises.

Joshua cleared a tickle in his dry throat. "We're mighty glad you came today."

She nodded. "Thank you for the meal, but I need to go home."

He couldn't stop himself. "Have you thought about what I said? We'd be happy to help with whatever problems you're having."

The animation in her face fell flat. "What problems could those be, Mr. Kerr? I'm gainfully employed, not committing any of those sins listed in that Bible. Jesus may be the way for sinners who need help. But believe me, I've seen sinners. And I'm not one of them. Not by a long shot."

With that, she headed out the door.

Joshua didn't move until she disappeared. He was worse than useless. *God, forgive me.*

Chapter 4

Goldie didn't know what she wanted to do with the rest of her day. She'd said she needed to get home, but they didn't expect her until the evening. Back home, people would be getting up, hungover, throwing up, reaching for the whiskey bottle. . .

A few years ago, Madame Amelia had experimented with closing the house on Sundays, in a short fit of appeasing God. The experiment didn't last long. She lost more than one day a week's business. Some customers went elsewhere permanently. They didn't like the implied criticism.

Us and them—that was the way Goldie had been taught to view the world. She'd hoped to find something different at church that morning. The way they had all those children and families of every sort had given her hope. But then the preacher had to ruin it, by suggesting she needed to change.

She knew she was being unreasonable. She'd sought him out after he offered to help and then got mad when he offered it. He'd help, all right. But would he expect something in return?

She'd recognized the signs. He'd noticed her, right from that very first day—and hated himself for seeing her as a desirable woman.

She didn't doubt his sincerity. Experience had taught her he'd fail when she needed him most.

The sermon kept running through her head. The Bible said Jesus was the Word. So what? She loved words, she loved reading, but no one single word was more important than another.

The Bible also said Jesus was the Water of Life, the Bread of Life, the Light of the World. Those things made a little more sense. This Jesus said He could provide the things people needed to survive. That He was those things. He was Life. If He was who they said He was, God Himself, that only made sense.

But a door? A shepherd? A vine? Those comparisons needed pondering.

That was the thing. She was intrigued and wanted to learn more. If only Joshua would stick to preaching and not meddling, they would be fine.

But he couldn't stop any more than she could stop singing. That day, and the next, and every day that week, snatches of the hymn singing came to her and she'd burst into song. Sunday morning, she found herself singing, "All hail the power of Jesus' name." She stopped right there. His name, Jesus, and all those other titles as well. No wonder everybody was falling at His feet, if he'd earned all those names.

It reminded her of a children's rhyme. . . and that reminded her of the children at the church.

She wanted to go back. Jane was kind, the way Goldie imagined a sister might be. And Joshua was. . .well, *Joshua*. Irritating and engaging, both at once.

But most of all, Goldie wanted to hear more about Jesus. She slipped into one of her workday dresses and headed down the street. Fifteen minutes later, she stood in front of the painted window. Jane was through the door and by her side in half a minute. Her face was every bit as pretty as her brother's was handsome, both of them strong, resolute, determined. A matched pair. "I'd hoped to see you again, although I didn't know it would be so soon."

Goldie didn't explain but followed her into the church. This time a few members nodded in her direction, as if welcoming her back. One of the children grinned at her. "Miss Goldie, will you be reading again today?"

More verses were listed on the chalkboard today. "That wouldn't be fair to everyone who worked so hard on them this week." Even so, Goldie read them silently when she sat down.

Goldie committed more of the hymns to memory that morning and listened with interest to the sermon. Joshua preached this Sunday, talking about a Comforter God gave to Christians and a special peace. Comfort and peace were luxuries she didn't enjoy most of the time.

Jane kept Goldie talking after the service and she wondered if they would invite her to join them for lunch again. Joshua smiled at her but didn't greet her, instead bidding good-bye to their other guests. Disappointed, Goldie decided she should leave.

Before she reached the door, Joshua stepped in front of her. "I'm sorry I didn't have a chance to speak with you earlier. I promised myself the next time I saw you, I would ask you to visit the hill where the nabobs live—up near California and Powell. We can throw some food into a picnic basket and walk up the hill. It's less than a mile from here, if you're willing."

Goldie stared at him, her heart racing as fear doubled her heart rate. "Women like me aren't welcome in places like that." She almost whispered the words.

She wanted to slip away, to escape. Joshua had stepped inside. Nothing prevented her from leaving—nothing except the kindness and compassion she saw in his eyes.

"That's not how God sees you."

She shook her head. "Maybe the folks on Powell Street aren't on talking terms with God." She stared at him, daring him to disagree.

"I can't speak for them. But I will tell you this: When I look at you, I see a woman created in God's image, precious in His sight. And I'd be proud to enjoy your company for the afternoon." He held out his hands in a pleading gesture, as if she held his heart in her hands.

"I think you mean it." She ran her hands down her dress, wishing she had worn her other dress, one she had purchased at the store.

"You look fine," Jane said. "And I've fixed a picnic basket for you. Maybe you can find an open spot where you can look down on the harbor and enjoy the food."

"I know just the place," Joshua said. "If you're willing."

Goldie had come this far, and she had a few more hours to kill. In Joshua's company, she might feel safe to venture so far from home. "Very well. I'll go with you."

A warm smile stretched Joshua's mouth and caused his eyes to crinkle. "That's settled, then. Let's get going."

The woman Joshua had dreamed of and prayed for had agreed to spend the afternoon with him. Inside his heart danced with joy. He wanted to believe it was because he would have another chance to share the Gospel with her, but he knew he wanted more than that.

When they left the building, Goldie took the lead, heading in the opposite direction of Geary Street. After a few steps, she stopped. "I'm sorry. I don't know where we're going, so I should let you take the lead."

"We can go this way. We're heading to Powell Street. The Colton mansion is less than a mile away." They turned the corner onto Powell. "It is a climb, however." A sneak glance at her feet confirmed she had on sensible shoes for walking and standing.

"Each house is fancier than the next," Goldie said. "The houses are big enough for a whole neighborhood. No wonder they're called nabobs."

"Everybody in the family has a room of their own, and then the servants, and one room to eat breakfast in, and another for formal dining, and another for music..." Joshua stopped when he realized Goldie was staring at him. He shrugged, embarrassed. "My father showed off his new wealth by building the biggest house in our town. Jane and I got lost a couple of times when we first moved in."

Goldie giggled. "I can't imagine living in a place so big you'd get lost." When her giggles died down, she grew serious. "And now you live at the church? Where do you sleep?"

"There's a couple of small rooms next to the kitchen. We divided the old storeroom into our living quarters. Once Matt and Jane have children, we'll need larger quarters. But until then—"

"But why?" Goldie stopped walking and turned around where they could see San Francisco Bay. "Why would you leave all of that and travel across the continent or by ocean to live in a tiny place near the bawdiest part of San Francisco?"

Joshua thought for a minute before replying: " 'The love of Christ constraineth us.' That's what the apostle Paul said, and that's the way we felt. That we had to preach Christ crucified, buried, and risen from the dead in San Francisco. To show His love to people who might feel God has abandoned them." He shrugged. "I can't explain any better than that. Some people feel compelled to go to China. We only came across the continent."

"I don't have any lofty reasons, but I sure would like to travel. I'm not so sure I would care to make the trip by boat around South America to make it to the East Coast, but traveling by train might not be so bad. See the farms in the middle of the country, cross the Mississippi River. Visit places like Washington, Pennsylvania, New York."

The water sparkled a dark blue, the ocean stretching west until it thinned into a line blurring sea and sky. "God's love is like the sea. Paul talks about that, too. How wide and deep and high God's love is."

"Do you always talk about God's love?" Goldie sounded peeved, curious—interested?

He laughed nervously. "Maybe I do. Because His love makes life worth living. And I am a preacher." He wanted to push but held back. Goldie teetered on the edge. "Come, let's go farther up the hill. I promise to stop preaching. You have to see the Colton mansion. You'll think you've gone to Greece or maybe a Southern plantation."

The mansion belonging to General David Colton, a railroad attorney, was one of fanciest houses Joshua had ever seen on either coast. Its classic white paint gleamed under the midday sun. Marble steps led up to a large portico with Grecian columns. Jane would know the name of the style, but he didn't.

For the remainder of the afternoon, Joshua avoided preaching, and Goldie managed to keep personal details to herself while sharing her opinions on a wide variety of topics. The sun hung low in the sky by the time they returned to the church.

"Can I talk you into staying for dinner?" he asked.

The later the hour, the more agitated she had grown. "I have to get home. They'll be looking for me." She stopped at the top of Morton Street. "I've had a wonderful time." She started to leave.

"Goldie."

She paused, still faced away from him.

"Will I see you again?"

She glanced over her shoulder. "Maybe."

He waited while she walked away, the sound of her footsteps growing softer and softer until he couldn't see or hear her.

God help him, Joshua cared about Goldie, although he didn't know why. They met only a week ago. Was he a fool, beguiled by a pretty face and a charming personality? "I can't care about her. Not that way. She's like a hundred other women I've met on Morton Street." He told himself.

Oh, no, she's not. His conscience answered back. God had put her in his path for a reason.

Goldie would have to make the next move. Whether she returned to Good Shepherd, or not. Joshua would count the days between now and next Sunday.

Chapter 5

No one commented on Goldie's absence when she returned to Madame Amelia's. They were used to her comings and goings, whether to Porter's store where she worked part-time, the book stall, or a few other quiet spots she had discovered throughout the years.

No one noticed anything different about Goldie, but a fundamental shift like the earthquake tremors the area felt from time to time had changed her. She no longer felt she could accept the status quo of life at Madame Amelia's. She was more determined than ever to escape.

When—she wanted to be gone by her seventeenth birthday, the day before Easter. But how—that question remained unanswered. If only Mr. Porter could give her a full-time job at the store, she might make enough money to move into a place of her own.

Would the folks at Good Shepherd help her? They had offered to, more than once. Goldie shook her head. Not yet. She wanted to believe Joshua, to trust him—but a lifetime with Madame Amelia had taught her to trust no man completely.

For now, she worked between eleven and two at Porter's Emporium, so all the employees could go to lunch. She also filled in when someone needed a day off, and most Saturdays.

Goldie thought about asking Mr. Porter to increase her hours as she walked to work on Monday morning.

She stopped by the front window, adjusting her skirt and her hair. With a smile on her face and a song in her heart, she opened the door. Today she sang the first line of "Amazing grace, how sweet the sound."

Employees and customers looked up at her approach, but she didn't spot Mr. Porter. Martha, the other lady clerk, waved to her from the register. "I'm taking first lunch." They exchanged notes and Martha left. Business picked up, and Martha returned before Goldie caught sight of Mr. Porter leaving his office with a guest.

The man with Mr. Porter looked familiar. Goldie averted her face, as she always did in similar situations. Few people wanted to admit the circumstances of their meeting.

Footsteps crossed the floor, strong boots, heading in her direction. "Miss Hatfield? Miss Goldie Hatfield?"

It couldn't be. She glanced under her eyelids. It was.

Joshua Kerr from Good Shepherd Church. "Welcome to Porter's Emporium, Pastor Kerr."

His face split into a wide smile, the corners of his eyes relaxed. "How blessed our paths should cross again. I didn't know you worked here."

She fought the urge to look away but kept her eyes fixed on his. "I fill in when there's a need. I loved shopping here, and I already knew the items available for purchase—you might say it was a match made in heaven." She almost batted her eyelashes. What did she think she was doing, flirting with a preacher, of all people?

"Do you think your job here is a match made in heaven?"

The man wouldn't let her get by with a figure of speech. She lifted her chin. "It was a piece of good fortune. One I sorely needed."

He cocked his head. "Whatever you call it, God was watching over you."

"Why?" she said. "Why would God watch over one solitary individual out of all the people on earth?"

"Why?" The preacher blinked as if the answer were obvious. "Because He loves you."

The doorbell jingled, and someone coughed. Other customers were waiting for her help. She put on her professional smile. "Can I help you find something, Pastor?"

He also noticed the line behind him. "I'll see if I can find it. Go ahead and take care of your customers."

Goldie apologized to the next person in line, a lady buying several yards of silk. Customers kept her busy until all three clerks returned from lunch, relieving Goldie at the register. Before she left, she checked to make sure Joshua had left already. She wasn't ready to face him again today, and not here.

Goldie didn't usually go back to Madame Amelia's right after work, but today they expected her for her dress fitting. She didn't know whether she was excited or scared about her birthday party. Madame Amelia never did anything without a reason.

Goldie slipped out the back door and took back alleys back to Morton Street. The farther she removed herself from the store, the more freely she breathed. Joshua hadn't followed her.

Instead he had gone ahead, waiting for her on Morton Street. She resisted the temptation to run away. She would have to face him. He was already walking in her direction.

"Miss Hatfield." He fell into step beside her as she turned down a side street, moving away from Madame Amelia's. "I was pleasantly surprised to see you at Porter's today. I hope I didn't create problems for you."

She tossed her head. "It worked out. I am always happy to help one of Mr. Porter's customers. I need to get home. My—guardian—is expecting me home to plan my birthday party." She stopped walking.

"Then let me accompany you to your home. You must realize this isn't the best place for a woman to walk alone. . . ." His voice trailed away.

Because she obviously was comfortable on Morton Street, which suggested a more intimate knowledge of its inhabitants than any churchgoing lady should have.

"You don't have to protect me. I am perfectly safe." She tossed her head. "But I will be in trouble if I don't get there in time."

Compassion she didn't want to see grew in his eyes. "I will let you go on one condition. Come back to Good Shepherd next Sunday."

Without a finger on her person, he compelled her to agree. "I'll be there. Now, please, let me go."

"Until then." Joshua remained in place, watching as she walked away.

Goldie took a few false turns to make sure Joshua didn't follow before she hurried home, arriving with fifteen minutes to spare.

As she tiptoed past the dressmaker's room, she heard low voices talking. When she heard her name, she stopped, curious about their plans.

"She has a spectacular figure. Are you certain you don't want something with a little more flare?"

Goldie winced. The flares the dressmaker suggested would identify her as a lady of the house, not as their singer. She held her breath. *Say no, Madame Amelia.*

"We don't want anything too revealing. But perhaps we can show a hint more here... and how about here?" Amelia replied.

Goldie fled up the stairs, more worried than ever about the coming fitting.

Joshua counted to one hundred while Goldie disappeared. He could learn her address from Mr. Porter if necessary, but he preferred to discover it on his own.

Their encounter today confirmed she lived somewhere on Morton Street. The thought sickened him. She wasn't a courtesan; he'd swear it on a stack of Bibles. But Morton Street was no place for a young girl to live.

Was her mother a working girl? Not impossible but unlikely that the mother of a girl Goldie's age would be working.

He stopped in his steps. Could she possibly *own* one of the houses?

He started walking again. What kind of woman would submit other women to that degradation, let alone raise a child in that environment? As unbelievable as it was, it did happen.

How old was Goldie? Eighteen at the oldest, maybe younger. Eighteen years ago, not many choices had existed for women in San Francisco.

Oh, goodness. He pushed his hair away from his forehead. He was thinking about Goldie like an exercise in logic, but she was an individual made in God's image and loved by Him.

Joshua stood at the top of the street, staring down the row of houses. A dozen other "Goldies" might live on Morton Street, but God had caused his path to cross Miss Hatfield's four times now.

Joshua recognized God's hand at work, but he didn't want to take anything for granted. He would need to be as wise as a serpent and as harmless as a dove. The Lord would reveal what He had in mind at the right time.

Maybe next Sunday, when Goldie had promised to return to church.

Joshua didn't tell Jane and Matt about the encounter, but he couldn't stop thinking about Goldie. After supper, he retired to his room and opened his favorite book. For twenty minutes, the struggles of the last Mohican kept him occupied. Then his thoughts returned to Goldie and her problems.

Jane knocked on the door to his room. "You've been quiet tonight."

He opened the door and Jane took a seat in his one chair. He said, "I've got a lot on my mind."

"I brought you a treat." She handed him an oatmeal cookie wrapped in a napkin.

He bit into the sweet crunch and let it slide down his throat. "Thanks."

She filled him in on the day's classes. When he finished the cookie, she said, "Brother, whatever is troubling you—talk it over with God until you've run out of words. Then the Holy Spirit can take what's left and take it to God, and maybe you can sleep." She patted his shoulder.

God bless Jane. His sister could point to the heart of a problem like William Tell shooting the apple off his son's head. He grabbed his Bible and headed for the corner stove in the main room. He opened the Bible but didn't know where to start.

Goldie Hatfield lived on Morton Street. She was associated in some fashion with the strange women who were the subject of so many of Solomon's warnings in Proverbs.

Goldie had never mentioned her family. Her parents might have died or abandoned her. She could even have run away. San Francisco was a good place to leave one life and start another.

Many runaways' hopes for a better life led them to even worse circumstances. Pretty girls like Goldie ended up snared by one of the houses on Morton Street. Where did he draw the line between immoral women and orphans and widows?

He started by listing verses about strange women and finished by searching for those that talked about helping the poor, the widow, the orphan. "Face it, Joshua. You're looking for a reason to rescue Goldie instead of avoiding her like the Bible says you should." He buried his face in his hands. "Just don't let me end up like my father. Getting so tangled in their skirts I get trapped in their debauchery."

Thinking and reading led him circles, leaving him as spent as man in the desert with no more water in his canteen.

What had Jane said? When he ran out of words, let the Holy Spirit do the talking for him while he slept?

He didn't think he could sleep. Not now. Even so, he closed the blinds against the streetlights and blew out the candle. He wrapped himself in a blanket and stretched out his length, half sitting, half lying on the chair. He tugged the blanket up a few inches, so that only the tip of his nose emerged far enough to breathe.

He counted his breath, ten, fifteen, twenty beats breathing in, breathing out. With each breath, another muscle relaxed. He was sleepy, so sleepy. . .

Before he knew it, two things jerked him awake: the aroma of strong coffee served with his sister's singing and knuckles rapping strongly on the door.

Before he came fully awake, Jane passed him and pulled the door open.

Goldie Hatfield stood at the portal, shrouded in darkness. The confidence that had marked her on her earlier visits had disappeared. A terrified woman, glancing over her shoulder as if more dangers awaited her on Union Square than on Morton Street.

"You promised you would help me."

God had answered Joshua's prayer. Now maybe He'd tell Joshua what he had to do.

Chapter 6

Goldie sat in the kitchen, hands wrapped around a coffee cup. After she heard the rest of Madame Amelia's plans for her birthday party, sheer terror had kept her awake all night. She had run to Good Shepherd Church as early as possible.

Inside the cozy kitchen, surrounded by friendly faces, Goldie wondered if she had made a mistake. Maybe she had asked for help too soon. Surely, she had misunderstood what she had heard. Surely Madame Amelia would let her go when she realized Goldie had other options.

As distant as Madame Amelia was, she had given Goldie a home. For that, Goldie would always be thankful. She had provided food and clothing and a roof over her head without expecting anything in return.

Until now.

At length Goldie lifted the coffee to her lips only to discover it had grown cold. Jane must have realized what happened, because she took it from her hands, dumped out the liquid, and poured a fresh cup.

Goldie drank a few sips, deciding what to do. She had time, a few weeks. Perhaps she should continue her ordinary routine. "I shouldn't have come this morning. Thank for you the coffee, but I'll be going."

Joshua flew to his feet and his hand landed on her shoulder, a gentle restraint. "You're not going anywhere until you tell us what's wrong."

He removed his hand and sat down again, but she couldn't have moved if she wanted to. His eyes locked her in place and hid the key.

"My—guardian—is planning a party for my seventeenth birthday. Easter weekend."

Three heads bobbed. She had mentioned her upcoming birthday on an earlier visit.

"She has been planning a new wardrobe for me for months. Beautiful things, straight from the pages of *Godey Lady's* or even Paris. Last night I had another fitting." Sitting here, in complete safety, her skin heated as she remembered their discussion about how much décolletage to display, perhaps whether to lift the hem above her ankle. . . Her breathing rate increased and she gulped down more coffee.

"Your guardian is generous," Jane said.

If only that were all.

Joshua lifted his hand. "You say your guardian is planning these events. Are you an orphan? Where are your parents?"

"My mother died when I was twelve. And my father. . ." Heat rose again, revealing the untold truth. "My mother never told me much about him. I like to think he died before I was born." The reality—her mother didn't know the identity of her father—was too painful.

"And you've been living with your guardian since then." Jane nodded, as if she didn't understand the undercurrents of the situation.

Joshua lifted a finger. "It's time we learn more about your circumstances. Let me tell you what I have guessed."

Goldie's insides twisted. He must despise her.

"From the day we met, I guessed you live on Morton Street, although you look like you belong in the schoolroom or a high society tea. No lady could walk down Morton Street without causing comment unless she lived there."

Her cheeks burned, but she nodded.

"You also obviously don't belong in the cribs. I doubt you're from one of the cow yards, either. You are too well dressed and too well spoken. You probably live in one of the higher-end houses. Your mother might have worked there when you were born, and they have kept you there since her death."

Goldie acknowledged the awful truth with a bare dip of her chin.

"You have a stage presence. You read with the skill of an actress and your voice matches Jenny Lind's. My guess is you work in the parlor of your house, giving it a sense of class but demanding no more of you than your God-given talents."

Oh, when he said it like that, she felt so ashamed. If her voice was a gift from God, the last place she should be using it was in a place like Madame Amelia's. Frightened, hurt, she struck back. "You speak as though you have been there."

Joshua's face blanched at her words, but he didn't release her gaze. "I haven't been, but our father knew it firsthand. He moved back East and made himself respectable, but Jane and I grew up with the rumors about his past."

Jane intercepted the connection between her brother and Goldie. "Please tell us where you live, Goldie. We want to help."

Goldie held back. Once she revealed her home, the last bit of her invisibility disappeared. They could—would, if Joshua had anything to say about it—march down Morton Street to claim her if they felt it was necessary.

But even if Goldie didn't tell them, Joshua might ask Mr. Porter. She gave in. "Madame Amelia's."

Everyone at the table relaxed.

Joshua drummed the table with the fingers before he continued his inquisition. "Something has changed. What happened at the dress fitting that frightened you?"

"I overheard them discussing whether to adjust the lines of my dress to make it more. . ." She moved her hands, letting them say what she didn't put it into words.

Jane's head lowered, as if anticipating Goldie's next words.

"Madame Amelia said to show just enough to give the customers a taste of the wares. To raise the price. She talked like I was an object on the auction block." Goldie rushed through the rest before she broke down and cried. "My birthday party isn't for me at all. She wants to put me to work, and she's inviting men to bid for the privilege."

With that, she crossed her arms on the table and pressed her face against them, unable, unwilling, to look the others in the face.

Joshua had guessed the end of the story before Goldie finished it. He wanted to scream, to carry on, to march down to Madame Amelia's house and demand she stop this abomination. He strangled the protests pushing out of his throat.

Jane spoke first. "Oh, Goldie. You must be terrified."

God bless Jane. He wanted to storm the brothel to save Goldie. Jane looked into her heart and saw her fear.

"Miss Hatfield." He used her surname to invest Goldie with respect. "You are welcome to stay here with us for as long as you need to or want to. We have a spare bed."

She shook her head, not speaking.

Jane's glare could have cut his arm off, and Joshua connected the dots. "But Madame Amelia would know where you had gone."

Let her come, he wanted to say, but the proprietress's power was real, financially, politically—emotionally. God was more powerful than anyone in all of San Francisco, let alone Madame Amelia, but Goldie didn't believe that, not yet.

Goldie nodded without raising her head.

Matt looked up from where he had been thumbing through his record book. "Is she Amelia Howell?"

Goldie lifted her head, startled eyes answering the question.

Matt grunted.

"Why? Is that important?" Jane asked.

He lifted his record book. "I've been digging into the financing behind the houses on Morton Street. If we can't make them feel guilty enough to quit, maybe we can find some other kind of pressure to make them close. That's what Wilberforce did in England, you know, to finally make slavery illegal in England. Diverted attention from the question of slavery and instead proposed a bill that made transporting slaves illegal, or something like that. My point is, they didn't make slavery itself illegal, they just made it more difficult." He shrugged his shoulders.

"It's a good idea. But more to the point, it doesn't address Goldie's immediate problem," Joshua said.

"Hold on a minute. If we could convince stores like Porter's to stop selling to Madame Amelia's until she . . ."

"Lets me go?" Goldie shook her head sadly. "That won't work. As long as they make money, the devil himself could look for a pitchfork, and they'd sell it to him." She straightened in her chair. "It's a grand idea, but nothing will stop the trade. It's the world's oldest profession, or haven't you heard? Even your Jesus made 'friends' with prostitutes."

Joshua grunted in surprise. "Where did you learn about Jesus and those ladies?"

"My mother," Goldie said. "She said she hoped God wouldn't be too mad at her, since Jesus forgave women like her. But what I want to know is, if God loved her so much, why did He leave us there?" Her face twisted. "Why did she have to die? She was still young."

Joshua chuckled, a miserable small affair. "I don't know the answer."

His chuckle brought a scowl on her face. "The professional preacher man doesn't know the answer? Then where do I find answers?"

"I can tell you what God says when people asked Him why bad things happen."

"And what is that?" She leaned forward.

"That He's God, and we're not."

"That's it?" Her voice rose at the end.

"He puts it in fancy language, but that's the gist of it. He knows what He's doing, He sees everything—and we don't. All that is true." He waved his hands around. "When I want God to connect the dots for me, He asks me to trust Him instead."

"Humph. If God was in control, He wouldn't let Madame Amelia have her way."

Joshua's eyes flew wide open. "And she won't. I don't know His plan, and we won't force you to do anything you don't want to do." He injected a confidence he didn't feel into his voice. "Even if it kills me to let you go. But God will make a way for you to escape."

She shook her head. "You mean well."

A late rooster crowed in the house behind their building, and the sky had lightened to early morning. Goldie rustled in her seat.

No. Everything in Joshua wanted to rush in, to ignore his promise to let her make up her own mind, to keep her at the church.

Goldie stood. "It is good to know I have friends. My birthday party is three weeks from Saturday. Nothing will happen to me before then. I'm safe, for now. I was foolish to get so worried this morning."

Would they continue to allow her to come and go until then? "I can't stop you. But—"

She frowned, hesitated. "What is it?"

"If you stop showing up at Porter's, I'll come looking for you."

Her eyes widened. "No one has said anything about stopping work."

Her voice cracked. *Good.* She needed to realize how serious her situation was.

Joshua looked at Matt and Jane, and the three of them nodded. "One of us will stop by the store every day. Not the same person, or else they'll get suspicious. And we expect to see you here next Sunday."

"Thank you." Her face looked brighter, more hopeful, than when she arrived. "Maybe God figures He doesn't have to explain why, when someone has good friends like you. Now I must go before someone comments on my absence."

With that, she disappeared.

Jane and Matt stood on either side of Joshua, their hands on his shoulders, watching until she disappeared.

"If she hasn't figured out how much you care for her yet, she will soon," Jane said.

Joshua sputtered. He wanted to deny his sister's words, but they were true. God help him, he was falling in love with a prostitute's daughter.

Chapter 7

Joshua took up residence in Goldie's mind. The man was so strong—physically, mentally, spiritually. He drew her attention in the way things were supposed to work between a man and a woman in the world where he lived.

When he didn't come to the store on Tuesday or Wednesday, she was disappointed. On Tuesday, only a few hours after Goldie had left the church, Jane showed up at the store. Matt came on Wednesday, and the husband and wife came in together on Thursday. Aside from checking out at the register, they hadn't spoken to her at all. Every day Matt or Jane came by, Goldie's heart dropped because she missed Joshua.

People had seen her with Joshua more than once. They were going about it the right way, but Goldie wanted to see him. If she had to wait until Sunday, she might go forward during the invitation just because she was so glad to see him. And even she knew that was the wrong reason.

By Friday she decided Joshua didn't care for her at all, except as a soul in need of saving. Then the door opened to his smiling face and he walked boldly to her station. "Miss Hatfield, it's good to see you doing well."

"You, too, Pastor. How is the Good Shepherd Church doing these days?"

"We're doing well. Our young people are working hard on an Easter program. Are you interested in taking part?"

Easter. He knew the reasons why she might not make it to church that Sunday. "If I can," she said carefully.

"I believe you will be there." He looked deep into her eyes. "I wrote down the verses we'd like you to read."

"You're sure of yourself." She looked at the paper. *John.* She recognized the name of the Gospel, followed by numbers. Jane had explained they referred to the chapter and verse.

"God will make a way. You need this." He handed her a thin volume. Black letters on the spine of the red book read *Holy Bible.* "Let me you show you a secret." He flipped through a few pages and then turned it around where it read *Table of Contents.* "This is a list of all sixty-six books of the Bible. There are thirty-nine books in the Old Testament, twenty-seven in the New." He ran his finger down the page, pointing out the two divisions. "John is in the New Testament."

"Page nine thirty-two," she read.

"It would be easier if they had an alphabetical list as well, but use this to find any Bible reference you want to look up." He glanced around, as if relieved no one had appeared yet. "And check out this feature. It's called a concordance. You can look up any word you might like to learn more about, like *faith*. It lists verses with the word *faith* in them."

She stared at the Bible. Something in her wanted to read it for herself, to see what God had to say about someone like her. But bringing it into Madame Amelia's house would invite every kind of comment. She bit her bottom lip. "Thank you. It's lovely, but I'm not sure if my guardian would let me accept it."

After a second's hesitation, he took back the Bible. A few people had come behind him, and their window for conversation had closed. "Don't worry. Perhaps we can fix the problem." He tipped his hat. "We'll talk about it the next time we meet."

Goldie pushed Joshua out of her mind until quitting time and as long as she was singing that night. As soon as her mind was free to wander, it sped down the maze to find Joshua at the center.

To her delight, he showed up at the store again on Saturday. The foot traffic didn't allow them to talk freely. He came to the counter to purchase a pad of paper. When he handed her the money, he slid a paper sack across the counter. "Will your guardian object to this?"

The plain burlap cover hid the same thin Bible. She flipped it open to be certain of its identity. "I don't see why she would. I will take it." She handed him his change. "Keep Porter's in mind for all your shopping needs." She pasted on her brightest smile.

"See you next time. Thank you for your help." He left without so much as a smile or a wave.

As the door closed behind him, Mr. Porter came up beside Goldie. "How are things going today, Miss Hatfield?"

"Quite brisk." She automatically handled the next customer and the next. He watched her for a few minutes and then left without saying anything further.

When her shift ended, she sought out her employer. "Do you have a few minutes?"

"For you? Always, Miss Hatfield."

"I have been working here for nearly a year now, Mr. Porter. I enjoy the work and would like to increase my hours."

His eyes shifted away from hers.

"In fact, I might like to work full days. Is that a possibility?" She held her breath. If she didn't have a means of support, how could she escape Madame Amelia, no matter how much she wanted to?

Mr. Porter wouldn't meet her eyes but kept his gaze on the floor. "I believe you have a birthday coming up in a few weeks, Miss Hatfield. Let's discuss the matter again after that."

Goldie's heart sank. Mr. Porter must know Madame Amelia's plans for her birthday.

Joshua walked slowly back to the church. Not even a week had passed since Goldie had revealed her deepest fears.

When she had shared her dilemma, Joshua's heart shuddered in sympathetic shock, but he wasn't surprised. Of course the madame wanted to put a beautiful girl like Goldie to work.

Joshua listed all the reasons they had to thank God. Goldie was still untouched. In other houses, she might have been put to work a long time ago.

"Trust Me." God's voice whispered into Joshua's heart. *"I am your Defender."*

"Are You Goldie's Defender?" Joshua dared to ask.

"I am the Defender of the orphan and the widow, of the powerless and those who are enslaved. Do your job. Speak of My love, My saving mercy, to those who need it most."

Joshua bowed his head. "Forgive me." Goldie's emergency had taken over his mind to the point where he was neglecting his ministry to others on Morton Street and throughout the Tenderloin District. His jacket pocket still held several pamphlets, unrumpled, ready to hand out. Designed for those with few academic skills—written in simple English, with more illustrations than text—he wondered how they had struck Goldie. She read well enough to study Jonathan Edwards's famous sermon, "Sinners in the Hand of an Angry God."

She might not have even read the pamphlet, but the address stamped on the back led her to the church. The simple piece of paper had done its job. "Thank You, Lord." With renewed enthusiasm, he retraced his steps to Morton Street, staying far away from Madame Amelia's. He patrolled the neighborhood, praying with each step.

Joshua strove to project a nonthreatening, nonjudgmental attitude, and his presence didn't pass unnoticed. Good Shepherd's ministry had earned a reputation as interfering do-gooders, a compliment and a complaint rolled up in one. Some were grateful for a man willing to give the help they offered to abused women and children, no questions asked. Others resented any interference in their business.

In the process, he had learned which people to avoid. Others sought him out. He strolled the street, keeping his eyes focused at eye level. He wished he could erase some of the images engraved on his consciousness.

Today he prayed God would lead him to people who would hold on to the pamphlet and read it, rather than toss it on the street to be trampled by horses' feet.

A druggist Joshua recognized passed him by, eyes fastened on the ground except for one quick glance at a clock tower. He increased his speed after that. A lunch hour assignation?

Another man caught up with the druggist and slapped him on the back in congratulations. Every time a man visited one of the houses for the first time, he stepped onto a slippery slope, one Joshua counted as a personal loss. He walked the same five blocks for two hours, praying for the men who passed by as if he were invisible.

"Hey there, handsome."

Joshua froze at the greeting and prayed for God to blind his eyes as he turned around. A young woman, close to Goldie's age, stood at an open door. "I've seen you walking up and down. Come on in and sit a spell. We'll take good care of you."

No lust stirred in his heart, only pity. "No, I'm not interested." With a wordless prayer to heaven, Joshua handed her a pamphlet. "But if you're ever looking for something different, stop by Good Shepherd Church. We hold classes every afternoon, services at night and on Sunday mornings."

"You're one of those folks who thinks God loves me." She tilted her head back, jutted her chest forward, and smiled. "He should. He's the one who made all of this." She gestured down her body.

He refused to acknowledge the heat spreading across his face. "That's true. God made you and He loves you." He nodded and prepared to leave. "Hope we see you sometime."

Joshua decided to head home. After days like this, he sometimes wished he had a wife. Someone who could work at his side in ministry and who would also encourage him and meet his needs.

His thoughts flew to Goldie, and then he scolded himself. Although sweet and pure, she wasn't a Christian. No believer should marry an unbeliever, certainly not a preacher.

Joshua passed by Porter's Emporium and went in. Although the storekeeper had never attended their meetings, he gave the church a discount. Joshua had wondered if he would support their cause in other ways, and Goldie's situation gave him a reason to ask.

After a pause in front of the store for a quick prayer, Joshua entered. Mr. Porter stood by the register, but when Joshua waved hello, he frowned.

Porter knew something, and Joshua wouldn't like the news.

Chapter 8

Goldie longed to escape into the arms of Morpheus until supper and her evening duties called, but she needed to think things over. What steps could she take? She sat in the rocking chair by the window open over the street where women greeted potential customers.

For years, she had been grateful for the private room, the fancy clothes, the facial creams and paints most women didn't use. She had chuckled at the remedies for pink cheeks and shining eyes she read in women's magazines. Give her the right bottles and tubes, and she could make herself look like a princess. However, most of the time she avoided using them.

Now Goldie realized all this—stuff—was meant to prepare her for the life Madame Amelia expected from her. That she would continue in her mother's footsteps. No one would spoil an orphan without expecting repayment, and Goldie should have anticipated the development.

How could she have been so blind?

Because she wanted to believe Madame Amelia loved her, although nothing she did had ever earned the affection she desired.

A sharp edge bit into Goldie's shin, and she retracted Joshua's burlap-wrapped Bible from her purse. He had written an inscription on the first page: *To Goldie Hatfield from Pastor Joshua Kerr. "For God so loved Goldie that He gave His only begotten Son..." God loves you. Read the Bible to discover more.*

If God loved her, He had a funny way of showing it. She put aside the Bible. She'd look at it later, when she wasn't fighting for her life. Now was the time for action: speak to Madame Amelia. She held on to a slim thread of hope everything would work out.

"God, if You are there, You can help me get through to Madame Amelia today." Goldie adjusted her hair. She debated about changing into clothes her guardian had provided. No, her store clothes were a visible reminder she had options. She could support herself. So was the Bible, which she wrapped in the burlap sack and hid under her pillow. The lump reminded her she had a place she could run to, if need be.

After she drank a glass of water to wet her throat, she headed for Madame Amelia's room. She hesitated for a moment, ready to walk away. A burst of courage enabled her to knock.

"Who is it?" A whiskey, smoky voice inquired.

"It's Goldie Hatfield."

"Goldie, my dear, come in."

The warm greeting should have encouraged Goldie, but uncertainty held Goldie back. She gathered her courage and opened the door.

Amelia's hair was the purple henna that came from a bottle, and her face was a white brought about by cosmetics, a life spent indoors, and, if gossip could be believed, from drugs she consumed. She held a slender cigarette in her left hand. Her silk robe left little to the imagination.

"I see you've been working at Porter's Emporium today." Amelia said it as if it were a matter of no importance.

"Yes." Goldie lifted her chin. "In fact, I have spoken with him about the possibility of increasing my hours."

"Nonsense." Amelia flicked a stray hair away from her face. "It would interfere with your responsibilities here."

Tell her. Goldie's stomach rumbled, but she drew a deep breath and projected her voice the way she had been taught. "I plan to work full-time, to move into a place of my own."

The madame took her time, twisting her hair into an extravagant knot. Goldie had conquered the hairstyle when she was twelve. Mother had taken it down immediately and braided Goldie's thick hair into two strands.

Madame Amelia smiled, the smile of a python or a black widow spider. She wrapped a long silk scarf around her shoulders and under her arm and sat back in her chair. "So, you're ready to fly the cage and make a life for yourself. Without a thought for all the money I've spent taking care of you." Amelia reached into her desk drawer and extracted a heavy blue ledger.

Goldie recognized the business ledger, which she had used to teach Goldie about numbers. Madame Amelia flipped through the pages. She reached a spot about a fourth of the way through the book and turned it around for Goldie's perusal.

"Goldie Hatfield" headlined the page. Red figures filled the columns. Food, clothing, education, singing lessons, classes in deportment—even Monday's dress fitting. The charges began at her birth. As long as her mother was alive, regular payments had kept the balance close to zero.

After Mama's death, the expenses had multiplied and the payments had stopped until Goldie started singing two years ago. Madame Amelia allotted her a small percentage from the nights she sang, but it wasn't nearly enough. The total due seized Goldie by the throat and squeezed it until she couldn't breathe.

"You won't be allowed to move from here until you have paid your debt. I have not required you to turn over your earnings from your employment at Porter's Emporium. Perhaps you have enough to pay the balance due?"

Of course Goldie didn't. "What do you want?" Fear and dread seared her throat as she forced herself to speak.

The python's smile slithered from Madame Amelia's face, replaced by a smirk. "You are old enough to work upstairs. I have allowed you to remain parlor entertainment for too long. You see, I've always had a soft spot for you."

She reached a finger out to caress Goldie's cheek. Goldie pushed away from the desk, and Madame Amelia laughed.

"You will start your new career on your birthday. You will not return to Porter's Emporium. Starting tomorrow, you will spend your free time learning the arts of pleasing a man."

Prison bars clanged in Goldie's heart with each word. She scrambled for an idea, anything that might help. "At least let me tell him I won't be returning." He might help her get word to Joshua.

Madame Amelia mouth twisted into an imitation of a smile. "That won't be necessary. He is aware of my plans for you."

I will not cry. Numb in mind and body, Goldie couldn't form a single thought.

"Come, now, Goldie. You must have been expecting this. Cheer up. You might even enjoy it. Some women do."

Saturday dawned early, and Joshua had no more inkling about how to help Goldie than ever. He joined the others for breakfast. "I want to go to the store today."

Jane and Matt glanced at each other. "But you were just there yesterday."

"And you went three days in a row. I'll buy some eggs while I'm there, like I went there to shop."

Jane nodded uncomfortably. "That should work."

Joshua's mind had raced ahead. "I might be late—I want to talk with Porter."

"Be careful, Joshua." They didn't discuss the dangers of their ministry very often, but snatching the goods from a popular brothel would bring danger to their doorstep.

Joshua jutted out his chin. "I choose to believe good of the man."

Jane shook her head. "I pray that is true."

Joshua wrote down *eggs* and underlined it to be sure he remembered. With that paper tucked into his pocket, he quick-stepped to the store. Too bad Goldie had already left for the day.

After Joshua gave the clerk his order, he looked around the store for a sign of the owner. A lamp burned in the room in the top right corner, Porter's office. Joshua paid the clerk and headed up the stairs.

When he reached the bottom step, Joshua halted. Was he doing the right thing? Before he could back out, Porter had seen him and motioned him to join him in his office.

"How can I help you or Good Shepherd Church? I've heard about the amazing things you're doing for the riffraff running around the neighborhood, turning them into productive citizens."

The words struck a nerve in Joshua, as if Porter were drawing a line. Did he think it was fine to take care of orphans but rescuing women from a life of prostitution was a different matter?

Joshua chose to believe the best. "Thanks be to God. He has allowed us to make some real progress. Today I'm not in need of your dry goods, however. There is no price tag for what I seek." He smiled, seeking to inject a note of humor. "I'm looking for information."

Porter's face went serious and he settled back in his chair. Tilting his head back until Joshua could no longer look him in the eye, he said, "What do you want to know?"

This was the moment. *Lord, give Porter a heart willing to share what he knows.*

"What do you know about Goldie Hatfield's situation? I'm—aware—she grew up in Madame Amelia's establishment. Her mother one was one of the ladies. I admire you for giving her a job here."

Porter brought down his massive head and peered at him through pensive eyes. At length, he shook his head. "She won't be working here much longer." He stood and walked around his room. "Do you drink whiskey?"

Joshua shook his head. "A few years ago, I would have accepted your offer but not any longer. Why did you say she won't be working here? I was under the impression she hoped to work full-time."

Porter drummed his fingers on his desk. "Miss Hatfield would make an ideal employee, but she has other obligations that make it impossible."

Obligations. Joshua repeated the word to himself, disturbed by the implications. "Please explain."

Porter blinked and then reached into his desk drawer for a slender file. "Madame Amelia informed me today Miss Hatfield won't be coming back. It was inevitable, after I received this."

He slipped a sheet out of the file. A rendering of Goldie jumped off the page but not the girl Joshua knew. In the picture, her face was made up, her dress pulled down, her hair styled to make her look older and more worldly—yet somehow innocent.

As arresting as the picture was—as disturbing as it was, with its suggestive expression—words in large print jumped off the page—A Birthday Auction.

The flyer announced an auction to be held on April 12—Goldie's seventeenth birthday. The winner would be her first customer. Goldie's worst suspicions were confirmed.

The words swam before Joshua's eyes. He closed his eyes tight until the circles stopped forming behind his eyelids. He forced himself to read the rest, the highlights of Goldie's résumé. She possessed a beautiful voice and body, her hair was the color of the gold that formed the city of San Francisco, and she had a sweet and willing spirit.

All the wonderful gifts God had given to Goldie, laid out to be twisted by the enemies' flaming darts.

At the bottom came the worst dart of all: Minimum bid: $500.

"I'm taking this." Joshua grabbed the flyer as if he could destroy its reality by tearing it to pieces. "Thank you for telling me."

He couldn't trust himself to say another word. Deaf to anything Porter was trying to say, Joshua stumbled down the stairs, remembered enough to grab the package for Jane, and headed home.

Chapter 9

Goldie had already dressed when Sunday morning dawned. She hoped to avoid Madame Amelia's plans for a few hours. She headed downstairs, eager for Li Min's company.

The cook had fixed Goldie's favorite foods, a sure sign she knew how upset Goldie must be. Goldie asked only one question: "Do you know who is doing my training?"

Li Min didn't pretend ignorance. "Missy Bessie."

The lady Goldie had hoped Madame Amelia would assign to her. Bessie worked with those women who promised the most payback but needed special handling. Stern, kind, and fair, she pulled no punches, but she did it without humiliating or hurting her students.

And she could be counted on to sleep until noon on Sundays.

"I'm going to church." Goldie covered up with a cloak. "I'll come back as soon as the service is over. Can you get word to me if they come looking for me?"

Li Min nodded her head. "You go. I pray."

Oh, how Goldie wanted to grab a small bag with some clothes, the one picture she had of her mother, and leave Madame Amelia's behind forever. But Amelia would send the police after her. She had done that to other girls—and always got her way. They had to live up to their obligations to a perfectly legal contract.

How could she have been so blind, not to realize what would happen?

She walked the route as quickly as she could, running ideas through her mind. Nothing practical had occurred to her before she arrived at the church building. The blinds were shut, but she saw light shining in the back. She rang the doorbell.

Quick footsteps, like a heeled shoe, crossed the floor. Jane opened the door. "Goldie! Come in."

Tears must have welled up in Goldie's eyes, because it looked like Jane was crying, too. "Oh, Goldie. Joshua spoke with Mr. Porter last night."

Madame Amelia's words came back to her. *"Mr. Porter isn't expecting you back."* "He knows about it?"

Jane opened her mouth and patted her arm. "I'll let Joshua explain."

Goldie didn't know how she could face Joshua. Shame, at her birth, at her employment, both present and future, the futility of her hopes her life could change. That God—

"—how can you still believe in a God who lets something like this happen? Most fallen women didn't start out that way. They were tricked into it or forced into it. Like me." Why had she come? There was no hope for her here, there was no hope for her anywhere. She stood, ready to bolt, before she got into real trouble with Madame Amelia.

"If you believed that, you wouldn't have come here," Joshua said. "Come in, take a seat."

"What choice do I have?" The words came out as a whisper. "I was going to go to Mr. Porter, but Madame Amelia said. . ."

Joshua looked to his sister and brother-in-law and they all nodded. "We know some of the plan, but why don't you fill us in?"

After much hemming and hawing, Goldie outlined Madame Amelia's plan for her birthday. "I don't think I can come here again. She's going to keep me busy morning, noon, and night, teaching me all those awful things."

Joshua looked at something he was holding in his hand. "You'd better see this." Before he handed it over, he added a final horrible fact. "I got this from Mr. Porter."

Goldie read the flyer, detail by lurid detail. The picture looked like her but not a picture any girl would send home to her family. Whoever had drawn it had imagined her like that—the thought sickened her.

She'd met men like that before. They'd always called her a pretty little thing, but the year she'd grown her womanly figure, their attitude had changed. "Pay no attention," Mother had said. "You are a good girl, whatever they say."

Her mouth quivered. "I wonder how much of that five hundred dollars will be applied to my debt total."

Jane jumped in. "Goldie, surely you realize—they don't intend to ever let you pay off the debt."

She refused to cry, so she simply nodded.

Joshua glanced at the floor. "I thought you would bring a bag with you."

Cobwebs cleared from her mind. "You think I came here this morning to stay? I can't."

"You can." Joshua the soldier refused to take no for an answer.

"I can't. Women have tried before. They're brought back by the police. Contractual obligations, they say."

"You haven't signed any contract. Have you?" Joshua's eyes widened.

"Not for. . .this. But since she was my guardian, Madame Amelia signed a contract on my behalf. That's all the courts care about." She looked at the ground, a lump in her throat. "I thought Mr. Porter was on my side."

Joshua shifted in his chair uncomfortably. "My opinion is he doesn't want this to happen." He turned the flyer over. "But he can't afford to offend the businesses on Morton Street." He scratched his head. "I don't know if anyone else would have given me that flyer."

He banged his hand on the desk. "There must be some way to convince him to drop his neutrality."

A small bell of hope rang in Goldie's heart.

Joshua wanted to bolt after Goldie when she left. No matter what she'd said about police and contracts, she must be able to escape. It used to be illegal to help slaves escape, but people did it because it was the right thing to do.

Matt sat in a chair that blocked the exit. Jane stood by his side, her back ramrod straight. "You hear me, Joshua Andrew Kerr. You are a servant of the Most High God who has all the angels of the heavenly hosts at His command. If He could keep Rahab safe when Jericho's walls fell down, He can take care of Goldie. You know it. Now act like you believe it. And if that's not enough—"

A bell rang at the front door.

"—God sent you to San Francisco for more than one lost soul. Feed the rest of God's flock today and let God take care of the one lost sheep."

Conviction fell on Joshua. Had he an idol of Goldie? The people gathering in their front room had come to worship. "Give me five minutes, ten minutes at the most." He went to his "closet" to pray—his room was a walk-in closet converted to a bedroom. He sank to his knees and lifted his hands to heaven. "Our Father in heaven, hallowed be Thy name." He repeated the familiar words, letting each phrase sink into his heart. God's will would be done on earth as it was in heaven. For now, God had given Joshua a message to share with the sheep of the Good Shepherd Church. When he said "amen," he felt ready to preach.

When Joshua joined the congregation, Matt was leading the church in singing hymns. The flyer called Goldie Madame Amelia's songbird, and Jane had mentioned her beautiful voice. His thoughts wandered away, but Joshua reined them back in. Making them obedient to Christ, as Paul said.

They strayed again when the children read the day's passage, and Joshua wondered if Goldie had read the Bible he had given her. Any of God's Word she hid in her heart armed her against attack.

The time had come for the sermon. Sometimes when Joshua preached, the words poured out of him easily, without effort. But not today. Although he had prepared as always, he kept referring to his notes. The subject, about how the Holy Ghost gave peace despite the trouble everyone experienced, had excited him when he studied it. But the words he spoke came out like wooden soldiers, and just about as useless on the battlefield. Hebrews talked about a sacrifice of praise. That's what this sermon felt like, a sacrifice offered out of obedience but without joy or power.

The side door opened, but Joshua didn't look. He couldn't afford distractions.

An eternity later, he reached the end of the sermon and offered the usual invitation while Matt led in a hymn.

A boy, one Jane had said was close to a decision, came forward. Joshua rejoiced for his sake.

An entire family came forward, the husband uniting with his wife in faith. The front row filled. They continued singing, repeated the verses—and another head appeared at the altar.

Golden hair appeared above a plain brown dress. It couldn't be. But it was. He knelt beside her, staring at her with astonishment.

"Li Min told me to come back and get things right with God. That I need Him on my side if I want to win against Madame Amelia." A warm smile showed through the tears sliding down her cheeks. "And somehow I agreed. She's covering for me, but I—"

"—can't stay long. But, Goldie. . ." Joshua had a hundred questions, but only one mattered. "You have asked Jesus to be your Savior and Lord?"

"I read the verses the Bible said about salvation and prayed. I need God to be my way, but I need Him as my Life and my Truth, too."

More than before, Joshua wanted to throw his arms around Goldie, hug her, and welcome her to the family of God. He resisted. They stood, looking at each other awkwardly.

Goldie looked at the clock. "I've already stayed too long, but I had to come back."

The door flew open and a shadow fell across the floor. "Goldie Hatfield, you're coming with me." Big Jim's brutish presence cast a pall over the congregation.

Joshua bristled. "She's not going with you."

"I am, for now." Goldie, so brave, took his hands in hers and squeezed tight. "Don't worry so, my warrior. I just know God is going to work everything out."

For the second time that day, Joshua watched Goldie walk away. She saw him as her warrior? She had that wrong. God was her Protector. He prayed God would set her high on a rock where neither Madame Amelia nor any of her associates could reach her.

If Joshua played a role in the process, he would dance down the street like King David.

Taking down a giant with a slingshot would be easier than facing Madame Amelia.

Chapter 10

A week later, after seven days when Bessie had taught Goldie every temptation known to woman, Madame Amelia dragged Goldie out of bed to join her in the office.

Amelia held a long-stemmed cigarillo and tapped it on her ashtray. "Bessie tells me you have cooperated in your lessons."

Goldie shrugged. If she feigned cooperation, she hoped to find some way to escape. If only she could unlearn them and wipe her memory clean.

"Such dedication should be rewarded. Bessie will accompany you to church this morning."

Goldie raised her gaze at that announcement.

"As long as they are willing to have you in the congregation, you and a companion may attend each week." She paused. "On Easter Sunday I expect you will be too tired for worship."

Goldie didn't know how to respond. She finally managed, "Thank you?" Was this the kind of thing God did for those who put their faith in Him? It was a first step, a small step, but an opening. Goldie prepared to leave, to salvage a few hours' sleep before the church service began.

"But Goldie?"

Madame Amelia's voice held her frozen at the door.

"If you go there without a companion, or at any time other than on Sunday morning, I will revoke the privilege."

"Yes, ma'am." Goldie fled up the stairs. As she slipped into her bed, she prayed silently. *I will praise the risen Savior on Easter Sunday, even if I go with my head hung low.*

Goldie had dressed conservatively for church, but Bessie hadn't. Did she have day dresses? She pulled the bodice strings together in an effort at modesty and added a coat to the ensemble. Without makeup, she looked older, more vulnerable.

Goldie's curiosity must have shown on her face, because Bessie chuckled. "Are you afraid I'll scare away your holy rollers? Don't worry. I'm not going in. I'll be sitting straight outside, where I can see every move. Don't try anything."

Goldie shook her head. She couldn't speak. As much as she told herself to be strong and courageous, she had a hard time believing it. When she came back from her lessons, she read the Bible in an effort to wash away the filth. She memorized verses about being strong in the Lord. She gobbled them as if they were as sweet as candy, as nourishing as mother's milk. Not a clue as to how they would work.

But today she would go to church. That was the first answer. She couldn't wait to see the expression on their faces when she walked in. Oh, she would love to spend the day in their company, share a meal with them, go on another stroll through San Francisco's neighborhoods with Joshua.

Maybe she could tarry. Since Bessie wasn't coming into the church with her, she wouldn't know when the service ended. But she could figure it out by looking through the window or when people left after the service. No, Goldie couldn't do much more than say hello. If she did more than shake Joshua's hand on her way out the door, Bessie would interfere.

She rubbed her forehead, hoping to clear away the tired cobwebs, and removed her Bible from the burlap sack. Since she had invited Jesus into her life, she had read the Gospel of John from beginning to end then gone back and read Matthew as well. The Jesus she read about in the Bible could do anything He set His mind to. She wished He walked the streets of San Francisco in 1873. But she didn't know how Joshua's God could solve her problem.

A piece of paper was stuck between the pages, where Goldie had written down some Bible verses she wanted to look up. She took lined paper and wrote a few lines, explaining the restrictions on going to church. "My training continues at a rapid pace. If not for the planned auction, I would already be put to work."

She crossed out those last two lines and rewrote the note, leaving out any mention of her training. "I want to believe God will deliver me, but I don't see how it will happen. They delight in tormenting me by reading the names of men who plan on attending the auction." Now she sounded like a whimpering child.

Before she could rewrite it again, Li Min knocked at the door. "Missy Goldie, I bring bread."

Goldie exclaimed. "My goodness. It's time to go." She threw her arms around the cook. "Thank you for the bread." She used the towel to cover her Bible and the note she had written as well. Bessie was dozing in a chair by the front door. "Let's go."

Bessie grumbled. "Slow down a bit."

Goldie took smaller steps to allow her guard to catch up. Better to arrive late than to be called back to the house for misbehavior.

If she could see Joshua every week, she still had hope.

Joshua headed for Porter's to pick up palm branches for tomorrow's celebration of Palm Sunday. Jane handed him the list of supplies she needed for the weekend.

"Here we are dying Easter eggs, and Goldie is counting the hours." Eight days, one hundred ninety-two hours, eleven thousand, five hundred twenty minutes. . .each passing minute ate one more piece from his heart, his concern, his faith.

"Christ is risen. Goldie reminds us why we must celebrate His victory now more than ever."

But. . .but. . .the promise of His resurrection felt hollow against the reality of Goldie's pending distress. Joshua was no closer to an answer than before. Previous hints to Porter had gone ignored. Today he would ask for his help outright.

"Joshua! I was expecting to see you today. We have the extra eggs you requested in the back room." Once they got away from the front room, he said, "If you can remain here for a few minutes, I believe I can arrange something of interest to you."

One thought jumped into Joshua's mind. *Goldie.* "I can wait." His heart sped up.

Porter brought Joshua up to his office. Twenty minutes passed while he prayed and imagined and wondered what he would do if Goldie walked through the door.

When the door opened, Goldie didn't come through. Instead, Porter held the door for an older, henna-haired lady in fancy dress. "Amelia Hamilton, please meet Joshua Kerr. Pastor, this is Miss Hamilton."

Madame Amelia. Joshua's heart raced as he sent a quick prayer to heaven. "It's good to finally meet you, Miss Hamilton."

She chuckled, a chortle from deep in her throat. "Mr. Kerr, we can dispense with the pleasantries. You would like to close the doors of my business."

Joshua did a double take. Straightforward, blunt—he would respond in kind. "I would like to see your business come to an end. However, I have nothing but the deepest regard for you and your situation. I care for you, if not what you do."

She waved that aside. "You are acquainted with Goldie Hatfield."

Joshua's heart thumped loud enough to echo in the room. "She's been worshipping with us for several weeks now." He held her gaze without looking away. *Good. Don't show fear.*

Mrs. Hamilton didn't blink, either. The staring contest lasted for thirty seconds. . .a minute. . .before the madame broke out in a smile. "I like you, Mr. Kerr. You have nerve. No wonder Goldie admires you."

Goldie admired him? Joshua refused to follow that rabbit trail. "I'm afraid I can't return the compliment."

Now the woman laughed. "Of course not." She breathed a smoke-laden aroma in his face. "You must know even if I closed my doors, a dozen more will spring up to take my place."

Joshua took shallow breaths. He refused to let her bully him. " 'The only thing necessary for the triumph of evil is for good men to do nothing.' Edmund Burke said that once. I will do what I can."

She inclined her head, as if accepting his position. "Let us get down to brass tacks. Miss Hatfield is a valuable asset to me. She possesses charm, beauty, and talent, as well as an amazing innocence for someone raised in her circumstances. I have poured money into her education and care for years, money she is obligated to repay."

Joshua glanced at Mr. Porter. "You wouldn't be here if you didn't have something to discuss."

She straightened in her chair. "I came to warn you. Don't interfere with my business. If Goldie is not in my house on this coming Saturday night, I will send the police to your church to arrest everyone we find on the premises. And if that happens, you will only be allowed to see Miss Hatfield if you can afford the price of admission."

The taste of sawdust filled Joshua's mouth.

Satisfied, she rose to her feet. "That is all I have to say. Thank you, Mr. Porter, for arranging this meeting. I can see myself out."

The price of admission. Thoughts whirled around Joshua's brain.

Heavy footsteps alerted him to Porter's return. "I'm sorry, Joshua."

"No. I appreciate your arranging this meeting. Now I can put a face to the opposition. But I do have some questions. Have you attended one of these auctions before?"

Porter sank onto the chair behind his desk, averting his face from Joshua's view. "I have, several times." Before Joshua could respond, he added, "But I do not plan on bidding on Goldie."

Joshua's stomach twisted at the possibility. "I leave that to your conscience and God's conviction. But I have questions about how the auction works. Does the five-hundred-dollar minimum work like a buy-in to a poker game?"

The red stain slowly faded from Porter's face as he explained the normal process. The answer to Goldie's dilemma became so clear Joshua scolded himself for not thinking of it before.

If only Matt and Jane would agree. They would have to. God willing, one day Goldie would be his bride.

Chapter 11

Sunshine broke through the window earlier than ever on Goldie's birthday, as if all the dirt and clouds had been scrubbed from the sky. She'd wanted to sleep a few extra minutes, even hours. The sunshine boring a hole through her window wouldn't let her.

She pulled the blanket over her head and reviewed the verses from Psalm 27 she had memorized. *"Thou an host should encamp against me, my heart shall not fear. . . . For in the time of trouble he shall hide me in his pavilion."* She kept repeating the words, hoping against hope. The psalmist said God would set her on a rock, but the only high point she saw in her future was sitting on the stage while men bid money for her. Unless Joshua, her hero, could rescue her.

"Now shall mine head be lifted up above mine enemies round about me."

As long as she kept repeating the words, the scary images stayed away.

Li Min disturbed her peace a short time later. "Missy Goldie, I bring you food."

Goldie groaned. "My stomach is too upset to eat."

"You feel better if you eat. Good food. Grapefruit. Eggs. Coffee."

Goldie hesitated to peel back the blanket, to admit her birthday had dawned. The savory aroma tempted her nearly empty stomach. She sat on the side of the bed and surveyed the tray. Li Min had prepared a little bit of everything.

"You like, maybe?" Li Min asked.

Tears swam in Goldie's eyes. "It's wonderful." She spread orange marmalade over the toast and swallowed it down with orange juice. Oh, how tangy and delicious. She ate more than half the food on the tray before Bessie arrived at her door.

"Li Min, so this is where you've been. Come now, we need bathwater. Chop, chop. Shame on you for stuffing Goldie today. Madame Amelia will be upset if she's bloated."

The food sank like coals into Goldie's stomach. *I am a child of God, a daughter of the King, precious in His sight.* God had already cleaned her spirit and her sins. The bathwater only touched the outside, which didn't matter to God.

The day dragged on. The bath cleansed every inch of her body, from her toenails to her scalp. Oils and perfumes softened her skin and brought her hair to a shining brightness. Bessie brushed, curled, and coiled her hair into layers of ringlets above, behind, beneath her neck.

At last she put on her new dress, a seafoam green with black stripes and ecru lace around the bodice, a large bow on the right hip.

"You should be more thankful to Madame Amelia for these clothes. She doesn't provide togs like this for the rest of us."

No, because Bessie wore red satins and lace, clothing that left no doubt as to her profession. Goldie's birthday gown was merely suggestive. She would rather wear a potato sack than pay for the new clothes.

Bessie put a towel around Goldie's neck for the final preparation for the evening: makeup, starting with a facial cream, kohl for her eyes, rouge for her cheeks and color on her lips.

Bessie inspected her work. "Try to look happy. Madame Amelia will be here to give us her opinion."

A rap on the floor announced the madame's arrival. "Stand up." She walked around Goldie with lips pursed. After her inspection, she tugged down the neckline by half an inch and adjusted the side bow.

"You've done well, Bessie," she announced. "Goldie, you will sing tonight, and you will sing as though you enjoy it."

Goldie's throat was a dry as the Sahara. If only singing were all Madame Amelia expected of her.

"Maybe 'Home, Home on the Range' or 'The Man on the Flying Trapeze.'" With that, the gorgon left Goldie under Bessie's watchful eye.

The hours dragged by. Goldie drank sweet tea and sucked on lemon drops to soothe her throat. Li Min arrived to remove the tea service. "I have message for you."

"The Lord your God is your strength and shield." The words were written in Joshua's spiky handwriting.

"Joshua was here?"

Li Min put her finger to her lips. "God is with you."

Goldie read and reread the paper before she crushed it and tucked it into a pocket. On the other side of the curtain she heard deep voices rumbling, the number and volume increasing. Likely alcohol was flowing freely to loosen purse strings and inhibitions.

Madame Amelia came up behind Goldie. "It's time." Satisfaction dripped from her voice. "You have captured the attention of our clientele. You should be proud of the number of men vying for your affection."

Goldie didn't speak. She didn't even nod her head. Where was the God she had counted on to deliver her?

Where was Joshua?

"Take your seat." Madame Amelia arranged the folds of Goldie's dress where she perched on a stool. The pianist took his seat.

"Good luck." Madame Amelia brushed past Goldie and through the curtain.

"A warm welcome to all of you. As you all know, tonight we are holding an auction to welcome the one, the only, Goldie Hatfield into the stable of my House of Pleasure."

Goldie's stomach soured.

Applause, catcalls, whistles increased in volume. One sliver of a face at a time appeared through the parting curtains. Beyond the spotlights, she'd guess at least thirty men waited for her.

The pianist segued from background music to the introduction of "Home on the

Range," but Goldie stayed silent.

"Sing," Madame Amelia hissed from the sides.

Goldie closed her eyes and opened her mouth, stumbling through the words.

Mild clapping greeted her performance. Anticipation mounted as Madame Amelia came back to the stage. "But you are not here tonight to enjoy Goldie's voice. We are here to celebrate her transformation from a sweet young girl to a beautiful and desirable woman."

Goldie breathed in through her nose, out through her mouth, trying to capture enough air to keep consciousness. The worst was about to happen.

"Come here." Li Min gestured to Joshua from the side door. "You sit here. You see them, but they don't see you."

Cries of "GOLD-ie, GOLD-ie" reached his ears.

He saw two dozen men through the door, but his eyes fled to Goldie. Ghostly pallor deadened her features under her makeup. *Lord, keep her strong.*

"Let the bidding begin!" Madame Amelia called.

"Five hundred dollars." The cry came quickly from all corners.

"Five fifty."

"Six hundred."

The numbers flew by at fifty dollars up a pop, quickly passing a thousand dollars.

Joshua wanted to rush the stage and rescue Goldie from the embarrassment, the battle she faced. But he must wait for the right time.

The bidders thinned out as the total rose. Goldie fixed her gaze on the floor. When they reached two thousand, three serious bidders remained.

At twenty-five hundred the number dropped to two.

Almost time.

At three thousand—"I'm out."

Joshua stood to his feet.

"The winner is—"

Joshua burst into the room. "I bid six thousand five hundred dollars."

Goldie's head flew up and color returned to her face.

The room had fallen silent.

"I bid sixty-five hundred for the night and for the contract," he repeated. A step at a time, he made his way through the chairs. He fixed his eyes on Goldie's, a triumphant smile on his face. "To pay off her debt and give you a tidy profit."

Madame Amelia crossed in front of Goldie, blocking her view of Joshua. "You have no right."

"In fact, he does." Mr. Porter emerged from a side room on the opposite side of the parlor. "We went to the lawyer who handles your affairs. He arranged for the transfer of the contract. It's here in writing, ready for you to sign." Mr. Porter slapped it in her hand. "Take it, Amelia. It's the best offer you're going to get."

Joshua walked forward until he stood between Madame Amelia and Goldie. He offered Goldie his hand. "Miss Goldie Hatfield, you are free to leave this place and never come back."

Joshua tugged her hand, and she took one step then another. Each step came a little quicker as they walked through the silent gathering.

Li Min waited at the door with a valise. "Clothes, Bible in here."

Goldie hugged the cook. "Li Min, will you leave this place with me?"

She shook her head. "I stay. Others need me."

As soon as they reached the street, Goldie's chest heaved as she breathed the free air. "I can't believe you. . .you shouldn't have. . ."

"Shh. Let's get away from here first." Jane had made arrangements for Goldie to stay at a friend's house, but they had another stop to make first. Within five minutes they entered the Good Shepherd Church. The room was as full as on Sunday mornings.

Jane swept forward. "Praise God, Goldie. We have been praying all night."

"But the money. . .it was a fortune."

"It was never ours," Jane said.

"We wanted to redeem the harm our father had done. What is more important than your life?" Joshua took Goldie's hands in his. "What could be more important to me than the woman I love? After the nightmare you have been through, it is too soon for me to ask you. But know I love you, and I will wait as long as it takes for you to love me back."

Goldie looked at him, his beautiful golden treasure, joy and laughter in her eyes. "That day will be soon, my warrior." She stood on her tiptoes and kissed Joshua on the cheek.

Bestselling author **Darlene Franklin**'s greatest claim to fame is that she writes full-time from a nursing home. She lives in Oklahoma, near her son and his family, and continues her interests in playing the piano and singing, books, good fellowship, and reality TV in addition to writing. She is an active member of Oklahoma City Christian Fiction Writers, American Christian Fiction Writers, and the Christian Authors Network. She has written over fifty books and more than 250 devotionals. Her historical fiction ranges from the Revolutionary War to World War II, from Texas to Vermont. You can find Darlene online at www.darlenefranklinwrites.com.

Through Stormy Waters

by Patty Smith Hall

Chapter 1

London,
1745

A crash of thunder boomed through the stony walls of the courtroom, the constant spray of rain hammered against the pane-glass windows as if God Himself was angered by the proceedings. Families of the accused stood huddled in the gray shadows, each waiting for a moment to whisper a brief farewell before their loved one stood in front of the magistrate to receive the sentence.

Captain John Randall sat back in the hard chair, his gut tied up in a series of intricate knots. How had he sailed men and women just like these across the ocean, away from everything they'd ever known and the people they loved, all for stealing a loaf of bread or a cup of milk? Why had he agreed, albeit grudgingly he noted to himself, to do this one last trip before he retreated to his farm in South Carolina?

Because it was either live up to his end of the contract or be thrown into prison himself. Granted, Newgate might be better than the guilt pressing down on him. Still, this voyage wouldn't be like past ones. The changes made on his boat these last few weeks had seen to that.

"It looks like we'll have a fine lot to choose from," the man beside John whispered as he scribbled furiously on his pad of paper. Martin Habersham was the leading broker of slaves and convicted prisoners in all of London, and one of the cruelest. "From the looks of things, these ladies haven't been in custody long enough to dirty their clothes. They still have some meat on their bones. Why, some are even round enough to draw us a fine price on the marriage mart."

John felt his temper rise. The lucrative deal he'd struck with the man several years ago—exporting prisoners and indentured servants to the colonies—now left a bitter taste in his mouth. Why had God been so merciful to him when he himself had shown so little to others? "It seems a bit much to sentence a lady to a lifetime of misery simply because she needed to feed her family."

Martin stopped writing and snarled at him. "I never expected to hear such from an earl's son. I thought your kind left those feelings to the gentler sex."

"Compassion isn't reserved only for our mothers and sisters."

"I see." The older man flipped the page of his notebook and began writing again. "I know you've lost your stomach for the business, but you gave me your oath and I expect you to live up to your end of the deal."

"I don't break my word," John answered. One more voyage, then he would sell his ship and settle on the land he'd bought outside of Charleston, maybe even help the very people he'd hurt over the last eight years. How, he wasn't sure, but he had to find some way to help these people after all the pain he'd caused.

A loud murmur rose in the courtroom, jolting John from his thoughts. He glanced over the bannister and saw a young woman, shackled at the wrists and ankles, being pushed into the defendant's box.

"Ah." Martin sighed beside him. "This is the jewel I've been waiting for. She'll fetch us a pretty shilling."

John craned his neck to get a better look just as the woman in question lifted her head and glared at her jailor. The brute of a man sneered back at her, his face turning more and more red the longer he stared. John slid to the end of his seat, gripping the arms of the chair so tightly they might break. *Dear God, don't let him hit her.* The brute of a man would kill her with one punch.

God must have heard his prayer, for the jailor snorted at the woman then laughed.

"Spirited little minx, isn't she? Perfect to warm a man's bed," Martin whispered.

John ignored him, concentrating on the woman instead. Despite her mussed hair and disheveled gown, her clothes and bearing spoke of a gently bred lady. "What is her crime?"

"Not hers, her father's." Martin stared at him as if waiting for him to respond. "Really, man, don't you read the newspapers? Some are even calling it the scandal of the century."

John shook his head. He didn't have much use for anyone who could be bought by the rich and powerful, particularly when they had the power to print stories that destroyed people's lives. "I don't read those rags."

The man shrugged. "Her father was a favorite with the ton until he was caught swindling money from several powerful members. Some say even the duke of Sheffield bought into his scheme."

Sheffield? The man was known for his investment acumen. John glanced down at the woman. Her father must have had a death wish to cross the powerful man. Still, Martin hadn't answered his question. "Then why isn't the man standing for his own crimes?"

"It seems someone decided to take their pound of flesh out of Singleton first." Martin made a notation in his notebook. "He was found in an alley last week with a bullet in his head. Lots of talk about who fired the fatal shot, but that's all it is. Talk."

"But why bring his daughter into this?"

The man coughed to cover his laughter. "You know these people, John. They do not like being made fools of. They want their revenge." Martin turned to stare at the woman. "And Charlotte Singleton provides the perfect means to that end."

Charlotte couldn't stop her teeth from chattering. She grasped the railing of the prisoner's box, her legs shaking so violently beneath her skirts, she feared she might crumble to the floor. But she couldn't, not until she knew the reason she'd been dragged out of her aunt Mary's house and thrown into Newgate prison.

What could I have done to offend these people?

It was a question that had kept her awake through last night. Her days basically consisted of caring for Aunt Mary with a weekly trip to St. Catherine's to deliver the baby blankets and scarves she knitted in the evenings as her aunt napped in the chair beside her. Her life was tidy and quiet, and she preferred it that way.

"Are you Charlotte Singleton, the daughter of Robert Singleton?"

Charlotte blinked. She could count on one hand the number of times she'd heard her father's name over her twenty-two years, and always with bad news. If her father was involved, it wasn't a good omen. "My father abandoned me in an orphanage when I was just an infant, sir."

"That is not what I asked you, miss," the man snapped, the powder in his wig forming a white cloud around his head. "Again, is Robert Singleton your father?"

The judge's sharp tone sent a shiver of fear down Charlotte's spine. "From my understanding, yes, he is."

The low mutterings of the crowd surrounded her in a sea of noise. Dear heavens, what had the man who'd given her life and his name done? "I have no memory of my father, sir. My aunt Mary brought me home from St. Catherine's when I was almost a year old. The only caveat to the adoption was that I keep my father's name."

The gentleman seemed to consider this. Maybe the situation wasn't as dire as she'd thought. Once they realized she was of no use to them, they would release her and she could go home to her aunt and her knitting and her quiet life again.

All her hopes went up in flames when someone from the gallery cried out, "She's Singleton's daughter. Bad blood, you know!"

Charlotte flinched. She'd been called worse, particularly when the other girls learned of her adoption during her first year at Miss Langley's School for Young Ladies. But to have her name tied to someone as villainous as her father? She could bear anything but that. Aunt Mary was the only family she'd ever known. Digging her nails into the wood of the railing, Charlotte took a steadying breath. "My lord, may I ask a question?"

White powder clouded the air around his head as he shook his finger at her. "Don't be impertinent. What kind of question could a woman like you have?" His mouth puckered as if the simple act of addressing her had left a bad taste.

"Why have I been brought before the court, sir?"

He stared at her suspiciously. "If this is a ploy to divert justice, miss. . ."

"No, my lord." Charlotte rushed to answer. "I truly don't know why I've been brought here."

"Don't you read the newspapers?"

A plait of hair fell over her shoulder as she shook her head. "We have more pressing needs for the money in our pocketbook."

The judge gave her an unconvinced look. "Robert Singleton, your father, extorted thousands of pounds from several prominent members of society, and they have brought forth charges."

Oh, heavens. So the little Aunt Mary had told her about her father was true. She'd prayed that her aunt's stories were scandalous embellishments of the old woman's imagination, but now she knew the truth. The man deserved to be locked up in Newgate and the key to his cell tossed into the Thames. Still, her question to the judge remained unanswered. Why had she been brought before the court? "If you were hoping to question me on my father's whereabouts, I can assure you, I have no inclination as to where he might be."

"We know where Singleton is." The man must have taken her silence to mean interest, so he continued. "He's buried in Potter's field."

Her father was dead? Charlotte stood, waiting for some emotion to overcome her at the news, but all she felt was sadness for her aunt. As much pain as the man had caused her, Aunt Mary still cared for her younger brother. Charlotte bowed her head. "Thank you for alerting me to this sad news. If you'll excuse me, I must inform my aunt of her brother's passing."

A titter of laughter broke out in the gallery, and she turned to look up at them. Most looked exceedingly amused by the proceedings, a few even looked bored and on the verge of sleep.

Then, there was *him*.

Charlotte focused on the man in the back row just to her right. There was a wariness about him, as if he'd experienced much sadness in his thirty or so years. The somber look in his eyes spoke of true heartache. What could cause such pain in a man? Why did he seem to sympathize with her circumstances?

"Miss Singleton, are you not aware of the law?"

Charlotte turned to face the magistrate again. "In what regard, sir?"

His mouth straightened into a frustrated grimace. "Someone must pay for Singleton's crimes."

How could a dead man atone for his sins? Unless they expected her. . . Terror unlike anything Charlotte had ever experienced tied her insides into painful knots. "But he deserted me days after my mother died giving birth to me. I wouldn't have recognized him if I'd seen him on the street."

"Yet, you share his blood." A second judge stared down his beaklike nose at her. "In accordance with His Majesty's laws, you will stand for your father's crimes and be sentenced accordingly."

"But, my lord." Charlotte hesitated for a moment to calm the hysteria gathering in her chest. Aunt Mary had taught her that while nobility loved someone groveling at their feet, they deplored complete desperation. "As I am not the perpetrator of my father's many crimes and have led a Christian life, could you please show mercy, if not for me then for my invalid aunt?"

"We are showing mercy, girl!" the lead judge spit out. "She should be thankful we left her in her nice warm house. We could have easily brought her up on charges, too."

Bile scorched a fiery trail up Charlotte's throat. They couldn't punish her darling aunt Mary! She'd never survive the dank cold cells of Newgate or a voyage across the ocean to be sold into hard labor in the colonies. These people wanted blood for her father's many sins.

And she was the sacrificial lamb.

Each man at the bench reached for a square piece of linen, placed it on his head, then focused on her. "Charlotte Singleton," the lead judge said, "as the sole living offspring of Robert Singleton, you are found guilty of theft and are hereby sentenced to deportation to the colonies, where you will be sold as an indentured servant for a period of no less than seven years."

The gavel came down, shattering Charlotte's heart. Seven years! What of Aunt Mary? The dear woman could hardly handle the stairs, her joints so swollen with arthritis. Who would bathe her knees in liniment or remind her to take her medicine? Who would make sure she was fed and warm?

A meaty hand closed over Charlotte's upper arm. She glanced up. The jailor glared at her, his lips pulled into a hard smirk. "Back to the cages with you."

Charlotte stumbled as he pulled her out of the box, but she caught herself, glancing around. There was no mercy or compassion in any of the observers' faces, just scorn toward her, as if she'd stolen their last shilling herself. Did they not see the injustice of her situation, or did they simply not care?

Only one gentleman had seemed concerned about her dilemma since she'd entered the courtroom. Charlotte glanced into the gallery. If she could only get a glimpse of his face, at least, and know there was someone who cared about what she must endure. But as she was dragged through the doors to the waiting prison wagon, tears stung the back of her eyes.

The gentleman, whoever he was, was gone.

Chapter 2

"Get up, you lazy wench!"

Charlotte pushed herself onto her hands and knees, her hair falling around her in a long stringy curtain. Four days pressed against the walls of the prison wagon, along with the unending sobbing of her fellow cellmates and their children had drained what was left of her strength. She tried to breathe, but the stench of unwashed bodies and human excrement choked any attempt to take a deep breath.

The beefy jailor grabbed the chain binding her wrists and jerked her to her feet. "I said, get up!"

Charlotte slammed her eyes shut. So far, she'd managed to avoid the back of his hand, but others had not been so fortunate. She stole a glance at Miss Hembree. A massive bruise lined the right side of her face simply because she'd asked for a cup of water. Now it was Charlotte's turn. What was he waiting on? Why didn't he just get it over with?

Instead of a punch to her face, a small hand slipped into hers. Opening her eyes, she found herself face-to-face with a little sprite of a girl, her somber face too wise for her meager years. "Mama said they won't hurt us anymore, not with the captain and the man who paid our passage looking on."

Charlotte watched as the jailor walked away. That made sense. Damaged goods wouldn't yield a high price, especially on the auction block. She glanced around. "Where is your mother, Donalyn?"

"Feeding Edward." The solemn-faced child nodded toward a small group of women huddled close together, their backs to the harbor as they shielded their babies from the bracing wind. Not for the first time, Charlotte wondered what would happen to the children once they made landfall in the colonies. Would they be allowed to go with their mothers, or would they be auctioned off and their families torn apart? She shuddered at the thought.

Pushing her questions aside, Charlotte ruffled the child's oily blond hair. "Have you ever been on a boat before?"

The girl shook her head. "Papa read me stories about pirates and such. It all sounded like a great adventure." She glanced up at the sails then looked back at Charlotte. "Do you think this will be an adventure just like in the books?"

Charlotte hesitated. From the little she knew on this subject, they would be fortunate to reach the colonies alive. But there was no sense in frightening the girl. She'd had enough tragedy in her young life, what with her papa's treachery. What kind of man sold his family into servitude an ocean away? Donalyn's mother, Sylvia, blamed it on the drink, but Charlotte knew her husband's betrayal broke the young woman's heart.

Charlotte knelt beside the child and pulled her close. "We'll make it an adventure, but for everyone's sake, let's pray that doesn't include pirates."

Donalyn rewarded her with a rare smile. "No pirates, then."

As soon as the prisoners had returned from relieving themselves, they were herded like cattle toward the lowered gangplank, a whip cracking over their heads to hurry them along.

A fresh wave of grief threatened to drown Charlotte. She'd never been more than five blocks from her home in Cheapside and now, she'd be half a world away from everything familiar, everyone she'd ever loved. Her fingers reached for the folded edges of the note she'd received from Aunt Mary in the days after her imprisonment. Though she had tried to obtain Charlotte's freedom, she had been unsuccessful. Their neighbor, Mrs. Shephard, had heard about their circumstances and had volunteered her daughter to check in on Aunt Mary every evening.

It was a kindness Charlotte had never expected and could never repay, though she did manage to send a note to the lady with her profound thanks. Still, seven years seemed like a lifetime before she could return home.

As she stepped onto the deck, the rocking of the boat made it hard for Charlotte to keep her footing, but the press of bodies kept her upright. How would this vessel accommodate all these people? Would they be locked in the cargo hold with barely room to breathe, much less sleep? The rumors she'd heard through her cell doors at Newgate terrified her. Prison transport ships in general were horrible, but Captain Randall's ship was rumored to be the worst of all.

The chains rattled their ghostly presence as the anchor was lifted from its watery grave. The sails above her gave a loud snap as the boat lunged forward. Charlotte planted her boots as much as her cuffs would allow, but Sylvia, chained to her, was caught off guard, tumbling into her, knocking them both to the floor. Charlotte scrambled to her knees, but the next wave knocked them out from under her.

"Men, remove those chains at once!" a man called out from above her. "The rest of you ladies, sit down before you fall down."

Charlotte looked up, but she couldn't see anything for the crush of people standing in front of her. Still, it must bode well for everyone on board that the captain, for she assumed it could only be he, had shown them this small mercy.

"What do you think he's up to?" Sylvia asked as she sat down beside Charlotte. "It can't be no good."

"Maybe he's just being kind."

The woman snorted, tightening her hold on her infant son until he let out a cry. "You've heard the rumors about these men. Savages, every one of them. No soul for God to save."

"God would have had to dig a little deeper, but I assure you, I do have a soul."

Charlotte jerked her head around as the man knelt and reached for the lock at her wrist. "You sat in the galley the day I was sentenced," she said.

Light caught the sun-bleached strands of silver in his dark hair as he nodded. "Yes."

"Probably there to see the goods," Sylvia spat out, jerking her away from the man. "If I'm not mistaken, this here's Captain John Randall."

Miss Singleton looked at him as if he were some mythical sea monster who had climbed on board to terrorize the passengers. John guessed he deserved as much. The last eight years of his life had been spent transporting prisoners to the colonies in cells and cargo holds, with the barest of rations. Some died from gaol fever, others, desperation, and he'd offered little comfort to their grieving souls.

But Meggie's death had changed him. He wanted to be a man after God's own heart, someone his sister would be proud to know. He had discharged his former crew and hired men who lived lives of kindness and compassion. At great cost, his ship, the *Margaret Grace*, had been refitted with cabins with beds, clean linen and washstands. His cook, Mr. Parker, would prepare nourishing meals, a rarity among most prisoners. John had even bought toys for the children, jacks and spinning tops and dolls for the little girls. What else would he need to do to rid himself of this mountain of guilt bearing down on him?

"A good reputation is earned, dear brother!"

John could almost hear the smile in Meggie's voice. She was right. Years of whispers and rumors could not be turned away with one brief kindness. His actions would prove that this voyage was unlike all the others that had gone before.

He gave them a friendly smile. "Ladies, may I show you to your quarters."

The woman with Miss Singleton blanched. "But me little girl, sir. I need to find her before you put us in the cages."

He took a deep breath to calm himself. "I have no intention of locking you up, madam. The holdings of this ship were recently converted into cabins to accommodate my passengers."

"You turned the cargo hold into rooms?" Miss Singleton asked. Her large expressive blue eyes seemed to stare straight into his heart as if searching for answers. "Why?"

His mouth went dry as dust. How did he explain something he was still trying to understand himself? Before he could answer, the woman beside her shook her head then laughed. "I'll believe it when I see it."

"Fair enough." He held out his arm to Miss Singleton.

But she didn't take his arm, instead taking the babe from her companion. "Mrs. Everett has been holding this child since we left London. Maybe she would enjoy an arm to lean on."

So, the lady had a kind heart, not that he didn't already know that. Her concern for her aunt during her hearing had touched even the most calloused heart. John turned to Mrs. Everett and offered her his arm. "Ma'am?"

The woman's eyes widened as she stared at his outstretched arm. Shyly, she slipped her hand under his elbow. "We haven't been properly introduced. I'm Mrs. Sylvia Everett, but me friends call me Syl."

"Captain John Randall at your service." He gave a slight bow then nodded toward Miss Singleton. "And your friend?"

Miss Singleton looked at him. "I thought you might remember my name from the court proceedings."

He couldn't disagree with her. Still, the lady deserved to be known by more than the horrible miscarriage of justice that brought her here. "I thought it might be best if we started over."

She didn't seem to know how to reply then smiled slightly. "You mean like a clean slate?"

John couldn't stop his own smile from forming. "Exactly."

She considered a moment longer then dropped a brief curtsy. "Miss Charlotte Singleton, sir."

Even with the grime and dirt from the four-day journey, Charlotte Singleton bore the markings of a gently born lady. She was a handsome woman with a grace and bearing that was sadly often missing among the ladies of the ton. Yet, here she was, a prisoner because of her family connections. What kind of justice was that? "May I show you to your rooms now?"

"Beg pardon, but I need to find my Donalyn. She'll need to know where I am," Mrs. Everett answered in her most proper tone.

"Of course. She's probably playing with some of the toys I brought aboard." John directed them to the makeshift nursery he'd created near the bridge. "I want them to enjoy the sea as much as I do."

"Me older brother joined the Royal Navy to have adventures. Is that what happened to you, Captain Randall?" Mrs. Everett asked. "Were ye looking for adventure?"

John chuckled softly. "No, ma'am. I didn't even see the English coast until I was fifteen. By then, I needed a profession, and being a sailor seemed as good as anything else."

"That must have been bad on your mum." The woman sniffed. "If me lad ran off and joined the navy, I'd be beside meself." She grabbed her baby from Miss Singleton and hurried toward a group of girls playing jacks with a sailor. "Donalyn! Stop pestering that man!"

John held out his arm to Miss Singleton and this time, she took it. "How long have you been a captain, Mr. Randall?"

"Eight years. I'd been at sea almost five years when my father died and left me the funds to buy the *Margaret Grace*." It felt like an eternity now, with nothing to show for it but the pain he'd caused.

"I'm so sorry for your loss."

He turned to face her. "As I am yours. It must have come as quite a shock to learn of your father's death that way."

"Not really." There wasn't any sadness to her voice, only resignation. "My aunt Mary always told me that my father would come to a bad end, and he did." Her slender shoulders rose with her sigh. "I sound quite heartless, don't I?"

For some strange reason, he wanted to comfort her. John laid his hand over hers. "It's understandable, really. As you said in court, you didn't really know the man."

Miss Singleton glanced up at him with eyes clouded with confusion. "Shouldn't a child love her father no matter what his faults?"

John didn't know how to respond. His own father hadn't been much better than hers, abandoning him and Meggie just days after they'd buried their mother. His only kindness had been in a small inheritance for John, and, for Meggie, a dowry that had led to her marriage to a wealthy landowner in the colonies.

John studied Miss Singleton out of the corner of his eye. All her father had given her was deportation and a prison sentence. "A man is not a father simply because he reproduced."

Her cheeks turned a pretty shade of pink. "I agree. I think of Aunt Mary as my mother, never having had the chance to know my real mother. I wonder how Aunt Mary is?"

John stared out on the horizon. Should he tell her that Mary Singleton had come to Habersham's office to offer to take her niece's place? That he'd been so moved by the love they clearly shared for each other, he'd offered his portion of the journey's receipts to buy Miss Singleton her freedom? When his offer was laughed off, he'd employed the older woman's neighbor to look in on the woman.

He couldn't tell her. She'd think it strange or worse. That he was some sort of leech rather than a man sincerely hoping to pay a long overdue debt.

Mrs. Everett bustled up to them. "Michaels said he would bring Donalyn to the cabin once the game is finished."

"My cabin boy," John said as he turned and led them across the crowded deck toward the stairs. "A fine young man from a good family just outside of Bath."

"A good boy, he is, teaching the girls how to play jacks. My heart would break if ever my son went to sea." Mrs. Everett looked down at the baby in her arms. "So don't you go getting any ideas, Eddie."

"Would you like me to take the baby for a little while?" Miss Singleton dropped her hand from John's arm and stepped toward the woman, taking the child out of her arms before she had the chance to answer. Did Miss Singleton not enjoy his company? They had managed to have an interesting conversation as well as share some private information about each other. But maybe that was the problem. Maybe she felt awkward about divulging such private thoughts. He would steer the conversation toward more amiable topics next time.

"How kind ye are, Charlotte." Mrs. Everett glanced up at the captain. "And you, too, sir. Yer mum must be so proud."

"I don't know, ma'am," John answered, opening the door to the stairwell. Hopefully, the woman would leave well enough alone.

"She's gone too?" Mrs. Everett blustered. "I never would have brought it up if I'd known."

He nodded in response. The last thing he usually wanted to do was speak of his parents, and yet he'd done so with Charlotte Singleton. Talking with her about the past had felt easy, natural, as if she'd always been a part of his life. John glanced back at her. Something about her made him feel as if she saw a great deal more than he was willing to reveal, yet she understood.

Of course she did. Miss Singleton's nonexistent relationship with her father mirrored his. In that sense, they were kindred spirits. He doubted they'd find much more in common.

Lantern light lit the long hallway near the hull of the ship. Once a cargo hold, the space had been transformed into small cabins that slept four, more if there were small children. As they moved down the narrow hall, Miss Singleton bumped into him. She mumbled an incoherent apology. John glanced over his shoulder. Pale as a bloody ghost and listing toward her bow.

"Mrs. Everett, you need to take your son now." John turned in time to keep Miss Singleton and the child from falling. Once the child was securely back with his mother, he raised Miss Singleton into his arms.

"What is it, sir?" The other woman stepped back against the wall. "She ain't got the fever, does she?"

"No need to fear, ma'am." He lifted Miss Singleton higher on his chest. "I believe it's just a case of seasickness. She'll be fine in a few days."

Still, Mrs. Everett kept her distance. She glanced at the sheet of parchment nailed to the nearest door. "This looks to be me cabin anyway. More crowded than I would have thought, but a far cry from the filth we had at Newgate. I tell you, we were crammed in so tight, there was not a breath between us."

"Please let me down, Captain," Miss Singleton whispered between fingers pressed to her lips, her head lolling to rest on his shoulder. "I'll be all right."

"And, Captain, I'm sorry I said you didn't have a soul worth saving," Mrs. Everett continued. Her fuzzy curls shook as she bobbed her head and let go of his arm. "This is far better than I could have hoped."

"Mrs. Everett, if you'll excuse me, I need to see to Miss Singleton."

The woman finally looked at the woman in his arms. "My word, she looks as green as the grass in Hyde Park."

"I'm sure it's nothing a little rest won't cure." Glassy blue eyes met his, and an unexpected surge of protectiveness welled up inside him.

"If you'll tell me which cabin is mine. . ." She drew in a deep breath through her nose. "Please."

"Mrs. Everett, would you look in on Miss Singleton after I get her to her cabin? If she needs anything, tell one of my men, and I'll make certain it's delivered to her cabin." He turned then hurried down the passageway, scanning each sheet of paper for Charlotte's name.

"Captain, please." The muscles in Miss Singleton's throat worked as she turned a deeper shade of gray. "Please."

"Here we are." John gently stood her on her feet then opened the door. "If you need anything, Miss Singleton, please let me know."

"Thank you, Captain." She rushed inside and shut the door behind her.

Poor woman! He wouldn't wish a case of seasickness on even his worst enemy, though today, it might be a blessing. It would be best if he kept his distance from Charlotte Singleton. She might prove dangerous to his heart.

Chapter 3

C harlotte opened her eyes and waited for the nausea that had been her constant companion the last few days. The foul stench of stale air filled her nostrils with every breath she took. She turned over on her bed to face the wall but found no relief.

Fresh air was what she needed after days of being cloistered in her room. Some broth would be nice or maybe a small bowl of soup. Her stomach growled at the thought of fresh bread or a strong cup of tea.

She sat up on the side of the bed and glanced around. The room was larger than she had expected with four bunks and a small writing table tucked away in the corner. Near the door, a wash pitcher and basin sat with a fresh cake of soap and clean towels nearby. Another kindness from the captain. Obviously, the rumors she had heard at Newgate were simply the figment of someone's overactive imagination.

Her legs wobbled slightly as she rose and walked to the washbasin. *Good heavens*, she thought as she stared into the mirror. She looked a fright. Taking the cake of soap in her hands, she did a quick wash then turned her attention to her hair. Her fingers worked through the knots, then she plaited a braid that fell to her waist. She smoothed the wrinkles out of her dress, the belt loose around her waist. She looked in the mirror once more. She would do, though her skin was still the color of baking flour.

Tiptoeing across the room so as to not disturb her ailing roommates, Charlotte opened the door quietly and stepped out into the hall. There was no one to be seen. The ladies must be upstairs with their children, enjoying the sunshine. The stairway that led to the deck felt as if it was an eternity away, but she managed it after several rest stops along the way.

The salty air filled her lungs as she stepped out on the deck. She closed her eyes to savor the moment, the last lingering effects of her sickness fading away. The sun danced across her exposed skin. *Thank You, Lord, for getting me through these last few days.*

"I see you've rejoined the living."

The familiar voice caused Charlotte's eyes to flutter open. There, leaning against the railing, stood Captain Randall, watching her, a bemused smile on his lips. Charlotte felt her cheeks go hot. This man had seen her in a most embarrassing circumstance, yet instead of being repulsed by her infirmities, he had sought to help her. "Do you always stare at your passengers?"

His smile widened. "Only the pretty ones."

Dear heavens, the man was too handsome for his own good—not that she should notice. Still, her fingers were singed when she pressed them to her cheeks. "You must not get ashore very much, Captain."

His warm laughter made her stomach flutter. "You have a sharp wit, a rarity in most women of my acquaintance."

Was this what flirting was? Surely not, but how would Charlotte know? "Then you're paying court to the wrong kinds of women."

"Maybe you're right," he replied as he approached her, his deep-blue eyes sparkling with untamed humor. "How is it that a woman like you doesn't have a husband?"

Such a personal question! But then, they had spoken about private matters earlier. "Are you a rogue, or have you forgotten the lessons your mother taught you regarding how to speak to a lady?"

"I would not call myself a rogue." The captain bowed slightly to her. "As for my mother, don't blame her for my mistakes. I was only two when she died."

Charlotte cringed. "You said something to that effect the other day, didn't you?"

"Not in so many words."

"I'm so sorry. That was rude of me to bring it up."

"No more than my question to you." He held out his arm to her and she took it. "So. That makes us even, wouldn't you say?"

The man really was the most charming creature. She nodded. "I agree."

"Good."

He walked with her around the deck. Now that the seasickness had passed, she could study her surroundings more thoroughly. Three masts shot into the sky, the large linen sails snapped tight in the afternoon breeze. A group of sailors gathered toward the front of the ship—the bow, she'd read somewhere—on the bridge. Women gathered in groups around the deck, watching as the children played with an array of toys. Anyone would think this was a passenger vessel, not a prison ship on its way to the colonies.

"Are you sure you're fully recovered?"

She looked up to find the captain watching her closely, worry creasing his brow. A man such as this shouldn't be concerned with the likes of her. He had bigger responsibilities than a convicted spinster. But it felt nice to know that, at least for the moment, she mattered to someone.

"Captain John, you promised to play jacks with us this afternoon." Girlish giggles filled the air around them. Sitting around a small circle of crimson yarn with pebbles spread around inside, four little girls looked up at them expectantly, awaiting the captain's response.

"I will, but first let me see that Miss Singleton gets a cup of tea." He winked at a set of twins in matching dresses except for the color. "We wouldn't want her to relapse."

"No, sir!" Donalyn Everett replied. She turned to the girl on her left and added, "Mama said she was sick as a dog!"

"Donalyn!" Heat crept up the back of Charlotte's neck. "I do not need a cup of tea at the moment. Besides, I'd rather see how the captain fares against you girls."

"Do you play, Miss Singleton?" The captain's eyes danced with mischief.

"I did when I was their age." She studied the smooth stones in the circle. "I wasn't very good at it."

"You can be no worse than I am." He held up his hands, wriggling his fingers in front of her face. "These have a tendency of getting in my way."

His were also strong hands that could save a lady from embarrassing herself at a weak moment. "I think you have nice hands, Captain."

"Really? Because I was just thinking that they could beat you at jacks." He winked at her.

The stirrings of a flutter started in her heart. "I don't know."

"Oh, come on, Miss Charlotte! Please play with us!" Donalyn stood and threw her arms around Charlotte's waist. "Mama hasn't been able to play with us in days."

Charlotte glanced over the child's head at the captain. "Sailing doesn't agree with her, either," he said.

Charlotte bit down on her lip to contain the bubble of laughter in her throat. Poor woman! And she had been so unsympathetic to Charlotte's own suffering a few days ago. She looked down at the child's eager face. Donalyn already had so little time with her mother, what with Baby Edward. She wouldn't disappoint her now. "I think I'm up for a game or two."

He was going to enjoy this.

John wasn't sure how a game of jacks could fill him with such anticipation. He'd never been fond of the game as a boy. The stones were hard to pick up and he never could time the movement of the ball. But Meggie had loved the game so he had played.

Why was this game different?

He glanced over at Miss Singleton sitting directly across from him, a small collection of stones gathered in the skirts of her dress. She'd only had one turn but managed to snatch up almost half the rocks in play. Yet it was easy to forgive her when her face glowed with such happiness.

"Come now, Captain Randall. It's your turn." Donalyn handed him a small wooden ball. "And remember what I said. Grab as many stones as you can."

He held the ball in his hand. "Thank you for the advice."

"Maybe we should give him something if he collects all the rocks," Daisy, one of the twins, said beside him.

"You mean how Mum always has a sweet for us when we bring home good grades?"

"Yes," the girl exclaimed. "But what could the captain want?"

John's ears perked up. The game had just gotten interesting.

"We could knit him a pair of gloves," Donalyn suggested as she lifted the edge of the yarn circle. "But we'd need yarn, and that would mean we couldn't play jacks anymore."

The other three girls shook their heads.

"Maybe Mum has one of her sweets with her," Maisy said. "She used to carry them with her all the time."

Her sister glared at her. "Don't you think she would have given us one if she'd had it back when we were in jail?"

Her sister frowned. "I guess you're right."

"What about you, Miss Singleton?" John asked, interested in what her answer would be. "Can you think of anything that could serve as an incentive to improve my game?"

"I'm not certain an incentive would work, sir." She sat all prim and proper, but there was an air of mischief about her. "As you told me when we began today, you're not a very good player."

He would take the bait. "Is that a challenge, ma'am?"

"Seeing as I'm the better player, it's not much of a challenge at all."

He turned to the girls. "Did you hear that? Are we ready to show Miss Singleton how it's done?"

"Yes," the girls squealed in unison.

Over the next hour, they played. Miss Singleton held her own against her young opponents, but finally the girls' practice paid off. As Donalyn picked up the last stone, Maisey cried out. "We won, we won!"

"Good game, ladies." Miss Singleton smiled. "And you, Donalyn, won fair and square."

"You play very good, Miss Charlotte," Daisy said then added, "You did better this game, Captain John."

"You're very kind, Daisy." The captain gave the girl's long braid a gentle tug then stood. "Now if you'll excuse us, I must see that Miss Singleton takes some nourishment before she perishes from starvation." He held out his hand to her. "My lady?"

Taking his hand, she rose with a grace he'd rarely seen, even among his father's friends in the ton. "Thank you, girls. I enjoyed myself very much."

"Maybe we can play again soon," Maisy said.

"Maybe." Miss Singleton offered them one last smile before turning to him. "If you would direct me to the dining hall, I would very much appreciate it."

"I can show you, if you'd like." He took her hand and placed it in the crook of his elbow.

"I don't want to take up your time. You must have more important things to do." She glanced around the deck as his crew went about their daily work.

"At the moment, my only concern is getting us both a cup of strong tea and a slice of sweet bread Parker made this morning. But if you'd rather not. . ."

She tightened her grip on his arm. "As long as you're going there, I could at least keep you company."

"How very kind of you." He struggled not to smile as they started across the deck to the stairs.

She walked quietly beside him, nodding to one woman or another. Though she had been gently born, she treated each as if they were a dear friend.

"Why do you tease me?"

"I beg your pardon."

Letting go of his arm, Miss Singleton turned to face him. "I've led a very quiet, solitary life with my aunt, but I do know teasing when I hear it."

"I guess I do it because you're easy to tease." He chuckled softly.

"It can be annoying."

"My sister felt the same way, but then, she was an easy target, too."

"Is that how you became such an expert at jacks?" She gave him an impish grin.

"Touché, Miss Singleton!" he answered with a smile. "Meggie loved to play, and as a dutiful older brother, I felt I should show her the pain of defeat."

"And when she won?"

Laughter mulled in his chest. "She'd crow about it until our next match."

"She sounds like a lovely person."

Pain twisted like a knife through his heart. Would the ache of losing her ever get easier? "She was."

Miss Singleton touched his forearm tenderly as if to reassure him. "I'm so sorry, sir. How long has it been?"

"Meggie died in childbirth along with her daughter almost a year ago."

"You must have loved her very much."

He nodded. "We were all each other had after our mother died. Our half siblings convinced Father to send us to his country estate in Sheffield. Meggie and I were inseparable until Father forced me to go to Eton." Why had he told her that? Very few people knew of his family situation or connections, yet he'd told Charlotte Singleton without a second thought. He might as well tell her the rest. "My father was the earl of Chesterfield. Mother was his second countess."

"You're the son of an earl?" She stared at him, her blue eyes wide with surprise.

Maybe he shouldn't have told her that part. The very last thing he wanted was to be kowtowed to by his crew and passengers. "Please, don't tell anyone. I couldn't stand all that bowing and scraping simply because of who my father was."

"But, my lord..."

He gave her a stern look. "I answer to Captain Randall. Or John."

Her cheeks flushed a bright pink. "Then please call me Charlotte."

"Charlotte." He opened the door to the dining area then stood back as she walked inside. "It suits you."

The earthy scent of the beeswax candles along with the delicious aromas from the kitchen filled the small area. Tables and chairs were scattered around the room while sunlight from a row of portholes on the far wall provided warmth. As a child, John always loved his visits to the kitchen on his father's estate, maybe because Cook had made him feel welcomed there. He hadn't felt at home anywhere in years.

Until today.

As John helped Charlotte get settled at a nearby table, Parker, his cook, poked his head out of the kitchen. "Something I can get for you, Captain?"

"Is there any more of that delicious split-pea soup you served at dinner last night?" John nodded to Charlotte. "Miss Singleton was unable to join us."

"Not many did." The man smiled at Charlotte. "Seasickness took down the lot of you landlubbers."

She shifted her gaze to John. "Landlubbers?"

John translated for her. "Someone who hasn't gotten their sea legs yet."

"Then I'm most definitely a landlubber." Her lips twitched into an amused smile. She glanced up to meet Parker's stare. "I'm so sorry I missed last night. Split pea is my absolute favorite."

Charlotte's heartfelt apology seemed to change the cook's opinion of her. "I have some warming in the kitchen. Maybe that and a pot of strong tea will help set you to rights."

"That would be lovely! Thank you so much, Mr. . . . ."

"Parker, miss."

"Yes, thank you, Mr. Parker." She smiled at him brightly.

Parker looked like some besotted swain. "If you need anything, just let me know."

"Thank you, Parker." John snorted, annoyed by the ease of their conversation. He couldn't quite pinpoint why he felt so bothered by his cook's attention to Charlotte. The man would have treated any other lady the same. But none of those women offered Charlotte's sweet smile.

Within a few minutes, a bowl of steamy soup and a tea tray was set on their table. Charlotte reached for the teapot, but John brushed her hands away. "I'll pour while you work on your soup."

"I don't mind. . . ." she started.

"But I do." Maybe if he teased a smile out of her, she would relax and enjoy her meal. "Besides, pouring gives me an extra piece of sweet bread."

Her lips turned up, and John's stomach did a funny little flip. "So you have a motive behind your kindness?"

Steam spiraled over her cup as John turned to his own. "If you'd ever tasted Parker's cooking, you'd be deviously plotting, too."

The sound of her laughter made him unexplainably happy. "Then why is he the cook on a ship rather than at one of the great houses in London?"

"He has two daughters. One in service back home, the other living outside of Charleston with her husband." John forked two pieces of the golden-brown loaf onto his plate. "His wife is gone, and he sails with me so he can see his children."

"That's so sweet." She took a sip of her soup, closing her eyes as she swallowed. "Mr. Parker should be paid a king's ransom." She drew in a deep breath. "This is excellent!"

Her obvious enjoyment pleased him. "The man is appreciated enough, especially when he makes a beef pie."

"That would taste like heaven! It's one of Aunt Mary's favorites." Her smile dimmed. "I wonder how she's coping with all of this?"

"I'm sure she's all right. Maybe one of her neighbors stepped in to help once they understood the situation." John could only hope Mrs. Shephard had honored their agreement to care for the elderly lady. Helping the older Miss Singleton was the least he could do after all the pain he'd inflicted on prisoners over the years.

A door slammed in the distance, followed by the sound of hurried footsteps coming toward them. Mr. Amos, most likely. His first mate was a good sailor but still required clarity on their position at times. But when he looked back, Michaels, his cabin boy, was running toward them. He stopped at the end of the table and snapped a salute. "Sir."

"What is it, Michaels?"

"Mr. Amos needs you on deck right away."

John figured as much. "Do you know what this is about, son?"

The boy nodded, his face suddenly pale as a ghost. He stared wide-eyed at them. Fear. "One of the children has taken ill."

Was that all? "Probably seasickness. Have the child's mother take him back to their cabin."

The boy shook his head. "This boy has a fever and a rash on his face. Mr. Amos says it looks like typhus."

Dear God, no! John's mind whirled in every direction. This would become a death ship if he didn't get the situation under control quickly. "Is it only the one child?"

Michaels nodded. "But he's been up on the deck playing with all the other boys every day since we set sail."

"Then there will be more coming down with the fever soon," Charlotte said. "We'll need to isolate them."

John nodded. She was right. He spoke to the boy. "Take Hollis and Waldwin and prepare one of the larger cabins for patients. And be quick about it! We don't have much time!"

The boy hurried away with his orders.

"All the children will need to be examined." Charlotte took one last sip of her tea then stood. "We'll need clean linens and toweling, as well as any water you can spare. And Parker will need to keep large pots of water on hand so we can boil the sheets and the children's clothing."

John studied her for a brief moment. "You seem to know a great deal about this."

Charlotte brushed past him and headed to the deck. "I spent time at Saint Catherine's whenever I could."

A child would fare better on the streets than that rundown hovel. It was so notoriously bad, the members of Parliament had tried to have it shut down.

Yet, Charlotte volunteered there. "Is there a reason you spent your time at that pile of sticks?"

She slowed then turned to face him. "It was where my father abandoned me after my mother died."

Chapter 4

It was much worse than Charlotte could have imagined. By the time she'd examined Henry Applebee, two more children had the fever and the telltale rash across their chests. By nightfall, ten more had been struck down.

Charlotte stretched her neck from one side to the other. It had been almost a week, yet the fever still held the passengers and crew in a deathly vise. And the losses!

Henry Applebee's raspy wheezing as his little body gave up his spirit haunted the few moments of sleep she'd stolen. The piercing scream from his mother, the heart-breaking pleas from his older brother, begging him to wake up. Others had followed, and their deaths had played havoc with her already shaky faith.

Are You even listening to me, Lord?

She wasn't sure anymore. All she could do was continue as she had before.

A woman in a bed nearby called out. "Water?"

"Yes, Mrs. Brooks." Charlotte stood then poured water from the pitcher on the bed-side table into a small cup. Sitting on the bed, she helped the woman sit up and pressed the mug to her parched lips. "Just a little bit now. I don't want you to get choked."

The woman nodded. She took two long gulps then fell back onto Charlotte's arm. "Thank you, miss." Mrs. Brooks was already asleep by the time Charlotte lowered her head to the pillow. Charlotte mopped the woman's fevered face then laid the wet cloth against her neck.

There was a quiet knock at the door. With a quick glance at her patient, Charlotte walked over and opened it just enough to peek outside and see John.

"How is she?"

"About the same," she replied. I fear if this fever doesn't break soon, we could lose her. How are the others?"

"Better, I think, though it's hard to tell at times."

"And Mr. Marcel?" Charlotte had taken a liking to the old sailor after he'd volunteered to help her nurse the sick. The stories of his adventures as well as his tenderness toward the prisoners had won her over quickly. But he had fallen ill early yesterday morning and she'd not heard a word on his condition since then.

Grief flashed across John's chiseled face then just as quickly was gone. "We lost him this morning."

"No!" Tears burned the back of her eyes. Mr. Marcel had been such a kind soul. Charlotte glanced up at John. If she grieved for the sailor, how much harder must it be for him and his men. She laid her hand on his arm. "I'm so sorry. He was a good man."

John nodded. "Yes, he was."

"He thought quite highly of you," she added. Mr. Marcel had shared the changes John had made in the months after his sister's death. The older man's stories of John's transformation from brutal mercenary to compassionate captain had caused a feeling of tenderness in her toward John that she hadn't expected. His caring for both his passengers and crew during the epidemic had only deepened her affection for him.

A silly schoolgirl infatuation, though it had been years since she'd stepped foot in a classroom. It might be ridiculous, but it was far better to think about that than what lay in her future.

"When was the last time you had a meal?"

John's question jarred her away from her lovely thoughts. "I had a bowl of mush this morning."

A scowl marred his handsome face. "That long ago?"

"What time is it?"

But he walked away without responding to her question.

Shutting the door, Charlotte checked on Mrs. Brooks and replaced the wet cloth at her throat. She had barely settled into her chair before the door opened again. It was the captain, accompanied by an older woman Charlotte didn't recognize.

"Mrs. Waters," John said, "this is Charlotte Singleton, the lady who nursed your daughter through the fever."

The woman bobbed a curtsy then stepped farther into the room, her gaze fixed on Charlotte. "Miss Singleton! How can I ever repay you? If you hadn't nursed my wee Daisy back from the clutches of death, I don't know what I would have done." Her face broke into a smile. "Thank you, miss. Thank you!"

Charlotte didn't know how to respond. She'd done nothing more than anyone else would have done. "I'm just thankful your daughter is better, Mrs. Waters."

"Yes!" The woman gave her a watery smile. "Praise be to God."

"Amen," John whispered then turned his attention back to Charlotte. "Mrs. Waters has kindly volunteered to sit with Mrs. Brooks while you have a meal."

"That's not necessary," Charlotte replied. How could she possibly eat when people were dying around her? "I do appreciate the offer, though."

Two sets of concerned eyes met her gaze. "But you look tired, miss," Mrs. Waters said. "We can't have you falling down on us, now, can we?"

Charlotte brushed a loose curl away from her face. She wasn't sure how she could rest until everyone was on the mend. "I'm fine, really I am."

"This isn't a suggestion, Charlotte."

She shifted her gaze to John, his expression as hard as granite. "Isn't it?"

"No," he said coolly. "It's an order."

Usually, such displays of power angered her. But John was doing this out of concern for her well-being. How could she be angry with him? Charlotte pulled Mrs. Brooks's sheet up a little higher then turned to Mrs. Waters. "Would you please send for me if her condition worsens?"

The lady glanced at the captain, who nodded. "I believe that can be arranged."

"Thank you."

John offered her his arm. "Shall we go and leave Mrs. Waters to her patient?"

Charlotte nodded. Bossy, wasn't he? He must be exhausted, not only having to attend to the sick but also to comfort those in mourning.

They were out on the deck before John spoke again. "You're a stubborn little thing, aren't you?"

Charlotte halted midstep. "Excuse me?"

He turned to face her. "You need to take care of yourself, Charlotte, or you will come down with the fever. And if you won't do it, then I will."

If he wanted a fight, she'd certainly give him one. "By bossing me around like a scullery maid?"

His mouth tightened into a straight line. "As captain of this ship, it is my duty to ensure the safety and well-being of everyone on board." He leaned forward until she could feel his warm breath caress her face. "That includes you."

"I'm a grown woman who can make decisions for myself, Captain."

He scrubbed a hand over his face. "Not when those choices risk your physical safety." He rested his hands on her shoulders and looked deeply into her eyes. "The truth is, I need you, Charlotte."

She swallowed, all the anger that had threatened to burst out suddenly banked. "I'm sorry. I'm just tired of seeing people suffer and not being able to do more to help them."

John's face relaxed. "I understand. It's one of the qualities I admire about you. It's one of the reasons I need to take care of you."

No one had ever been her champion before, although Aunt Mary had tried at times. Still, to have this man determined to take care of her was a very heady feeling. "Then I guess we should go to supper."

"Good." His breath was warm against her cheek. "I think you're going to enjoy what Mr. Parker has prepared for you tonight. An apple tart."

"Truly?" She'd heard so much about the cook's pastries but hadn't had time to sample them herself.

"He wanted to thank you for nursing Beasley back to health, not that he would ever tell you that."

She chuckled softly as he led her into his private dining room off the kitchen where those well enough had been taking their meals. "Parker thinks of that boy like a son. How old is Beasley, anyway? Fourteen or so?"

"Fifteen, I think. He's been sailing for three years now."

"The sea catches them early," she replied as he held out her chair.

"And most times refuses to let them go."

The question was out before she'd even realized what she'd asked. "What about you? Will you spend the rest of your life at sea?"

"No," he replied as he laid his napkin on his lap. "In fact, this is my last voyage."

His answer surprised her. "But I thought you enjoyed your life at sea."

"I did once, a long time ago, but for a while now, I've felt the need to put down roots. Right after Meggie died, I bought a small farm outside of Charleston, and I plan to sell my ship once we reach port. I'll use the proceeds to support my household until the farm turns a profit."

"I always wanted a small cottage in Sheffield or York. Just a little place where I could grow a garden and maybe have a chicken or two." But that dream had died when she'd been deported. All she had to look forward to was seven years of drudgery. Still, it was lovely to think of John out on his farm.

"Shilling for your thoughts."

She couldn't tell him the truth. "I think they're worth more than that."

"Without question." He lifted the pot and poured her a cup of coffee. "But I do wish you'd tell me what you were thinking about so hard."

Maybe it would help to talk about it. "I was just thinking how much I envy your future."

"Charlotte, I never meant to. . ."

"Oh, I know you didn't." She chuckled softly. "I just never saw my life turning out this way. I wish I understood why God would allow this to happen to me."

"I've been wondering that same thing since the moment I saw you in the courtroom. Meggie once told me that the Lord has a purpose for every situation, the bad as well as the good." Warmth radiated up her arm as he took her hand in his. "This past week, your presence has been a blessing through this storm."

She had never received many compliments, and she'd all but begged for this one. Charlotte withdrew her hand from his, feeling somewhat bereaved by the loss of his warmth. She shouldn't allow herself to enjoy his company so much. He was the son of an earl, for heaven's sake! And who was she, but a doomed prisoner with no future. The thought left a bitter taste in her mouth.

The dinner was excellent, the apple tart better than any Parker had baked before, yet the meal John had looked forward to all day long was not what he had hoped.

He should have never mentioned the farm.

Of course, Charlotte had asked, but he'd answered without any thought to what her future held in South Carolina. A seven-year prison sentence at the hands of her new master. And if she survived that, then what? She would have learned a trade, but what kind of life would that be for a gently bred woman such as Charlotte?

And what if she was put on the marriage mart?

He couldn't bear the thought of it. If ever Charlotte should marry, it should be to a man who would understand what a rare gift he'd been given, not someone just wanting to get her with child then cast her aside. She needed a man who would love her with his entire being, even when she was being stubborn. She needed a man like. . .

Me.

For some odd reason, the thought did not shock him as much as he expected, but then, his admiration for Charlotte had been slowly growing for several days now. She would make a fine mistress for their home, and he would make her a good husband.

But how? Habersham had already refused his offer for her. What little money he had had been used to pay a nurse for her aunt, and the purchase of his ship would not be finalized until they pulled into port. By then, it would be too late.

"A shilling for your thoughts."

John glanced over at her as Beasley cleared the last of their plates. Heavens, but she was lovely. After their dismal dinner conversation, he decided to lighten the mood. "Do you have a shilling?"

Her mouth turned up into a soft smile. "If I did, I'd save it to pay off my father's debt."

He hadn't expected that answer. "You would do that?"

Charlotte nodded. "The people my father swindled deserve to be repaid."

"But most of them have more money than they could possibly need."

"Maybe." She sighed. "But it still belongs to them."

"You're not here because of the money, Charlotte. You're here because they were duped." The thought of her trying to pay back everything her father had taken irritated him. "They had you arrested so they could save face."

A loose curl clung to her throat as she tilted her head to one side. "I never thought of it that way, but you're probably right."

"The charges should have died with your father. Then you would still be in Cheapside, living with your aunt, where you belong." But did she belong there anymore?

"Instead, I'm here, caring for the sick and having supper with you. On my way to the colonies to serve my father's prison sentence." She closed her eyes as if she'd just realized the enormity of her situation. "How is this justice?"

Heavens, how he wanted to take her in his arms and comfort her. Protect her from all the spiteful people of the world. Instead, he led her out of the dining room to a nearby bench for a breath of fresh air. Once they were seated, John took her cold hand between his. "The ton was out for revenge, and with your father gone, they sought their pound of flesh from you."

"And in the process, condemned not only me, but my aunt Mary." Charlotte's voice broke at the mention of her beloved relative. "I don't know how she will survive this, John. She is so frail and dependent upon me."

"She told us as much."

The bluest eyes he'd ever known stared back at him. "You've met my aunt?"

He hadn't intended to tell her about their meeting in Habersham's offices, but the pain Charlotte felt had become much more personal. "Your aunt was waiting when Habersham and I arrived at his offices the day after your sentencing. She had a proposal for Habersham."

"What sort of proposal?"

A small group of ladies chose that moment to stand at the railing in front of them. He leaned closer so only Charlotte could hear. He wouldn't allow her to be fodder for gossip. "Your aunt suggested that Habersham take ownership of the house in Cheapside in return for your freedom."

"She was going to give up her house for me?" Charlotte's voice wobbled as she spoke.

He squeezed her hand. "She would have given up a great deal more. When Martin refused, she offered to go in your place."

A cry burst from her lips. "Why would she do that? I'm not worth that!"

He hesitated. How could Charlotte even think such a thing? Didn't she know how truly special she was? "When I spoke to her, she introduced herself as your mother."

"She is my mother in every way that matters." Charlotte sniffed. "I guess you can understand why I want to get back to her as soon as I can."

His heart twisted like a dagger had been plunged into his chest and turned. Had no one explained the particulars of her punishment? That there was more to her sentence than seven years in service?

"John?"

He had to tell her the truth, though it killed him to do it. John drew in a deep breath and straightened. "You can't go back home to London, Charlotte. Not ever."

"I don't understand."

There was a note of panic in her voice, but he had to press on. She deserved to hear the entire truth of her situation. "When you were deported, as part of your prison sentence, you gave up your rights as an English citizen. If you go back home, they won't send you to back to jail. You'll swing from the gallows."

Chapter 5

She could never go home!

The dam broke, and suddenly the tears Charlotte had struggled to keep at bay couldn't be held back any longer. There would be no more mornings of sharing a cup of coffee with Aunt Mary. No more visits to Saint Catherine's. No more cozy evenings by the fire, reading a book out loud as her aunt sat close by. No more worshipping together at the little church around the corner from their home.

She had been given a life sentence, with no possibility of a reprieve.

The thought robbed her of breath. How would she ever survive this? What would become of her now? Without thinking, Charlotte bolted from the bench.

"Charlotte!"

She flung open the door to the lower deck and stumbled down the stairs. The only home she'd ever known was with Aunt Mary. She was alone in a world she didn't recognize anymore, and her aunt? Charlotte's legs gave out beneath her and she sat down on the steps.

"Charlotte!"

The sound of John's footsteps vibrated through her body and then he was there, pulling her into his arms, pressing her head to his broad shoulder. There, in his embrace, she felt warm and safe, protected against the cruelty of the world.

"It will be all right."

John was wrong. Nothing would ever be right again. She buried her face in his neck as a fresh wave of tears bombarded her. "How could it be?"

He rocked her gently. "You're right. Nothing will ever be the same again."

She sniffed. "You're not very good at this."

"I haven't had much practice with this sort of thing." His voice rumbled softly through her. "When Meggie died, I thought nothing would ever bring me joy again, but I was wrong. Watching the faith my sister had as she lay dying helped me find God again and that gives me great joy."

She lifted her head to look up at him, but his face was in the shadows. She once had a relationship with God like that. What had happened? "I've always tried to be a good person and to live out my faith in God." She didn't know if she had the courage to confess what she had been feeling since her arrest. But this was John. She didn't know how, but he would understand. "So why does God hate me so much?"

"Why would you think that?"

Charlotte drew in a shaky breath. Was she brave enough to tell him? "When I was five or so, Aunt Mary decided my father should visit me and sent him a note requesting that he come. Of course, he never came, but I found his reply in one of Aunt Mary's books." Her eyes began to burn again. "He wrote that he had seen me and I didn't look to be very loveable."

His arms tightened around her. "If your father wasn't already rotting in his grave, I'd kill him with my bare hands."

She didn't doubt his words. She snuggled deeper into his arms. "That's kind of you, but I'd rather not see you hang from the gallows."

"Thank you for that." He rested his chin on top of her head. "In some ways, my father was cut from the same disgusting cloth as yours."

"How so?"

His solid chest expanded beneath her hand as he sighed. "He was forced to marry my mother after they were caught in a compromised position, but he never forgave her. He'd had his heir and a spare with his first countess and never intended to marry or, as he loved to tell me, bring any more 'brats' into the world. Our situation was particularly hard for Meggie."

His poor sister. "I wish I could have met her. It sounds as if we'd have a lot in common."

"You're alike in many ways. She was a very good woman who thought nothing of putting others' needs before her own."

Charlotte rested her head on his shoulder. "Maybe you're not as bad at this as I thought."

"Is that another compliment?" He released her then reached for his handkerchief and handed it to her.

"It depends." She blotted her cheeks and nose. "Are you the type of gentleman who allows the smallest compliment to go to his head?"

He shook his head. "Only when given by a lady I respect and admire."

"Yes, well." She would savor his compliment during the cold lonely years ahead. Charlotte reluctantly released him and stood. "I should be getting back to Mrs. Brooks."

"Charlotte, would you have supper with me on my private deck tomorrow night?"

She should refuse. These feelings she was beginning to have for John should not be encouraged. In just a few short weeks they would part ways, never to see each other again.

But she couldn't find the strength to say no. "I would love to join you, Captain."

Again, supper didn't go as John had planned. It had to be postponed for a week when a second outbreak of the fever blindsided them. This one was more virulent, preying on those weakened by illness or those exhausted from nursing the others. By the time the second round of typhus had run its course, twenty more had been buried in a watery grave. But even though the last patient had recovered, John kept a watchful eye on Charlotte. The shock of learning she could never return to England had taken its toll on her. Still, she worked hard to save as many passengers as she could. It was backbreaking work with more losses than victories, yet she never gave up.

Charlotte deserved this supper. John had instructed Parker to use the best china and silverware as well as the linens his sister had purchased for him when he'd first become captain. A beef pie and fresh bread as well as another one of Parker's fruit tarts were on the menu.

It was perfect.

John pressed his fingers to his forehead and tried to concentrate on the columns of figures he'd been working on. He intended to woo her tonight. Maybe they could put their heads together and come up with a plan that would see them married and settled on his farm.

What in blazes was wrong with these figures? The lines wiggled on the paper like a desert mirage from one of the stories in *Arabian Nights*. Exhaustion could do that to a person, but nothing had interrupted his sleep for the last two days. Maybe he deserved this dinner with Charlotte as much as she did. John reached for the water pitcher sitting on the corner of his desk. It was bone dry. "Michaels!"

The young boy came to the door. "Yes, sir?"

"What have I told you about keeping this pitcher filled?"

"I don't understand." The boy looked at him in confusion. "I filled that pitcher not even an hour ago."

John seemed to remember the boy in his quarters when he pulled the books down to balance them. Had he drunk that much water without even realizing it? He tried to remember, but it made his headache worse. "Please, fill it again."

Michaels grabbed the pitcher then stepped back. "Are you all right, Captain? Because you don't look well."

"What do you mean by that?" John rubbed the back of his neck, only to find the hair at his nape drenched. He pressed a hand to his forehead. Could he have a fever?

"Nothing, sir. You just look kind of flushed. And your neck." He pointed to John's open collar. "It looks odd."

"Odd?" John rushed to the looking glass over his washbasin, plucked the ends of his shirt out of his pantaloons and tugged it over his head. An angry rash spread across his upper chest and neck. He knew he didn't have much time before the fever took hold. "Prepare my bed, Michaels. Then find Parker and Amos and tell them to come to my quarters." He hesitated. "And find Miss Singleton." This was most definitely not what he'd planned for this evening. Even now, he could feel his skin growing hotter. "Tell her I need her, now."

Chapter 6

The sound of children laughing felt like music to Charlotte as she enjoyed the afternoon sunshine. The slight breeze felt good against her face after so many days in the sickrooms. Seagulls crowed overhead, then one would separate from the group and dive into the water then resurface with a fish in its bill.

She stopped to watch Daisy and her sister playing jacks with Donalyn. Who would have guessed Charlotte would find happiness in watching little girls play a game? If the last few weeks had taught her anything, it was to take pleasure in the ordinary moments, for they become the stuff of treasured memories. She still mourned the loss of her home, and she missed Aunt Mary horribly. But she still had her life while others on this trip had lost theirs.

This voyage had turned out nothing like she had expected. But then, she hadn't known what to expect. The rumors she'd heard whispered in the darkness of her cell at Newgate had been far removed from the reality of this journey. John had made certain of that.

"You have a lovely smile, Miss Singleton."

Charlotte turned to find Mrs. Waters walking arm in arm with Mrs. Applebee. Though pale from her own bout of fever and still mourning for her son, Mrs. Applebee looked remarkably well. "Thank you. I like to watch everyone enjoy the fine weather."

"Yes." Mrs. Waters glanced over to where her twins were playing. "There's been so little to smile about these last few weeks. But God has been good."

"Yes," Charlotte answered politely. Whether she believed it or not was another story. Though John had told her repeatedly that her father had been wrong, that God loved her, she still had her doubts. If God loved her so much, why had He allowed her to be banished from the only home she'd ever known?

Daisy ran up to them, winded and breathless. "Mama, the sailors are teaching the boys how to fly kites and asked if we'd like to come along. Could we, Mama? Please?"

"I don't know, Daisy." Mrs. Waters looked at Charlotte. "What do you think, Miss Singleton?"

Charlotte studied the child's bright eyes and the light spray of freckles on her nose, then nodded. "I think an hour flying kites would be good for her. But stop if you feel tired, all right, Daisy?"

"Yes, Miss Charlotte." Daisy skipped off in the direction of her friends.

"Children." Mrs. Waters chuckled. "Always into something."

"I'll have to take your word for it," Charlotte replied. "I was raised as an only child by my aunt."

"As I fear my boy Charlie will be." Mrs. Applebee lowered her voice. "His father died in Newgate before he could be deported. Now that Henry's gone, I don't have anyone except me Charlie." She shrugged. "But I may not have a choice."

Charlotte was confused. "Why wouldn't you have a choice?"

The women laughed. "Because there's a good chance we be all headed to the marriage mart." When Charlotte didn't respond, Mrs. Waters added, "But you don't need to worry about that. We've all noticed how the captain looks at you. I'd be surprised if you're not married before we reach the coast."

Married to John? What a lovely thought! But there was still the matter of her prison sentence, and what was she to do about Aunt Mary, and. . .

"Miss Singleton!" Michaels, John's cabin boy, ran toward them, looking as if he'd stood in the crow's nest for the better part of the morning. When he finally reached them, he doubled over, drawing in big gulps of air before he could continue. "It's the captain, ma'am. He needs you, bad."

But John was supposed to collect her for dinner at six bells. "Michaels, do you know what this is about?"

Worry flashed in the boy's gray eyes but he shook his head. "All I know is the captain sent me to escort you back to him."

Mrs. Waters gave her a knowing glance. "I told you, missy. The captain's sweet on you."

Charlotte chose to ignore her. "If you'll excuse me, ladies, I must see what the captain needs." She nodded to the boy. "I'm ready, Michaels."

The boy set a fast pace as they hurried toward the bow where the captain's private quarters was located. Something was terribly wrong. John would never risk her reputation by entertaining her in his rooms. Charlotte hesitated at the foot of the stairs. "What's wrong, Michaels?"

The pain she saw in his young face gripped her heart in a tight fist. "It's the captain, ma'am. He has the fever."

Charlotte's world tilted. "How could that be? He was fine this morning." Though now that she thought about it, he did seem off his breakfast. Otherwise, he'd been happy that the sickness was over and was looking forward to their supper.

"It started right before lunch. He was thirsty, and when I went in to refill the pitcher, I noticed the rash on his neck." The boy chewed on his lower lip. "He sent me to find Mr. Amos and Parker then told me to fetch you." He hesitated. "Is he going to die?"

She wouldn't know how bad it was until she examined him. "Is he in his bedchamber?"

Michaels nodded. "Parker stayed with him when I came to get you." He glanced at her. "The captain was so looking forward to your supper this evening. He even had Parker make one of his beef pies."

Her heart melted. John had remembered how much she'd longed to try one of Mr. Parker's specialties. No one, not even Aunt Mary, had ever done something like that for her. He had to get better, he just had to. Lifting her skirts, she climbed the steps to John's quarters. "Could you have the men bring up a barrel of fresh water? And I'm going to need some clean toweling and linens. Beasley will need to boil water for the captain's clothes and linens."

"But we're down to the last of our water as it is, with all the sickness we've had."

"I'm aware of the situation." John had discussed his concerns with her, but if his calculations were correct, they'd dock before the last drop was gone. "We'll ration if we have to, but I need that water to nurse the captain back to health."

"Aye aye, ma'am." The boy paused. "What should I tell the men?"

"Let's leave that decision up to Mr. Amos. Thank you for everything you've done, Michaels. I'm sure the captain will be quite proud of you when he recovers. Now, if you could get me those items I asked for, I would appreciate it."

"Anything for Captain Randall." The boy rushed out of the room.

Charlotte hesitated at John's bedroom door. How would she find him? Would he tease her for making more of the situation than necessary? Or would she find him abed, just a hair's breadth from meeting his Creator? Her lungs refused to breathe. She couldn't bear the thought of losing him, not when she. . .

I love him!

She gasped. When had that happened? But did it really matter when the man she loved might be dying in the other room? Charlotte walked into a small parlor and was instantly greeted by Mr. Parker. "Miss Singleton, thank God you're here. I just came from the kitchen. Beasley's handling the washing."

"Good." She drew a steadying breath. "Where is he?"

He nodded toward an open door to her right. "I've never seen the captain like this before. When Amos and I helped him into bed, his skin scorched my hand as if I were holding a hot coal."

That didn't bode well for John's prognosis. If she didn't get him cooled down soon, he ran the risk of having a seizure. If his fever was as high as she feared, she may have to do something drastic. "Is there a washtub on board?"

"I believe the crew has one in their quarters."

"Could you bring it to me? We may have to soak the captain in it if his temperature climbs any higher."

"Yes, ma'am." Parker took her hand and kissed it. "The captain wasn't mistaken when he said you were a remarkable woman." He straightened. "Once I arrange everything, I'll be right outside the door if you need me.'

"I'll remember that." She waited until he left then hurried into John's room, hesitating just inside the door. Even from this distance, she could see the angry rash across his chest and shoulders. His dark hair, usually so tidy in a queue at the nape, lay plastered against his head and face. Sweat beaded along his upper lip and nose. His cheeks were purplish-red. His sheets clung to him like a death shroud.

She splashed some water in the basin then carried it to his bedside, drops of water pouring out on the floor like a burst of rain. She had to get his fever to break before he seized. Grabbing John's discarded cravat from the floor, she plunged it into the water, then laid the soaked rag against his neck. He moaned.

Charlotte took in the aristocratic curve of his nose, the tiny laugh lines around his mouth as she leaned over him. "I'm here, darling. I'm trying to get your fever down."

"Water," he croaked.

She poured a small glass of water then sat down on the bed next to him. Sliding her arm around his back, she braced him against her as she lifted him. "Only a few sips, just enough to wet your mouth." She pressed the cup to his lips.

John took a small sip then another before settling back against her. "Do you call all of your patients darling?"

Charlotte tensed. The word had popped out without her thinking about it. "I thought you were unconscious."

His lungs wheezed as he drew in a shallow breath. "You didn't answer my question."

And he'd called her stubborn! Didn't he know what grave danger he was in? If she'd learned anything about John over the last few weeks, it was that when he set his mind on something, he pursued it relentlessly. "No, I don't call any of my patients darling."

"Good." His face relaxed into a dreamy smile before he fell back to sleep.

She lowered him gently to the bed then pushed the damp hair away from his face. He was on fire! Charlotte wet the cloth again and mopped his face and arms. *Dear Lord, please! Make John's fever break soon. Please!*

A knock at the door startled her. Two men entered carrying a large wooden barrel. "Where do you want us to put this?"

Thank You, Lord! Charlotte nodded toward a nearby corner. "If you could open it..."

"Yes, ma'am."

"I found the washtub," Mr. Parker called out as he carried a large brass tub into the room. "Some of the men had hoped to use it before we land next week."

"We need to fill it as quickly as possible." Charlotte grabbed a small kettle that hung by the stove and plunged it into the water barrel. "We don't want it too cold. Just enough to cool him down."

The next half hour was a whirl of activity. Charlotte continued to sponge water over John's neck and chest as the men carried pans of water to the tub. As the last steaming kettle was poured into the bath, Michaels arrived carrying a bundle of clean towels.

It was time. Charlotte bent close to John's ear. "We have to move you to the bathing tub."

"No," he wheezed.

Her palms burned as she cupped his face in her hands. "Please, darling. You have a high fever. There is no other way to bring it down."

The muscles in his throat rippled as he swallowed. "All right, but you must promise me something."

Charlotte would vow to swim like a mermaid in a school of sharks if the man would cooperate. "What is it?"

Fevered blue eyes pinned her, and for a brief moment, it felt as if they were the only two people in the room. "Promise to call me darling for the rest of our lives."

A bolt of joy shot through her then and just as quickly flamed out. John was out of his senses, his proposal just the babbling of a very sick man. But, oh, how she wanted it to be real! No, it hadn't been a true proposal, but she would promise John anything to see him well again. Charlotte leaned down and kissed his forehead. "You have my word."

He didn't hear her. He'd passed out.

Chapter 7

John lifted the mug of broth to his lips as he watched Charlotte discuss the next day's menu with Parker. She looked a bit tired—but nothing that a good night's sleep and one of the cook's apple tarts couldn't put to rights. Yet even now, mussed and with dark circles under her eyes, Charlotte was still the most beautiful woman he'd ever known.

It had been five days since he'd taken ill. Five days since Charlotte had left his side. Even in his febrile state, he had recognized her selflessness and sweetness. She was everything he desired in a wife. Strong, yet tender; confident, but not afraid to ask for help from others. Compassionate to a fault. He loved her, and that love grew with each passing moment.

He set the cup on the bedside table. He'd known exactly what he was doing when he'd asked her to call him darling for the rest of their lives. Marriage, and the sooner the better. He could have Mr. Amos perform the ceremony before they reached South Carolina. No, he'd need to get back to London to fetch Charlotte's aunt, and if he did, Habersham would most certainly swear out a warrant for his arrest. John could only hope Mr. Morris of Richmond would be in Charleston to buy his ship before Charlotte went to the auction block.

"Are you warm enough?" Charlotte walked over to where he sat and tucked the blanket in around him. "You could catch a chill."

"I'm not going to catch a chill." He took one of her hands in his and tossed the blanket to the floor. "Good thing the Royal Navy doesn't accept women into their ranks. You'd be an admiral by now."

Charlotte straightened. "What does that mean?"

John brought her hand to his lips and brushed her knuckles with a kiss. "Only that if you ever decide to take to the sea, you'd make a first-rate captain." He smiled up at her. "From what Parker has told me, you've kept everything running smoothly while I was indisposed."

"I might have to have a word with him. He was supposed to let you rest."

"Don't throw him in the brig. I ordered him to tell me."

She snorted softly. "John."

He knew she was only looking out for his best interest. Another quality he loved about her. But she needed to understand that the life of every person on board was his responsibility, not hers. By his calculations, they should be entering the waters of South Carolina any day now. "Mr. Amos is not familiar with the choppy waters and sandbars along the coastline."

She hesitated for a moment then nodded. "I understand. You have a duty to your passengers and crew."

"Good." He stood, the floor unsteady beneath his feet. Once he gained his balance, he continued. "Then you'll understand why I'd like to go up on deck."

"No, John." Charlotte's mouth flattened into a somber line.

What would it be like kiss those lovely lips, to feel them become soft and yielding under his? But he had no right to a kiss yet, not until he was certain he could rescue her. Even if it meant selling everything he owned, he'd do it. His life would be empty without Charlotte in it. She was his friend, his love, and hopefully soon, his wife. Mr. Morris had to be in Charleston when he docked. It was the only way.

First, he had to settle things with Charlotte. "What if we go up to my private deck? It would give me the opportunity to check out coordinates without running into the crowds downstairs."

She studied him for a long minute, then, as if she'd made her decision, breathed a deep sigh. "All right, but only as long as it takes to settle your concerns. Then we come back inside. Agreed?"

"Agreed." John felt a smile lift at the corners of his mouth. Would their children be as stubborn as their mother? He certainly hoped so.

After a short discussion on the merits of wearing his heavy overcoat—they finally agreed on a thick woolen shirt—he led Charlotte up to his private deck.

"What is this?" she asked, glancing over the simple yet elegant table Parker had set for them.

"I thought you might like to have that supper I promised you, only now, it's lunch."

She delicately touched the silverware then traced the outline of a plate before turning to face him. "But you wanted to check on Mr. Amos's progress."

"Yes." He walked over and pulled out a chair for her. "I may have had something else in mind, too."

Once Charlotte was seated, he sat down across from her. How wonderful it would be, to look across the breakfast table every morning and see her lovely face. Still, he mustn't get ahead of himself. There was the matter of her sentence to consider. For the moment, he simply would enjoy this time with her.

Charlotte unfolded her napkin and laid it across her lap. "It seems unfair to have all this and not share it with the others."

"I thought you might say that." John took a sip of his lemonade. "I asked Parker to prepare a special meal for all the passengers and crew. I figured they deserved it after this plague-infested voyage."

"That's very kind of you." Charlotte lowered her gaze to study the intricate design on the table linen. "Nothing like the rumors about the dreaded Captain Randall."

John's gut clenched. He couldn't propose marriage without Charlotte knowing exactly who he once was. He folded his hands in front of him. "I was that terrible man at one time, Charlotte, but my sister's death changed all that for me." He pressed his lips together as he collected his thoughts. "Do you know what Meggie said to me before she died? She said that the first thing she would do when she stood before God would be to ask him to save her brother's horrible soul." He sighed. "On her deathbed, she was concerned for me. It wasn't too long after her death that I discovered my faith again."

"Your sister must have presented a very good argument."

He chuckled. "She loved a good debate. After my decision to follow Christ, I didn't want to continue transporting prisoners with Martin Habersham, but I was under contract. So I outfitted my ship for passengers, not convicts."

He felt her delicate hand through the sleeve of his shirt and looked up. "John, your sister would be so happy with the man you've become."

John covered her hand with his, her warmth filling up all the lonely spaces of his heart. "What about you, Charlotte? Could you love a man with such a wicked past?"

Her smile wobbled slightly. "Why do you ask?"

He chided himself. Charlotte needed to know his heart before she'd feel comfortable revealing her own. "I love you, my dearest, and only want to make you happy for the rest of our lives. Will you marry me?"

"Oh, John, I love you so very much." She slipped her hand from his grasp and sat back. "But this can't be. Once we dock, I will be sold and begin my prison term."

"Not if I win the bid myself."

The shocked revulsion in her expression warned him he was in dangerous waters. "You would purchase me?"

"No. Yes." He needed to make her understand. "Someone is going to buy you. Why not me?"

"No!" She stood and moved over to the railing as if the stench of their conversation had her gasping for fresh air.

John watched her for a moment then stood also. "I know it sounds coldhearted, but this is the only option we have at our disposal. I tried to buy your contract from Habersham after your aunt's visit, but he wouldn't hear of it. He wanted more than I had."

Her back stiffened. "Why would he think I was worth so much in the colonies?"

He walked to her and raised her chin until her gaze met his. "You really have no idea just how wonderful you are." He rested his forehead against hers. "A man would have to be a fool not to fall in love with you."

"And you're no fool," she whispered.

"No." He kissed her then, as he'd dreamed of doing for days now. She tasted of sunshine and sweetness, his true North Star. But as he reluctantly lifted his head, he sensed a resignation in her he had not foreseen.

Charlotte stepped from him, her hands fisted in the folds of her skirts as if to steady herself. "I love you, John. Really, I do. But you already said Habersham wanted a large sum for my contract. How could you afford it?"

"I'm to sell my ship once we reach port. That should be enough."

She shook her head. "No, John. You had plans for your farm with that money. I wouldn't feel right if you spent it to free me."

"But dearest. . ." There was no use in arguing. She had made her decision, stubborn woman that she was. Well, he refused to let her throw her life away over unfounded fears. He'd purchase her contract then free her to make her own decision about his proposal.

The shuffle of boots and shouts from below drew John's attention to the bridge. He found Mr. Amos in the midst of the chaos, his spyglass pressed to his eye. John lifted his gaze to the horizon. A haze had settled over the water, blurring the lines between sky and sea. But there, off the bow. John felt his heart pummeled.

"What is it, John?!"

He turned to the woman who held his heart. The only woman he'd ever love. "Land."

Chapter 8

Land.

Charlotte stared as the outline of the South Carolina coast grew closer with every passing second. Soon John would be needed on the bridge to safely sail the ship into port. Once there, she would be chained along with the others then herded down the main street to the city square where she would be sold to the highest bidder.

This was truly good-bye. This moment felt like her life had been divided by the sharpest of blades into two parts: the days with John and what came after. Years of loneliness suddenly spread out before her, robbing her of hope.

"Charlotte?"

Her name on his lips would be a sweet memory she'd carry for the rest of her days. For now, she had a new life she needed to prepare for, one that only promised years of work and heartache. "I should go."

"No! Wait!" He wrapped a strong arm around her waist and pulled her close. "I won't allow someone to own you, Charlotte. Do you understand?"

Rather than argue with him, she nodded. Whether he accepted it or not, these would be their final moments together, and she wanted to make one last memory. "Please, kiss me."

His kiss was possessive, filled with all the love and passion a young girl dreams of in the man she loves. But John surpassed her silly girlhood dreams. He was flesh and blood, and more than she ever deserved.

He lifted his head when a knock rattled the door. Parker stuck his head in. "Excuse me, sir. You're needed on the bridge."

"In a minute."

Charlotte stepped back out of his reach, her hands clenched behind her back to keep from reaching out to him. It was time to let him go. "I need to get back to the others. I'm certain Mr. Habersham's associate will want to claim his merchandise as soon we dock."

"I love you, Charlotte. Do you hear me? I love you!"

Those were the last words she heard as she rushed out of John's life.

Two hours later, the *Margaret Grace* docked in the port of Charleston. True to Charlotte's suspicions, Mr. Habersham's associate, Mr. Greystone, was waiting when the ship made anchor. Whispers spread that an auction had been scheduled at a horse barn right off the town square and that the auctioneer needed merchandise.

"This isn't the marriage mart," Mrs. Applebee whispered to her after they'd been placed in chains. "He must be selling us for household staff or kitchen help, not that I mind either as long as I can keep my Charlie."

Mrs. Waters added, "At least we'll have a roof over our heads."

"Yes." Charlotte supposed there could be worse things in this life than being in service, but at the moment, she couldn't think of any, not when all she could think of was what she'd lost. *Lord, I feel lost and all alone. I want to believe You have better for me, but I'm struggling. Please help me have faith.*

The next few hours were the longest of Charlotte's life. Chained at the wrists, waist, and ankles, the prisoners were forced to parade through the center of town, a crier at the head of the group calling out their names along with the crimes they committed and their prison sentence. Men gawked at them while the women turned their backs on them. And children! Charlotte's heart broke over some of the rhymes the children yelled at them.

By the time they arrived at the stockyard, the sun had mercifully dipped behind the trees. The women were shoved into animal pens so tightly, Charlotte could barely breathe. They stood in pig slop and horse dung for hours, it seemed. Then, in sets of four, they were shown to the platform. Some were beaten and dragged when they didn't follow the jailer's orders, but most went quietly to their fate. An eerie silence fell over the pen until the bang of the gavel pierced the yard. The sound grew no easier as the evening wore on.

Suddenly, it was Charlotte's turn. A spry older man grabbed the chain between her wrists and gently tugged. "Come." He walked them up a short path to the wide-open door of the barn. Through the center of the room, a long wooden platform stretched from one end of the barn to the other with large groups of men on both sides.

As she glanced out over the crowd, she couldn't find John. He had to be here. He told her he would come.

"You're next, miss."

Dear God, this isn't happening. Charlotte slammed her eyes shut. How could she bear this? How would she survive?

A gentle hand came to rest on her shoulder, and Charlotte looked up. It was the old guard. "Would you like me to pray with you, miss?"

Charlotte was too frightened to speak, so she merely nodded. The man bowed his head, then, whispering so only Charlotte could hear him, he said, "Precious Lord, You know the worries of this young woman's heart. Give her the strength to handle what is to come. Let her find freedom in You. Amen."

Tears pricked the back of her eyes as Charlotte looked up at him. "Thank you, sir."

He nodded then whispered, "A word of warning. The auctioneer—Wilkinson—he doesn't like when the prisoners speak, so stay as quiet as a mouse, you hear?"

She nodded.

Charlotte didn't remember climbing the three steps to the platform until she was shoved into place by the auctioneer. He walked around her, his smile growing into a ruthless snarl. "Gentlemen, we have some fine stock to offer you this evening. A gently reared lady, all the way from London. She'll make a fine house servant or lady's maid." He chuckled. "Maybe you're looking for a woman to bear your children. A good breeder, if that's what you're looking for."

"I need to see her teeth and legs," a man from the back of the room yelled.

"Me, too. Want to see what I might be purchasing." A man from the front gave her a wicked glare.

This was madness! Inspect her teeth like she was a Jersey cow or a horse! And her legs! Charlotte's face burned from embarrassment. She'd worried about lifting her skirts to walk up the stairs for fear of showing too much ankle, yet these men demanded they see her legs!

The auctioneer waved to the men in the crowd. "Come on up, gentlemen, and take a look. I'm sure the lady will oblige." He walked over to her, still smiling, but his words were menacing. "Better lift those skirts as high as you can or it will be the cane for you."

"But..." Too late, she remembered the old jailer's warning. Her next words were lost as the crack of a cane exploded across her shoulders. Charlotte crumpled to the floor on all fours, fighting for her next breath.

"I bid fifty pounds."

Charlotte forced her head up. Who would pay such an enormous amount of money for her? Only one person she knew—John. But it wasn't his voice that called out from the back of the room.

The auctioneer stepped away from her, a huge smile on his face. "Mr. Berrell, sir. It's always a pleasure when you grace our auction."

Charlotte strained to get to her feet as the crowd parted to reveal a tall, middle-aged man. His silver hair was queued in a tie at the nape of his neck. His clothes were well made as were his leather boots. When he stood in front of the auctioneer, he exuded power and position.

A chill ran down Charlotte's back. Why would such a man want her?

Finally, Mr. Berrell spoke. "Do we have an agreement, Mr. Wilkerson?"

Mr. Wilkenson nodded. The gavel came down before Charlotte's next breath. "Sold!"

The bang of the gavel smashed what was left of John's heart. He was too late. He had lost Charlotte.

He collapsed on a bale of hay outside the barn door. The transaction with Mr. Morris had taken longer than he had hoped. By the time all the paperwork on the ship was signed and the banknote safely in his pocket, it was almost seven o'clock.

Five hours after they'd docked.

He felt empty inside, as if Charlotte had died and a part of him with her. How could he build a life without her in it?

"Captain Randall?"

John glanced up at the finely dressed man. It was him, Berrell. The man who'd taken Charlotte away. John glanced around, hoping to see her.

"Charlotte is with my wife, being fitted for a new dress." Berrel sat down on the bale with him. "They'll be joining us shortly."

John had more questions than answers. "What do you want with her?"

The man folded his hands together and leaned back. "I guess I should tell you the whole story. When I was a boy, I was caught stealing a loaf of bread for my sisters. Our parents had been taken off to debtors' prison, and we were left on our own. I was tried and deported to Charleston, where I went to work under Samuel Smith. He treated me more like a son than a convict, and through him, I learned about the saving grace of Christ."

John felt comforted, knowing that Charlotte's new master would at least be kind. Still, his heart ached. "What has that got to do with Charlotte?"

"Ah." The man smiled. "Samuel passed away, leaving me a very wealthy man, but no amount of money can replace the love of a child. My wife and I have been unable to have children of our own, so years ago we decided to help those folks like me who'd been convicted and forced to leave everything they've ever known." He pulled a newspaper clipping from his coat pocket. "A few days ago, my wife read about Charlotte's trial. It seemed unfair to us that she be convicted of her father's crimes, so we decided to buy her freedom."

John wasn't sure if he'd heard the man correctly. "What did you say?"

The man slapped him on the back. "Charlotte's free, John."

John jumped to his feet. "Charlotte's free?"

Berrell smiled at him. "Yes, son, and it appears she wants to marry you."

He thought his heart might burst. Charlotte free! "I want to marry her more than I want to take my next breath."

The man studied John for a long moment. "I have heard of you, Captain Randall. Before I agree to let Charlotte enter into this marriage, I must know if the stories are true."

"Of course." He didn't blame Berrell for having concerns. His former reputation had been well deserved. Praise God for second chances. "It would seem our heavenly Father has been at work in me as well."

Over the next hour, John explained his renewed faith after his sister's death as well as his plans for the farm. Finally, Berrell nodded. "You've satisfied all of my concerns, Captain." He looked up at the clock tower in the square. "The ladies are probably waiting for us at Pastor William's home by now."

"Sir?"

"I've arranged for a preacher friend of mine to perform the ceremony at his home just down the street." The man gave him a troubled look. "That's all right, isn't it?"

John couldn't help the smile on his face. "As long as I get to marry Charlotte, you can plan any kind of wedding you want!"

A half hour later, John stood in the front parlor of Reverend Hubert Williams, waiting on his bride. When she came to the doorway, John could barely breathe. Years from now, he wouldn't remember the color of her gown or if she wore a hat. No, he would remember the sparkle in her dark-blue eyes and the way she glowed when she finally saw him. He rushed past the Berrells to where Charlotte stood waiting.

He took her hand in his. "I'm sorry I wasn't at the auction. I tried. . ."

"Don't." Joy flooded through him when Charlotte smiled up at him. "Things turned out exactly as they should. All that matters now is that we're here, and I'm free, praise God."

"Amen." John smiled back at her. Though Charlotte hadn't said anything about it, he knew she had made peace with the Lord.

She worried her lower lip. "If you still want to marry me. . ."

He lifted her hand to his lips. "Always, dearest."

Then John led her across the room to the preacher who would pronounce them man and wife.

A multi-published author with Love Inspired Historical and Barbour, **Patty Smith Hall** lives in north Georgia with her husband of over 30 years, Danny, two gorgeous daughters, her son-in-love, and a grandboy who has her wrapped around his tiny finger. When she's not writing on her back porch, she's spending time with her family or reading on her front porch swing.

Moira's Quest

by Cynthia Hickey

Stand fast therefore in the liberty wherewith Christ hath made us free,
and be not entangled again with the yoke of bondage.
—GALATIANS 5:1

Chapter 1

New York,
1869

Moira Callahan stared from the stage at the sea of men's faces. She cast an imploring glance at her uncle. How could he sell her to the highest bidder as if she were a cow? She clenched her fists to keep from fidgeting with the jewel pinned to her shift.

Holding her breath to keep from keeling over from the strong fumes of whiskey and unwashed bodies, her gaze fell on a man in the back of the room. He looked on her with pity and...something else, something that made her squirm under his intense stare. She lifted her chin and stared over his head. She would not suffer the pity of anyone, nor would she allow anyone to make her feel less than she was.

Uncle Liam stepped forward. "All right, gentlemen, let the bidding begin. You can see she's a comely lass, healthy and spirited. She's a strong worker and will make any man a fine wife. Let's start the bidding at fifty dollars."

"Fifty dollars! Who has that kind of money?" one man called, and was echoed by others. "This is Five Points. No Irish man has more than two copper coins to rub together."

"Very well. One dollar." Uncle Liam's face reddened. "She's worth ten times that."

Just ten times? Moira thought. What did Uncle Liam think? He had to know there was no money in the slums. She'd be sold for a degrading sum and forced to care for dozens of children for a man who would age her beyond her years. The luck of the Irish, at least in her case, usually meant bad luck.

The man in the back of the room moved forward, shoving through the crowd. A muscle ticked in his square jaw. His dark hair caught the light from the oil lanterns. Piercing blue eyes flashed. "I'll pay ten dollars."

The room gave a collective gasp.

"Very well, sir." Uncle Liam beamed. "You just bought my niece."

The man's eyes narrowed. "Your niece?" He shook his head and offered his hand to Moira. The disgusted look on his face spoke clearly of his thoughts regarding the auction.

She took his hand, feeling the calluses of a working man. After he practically had her running from the building, she yanked free once they stepped outside. "I am not a loose woman, sir. If you think you can purchase me, use me—"

"I'm going to marry you, miss." The corner of his mouth quirked. "I would never debase a woman in the way you suggest."

"You're going to marry me? We don't even know each other." There had to be another way. "Let me pay you back. Then we can both go our separate ways."

He shook his head. "No, ma'am. You'll end up back in that scoundrel's hands. It's best we get hitched so you'll be safe. Follow me."

So, she was to be his prisoner. A captive bride, married to a stranger. Well, Moira was a strong woman. She always had been. Especially since the death of her parents ten years ago. She'd done nothing but be at Uncle Liam's beck and call since then.

She'd make the best of the situation and would not cry. She blinked back tears. Neither would she exercise her wifely duties! She'd find a way of earning back the ten dollars and have the marriage annulled. But first, she'd have to find Leah, the young girl sold to the highest bidder just yesterday. They'd leaned on each other, shared each other's burdens, until Leah had been whisked away under the cover of darkness.

The handsome stranger stopped in front of a redbrick building. "What's your name?"

"Moira Callahan."

"I'm Sean McGowan. Pleased to make your acquaintance." He opened the door for her.

Moira eyed the brown wool skirt she wore and faded yellow blouse. "I'm not dressed to get married."

"You're fine." He waved her in ahead of him.

She stepped into a cavernous room. Her shoes clicked on hardwood floors as Sean led her to a counter and asked for a justice of the peace. So, they weren't even being married by a priest. Her spirits dropped further as a portly man with stained teeth read from a worn Bible. A harried woman acted as witness. Ten minutes later, Moira Callahan was Moira McGowan.

"Where are your things?" Sean glanced down at her.

"I have very little, but my bags are back at the pub. I don't want to go back there."

He studied her for a moment then nodded. "I'll send for them." He stopped a lad on the street, promised him a coin in exchange for the job, and linked Moira's arm in his.

They headed to the far end of Five Points where the poverty didn't seem as desperate. Sean unlocked a door in the side of a building. "Welcome home, Mrs. McGowan."

She entered a two-room apartment with a small cooking area in one corner. The room was clean, the one window unbroken, the floor clear of debris. It would be heaven compared to the hovel she'd shared with her uncle. She eyed the one door where a corner of a bedstead could be seen. "I won't sleep with you."

"You will." He removed the leather vest he wore. "We do not have to consummate, being strangers, but neither of us will sleep on the floor. It gets cold come winter."

She whirled and planted her hands on her hips. "You, sir, are used to getting your way."

"Yes, I am." He gave the first smile since they'd met. A crooked grin that did funny things to Moira's stomach. "I'm a cop. I'm used to giving orders."

"I'm not good at following them."

She turned and surveyed the small table, two chairs, and leather chaise in front of a wood-burning stove.

"It's bare, my apologies. It needs a woman's touch." He changed from his white shirt to a dark blue one and pinned on a copper star. "I'm headed out. Once you inventory the pantry, let me know if there is anything you would like. I'm not a rich man, even poorer now, but we'll get along fine. I should be home by dusk." He slapped a hat on his head, gave a curt nod, grabbed a coat from the back of a chair, and then left her alone.

Moira sagged into the nearest chair, covered her face with her hands, and wept.

Sean was plumb crazy. What business did a law enforcement officer have taking a wife? Most likely, she'd be a widow within the year, especially with Sean pounding the bricks to oust the newest gang to set up shop. A gang run by none other than her snake of an uncle.

When he'd seen the beautiful, spunky woman with red-blond hair and hazel eyes, he'd lost his mind. Ten dollars! He'd have to find a second job to make back the funds or chance not having enough to pay rent.

Still, no matter how hard Moira had tried to hide her fear, he'd seen it in her wide eyes. No respectable man could have done any differently than he had. At least now, she was safe.

He shrugged into his coat to hide his star and headed for the worst section of Five Points. Entering the building once known as the Old Brewery, he climbed to the fourth floor and knocked on the door of his informant.

"Man, you want me dead," a shriveled young man with a hunched back said. "I asked you not to come here."

Sean glanced around the thirteen-by-thirteen-foot room. Twelve pallets filled the floor space with a couple of bunks providing another layer of beds. A rat scurried across one of the pallets. He would never get used to the tenement poverty and thanked God every day that, while small, his apartment was clean and free of rodents.

"You work for Liam Callahan, right?" Sean had never asked the young man's name, not wanting to put him in greater danger than he already was.

"Yeah, I dump his slop."

"What do you know about his niece?"

"Pretty Moira?" The young man rubbed his chin. "The man wouldn't let anyone near her. He kept her behind the bar serving drinks. She always had a smile and a kind word for me. What's your interest in her?"

"I bought her and married her today." The words left a sour taste in his mouth.

"You likely saved her life. It was only a matter of time before some lout crossed the line."

Sean tossed the young man a coin. "Thanks." He left the tenement apartment and headed for Paradise Square, the best place to watch the goings-on of the young boys doing the work of the gangs.

He felt better about his impulsive marriage. In his five years as a cop in Five Points, he wanted to do something to ease the plight of the city's women. He couldn't marry them all, but doing his part to shut down the gangs would benefit not only the women but children and law-abiding men as well.

Finding a spot in the shade of a large tree, he leaned against the trunk, pulled the brim of his hat low, and watched small children in tattered clothing pick pockets. They weren't his target. No, Sean was after bigger fish.

A man in a tweed suit and twirling a cane marched down the sidewalk. He threw out a handful of coins and laughed as the children pounced. Then, belying his kind gesture, he approached a young prostitute who couldn't be more than fourteen years old and slashed her across the back with his cane.

She screamed and cowered.

Sean rushed forward and twisted the man's arm until he dropped his weapon.

"Mind your own business do-gooder!" The man struggled, catching Sean in the cheekbone with his elbow. "This girl belongs to me."

"I'd run if I were you, young lady," Sean said. He placed his foot in the bend of the man's knee and forced him to the ground.

Eyes wide, she did as instructed. With her flight went Sean's opportunity for answers to his questions. He cuffed the cursing man and dragged him to the precinct where he put him in the capable hands of another officer. "Book him on assault. I'll do the paperwork when I come in the morning."

"Heard you got hitched today."

Sean raised a hand on his way out the door. The man's congratulations reminded him that he did, indeed, have a wife waiting at home for him.

He opened the apartment door to the sight of Moira stirring something over the stove and the aroma of roasting potatoes. "Smells good."

"Shepherd's pie. Sit." She lifted the pan with the hem of her skirt, giving him a glimpse of a tattered petticoat as green as Irish grass. "Your face!"

"It's nothing." He touched the aching lump on his cheek.

"I've witch hazel in my bag." She dashed to the bedroom and returned with a dark-colored bottle and a rag. After filling a bowl with water and adding a few drops of witch hazel, she bent and tended to his face. "Does this happen often?"

"More often than not." When was the last time a female tended his wounds? Not since his sister ran off a year ago. "I'm glad your bags came."

"A little while ago. I was going to fetch them myself, thinking the lad made off with your money."

He grabbed her hand, stopping her ministrations. "Don't. Do not leave this apartment without me knowing your whereabouts. It isn't safe."

"I'm sure I've been taking care of myself for a good long while," she said, her brogue more pronounced.

"I'm sure you have. Are you aware of who your uncle is?"

"Liam Callahan. I've known him my whole life."

"Were you aware he's the leader of one of New York's most notorious gangs? That he kidnaps young women and forces them into prostitution? That he beats boys into doing his bidding, cutting out their tongues if they squeal to the cops?"

She shook her head and stepped back. "No, he's gruff, but—"

"He's one of the most despicable men in this city, and he's the reason my little sister is missing."

Chapter 2

Moira spent the night very aware of the man who slept next to her. Instead of closing her eyes, she had stared at the ceiling, thinking over what Sean had said about her uncle and trying not to think about being married to a handsome stranger who seemed to have an agenda of his own. One that meant keeping her in the apartment.

Questions peppered her mind. She hadn't been completely truthful about not knowing the type of man Uncle Liam was. She knew full well he was capable of murder and intended to find evidence that he had killed her parents. Their carriage accident had been no accident. Da had been under Uncle Liam's thumb for as long as Moira could remember. He'd wanted out of the unlawful doings forced upon him. She was sure the brake had been tampered with, causing the wagon to go into the ditch, throwing her parents. Moira had vowed at their graves that she would not be under anyone's thumb.

She should have been in the carriage that day. It was her job to go to market and sell the shawls her mother knitted. But that day she'd asked to stay home, letting them know the night before that she wanted one lovely afternoon to dig into the latest tattered novel she could get her hands on. It should be Moira that was dead. . .but that wouldn't have served her uncle's purpose. No, she was worth more to him alive.

She climbed out of bed, Sean having already woken, and headed to the stove to make coffee. Dismay filled her at the sight of her husband sitting at the table, paper in one hand, coffee cup in the other. "I'm so sorry I didn't wake sooner." She grabbed her apron.

He glanced up. "It's no problem. I'm capable of fending for myself."

After pouring herself a cup, she sat across from him. "What is your sister's name?"

"Excuse me?" He set down his paper.

"I was thinking of your comment last night, and—"

"Leah. She has hair the color of a crow's wing and eyes as blue as the sea. A pretty lass."

The blood drained from Moira, settling in her toes. "Leah?" Why hadn't she put the pieces together when she'd heard Sean's last name? Not that it would have mattered. Leah was long gone by now, hidden away somewhere in a Five Points brothel.

Sean's eyes narrowed. "You've seen her?"

"Uncle Liam sold her to some man the day before you purchased me."

He leaped to his feet and shook her. "To whom? What's his name?"

"I don't know. Sean, please, you're hurting me."

He stepped back, eyes wide. "I'm sorry. I would never—" He slumped back into his chair and rubbed his hands over his face. "I've been so worried about her."

"I think he was well-to-do. His suit looked tailor-made. He was a bit older and slipped her hand in the crook of his arm as they left. Perhaps he's kind?" Oh, how she wanted to erase the look of pain from her husband's face. If skirting the truth did that, then that's what she would do.

"I'll ask around." He sighed. "She was so close, yet I couldn't find her. Practically right under my nose."

"I could ask Uncle Liam—"

"No! Stay away from him." Sean stood and grabbed his coat. "I'll take care of him and Leah. You stay here where it's safe."

"A prisoner, you mean." She lifted her chin.

"That's not what I mean at all. If you feel the need, we'll discuss this further when I return."

"Don't you want breakfast?"

"I'm fine. Have a good day, Moira." He left.

She jumped from her chair, grabbed a couple of day-old biscuits, and wrapped her shawl around her shoulders. If Sean thought she would be a bird in a gilded cage, he had another think coming. Outside, she glanced up and down the street and set off for Uncle Liam's pub at a fast pace. Her uncle would most likely be sleeping, but Johnny would be hard at work mopping the floors. The disfigured young man knew everything that went on at the pub. If anyone knew where Sean's sister had been taken, Johnny did.

She took another cautious look around and opened the pub door. "Johnny?"

He popped up from behind the bar. "Moira." He grinned, transforming his homely face into something beautiful. "I know your copper husband."

"How?" She cocked her head.

"Oh, uh, I can't rightly say, outside of breaking my oath. What brings you back to this den of iniquity?"

She stepped closer and lowered her voice. "Do you know where Leah was taken?"

"Please tell me you aren't going off on a crusade to rescue the girl."

"What if I am?" She crossed her arms.

He sighed and cast a furtive look toward the stairs leading to Uncle Liam's apartment. "She was bought by the most infamous brothel owner in Five Points, a man by the name of Dan Lambert. You can't save her. Not without endangering yourself. Of course, if Leah causes the man too much trouble, he'll sell her as a bride to someone out West. Pray she's as strong as you."

"How long would that take?"

He shrugged. "Depends on how patient Lambert is. Leah is a comely girl, so he'll hold on to her as long as possible."

That's what Moira was counting on. She planted an impulsive kiss on Johnny's pockmarked cheek. "You're an angel."

"One that will be lighting many a candle for you, Irish gal." He winked. "Now, go, before your uncle wakes and causes a ruckus."

With a smile and a wave, Moira dashed back out to the street. Leah had been her only friend, other than Johnny, since Moira landed on American soil. If she could rescue the girl, Sean was bound to be so grateful, he'd let Moira out of their marriage. It was a good situation for all of them.

She never should have allowed her uncle to drag her to America. She should have run off and hidden in the green hills of Ireland or the alleys of London. Nothing had gone right since they'd left. Now, she found herself married to a stranger, trying to avenge her parents' deaths, and save a young girl from a disastrous life.

God help them all.

Why did Moira look on him as her captor? All Sean wanted to do was keep her safe. He'd failed in regard to Leah and his mother; he wouldn't fail his new bride. He'd save every girl from every brothel in town if he could. Growing up as the son of a prostitute who'd spent more time beaten up and drunk than caring for her children had set him on a path he couldn't veer from. Not for anyone.

Speaking of his wife, he spotted her darting around a corner. Sighing, he set off in pursuit. She wasn't going to make his job of protector easy.

His jaw dropped when she stretched out a hand to open a faded red door known throughout Five Points for the entertainment within. "Moira."

She whipped around to face him. "Hurry. This is the man who bought Leah."

Those were the words he least expected to come out of her mouth. "Are you sure?"

"Johnny told me, he works for—"

"Who's Johnny?"

"A young man with a bowed back, he works—"

"I know him. Stay out here." Sean reached for the door handle.

"But. . ."

"I mean it." He stepped inside and slammed the door, hoping, praying, she'd follow his orders.

He was immediately greeted by a buxom woman in a deep purple dress and a low neckline that showed off too much freckled skin. She trailed a finger down his cheek. "You're a handsome one."

He pulled aside his coat to show his badge. "I'm looking for someone. A girl."

She frowned. "Well, we don't often get coppers in here, but do on occasion. Step up to the glass and I'll show you who's available." She pulled aside a curtain and revealed several girls lounging in a small room. None of them was Leah.

"The girl I'm looking for is new, purchased just two days ago from Liam Callahan."

"I'm sorry, but it requires several days to train these girls to know their place. Perhaps next week?" She raised her eyebrows. "Or one of these?" She motioned toward the window.

"May I see the new girls?"

She shook her head. "No, I'm afraid they are kept away until they're ready."

He nodded. "I'll be back."

He stepped outside. Moira was nowhere in sight. He groaned and leaned against the side of the building. Where would a headstrong Irish woman go? The market? One of the factories? He pushed off with his foot and headed around the corner. A clanking overhead drew his attention to the fire escape.

He caught a glimpse of an emerald-green petticoat before it disappeared through an open window. Moira was going to be the death of him. Shaking his head, he climbed after her, whispering her name.

Her pretty face fell as she looked back and caught sight of him stepping through the same window. "You're everywhere."

"So are you, it seems. What in tarnation are you doing?"

"Looking for Leah. I know she's here."

He grabbed her arm. "Let me handle this."

"You can use my help." She yanked free. "We can work together or you can keep following me and not doing your job."

She had a good point. "Fine, we work together, but we do this my way."

She opened her mouth as if to argue then snapped it closed and nodded. With a bow, she waved her arm for him to precede her.

They needed to have a serious conversation when they returned home. Moira needed to learn to listen when he told her not to do something. The city was not safe for a beautiful woman to wander alone. Somehow he needed to convince her of that fact.

They moved down a hall with several doors branching off each side. Every handle he tried was locked. "Leah." He didn't want to shout, but a whisper wouldn't penetrate through the door.

"Maybe she's in a room downstairs or in the basement. I saw stairs off that way." Moira pointed to another hall on their left. "We need a story if we're caught."

"Well, I'm a cop. You're a trespasser. That should be simple enough."

"Very funny." She turned to the left, taking his hand.

His large one closed over her smooth one. Her climb through the window had knocked hair as fine as corn silk from its bun down to her shoulders. He guessed if fully released, the strands would fall to her waist. He shook himself. Wake up! They could very well be walking into a dangerous situation, and here he was thinking of how soft Moira's hair would feel to his fingers. Maybe it wasn't a good idea to look for Leah with her. Moira was too distracting. He couldn't afford a distraction right now.

"There. See that door. I'd bet my hat your sister is in there. Uncle Liam has kept other girls there in the past."

Sean rushed toward the heavy wooden door. "Leah."

"Sean? Is that you?"

He closed his eyes in relief. "Are you all right?"

"Yes. Get me out of here. I cut him with a piece of glass. He's mad and is going to ship me west."

Not if Sean could help it. He glanced around the room for something to bring down the door with.

"Move aside." Moira pulled a hat pin from the floppy hat on her head and jiggled it in the lock until a definite click sounded.

His bride was full of surprises.

Leah flew out and into Sean's arms. "I knew you'd find me. Hello, Moira." She tilted her head, a questioning look in her eyes. "How—?"

"Questions later," Sean said. "Let's get out of here." He took each woman by the arm and rushed toward the fire escape. They couldn't be seen. He couldn't risk gunfire while they were with him. Once home, Leah needed to stay out of sight. No one could find out where she was.

"Straight to the police station," Moira said. "Leah needs to testify against my uncle."

"She needs to hide."

Moira stopped. "No, my uncle needs to be locked up." Tears shimmered in her eyes. "He can't be allowed to roam free. Him, and men like him, need to hang."

"We'll talk about this at home."

"Home?" Leah glanced from him to Moira.

"Your brother purchased me yesterday. We're married." Moira swiped her hands across her eyes.

"Sean, you didn't!"

"Please. Let's go." He dragged them after him. What was wrong with women? They were full of haste in one moment, and full of righteous indignation that slowed them down the next.

As they raced for the fire escape, a man stepped from one of the rooms. "Two? Lucky man." He grinned and continued downstairs. "I'm going to let the madame know how unfair that is."

Sean's heart pounded. They'd be discovered for sure the moment the man entered the downstairs parlor.

Chapter 3

Moira plopped on a straight-back chair and glared at Sean. "Uncle Liam will be even more suspicious of you as soon as he knows Leah escaped. It's going to be that much harder to catch him." She felt through her blouse for her mother's brooch. What would her uncle do if he knew she'd had it all these years?

Sean sat across from her. "It's answer time. Why are you determined to defy me and put yourself in danger?"

"He killed my parents. I know he did." Tears burned her eyes. "I may not be able to prove the accident was at his hands, but I'll have him behind bars any way I can. You keeping me prisoner here thwarts my plans."

"I'm not keeping you prisoner! I'm trying to keep you safe." He exhaled heavily. "Leah, are you. . .unharmed?"

"Yes." A sly smile stretched her lips. "I believe that no-account seller of women was a bit afraid of me."

Moira laughed. "Let's take him and the man who bought you down together."

"You two will do no such thing." Sean lunged to his feet. "That's my job. If I didn't have to run after the two of you at every turn, I might accomplish that deed. Once I do, both men will be behind bars until they hang."

"We can help you." Moira stood and placed a hand on his arm. "We can go where you can't."

"No. Sit down. I need to tell you something."

Her gaze not leaving his face, Moira resumed her seat.

"This is not something you can talk about," he said. "I'm trying to bring down the Lambert gang and Callahan's. In order to do that, I cannot have the two of you leaving this apartment. What if you're taken and shipped west? I'd never find you again."

Moira exchanged a glance with Leah. It was clear his sister felt as she did about putting these men behind bars. Sean needed their help whether he knew it or not. "I can get a job working the bar in Uncle Liam's pub. He won't harm me since I belong to you now." The words threatened to choke her. While she liked her husband, his integrity, his looks, she couldn't get past the fact that he'd purchased her like an animal at the market.

"Stop looking at each other that way." Sean got to his feet again. "Maybe I should lock the two of you behind bars so you can't interfere. God save me from Irish females." He grabbed his hat and stormed from the apartment.

"What's on your mind?" Leah scooted her chair closer. "I think the first thing we should do is pray. . .for wisdom and Sean's safety."

Moira picked at a loose thread on her shawl. "I don't think God listens to me anymore." She'd felt His absence since the death of her parents. If God cared, why did He allow her to suffer at the hand of Uncle Liam, her appointed guardian?

"What's bothering you?" Leah placed a hand over Moira's.

"I feel very alone." Tears pricked her eyes. "My parents were murdered, I was sold like used goods, and Uncle Liam treated me like a slave. My back carries the scars of his abuse. If God cared, why did He allow that? You were sold to a brothel, for goodness sake."

"At the hands of men who don't follow God's ways. Remember, humans have free will. Did it occur to you that maybe Sean's buying you was God's way of rescuing you? Then God used you to save me? There are far worse fates than being wed to my brother, I assure you. He's a fine-looking man, am I right?" She grinned.

"Perhaps." Her friend's words definitely gave Moira something to consider. She took Leah's other hand. "Go ahead and pray."

Leah spoke as if God were a person sitting in the chair next to them. She prayed first for Sean, then for wisdom, then gave thanks that she and Moira were free.

Was Moira free? She was married to a stranger who wanted to keep her under lock and key. For her safety, he said. Wasn't being married to a copper safety enough? No one would dare harm her.

"Amen."

Moira jolted back to where she was. "Amen. Thank you. Now, we need to make a plan. I'll get a job at Uncle Liam's pub. I do agree with my husband that you remain in hiding. If Callahan sees you—"

"I need a disguise. It wouldn't be hard for me to look like a boy. I'm small enough. Then I could roam the streets and gather information for Sean. I'm sure he won't be happy about you working in the pub, but he's gone all day. He can't watch you every moment."

Moira studied the girl in front of her. Small chested, thin, but very pretty, with a mane of hair halfway down her back. "You'll never get all that hair up under a peaky cap."

"I'll cut it. Right now." She jumped up and grabbed Moira's sewing scissors from the counter and started snipping.

Moira gasped as dark curls fell to the floor. "Sean will have apoplexy."

"I'll say it's to make me harder to recognize. It won't be a lie." Soon Leah's glorious hair lay in a dark puddle at her feet. Moira's hands trembled. "I haven't thought of my husband as a violent man, but this might drive him to punching holes in the wall."

"No, not him." Leah grinned and ruffled her curls. "I feel so light. Now, let's go borrow me some boy clothes."

The weight of responsibility sat on Sean's shoulders like a woolen blanket soaked in the sea. He thanked God for his sister's freedom and wished for a way, a place, anywhere to send her and his wife to keep them from the gangs of Five Points.

He leaned against a tree in the park, careful to keep his badge hidden, and watched several young lads dart in and around the more wealthy strolling there. Several walkers would be lightened of a wallet or a watch by the time they returned home. That wasn't why Sean was there. He needed to know where the gangs holed up.

"Hey, Copper." A boy peered around a tree trunk. "Yeah, I know what you are. Lookin' for someone? I'll tell you anything you want for a coin."

"Run away, lad. This isn't your business." Sean glanced down. How had the boy known his profession? His jacket completely covered his badge.

Instead of leaving, the boy came closer. "Word on the street is that you're looking for Lambert and Callahan. There's a fight tonight at the Old Brewery. Eight o'clock." He held out his hand. "They'll both be there."

"Are you certain? I won't have you lying to me." Sean tossed him a coin.

"You'll have to dirty yourself up some if you want to get in undetected. . .Copper. If they catch you, they'll hurt you." The lad laughed and raced away.

That Sean knew for a fact. The last time a police officer stepped in to watch a fight without placing a bet, he'd been dumped in an alley with broken ribs. He sighed and pushed away from the tree. It looked as if he had plans for the evening. But not before he had dinner with his wife and sister.

He stepped through the door of the apartment and smiled at the homey scene. Moira and Leah chatted and giggled while Moira stirred a pot on the stove and Leah set the table. Leah! So engrossed was he in the scene before him, it took a moment for Sean to notice what was different. "What in the name of our mother did you do to your hair?"

"I cut it so Callahan wouldn't recognize me easily." She patted the curls that sprouted around her head. "Genius, if I say so myself."

"It's scandalous." He frowned. "A woman's hair is her crowning glory." He glanced at Moira to make sure she still had hers. Yes, every silky strand seemed to be in place.

"Sit down, Sean." Moira plopped a bowl of thick potato soup with cheese in front of him. "The deed's been done. No changing it now."

The tantalizing, rich smell of his dinner almost made Sean forget his disappointment in Leah's actions. He grabbed a slice of fresh baked bread from a basket in the center of the table and dunked it into his soup. His sister was right. She needed to keep from being recognized. Still, the sight would take some getting used to. What didn't take getting used to was how much he enjoyed having a beautiful woman waiting on him when he returned home at the end of the day. Marrying Moira had been one of his finest ideas.

"I still don't understand the reasoning, Leah. Wouldn't a hat have done as well, or better yet, follow my instructions and stay in the apartment?" He bit into the sopped bread and closed his eyes in ecstasy. "You're a right fine cook, Moira."

She blushed and ducked her head. "Thank you."

Sean smiled. He concentrated on his food as the women joined him at the table. "Before I take another bite, I'll say the blessing." He held out his hands, enjoying the feel of Moira's small one in his as he prayed. When he'd finished, the women dug into their soup, sending each other a suspiciously conspiratorial glance once in a while. Sean would have to keep an eye on them. As sure as the sun set in the West, they were up to something.

When he'd finished eating and pushed his bowl aside, he folded his hands on the table and fixed a stern glance on his wife. "What are you two planning?"

She choked on her bread.

Sean bolted to his feet and pounded her on the back.

Once she had her breath, she waved him aside. "Thank you. We are only talking women things. Nothing for you to trouble yourself over."

"Hmm-hmm." He sat back down. "That's a falsehood, dear wife."

Her face colored prettily again. If that's all it took, he'd call her dear more often. "You two are up to something and I don't think I'll like whatever it is."

"Don't worry." Moira patted his hand as if he were a child. "We aren't doing anything that doesn't need doing."

It was worse than he feared. They were going after Callahan and Lambert. He needed a plan to keep them away from the dangerous men.

"I see the wheels turning in your mind," Leah said, "and you can stop it right now. You don't own either one of us. We're free to do as we please."

"I'm responsible for you two." He glanced from one to the other. "I care about you both. I can't let you roam the streets after these men."

"Short of locking us in and taking the key, you can't stop us. Even then, we'd climb out the window."

Moira stared at him with wide eyes shimmering with unshed tears. "I don't want to disobey you, but this is something I must do."

He sighed. "Then we have to work together. It's my best chance at keeping you safe." He stared at a spot of spilled soup on the table. How could he work efficiently and keep them safe? The only way was to keep them with him. "There's a fight tonight. I'll see to it that you're hired to serve drinks, Moira. You, Leah—"

"Will be dressed as a boy," she said with a grin. "Taking bets."

Chapter 4

Moira entered the large, dank room from a back door and set off in search of her uncle. She glanced over her shoulder to where Sean, dressed as a ruffian, and Leah, as a scruffy boy, watched her leave them. It couldn't be helped. She couldn't approach Uncle Liam with them in tow. Not if her story was going to work.

She found her uncle behind a makeshift bar screaming at a cowering girl in a stained apron. "Uncle Liam, I'll tend the bar."

He whirled, eyes narrowing. "Why? Doesn't your husband make enough to support you?"

"Certainly." She stiffened. "But until we have children, I've little to occupy my time."

"Fine. This girl is an imbecile." He raised his hand as if to backhand the poor lass. "Go sweep the floor and stay out of the way."

The girl scurried out of the room. Uncle Liam tossed Moira an apron. "You know the drill."

She held the dirty apron away from her with two fingers. "Don't you have a clean one?"

"That's it." He marched away.

Moira sighed and took her place behind a makeshift wooden counter as Sean and Leah entered with a group of men who volleyed for position around the boxing ring. She hated boxing. What a barbaric pastime.

Sean glanced her way and raised his eyebrows.

She nodded and turned to pour a pint of ale to a customer. The familiar action brought back all she hated about living with her uncle. She held on to the idea that together, she and her husband would soon have Uncle Liam and his kind behind bars.

Husband. The word still tasted strange on her tongue. But she'd married a kind man with convictions. A handsome man who loved God. A man who could, if she would let him, win her heart. Things could have been a lot worse.

"My pockets are bulging with bills," Leah said, leaning on the bar. "Too bad I can't keep the money. It's enough to fund a new life out West. I need three beers."

"I'm surprised they let you keep the money on your person."

Leah shrugged. "They know that I know they'll kill me if I run off or lose a cent." She set the poured drinks on a tray. "My brother is trying to stay out of the eye of the crowd, but several men have been staring at him. I hope they don't know he's a copper."

"Shh." Moira frowned at her. "If they find out, they'll kill him." There wouldn't be a thing she could do to save him.

She searched the room, growing concerned until she spotted him, peaky cap pulled low over his eyes, lounging in the corner. She set a beer on a tray and headed in his direction. "Care to buy a pint?"

"Thanks." He dug a few coins from his pocket, dropped them on the tray, and pretended to drink.

"Leah is worried some of the men know your identity."

He glanced up, worry creasing his face. "No matter what happens, stay behind the bar."

"You're my husband. I won't stand back and let harm come to you."

"And I can't let it come to you." His eyes darkened. "I appreciate your concern, Moira. Please return to the safety of the counter." Holding the beer, he sauntered away.

Despair filled her heart as several men watched Sean head to the opposite side of the room. She headed toward them, transferring their attention to her. "Drinks before the fight starts?"

"I thought you got hitched." One man crossed his arms. "What are you doing here? Ain't your husband a copper? Is that him?" He motioned his head toward Sean.

"I've never seen that man before. Do you want a drink or not?" She held his gaze, hoping he hadn't been present when Sean bought her.

"Sure. We'll all take one." He tossed money onto her tray. "Keep the change and enjoy the entertainment."

They knew. She had to get Sean out of there. She continued to travel the room, taking orders until she stood in front of him again. "They know who you are. You have to leave."

"Not without your uncle."

"Please." Tears welled in her eyes.

A commotion sounded from behind as four men shoved past her. They grabbed Sean, knocking the hat from his head.

"He's a cop!"

"Toss him in the ring!"

"Make him fight to leave!"

"No." Moira dropped the tray, coins scattering, and tried to force herself into the fray. "Stop."

Someone shoved her, sending her to the floor. Hands grabbed her arms, dragging her to a cleared space.

"You can't help him if you're trampled," Leah said. "Sean can hold his own in a fight."

"He's outnumbered."

"It will only be him and one other in the ring. They won't kill a cop with so many witnesses." She helped Moira to her feet. Together, they found a spot next to the ropes. "It's a game they play. He'll win a few dollars if he stays upright long enough."

Sean's shirt was torn off him, then he was shoved into the ring to face a pug-nosed man who outweighed him by at least twenty pounds. The man, light on his feet for one so big, bounced lightly, taunting Sean.

A third man entered the ring and stood between them. "Last man standing is the winner. No gouging, no weapons, no scratching." He stepped back and waved his hand.

Sean circled around the larger man then threw a punch that caught the fighter in the rib cage.

Another punch, and another.

Then the man threw a right hook that snapped Sean's head back.

Moira clapped a hand over her mouth to stifle a gasp.

Sean looked her way.

An uppercut split his lip. The metallic taste of blood filled his mouth. *Pay attention, man! You can't have your wife and sister watch you pummeled.*

Sean moved back, trying to stay out of arm's reach of his opponent. It wasn't easy. The man was an experienced fighter and had the scars, and experience, to prove it.

Another swing caught him in the face. Within seconds his left eye was swollen almost shut. Taking a chance, Sean ducked and came up swinging. Punch after punch struck the man's ribs, jaw, and cheekbone. Again and again, until Sean backed up panting for breath.

The other man charged, bellowing like a bull. He grabbed Sean around the waist, lifted him, and slammed him to the floor.

Sean's breath left him in a whoosh. He rolled as the other man tried to stomp on his face.

Moira screamed as the man's foot landed on Sean's arm. He heard the bone snap.

Agony burned through him.

Shouts filled the room as Sean's cop buddies finally arrived.

Someone fired a gun.

Moira squeezed through the ropes and knelt next to him. "Oh, husband." She took off her dirty apron and fashioned a sling. Before she could hand it to him, Sean's opponent hefted her off her feet and tossed her aside. She crumpled to the floor.

With a screech, she launched herself at the man's back.

Another gun fired and a cop pulled Moira free, handcuffing her.

"That's my wife!" Sean struggled to his feet.

"Sorry." The cop freed her hands and pushed her toward Sean.

With his good arm, Sean led Moira to a corner away from the chaos. "Where's Leah?"

"I don't know. Let me get this sling on you. Then you can find her and the three of us will find a doctor." Her words told him she wouldn't accept an argument.

As the adrenaline drained from his body, the ache of his broken arm consumed him. Nausea rose in his stomach and he slid down the wall to sit on the floor. His left eye was now totally swollen closed. He'd failed again to take down Callahan.

"Stay here." Moira patted his cheek. "I'll find Leah." She raced away, returning a few minutes later with his sister in tow. Leah sported a black eye.

"Sometimes I think I have a brother instead of a sister," he muttered.

"I just got in the way of a fist," she said, propping her shoulder under his good arm. "I wasn't fighting. Moira, can you clear us a path?"

Moira put two fingers to her lips and gave a very unladylike whistle. The men parted like the Red Sea. Head held high, she led the three of them out of the room and onto the street, but not before grabbing a few bills from a waiting man. "I'd say my husband earned these fair and square." She led them to the right and down another street until she stopped in front of a faded green door. She knocked then pushed the door open and ushered them inside.

"In here." An older man led Sean into a small bedroom. "On the bed there. I'll have you fixed up in no time, sir."

"Who is this?" Sean directed his question at Moira.

"A doctor Uncle Liam uses. He's used to working without asking questions." She collapsed into a chair opposite the bed.

Sean closed his eyes and endured while the doctor set his arm. Sweat beaded on his lip. By the time it was finished, he'd lost his dinner in the nearby chamber pot.

The doctor declared the job done and Moira paid his fee then supported Sean's weight home.

When they arrived, she laid him on the bed and started wiping the blood from his face. "Witch hazel will help the lip. I'm so sorry I distracted you."

"Moira." He caressed her cheek. "This wasn't your fault. I was not going to win the fight. I just had to keep going until help arrived. I managed."

She shook her head, tears coursing down her cheeks. "No, I accept full responsibility."

"You, Moira McGowan, are a stubborn woman."

"Guilty." She gave a tremulous smile.

"It seems you may care for me, a little?"

"Perhaps." Her cheeks darkened. "I do believe you might be growing on me."

"You no longer feel as if you're my captive?"

She chuckled and wiped the back of her hand across her face. "Sometimes I still do."

"We'll learn this marriage business together, if you're willing." He took her hand. "I know you've considered an annulment, but I'd like to give us a try." He patted the side of the bed. "Lie with me."

"You're injured!" She clutched the neckline of her blouse.

"Just lie here and keep me company. I'm weary."

She nodded and lay next to his good side. "You let me know if you need anything."

"I will." He closed his eyes, breathing in the faint scent of lilacs from her hair.

When his opponent had tossed Moira aside like a rag doll, Sean had tried to go to her aid. His broken arm had made that impossible. He smiled, remembering the way she'd attacked back. Like a mama bear defending her cub. Maybe they had a chance at love with each other. Plenty of marriages did quite well on friendship and respect. They were well on their way to more than that.

Soft snores signaled she had fallen asleep. He turned his head to gaze on her lovely face. The curve of her cheek. The shadow of her dark lashes against her skin. His wife was a beautiful woman.

"Do you need anything?" Leah stood in the doorway.

"That quilt over there, please." He pointed to a chair in the corner.

She took the quilt and placed it over him and Moira. "She's quite a woman, your wife. I like her."

"So do I, sister. So do I."

Chapter 5

Moira woke and stared at her husband's battered face. What possessed a man to rush headlong into danger for the sake of others? They were more alike than she'd thought. They both wanted to put a stop to the violence of Five Points. The difference was...Moira thought only of putting away Uncle Liam, who had changed her world the day he killed her parents. Sean thought of the slum's population.

Slipping slowly from under the heavy quilt, she then tucked it around his shoulders and headed for the stove. She hadn't intended to fall asleep last night, but waking up next to Sean had felt more comfortable than she could imagine.

She found a few eggs in the pantry and some leftover ham. Soon she had breakfast ready and carried a tray to Sean.

He groaned as he got to a sitting position. "I feel as if I've been dragged behind a wagon led by runaway horses."

"I'm guessing you'll be off work for a while." She placed a pillow behind his back to support him. "What will that do to your investigation?"

"I'll still pound the pavement looking for evidence. The difference is, I'll have to have someone else make any arrests." He peered up at her with one eye. "A lot of men were taken down last night, but I saw your uncle duck out a back door when the cops arrived. You'll need to be extra careful. He'll think you've betrayed him."

"He won't harm me. I have something he wants." She unpinned the emerald brooch from her chemise and handed it to him. "This belonged to my mother. It's worth a small fortune."

"It's beautiful." He cocked his head and handed it back to her. "Most people would have sold it or turned it over to a man like Callahan."

She re-pinned it to her chemise. "It's all I have left of my ma. I still believe he caused the accident that killed my parents, and I intend to prove it. He forced my da to do his bidding, some of it illegal. When Da wanted out...well, my parents died soon after."

"How will you prove he's responsible?"

"I don't know." The accident had happened close to her village. There was no way to prove her instincts wrong or right. "I'll have to be satisfied to see him behind bars."

He took her hand. "I'll do my best to see that happens."

"With my help." She smiled. "Since you only have one good arm, I'm going back to work at the pub. I know how to be invisible when I need to. The men say things."

"A woman with your looks can never be invisible."

She flushed. "Flattery will get you nothing, sir. Do I need to feed you?"

"No, it's my left arm that's broken, and I'm right-handed." He lifted his fork. "Where's Leah?"

"She wasn't here when I woke." Moira had wondered the same. It seemed as if the girl's disguise had worked the night before, but she still shouldn't wander the streets alone. "I need to go to the market. I'll keep an eye out for her."

"Take what you need from the crock, and be careful."

"I will." His caring warmed her all the way through. Since the death of her parents, no one had cared for her the way Sean seemed to. Watching him walk in the door at the end of the day was becoming as familiar to her as the sight of her reflection in the mirror.

After taking money from the crock, she grabbed her shawl and a wicker basket then locked the apartment door behind her. On the street, she headed to the market, studying the crowd for Leah's dark head. Where was the headstrong girl? There. It wasn't until Moira grabbed the lad that she realized it wasn't Leah. "My apologies."

She couldn't return home without Leah. Spotting another person she thought might be her sister-in-law in disguise, she set off down a side street. "McGowan!"

Leah turned. "I'm Lanny today," she said, grinning.

"What are you doing? Sean is beside himself because you weren't there when he woke."

She shrugged. "He'll survive. Come with me." She took Moira's hand, dragged her into an alley, and pointed to a ramshackle building. "Lambert hides there when the cops are out in force as they are after a fight. That's what I've been doing. Trying to help my brother."

"How do you know he's in there?" Moira peered at the dirt-covered window.

"I went inside. He didn't recognize me. It's easy enough to act as a delivery boy no one pays much attention to."

Moira nodded. "I'm getting my old job back at Uncle Liam's. I doubt he'll pay me, but I can keep my eyes and ears open. Sean won't be able to do his job for a few weeks. It's up to us now." She didn't like Leah wandering the streets alone, dressed as a boy or otherwise. There had to be another way to keep an eye on Lambert. "Come with me to the market. We'll make our plans."

Leah fell into step with her. "Delivery boy is the perfect ruse."

"I have to agree with Sean on this one."

"Too bad for the both of you that I'm no longer a child." Leah tugged her hat tighter on her head.

Moira stopped and planted her hands on her hips, amused at the girl's indignation. "I'm not saying you shouldn't help. I can't do that when I'm just as convinced as you are that Sean needs us. What I'm saying is. . .walking right under the nose of the man who sold you into prostitution isn't the wisest choice."

"It's no different than your uncle selling you. You got lucky that my brother purchased you."

"Agreed." Moira sighed. They had no choice other than to go into the lion's den.

Refusing to stay home while Moira worked her uncle's pub, Sean hunkered over a scarred round table and pretended to nurse a glass of whiskey. The ache in his broken bone spread tentacles of agony into his shoulder. But he was here to keep an eye on Moira for what little he could do.

"How's marriage to my niece?" Callahan sat in the chair across from him. "You took quite a beating at the match. Why were you there? We weren't doing anything wrong."

"Fighting for money is against the law. Plus, I was keeping an eye on my wife, same as now." Sean met the other man's hard gaze. "We're doing fine. She's a good woman."

"She's a thief."

"That comment needs an explanation." Ignoring the pain in his arm, Sean straightened.

"She has something that belongs to me. I've let her wear it, because I know what it meant to her, but now I want it. I owe someone a lot of money, and that brooch is more than enough payment." Callahan crossed his arms. "It seems to have disappeared."

"Do you have proof it's supposed to be yours?"

"Just the word of her dead father."

"That won't hold up in a court of law, sir." From the look on Callahan's face, Sean didn't believe the danger to Moira would ease any time soon. "Perhaps it's best if you cut your losses."

"That won't happen, Copper. I intend to have what's mine." He glanced to where Moira wiped down the bar. "She has it, and I will take it soon. It's a matter of time."

"Is that a threat?"

"That's a promise." Planting his hands flat on the table, Callahan stood and leaned close. "Mind your back and hers. Enjoy the whiskey. It's on the house." He strode up a nearby staircase, whistling an Irish jig.

Sean sat back. The brooch needed to be somewhere other than pinned to Moira's underclothing. The bank was out of the question. At least the local branch. The manager was as crooked as the gang leaders.

The apartment wasn't the solution, either. Perhaps the safe at the precinct? He could hide it in the evidence room. He hoped Moira would agree to let the jewel out of her possession for a while.

He waved her over. "Do you have a minute? There's something I need to speak with you about."

"Sure." She sat and fixed her gaze on him.

He reached his good arm across the table and took her hand. "Your uncle approached me about the brooch. I think we need to stash it at the precinct for your safety."

She pulled away. "No. I keep it close."

"If he were to search you. . .well, you could be in more harm than you are now."

"It won't happen. He's never laid a hand on me."

"Moira. I haven't told you this, but as powerful as your uncle is, he's broke. Bankrupt, if he doesn't come into some money. That brooch is his ticket to some money."

"He can't have it, and neither can you." She jumped to her feet. "It stays with me."

"Then I pray God looks out for you when I can't." Why couldn't she see reason?

"I've been doing just fine on my own. Stop trying to control me!" With a swish of her skirts, she marched away, just as Sean's mother had the last time he'd seen her alive.

As the son of one of Five Point's prostitutes, he'd spent his childhood looking after his mother and sister. But his thirteen-year-old self hadn't been able to keep his mother from stumbling drunk in front of a train. He'd begged her not to leave that night, but she had a boss who wouldn't go easy on her if she missed a trick. He'd vowed right then and there that he wouldn't let that happen to another woman if he could help it. The problem was, Sean wasn't very sure he was capable of saving even one.

He'd thought becoming a cop would help. What a delusion. The people of Five Points hated law enforcement, same as his mother had. Every day of enforcing the law was like swimming upstream in a raging river.

He glanced back to where Moira slammed a glass of beer onto the counter. What was really behind his wife's determination to hold on to a piece of jewelry at the expense of her life? She blamed her uncle for killing her parents. That should make her fearful of the man. Instead, she seemed to want to provoke him.

He saw Leah duck in through a back door. There was another concern. While she'd been saved from the fate of their mother, thanks to Moira, Leah's wildness kept Sean worried every moment of the day. He could very well lose the two women in his life. He sat there beaten and broken while they seemed determined to take over his job.

"Psst." Leah waved at him.

With a groan, he pushed out of his chair and joined her in the shadow of an alcove. "What in heaven's name are you doing here?"

"Chasing down Lambert. He's upstairs with Callahan. The two are plotting something." Her eyes flashed. "I thought you might want to know."

"I do. Can I get you to take a message to the precinct?" He grabbed a scrap of paper from a nearby table and with the stub of a pencil he kept in his pocket, scribbled down a message for help. "Take this to the captain. Tell him to make haste." He flipped a coin in the air, which she deftly caught.

Once she'd left, he stormed over to a table nearest the stairs and told the drunken man sitting there to get up and get out. He then pulled the brim of his hat low over his face and sat back to wait.

Chapter 6

W hat a waste of time." Sean nursed a cup of coffee after breakfast the next morning. "Callahan and Lambert must have been tipped off that the police were on their way."

Moira had seen her husband waiting at the bottom of the stairs and watched with trepidation as he'd thundered to the second floor behind the other police officers. Then she'd offered coffee all around when the officers tromped back down after finding out their prey had disappeared. "But who would have told them?"

He shrugged. "Maybe Callahan suspected something. Next time there will be men posted next to the fire escape."

She patted his shoulder, wishing she could do more to console him. "We'll catch them." What they needed was a trap. "I'll lure my uncle with the brooch. We can set up a meeting place. When he arrives, you can arrest him."

"If the plan fails, you've lost your mother's pin." He shook his head. "Things are going to escalate, Moira. I don't want you anywhere close when we bring him down." He put his hand over hers. "I couldn't bear it if something happened to you."

"It won't."

"It could."

"It won't." She sighed and refilled his drink. "Relax and trust in the God you pray to." The one she struggled daily to trust. As willful as Leah was, her faith was steady. As stubborn as Sean was, his faith was rock solid. Why couldn't Moira step back and let God serve justice on her uncle?

Still holding her hand, Sean stood. "Let's get out of here. Take a walk around the green area and get to know each other. Will you come?"

Face heating, she nodded. "I'd like to take a stroll with you." She grabbed her shawl on the way out the door. Maybe she'd get to know this man who was her husband a bit better.

With his hand on the small of her back, Sean kept her close as they strolled to the small grassy area designated as a park. It was nothing like the green of Ireland, but in the squalor of Five Points, it was as close to nature as Moira was bound to get.

Sean motioned to a crude bench. "Sit, please. Are you cold?"

She shook her head. "Not at all." How could she be when the look in his eyes as they rested on her heated her blood as hot as a coffeepot on the fire? How could she be chilled when she woke early each morning just so she would have the opportunity to watch him sleep?

She glanced up and their eyes met. His darkened. What would it take for him to kiss her? Silly girl. They barely knew each other, yet her heart rate quickened when he stepped through the door at the end of the day. Moira McGowan was a ninny. Would she really fall in love with a stranger at the slightest gesture of kindness? Yes. Kindness had been sadly lacking in her life for the last ten years.

Sean sat next to her, his shoulder brushing hers. "Tell me about growing up in Ireland."

"Da was away in London a lot, but the times were good when he was home." Tearing her gaze away, she stared across the lawn as a boy in patched clothing tossed a ball for a dog to chase. "If I close my eyes, I can imagine I'm there. We had a cottage near the sea, on a bluff overlooking the waves. My parents loved each other deeply, yet Da got involved in the wrongdoings of his brother. Out of obligation to help, I think. After a few months, he wanted out." She plucked at a string on her shawl. "Before the...accident... life was idyllic. I was very loved. We didn't have much, but love was something we had in abundance. Shortly after my parents died, Uncle Liam took me to London and later brought me here." She glanced up. "What about you?"

"I grew up here." He sighed. "I practically raised Leah. Sometimes, I think I did a terrible job. Our mother, a prostitute, was never home. She arrived on these shores lost and alone. When she died, I vowed to save as many women from her lifestyle as I could."

"Which is why you bought me."

"Yes." He took her hand in his. "I couldn't bear for any woman to be sold into that kind of life. And when I saw your spunk and determination in your uncle's pub, I couldn't bear to see that spark extinguished."

"Thank you."

The corner of his mouth quirked. "Really?"

She laughed. "Yes. I wasn't happy at first."

"I noticed. Are you happy now, Moira?"

"More than I've been in a very long time. You're a good man, Sean McGowan. You've a good heart. Don't despair. You did a fine job raising your sister."

"May I kiss you, Moira? I've wanted to for a very long time."

"Yes." She lifted her face.

He cupped her cheek with his good hand and tenderly kissed her. She sighed and leaned in, deepening the kiss. It was everything she'd dreamed in the early mornings as she watched him sleep.

Moira's lips were as sweet as a spring day. He wrapped his good arm around her shoulders and rested her head against him. "Thank you."

"Silly man. No reason to thank me for a kiss that I enjoyed."

He chuckled. "You just might be worth more than ten dollars."

She slapped his arm. "Of course I am."

They sat in the autumn sunlight and watched as lovers strolled hand in hand, loose women plied their trade, and pickpockets darted here and there. Not a place Sean wanted to raise a family someday. "Have you ever considered going west?"

"I have. I'd love to go to Oregon or California and feast my eyes on the ocean. I'd love to walk along a beach not strewn with waste. Why?"

"I thought maybe…when I'm finished with my job here…we could go." He straightened and searched her face for an answer. "Would you come with me?"

Her eyes widened. "I think I'd follow you anywhere."

A commotion to their left had Sean jumping to his feet. He stood in front of Moira, shielding her from two groups of men squaring off for a fight. "Go to the precinct and get help."

"I can't leave you here." She clutched his arm. "If they turn on you—"

"I'll stay here, behind the bushes. Hurry, before someone is hurt or worse."

She hitched up her skirts and raced away.

Now that Moira was out of harm's way, Sean crept closer to the two gangs and hunkered behind a bush within earshot. Callahan and Lambert were not there, but he'd bet his badge these were their gangs up to no good. He breathed a quick prayer for safety. Then he spotted Leah circling the shouting men.

He ought to ship her west right this minute. As soon as she ventured close enough, he grabbed her and dragged her into his hiding place. "What in tarnation are you doing?"

"Spying." She brushed his hands away. "Same as you, only I can do it in the open. Where's Moira?"

"I sent her to the precinct for help. What do you know?"

"Something big is going down. I think Callahan and Lambert had a falling out the other night. That crowd out there is not friendly. If they go to war, no one in Five Points will be safe. I've heard talk about a brooch that Callahan owes to Lambert."

Sean's heart dropped to his stomach. If Leah was right, Moira was in more danger than he'd thought, and he'd sent her off alone.

Grabbing his sister's hand, he led her away from the increasingly angry crowd. "We have to find Moira."

They made haste for the precinct. Sean's legs almost gave way with relief when he spotted his wife speaking to the police chief. Sean joined her, still keeping a tight hold on his struggling sister.

"McGowan, I didn't expect to see you out and about for a few weeks." The sergeant's heavy brows lowered.

"Some things can't wait. There's trouble brewing at the green area. A fight, most likely."

"So your lovely wife said." The sergeant gave a shout and several officers came running. "I doubt they'll be there when we arrive, but I appreciate the heads-up."

Sean nodded. "I'm getting my family home where it's safe. Please keep me up to date." He released his sister and pulled Moira close. "I was so worried."

"Why? I know my way."

"Leah told me she overheard Lambert telling your uncle that he wants the brooch."

She paled. "They both want the jewel."

"It appears so. We've got to get you somewhere safe."

"There is nowhere safe in Five Points. I'll turn it over. The two of them can fight over it until they kill each other." Tears welled in her eyes.

"I'm sorry, Moira. I know how much it means to you. Perhaps, once they're behind bars, you'll have it in your possession again." It pained him to see her so upset. "Forget it. I'll think of something else."

"There is no other way. I'm not the only one at risk here. You and Leah are in the same danger now." She stepped back and unpinned the brooch from inside her blouse. "I'll head to the pub to see if Uncle Liam is there."

"Not by yourself." With the two women flanking him, Sean led the way out of the precinct. Handing over the brooch wouldn't guarantee their safety, not with them knowing about the jewel, but it would help.

When they reached the pub, Moira asked him to wait outside.

"Not a chance. Where you go, I go."

She smiled. "Like Ruth in the Bible? I do believe those words should fall from my lips, not yours."

"As the time fits, dearest." He opened the pub door.

"I'll stand guard," Leah offered. "No one will pay me the slightest attention. If that rowdy crowd heads this way, or Lambert, I'll whistle a jaunty tune."

Sean didn't like the idea, but having someone keep watch was a good idea. "You run at the first sign of trouble."

"I will." She pulled her cap low and leaned against the brick wall.

Moira took a deep breath, her back expanding under Sean's hand. "Here goes everything."

Sean wished he had the funds to pay Callahan for the jewel, but that was a fool's dream. He had nothing to offer that would put a smile back on his wife's face. No words to say that would make her feel better about her decision. Instead, all he could do was pray that things would be all right.

Chapter 7

The thought of handing over the last piece she had of her mother caused Moira's stomach to churn. Who was she to think she had ever deserved something so priceless? If she had gone to town that day, none of this would have happened. Her parents would still be alive.

She couldn't do it. She glanced to where Leah waited on the other side of the door. Then, without a second thought, she walked through the pub and out the back door. The slums was large enough, crowded enough, she ought to be able to hide until she could purchase a ticket back to Ireland. Once Uncle Liam knew she was gone for good, he'd leave Sean and Leah alone.

The brooch hung heavy on her chest. A reminder that she left what promised to be a wonderful future with a man who might, in time, come to love her. Still, his safety was more important.

"Well, well." Uncle Liam ground a cigarette under the heel of his boot. "Have you come to give me what's mine?"

She startled then shook her head. "I've told you, I don't have a brooch."

"Then perhaps you have the pearl necklace? The diamond earrings? No?" His eyes hardened. "Oh, yes, my dear niece. I happen to know an emerald brooch wasn't the only thing your father kept from me. He was quite the able thief, you see. I know he left you in possession of the jewelry."

There was more? Her knees weakened. It was more imperative than ever that she escape Five Points. Her uncle would never believe the brooch was all she had.

"If you don't turn it all over to me, I'll kill your husband and give his pretty little sister back to Lambert." He grabbed her arm and squeezed. "Either way, I will get what is owed me."

"Please. On my mother's grave I don't know what you're talking about. What sister? What brooch?" Pain radiated up her arm.

"Don't play ignorant with me. You know exactly what I'm looking for. As for your husband's sister, you two were spotted sneaking in and out of the building together. Look harder!" He tossed her aside as if she were nothing more than garbage. "Make it quick, dearie. My patience is running out." He stormed into the pub.

A sob caught in her throat. She couldn't leave now. Either way, Sean and Leah were in danger.

Why did her uncle think she had more jewelry? *Oh, Da, what did you do?*

She got to her feet, brushed the dirt from her skirt, and rounded the building to where her husband waited. "I didn't give it to him."

"Why not?" Sean frowned.

"He thinks I have more." She gripped his good arm. "If I don't find the other jewelry, he'll kill you."

"Let him try." A muscle ticked in his jaw.

"Let's go west now, Sean. This very day."

He studied her. "We can't. Not until this is resolved."

He would die. As sure as the sun rose each morning, Uncle Liam would kill him. "I don't have what he wants."

"Maybe the brooch will satisfy him."

"He said he wants it all." She whirled and barged back into the pub. "Here." She ripped the brooch from inside her blouse. "I swear, it's all I have."

"You're a liar like your father." He took the brooch and dropped it into his pocket. "You have one day, Moira, to find the rest."

"How do I find something I don't have? I'm sure Da left them in London."

"For the sake of your husband, I hope not. The man has been a thorn in my side, trying to get clear evidence against an upstanding citizen such as myself." He smiled without humor and brushed an invisible speck from his brocade vest. "Hurry along, dear. You haven't much time."

She exhaled sharply and stomped from the pub. "I hope the gangs kill each other off and spare us the trouble," she said to Sean. She leaned against the warm brick of the pub. "Why did Da get involved?" What if Uncle Liam wasn't responsible for her parents' death? The more she learned, the less sure she was. If Da had been as good a thief as her uncle said, anyone with a grudge could have caused the accident. Maybe it wasn't her fault her parents died. If Da had stolen from the wrong person, they would have found a way to kill him. Then again, maybe the accident really was what it appeared to be—an accident. Was it possible she'd been trying to right a wrong that only existed in her mind?

She blinked away the tears pricking her eyes. Crying like a wee lass wouldn't bring her parents back. She needed to keep her new family safe.

But how? All she'd brought with her from Ireland was a large carpet bag and a cedar box the size of a loaf of bread. The box. . . She gasped. "I need to get home." She hiked up her skirts and dashed away.

The pounding of footsteps behind her told her Sean and Leah followed.

She burst into the apartment and pulled her things from under the bed. With the box in hand, she sat on the edge of the mattress and studied the design. Da had told her when he'd given it to her as a little girl that it was a magic box that could hold many secrets.

"What are you looking for?" Sean sat next to her.

"A hidden compartment."

"Let me see."

She handed the box to him. He ran his fingers along the sides and bottom. Finally, a small click and the bottom opened. Inside, nestled on green velvet, rested a pearl necklace and diamond earrings. Moira could save her husband.

"I have to take these to Uncle Liam."

"Wait. How long do you have?"

"A day."

"Let me talk to my captain at the precinct. Maybe we can set something up." He closed the secret compartment and planted a warm kiss on Moira's forehead. "I'll do my best to get your brooch back."

"We need to locate the owner of these."

"I'll send a telegram. Stay here. I'll return in an hour or so."

She nodded. "I'll have supper waiting." Her heart leaped at the look in his eyes.

He smiled. "We're nearing the end, darling." With a wink, he left.

Despite his soft words to Moira, Sean was finding it hard to believe she hadn't had a clue about the jewelry she'd brought with her. It was hard for him to believe that she hadn't known the depth of her father's transgressions. What kind of father put his daughter in the danger Moira had been thrust into? He couldn't shake the niggling thought that his wife knew more than she let on. She'd gone straight to the box after her visit with Liam. Who was the woman he'd married?

He shoved through the doors of the precinct and headed for the chief's office.

"I'm surprised to see you, McGowan." Chief Larson leaned back in his chair. "You can't return to work with a cast."

"I know." He sat in the chair across from his boss and explained the predicament. As he talked, the chief's eyes narrowed.

"Stolen jewelry. Are you sure your wife isn't involved more than she says?"

"I'm not sure of anything other than the fact she's willing to hand the things over. I was hoping we could use this to our advantage. Callahan will sell the jewelry, most likely to Lambert, to pay off his debts. If we can set them up, we can arrest both at the same time, recover the stolen items, and put two very dangerous men behind bars."

"How will we know where they'll meet? Every time we show up, they disappear."

Sean rubbed his chin. "We need someone undercover. A man that can infiltrate one of the gangs." Or maybe one Callahan already trusted. Would young Johnny be willing? It would be dangerous, but for the right reward, he might.

"I see from the look in your eyes you have someone in mind?"

"A young man that already works for Callahan. I'll let you know. We'll have to move fast." Sean stood. "I'll send a messenger to you."

After exiting the precinct, Sean headed to Johnny's tenement apartment.

The young man shook his head at the sight of him. "Why do you insist on coming here?"

"I can't talk to you at the pub." He pushed his way into the squalor. "I have a proposition."

"Not here. The walls have ears. Meet me in the alley behind the butcher in fifteen minutes. And for the love of Pete, don't let anyone see you leave my building."

Sean nodded and peered into the hall. All was quiet. He hurried to the designated meeting place and waited.

Johnny was right on time. After Sean explained what he needed, the young man stepped back. "You're trying to kill me. A bullet would be faster."

"Don't you want Callahan stopped?"

"Sure I do, but not at the expense of my life." He sighed. "But I'll do it for Moira. She's been kind to me. If I die, it's on your head." He scampered away, his back hunched under the ragged coat he wore.

Sean scribbled a note on a piece of paper from his pocket and paid a scruffy street boy to deliver it to the chief. There was nothing more he could do but hope and pray. Not quite ready to return home until he gathered his thoughts about Moira, he headed for the so-called park.

Finding a spot on an empty bench, he sat and stared across the area, his eyes not seeing, his mind focused on his wife. Could her innocent facade be real? *Lord, let it be real.* She'd been open and forthcoming about the brooch. Was it too many years as a cop that had him suspicious of her motives? He bowed his head and prayed that she was honest. He also prayed for Johnny's safety. Johnny was right. If anything happened to him, it would be on Sean's head.

Steps heavy, he headed home to question Moira.

The aroma of beef stew and baking bread greeted him at the door. Moira sat in a chair next to the stove, darning a pair of his socks. Leah's head bent over a book as she sat cross-legged on the floor. A homey scene he had no desire to ruin, yet his questions needed answering.

"Leah, could you give Moira and me a few minutes alone?"

She got to her feet. "Sure. I'll go check on Mrs. Ryan. She's been feeling poorly."

"Take my medicine box," Moira said, her eyes on Sean's face. "You're later than you said, husband."

"My apologies." He motioned for her to join him at the table.

"Did you and your chief come up with a plan?"

Sean nodded. He opened and closed his mouth several times, knowing his question would either wound Moira or push her away because of his distrust. He took a deep breath. "Did you know about the jewelry in your box?"

"No." Her brows lowered. "All I knew of was the brooch. It was my mother's. Of that I'm certain. She wore it pinned to her blouse for as long as I can remember. You don't believe me?"

"I find it hard to fathom that you could have come across the ocean with your uncle and not have known you had a fortune in your possession."

"If Uncle Liam had known, I wouldn't have had it in my possession." She pushed to her feet. "My da must have hidden it there for reasons that died with him. I'll never know why he put me at such risk, but I promise I had no idea the jewelry was in that box."

"You knew where to look easily enough."

Her face reddened. "It could only have been there or in the carpet bag. Supper's on the stove. Feed yourself." She stormed to the bedroom and slammed the door.

That didn't go well at all. Sean ran his hand through his hair. He had no choice but to believe she told the truth. With a sigh, he removed the bread from the oven and set it on the sideboard. He didn't need to add burning supper to his list of faults for the day.

He glanced at the closed bedroom door. He'd be sleeping on the floor next to the stove that night.

The bedroom door opened. Moira stormed out. "Apologize right this instant."

His heart lurched at the sight of her red-rimmed eyes. "I'm sorry. Sometimes my cop mind goes in directions it shouldn't." He held out his hand. "Please, sit and eat with me."

"Only because I'm hungry." Her gaze met his. "If I had known the other jewelry was there, I wouldn't have handed over the brooch so easily. I would have fought harder to keep what I had left of my mother. Don't you see, Sean? I turned it over to save your life. Not because I was hiding something else."

He was a cad. Plain and simple.

Chapter 8

Y ou want me to do what?" Moira planted her fists on her hips.

"Give the jewelry to Callahan then stay in the apartment while he meets with Lambert tonight." Sean drained his coffee.

"You're forbidding me to see this through to the end?" She couldn't believe the audacity. "By giving up all that I have, you can't seriously think I don't want to witness his arrest."

"What if there's shooting? You could be hurt."

"I'll take that chance. How about this? What if I tell my uncle that I'll give it to Lambert myself?"

"You aren't supposed to know about his financial state." Sean set his cup down with a definite thump. "I've been more than tolerant with your 'help.' I won't give in on this."

She'd see about that. She'd sneak out while he was at the precinct. One way or the other she would be there.

Sean stared, unspeaking for several seconds. "Everything you're thinking is showing on your face. Come with me."

"Where are we going?"

"To the precinct to speak with the chief."

She grinned. All it took for a woman to get her way with a man was for her to stand her ground.

She followed along as Sean marched to the police station and held the door open for her. Smiling at the other officers, she waited next to the reception desk while Sean disappeared down a short hallway. When he returned, another cop accompanied him.

"Turn around, Moira," Sean said.

"Why?" She frowned.

"I'm locking you up for impeding an investigation." He turned her so the other officer could cuff her.

"Are you serious?" Her voice rose. "You're putting me behind bars? I'm not the criminal here!"

"It's for your own safety." Her husband turned away and left her.

The other cop led her to a small cell, removed the cuffs, and motioned her inside.

Tears blurred her vision as she sat on the hard cot. Betrayal filled her, as bitter as medicine. Her throat tightened and she refused any water or food. She lay down on the thin mattress and curled into a ball. *Good luck, Sean.* A sad smile curved her lips as she shoved her hand into her pocket.

Sean sat on the edge of the bed. The jewelry was gone. The little minx! Where could she have hidden it?

The clock was ticking and he was at the starting point. . .again. He'd wring her pretty little neck.

Once he arrived back at the precinct, he marched straight to Moira's cell. At the sight of her curled up on the cot, he fought back the yearning to take her in his arms. If she'd only let him do his job, this would all be over.

"Where is the jewelry?" he asked.

"I won't say unless you release me."

"I won't release you unless you tell me." He could be as stubborn as she. In fact, his wife had no idea how he could stand his ground.

"Stalemate." She turned and faced the wall.

Sean rattled the bars of her cell. "Why are you being so obstinate?"

"Why?" She faced him. "I'm owed watching my uncle get what's coming. Even if he didn't kill my parents, he's still the reason my da worked on the wrong side of the law."

"Don't you think your father might have had some say in his job of choice? He couldn't be as innocent as you want to believe." *Nothing, absolutely nothing*, Sean thought, *would make me do anything unlawful.*

"What would you do to put food in your family's mouth? What if you and I had a child and she was starving? What if the only other choice we had was for me to sell myself?"

Oh. Maybe he wouldn't be much better than her father after all. "Did your father explain anything to you? Leave a note about the jewels?"

"You were there. All we found was the jewelry."

"I'll look closer. Maybe the answers to the questions in your mind are waiting for you at home."

"You do that." She looked away.

Sean groaned. The woman could be impossible.

An hour later, he returned, a sealed envelope in his hand. He held it through the bars of Moira's cell. "I found this in the lining of your carpet bag."

Moira rushed to take the envelope then ripped it open and read:

Dearest daughter,
If you find this, your mother and I are both gone and you are living with your
aunt. I realize you're little more than a child and may not understand. Inside the
magic box is some jewelry. I regret to say I stole it from the house in which I'm a
gardener. I intended to return it almost immediately, but Liam threatened to have
me arrested and you thrown into an orphanage. I fear he may plan to do us harm in
order to obtain the jewelry. I stole them because he was going to evict us. His own
brother!

Nevertheless, what I did was wrong. If you should find these things, please find a way to return them to the rightful owners with my apologies. Under no circumstances should you give them to your uncle.

Moira choked. Another lie from her uncle. He was never intended to be her guardian.

Your uncle is a bad man, daughter. He plans on heading someday to America where he vows to be a man of power. I've done my best to slow down his plans, but I fear I've failed. He will come looking for the jewelry. It's best you do not have it in your possession.

Your loving father

Tears rolled down her face as she folded the letter and tucked it into her pocket. Then she pulled out the jewelry and handed it to Sean. "My father did not want this to go to Uncle Liam. He wanted it returned to the people he stole it from. It doesn't matter now. This should have all been resolved ten years ago." She went and sat back on the cot. "You can go now. I'll be here when you return."

"Moira."

She wouldn't look at him. Every man in her life had done nothing but disappoint her. "Just go. Finish this."

His footsteps moved away.

She dissolved in tears. How could the burgeoning love she felt for Sean recover from such betrayal?

"Hey, Moira."

She looked up to see Johnny, face pressed to the bars. "What are you doing here?"

"Your uncle is coming. You have to get out of here."

"He's coming for me?"

Johnny nodded. "I heard him talking."

"You have to find Sean. He left a few minutes ago. I think he's headed for the pub. They won't release me without his say-so." Why would her uncle come there? The cops wouldn't let him take her, would they?

Loud voices sounded from the front of the building. "You have to leave, Johnny. They can't find you here."

Shots were fired. A woman screamed.

"Go, Johnny!" Moira stepped back from the bars of her cage.

He glanced behind them, then at her. With a nod, he raced in the opposite direction from where he'd entered.

With her back against the wall, Moira waited for her uncle to come. She wanted to pray, so badly did she want to. But God had turned His face from her years ago. She couldn't come to Him now. Not when she'd made no moves to reconcile with Him. She took a deep breath and kept her gaze locked on the opposite wall.

"My lovely niece. Behind bars." Uncle Liam laughed and pointed his gun at the head of a young copper. "Open the cell, my good man."

The officer inserted a key in the lock and pushed the cell open. "Sorry, miss." He ducked away.

"Even the coppers can be bought in New York." Uncle Liam smiled. "Now, where is my jewelry?"

"I don't have it."

"But you know where it is." He pointed the gun at her. "Don't you? Is it possible you gave it to your husband? Ah, I can tell by the look on your face he has it. Well, come along, then. We've a meeting to attend. You, my dear, are leverage."

Head high, she marched from the cell. "Where are we going?"

"Where all things happen in Five Points, of course. At the corner of Orange and Cross Streets." He pushed her along, past the bleeding receptionist and one dead policeman. Outside, his gang stood waiting. "I've brought my friends. See, I've no intention of turning the jewelry over to Lambert. But, as it seems your husband is most likely headed to see him, I've no other option but to see this through. Should we live through this, I'll give you back your mother's brooch and set you free. I've let you keep it all these years, and I don't need it once I have the necklace and the earrings. I'm not completely heartless."

"I hope you die." Moira marched through the waiting crowd. She spotted Leah with a group of other street kids. Hope leaped in her heart. "Did you say Orange and Cross Streets?" she asked loudly. Leah ducked down an alley.

"You heard correctly. Now walk."

Uncle Liam's gang followed as Moira moved ahead of the pack. If she slowed, she got jabbed with her uncle's gun. They reached the designated intersection. The street was empty, as if the residents knew a brawl was going to take place.

A woman in an upstairs apartment cast Moira a worried look before she pulled her shutters closed.

"The meeting has moved again," Leah said, running to where Sean waited in the Old Brewery. "Callahan took Moira from the jail. He's taking her to Orange and Cross."

Sean's heart leaped to his throat. His efforts to keep his wife safe had failed. He could no more keep her from harm's way than he could have saved his mother years ago. "How did he get to her?"

"His gang took over the precinct. Most of the cops were gone, but at least one is dead."

God help them. "Please stay back, Leah. I need someone to come home to."

"What you need is someone to watch your back. I'll stay on the outskirts, I promise. If I have the opportunity to grab Moira, I will." The hard glint in her eyes told him she wouldn't stay behind. He handed her the extra pistol in his waistband. "I trust you remember how to use this."

"I do."

"Then head to the pub and tell the cops waiting there to meet us at Orange and

Cross. Tell them to hurry."

Sean turned down Little Water Street then to Cross Street and over. By the time he arrived where five streets converged to one point, the rival gangs had squared off.

Right in the center stood Callahan, one hand gripping Moira, the other a pistol. Facing him was Lambert.

"You needed to bring your niece to this fight?" Lambert laughed and glanced at his men. "Can't come without a woman to give him courage."

"She doesn't have the jewelry," Callahan said. "I'm giving her to you to pay my debt."

Lambert grew serious. "She's a beautiful woman, but not worth the price of what you owe me."

"I'm good for it. I just need more time."

"You're out of time, Callahan. I'll take the woman and your head." He motioned for two men to move forward and take Moira.

"Wait!" Sean stepped around the corner. "I have what you want, Lambert. Let her go."

"So, the cop is willing to make a trade." Lambert drew the back of his hand down Moira's cheek. "She is quite lovely. Perhaps I'll take it all."

"Over my dead body." Sean clenched his fists.

Chapter 9

N*o, Sean.* Moira's legs threatened to give way. What was he doing? These men wouldn't think twice about shooting him. He should let her go. Maybe she would find a way to escape.

To her horror, her husband marched between the two gangs and held up the pearl necklace. "Let her go and it's yours."

Lambert laughed, the sound hard and cruel across the road they stood on. "You have the thickest head of any copper I know. We'll take the jewelry, your wife, and leave you in a heap on the pavement. Don't think because you wear that copper star that we won't shoot you."

"I don't think so." Uncle Liam stepped forward. "Take the woman, but the necklace is mine. You can have the earrings. My debt is paid." His men shouted taunts to the other gang.

Soon the air rang with their cries. The rioting mood was escalating, and Sean would be caught in the middle. Moira called to Lambert. "Let me speak with my husband."

Lambert's hard eyes clashed with hers. "You may join your husband, in fact. Women who are no longer pure don't bring top price. You have little value to me. It's your uncle you need to speak with. Otherwise, we'll take the jewelry by force. I'd hate to see that pretty face of yours marred because you were caught up in this. Once I've finished with your uncle, I intend to come for the rest of the jewelry." He shoved her toward Sean.

Sean, still clutching the necklace, wrapped his good arm around her and pulled her close. "What are you doing? You were safer over there."

"I was trying to save you." Now, they both stood between two increasingly angry gangs. "What do we do?"

"Stall until backup gets here. Most of the men are armed with knives. Pistols cost too much."

Her heart beat so hard she thought it possible it could be heard above the shouting men. How long until help arrived? "Let me talk to my uncle. Maybe I can diffuse the situation."

"Don't leave my sight." He gave her a squeeze then released her. "And whatever happens, do not leave this spot. If you do, I won't be able to find you."

Trying to be more courageous than she felt, she approached her uncle.

His eyes narrowed. His lip curled. "You won't change my mind. I've never had any use for you, the daughter of my brother. The man who tried to betray me."

She lifted her chin. "I've always known you held no fondness for me. I've also learned you were never meant to be my guardian. Take the brooch and go. Let Lambert have the rest. If not, you may not leave here alive." Regardless of his treatment of her, he was family. She didn't want to watch him die in the street.

"I'll not be the one dying today." He shoved her aside and motioned for the men with him to converge on the others. With shouts and knives held high, the two gangs charged.

Moira lost sight of Sean in the whirling mass of men. How could they tell who was friend or foe?

Several men, throwing punches, stumbled her way. She leaped to safety, pressing her back against a wall. A young boy peered from the open door.

"Get inside and lock that door!" Moira waved him back. At least most of the residents of Five Points had the sense to stay out of a gang war. No innocent blood should ever be shed over men's egos.

One of Uncle Lambert's men, hands wrapped around his bleeding middle, hit the wall and slid to the ground. "Help me," he said, his voice hoarse.

What should she do? Moira knelt next to him and pressed the hem of her skirt against his wound. From the amount of blood pumping from his body, he wouldn't live long. "I'll find help."

She stood and motioned to a woman peering from an upstairs window. "Do you have clean rags? Perhaps someone could bring me hot water?" If only she had her medicine box. Thanks to a kindly elderly woman in London, she had a few skills, but not enough to save the most gravely hurt.

Soon, white strips of linen rained upon her head. She took the longest piece and wrapped it tightly around the dying man's stomach. Maybe, if God had mercy, He would spare the fool lying at her feet.

God. Where was He in the madness ripping through Five Points as more men joined in the fray and more fell to the bricks, bleeding?

Where was Sean? She stood on tiptoes, until she spotted him off to the side in what seemed like a heated conversation with a man.

Following the order he'd given her to stay put, she dragged a fallen man from the chaos to tend his wounds. She bound a bleeding arm and watched in disgust as the man then darted back into the fight. Did they know why they were fighting? Did any of them expect a cent of the worth of the jewelry the two leaders fought over? Fools, every one of them.

The sun started to set, casting the area into shadows. As time passed, and Moira lost sight of her husband, she grew more fearful. Where were the other officers?

She stood and popped the kinks in her back as a commotion in the alley told her help had finally arrived, led by none other than Leah. Moira grabbed the girl's arm. "What took so long?"

"They'd been lured into a building and chained in. It took me a while to find a saw and hack my way through. Where is Sean?"

"In there...somewhere." Moira waved an arm covered in the blood of others.

Sean shoved the necklace into his pocket the moment the fighting broke out. It wasn't easy punching with one arm, but he managed to connect with a jaw or two in order to fight his way free of the melee. Unfortunately, he found himself on the opposite side of the street from where he'd last seen Moira.

He'd also lost sight of Callahan and Lambert. If those two escaped again, he'd give up. He'd have to go west without reaching his goal. He'd fail again. Still, he wanted a normal marriage with Moira, and not in the squalor and violence of Five Points. A life with her was far more important than spending more time in a city he detested.

Someone hit him on the back of the head with something hard. Then a knife jab to the side brought him to his knees. He pulled a knife of his own from his boot and turned, stabbing upward. Lambert's eyes widened before he fell, taking Sean down with him.

Sean squirmed his way free and got to his feet, staggering farther from the fighting. One gang leader down, one to go. Clasping his hand to the cut across his rib cage, he blinked away stars and tried to locate Callahan, praying all the while that Moira was out of harm's reach. He'd feel a lot better if he could see her face.

"I want that necklace." Callahan charged through the crowd, tackling Sean to the ground.

Sean's broken arm hit the pavement, sending pain shooting into his shoulder. He pressed his palm against the other's man chin and shoved his head back. Pulling his legs to his chest, he thrust Callahan off him and struggled to his feet. Knife clutched in his good hand, Sean circled the gang leader.

"You're losing a lot of blood, Copper." Callahan grinned. "All I need to do is let you dance around me long enough for you to pass out. Then I'll slit your throat and leave you lie."

"We'll see." Sean blinked away the perspiration running into his eyes. Callahan was right. He was growing weaker by the minute. He propped his shoulder against a wall, keeping his gaze on the other man. "I've still some fight in me."

"Brave to the end. Just like my brother. Did Moira tell you she wasn't meant to come with me?" Callahan laughed. "Another part of my great plan. But then, you so nobly purchased her from me. I wager you fell in love with your captive bride, am I right? If only she were here to see you die."

"I'm here." Moira, her hands bloody, stood behind her uncle, a broken board in her hands. "Step away from my husband."

"You don't have it in you to fight me, little girl."

"What about two of us?" Leah stood next to her and handed Moira an iron pipe to replace the board. "In Ireland we fight for what is ours."

Callahan shrugged. "Irish women never did learn their place." He pulled a derringer from inside his vest and pointed it at Sean.

Sean squared his shoulders and met Moira's wide-eyed gaze. He'd go to his death with her beautiful face the last thing he saw.

"No." Moira stepped forward, raising the iron bar. Before she could bring it down, three cops rushed forward to disarm her uncle.

Callahan pulled the trigger.

One of the cops fell.

He swung his gun hand back to Sean.

Moira let the bar fall, and her uncle crumpled to the ground.

Leah removed the gun from his hand and handed Moira a length of rope. Soon, the two women had the man trussed up like a hog for slaughter.

Sean slid to the ground. His wife was some woman.

"Sean? Look at me." Moira knelt next to him. "Keep your eyes open. Let me tend to your wounds."

"Get your brooch first, please. I'm fine."

"You silly man." She left him and rummaged through her uncle's pockets, emerging with the beautiful jewel.

"I want to make that into a ring for you," he said, doing his best not to lose consciousness. "Then you'll have something that symbolizes your old family and your new."

"I'd like that. Now hush." She tore a strip from her green petticoat and wrapped it around his waist. "Leah, find some men to help us get him home, quickly please. Now, Sean, where else are you hurt?"

"I took quite a knock to the head."

She ran light fingers across his scalp. "You'll need stitches. Stay awake."

"I can't." He closed his eyes. "Let me rest for just a moment."

"If you sleep, you might die. I can't have that." She slapped his cheek.

His eyes snapped open. "Cruel woman."

"That's right. I'll hit you harder if you close your eyes again." She glanced over her shoulder but not before he saw the worry in her eyes.

So, he was going to die. He sighed. "Kiss me, Moira."

She faced him and frowned. "What?"

"I want a kiss before I die."

Her eyes shimmered. "I won't let you die."

"Kiss me just in case God has other plans."

She leaned forward, pressing her sweet lips to his.

He tried to raise his arm to hold her close, but his limbs failed him. He sighed again and blackness took over.

Chapter 10

Moira wiped Sean's brow for what felt like the hundredth time. For two days he'd slept while her heart lost hope with each set of the sun. The magic box her da had left her held the jewelry in the hopes the authorities could locate the rightful heirs. Pinned now to the outside of her blouse was the brooch. Uncle Liam sat in jail awaiting trial along with those who had survived the gang fight.

"Our deal isn't complete, God. My love may still die," she whispered. Funny how she continued to speak with Someone she wasn't sure would listen. Since men had carried Sean home, she'd started talking to God, only to have the spark of faith that had shimmered with their kiss begin to fade.

"How's he doing?" Leah, now back to wearing dresses, carried in a tray with a teapot and two cups. "The doctor said there's no infection."

"It's the head injury that worries me." Moira gratefully accepted the cup of hot tea. "He spoke once of us moving west. I'd like that."

"A new adventure." Leah smiled. "Maybe I'll find a man worthy of me out there. One that can put up with my less than ladylike ways."

"I'm sure you will."

Leah stayed for a few more minutes then left to fix supper.

Moira set her cup down and rubbed her hands roughly over her face. *God, don't take him from me.* She leaned back in her chair and stared at her husband's face. Foolish man. Other than their wedding day, his face had sported bruises more often than not. Mostly on her account. "God, if You let him live, I'll not give him another moment's worry for the rest of his life."

"That. . .would be. . .boring, darling." Sean cracked open an eye. "You keep life. . . interesting."

"Oh, Sean." She sobbed and grabbed his hand, bringing it to her cheek. "You've had me worried for sure."

"It takes more than a knock in the head to finish me off. Help me sit up."

She hurried to prop pillows behind him. "Do you need anything? Tea? Toast?"

"Tea and you. That's all I desire." He closed his eyes for a moment then opened them again.

"I thought I heard a man's voice," the doctor said, entering the room. "It seems you'll live after all. Good job, young man." He took Sean's temperature and shined a light in his eyes then checked his wound. "A few more days in bed, and you'll be on the road to recovery."

"Thank you." Moira clasped the doctor's hands in hers. "More than I can say."

"My pleasure." The doctor nodded and left.

"It looks as if you owe God your part of the agreement," Sean said, holding out his hand. "I clearly heard you strike up a deal with our heavenly Father."

"I did." She squared her shoulders. "I intend to keep my word. Daily prayer and Bible readings. No more headstrong actions. I intend to devote the rest of my life to you and Him."

"While I love the idea, I have to say I hope you fail in regard to being headstrong." He brought her hand to his lips and kissed the center of her palm. "I didn't marry a meek woman, Moira. I rather like the one I wed."

She laughed. "I suppose there are all kinds of trouble out West for me to get into."

"With all certainty there is." He grinned. "Let me rest a bit more and then we'll make plans." He closed his eyes, keeping her hand folded in his.

She traced the lines in his palm, marveling at the strength of her husband. What a ninny she'd been to think her his captive. Oh, the trouble she'd caused in her course of wanting vengeance. She glanced at the wooden box. What would they do with the jewelry if there was no one left to claim it? Perhaps they could build something in the West to help immigrants like herself.

Now that she knew Sean would live, there was one more thing she needed to do. She collected her shawl and reticule, informed Leah she would return shortly, and then set off for the jail to confront her uncle for the last time.

He was clearly not happy to see her. "Ungrateful is what you are. I provided for you the last ten years, and now I'll hang for my trouble."

"You'll hang for your unlawful deeds." She folded her hands in front of her. "I've come to say my good-byes. We'll be heading west in the spring to begin a new life away from here. If no one claims the jewelry, we'll put it to good use helping the unfortunate in a new land. I pray that brings you a measure of peace."

"Peace? What is this religious talk? Have you found God?" His scornful laugh bounced off the walls. "I've heard it all now. A religious Callahan."

"Da believed, at least toward the end. I had hoped you would come to know God before your death."

"Not a chance." He turned away from her. "Have fun among the savages."

They were bound to be better than the years spent with him. "Good-bye, Uncle." She turned with a heavy heart, sending a prayer heavenward for mercy if God should see fit.

Sean sat up in bed, surprised to see his police chief sitting in the chair Moira had been in. "Hello."

"Good to see you're going to make it, McGowan. Thanks to you, we've shut down two gangs. Sure, more will pop up. I'd like to promote you, once you're up to the task."

"No, thank you, sir. I'm heading to California. Maybe I'll run for sheriff in a small town along the coast. I miss the ocean, and I'd like to raise my children in clean air." He pushed himself to a sitting position.

"Any place you settle will be lucky to have you." The chief grinned. "I heard talk of a young man named Johnny taking over Callahan's pub. Seems the rascal managed to squirrel away a pile of coins."

"That is good news." Sean grinned. "I'm glad to know he survived the fight."

"Well." The chief stood. "I'd best be getting on. I do hope you'll continue working until you leave New York."

"With pleasure, sir." Sean held out his hand.

The chief shook it and left, calling out a greeting to Leah on his way.

Sean took a deep breath, pulling against the stitches in his side. A new life with Moira. One where the ocean waves crashed against the shoreline and gulls screamed a warning when they walked too close. He glanced at the nightstand where his copper star rested. He'd managed to do some good wearing it after all. He smiled and called for Leah to bring him some soup.

"It's pleased I am to see you up and hungry." She brought him a bowl. "Do you need help?"

"Just give me something to set the bowl on and I'll manage."

She set Moira's wooden box next to him then set the bowl on top. "Don't spill it or I'll not live long enough to see the coast. Your wife does treasure that box."

To think he'd once thought her as guilty of theft as her uncle. Moira was very far from a criminal. He'd heard bits of conversation during his illness of how she'd doctored those injured in the fight, not caring that they were criminals or which side they'd fought on. She was more rare than the emerald she wore on her blouse.

"You're eating." As if his thoughts had fetched her, Moira strolled into the room, giving Leah leave to go.

"Do you still feel as if you're my captive?" His gaze searched hers.

She sat in the vacated chair. "A bit. It seems you've captured my heart, Sean McGowan. I hope you keep it enslaved for all the days left to us." She leaned forward and kissed him.

Epilogue

With his arm wrapped around Moira's shoulders, Sean glanced up at the run-down two-story building in front of them. "Are you sure you want to purchase this place? It will require a lot of work."

"It's perfect." She rubbed a hand over her rounding stomach. "There's a lot of room on the upper floor for us to raise a family, and the other two floors will provide rooms for women wanting to leave a life of prostitution. You'll be able to help women after all." Since every remaining heir of those Da had stolen the jewelry from were gone, Moira had sold it. They would use the money for good rather than the evil the theft had been intended for.

"We'll hire a cook and a maid. Send Leah to finishing school. I've heard they're all the rage in America." She smiled as her sister-in-law frowned.

"I'm not going off to some fancy school. I'm sixteen. Too old for more schooling." Leah glanced in the direction of the sprawling city. "I plan on finding me a wealthy man to marry so I can travel the world."

Sean laughed. "Always looking for the next adventure. Wasn't the wagon train here enough for you?"

"That's over with." Her eyes sparkled. "I've years ahead to discover new things. Just because you're ready to settle down and have bairns, doesn't mean I am."

Moira smiled. "Life has a way of changing a woman's mind. Watch and see. Some handsome lad will steal your heart one day."

"I'm not marrying for love. Money is the way to go." Leah skipped away from them, her hair lifting in the ocean breeze.

"That girl will be the death of me," Sean said.

"Not so much, dearest. I'm afraid the little one coming soon will be more than enough worry for you." She slipped her hand in his. "I want to feel the water on my toes. Will you come?"

"Anywhere you lead, darling."

Moira could never have imagined the happiness she felt at that moment. With a bairn kicking inside her, a man who loved her at her side, and a promising future...well, the last ten years almost seemed worth it. She glanced at the brilliant azure sky overhead where seagulls soared, and thanked her heavenly Father for his overwhelming gift.

"What are you thinking?" Sean smoothed a wayward strand of hair from her face.

"How lucky I am." She laughed. "I'd always thought the luck of the Irish had passed me by. Now, I realize I was looking in all the wrong places."

He turned her to face him, wrapping his arms around her waist and pulling her close. "Will you kiss me, Moira?"

"Another kiss before you die?"

His lips curled. "A million kisses before I die." He lowered his head and kissed her, and the seagulls screeched in song.

Dear Reader,

Being a descendent of Scottish immigrants, I've always been fascinated by the strength and fortitude of those who fled to America in search of a better life. So many ended up in the notorious slums of Five Points, finding out that life in the new world wasn't a lot better than where they'd come from.

I hope that Moira's story helps draw you closer to God when trouble strikes or things seem too hard to conquer. I pray that you lean on His understanding and let Him guide your paths. If you find yourself more like Sean, who carried a heavy burden for his neighbors, I pray that you let God help carry that burden.

Forge ahead into new worlds of your own knowing that there is One who walks beside you that will never leave or forsake you.

Blessings,
Cynthia Hickey

Cynthia Hickey grew up in a family of storytellers and moved around the country a lot as an army brat. Her desire is to write about real, but flawed characters in a wholesome way that her seven children and five grandchildren can all be proud of. She and her husband live in Arizona where Cynthia is a full-time writer. Visit Cynthia at www.cynthiahickey.com.

Love's Escape

by Carrie Fancett Pagels

Dedication

To my family: Jeffrey, Clark, and Cassandra Pagels.
And to Avis Fretz, who was a fantastic teacher,
encouraging and nurturing my childhood creativity.

Acknowledgments

To God—You know I couldn't do any of this without You. My husband and son, Jeffrey D. and Clark J. Pagels, for putting up with my writing life and supporting me in my efforts. Kathleen Maher, who is like an angel sent from God to help me with her amazing critique partnering, brainstorming, and fund of information! Julian Charity, Shirley Plantation's historian, for sharing with me about slaves being smuggled out of some plantations via caskets. Libbie and Mack Cornett for discussing her family's funeral home business with me and about the history of the Shockoe area in Richmond.

Thank you to my mother-in-law, Joan Pagels, for help with corrections during a very difficult time. God bless the 1K1HR Facebook Group members for support and encouragement, particularly Deb Garland, and the Pagels' Pals members. Thank you to Rebecca Germany for this collection's seminal idea, to Cynthia Hickey inviting me to join in, and to my editor, Becky Durost Fish.

Prologue

Charles City, Virginia,
1850

Today, Nathan Pleasant would put an end to Letitia's nonsense if he had to shackle her himself. His face burned at the uncharitable and wicked thought. If not enslaved, the beautiful young woman wouldn't be in the predicament of trying to escape her plight. But she must be more prudent. He scanned the fields of winter wheat as far as the eye could see. How did those slaves who simply ran without the benefit of a "conductor" manage? *They didn't.* Most were returned within a day of having escaped. A shudder moved through him and coursed to his broad hands. He tugged at the reins, slowing his bay mare. Birdsong rose above the gentle *clip-clop* of his horse's hooves on the hard-packed road, but did nothing to calm his taut nerves.

Ahead lay Burwell Plantation, its great house dominating the gentle hill. A mockingbird imitated the shrill of a child's tin whistle. Nathan pulled the reins to halt his mount and listened. Letitia had been careful so far. She'd shared her desire to escape only with him. But what if she became desperate and loose lipped? What if she mistook an evildoer for a helper? What if some human mockingbird imitated a conductor? *Dear God, help her.*

On each trip to the Charles City plantation, he'd managed to speak to Letitia alone, but only for a short while. But when she'd secretly accompanied the elderly Mrs. Burwell into Richmond, Nathan had been able to spend much more time with her. On the last trip, he'd insisted on accompanying them home, when their driver fell "ill" after spending a little too much time in Shockoe's taverns.

As he neared the plantation buildings, a groom ran up from the stable. After he handed off his mare, Nathan strode across the green to the big house. Today he'd tell Letitia his plan and urge her to do nothing to alter her circumstances until he could set everything in place. Would she trust him?

The scent of woodsmoke, ham, and spicy apples wafted from the kitchen house as he passed.

"Lettie! You gets back in here now, girl!"

Stiffening, Nathan turned to face the two-story brick building to his right. A slender, light-skinned servant stood framed in the entryway, her head covered by a bright cloth, her shabby dress too short over her bare feet. She met his eyes.

"Letitia?" His voice was barely a whisper, and she couldn't have heard him, for a plump, dark-skinned woman jerked her arm and pulled her back into the kitchen.

What was Lettie doing in the kitchen? And why wasn't she wearing attire suitable for her position as a house servant?

Sweat broke out on his brow. Visitors weren't normally allowed near the kitchen house. How would he speak with her?

"Mister Pleasant!" Burwell's eldest daughter, Phebe, bedecked in a blue-and-purple-striped gown, stood on the front porch, twirling a parasol over her dark head—unnecessary since she was in the shade of the portico's overhang.

When he joined her, Miss Burwell linked her arm through his and ushered Nathan inside. "Papa will be so glad to see you. Wants to thank you properly for bringing Grandmama home, and that slave girl, too."

"No trouble at all." At least for him. But had the Burwell women sensed something between him and Letitia? "Is your house servant now moved to the kitchen?"

Phebe cast a sidelong look at him. "We'd had enough of Lettie's uppity ways."

Nathan stiffened and averted his gaze, not wanting her to see his anger.

"Now Mr. Pleasant, why don't you tell me why you're *really* here?" Her coy voice irritated, yet never had he been so grateful for the vixen's misconstrued notion that he held an interest in her. But her jealousy of Letitia now put the one who he truly sought almost out of his reach. "A gentleman doesn't play all his cards at once, Miss Burwell."

Laughing, she twirled her parasol. "Why, Mr. Pleasant, does this mean you intend to court me?"

If it got him out there again and close to Letitia, he'd do it. But his gut rebelled.

When he didn't respond, she tilted her head back and laughed. "You'll have to fight David Bryant for that chance."

His shock must have shown on his face because she giggled. His closest friend had never mentioned an interest in Phebe and had his own plans. "Will Captain Bryant be bringing you out our way when he comes back into port?"

What game was Phebe playing?

Chapter 1

How dare the stars still light the night and the James River continue to flow, when the one who made Lettie's life bearable was gone? *Oh, Mama.* Lettie wailed again, catching her tears with her dirty apron. She sank down onto the oak bench, shoved against the plastered wall. The cool rough surface nudged through the thin cotton of her work shirt, but she didn't care. How much pain had her mother endured before she'd finally fainted? And then died, within hours. Lettie trembled and fisted her hands. Revenge should be hers—not the Lord's.

A candle flickered as a lithe figure descended the kitchen-house brick stairs. "You all right, Lettie?" Her friend Nestor extended a dark hand, and Lettie clasped it.

"No, I'm not fine at all." Wouldn't ever be again. Lettie hiccupped a sob. Her lovely mother was gone. But what good had her beauty brought? Her mother was far prettier than their mistress, and that had resulted in Mama being kept in the kitchen and never allowed inside the house. Lettie had been proclaimed better looking than the Burwell daughters, who continually sought to insult her or get her in trouble. But it was their wicked overseer who'd brought about her mother's downfall, despite the master being the one who had allowed the whipping.

The fellow slave girl sat down beside her. "It ain't right what they done. You knows it, and I do, too."

"No, it was evil." A knot had formed in her throat, and she choked with emotion.

Nestor set the candlestick down and pulled her into a shivering embrace. "What you gonna do, Lettie? About that overseer?"

She shook her head. If she could, she'd kill Durham in his sleep. But with Satide likely sleeping right in there with him, she daren't try.

"You think Satide mean what she say?"

Satide was the overseer's favorite slave and his mistress. Which had given the young woman powerful sway over him—except when it came to other slaves he wanted to subject to his perverted desires. Only Mama and Satide's influence had stood between Durham forcing Lettie to come to his cabin once she'd been moved out of the big house. Before then, she'd been protected. He'd never have dared grab her in the house.

"I don't know." Lettie sniffed and wiped at her eyes. With Mama gone. . ."

"Satide was right about what nasty ol' Durham would do first." Nestor's eyes widened. "She say he gonna get your mama out of the way."

Lettie sucked in a hard breath and held it, before releasing a slow exhale, willing herself to chase away the terror that Satide's words had brought her. "But Master Burwell allowed it."

"I hear it was the missus who gave Durham permission."

"No." Lettie had been delivering a pot of tea to the master's office and was in the hidden alcove outside when the overseer had stomped in, bellowing about her mother and her supposed defiance. Lettie should have done something. She should have gone in and contradicted Durham. Should have. . .

Nestor's eyes filled. "Well, you gonna die, then, girl, just like your mama done, 'cause I know you ain't givin' yourself to that piece of trash."

A long shudder coursed through Lettie. She was going to die. Just like her mother had. Lettie would refuse him. Then he'd concoct a story about her, lie to the master, and that would be the end of her, too. She sobbed.

"Girl, don't even think about givin' yourself to him, 'cause Satide already say she gonna stick a knife in your heart if you lie with her man."

Lettie dug a rag from her apron pocket and blew her nose. This had been the only home she'd ever known. The kitchen house stood northeast of the big house. The brick building, with its two stories, would be a beautiful home if she were free. But Letitia wasn't. She was Mr. Burwell's slave. As had been her mother. But Parkes was Mama's surname, taken from old Mr. Parkes who'd first owned her. The only reason her mother hadn't been tossed in the ground like dirt was because of Mr. Parkes, who'd sent his boy over to tell the Burwells he wanted Mama buried on his property.

"I hear Mr. Pleasant gonna put your mama in a fine box."

"Mr. Pleasant?" Hope nudged its blossom upward, pushing aside her soul's hardened soil. She might have one day, maybe two, before Durham would come looking for her, if she was lucky. When Nathan Pleasant heard of her plight, would he make his offer again?

"That's what I heard. Ol' Mr. Parkes, he gonna pay for it."

Her heartbeat skipped and jumped. "Nestor, make me a promise."

"What?"

Lettie pressed a hand to her chest. "When Mr. Pleasant arrives, come and get me no matter where I am."

Nestor nibbled her full lower lip. "I do my best, but there's a new girl comin' tomorrow, too, I heard."

"Oh?" They were replacing Mama already? Lettie frowned.

"The Dolleys' town girl—whose fancy owners treated her like she their own child."

"Not Beneida?"

"That be her name."

"But she was supposed to be freed." The last time Lettie had seen her, Beneida confided she planned to get free in England, when her owners were there. But the Dolley family had recently returned with her in tow. "Her owner just died. He said—"

"It don' matter what he said—only matters what be. And she be sold to Master Burwell."

What heartache her friend must be suffering. And what danger Beneida would encounter with Durham once he caught sight of the young woman who outshone all the beautiful belles in Virginia. They had to get out of here. *But Lord, how?*

Pleasant Funerary, Richmond, Virginia

Nathan paced the outer corridor's stone floors, eyeing the scuff marks of the many who'd lived, and died, over the years. White people. But in the back—that was a different matter. Not one of their white patrons suspected that an Underground Railroad link stood right under this roof. And more would be freed soon, if the new coffin design worked. He and his brother Jules would be convincing some wealthy Virginians to purchase a much more elaborate coffin, one that possessed a secret compartment.

The interior door to the blue-and-gold wallpapered viewing room opened, and his father slipped out. At sixty-five, Martin Pleasant's face glowed with good health. Father clapped Nathan's shoulder. "Have you set up the viewings for the Alderman family?"

"Yes, sir. All taken care of."

"Good." Father stroked his clean-shaven chin, beneath his heavy white mutton-chops. "And you'll be going out to Burwell's in the morning?"

"Yes, sir." He must see Letitia again while he was there. But he had to be very careful. The Burwell Plantation in nearby Charles City was home to the woman who'd turned his life upside down from the first time he'd met her, thinking Letitia was one of the master's daughters. Never had he laid eyes on so beautiful a creature. So comely. With a lovely heart-shaped face. When he'd been informed the angelic girl was, in fact, a slave, his notions of what his life would be like had turned upside down.

Behind them, one of the entry doors opened.

Father's quickly affixed "funeral home" face slipped off, and he quirked an eyebrow. "David. Welcome."

Nathan turned to find David Bryant, hatless, his dark hair shooting in a dozen different directions, his ascot askew. "Have you a moment for a friend?"

Father gave a quick nod of approval and headed off toward the office.

"Are you unwell, David?" Nathan gestured for his friend to go into the casket room.

"No." The boat engineer's voice was hoarse. "Beneida has been sold."

"What?" Nathan's hushed voice flew out as a hiss. "But she was to be freed." And she and David were to run off together, if his friend had his wish. A heavy weight settled in Nathan's chest as he opened the walnut-paneled door and stepped into the very room where Beneida's mistress had just that morning selected a casket for her husband.

He closed the door behind him. "What happened? Where is she going?"

"She's been sent to Burwell's."

"Oh, Lord, be merciful." He knew what a hard taskmaster Burwell was and that his overseer was notorious for brutality. Nathan pressed his eyelids closed. Rebellious notions of rescuing Letitia, fed by seeds of David's discontent and plans to one day begin a new life with Beneida, had blossomed in Nathan months earlier. But Letitia had rejected his plan as being too dangerous. He'd vowed that the next time he saw her he'd disclose his family's part as conductors in the Underground Railroad.

"I believe the Lord is telling me to act, Nathan."

He met his friend's dark eyes. "What are you thinking?" He and Father had discussed a plan to get David's sweetheart onto a ship, but then Beneida had gone to England with the Dolleys, and they'd shelved the notion.

"I want to go out to Burwells and buy her contract."

Nathan couldn't stop the curt laugh that burst out of him. "You know Burwell would never do that. What is *his* is always his."

David ran a broad hand beneath his vest, over his heart. "I gave Beneida money to escape when she was in England. Told her to disappear into the countryside."

"But she returned. Why?"

"She couldn't get out... hadn't been able to sneak past Lord Armstrong's household manager." David groaned, sweat breaking out on his brow.

"I'm sorry. She thought she'd be freed."

David's dark eyebrows rose high. "And now she isn't. So I need your help."

"How so?"

"You asked me to pay a visit to Phebe Burwell, didn't you?"

"Yes, but—"

The door to the room opened. Father slipped in, closed the door behind him, and blinked at Nathan. "I've just gotten word that you'll need to travel both to Burwell's place and then to Parkes's."

"Did he pass?" The frail elderly Mr. Parkes had once been a terror to both his family and his slaves, but in his elder years he'd become more active in his church parish. He was one of the few voices in Charles City calling for a change to utilizing freemen working the fields. His neighbors expressed that they believed he'd lost his reasoning abilities but Nathan believed the man was finally coming to his senses.

"No, son. It's a little complicated." He cast a glance between the two men. "He asks for the Burwell's cook to be transported to his land."

"Cook?" Letitia's mother was their main cook.

"She was beaten badly and died."

"Oh, no." What did this mean for Letitia? Would she change her mind and take a chance? How she must be grieving. If only he could go to her sooner than in the morning.

"Mr. Parkes said to spare no expense for the casket."

Nathan and David exchanged a look. The Burwells' cook possessed the same emerald-green eyes that Parkes had.

"Said Burwell wouldn't return his daughter to him in life. But Mr. Parkes said he'd go through hell and high water to bury her at his place."

Nathan swallowed. Would there come a day when love alone, and not one's skin color, could allow people to marry whom they willed? And for slavery to be outlawed?

Father cleared his throat. "Did you show David the newest design?"

"Not yet."

Six coffins were lined up in the room, with the newest, finest one prominently displayed. Father gestured to their creation—what might prove to be the way to smuggle slaves to freedom.

"Isn't it beautiful?"

David ran a hand over the glossy, dark wood. "The walnut is superb."

"And extra cushioning with deep satin pillows." Nathan pushed against the sides and bottom of the casket.

"Stained a rich dark color, too." David patted the casket, bending low. He circled the base.

Father crossed his arms. "The air holes have to be pushed out from the inside. They're only partially cut."

"Genius."

"So they're not visible on the outside." Nathan took a few paces, trying to pull his plan into better formation.

"And once pushed free, there is dark cloth behind the small holes so they won't be easily detected." Father grinned.

But with only one hidden compartment, how could they get both Beneida and Letitia out? Nathan swallowed back bile. Letitia had continued to occupy his thoughts, despite the impossibility of a relationship between the two of them. David, edging up on thirty, had waited all these years for Beneida to be freed. With only room for a single soul to escape, must one couple's happiness and freedom be forever sacrificed?

Chapter 2

The stench of slave broker Hiram Cheney's tobacco, sweat, and alcohol was only intensified by his heavy use of bergamot oil. Lettie held her breath as she backed away from the open entryway, through which the paunchy man was shoving Beneida, the Dolleys' servant. Lettie released a gasp. She'd met the beautiful young slave several times—the first time when Lettie accompanied old Mrs. Burwell to see her dressmaker in Richmond.

Today Beneida wore a pink-and-yellow-checked day dress that was as fine as any Virginia society belle's. Lettie pressed a hand to her throat. She couldn't voice her question: What was Beneida doing in their kitchen?

"Where's Burwell?" The irksome man pulled a heavy watch from his purple-and-sky-blue plaid vest.

Lettie backed up to the kitchen window and startled when her apron strings tapped against the glass.

Nestor dipped a little curtsey and ducked her head. "He where he usually be, Mr. Cheney. Up in the big house."

The man grinned, his pockmarked ruddy face one Lettie had encountered in her nightmares. The other slaves told stories of the man as though speaking of the devil himself. No one wanted to be taken from Burwell Plantation by this man and sold elsewhere. Who knew what all he would do before they ever reached their destination?

"Why, lookie here." He chucked Nestor under her chin. "Things has worked out fine for ya here, ain't they?"

"Yes, sir."

Lettie must have been staring, for Cheney growled as he looked at her. She quickly glanced away and moved from the window to the stove.

"I'd say I was sorry about your mama, Lettie, but I ain't a man to lie." He patted the pockets of his burgundy coat.

She chewed her lip, willing the tears to stay put.

"Fact is, I was surprised it ain't happened earlier."

"Mr. Cheney, you want to try my new sugar biscuits?" Nestor's voice was tight.

Lettie heard the man's boots ground into the brick floor. "Why, if I had more time, I'd gladly savor some of your sugar biscuits, Nestor."

Lettie cringed at the insinuation in the insufferable man's voice. Beneida's sniffles carried from the corner.

"But I got to hand off this handsome gal and git on back to Richmond afore the boat departs. Got me a hundred. . ."—he used a derogatory term that set Lettie's teeth on edge—"to take down to Charleston."

Lettie turned to cast a sideways glance at the man, who was touching Beneida in an all-too-familiar manner. "Just remember your place and don't be puttin' on no fancy airs here, girl, and Miz Burwell might keep you."

As beautiful as the young woman was, who knew what shame Beneida would know at this plantation? Or had already suffered at Cheney's hands. Mama had somehow been able to keep the young Burwell men from her and had prevented Durham from getting near her, but now. . . Tears flowed down her cheeks, and Lettie bent to stir the stew simmering on the hearth.

"Goin' up to the fields. Burwell wasn't at the house when I stopped." Cheney spit a glob of tobacco onto their clean kitchen floor. "Wipe that up, girl."

He pushed Beneida toward the filth. When she hesitated, he kicked her. "Use that fancy gown of yours. Ya won't be wearin' it here."

Beneida grabbed a handful of the taffeta fabric but found what Lettie knew—the stiff fabric wouldn't pick it up—it merely smeared the foul substance around.

Spinning on his heel, Cheney cackled as he heavy-footed it out of the kitchen.

Lettie whooshed out a breath. She grabbed a wet rag and brought it over to wipe up the tobacco clump.

Nestor offered their newcomer a hand up. "You be Beneida?"

"Yes."

Lettie bent and wiped up the dark stain. If only life's messes were that easy to clean up. If only God could blot out the sins of men and restore them to right reasoning. Would they realize enslaving people was wrong?

"I heard about you." Nestor plucked at her shabby gray cotton skirt, beneath her stained apron.

"How so?" Beneida nibbled her lower lip.

"Lettie say you gonna be free. That you go to England."

Her oval face paled. "I did. But we returned. Mr. Dolley died. And his wife sold me to the Burwells." Tears streamed down her face, and little Nestor patted her arm.

Beneida stared out through the windows. "I've never lived anywhere but in town."

Lettie followed her gaze. Outside, well-muscled field slaves pushed carts of produce to the back of the kitchen house. A number of men sat on the ground by the well, drinking their fill of water before they headed back. Across the yard, female slaves carried baskets of laundry atop their heads and into the laundry building. Smoke curled up where huge pots of water boiled for the task.

Chauncey Burwell rode up the center lawn astride his white gelding, waving his hat high. He circled the square, and the kitchen workers all quickly turned their attention to chopping vegetables on the counter. Even Beneida picked up a knife, in pretense.

"You look ridiculous in that outfit, in here." Lettie pointed to the hall.

"Everything I brought in my bundle is this fancy or more so." Beneida gingerly fingered the glossy bow on her right shoulder.

"I've got extra clothing upstairs you can use."

"She got more problems than clothing if she stay here." Nestor pointed toward the overseer, who was ducking into the laundry building. Where he had no business to be.

Sweat rolled down Nathan's neck into his ivory linen cravat as he brought the Pleasant Funerary's conveyance to a halt midway up the Burwells' circular drive. "You go up to the house and distract them while I speak with Letitia and explain our plan."

A muscle in David's cheek jumped. He looked as nervous as Nathan felt. "All right."

Slipping from the wagon, Nathan jogged up the stairs of the kitchen house. To the right, several women worked chopping vegetables. Letitia bent over a board, her face wan and tear-streaked.

The scent of onions caused his eyes to water. *That must be it.*

The beautiful woman looked up and gasped. "Nathan?"

"Can I get a cup of water?"

She wiped her hands on her apron and grabbed a tin cup and headed toward him. What would it be like to grab her up into his arms and carry her off? Wasn't that what he was about to do?

A dark-haired woman, attired in a dress more suited for the drawing room, swiveled to face him. "Mr. Pleasant!"

"Good day, Miss Dolley." How strange to act as though all was normal. As though they were in town and he'd passed her in the street.

Lettie joined him and pressed the cup of water into his hands, their fingers touching briefly. She looked up at him, pleading in her eyes. How he longed to comfort her. She broke the connection and turned to face a short servant behind her.

"Nestor, would you please finish your chopping out back for a moment?"

The younger woman scooped up her bowl, a knife, and a small board and passed them, eyes downcast.

"I trust her, but we need privacy, don't we?" Lettie's breathy words stabbed his heart. "Oh, Nathan, I'm not safe here."

"I know, that's why we're here."

Beneida stopped chopping. "Is David here?"

"He's at the big house right now."

"Oh!" She pressed a hand to her mouth.

Taking Lettie's hand, Nathan led her out to the passageway between the two large rooms on the building's first floor. He'd already closed the front entryway door on his way in, so they were less likely to be seen.

"Thank God you're here, Nathan. Praise be to God." Tears rolled down her cheeks.

"I know about your mother." He took her hands and rubbed his thumb over her knuckles.

"But do you know who and why?" The pain in her eyes made him long to soothe it away.

"We heard rumors."

Letitia's thin cotton dress shook in ripples as she trembled. "The overseer is straight from the devil."

If he could, Nathan would pummel the man. But such would not be tolerated. "We have to get you out of here. We don't have a lot of time, so listen."

"All right."

"Mr. Parkes has paid for your mother to have a special casket and to be transported to his plantation for burial."

"No wonder, then, that they put her there"—Lettie's lower lip quivered—"in the icehouse."

"But you're coming with us."

"How?" Someone in the next room sang a spiritual in a low voice.

"You'll accompany me to get your mother's body."

She nodded. Chopping noises in the adjacent preparation room made her flinch.

"Then you'll slip into the back of the wagon."

"All right."

"Then you'll climb into the bottom of the casket."

"What?" she lifted her head and raised her voice.

"Shh!" Nathan squeezed her hands. "Do what I say and all will be well."

"Lord Almighty knows I'm gonna die here if I don't do somethin' quick." Letitia released his hands and swiped at her tears.

"We're trying to get Beneida out soon, too."

"If you take me, you gotta take her, too, or that overseer will have her, he will."

How Nathan longed to hold Letitia, to assure her. "We have to see what we can do."

The front door to the building opened and a young slave carried in a basket of kitchen rags and towels. Letitia took the willow basket from her. "Thank you."

Without a glance at Nathan, the servant turned and departed, leaving the door open to the cool river breezes.

Wagon wheels rolling over the crushed oyster shell drive sounded outside.

A fine burgundy coach stopped in front of the kitchen. Letitia took several steps, her thin shoes' soles shuffling over the brick floor. She leaned out of the door frame then returned to his side.

"It's Master Parkes, my Mama's father, if rumors be true." She nibbled on her lower lip, as if resisting saying more.

No wonder the man had requested the body, which would otherwise have been ignominiously thrown in the ground by the Burwells. "Thank God for his mercy."

"What?" Letitia blinked at him.

This wasn't the time to get into conversations about masters sleeping with their servants. But blast the man. Parkes could disrupt their entire plan.

"Let me go out to him." As he turned, Nathan spied David exiting the house, frowning. Nathan gestured for David to join him as Letitia scurried off to the kitchen. David jogged across the lawn.

"Seems Miss Burwell only told you we were courting to see if you'd inform me." David gave a lopsided grin. "But now I have an invitation to return."

"Won't be doing that."

His friend's dark eyebrows drew together. "Did you see Beneida?"

"Right." He rubbed his aching jaw. "Plan B. We need to get Beneida out of here, too."

"Today? How?" David fixed his gaze on Parkes' carriage.

He drew in a deep breath. "I don't know. But God does. And we need Him now more than ever."

From the kitchen, Lettie eyed the Pleasants' hearse wagon. They'd have to take it to the icehouse for Mama's body. She let the tears run down her face then wiped them with the back of her hand. A hand as pale as any of the Burwells'. And now she knew why she'd resembled them so much. Which made her father's betrayal all the more cutting. He'd allowed Mama to be whipped to death to put an end to his wife's nagging that she didn't want her or her daughter there on the property. Could she blame Mrs. Burwell for not wanting to accept her husband's behavior and the result of his sin—her, Lettie?

But she had to get Beneida out, too. How could she do it? That girl wouldn't last at Burwell Plantation for more than a few days. Too beautiful for the big house, too incompetent for the kitchen, how would the woman—who should have been freed—last in the fields? How long before Durham made her his next target?

Lettie moved into the opening to the preparation room, which now held a dozen slaves preparing for the midday meal, hoping to catch Beneida's eye. With her mother now gone, and no one really in charge yet, Lettie clasped her hands at her waist, as Mama had done, and stood, shoulders squared. "You come on with me now, Beneida. I got work for you elsewhere."

The others quickly raised their eyes in disbelief but resumed their efforts when Lettie gave them a curt nod.

The newcomer dragged her knife across the chopping board, pushing cut carrots into a large blue bowl, then set the bowl atop the table, wiped her hands on her apron, and joined Lettie.

Turning, Lettie led the woman upstairs to their rooms. "If you have anything at all you need to take with you, stow it on your person now."

"Why?"

"We leave soon." Heart hammering, Lettie pushed open the rickety door to her room. It squeaked in protest. She was lucky to have a door.

Beneida hauled up a canvas bag from beside her pallet.

"You can't take all that. It won't fit in a casket, I'm guessing."

"What?" The other woman's squeaky voice grated on Lettie.

"I'm already shaking in these here house shoes, so don't make things worse."

Beneida bobbed her dark head and pulled a few things from the bag. "Where are we going?"

"Don't know." Lettie scanned the room, dizziness threatening. *Be strong.* She had nothing of value. She examined the window's ledge where a string of the Burwell girls' cast-offs trailed. Once she'd thought the silvery button, the piece of yellow ribbon, the bit of lace, the satin rosebud all treasures. Not now. She had nothing. Except her mother's love. God may have let her down, but no one could take Mama's love away. At least she had that. She turned on her heel. "We need to go."

The two women rapidly descended the stairs and then exited the back. "Keep your head down," Lettie cautioned, as they passed two of the Burwell sons.

With Beneida's beautiful hair wrapped around her head and covered in a turban, she almost blended in. Could they get past? The James River's breeze carried the brackish scent of the water and the promise of spring.

"You there. Lettie!" Hampton Burwell called out half playfully, half in earnest.

"Keep going, Beneida," Lettie ground out between clenched teeth. She squeezed the other woman's hand, and then her friend continued on toward the icehouse.

Grief suddenly washed over her, with the fear that one of these young men, her actual blood brothers, might inquire about Beneida. Might plan to. . . She forced the horrible images from her mind. "Yes, sir, Mister Burwell."

Keeping her eyes to the ground, she waited. Birds tweeted to one another nearby, some chirping in a sound so cheerful it set her teeth on edge.

"Come here." The elder of the two drew in a deep intake on a cheroot and then exhaled, the scent of tobacco carrying on the light river breeze.

She would leave here. She'd die trying. She'd get into a casket, despite her fear, if it meant the end of this constant agony of the never knowing. The never knowing of when someone might strike her, as had been done the previous spring when she'd not immediately obeyed one of the other brother's commands.

"Is the new girl fitting in?" Reilly Burwell's voice was hard and cold, sending a shiver through her.

"Yes, sir, she is."

"Good."

She lifted her chin slightly and saw the two men exchange a glance. "We've told Durham to leave you alone."

She sucked in a breath.

Hampton placed a smooth finger beneath her jaw and lifted. His eyes were the same icy blue as his mother's. "So have no worries."

Reilly tossed his cheroot stub to the dirt and ground it out beneath his heel. "We told him the new girl was his."

Beneida. No. Dear Lord, no. Face hot, Lettie forced herself to nod in understanding.

"Go on, now. Help Mr. Parkes and that undertaker get your mama out of here."

Again, she nodded and turned, fighting the tears and the urge to run.

Nathan listened, mouth agape and disgust mounting, as Letitia explained in detail what would happen to Beneida if she didn't get into the false bottom of the casket. Letitia had been silent since he had suggested that she hide in the back of the wagon beneath some burlap sacks and hay.

Beneida stood behind the wagon, shaking like a dogwood tree in a hurricane.

"I can't do it." The beautiful woman clasped David's lapels, but he pushed her away and grasped her hand.

"You have one minute before I stuff you in there myself." His friend sounded serious.

To Nathan's surprise, David pulled a flask from his coat pocket and handed it to his sweetheart. "Here, take a few swigs."

David pressed the silver flask into her trembling hands and Beneida gulped greedily, eyes closed, before handing it back and wiping her mouth.

"Get in." David did sound like a captain, with that stern voice.

Beneida climbed up on the back of the wagon and then crawled into the bottom of the casket, before Nathan joined David and lowered the top section.

Then the two men set about transferring the chill, blanket-covered form of Burwell's deceased cook from where she'd been laid in the icehouse. In death, her face was serene, reflecting a peace she'd likely never known in this life. How could God allow this travesty to continue?

How can man?

The two men carried the body to the wagon, set it gently into the top portion of the box, and then closed the casket.

Letitia stood, arms clasped across her bosom, trembling from head to foot. She stared at them, as though unseeing.

"We must go." Nathan pointed inside.

When she made no move to join them, Nathan jumped down from the wagon, heart pounding. They had to get out of here before anyone noticed the two women had not returned to the kitchen.

"You have to get in."

Letitia shook her head.

"You must jump up in the back."

"No she doesn't." A commanding, but tremoring, voice sliced the chill air.

Heart sticking in his chest, Nathan whirled around.

Chapter 3

Lettie bit back a cry as silver-haired Rushworth Parkes stabbed his cane into the hard-packed dirt floor, covered with straw, and lurched forward toward them. As he neared, he pointed to her. "My eyes were once as green as yours."

Lettie returned her gaze to the ground, hadn't realized she'd been staring at the man who was purported to be her grandpappy. But she'd taken in his frail appearance quickly: large feet like Mama and she had, large hands like Mama, tall if he could straighten.

The man shuffled nearer, both Nathan and Mr. Bryant closing up the casket. Beneida's soft sobs carried out.

Mr. Bryant tapped the side. "Hush now, Beneida."

Dry, paperlike skin covered the fingers that lifted Lettie's chin. "You're so beautiful—the image of my mother."

No wonder Lettie had never been allowed in the house when the Parkes family had visited. She'd relished those times when she and Mama had stayed upstairs in the kitchen house, out of view.

The elderly man's eyes were filmed over with age. "Even with my bad eyes, I can see your hair is the exact shade of auburn mine once was." He fingered a stray curl by her ear.

Nathan jumped from the wagon and joined them. "We best get going Mr. Parkes."

This man, her grandpappy, extended an arm to Lettie. "She rides with me."

"Sir. . .please." Nathan's eyes widened in dismay. "We can't do that."

"Better ride right out in front of their noses." The elderly man slapped his hat back on his head. "Any of these wicked Burwells try to stop me, I'll shoot 'em dead."

When he patted a bulging pocket, Lettie understood that he meant his words.

Mr. Bryant closed up the wagon and hopped down. "Clever idea, sir. Capital!"

"What?" Nathan's eyes narrowed into slits. "It's ludicrous."

Bryant wiped his hands together. "No. Mr. Parkes can say he demands for Lettie to be there."

"Exactly." Mr. Parkes tugged Lettie's arm. They moved forward, the straw crunching under the thin soles of her house shoes.

So soon, Lettie found herself riding beside Charles City's notable plantation owner, clinging to the bench as the man drove at a breakneck speed over the ruts of the country lanes. They drove past Burwell Plantation, the overseer scowling and yelling something at them, but her grandpappy didn't slow at all, instead hooted in glee. "He'll be dead before morning."

Lettie wasn't sure she'd heard correctly. Did he mean Mr. Burwell?

"You don't mess with a Parkes unless you dare take on the consequences."

"Sir?"

He transferred the reins to his other hand and tried to retrieve something from his navy-striped silk vest, a handsome garment. "Grab my flask, would ya, girl?"

Spying the silver cap, Lettie tugged it free.

"Open it."

Spirits did awful things to white folks. But she did as commanded and handed it to him, still holding the cap.

"This here was from my great-grandfather. He fought in the American Revolution." Mr. Parkes drank from the container, gulping greedily. "He wanted freedom, yet he enslaved others."

Not knowing what to say, Lettie nodded then accepted the engraved flask back from him. She ran her finger over the figures of soldiers attired in breeches and hunting shirts, their muskets raised high.

"You keep that."

"I can't." Oh, no, she shouldn't have contradicted him. Would he hit her? She'd only twice talked back to the Burwell sons, and she'd paid for it with her flesh. She cringed at the memory and ducked, preparing for a blow that never came.

"It's yours. And much more." He directed the horse around a deep puddle in the road and slowed the wagon.

"What do you think Rush Parkes is telling Letitia?" The old man had surprised Nathan at every turn.

David, who'd not appeared this tense since the very first steeplechase they'd engaged in at school, shook his head. "I hope he's saying something good."

"We cannot linger. We must get Letitia's mother buried and then be off."

"Humph! Try telling that old codger and see what he says." David shook his head.

They drove on past slaves toiling in the fields, the sun beating down and evaporating the recent rain into a fog of steam. "How do they manage in this heat?"

"I don't know. It's unconscionable." Nathan loosened his collar.

"Yet our peers would continue this practice."

Nathan directed the horses to swerve around a deep rut. "Not only continue but pursue their 'property' up into the northern states and put teeth into the Fugitive Slave Act with hefty fines."

David grabbed the edge of his seat as the carriage slowed and dipped into the edge of the low-lying trench. "Do you believe the North will willingly cooperate with this new legislation?"

"It's not really new law but upping the ante for an old law on the books. And enforcing it."

"But will we get the ladies North only to have someone grab them and bring them back?" Hearing David give voice to the nagging worry aloud only made Nathan feel worse.

"What kind of faith do we have if we can't trust God in every situation?" But his words sounded hypocritical. Hadn't Nathan expressed his concerns to David the entire way to Charles City? His face heated in embarrassment.

"We're told God can meet every need. But have you ever been tested before?" The wagon wheels churned on, the horses' hooves plodding through the thick Virginia soil.

Nathan had recently been nominated for deacon at Shockoe Baptist Church in Richmond. He'd grown up part of every activity offered in the church, home to some of Richmond's oldest and wealthiest families. What would the others say if they ever learned that Nathan had helped a slave escape and later married her? That *was* his plan, wasn't it?

He exhaled a sigh.

"Beneida must be terrified in there." David flicked the reins, and the matched pair of bays picked up their pace.

"I have an idea."

Mr. Parkes, who'd insisted Lettie call him "Grandpappy," had sent two house servants to pack a trunk for her and Beneida and had sent them to change in a spacious room upstairs. The armoire held his daughter's and some of his granddaughter's clothing, all faintly scented with cloves.

"We need to hurry, Beneida." Lettie longed to spend time gazing at her transformation in the long, silvered mirror in the blue, flocked–wallpapered room. She fingered the gold necklace that her grandfather had pressed into her hand and that now hung from her neck, beads of deep blue lapis lazuli hanging in layers from the golden chain.

A knock on the door interrupted her reverie. "Time to go." Mr. Bryant's firm tone allowed no argument.

Beneida and Lettie grabbed their borrowed reticules.

Soon they'd descended the winding staircase, portraits of Lettie's ancestors, free people who seemed to watch her escape. Were they nodding in approval? In the heavenly realms, did they watch like a great cloud of witnesses? She hoped so.

Nathan met her in the marble-floored entrance hall. "We have a plan. We can't waste time arguing."

"What?"

"Letitia, I'll need you to get into the coffin."

"No." Lettie shook her head so hard that the curls the Parkes' servant girl had coiled on her head began to loosen. She swiped at the coral-and-yellow-striped damask gown Mr. Parkes had given her—one of his granddaughters', one of her cousins by blood. "I'm not climbing into that casket, Nathan."

Beneida pushed a curl beneath her black bonnet. She patted the netted veil, held back by shiny ebony hat pins, and tied the ribbons at her chin. "It's not so bad."

"Then why were you white as a ghost when you got out?" Lettie fisted her hands on her hips, which were now almost twice as wide as normal, due to all the underpinnings she had and the extra material in the gown.

"At least you'll have more room up top." Beneida tugged at her black moiré sleeves. "I could hardly move at all in the bottom."

"I hate to ask this, but it's the best we can figure." Nathan's fond gaze stirred something in Lettie. Could she trust him? "And we must travel quickly."

"All right, then." Lettie lifted her skirts. Thankfully the shoes she was given were only a little tight.

"We've put your bags in the hiding spot in the coffin." Mr. Bryant took Beneida's hand.

Nathan tucked Lettie's arm through his. "Let's practice descending the stairs together. We'll be doing this soon enough at the wharf."

Her cheeks heated as he drew her close to his side. His scent of leather and bayberry would be with her long after they parted. For no matter what he said, she'd not believe he would offer marriage to her. Not to an escaped slave. Still, they had to get to freedom. "Yes, let's do, for I'm afraid I may trip in these heels." And being treated like a lady felt altogether foreign.

Before long, they'd said their goodbyes to her grandpappy. How good of him to bury Mama in a proper manner. Now Lettie faced the wagon—and the coffin.

"Just jump on in the back."

How could she? Her dead mother had lain there.

"Do you know how many people have been conducted to freedom through our funeral parlor, Lettie?"

She waved Nathan's comment away. "I don't care. I can't."

"You can do this." The soft voice whispered to her soul.

Tears streaming down her cheeks, Lettie began to hum one of her favorite songs from church. And in no time at all, Nathan was assisting her into the box. His firm warm hands held hers as he tried to help her in.

"I need to lift you in." He released his hold and scooped her up, one strong arm beneath her legs and the other behind her shoulders like she was a bag of goose down.

She sucked in a breath and stared up at him as he lowered her into the fancy coffin. The padded satin lining felt cool, but Nathan's lips as he pressed a kiss to her forehead were hot.

"You'll be fine, Letitia. I'll be right here."

"Ready?" Mr. Bryant called out as Nathan rolled a blanket up and lowered the coffin's top onto it, leaving space for air to circulate.

"Roll on!"

Within minutes, the carriage shuddered to a start, and Lettie slid slightly in the box. She cried out.

"Are you all right?"

"I'm fine. It's just slippery in here."

Nathan's fingers slid over the side and she reached out and grasped them. While she yearned for the strength she felt there, she also knew her ideas of romance were foolish. But for now, she could pretend. She thought of the stories the Burwell sisters had enjoyed, many they'd read aloud while she dressed them or cleaned up after them. One was about a noble lady who was set adrift in a boat, and whose true love—a troubadour—found her and saved her from drowning in the shining lake. If she pretended she was that lady, then maybe she'd not think about Mama lying on these same cushions.

They rode on, the sound of the wheels on the road faintly carrying into her hiding place.

Whose crazy idea was this? Nathan's back ached from sitting in the rear of the wagon on the ride to Richmond. Beneida, attired in a mourning gown belonging to one of the Parkes women, sat in the front with David, while Letitia lay in the top half of the coffin. This was his own notion, and a poor one.

"You there, Nathan?" Letitia's voice carried from the coffin. The bottom section had small holes drilled into it, but not the top—a defect Father would have to fix if they were to use this design again to carry a live person.

"I'm here."

Almost to Richmond, now, they'd not been accosted by anyone. Tomorrow, though, surely Burwell would seek the women out and demand to know where they were. Parkes swore he would claim that he had Letitia locked in his house and wasn't letting her out, and he'd deny knowing anything about Beneida. That might work for a few days until the sheriff was brought in to search.

The scent of damp earth and brackish river water intensified as they neared the river. "We'll be there, shortly."

Soon, he'd be saying goodbye to his father, to Richmond and the South. He and David would take the two young women to freedom. First, though, they had to get safely home and then to the boat.

The carriage slowed. "Riders!" David called from the front.

Nathan jumped up, got his feet beneath him as the wagon swayed, and then pulled the blanket out that was holding the coffin open. "Just for precaution, Letitia."

"I'll lie real still."

"Sheriff!" David's overly cheerful voice didn't hide the warning Nathan heard as he gently closed the coffin cover and sat on the blanket, on the wagon's bed.

They slowed to a stop.

"What are you doin' in the Pleasants' wagon?" Nathan strained to discern the owner of the stern voice. His heart hammered.

David said something back that was undecipherable.

"How you doin', Captain Bryant?" The other rider's voice resonated. It was Sheriff Digges of Richmond.

"Doing fine. Helping out Nate. He's in the back with this dear lady's departed kin." David's voice deepened in faux sympathy.

"My condolences, ma'am."

Thankfully, Nathan didn't hear Beneida reply, as they'd instructed her if they ran into any trouble.

"Her family asked if we'd allow her to ride with us to Richmond, so she could be there early. They'll be a few hours behind us."

"Checkin' in the back, Sheriff." In a moment, a mustached, ginger-haired man about Nathan's age peered in at him. He dismounted from his sorrel mare.

"Hello there. I'm Nathan Pleasant." He extended his hand, but the man narrowed his gaze.

"What ya got in that coffin?"

Nathan raised his eyebrows, feigning surprise. "A corpse."

"Don't suppose you'd mind if I looked?"

"Not at all. She doesn't stink." He winked. "Not yet."

The man blinked a few times. "I'm the new deputy. Barnes."

"Good to meet you, Deputy Barnes." A lie if ever there was one.

Barnes patted his mount's neck. "I heard one way to tell if the person in a casket is really dead is you can put a flame to their toe."

Hearing the muffled words, Lettie gasped. Would the deputy open the casket, remove her shoe, and place a flame on her foot? Would her gown light up in flames?

"That's right." Nathan's voice was even. "If the person is still alive, the burn will fill with fluid."

"Good way to check, ain't it?"

"It is. And my father does so as soon as we get the bodies to him, which you're preventing right now."

A long silence followed.

Finally, the sound of a second horse's hooves carried toward the back. Lettie shook from head to toe. Did she shake the wagon? She tried to breathe shallowly, but it was hard.

"What you yammerin' on about back here, Barnes?" The man's deep voice held authority.

"Just discussin' things." The deputy coughed.

"Time to get on our way as I'm sure these men ought."

"How's Mrs. Digges doing, Sheriff?"

"Fine, Nate. New baby is fine, too. Gracie won't be happy if we return after dark, though."

Nathan's laugh sounded genuine enough. "I'm just hoping my hindquarters aren't battered by the time we arrive in Shockoe."

"I'll take a long day on horseback over an afternoon in the back of a wagon any day."

"At least I'm not traveling that way!" Nathan's laughter was joined by the others. He must be pointing at the coffin. Lettie wished she didn't have to travel this way, either.

"That's right, Nate. Now you stay outta that coffin, ya hear?"

"Sure thing, Sheriff. Have a safe journey."

"Safer than the ones we're going to get." Deputy Barnes' tone sent a chill down Lettie's spine.

"Mount up, Barnes."

The rustling of a saddle carried, and the horses whinnied. She needed air. She'd wait a moment before calling to him.

"Letitia, I'll open that top just as soon as they're out of sight."

"Soon. It's hard to breathe."

"How do you feel about being a widow, Letitia?"

"What?" She wasn't even married yet.

"I meant dressed in mourning—like Beneida is."

She'd not wanted to ask where they went next. Was afraid to hear the plan. Lettie ran her tongue over her lips to moisten them. The hearse bed creaked and the top of the coffin opened, as Nathan peered in. If that didn't squelch any romantic notions he might have, then she didn't know what would.

He pressed a cool hand to her cheek. "Are you all right?"

"Yes," she whispered, sucking in the air, not minding the earthy smell of the dirt being kicked up behind the conveyance.

Nathan relished the feel of her soft skin. "I can't believe we did it."

"What?"

"Got both of you out of there." He bent and grabbed the blanket.

"I've been praying you'd come back for me." Letitia exhaled a sigh and a sob. "I'd just about given up. Was thinkin' about runnin' on my own."

"Glad you were there." What would he have done if she'd not been? "David never expected Beneida to return. I've never seen a man more heartsick—until he'd heard she'd been taken to Burwell Plantation." He grazed his thumb slowly near her perfect lips.

"Would you have been heartsick if I'd left?"

His words stuck in his throat.

When he didn't reply, Letitia closed her eyes, as though shutting him out. "You best sit down, Nathan."

"Yes." He gently closed the lid onto the blanket. "With two of you women, it will be a little more difficult, but David and I discussed a plan."

"We don't have to stay in this coffin, do we?"

"No." He exhaled sharply. "We considered that, but it would be too difficult. And risky."

"And I ain't doin' it."

He couldn't help laughing. "Well, let me tell you how things will go, once we get to my father's funeral home. He's affiliated with all of the larger churches in Richmond, and we conduct services and burials for those without any specific faith, as well."

For the next half hour, he explained what would transpire. Then, when they arrived, his father and brother flew into action, helping the men transfer the casket inside, locking the room, and assisting Letitia out. Brief introductions were made.

Father's eyes widened as he took in Letitia's appearance. "With her light coloring, she could easily walk through Richmond on your arm and no one would know she was a slave."

"We're not risking anyone recognizing either of our precious ladies." David lifted a deep purple gown from the trunk. "Have you got another heavy veil here, Mr. Pleasant?"

Everything happened in such a rush that Lettie felt dizzy as the two couples were soon outside again, this time heading toward the wharf and a ship that would carry them to freedom. She tugged at the bottom of the scratchy black veil that smelled of someone's face powder. She fought the urge but then sneezed through the face covering, sending a tiny puff of white powder forward. Nathan squeezed her hand.

"Mrs. Shoultus," Nathan said her fake name so convincingly, Lettie almost believed she was the widow Shoultus. "We'll get you down to the boat, where you'll soon be home to your family."

"I do miss Philadelphia." A place she'd never been and could scarcely believe she would soon see.

Nathan brushed a piece of lint from his navy-and-gray herringbone wool suit. "Pity it's not for a leisurely visit."

Beneida slowed, ahead of them. "Will your father be able to get our belongings to the ship?"

"He's already sent the carter with them, but they'll be traveling on the main road while we're taking these two backstreets for the moment."

Soon they turned up a side street toward their destination. The brackish water of the river filled the air, dampening clothes, but not Lettie's rising hopes. Her heart beat time with their quick footsteps as they stepped up onto the wooden walkway.

"We won't be on this long. There's a step down ahead." Nathan pointed to where the walk ended and a bricked path extended to the wharf.

Pipe and cigar smoke wafted up from a side green, where a group of a dozen men, all similarly attired in vest and waistcoat, slim trousers, and buffed shoes, gathered. Southern men who would seek to keep her enslaved. Yes, many spoke out against slavery, but the plantation owners' voices prevailed. They needed the slaves to hold on to their livelihoods and prosperity.

Just ahead of them, Captain Bryant and Beneida strode more quickly, the thick, dark mesh of her veil covering her face and neck and the extra padding in her gown making her appear more a matron than the young woman she was.

"It's all been so tedious. So tiresome." Beneida's affectatious voice sounded a cross between a Southern lady and a rich Northerner. "I'll feel so much better when we've put this ordeal behind us."

Lettie clung to Nathan's arm, periodically glancing around them. Ahead, ships six deep stood over two-stories high on the water. She'd never been on a ship before. Would they sink in a storm? She bit back the urge to laugh. For she could smell freedom. It smelled a little like horses, straw, the wool of another's fine garment, and the spicy scent of Nathan Pleasant. She lifted her head higher. She was a lady. A grieving lady. It didn't take much for the tears to stream as she remembered what her mother had endured. She reached into her reticule for a handkerchief. A real linen handkerchief. Embroidered with someone else's initials, but it didn't matter.

As they neared the dock, a stream of dark-skinned slaves were unloaded, some barely dressed and then only in rags. Lettie gasped. Nathan patted her hand.

"Don't be alarmed, dear. I'm sure there's no problem here."

Did Beneida's face pale beneath her heavy veil? She, too, held fast to her escort's arm.

"There's the passenger's queue." Nathan pointed ahead to where a line of men, women, and children slowly moved forward toward a ship where all manner of crew were running up and down the boarding planks and hauling luggage back on.

Mr. Bryant turned and smiled over his shoulder. "I was told they intend to depart promptly."

Good. The sooner they left, hopefully the quicker this churning in her gut would stop.

"You there!" A man's low voice called out behind them.

Nathan continued walking. "Keep going," he hissed. "Just ignore them."

Mr. Bryant stepped aside, with Beneida. "Get onto the ship, you two. Remember our plan."

"Bryant!" The man behind them called more urgently.

Nathan grasped her hand and pulled Lettie onward, toward the gangplank. Soon the line slowed as tickets were collected.

"Ticket?" The swarthy man, a head shorter than Nathan frowned at Lettie, who was dabbing at her cheeks beneath the borrowed veil.

"Here you are." Nathan passed them to the man.

As they were waved on, Lettie tugged at Nathan's arm. "We can't leave Beneida and Mr. Bryant."

Nathan grinned at her. "They can't leave without the captain aboard." But sweat trickled down his brow.

Lettie turned to see a red-faced man shaking a finger at David Bryant, while Beneida took a step backward.

Chapter 4

Atlantic Ocean, off the Eastern seaboard of America

Lettie cradled Beneida's head in her lap and pushed damp curls away from her flushed forehead. "You'll be all right soon enough." As soon as this ship came ashore. But then there'd be another host of problems.

"You feeling better, yourself?" Her friend's whisper was raw.

"Yes, thanks to you." Lettie grabbed the nearby cup of ginger tea. "Sit up a little bit and drink."

The ship's gentle rocking motion sloshed a bit of liquid onto the pastel quilt that covered the women. But the ginger tea's action was nothing compared to the terrifying waves they'd tossed through the previous night. Only Captain Bryant resisted the ocean sickness that had overcome the rest of them. How was Nathan faring today? They'd sent a man in to sit with him but had heard no word this morning.

Beneida took a few sips but then pressed the cup back into Lettie's hand. "Thank you."

After setting the medicinal drink back on the small mahogany table next to the bed, Lettie assisted her friend in lying back down and pulled the coverlet up over her quivering shoulders.

"I think I can sleep now, Lettie."

Would her friend's dreams be filled with Captain Bryant as Lettie's were with Nathan? All of their promises seemed to be coming true. She couldn't help dreaming that one day she might have a husband as kind as Nathan Pleasant. What would it be like to be Mrs. Pleasant? A tear slipped down her face. He'd never said he loved her—only that he cared for her deeply. And the brave man had never promised her more than assisting her to escape, unlike David Bryant had Beneida. The dark-haired man had dropped down on bended knee the previous evening and presented her with a beautiful garnet ring. The pursuer who'd flagged them down at the wharf was the jeweler who had taken the captain's order months earlier, before Beneida had departed for England. The shop owner had certainly given them all a good scare, chasing after the captain like that to make sure he took possession of the ring.

Lettie waited, and when Beneida's breath became more gentle and even with sleep, she rose and quietly washed up, using one of the fresh towels that the captain had sent in that morning. How nice to have a clean, fresh cloth and soap that smelled of lemons. Lettie lifted the soap bar to her nose and sniffed. She smiled. As the ship rose on a swell, she braced her feet, glad she'd remembered to fill the water basin only shallowly for just this reason.

She slowly opened the lid of the black leather–wrapped trunk that her grandfather had sent with them, which squeaked a slow moan. When Beneida stirred in the bed, Lettie held still, praying the woman would not awake. After a moment of silence, save for the groaning of the ship, Lettie pulled a chemise; an overblouse in an interwoven lavender, black, and deep purple linen with ribbon trim; and a matching plum-colored skirt from the trunk. Mr. Parkes's daughters had owned beautiful clothing. Even with these colors of late mourning, the ensemble was stylish. With a little stitching, Beneida and she could alter the clothing to fit them. If they stopped at a millinery shop, they could even choose updated ribbons and laces to bedeck their gowns. Lettie ran her hands over the finely woven chemise and pulled it over her head, recalling a visit to Richmond during which Mrs. Burwell had allowed her to select a satin ribbon for herself. She'd chosen a narrow burgundy strand, which she gave to her mother. Mama had cried when Lettie pressed it into her chafed hands.

Tears streamed down Lettie's face as she dressed herself. Here she was wearing a lady's clothing. Her mother lay dead. These garments had been worn by her cousins. Women who solely by birth were free, while Mama was enslaved and then sold off to the neighbors.

Mama would have said, "Ain't no use worryin' about what has gone by. Trust the good Lord. One day we will all be free in glory." Lettie wiped away the tears and sniffed before glancing in the mirror. Her cheeks, as pale as any white woman's, were streaked with red from crying. Her hair needed a good brushing. She reached for the brand-new, boar-bristle brush that sat atop the dressing table. There was a matching one for Beneida. Each had their own. Lettie ran her fingers over the rosewood handle—as fine as Mrs. Burwell's brush.

Hope, like a kindling, a tiny spark lighting the hearth, rose up in her. Something she'd never felt before bubbled in her. What was it?

Joy. Joy despite the hardships. Joy rising above the fear.

Lettie blinked back more tears and raised a hand to her lips to stifle a laugh. Beneida had been the only enslaved young woman Lettie knew who seemed happy. Who spoke of joy. At least she had, the few times they'd met in Richmond.

She set the hairbrush back down and retrieved a handkerchief, blowing her nose as quietly as she could. The new emotion made her suck in a breath. From her first memories, all she had known was bondage, of being made to sit still and watch as her mother worked. To stay out of the way. To see her mother mistreated by people who said they owned her. And look what Beneida's owners had done.

"Only I own you. If you choose."

There'd been no audible voice. Just a whispering inside her. In her soul. She sighed and lifted the hairbrush to her head, removing tangles as quickly as she could. She gathered and pinned her hair into what she hoped would pass for a lady's hairstyle. She'd often done the elder Mrs. Burwell's silver tresses in such a fashion. She didn't mind being considered dowdy, as long as she wasn't caught as an escaped slave.

Soon she was ready to check on Nathan. First, she leaned over Beneida, then extinguished the oil lamp before leaving the room and locking the door. Outside, the skies were heavily overcast with thick gray clouds piled up on top of one another like pillows awaiting a good beating. She held the railing affixed to the ship's side, as Captain Bryant had instructed her to do, even though the waters were calm.

A worker walked by, balancing a tray in one hand. He nodded and bowed his head in subservience, avoiding her inquisitive glance. How strange to have a servant treat her like a superior. She wasn't, of course. How strange to be treated as a free woman. Could it last?

Between the bell clanging, a horn tooting from the Philadelphia harbor, and the noise of shipmen clattering up and down the stairs, Nathan's ears rang.

Porters rushed past Nathan, their carts piled high with luggage. "Make way! Make way!"

This was real—they had sailed upriver into Philadelphia's fine harbor, its long, wide wharf a welcoming beehive of activity below.

David strode toward him, still attired in his captain's clothing. He clapped his hands together. "I'm ready for some good Philadelphia cooking." Only the tic near his left eye gave away his anxiety.

"Let's gather our good ladies, then."

The two of them carefully wove between the passengers and crew members, most making way when they eyed David's uniform. The captain grinned and tipped his hat at all the ladies as they passed.

Finding the appropriate cabin, Nathan knocked on the escaped women's door. In a moment, it opened, and the two, their faces obscured by the heavy black veils, emerged from the cabin. He tucked Lettie's gloved hand into the crook of his arm. "Ready?"

"You have no idea how ready I am."

He chuckled. "I believe I have a notion."

Beneida looked up at Nathan. "You're looking mighty spry for having been so ill, Mr. Pleasant."

"That's because you're viewing my friend through a veil, my dear." David patted his sweetheart's arm. "He's still a dull shade of gray-green."

"Much like the skies, then." Letitia pointed overhead to where the dark clouds gleamed the sickly color.

Soon they descended from the ship. The sun forced its way out from beneath the banked rain clouds, the fragile rays illuminating the small group. "A good omen, I pray." Nathan resisted the urge to pick Letitia up and swirl her around.

David bent and embraced Beneida. "We're here, my beloved!"

Looking up through green eyes expectant beneath the dark veil, Letitia gave a tremulous smile.

Nathan gently lifted the veil and pressed a kiss to her smooth forehead, enjoying her soft gasp of surprise. He quickly lowered the dark mesh, again. "The city of brotherly love."

Letitia cocked her head at him.

"That's the meaning of the city's name."

"Oh."

David leaned in. "How does it feel to be in one of the largest cities in our great nation? Over a hundred thousand people live here, I've heard." Fantastic? Frightening? Freeing?

"Good place to disappear." Letitia's soft voice barely carried over the loud noises of the carters as they rolled baggage from the docks, the passengers conversing loudly with one another, and street vendors hawking wares.

The scent of sausages cooking over charcoal drew Nathan's attention. He jerked a thumb toward them. "Shall we?"

No doubt the women wished to flee the wharf as quickly as possible. But he and David had cautioned them that they must act naturally. But his friend continued to scan faces at the dock. "I saw no one I recognized on board nor on the roster of travelers."

"I'm not yet well enough to eat. I'll leave my veil on." Beneida turned from David to watch the passengers streaming past.

Letitia jostled his arm. "Why don't you men have your sausages, and then let's go on to the inn."

"All right." Nathan's stomach rumbled, and despite his seasickness, his empty gullet begged to be filled. "And we'll have something sent upstairs for you ladies when we arrive at the inn."

They all stepped closer to where a man, attired in heavy dark navy wool garments, poked at the sausages sizzling on the grate over a bed of coals. Nathan held up two fingers and pointed to the sausages.

When the vendor muttered something back in what sounded like German, Nathan looked to his friend. David, however, was already fishing money out of his embossed leather wallet and handing it to the man.

"I've never seen sausages served like this." Letitia pointed to the thick split rolls that the vendor placed the sausages upon.

Nathan grinned at her. "Do you want to try it?"

"Maybe a bite?"

"Here, take your gloves off. Then you can manage if you push that veil up." He assisted her in unbuttoning the wrists and tugging each tight finger free from the gloves. Even with all the bustle of people coming and going on the wharf, the act felt intimate. But this was as a husband should do for his wife, was it not?

"Thank you." Letitia's throaty whisper caused his cheeks to heat.

"You're welcome, my love."

Her eyes widened in surprise. It was the first time he'd used that word with her. Was it possible that she might welcome a life spent with him? Did she care for him more than just as a friend who'd help her escape to freedom? He raised her hand to his lips and pressed a kiss to her hand, inhaling the sweet scent of lemons.

"Why, Nathan. . ." Letitia's accent grew more affected.

So, she was just playing the part. Disappointment riffled through his belly, souring his lunch.

From a nearby bank of low wooden structures, a man attired in a loose-sleeved shirt, a snug brown vest, and matching pants exited and jogged in their direction. Nathan's heartbeat ratcheted up.

"It's just one of our shoremen," David muttered. "Be calm."

The tousle-haired man slowed as he neared. Breathing heavily, he shoved a telegram at David. "Captain, this just arrived for you."

His friend scanned the message. "It's from your father, Nate."

Letitia nibbled on her lower lip. Nathan's heart went out to her. "What does it say?"

"He says your two stray cats want sardines, but he fed them Irish stew and he'll keep doing so."

Beneida snorted. "What kind of crazy talk is that?"

"It's a coded message." Nathan rubbed his temple. "A warning."

Chapter 5

Nathan's chest squeezed. "It means two people were looking for you ladies and that Father was giving them malarkey, a bit of the Blarney stone, to deter them." The German vendor glanced up, brows drawn together. Did he understand English? He'd have to be more careful what he said in public.

"Did he say anything else?" Letitia wrung her hands.

David lifted the telegram. "He hopes your holiday to Boston gives you a little rest."

Boston meant they couldn't stay on the Eastern seaboard but to continue on to Buffalo. And a little rest meant they might have pursuers a few days behind them.

"Boston?" Beneida clutched her reticule tighter.

He and David would have to discuss their change of plans in private. They would have to be very careful. They'd discussed David obtaining a sailing position to France, but he wasn't sure he could find a ship quickly enough. And Nathan wasn't quite ready to commit to marriage and to leaving America. Letitia might want to fully drink of the freedom she could find, including her choice of future husband. But she'd need someone special who wouldn't abandon her if he learned of her past. Nathan longed to be the one who could care for her. But he had no means to support them beyond the savings they'd use to get them to Buffalo and for provision for several months afterward.

"Let's all have a sit down." David pointed to two benches in a small grassy area ten paces beyond the vendor's cart.

After they'd finished their sausage rolls, the foursome found a coach and were transported to *Das Geheime Inn*.

"I've stayed here many times, and even I didn't know this was a conductor's safe place until you told me, Nathan." David disembarked from the carriage and assisted Beneida then Letitia down, followed by Nathan.

The skies had darkened again. "Let's get inside before it pours." Raindrops began to plop onto the brick sidewalk that led to the two-story, square inn sided in white clapboard. Heavy dark green shutters, held open by S-shaped brass holders affixed to the house's exterior, reminded him that this port, this city, like Virginia, also experienced hurricanes. At least they didn't have to go back out onto the ocean again. *Thank God for that.*

They stepped into the building just as the clouds opened and poured their contents down. Nathan quickly secured the front door, inhaling the heavy fragrance of apples and cinnamon inside.

To the left, tables and chairs filled a small room that could hold perhaps twenty people but was currently empty.

David swiveled to face him. "They serve only breakfast and dinner here, but I'm sure Mrs. Frohlich will have the kitchen send something up."

"I can wait." Beneida placed a hand on her padded stomach. She certainly looked the part of a matronly woman.

"Me, too." Letitia tugged at her hat strings. "I have got to get this contraption off my head."

The wide-brimmed black bonnet, to which the veil was affixed, did look heavy and uncomfortable.

Footsteps sounded on the nearby staircase. A blue shirt strained across the chest of a blond workman. He looked half a head taller than both Nathan and David. "Travelers?"

"Yes," all four exhaled the word simultaneously.

Morning light filtered through the broadcloth curtains that ran from ceiling to floor. Behind the ugly brown cloth, harbor winds rattled the two tall windows. Lettie bent over the basin and washed with the chill water she'd poured from the chipped, cream-ware pitcher.

"Where will we go today?" Beneida threw back the down-stuffed bedcovers and stretched, her mussed hair trailing down her slim back. She tugged at the shoulders of her linen gown.

Lettie eyed the dresses hanging in the open mahogany wardrobe. Never in her life had she owned so many clothes. But when she wore them, she would have to settle into them so she didn't appear as though she was uncomfortable.

A gentle tap at the door startled her and Lettie sloshed water onto the front of her chemise. She dropped her rag into the water and leaned heavily against the washstand. Had someone discovered them? "Who be—"

"You know," the low, deep voice was unrecognizable and her heart lurched in her chest.

"Who?" she managed.

"It's me, David," the captain whispered through the door. "We'll meet you in the dining hall in twenty minutes."

Beneida ran to the door. "Yes, dearest." Her singsong voice made Lettie laugh.

"We'll eat without you if you're late, so no dawdling." *My, he sounded stern.*

But Beneida just laughed.

The captain's footsteps echoed down the hall.

After they'd dressed and donned their matching velvet hats with feather plumes, the two women descended the stairs to the dining room.

Both men rose from the table overlooking the street. Outside, early morning street sweepers worked, and carters hauled luggage, vegetables, and all manner of caged animals up the busy street. As a goose determinedly flapped its wings inside a crate, Lettie shivered. Nathan followed her gaze, his eyes half closing, as though realizing the reason for her distress. He pulled her chair back and assisted her into it.

Leaning close, his warm breath caressed her ear. "We depart earlier on the train than planned."

Lettie stiffened. "For Boston?"

"Buffalo."

Across the table, David assisted his "wife" into her spot and gave her a husbandly peck on the cheek. "How are you feeling this morning, my darling?"

Heat flushed Lettie's cheeks. Nathan took his seat next to her. He pressed an unusually chill hand over hers. "We believe we've attracted attention."

Lettie drew in a full breath; glad she'd not had time to don one of the infernal corsets that Beneida insisted upon her wearing.

Captain Bryant leaned in. "We saw two men lingering outside the hotel this morning."

"I thought I recognized one." Nathan released her hand. "I can't place him, though."

"I'm hoping he's a doppelgänger."

"A what?" Lettie scowled but then forced her features to relax. Ladies didn't scowl. At least not in public they didn't. So many new rules she'd needed to learn.

"It means a person who looks like you."

"Like a cousin?"

"Like that, but it usually means someone who looks like a double of you but is of no relation."

Who were her relatives? The Burwells faces danced through Lettie's mind. What common features did they all share? But they were not related for purposes of the world. She was a slave. And they her owners. Moisture pricked her eyes, and she swiped it away with the back of her hand.

"Here." Nathan tugged a creamy handkerchief from his jacket pocket and passed it to her, his touch definitely cool. He must be frightened, too. But a man wasn't allowed to show it.

"The proprietor wasn't here when the two gentlemen were lingering, so we couldn't ask him who they might be." David ran his hand over his jawline. "But we'll take the train as soon as possible."

"Couldn't we at least do a quick tour of the Philadelphia sights?" Beneida leaned in toward Mr. Bryant. "Isn't this city one of the seats of freedom for this country?"

Not for slaves.

"Let us out at Independence Hall." Nathan instructed the cabdriver before they got in. Soon, they'd arrived at the imposing building. A thrill shot through him at the thought of bringing independence to these two women.

"The bell is in the Assembly Room downstairs. Just follow us." David took Beneida's arm and entered the brick building.

"Mr. Burwell used to say they ought to crack the bell all the way through now that people are using it as a symbol of freedom from slavery." Letitia's voice held barely repressed anger. What must it be like to have a father who was your owner and kept you enslaved?

Nathan cleared his throat. "The abolitionists have, indeed, grasped onto the bell as a symbol of their cause." Which made it all the more fitting that they view this symbol before departing.

"I'm glad they moved it to where more people can now behold it," David called over his shoulder.

They moved toward a queue of visitors. Before too long, the four stood before the icon. Displayed on an ornate sculpted eagle stand, the cracked Liberty Bell rang something true, something real, within Nathan's heart.

"Do you feel it?" Letitia whispered.

"I do." He wrapped an arm around her.

Beneida and Letitia stood stiffly, staring at the large bell.

"Not particularly so beautiful to look upon but altogether lovely in what it represents." David placed his free hand over his heart.

"It is lovely, Captain Bryant." Letitia's eyes glistened.

"Please, call me David." He smiled. "I am, after all, betrothed to your best friend."

"Thank you. . .David."

Behind them, the voices of those awaiting their turn rose slightly, likely signaling their impatience.

"Well, although I hate to do so, I'll need to leave you now to get our tickets." Nathan took Letitia's arm and led her away from the symbol of precious liberty, with David and Beneida following.

"I'll keep my eyes open for those men. And if I see them, we'll take refuge at the Quakers' Hall."

"I'll stop to look for you at the Merchants' Exchange first, though." Nathan nodded to David, who had suggested the beautiful building would be a good stop, and he could check on his stocks while he was there.

Nathan hurried through the morning crowds to the train station. The bespectacled ticket booth clerk tapped his black visor. "This one departs at 1:00 sharp, young man. This day only." His light eyes fixed on Nathan's. "You can make changes farther up the line."

"Yes, sir." He paid. But they had much farther to go from that stop.

Nathan first checked the Merchants' Exchange, dodging passengers and traffic as he crossed one busy street after another, narrowly missing a dray that pulled out from the curb as he made it to the other side. Wouldn't that be something? Mowed over by draft horses before they could ever get the women to safety.

Nathan tugged at his cravat that had come loose from its butterfly tie and tapped his top hat as he reentered the building, which was crowded with businessmen.

Standing by the far wall, Letitia, attired in a dusky lavender dress, turned from admiring a painting of a patrician Philadelphian and met his gaze. His breath stuck in his throat. Her auburn curls trailed down her creamy skin, visible above the bodice of her waist-nipping jacket. *Dear Lord, You've made her so beautiful, so kind, so persistent, and filled with a passion for knowing You better. How could You allow her to be enslaved?*

All were God's children. What would it take? Talking hadn't worked. With this new act, or rather the enforcement of an old law, would words turn to something worse? Could reason not prevail?

David and Beneida rose from where they sat at a low divan. "Isn't it grand, Nate?"

"An imposing building to be sure."

From the corner of his eye, Nathan sensed movement. He swiveled, expecting to spy the two men whose path crossing theirs earlier. Instead, a well-dressed older man locked eyes with Nathan. He smiled and cocked his head before lifting his bowler hat in acknowledgement and then gazed at the handkerchief peeking from Nathan's pocket.

Who was Nathan chatting with? Lettie lifted the watch pinned on her bodice. It felt so strange to have the heavy timepiece there. They hadn't much time to spare, did they? Should she play the adoring wife and join Nathan? Before she could decide, David and Beneida joined her.

David smiled down at her. "Have no worries. That man poses us no harm."

"Who is he?"

"Do you see the daffodil embroidered on his handkerchief?"

Lettie peered around David's broad shoulders. "I can't tell from here."

"Well he has one. As does Nathan, if you've ever looked closely on this trip."

"I hadn't noticed."

Beneida leaned into the captain. "Is he a fellow conductor?"

"Yes."

David Bryant took their elbows and steered them toward the exit.

Lettie stopped walking, and he released her. "You're leavin' him here?"

"Only for a moment."

She puffed out an exasperated breath as they exited the building and went out near the street. Wagon wheels rattled over cobblestones. Vendors called out their wares. Men and women ambled, arm in arm, some veering from beggars with hands outstretched.

A flaxen-haired girl ducked in front of Lettie, front teeth missing in her dirt-streaked face revealing her to be about six years old. "Got a half-penny, lady?"

David scowled as Lettie struggled with her pouch and fished out a coin. As quickly as the half-penny had dropped into the tiny palm, the child was gone.

"Mind yourself, Miss Letitia, for some of these urchins will rob you just like that!" He snapped his fingers.

"I've only seen such children at the wharves." Beneida's eyebrows rose high. "Never in Richmond proper."

The few times Lettie had been to the Virginia capital, she'd been more concerned about how to escape than she had been about noticing any of the unfortunate children. Old Mrs. Burwell remarked that at least the slaves were fed and housed and clothed, unlike the cast-off children who'd likely die in a gutter before they'd reached ten years. Lettie's hands trembled, recalling her thoughts that she'd rather be free like those urchins and live a short life than to die a slave. *Was such a thought wicked, Lord? Do You have a reason for my life?*

"I've asked the hotel porter to transport our luggage to the railroad. But we paid for an extra night."

"What of the porter? Did you pay for his silence?" Beneida gazed up at David.

They stopped walking and stepped aside so an elderly couple could pass, the silver-haired gentleman giving David a sharp look.

"What have we to keep silent, wife?" David issued a short chuckle.

"True. We are simply a couple traveling with our friends on holiday."

"And if we act as if we've changed our minds, that is fine."

"But the hotel fee?" Lettie frowned.

"Ah." David stroked his chin. "Better a happy and *quiet* innkeeper who has received his full pay for our board than one vexed at losing the income from two days' rent."

"Even if he is a cooperator, and an abolitionist, he must earn a living." Beneida bobbed her head as if agreeing with herself.

"I'm grateful, David, that you know about such things." As much sorrow, as much toil, as much denial as she'd experienced, Lettie was as wise in the way of the world as a baby lamb.

When they continued on and reached the intersection, David led them away from the railroad station. "We're to take lunch at the Philadelphia Tavern."

"I don't know if I'll be able to fit in these fine new clothes if the food at the tavern is as good as you say."

"Do we have time for this?" Beneida glanced to the left and right.

Carefully, Lettie took in the approaching walkers. Two women who looked to be sisters, with identical light brown hair curling around matching round, thin-lipped faces briskly strolled past. Next a Quaker minister, wearing an odd-looking hat, turned down a walkway to the meeting hall. Then they shared the walkway with a woman dressed in brown homespun fabric holding tightly to the hands of two dark-haired boys attired in coal-black knickers and white cotton shirts who alternately struggled to pull free from her, one now lying on the ground in front of them.

"Sorry," the plain woman muttered up to them as she sank to retrieve the child.

"Do ya, do you need help?" When the woman didn't respond to Lettie's question, being focused on the flailing child on the ground, Lettie opened her arms to the other child. He broke free and ran to her.

He clutched her knees and gazed up. "Pretty. Like Mama."

The boy had dark waving hair and striking blue eyes in his rosy face. Could she have a child so handsome? Lettie lifted him up onto one hip, as she'd done with the Burwell children, and jostled him there. He placed his hands on her cheeks and pressed them, intently examining her face. "Mama's gone."

Tears clouded her vision. Her mother was gone, as well.

"Miss Letitia," David hissed, his face flushed.

The stranger gathered the other child up. "I'm sorry. They're due for a nap, and I kept them out too long."

"Can we help get them home?" Lettie avoided David's gaze but heard his loud sigh.

The woman, who must be the boys' caregiver, glanced at them but shook her head. "My employer wouldn't be happy."

With the boys settled again, the nanny walked off.

The captain turned on Lettie. "What were you thinking?"

She shrugged.

"It's thoughtlessness like that that will derail this journey."

Beneida gave a curt laugh.

"What's so funny?"

"Letitia was being thoughtful, yet you called her helping that governess a thoughtless act."

He curled his lips together. "That isn't what I meant, and you know it."

Footfall on the cobblestones behind them carried toward them. The trio turned. Nathan ran to catch up. "Did you see them?"

"Who?" David tilted his head and looked back.

"The two men from this morning."

Lettie lowered her head and sent up a quick prayer. "No."

David shook his head. "Didn't see them."

"They are definitely following in our footsteps."

"Let's take the back alley to the tavern." The captain took Beneida's hand and quickly turned the corner.

Chapter 6

Pennsylvania Canal System Railroad, Central Pennsylvania

Tell it again, David." If Lettie could hear about the Englishmen again, maybe it would assuage her fear that bounty hunters might still be waiting for them at the end of this long journey by railroad and canal across this large and mountainous state.

Beneida squeezed her sweetheart's arm as the train rumbled over the tracks. "Yes, tell us again."

Nathan rolled his eyes. "I could likely tell it for him."

Lettie laughed. "Then do tell."

Seated across from her, David Bryant raised a broad hand. "When I sent you out the tavern's back door and on to the railroad by yourselves, the two men following us had just entered the tavern. I asked them to sit with me and told the waiter to have your lunches placed in tins."

Nathan patted his slender midsection. "Of course, you'd think of your victuals."

"I was only thinking of the three of you." He grinned.

"And nearly missed the train!" Beneida swatted at his knee.

"But I didn't, did I?" David kissed her cheek. "Anyway, I detained them there and demanded that they tell me why they were following us."

"I can't believe they'd just sit there." Beneida cocked her head at him.

Lettie frowned. "How did you convince them? You've left that part out."

The captain patted at a lump in his right waistcoat pocket. "I have a friendly implement that helps on such occasions."

"A gun?" Beneida's eyes widened.

"I'm not sure they would have listened otherwise." The captain quirked his eyebrows.

"I can't imagine those men chasing across the ocean for Beneida." Would Nathan ever care for Lettie like that? Was he already falling in love with her?

Nathan gazed at her with an intensity that made her cheeks heat. "He was besotted beyond all reason."

"I believe it was more lust, than love, that motivated Lord Wrenwick to pursue my beloved." David frowned. "Or I might be without a bride."

All that—sending men to find Beneida and bring her back to England—merely to be the man's mistress. How was that any different from being sold by one's master into sexual slavery? At least the mistress had freedom.

Beneida's face flushed. "Even if Wrenwick offered marriage, I'd not have accepted."

"And who's to say those two gents would truly have conducted you back to England,

324

had you agreed to be set up as the Englishman's mistress?" Nathan expressed a worry that Lettie, too, had considered. What if they'd brought her friend back to Virginia and into a life of slavery again?

Lettie shivered.

Nathan took her hand. "You're cold."

"I warned you that rail and boat travel might make us miserably cold for some time." The captain sounded peevish.

Nathan settled his wool lap blanket around Lettie first and then himself. "Better?"

The warmth of the covering was nothing compared to the light in his eyes. That look said that he loved her. And she could no more part with Nathan when they arrived in Buffalo than she could survive without her heart.

Patriots' Inn, Northern Pennsylvania

Outside Lettie's second-story window, icicles hanging two-feet long slowly dripped from the eaves of the inn's roofline. If freedom felt this frigid cold, could Lettie stand it? Still, a little song bubbled up from within her heart: "Blest Be the Tie That Binds." Just like in the song, she, Beneida, Nathan, and David were bound together on this journey, bearing one another's burdens and woes. That morning, they'd all attended services, where with one voice they'd sung the verses of the beautiful song. No wearing veils, no one pursuing them, simply a celebration of life.

"Ready for lunch?" Beneida lifted a long ebony curl from her neck and pushed it back. Her rose-and-yellow-plaid day gown flattered her coloring. "No disrespect to your mother, but I was ready to be out of mourning clothes many miles ago."

Lettie gave a curt laugh. "Slaves don't have the privilege of mourning. And clothing in a certain color doesn't tell how I'm feeling inside." Surprisingly, she'd felt her mother's presence, not in a physical way but in her heart—Mama would have been so thrilled that she'd made it to freedom.

Beneida grabbed the key from the vanity table. The two went outside the small square room, and her friend locked the door behind them then placed the ornate key in her reticule. "This is an old place."

"From the American Revolution." A war for independence, but not for all.

As they descended the stairs, the sweet scent of vanilla and cloves mingled with roast beef and yeasty bread. "Sure smells good."

"Um-hum, we haven't eaten this well on this entire trip." Beneida patted her middle.

Without the padding, and with their rations being sparse, her friend looked like she was wasting away.

Both Nathan and David rose when they arrived in the dining room downstairs. Only about sixteen paces in either direction square, the room held a surprising number of guests—at least twenty people were seated at the tables.

"Letitia?" Nathan pulled back her rush-seated chair, and David did the same for her friend.

Beneida made a show of sniffing the air. "If it isn't roast beef, I may die."

"Maybe you should take up work onstage," David muttered. "You're sounding rather theatrical."

Nathan stifled a chuckle, as did Lettie.

At a nearby table sat a ginger-haired man attired in a navy brocade vest spattered with mustard-yellow dots and contrasting brown pants with a seam ribbon of tan. He peered over his newspaper at his companion, a tiny woman wearing clothing as drab, yet refined, as the man's was garish. "My dear, they are yet driving that law through— the Fugitive Slave Act."

The woman sniffed. "It's all botheration."

"Indeed." He leaned in on his elbows and folded the paper down. "Why do the denizens of our fine state need to have the federal government dictating what we are to do about those so fortunate as to escape their plight?"

A man at an adjacent table, whose sparse, mouse-brown hair was plastered across his balding pate, cleared his throat, catching the other man's eye. "Why do you care if those Southerners willing to track down their property do so?"

Around them, a few ladies' eyes widened, and Lettie forced herself to exhale the breath she held. Nathan cast her a warning glance, but David glared at the man.

The ginger-haired stranger stopped slicing his roast beef. "Sir, you forget yourself. You are in Pennsylvania—not in Georgia or Mississippi!"

Nathan leaned toward her and whispered. "Pennsylvanians have enacted all kinds of statutes to prevent slaves from being returned."

The balding man stood, pulled off his gravy-stained napkin from his neck, and placed a fist on his narrow hip. "Soon, Pennsylvanians will be forced to comply or they shall pay the price."

Around them, other men rose from their tables and made shooing motions toward the horrid man. "Be off!"

"Go!" a chorus of voices raised up.

Grabbing his coat and hat from a peg, he soon scurried out to the hisses of the others. Lettie's heart beat hard in her chest.

"Pray God they don't push that bill through." Nathan took her hand in his and squeezed.

What if they did? Would these brave men be willing to leave their country behind? Did she and Beneida have the right to ask them to do so?

No.

Chapter 7

N athan stood and stretched as the canal boat came to a full stop, the workers securing it. His muscles ached and head throbbed. "Ships, trains, canal boats, stagecoach—I think the only thing we've missed out on is horseback."

The canalman strolled through, grinning. "Buffalo, folks."

Nathan stroked his thick reddish beard while David scratched his straggly more pepper than salt goatee.

"Stop doing that," Beneida hissed at his friend as David helped her from her seat. With light powder, a mole near her eye and one on her chin, and her eyebrows broadened and darker, she wasn't the stunning woman she normally was.

Letitia, her hair tinted with henna, and covered with some sort of turban-looking wrap, stood with shoulders squared. "It's mighty pretty here. I can say that!"

Tall oak and maple trees were covered in new leaf. Narcissus, serviceberry, and flowering plum trees covered the park near the canal's wharf. On their way in, they'd viewed farm fields freshly tilled and edged by thick towering pines. New construction of homes and businesses bespoke the area's prosperity.

Nathan pointed to Letitia's feet, which were shoved into some tight, high-heeled satin pumps. "Those won't last more than a half mile if we must walk."

She looked down her nose, the low-cut bodice of her gown revealed she was more amply endowed than he'd imagined. The half-dozen gaudy necklaces strung around her long neck dangled into her cleavage, drawing the eye there. Beneida had insisted, at the last stop, that this getup would be perfect. Still, Nathan felt uncomfortable seeing Lettie attired in what he considered to be more appropriate for a trollop.

David pulled his watch from his vest pocket and examined it. "I'd like to run down to the port, if you don't mind. I want to check on the position I telegrammed them about."

"You go ahead, then." Nathan inclined his head toward the departing travelers. "I'll get the luggage, and we'll go on to the hotel."

"Are you sure?"

"Yes. Now go." Nathan and the ladies lingered in their spot, allowing David to move into the crush of people departing. "I hope there are taxis around when we get out."

Within the hour, they'd retrieved their belongings and had been brought by carriage to their hotel, not far from the wharf but in a questionable part of town. Were David's funds running so low? He'd been the one to make the arrangements and hadn't said anything about there being a problem. Now that they were in port, perhaps Nathan should take a chance and wire his father.

Thankfully, the rooms were immediately adjacent one another, so Nathan could listen for any signs of trouble for the women. He quickly unpacked his satchel and then washed up. Were they really here? His head felt clogged with cotton balls. He laid down on the bed to take a quick nap.

A loud rap roused Nathan from slumber. Where was he? He tossed aside the thin covering and rose, the bedsprings creaking.

"Nate, it's me."

He pulled his suspenders over his shoulders and went to the door and opened it. "I fell asleep."

David strode in, his eyes red as though he'd been crying, and slumped into a ladder-back oak chair by the wall. "They have no positions for me."

"What?"

"I was counting on this—that there would be a shipping job. And there is none."

Had she heard right? Lettie pressed her ear to the thin wall.

Nathan's fragmented voice carried in fits and spurts. "How. . .support. . .all? Cash. . . that tight?"

"Someone will hire." David Bryant's bass voice held false confidence.

"I can. . .work. . .Great Lakes."

Nathan had been so ill aboard the ship, how could he be employed on a boat?

The two men's voices lowered, and Lettie could no longer understand them. A knock at the door startled her. But then the key rattled in the lock. "I've got the water," Beneida called as she opened the door and carried in a pitcher.

Lettie took it from her and set it on the wobbly washstand. "We need to go ahead with our own plan."

"To support ourselves?"

"Yes."

Beneida slumped onto the bed, the springs creaking loudly. "Where?"

"Wherever we can get work." And she'd saved up enough money so that when she needed to depart for Canada, if and when Congress passed that wretched law, she could leave Nathan to remain in his own country. To return to his family in Virginia and resume helping others to freedom. But how could she go on without him at her side?

Somehow she'd have to. If work was hard to come by here, how much more so in Canada? Abolitionists might be sympathetic to Lettie and Beneida's plights, but would they really put themselves out to help two white Southern men?

Tomorrow she'd get up and find whatever work was available. She was no stranger to toil. But she was free. And if freedom meant working sunup to sundown with no master owning her, she'd not complain.

Both Nathan and David had slept through much of their second day in Buffalo, much to their chagrin. At dinner the previous night, their only meal of the day, Nathan and his friend had apologized to the women, who both seemed very subdued. Neither he nor David had been able to get the ladies to share their concerns, nor what they'd been doing that day.

Now, Nathan pushed through his morning ablutions, readying for the day.

Determined to get to the docks at first light, he dressed with the aid of the flickering single lamp. Then he tucked a hard roll in his pocket and headed out. Street sweepers, carters, women selling muffins from piled-high baskets, and maids attired in stark black-and-white uniforms populated the walkway. As he neared the dock, he passed groups of fishermen and uniformed boatmen who smoked pipes outside the boatyard.

Nathan smiled and nodded to the well-dressed man whose dark hair and eyes, combined with golden skin suggested he was at least partly of Native American descent. The stranger carried boxes. "Are those filled with paperwork?"

"Yes."

Not long ago, Nathan had been hunched over a desk managing Father's ledgers. Now, though, he'd take any work he could get, including deckhand even if his constitution rebelled. "Can you direct me to the hiring office for Blue Star Line?"

"They have an office dockside in that building there." The tall man, wearing a navy suit, inclined his head toward a long shingled building adjacent to the water. "I'm heading that way, so join me."

"Thanks." Something about the man, who was perhaps five years older than himself, seemed familiar. His voice, too, was reminiscent of another man.

"Where're you from?" The man shifted his load, which looked heavy.

"Virginia. And I'd be glad to help you with one of those boxes." Nathan extended his hands.

He passed him a sturdy box, which weighed about ten pounds. "Normally they wouldn't bother me, but I've been moving our office from across town a little at a time."

Nathan and he fell into step beside each other. "Where do you work?"

"At the ferry to Canada."

"Do you like it?"

The man laughed. "I can't wait until they put me back on the water again."

"I think my friend David feels that way, but his promised captain's position was gone when we arrived."

"What about you? Are you a Virginia waterman?"

"No. Not sure I have boat legs." Nathan didn't normally share that he was a funeral home clerk. "I'm an office worker and happy to tally numbers."

The other man chuckled, a sound so deep in his chest that it rumbled, again recalling another gentleman. Someone kind.

"You should talk with the stevedore's manager, then. Wellington is looking for someone."

"Certainly." He had nothing to lose. Unless he was required to frequently be aboard a ship. "What does a stevedore do?"

Again the ferryman laughed. "The stevedores haul stuff on and off the ships. But the manager tracks those materials. And the men. Some of whom can be, well, a trifle. . ."

Nathan gave a curt laugh. "I think I understand."

The man turned his head toward Nathan and smiled, his large white teeth gleaming against his tan skin. "One must be wise in the ways of the world to manage those stevedores!"

As if to illustrate his point, a group of men ahead began pushing one another and cursing loudly. Then one spit a stream of tobacco so close to them, they had to step back to avoid being hit by it.

"As I was saying. . ." The man shook his head, a dark curly lock falling against his forehead in the same way Nathan's often did.

Letitia would push Nathan's errant sandy-red curls back in a gesture that was quickly becoming familiar and heartfelt. If he could land a job. If they could get settled. What would life be like as her husband?

Soon they neared the dock and the whitewashed building. "This way."

Nathan followed his companion into the building. Removing his hat, he ducked beneath the low entryway and went inside, hat in hand, box in the other.

The left of the building was comprised mostly of large windows, which allowed light to stream into the long hallway that fronted the offices. Cigar and pipe smoke formed a gray cloud that was barely diminished with the opening of the entry door. Sturdy oak chairs were occupied by men whose attire ranged from that of dockhands to the more refined businessmen wearing suits, loose ties, and shoes buffed to a shine.

The stranger paused by an open door and rapped on the frame, grinning at whoever sat inside. "Have you got a moment, Mr. Wellington?"

"Certainly," a deep voice boomed from inside. "Always time for you, Marrton."

When motioned forward, Nathan stepped into the room. A glass-fronted filing cabinet to the right was crammed so full that the brass fastener looked as though it might pop free. The narrow oak desk had three piles of paper in stacks and a spindle half full. To the left were two wide-seated Windsor chairs, covered with boxes. The man behind the desk rose. He stood close to their height, with a head of hair almost as dark as David's and nearly as wavy. His dark blue eyes reminded Nathan of deep ocean waters, but his broad smile immediately put him at ease.

"I'd ask you gentlemen to sit, but as you can see. . ." He pointed to the clutter surrounding him, "I'm in the midst of a pile of paperwork."

A box marked "Bills of lading" teetered at the edge of the desk, and Nathan was sorely tempted to push it back.

"Did your assistant quit, then, Welly?"

Wellington exhaled loudly. "He did. But I'm sure that's not why you're here, Marty!"

"No, indeed. I met this man on the way in. And he has office experience."

Nathan stepped forward and extended his arm in a manner that wouldn't topple the piles. "Nathan Pleasant, sir."

"Good to meet you." He extended a broad hand. Mr. Wellington possessed a grip so strong that Nathan fought the urge to wince.

Beside him, he sensed Mr. Marrton shifting his weight. Probably needed to leave. Instead, he removed the boxes from one of the chairs and settled into it, as though planning to stay. Finally, Wellington released Nathan's hand.

Framed documents and certificates dominated the wall behind the agent. A newspaper clipping, peeking from the edge of the man's papers, had the bold headline "Another freighter sunk outside Milwaukee." Apprehension chipped away at Nathan's resolve to take whatever work he could. But he had Letitia to think of and their future together.

"Sir, you say you require an assistant?"

"I do. And you performed accounting and general paperwork elsewhere?"

"Yes. In Virginia."

"That's good news to me, Mr. Pleasant."

"I'm glad, sir."

The shipping agent rubbed his cleft chin and aimed his gaze at Marrton. "The Frenchmen and métis in these parts, like you, would pronounce his name as Plez-awnt." Wellington accented the second syllable instead of the first.

"Yes. *Plaisante* is how my mother's tribe pronounced my English name, Pleasant."

Marrton—was that his pronunciation of *Martin*?

Wellington glanced between them. "Do you have family in these parts, Nathan?"

He cleared his throat, suddenly uncomfortable. "Thirty-eight years ago, my father fought in the War of 1812, after rebelliously running away from home to join the navy."

"His name?" The ferryman's deep voice commanded the same attention Father's always had.

"Martin Pleasant."

"Martin Pleasant, *Senior*?" With Father's same mannerism of tugging at his tie when stressed, the man stood and drew in a heavy breath.

Nathan stared, recognizing the truth. "He's looked for you for so long."

"He left me behind."

"He had to."

Mr. Wellington came around the side of the desk and clapped Martin Pleasant, junior on his shoulder. "My friend, thank you for bringing Nathan to me. You may continue this family conversation when I'm done with our interview, all right?"

Nathan's half brother nodded curtly. Would he come back? From the angry look on his face, likely not. He spun on his heel and departed.

Wellington's eyebrows rose nearly as high as the fringe of bangs that bobbed on his forehead. "Well, that was interesting but not what either of us needs to address at this moment. Sit down and tell me about your skills."

The whole time they talked, Nathan's mind kept wandering to the chance encounter he'd had that had brought him full circle from where his father had begun. Father had headed as far north as he could to get away from his own controlling father. And from Richmond. But when his Chippewa wife had died, in Michigan, the tribe had insisted he leave his son with them. Would his half brother believe him? Did he even know what had happened?

Like the rushing water of the Niagara Falls, the week had burst past, with each of them heading out in a different direction each morning after a quick breakfast downstairs.

Lettie alone sat by the window, sipping her dark coffee, savoring the quiet moments. She had the luxury of leaving last, for her work at the new hat shop just down the street. Nathan and David headed off to the wharves first, followed by Beneida who'd found a position at a dressmaker's shop.

God had brought her out of slavery. But a glance at the *Buffalo Journal*'s headline announced just how tenuous her situation was—"COMPROMISE GAINS SUPPORT." What kind of compromise was it to penalize people a thousand dollars for aiding enslaved people to freedom and then returning the "property" to owners?

Rise up, girl. Mama would have told her to rise and let God's light shine through her. Lettie hadn't really understood that until recently. She lowered her head and closed her eyes. *God, I'm trusting You. You know I want to be free.* She'd always feel chased unless the Lord lifted this burden.

"Miss Lettie?"

She looked up at the maid, whose beautiful bronze skin reminded her so much of Mama's. "Yes?"

The young woman fished a cream-colored envelope out of her pocket and handed it to Lettie. "This be for you, miss."

"Thank you." She accepted it and laid it atop the blue gingham tablecloth before opening the missive. She recognized that it was from her grandfather, with *Parkes* scrawled across the back of the envelope. Could her limited reading skills allow her to read it? She sounded out the top section. *Dearest Lettie, My grand. . .*

"Lettie!" Beneida swooped in to her table, eyes wide. "I wasn't expecting you here."

"I have a letter."

"Yes, and David received a telegram, and I suspect Nathan may have gotten something, too. We sent an errand boy to him at the wharf to see."

Face pale, Beneida pressed a palm to her chest and sank into the chair beside Lettie. "We're to be married this afternoon, and David will try to be transferred to the Canadian line."

"What?"

"We think Nathan's half brother contacted his father by telegram, and he, in turn, went to David's father. So if Burwell discovered where we are, then we may be in danger. David sent me a message to go and get ready."

Lettie's heart beat so hard in her chest she could scarcely breathe. "I'll go to Canada, then, as I planned."

"What does your letter say?"

Lettie pushed the letter to her friend. "Would you read it?"

"Certainly." Beneida quickly scanned the letter.

"I meant read it aloud to me."

Smiling, Beneida turned to her, eyes filled with happy tears. "You're free! Your grandfather purchased your contract."

She sucked in a breath. "How?"

"Master Burwell was convinced by your grandfather's gun."

Lettie gasped. "Did he shoot him?"

Laughing, Beneida pointed to the middle of the page. "He says he opted to let the miscreant live but made Burwell sign over a bill of sale for you."

"Oh, Lord, have mercy. . ." A shudder of relief course through her down to her laced-up work boots.

"He adds, however, that the slave broker, Cheney, has gone missing." She looked up. "And that the overseer, Durham, met his end in a way he'd not wish upon anyone."

"Oh, my! Was it Satide?"

"I guess so, because Cheney was transporting Satide to Richmond, for sale, but neither made it there."

The two sat silently for a moment.

Lettie shivered. "There will always be more Cheneys and Durhams out there to replace those wicked men."

"But there are good men like Mr. Parkes." Beneida smiled. "He promises to send your freedom papers by special courier and is having copies made."

Free. "I can hardly believe it!" And Nathan would be free to marry whomever he pleased. He'd not have to feel bound to protect her anymore.

"It's true. Says so right here."

Lettie sniffed back tears. "But, Beneida, what about you?"

"Let me finish reading and see if he says." She bent over the letter and quickly moved from the first to second page. Her expression changed from one of awe, to confusion, to sadness. "Mr. Parkes just says Burwell told him that Lord Wrenwick would be happy with me and to not concern himself."

"Oh, Beneida, Mr. Burwell must have known about Wrenwick's two men pursuing you, then."

"Probably aided them."

"No doubt."

"It's all right." Her friend brushed moisture from her face. "David and I will marry and get on with our new life."

"But you'll be gone to Canada. And sailing on the Great Lakes."

"Yes."

Lettie, too, would be gone as soon as her papers arrived. But, oh, how her heart would grieve her loss of her friends, and of the man she loved.

By the time Mr. Wellington could release him from work, Nathan had himself worked up to give his brother, Martin, an earful. Hadn't the man even thought of what his careless telegram could have wrought? At least there would be some good that could come of this for Beneida.

"Mr. Pleasant?" The dirty street urchin that he'd sent to the inn with a message, stood in the doorway. "Do I still get my money even if I couldn't find 'em?"

Had they already gone? David may have panicked. "Did you stop at the millinery shop?"

"Yes, sir, but they said she'd drawn her wages and left."

"Left?"

"Yes, sir." The boy held out his grimy hand and David placed several coins there. With wide eyes, he counted the amount aloud and grinned. "Thanks!" He sped out of the building, brushing past Wellington as he went.

Nathan rushed to the inn. Where would Lettie have gone? Was she in hiding? They'd agreed to meet at the church they were attending. Surely Pastor Maher or his wife would know. And what of Beneida and David? Would they still marry when they learned that she was free—that Miss Dolley should have been free all along? Amazing what evil that money slipped into the pocket of a greedy judge would do. Father had included a clip from the *Richmond Times* in with his letter, that explained how Lord Wrenwick had arrived in town in high dudgeon and had pursued the matter until Mr. Dolley's will was produced and legal documents clearly showed Beneida should have been freed upon his death. How would David react if Beneida now refused to marry him? Would the ebony-haired beauty no longer need his friend once her freedom was secure?

Once inside the building, he clattered up the stairs to their rooms. No one answered at either door. He unlocked his room. All of David's belongings were gone. Inside Letitia's room, a maid was dusting the bare room.

"They at church, sir."

"Thank you." They were at church, but all their belongings were packed. Would they have already gone on?

When he arrived at the Church of Eternal Salvation, an abolitionist meeting place, he tried the sanctuary door. Locked. He knocked. No one answered. He pounded louder.

A metallic clicking sounded as someone inside unlocked the door and pushed it open. Mrs. Maher, a pretty blond woman about Letitia's height, placed a finger by her lips. "We have a wedding going on here."

In the front, Pastor Maher held his Bible and spoke to Beneida and David. Where was Letitia? He scanned the square sanctuary, all ten rows of benches empty.

"Would you like to witness with me?" Mrs. Maher asked softly.

"Where's Letitia?"

At the ferry, Lettie sought out Martin Pleasant. She spied a man of Nathan's height and similar build, his back turned to her, attired in a dove-gray long coat and matching trousers, and a top hat. When he turned, Lettie couldn't suppress her surprise and gave a little gasp. The man resembled an image of Nathan but dipped in caramel. This had to be his half brother. Nathan had met with Martin once and had shared about their past but hadn't seen him again. While she was grateful his telegram had helped her grandfather find her, he may have imperiled her friend.

She strode toward the man. "Mr. Pleasant?"

He tipped his tall hat. "May I help you?"

"I'm Lettie, Nathan's. . ." What was she to him? His friend?

"His fiancée?" Martin grinned broadly, revealing large white teeth. "No wonder he fell so deeply in love with you."

Lettie couldn't manage a response. Her heart sputtered in fits and starts. Was that really what Nathan had told him?

"Glad to meet you, Letitia. And happy for what little part I may have had in bringing you two together, or possibly my grandmother's influence."

She frowned. "What do you mean?"

"My father, too, married the descendant of a slave—in his case, a Sioux maiden captured and given to a French lieutenant at Fort Mackinac." He rubbed his chin. "When the English came in, my grandmother escaped with my mother and obtained work at Fort Detroit. Nathan told me that our father shared this history with him as the reason that drove him to support abolitionist work in the South. He'd seen firsthand how slavery had affected my mother and grandmother."

She felt a strange kinship to this man. An understanding. "I thank you for sharing. But I'm here for help."

"In any way." He extended his hands as passengers streamed toward the wharf and the ferries.

"You see, your telegram to Mr. Pleasant may have alerted slave catchers to our location."

He pressed his dark eyes closed. "I wasn't thinking. I was just so anxious to contact him."

"Yes, well some good came of that, for me." The wind rustled her skirts. "But my friend may be at risk."

"I'm so sorry. Tell me what you need."

Their carriage stopped by the Blue Star Line Ferry, and they got out, Nathan first. David paid the driver and grinned at Nathan. "My father's a gem. He transferred funds for me, and now we won't have to worry. Nor live in that squalid inn."

Nathan scanned the queue of passengers but didn't spy Letitia.

"There she is!" Beneida waved, jumping up and down like a child.

"My darling, we're in public."

But Beneida ignored David and ran off ahead of them.

"No doubt happy to share her news." David sighed. "Let's hope Lettie likes your idea."

His neck suddenly hot, Nathan loosened his cravat. If all went well, tonight he'd have a bride.

"Come on, Nate!" David darted ahead, dodging through the line.

"Excuse me," Nathan repeated over and over again as he wove through the groups of passengers, in pursuit of his friend and on to his future wife. If she'd have him.

When he finally reached her, Letitia and Beneida were hugging and crying. David stood behind them, arms crossed. From a small whitewashed building to the right, Martin emerged, holding up what looked like tickets. Nathan inched closer to Letitia, waiting for his moment.

"Who's going to Canada?" Martin asked.

Letitia glanced from his brother to him, a question in her eyes.

Nathan swooped upon her like a bird of prey, possessively wrapping his arms around her and kissing her so soundly, Lettie could barely breathe. The dock seemed to fade away, the passengers' voices dimming, as she sank into the warmth of his promise. His lips covered hers and then moved to her cheek and then to her neck. Her breath stuttered.

"Will you have me as husband, even though you are free to choose whoever you want?" Nathan's lips traveled up her cheek to her mouth again before she could respond. Then he embraced her and held her so tenderly that she buried her face in his jacket, wanting the moment to never end.

David cleared his throat. "I think we'd better get them back to the church before Pastor and Mrs. Maher get busy with tonight's meeting."

"And before they make any more of a spectacle of themselves on my wharf." Martin laughed, and Lettie broke free from his brother's grasp.

"Sorry." Face flushed, she tried to straighten her cap, which had been knocked askew.

"I'm not." Nathan grabbed her hand. "I love you and want you to be my wife."

"I love you, too." She closed her eyes and tipped her head back and was rewarded with another delicious kiss.

"We don't have the licenses yet, but we do have a church, a pastor, and can be your witnesses." Beneida's face glowed.

"And we're free."

Nathan turned to face his brother. "I don't think we'll be needing that ferry ride to Canada, now that both have their papers coming. Thank you for your unintended wedding gift."

"Anytime." Martin winked at him. "And a ride on the ferry just for fun is yours for the asking. Several nice private inns over there."

"We'll be back in an hour, then, after we see the preacher." Nathan laughed.

Heat crept into Lettie's face. "I don't think I agreed to anything yet."

"Will you say your vows?"

"If you'll say yours."

Martin wrapped an arm around Nathan and around Lettie. "I'll see you back later, then, and I'll send word for a cottage to be held for you on the other side tonight."

The other side. The other side of slavery was freedom. She'd finally arrived in the promised land. And she didn't have to wait for heaven to be there.

Author's Notes

The daffodil was being cultivated more widely in the Mid-Atlantic area at this time. There was no known symbol of the daffodil being used to identify "conductors"—I just made that up. And it's hard to believe that our Eastern seaboard wasn't highly populated. In 1850, our cities were the size of many of today's suburbs or smaller. In the 1850 census, slaves were included on the household lists. I think of my heroine and her friend and can only imagine how horrible it would be to have one's name listed as property.

Train travel was taking off during this time. Likewise ship travel was changing drastically with the transition from sail-powered to engine-powered ships (steamboats). There were even hybrid ships, which were a combination of both. Due to the short length of this novella, I did not elaborate upon the details of travel. A great reference book you may want to read is *Wet Britches and Muddy Boots: A History of Travel in Victorian America* by John H. White Jr. (Indiana University Press, 2013).

As mentioned in the story, the Fugitive Slave Act of 1850 was part of the Compromise of 1850. During the Mexican-American War, as new territories were acquired, there was acrimony between slave owners in the South and abolitionists in the North. In addition, those who favored states' rights to enforcing or not enforcing the return of slaves didn't want the federal government to enforce the return of "property." Unfortunately, the new act made slavery a protected institution and set up the beginning of the buildup to our Civil War. As slave catchers swarmed the North and states fought back against legislation, abolitionist sentiment burgeoned. My hero and heroine live in a time on the cusp of tremendous turmoil.

ECPA-bestselling author, **Carrie Fancett Pagels**, Ph.D., is the award-winning author of over a dozen Christian historical romances. Twenty-five years as a psychologist didn't "cure" her overactive imagination! A self-professed "history geek," she resides with her family in the Historic Triangle of Virginia but grew up as a "Yooper" in Michigan's Upper Peninsula. Carrie loves to read, bake, bead, and travel – but not all at the same time! You can connect with her at www.CarrieFancettPagels.com.

Waltzing Matilda

by Lucy Thompson

Stand fast therefore in the liberty by which Christ has made us free,
and do not be entangled again with a yoke of bondage.
—GALATIANS 5:1 NKJV

Chapter 1

The Bolter
Parramatta, Sydney 1821

Matilda Brampton took one more look at the walls of the Parramatta Female Factory and vowed it would be her last. Clutching month-old baby Charlotte close, she skipped across the rutted street, bold as any freeman and hustled to the wider main road that led out of Parramatta.

Several streets over, she passed her place of work since landing in Port Jackson, a hastily built house of wattle and daub where she'd ordinarily spend long hours bent over a needle.

"Not today, lass," she muttered. She skirted the building and hurried to join the smattering of people hustling along the street.

First, she needed to change out of this kit and find some new clothes to wear. The yellow calico of her dress stood out like a ticket of leave on the governor's table. Though she might be a bolter, she'd rather not be so obvious. The next item on her hasty list would be to join the safety of a group headed over the Blue Mountains toward Bathurst. No one would look for her there. Or so she'd heard. Much as she'd like to rely on no one and do things herself, fear of native attacks demanded she be sensible.

"Be careful, miss!" a man shouted.

At the warning, she stumbled back against a rough brush fence, her skirts buffeted by the sheep that ran past.

Sheep. In town? And not just in town—in her way. Matilda clutched Charlotte and glanced down the wide track that passed as the main thoroughfare. A bleating, haphazard wall of sheep surged toward her, driven forward by a group of men and several dogs, occasionally yipping at their heels.

"Sheep," she muttered, edging along the brush fence until she came to a small laneway. "Of all the times I need to leave unnoticed I would get waylaid by something as absurd as sheep."

She needed to hurry before she was missed and reported. Weighed down with Charlotte, she could never outrun a group of soldiers. Not just hurry. She needed to leave *now*. Matilda stamped a foot, the rough stone stabbing through the thin soles of her shoes.

Charlotte squirmed in her arms, snuffling in her sleep. Matilda adjusted the baby's clothing, sweat sticking the nightgown to the baby's back. Sickly as Charlotte was, staying in Sydney was not an option.

She headed to the end of the laneway. Sheep continued to trot past, oblivious to her and the fact they were in her way.

"Shoo," she said.

They ignored her.

No matter how cute their fluffy little faces were, if one of them so much as decided to try and knock her down. . . She sucked in a breath. 'Twas unthinkable. If she fell and crushed Charlotte, no one this side of the equator would care.

Dander raised, she grasped a handful of her voluminous skirt and flapped it. "Shoo!"

Still they continued to hurry past her, oblivious. A dog of dubious heritage nipped at one sheep's heels, briefly pausing to eye her curiously.

Confound it. Did no one care that if she stayed, Charlotte would be taken from her and placed in an orphanage? The prospect was nigh on three years away, but with the ever-changing laws in this new land of Australia, it wasn't a risk she was willing to take. She couldn't lose the one piece of good left in her life.

They were leaving Sydney that very moment and that was that.

She charged to the end of the laneway, flapping her skirt wildly. "Move your wooly buttocks the cursed lot of ye!"

Just as she'd hoped, they swerved away from her and ran this way and that, their spindly legs barely able to hold up their wool-laden bodies. Within moments, the men herding the sheep began shouting. Short whistles pierced the air as they commanded their dogs.

"What do ya think you're doing, lass?" a man called out from atop a sturdy bay horse.

His red flannel shirt and brown trousers proclaimed him to be a freeman—one who'd served out his sentence. The black bandanna tied sailor-fashion around his neck and the wide grin on his clean-shaven face pronounced him to be the cheeky sort she'd best avoid.

"Trying to get past these sheep," she yelled back.

" 'Tis that what you're doing?" He heeled his horse into the middle of the mob and began moving toward her, a light brown dog following close behind.

"No, don't come over here," she muttered, backing away.

The sheepherder broke free of the sheep and stopped before her. "Are you all right? Nearly got yourself hurt."

Briefly, Matilda glanced at his face and caught sight of his laughing blue eyes and the shock of light brown hair that fell over his tanned face.

"I'm fine. No cause for concern." She kept her gaze upon the ground, fear of recognition weighting her head.

"May I offer some assistance to cross the road? A woman with such pretty locks ought not be subject to those perils, unaccompanied."

Ach, he was a smooth-tongued devil, and she'd not believe his lies. Still, she couldn't help but reach up to touch the strands of black hair that escaped her plain bonnet.

"No." Head down, she bit back the fierce words upon her tongue. The last time a man offered her a *helping hand* she ended up pregnant aboard a transport ship bound for

Australia. She'd not mistake anyone's gilded kindness again.

The brown dog sniffed at her skirts, tail wagging. At that moment, Charlotte stirred, preventing Matilda from stooping to pat the dog and offer a reward for his honest affection.

"Take care, milady. I'll not have it said that Henry Powell is going about knocking good women over." His carefree laugh followed him as he wheeled his horse and, with his dog, dashed to round up the straggling sheep.

Good women. That did not apply to her. No, she was made up of words such as *thief, liar,* and *escapee convict.*

God seemed to have turned His face away. To have forgotten her. She couldn't trust Him with her daughter's future when her past was so far out of His hands.

"Pay him no mind," another sheepherder said as he pressed by with a laugh. "He's an incorrigible flirt. Has half o' the Sydney girls hanging off his words."

If that's what Henry Powell was like, the Sydney girls could have him. Foolish chits. She had bigger worries.

Once again, she eyed the passing sheep. Maybe they could provide enough distraction to cover her. Perhaps once she'd found suitable clothes, she could join the sheepherders and follow them out of town.

Charlotte began to cry, small whimpers huffing past her tiny mouth.

"Hush, darling. Mama nearly has found a way free for us." Matilda rocked the baby. "Look, there are several sheep who've gone down the wrong street."

Taking advantage of the confusion, Matilda scurried down the lane, away from the main road, pausing to dart through somebody's back garden, and pilfered a long pair of men's trousers and a faded shirt. Ahead, on the outskirts of town was a thick stand of trees, eucalypts hemmed in by scrubby underbrush. Shielding Charlotte, she plunged in, not stopping until she was sure her presence would not be detected from the road.

Laying Charlotte on her bundled-up shawl, she hurried out of her convict-issue clothes and into the men's trousers and shirt. Hastily tearing one of her petticoats and arranging her apron, she made a makeshift sling for the baby. Tucking in the ends, she tried as best she could to disguise the sling as a provisions bag.

After feeding the lethargic baby, she laid her in the sling and tried it on. Not perfect, but it would have to do. She'd take her chances, face whatever perils came her way. Charlotte depended on her to be successful.

What had that man said? Something about her *pretty locks* and being subject to *perils unaccompanied.*

Would her hair give her away? Could she get away with this deception? She was going to be detected and dragged back if she didn't do something to disguise her hair.

Already she could feel their gazes crawling over her, could feel hands grasping her again, fettering her limbs as dank water sloshed over her bare feet.

"No," she whispered. "I can't go back to that. Please, Lord, if You're there, make a way for us to be free. Truly free."

Chapter 2

The Choice

W hen are you going to settle down and think about taking a wife?"
Henry Powell looked to the left, to the man riding next to him as they
pushed the middle group of sheep onward. "Oh, I dunno. How about in a
week or so?" he called back to his longtime friend and constant source of teasing.

John Phillips laughed, and Henry joined him, the sound echoing down through the
valley that led the way to the Blue Mountains.

"That flirting will get the better of you one day, friend."

"Not so long as I have a merry tune to tire them and a fleet horse at hand." Henry
clamped his hat to his head, dodging the low tree branches that arched over the narrow
track, and stood in the stirrups.

Not far ahead, the track dipped steeply over a hill and already he feared the sheep
would struggle despite two solid days of trekking.

John nudged his horse closer to Henry's. "You could have had your pick of all the
girls in Sydney. Why didn't you choose one before we left?"

Henry shook his head. "They are convict girls. Most are as lewd and brash as any
on a street corner at night." He whistled for his dog and waited for the last wagon to
catch up. "I'm praying for a God-fearing wife. The Lord will send her along when the
time is right."

"Praying?" John sputtered the word like it was a mouthful of pease porridge. "You
take your religion thing far too seriously."

"Jesus took—"

"I don't want to hear about it." John shifted in his saddle for a moment and then
brightened. "What did you pray? How will you know the good Lord has sent this par-
agon of virtue?"

"Jeremiah 29:11 'For I know the thoughts that I think toward you, saith the Lord,
thoughts of peace, and not of evil, to give you an expected end.'"

"Might as well be Dutch to me."

"It means," Henry said, catching sight of the last wagon to pass over the hill, "that
she'll be peaceful, pure, and will fit into my life perfectly."

"Well, when you find her, ask if she has a sister." John's gaze shifted behind them.
"Better keep an eye on those shepherds on foot. One in particular is having trouble
keeping up. We might need to turn him back."

Henry nodded then whistled for his dog. "Hiyup, Dodger. Bring them up."

Dodger gave a delighted *woof* and loped her way to the back of the sheep, herding wayward sheep into a more compact formation as she went.

Ever since the feisty girl in Parramatta had spooked the sheep, the wooly beasts had been more flighty than usual. He'd be glad when they got over the mountains and could settle them on some good pasture on his sheep run near Bathurst. In the meantime, he'd remind himself that the Lord was thinking of him, would look after him. He need not fear.

Shading his eyes, Henry scanned the remainder of their convoy. A storekeeper and a publican trudged alongside their loaded wagons, each with his allotted convict slaves strung out in front, a motley crew made up of men eager to be rid of the starving rations in Sydney. He would gladly work alongside these enslaved men as they conquered the inland of this wide brown land that so differed from England.

Henry squinted against the deep afternoon shadows, trying to catch a glimpse of the man John had mentioned.

A pistol shot rang out, its echo ricocheting along the valley for several seconds. The sheep parted like the Red Sea.

Two men ran toward Henry, veering left and right and continued to shout, "Snake!"

Henry wheeled his horse around to meet the men.

"Cor blimey. He's dead," a voice said in wonder.

Henry held his horse still. "Who is?"

A small circle of onlookers peered intently at the ground. If they'd shot a person, Henry would have the entire New South Wales Army Corps on his head.

"Brown snake, gov." One of the onlookers, the ruddy publican, looked up with a grin. "A six-footer, to be sure. Glad we got 'im afore he bit someone, and they was kilt."

Henry stepped off his horse and got a closer look. The snake writhed on the ground, the head missing from his coffee-colored body. The onlookers pressed closer, snippets of their conversation floated on the still, afternoon breeze as they offered advice on what could have and should have been done differently. A short man in a wide hat that was tugged low, his shirt bagging at the waist, clutched at a lumpy provisions bag and visibly shuddered.

"Watch 'im!" someone shouted.

The snake whipped around, almost the length of his body and wrapped around the ankle of the man clutching his bag. He screamed. A long, high-pitched scream that rang Henry's ears. Either the man's voice hadn't broken yet—or he was deathly afraid of snakes.

"Get it off! Get it off!" the man continued to squeal. "Somebody help before it hurts my baby."

"Baby?" Henry stared at the man. What was a man doing with a baby? All his workers were single and eager to work hard to provide for any future families. Future. Not now. Not here.

The man screamed again, dancing on one foot.

"Stand still," Henry ordered and then jerked the coiled snake off the man's leg. He hurled it into the bush and propped his hands on his hips. "Somebody want to explain to me why we've got a baby in our convoy?"

"No," the man mumbled, head down.

Henry tapped his chin as he considered the man's stance. He was no mathematician and could barely write his own name, but something wasn't quite adding up. "Take off your hat."

"No."

The voice was quieter. More determined and yet—somehow, more defeated.

Henry motioned to John to round up the sheep and their hired crew. With a whistle, he directed Dodger to assist John. If they didn't keep the herd together, the sheep would wander off into the bush and be lost to the natives and wild dogs. Not to mention that Henry would like to make camp by water tonight, which meant still keeping a forced pace.

The man who'd screamed started forward, but Henry grabbed his arm, stopping him. "Not you." Once everybody had passed, he released the man and gentled his tone. "Remove your hat, please. If you're who I think you are then you're going to need my protection."

That brought the man's chin up. Green eyes shone fiercely over a slightly upturned nose and full lips.

Female. Most decidedly female.

She yanked off her hat, revealing black hair twisted tightly around her head.

Not just any female. The woman who'd stampeded his sheep in Sydney.

"I don't need protection from any man—jack-a-dandy or otherwise."

Dandy? Just because he combed his hair at least once a day didn't qualify him for the term. Perhaps she was simply exhausted, the circles under her eyes spoke of that. Or perhaps the heat of the day had left her parched. There was no time to sit and rest, but he could offer her what little provision he had.

"My name is Henry. Henry Powell. Would you like some water, milady?" He retrieved a water pouch from behind his saddle and held it out.

Something akin to grudging acceptance flashed in her eyes. Yet she took the pouch.

"Now, let's see this poor mite." Careful to keep his movements slow, Henry motioned to the sack she had slung over her shoulder. "I, ah, take it he's—"

"She," the woman interrupted. "She's a girl." Carefully, she lifted the baby out of the sack.

He'd seen bigger kittens. And with less hair. At least a third of the baby appeared to be a shock of thick black hair, the rest of her tiny body covered in a thin gown.

Weakly, the baby began to cry, her sweat-streaked face nuzzling into her mother's shirt.

Not for the first time, he wished his mother were near. If she were, she'd know what to do, not stammer and blush as he was.

"Turn your back, please." The woman rocked the baby, doing little to quiet her husky mewling. "I need to feed Charlotte."

Pivoting on his heels, Henry considered the track his sheep and men were gradually making their way down. "Charlotte. . . Was that the ship you arrived on?"

Silence at first, followed by the rustling of clothing. "No. 'Twas the *John Bull*."

"Mine was the *Somersetshire*," he said absently. "A lifetime ago, really."

"Too long ago," the woman said wearily. "All I know is I'm not going back to Sydney. Ever. They'll have to drag me back in irons."

A sudden image of the clothing she'd worn the first time he'd seen her reemerged, and he laughed. "You're a bolter."

Silence.

"An escapee prisoner." He had to remain matter of fact. Not let his heart be wrenched by the tenderness she'd shown her baby. He'd give her a second chance in a heartbeat, but it was the authority's place to deal with runaways. "I'll take you back to Sydney."

More silence. He waited several moments longer. The silence seemed, well, too *silent*. He spun.

The track behind him was empty.

He shook his head and moved to get his horse. At least she'd had the good sense to take his water pouch.

Chapter 3

Milady's Name

Matilda crouched in a shallow depression at the bottom of the hill they'd just climbed. Already, the shouts of the men and noises of the sheep had begun to fade.

She'd run as fast as she could without making too much noise, but was it far enough?

The man who'd offered her water, Henry, had seemed nice enough. He'd made no overtures nor pressed for details she was not prepared to give. Still, she refused to let her guard down, to trust. No. The only person she could rely on was herself, and no one—no matter how kind his blue eyes had appeared—would change her mind otherwise.

Tiny black ants climbed over her ankles and crept inside her pant legs. Matilda tucked the water bag under her arm. She slapped at the ants while trying to keep her ears attentive to any other noises.

A flock of white birds flew overhead, squawking loudly. They settled in the tree above her and began a noisy conversation, yellow crests rising as they complained about her presence. Cockatoos, she'd heard someone call them. Much as she disliked the lack of civilization, she'd do her best to be brave, to endure. Best to keep moving. Now that Charlotte was fed, she slept, body limp. Already sweat dampened the layers of clothing between them.

Matilda shielded the sling from the low branches of the bushy undergrowth and carefully picked her way forward, following the trail of horses and livestock from along the bottom of the ridge. She'd slip past them and, when they stopped for the night, try to catch up with the bigger group of settlers journeying several miles ahead. Surely, there she could hide.

She paused at a group of squat sandstone boulders, layered with grainy bands of white and red. Another twenty feet of uphill climb would put her back on the trail. Once she'd caught her breath, she'd press on. Upward and onward.

"Need some assistance?"

Her gaze snapped up.

Henry.

He stood, one hand grasping a small sapling as he leaned down the slope, his free hand extended to her. He smiled, those blue eyes twinkling at her again. "It's a bit of a steep climb. Come on. Up we go."

Could she ever be rid of his help? The day's events pressed in. The heat. The need for rest. Why did everything she attempted have to be so *hard*? Curse her vulnerability. Perhaps she was better off facing the dangers she could actually see. To give this man and his sheep a chance, albeit at a good distance. Surely, that was better than deadly snakes, noisy cockatoos, and goodness knew what else that lurked in the scrub.

With a sigh, she held out her hand.

He took it, holding her weight easily as she struggled up the leaf-slick slope. At the top of the ridge, his horse and the trail came into view. Her knees shook as she took the final step onto firmer ground.

Once on the trail, she tried to tug her hand free, but his fingers held fast around her wrist.

"What's your name, lass?"

Clamping her lips tight, she tugged harder.

"What 'tis the matter?"

"I'm not going anywhere with you. I heard what they call you." Matilda worked her mouth around the word before spitting it out. "A flirt."

"Is that all?" His grip softened, fingers sliding from her wrist to briefly clasp her fingers before letting go. "I thought it was some beastly name."

Her eyes narrowed. "An incorrigible flirt."

He laughed, then, the soft sound barely reaching her ears. " 'Tis true that I flirt. Life is meant for having fun, laughter, and dancing."

"So you admit it, then."

"Mm-hmm. But I never trifle. *That* would be beastly. Your affections will remain unchanged, milady."

He could wager his worn saddle on that surety. She'd make sure her heart remained firmly behind the bars of her good sense.

"I mean you no harm. 'Tis only your name I seek."

A search of his face and the way he stood casually attested to that. He didn't crowd her nor try to win her with smooth words. Oh, his words were smooth enough. . .but somehow. . .different.

"Why? So you can turn me in?"

"Not today."

"Then I cannot trust you." Matilda backed up a step, eyeing the embankment she'd just ascended. Better her chances on her own, not with someone who was untrustworthy. "You know what I am. I heard you say so—a bolter."

"Yes. I did say that."

Henry brushed his hair from his forehead, giving her a better glimpse of his eyes.

"That's what you've done, not who you are. Each of us—you and I and half of the men taking care of these sheep—is a convict who has a story to tell. What's yours?"

"My story?" Matilda licked her lips. "I don't have one. What you see here is who I am."

"Ah. The lady hides herself well." Henry scooped up the reins to his horse and strode forward several steps. "Fear has taken her captive."

"I'm no one's captive." Matilda turned her back on him and marched down the track. "I need only rely on myself, thank you very much."

"Like you did with that snake?"

She halted, glancing at the sides of the narrow track. The snake had slithered over the track right in front of her, giving her no time to react. The memory of the thick coils squeezing her ankle, smooth, warm scales sliding to form a tighter grip. *Ugh.* Matilda danced sideways, shaking the numb sensation from her foot.

"Is it so hard to share who you are and why you are here?" Henry asked.

"Yes." Matilda swung around, hands propped on her hips. "Anything I tell you can and most possibly will be used against me. Against Charlotte."

"What have you got to lose?"

"Everything!"

At her yell, Charlotte jolted, lips smacking together. Matilda ran a hand over her daughter's back, soothing her to sleep again.

"And what have you to gain, hmm? Have you not thought that through?"

Gain? But at what cost? Laying her soul bare? No, thank you.

"What about you? What do *you* gain, Henry Powell, the notorious flirt?"

"A little peace for my soul."

"Ha." Her huff of laughter quieted at his pensive look. "I almost believe you."

He gave himself a shake and took a step forward. "I was once like you. Bold. Brash. Outspoken."

"I'm *not* b—"

He held up a finger. "You are. And it's admirable. It's also an excellent way to get yourself in trouble, but still I admire your spirit. Chains do something to a person, to a soul." He held up his wrists, shoulder-width apart. "I became obedient. Compliant. In reality, I was a coward. I'll not do that to a person."

Coward? This confident freeman with his herd of sheep, friends to laugh with, and dog at heel was a coward?

His humbleness sparked a need, no, a desire, to speak.

"I stole four spoons."

There it was. Her sins laid bare. Reason enough to send her back to good ol' Botany Bay.

"Only four?" His eyebrows rose.

"Well, they were silver," she huffed. "And they were found in my possession. I didn't steal them. 'Twas the other maid. The lying, cheating hus—"

"Hungry servant?"

Matilda snorted. "Or that word. Still, I'm the one with a seven-year sentence. Who was transported. Ended up pregnant. Who will have my child taken from me."

Henry regarded her, gaze steady. "See now. Was that so hard to share your story?"

"Yes!"

He had no idea how exposed she now felt. How vulnerable.

She glanced over her shoulder, retracing the cloven prints left by the sheep. "So. . . are you going to turn me in now?"

"Not today." He winked. "How can I when I don't know fair lady's name? Reason enough to know it, seeing as we'll be journeying together."

"Journeying?" She eyed him through narrowed eyelids, mouth pursed.

"Yes, yes. The act of traveling from one place to another. Marvelous activity. Also known as a long and oft difficult process of personal change. However, I suspect we're talking about the first instance—traveling together."

"Together. . .what do you mean by that?"

He gestured, indicating the blue haze that hung over the mountains ahead of them, the soft green of the eucalypt tree canopy, the white-pink of the tree trunks flashing through the dense forest that spread on either side.

"As we journey together across this sunburnt country, milady." He strode forward, confidence practically dripping from him. "Until we arrive wherever the horizon will take us."

"Us?" She eyed him suspiciously and then trudged to catch up to him. They headed away from Sydney. Did that mean he'd found his peace and decided against turning her in?

"Yes." He nodded, before relieving her of his water bag. "You, baby Charlotte, my best mate John, then there's—"

"I understand. No need to go on."

"And go on we must if we are to make camp before nightfall." He grimaced. "I don't know about you, but I'd rather have the company of a blazing fire and some nice music than the howls of the dingoes."

"Dingoes?"

"The native dogs. Sneaky as sin, they are, and just as fatal."

"In that case, a fire sounds right nice." As did the notion of finally sitting down. She'd not yet recovered her strength from the months of travel at sea and then the strict regime of work once she arrived at the Parramatta Female Factory, followed by the birth of Charlotte. The last two days of constant walking hadn't helped, either.

"May I offer you my horse—?"

"Matilda." Her name was the least she could offer in return. It was a small token, but the only she'd give. "Matilda Brampton."

"I remain your humble servant, Miss Brampton." He glanced at Charlotte, a small frown forming. "It *is* miss, is it not?"

"Yes," she answered shortly.

He nodded, apparently content not to pursue the matter.

Sydney was filled with babies and small children with no fathers to claim them. It wasn't like she was an oddity. The governor had even commissioned an orphanage to contain, educate, and otherwise control the effect the convict parent might have on their children. Convict parent she may well be, but she'd be the one to influence her child, not a harsh governing authority, no matter the costs.

Henry stopped to mop his brow with a snow-white handkerchief. She paused, lost for words as she took in its color and clean condition, so at odds with the dusty surroundings. Many an Englishman now called Australia home for stealing handkerchiefs only half as nice as this one.

He caught her staring and smiled. "My mother's parting gift."

She nodded, a lump forming in her throat. Her last memory of her mother was a thin figure waving from their wicker gate in Kent. Mother would not have known of the supposed theft of the four silver spoons, the short trial, nor her stay aboard one of the floating hulks. More than three years had passed now. Who was to say whether she was even still alive on their tiny farm?

"Milady?"

Henry's voice held the patience of one who had repeated himself more than once.

"Yes?"

"My men will be wondering what has happened to me. We need to rejoin them as soon as possible." His gaze darted past her. "These trees may appear empty, but who is to say if we've angered the Wiradjuri people? Too many white men have hurt the native people here. Tensions are high, and we are safest where we have firearm protection."

He mounted his horse then leaned down, hands extended. "Pass Charlotte to me, and then I'll settle you behind my saddle."

Reflexively, she hugged Charlotte closer. The tiny rosebud mouth worked in her sleep. Could she trust another to hold her?

"Miss Brampton." He waited until she met his eyes before continuing. "As the Lord Almighty is my witness, I'll let no harm come to her. And if I somehow inadvertently do, I'll hand you my pistol myself, and you can shoot me."

"You wouldn't."

His eyes twinkled a moment before he laughed. "How about we trust each other— just for today."

"No lies?" She frowned at his hand as if it were the snake that had chased her.

"Nary a one."

"For today, then," she agreed and lifted the sling containing Charlotte from her shoulder.

Today, and only because she was so very tired, she would let her guard down. She'd have her rest, and Henry would have his peace.

He laid Charlotte in the crook of his elbow, his tanned forearm contrasted against her much paler skin. Matilda swallowed against her tight throat.

Was that how Charlotte would have looked, tucked in her father's arms?

If only God had listened to her prayers, had turned His ear to her sobs, her baby would have had both her parents. Tears wet her lashes as Henry gently tucked the muslin gown over Charlotte's exposed skin.

If only.

Henry removed his foot from the stirrup. "Put your boot in, and I'll swing you up. You're already wearing trousers, so riding astride should pose no problem."

Yes. No problem. If one had trust. If one had faith.

"Trust," she whispered as she grasped his wrist.

A short tug later and she was seated behind him, his wide shoulders blocking most of her view.

With a click of his tongue, he set the horse in motion. For the first time in her eighteen years, she would have faith that someone would protect her.

Yes, she would trust him.

But could he be counted on when—not if—the soldiers came for her?

Chapter 4

Shall We Dance?

Matilda threw another armful of branches on the campfire. It crackled, sparks showering upward and glinting red against the stars that made up the Southern Cross.

Picking her way past several sheepherders that slumped on their bedrolls, she ignored their soft snores and quiet conversation as she made her way back to where Charlotte slept fitfully in a bundle of blankets.

First chance she got, she'd try to reach the other group of travelers. The larger group promised anonymity, no second looks, and no knowledge of her name.

"Miss Brampton?"

She brushed dirt from her fingers and looked up. "Yes?"

Henry extended his handkerchief, one corner translucent and damp. "Perhaps this might cool your wee one."

"I can't touch that." She tore her gaze from the fine lawn and lace edging. "It's your mother's."

"Aye. With a heart as wide as Port Jackson Harbour." He pressed the handkerchief into her hand and curled her fingers around it. "She'd be most emphatic that your babe be comfortable, as am I."

"If you insist." She gently wiped the cloth over Charlotte's face and neck, cooling the delicate skin. Already she slept more soundly.

"I'm going to fetch more water," Henry said. "Help John keep a watch out for snakes or wild dogs or anything else that might pose a threat."

She quickly finished wiping Charlotte down and sat, hands clenched between her knees as she scanned the perimeter of their small camp. A slight breeze tousled the low branches and rustled through stubbly grass. Quiet sounds. Restful. Enough to put aside her fears of brown snakes—at least for the moment.

Across from her, Henry's friend John alternated between glancing at the scrub and absently scratching on a ragged piece of paper with a pencil. A sense of quiet stole over the camp, so much so that she could make out the sounds from the larger camp several miles away.

Henry reappeared out of the darkness, a water bag slung over each shoulder. He slapped the canvas bags, sending their contents sloshing.

"What's this?" he boomed. "I go away for ten minutes, and the entire camp is in the doldrums. We've got men already rolled in their blankets, John over here with the long face, and Miss Brampton with nary a smile. No, no. This won't do at all."

"Ach. Quiet yourself," John said. "Save your sweet-talking for another time. Some of us have had a hard day."

"All the more reason for some music." Henry dumped the water bags at the base of a nearby tree and stalked to his saddlebags. Rummaging through the bags, he emerged waving a violin case.

"Music?" Matilda said, checking that Charlotte still slept beside her in her bundle of blankets. "But how did you obtain a violin?"

"Exchanged my rum ration for it." He tucked the violin under his chin, adjusted the pegs, and tuned up. "A man can live without rum. But music? No. One must have food for his soul."

"You and your poetry," John said. "I think we're better off sleeping. There's another long day ahead of us tomor—"

His words were drowned out as Henry ran his bow over the strings. Mincing his steps, Henry made his way around the campfire, playing low and slow then faster and faster once the men had rolled to their feet. He played a rollicking tune that wound through the gum trees, encouraging the men to dance, stamp their feet, and link arms as they sang about leaving lasses and the homes they loved.

Henry came to a stop, the bow resting against his knee. "Milady?"

Matilda turned her face away. She was no lady. Nothing about her qualified her to dance or to join in their revelry. Her convict status, the lack of proper attire, a heart that felt heavy as sandstone all weighed against her. She'd watch from the sidelines, and that would be enough.

The violin sounded again, a series of haunting notes that, despite her best attempts to suppress it, caused a smile to appear and her head to turn.

She'd missed this. Missed the way her da would play in the evenings, the notes lifting the smoky gloom from their tiny one-room dwelling. Longed for the feeling of belonging singing together evoked. She drew in a shaky breath. She missed her family.

"Milady. . ." Henry drew his bow long and low, underscoring his words. He raised one eyebrow and grinned boyishly. "May I have this dance?"

"But I—"

"Up, up. On your feet." He walked backward for several steps as he played a lively tune. "For the night is young and the company sweet."

"You got that right," one leathery sheepherder called out. "Just look at *my* face."

Laughter rang throughout the camp.

She rose to her feet, Henry's handkerchief still clenched in her hands. She'd join in just this once. She may not be in a ballroom, but a wallflower she was not.

Henry continued to play as he moved around the camp, occasionally joining in with John's crow-hopping dance or singing loudly. He made his way back to her, blending the end of his lively song into the opening bars of a waltz.

"Milady, shall we dance?"

On the second beat, she stepped into position, one arm curled in front of her, and the other hand extended, pretending to partner with him as she still clutched Henry's handkerchief.

Their eyes locked. He continued to play as he moved forward. She stepped back on her right foot then slid to the right, feet coming together. His steps mirrored hers, never too hurried, never too close. A smile lit his eyes as he advanced, this time pressing her to step back on her left foot, slide to the left, and then bring her feet together.

The firelight glowed golden, casting their shadows against the white trunks of the gums. Around and around the fire they danced, raising soft puffs of fine dust around their boots.

How long since she'd last danced? Two years? Three? In England, her life had been weighed down with working from dawn till the streetlights were lit. No time was spared for frivolities, for fun.

"Miss?"

Losing count of her steps, she stopped and turned to see a weather-beaten worker extend a hand.

"May I cut in?"

"Cut in?" She blinked, the hazy glow lost now that she wasn't so focused on Henry. "No, I'm not much for dancing."

"Could have fooled me," the man said, moving closer.

The music stopped abruptly.

"The lady said no," Henry said.

This time her *no* would be heeded. Someone would listen—and protect her.

The man brushed off the front of his shirt with exaggerated movements. "See if I care. Didn't really want to dance, anyways. Just felt sorry for the girl."

Her pent-up breath escaped in a soft *humph*. Sorry for her? An unnecessary sentiment.

"Miss Brampton?" Henry said. "Shall we dance another time? Without the fiddle between us?"

She searched his face for signs of hardness, of ill will toward her, and found none. Still, a warning pealed at the back of her conscience. He was an ex-convict, too. Had been tried and found guilty. She'd do well to take heed of that.

Chin lowered, she pressed his handkerchief into his pocket and stepped back. "Here. You'll want this back now."

The handkerchief unfurled from his pocket and fluttered to the ground, settling over the dust like a miniature picnic blanket.

Her hands flew to cover her gasp. "I'm so sorry. Please forgive me."

"No harm done, lass." Henry scooped it up and shook out the dust.

"Pshaw." John let loose with a loud laugh. "No 'arm done? You'd best be glad they didn't catch you doing that down in Sydney."

"Doing what?" Matilda said. "I didn't steal his handkerchief, only dirtied it."

John laughed again. "Dropping a handkerchief at someone's feet is practically a marriage proposal. Be glad you weren't in the women's factory in Parramatta when you did that."

"Why's that?" Matilda asked.

"Or you'd be married before sundown."

Chapter 5

Dare to Dream

Henry hummed as he herded sheep the next day. Waltzing Matilda, what was he thinking? And offering her the last link he had to England—his mother's handkerchief? He may as well paint *I fancy Matilda* on the sheer rock face they passed, judging by the sly grins his workers sent his way.

He nudged his horse off the trail, dropping back to circle the herd. He didn't fancy the girl. Couldn't fancy her. No, 'twas the wistful look on her face. The sadness as she tenderly cooled her babe with the cloth. His mother had warned him of lame ducks—and Matilda Brampton was in sore need of binding up the wounds that transportation had left on her soul. She needed the Lord.

Spying Matilda walking slowly behind the herd, a thin stick dragging from her hand, he stopped and waited for her to catch up.

"Top of the morning to ye, Miss Brampton. I trust you—"

"Slept well. Yes." She rounded his horse and kept walking, her steps almost a stomp.

Henry kneed his horse and soon caught up. "And how is Miss Charlotte this lovely morning? What contraption is that she's in?"

"She's fine. Sleeping in her sling." Matilda used her stick to prod a few sheep forward and kept moving.

Resting his hand on his thigh, Henry let his horse amble after her. "Are you determined to ignore me, then?"

"I am not ignoring you. I answered your questions."

"So you did. Now how about telling me what's wrong. What have I done that's put you out of sorts?"

"Nothing."

He smiled at her short answer. "Does this have anything to do with dancing with me last night?"

"No." She tossed the stick away and wrapped her arms around the sling holding Charlotte, her fingers restless on the crossed straps.

"I told you I don't trifle."

Her face tightened, her grip on any emotions iron tight.

He slid off his horse and jogged to stand in front of her. "Jeremiah 29:12."

"What?" She stopped and stared at him like he'd been kicked in the head.

"Then shall ye call upon me, and ye shall go and pray unto me, and I will hearken unto you."

"What is that supposed to mean?"

"I sense you are afraid." He reached out and gently halted her forward march. "The Lord wants you to call on Him—to pray. He hears you."

"Then you would be wrong. I don't fear anything." Her hands clenched the straps. "I rely only on myself. And as for God—I no longer talk to Him."

Henry searched her face and found hurt lurking in the depths of her green eyes. Could he make her smile again, put a sparkle in her eyes? Convince her of the truth seated deep in his heart? He knew the Lord *was* good, and He *was* ever close to the brokenhearted. He'd shown up too many times in his life to ever be doubted.

"Sometimes," he said slowly, "we need others to help, to share our life with."

"We? You mean yourself?" Matilda sidestepped him and continued to herd the sheep—his sheep.

How could he be jealous of the attention she paid his animals? Not that he wanted her to prod him with a stick, but he'd take any scrap of attention she tossed his way.

"Yes. I suppose I do mean myself also." Henry collected his horse and hurried until he strode shoulder to shoulder with her. "I know what it's like to be in chains—both literally and spiritually. To have plenty as I did in England. To be on starvation rations in the colony. Through all that, I've learned we aren't made to live solitary lives, and the good Lord has made us to be free. Free to choose companionship or the company of good friends."

"So you can flirt and dance with every girl in Sydney?"

"Is that what's bothering you? The thought of me—"

"No!"

The sheep startled at her yell, hurrying forward for several paces before settling into their methodical plod.

"That's *not* what is bothering me. I think I want—no, I *know* what I want. To be free," she said brusquely. "Not just for me, but for Charlotte."

"Ach. The currency, lass," Henry said. At her frown, he elaborated. "That's what I've heard others call a child born in Australia."

Matilda brushed damp hair off the babe's forehead, her touch gentle. Henry was reminded of his earlier prayer. *Thoughts of peace. . .not of evil. . .to give you an expected end.* She'd arrived in his life so soon after that prayer. Could this spitfire be his future wife? Did the Lord intend her for him?

No.

No matter how much he was beginning to hope otherwise. Regardless of her determination to be free, her sentence—whatever that was—needed to be served. Otherwise, their future would forever hang in the balance. The Lord would bring about *his* expected end. And that end meant traveling to Bathurst and settling on his sheep run, not harboring escapee convict women or even considering a future with one. He'd have to work harder to guard his heart and not let this feisty lass steal her way past his defenses.

"I apologize if I've misled you, milady."

Her steps slowed as she turned to him. "How so?"

"By dancing I simply meant to lift your spirits, the entire camp's spirits, not lead you to think ill of my intentions."

"Henry Powell, let me assure you I did *not* think ill of you." Her eyes sparked a warning. "Nothing but a bit o' fun for you and your men, was I?"

"No." His head shook vehemently.

"Thought you'd all 'ave a laugh at the girl in trousers, did you?" She raised her chin, throwing down a gauntlet he couldn't avoid.

" 'Twas nothing like that, milady."

"And stop calling me *milady*." She gave a short, bitter laugh. "I'm no lady."

"Outward appearances only. To me that is what you are. As does your heavenly Father."

"Oh, Henry." She rolled her eyes. "Henry, Henry. . . You are so"—she nipped at her full bottom lip, nose wrinkled—"so *different* from anyone else."

He couldn't resist teasing her. "So different that you won't waltz with me again?"

"Mayhap." She met his gaze, no coyness present. Just raw honesty. "No laughing?"

"Only together, mi—"

"Matilda. Call me Matilda."

"Oh, no. I cannot do that. 'Twould not be proper."

"Proper? Henry, look around you." She swept a hand, encompassing the winding track behind them, the light brown of the sheep ahead, and the stringybarks and saplings that made up the bush around them. "We're *days* from civilization, and right now no one except the *sheep* can hear you."

One of the sheep turned to bleat at them as if indignant at being mentioned.

"All right, all right. Calm down. You'll wake the baby," Henry said.

Matilda shooed the sheep back into the herd. "I *am* calm. Passionate—but calm." Her frown smoothed out as she stroked a hand over the baby's back. "I worry for her. She's so tired all the time. I don't think she gets enough nourishment from me."

Nourishment? Henry gained a sudden interest in his boots as warmth singed his ears and cheeks. That was his Matilda—honest and straightforward.

His Matilda. When did he start thinking of her as his? Already he'd failed to keep watch over his thoughts. He'd have to apply himself with more vigilance.

She was the Crown's to do with as they pleased. He had no claim to her, and he'd best remember that.

He focused on Charlotte, turning the problem she presented over and over in his mind until an idea introduced itself.

"Aha! May I suggest a solution?" he said.

"Of course."

"Milk."

Matilda looked at him from under raised eyebrows. "Really? That's your solution?"

"More specifically, sheep's milk."

"Ugh." Her gaze slid from his to the tightly packed sheep ahead of them. "Is that even possible? I mean, they are so wooly, and do any of them even have lambs? Or milk?"

"Yes, there are some lambs. Leave it with me. I'll figure out a way to feed your babe."

Henry tapped the side of his nose. "Now, how about you ride my horse. Rest your legs. Tend your babe. Save your strength for dancing."

After assisting her onto his horse, he took her place herding the sheep.

He might be a known flirt, but he'd not have it said he wasn't a gentleman.

Chapter 6

You'll Come A-Waltzing Matilda

A sense of excitement gripped Matilda as she rounded up the last of the stragglers and turned them into the pasture near the Fish River. *Not excitement*, she told herself. Dread. *Yes.* That was more like it.

"Now, Matilda Brampton," she whispered to herself, "you hate lies, so stop it at once. No shame in being excited at the day's end about a spot o' fun."

An image of Henry's smiling eyes and saucy violin came to mind. She'd not be wooed by fancy playing and laughing blue eyes.

She slid off Henry's horse, knees threatening to buckle once she landed. Charlotte startled and began to cry.

John approached, hat tilted back on his forehead. "Here, I'll unsaddle 'im for you. Go see to that baby of yours."

"I c—" The words died on her lips.

She rubbed the horse's neck. He'd have to be as tired as she was after the miles they'd covered that day. What did it matter if John wanted to help? It was his friend's horse, after all.

Stepping aside, she allowed him access to the horse. "Thank you."

Charlotte thrashed her arms, face reddening as she began to cry harder. Already, Matilda could feel her shirt dampen with milk.

"Hush, my darling. It's all right. Mama will feed you." Ducking behind a small stand of trees, she kept within yelling distance of the camp and found a log to sit on.

Several moments later, Charlotte was happily feeding, her cries silenced. Matilda tilted her head back, easing the ache in her shoulders. Worries pressed in on her. Her ability to satisfy her baby's appetite, the constant looking over her shoulder for soldiers, being wary of the others in camp. She held no faith in their trustworthiness. After all, a pardon in return for turning her in was bound to be tempting.

But would Henry do that? Could she trust him? If only her heart and her head would call a truce.

She pulled Charlotte into a sitting position. Propping the baby's small chin between her thumb and forefinger, she adjusted her clothing and began patting the small back. Within seconds, she'd coaxed a burp from the baby.

"Good girl. Full now, are we?" She pressed a kiss to the baby's nose before settling her against her shoulder. Hopefully, she had sated the tiny appetite, for she had no more to give.

With a frown at the deepening shadows, she hurried to the safety of the fire. The camp was busy with men bustling to and fro. Several carried slack water bags over their shoulders, obviously headed for the river. Henry and another man squatted near the fire, mixing flour and water in a large cast-iron pot.

He looked up as she approached, hair bearing recent comb marks and his face cleaned of dust. "Good morning, ladies."

The man beside him laughed, shaking his head. "Look at him—addled already. Been struck by Cupid's arrow for sure."

Matilda glanced away, her gaze hunting for the fastest path away from them.

"Evening." Henry's voice firmed, whether for her or his companion, she wasn't sure. "Evening, Matilda."

Unable to leave or ignore him without being rude, Matilda returned his greeting.

"How's the little lady?" he asked.

"Fine." Matilda jiggled her as if to prove her point.

Still her traitorous feet refused to step away. Diverting her attention from the way Henry's curls brushed against his collar, she pretended interest in what the men were mixing.

Charlotte shoved a small fist into her mouth and noisily sucked on it. Several men frowned her way, presumably irritated at Charlotte's slurps. Matilda glared at them until they looked away. Blighters, the lot of them. Rocking her, Matilda began to pace around the camp.

Henry placed the lid on the pot and buried it in the coals. Moments later, he caught up to her.

"Hungry?"

She swung around. "Not at this moment, thank you."

His eyes twinkled. "Not you. Charlotte."

"Oh." She rocked the baby, who was still working on her fist. "Yes, she is."

"Did you want to try that sheep's milk?"

No. No she did not. She was the mother. Was solely responsible for her baby's well-being, not some smelly, bleating sheep.

She glanced at Charlotte, taking in the wide eyes and full head of hair. The baby paused to give her a gummy grin before returning her attention to her hand.

"Yes," she said, "let's try it."

While she continued to pace with Charlotte, Henry organized his men to help milk a very reluctant sheep and then approached, a small cup in hand.

"Here we are," he said a few minutes later, "warm sheep's milk. Doesn't that sound positively delicious?"

"Positively," she agreed, scrunching up her nose.

They sat at a safe distance from the fire. Henry shook out his handkerchief, its snowy appearance standing out against the dark material of his trousers.

"In case you are wondering, I washed it earlier." He smiled. "I even used soap."

He dipped one corner in the cup of milk wedged between his knees and offered it to Charlotte. The baby stared at it cross-eyed.

"Hmm." Henry poked the handkerchief closer. "I saw this done with kittens once.

She needs to suckle the cloth."

Matilda leaned in and held Charlotte's head steady while he dabbed the cloth to her small rosebud lips. The baby screwed up her face but began to suck.

Henry dipped the handkerchief back in the milk and continued to feed her. He leaned in, and Matilda had to fight against the pang that shot through her, squeezing the air from her chest and causing her hands to fumble.

How easy it would be to imagine them as a family. An *us*. No longer mother and babe. Not a single, struggling half, but a whole. A mother, father, and baby whole. Dare she pray it could be so? Earlier, Henry had said something about praying to God. Said He would listen.

Henry, always Henry.

Unable to resist a second glance, she peeked through her bedraggled bangs. Henry was a study in concentration as he cupped Charlotte's chin, guiding the cloth to her tiny mouth. His long, tanned fingers brushed against the baby's face, encouraging her to kick her arms and legs. At some point in the day, he'd unbuttoned the top button on his shirt, the tiny triangle of exposed skin begging a closer inspection. Matilda dragged her gaze away, following the hand-stitched seam on his shirt to the cuffs he'd rolled up, revealing muscled forearms. Starvation rations obviously hadn't affected him.

Charlotte waved her arms, smacking Matilda and jolting her attention away.

"Have you finished, my darling?" With a smile, she wiped the droplets of milk away from the baby's chin.

"She has a hearty appetite," Henry said. "She'll be out of that nightgown and into short dresses before you know it."

Matilda raised the baby to her shoulder and gently patted her back. "I'm focusing on the present, savoring every moment I'm with her. Treasuring memories in my heart."

"Don't you dream? Think about what it would be like to have your own home among the gum trees?" He spread his arms wide, grin boyish. "Cups o' tea in the morning on the veranda. Wallabies eating grass nearby at dusk. A pair o' rocking chairs to enjoy the evening breeze. Ah, yes."

A flock of cockatoos flew overhead and settled in a tree close by. Their harsh squawks echoed through the darkened treetops. If only she could be fully included in a group as they were. To be free to chatter and talk with no fear of being discovered.

"I can't think like that. You know what I am—a convict. A runaway. If you don't turn me in, someone else will."

She slid him a glance out of the corner of her eye. He stayed silent, head tilted to the side as he considered her. Still, he offered no further promises of her safety.

She pursed her lips at the notion of him turning sour. "My future isn't secure until I've put a hundred miles between here and Sydney. Then can I think about a more permanent home for us or a job."

"Surely, there's another way?" he said.

"Believe me, if there was, I'd have taken it."

"Not even"—he glanced away, a blush the color of a gum blossom staining his cheeks—"marriage? I've heard tell of women marrying to earn themselves a pardon."

"No. If you'd seen the men eyeing us like we were nothing but cattle, you'd no' consider marriage an option." She blew out a puff of air, remembering the oily men with their busy, grasping hands and loud criticisms of each woman in line. "For some women, marriage wasn't even an escape from the factory. They'd leave one day and be back by the third. Exchanged with no more consideration than a sack of flour."

Henry's hand settled over hers on Charlotte's back. "Hush. You're becoming passionate again. You'll wake the baby."

"Oh." Turning sideways, Matilda presented Charlotte's face for his consideration. "Is she asleep yet?"

Henry nodded. "Like the proverbial babe."

Matilda laid the baby on her bedroll—a gift of assorted blankets from other members within the camp—and stood.

Henry whistled his dog over, and after directing Dodger to guard Charlotte, he joined her, keeping one hand behind his back. "I'd like to encourage you to trust the Lord for your future. He will make a way. But for the present, I've just the thing to ease those doldrums."

A giddy sensation swept over Matilda. Her toes tapped at the mere suggestion of his music, and her cheeks filled with heat. She fought the urge to tidy her hair and brush at the wrinkles in her clothes.

Slowly Henry pulled his hand from behind his back, exposing his violin. "Matilda?"

"Yes?" Her voice came out soft and breathy. She cleared her throat and tried again. "Yes."

"Will you come a-waltzing with me?"

Henry quickly tuned his violin. The heat and humidity played havoc with the wood, necessitating adjustments every time he lifted the instrument to play.

Still waiting for Matilda's response, he ran through the first few bars, hoping for her response.

Matilda shot to her feet so suddenly he took a step back. "Henry, I've deliberated long enough." Tugging her hat free, she let her pinned-up hair fall free. Leaning back, she shook her dark hair out and finger-combed it. "I accept your offer to dance."

He'd planned on playing something lighthearted. Frivolous even. But the hesitancy in her movements, the way her gaze skittered from his led him to draw the bow across the strings, almost in a caress.

Humming under his breath, Henry focused on playing, on winning her trust and getting her to soften.

He frowned, plying his bow with more pressure. No, not soften. That was the Lord's job. His was simply to be obedient. He nodded, careful to time it to the music and not look like he was giving himself a stern talking to.

Playing the second stanza with more fervor, he glanced up. Matilda hadn't moved from her place where they'd fed Charlotte. Her boots tapped in time with the music, as she stood, eyes closed.

Charlotte was safe only a few steps from where they stood, and his faithful Dodger would protect her to his last breath. What was holding Matilda captive?

His hand faltered on the bow, and she opened her eyes, her gaze meeting his. Immediately, her eyes shuttered, hiding their sparkle from him.

Well, now. He couldn't have that.

Playing faster, Henry stepped closer. Matilda colored, tilting her face away.

Henry couldn't resist raising an eyebrow and began slowly circling her, playing as he went.

"Milady," he said softly, "where is your courage, your fire?"

She faced him straight on, eyes snapping. "I am plenty—"

He stepped closer, remaining easily within arm's reach. "Come waltz with me."

"You're flirting again."

"Only a little. Is that all right?"

He set the violin to dancing again as his grin belied his words.

Someone tapped him on the arm. Henry turned to find John standing there, arms outstretched.

"Allow me."

"With pleasure."

In the space of a few missed notes, Henry handed the violin to John, who ran a few experimental bars before again taking up the tune.

Waiting for the right note, Henry stepped to Matilda and bowed deeply. He straightened to find her watching him, lips forming a tentative smile. The music faded into the background as he moved closer, basking in the glow of her smile.

He captured her hand, lifting it to within an inch of his mouth. Raising an eyebrow, he pressed a slow kiss to her knuckles. "Shall we?"

She stepped into his arms, her small hand fitting into his like a smaller template of his own.

He wanted to hesitate, to savor the moment before she pulled away and hid, or worse—scoffed at him for even trying. But the music swelled, and her fingers began to tap impatiently on his upper arm.

"Ready," she whispered.

"Annnd one. . .two. . .three," John called loudly, doing his best to imitate a nasally dance instructor. He winked as Henry waltzed Matilda past. "You said a week, right?" He worked the bow, keeping the music lively. "Two. . .three."

"Oh, go eat a stocking." Henry turned Matilda, lengthening his steps to put them out of earshot of his friend's attempts to rile him.

No need to remind him of his joke to be married by the following week. Even if Matilda was someone he could marry, Reverend Marsden was several days away and as for himself, he had obligations to meet, sheep to herd, and men to oversee.

Matilda gripped his waist tighter, forcing his attention back to her.

"Why the pensive look?" she asked.

He swallowed. How to answer? He couldn't share the truth with her, couldn't leave himself open to the very *trifling* he promised to avoid. Still, her patience demanded an answer.

"Obligations," he said, stepping to the side on the second beat.

"Your men?"

He nodded, thankful that she understood.

"Although I am free, sometimes I am not free to do as I would please." He squeezed her fingers gently, willing her to understand. "Does that make sense?"

"Perfectly." She followed his lead, for once not questioning everything he said.

He searched her eyes, silently begging her to understand, to wait. She bore his scrutiny without flinching, holding nothing back.

She patted his back, her hand pressing his shirt firmly against his skin and heating it. "Henry, you are a good man."

"No, milady." If only she could see otherwise.

"You are. I've known men, other men, who are not. I see who you are—and you are good."

If she didn't stop, he'd be reduced to a blushing idiot, a malleable lump of clay in her hands, or worse—a besotted fool.

"I once was a fool." He paused to let that sink in. "A browbeaten fool who thought life had him licked. That my chains meant I was nothing."

She watched him carefully, no condemnation lurking in her pretty face.

"Don't get me wrong, I was obedient—on the outside. Regular whippings made sure of that. But on the inside, I hadn't fully grasped that I have a right standing with the Lord. That I am who *He* says I am and need fear nothing—not even a whip. He is my goodness."

"Like I said. You are a good man." Her hand brushed over his back again. "You go and fulfill your obligations. Don't worry about Charlotte and me. We'll be just fine."

She reached up on tiptoe, mouth hovering near his. "A good man."

He clutched her close, turning his head so they rested cheek to cheek. She smelled of milky tea, the floury campfire damper he'd mixed earlier, and melted butter. *A good man.* The surety of her words settled over him.

So much hung in the balance. Her past and when it would catch up with her. Whether his sheep run would be a success. Baby Charlotte's survival in this often times dangerous land.

So much to consider. So much to weigh. Her questioning faith. His firm beliefs. But just for this moment, he would savor her, nurture their fledgling relationship. Would focus on the present—not the future.

Clutching her shoulders, he redirected his thoughts. He tucked her head under his chin, and they swayed in place for several moments before he gently held her at arm's length.

"Matilda, I—"

"Want to dance?" She nodded and placed her hands back into position. "Yes. I do."

Henry traced the features of her face as he gripped her hand. With a faint nod, he let the music guide him and followed the steps of the waltz. Forward on the left foot, slide on the right foot, feet closing together. Then forward on the right foot, the actions mirrored.

Their steps reversed. Their situations reversed.

At this point in time, she was the one freed, and he was weighed down by the chains of duty. She could go where she liked, even disappear into the trees like a morning mist, but he was chained to his responsibilities.

"I find myself wishing, hoping even, that things could be different." Why he wanted her to know that, he wasn't entirely sure, but it seemed somehow important that she be privy to how he felt.

"But things are not. And that's how it is. I understand." She smiled, her eyes sad. "If I recall correctly, you said that life is meant for having fun, laugher, and dancing. We have tonight. Let that be enough."

"Then tonight 'twill be enough."

But it wasn't enough. Would never be enough. He forced himself to wink, a token gesture to the man and actions he was known for.

Her lips parted in a slight gasp at his impudent reminder. He forced his gaze away from the fullness of her lips. If only things could be different.

The music abruptly fell silent.

Henry dropped Matilda's hand and swung around. "John, what the dev—"

Two soldiers rode into the camp, muskets across their laps. He turned, catching sight of one, two, no—three more soldiers emerging out of the night like dark angels.

They were surrounded, no doubt about that. Henry fumbled for Matilda's hand, pulling her to his side as he turned back.

It was too late to run—and only the Lord knew if that was a good thing.

Chapter 7

Catch Me Alive

Matilda clung to Henry's hand, sweat making her grip slick. Every part of her body screamed at her to *run!* To snatch up Charlotte and run as fast and as far as she possibly could. To leave, to try with all her being to get away from men in uniform, from their hardened eyes and constricting manacles. Escape from the belittling and abuse that would await her at the Parramatta Female Factory.

Seven more years of her sentence remained. She wouldn't live to see the end of it. Her breathing increased as she counted the soldiers until black spots danced before her eyes.

Five men circled the camp, horses snorting as they formed a solid barrier between her and the scrub. No doubt there were more men hanging back out of sight, lying in wait in case she bolted.

All for her. Was she really worth all this trouble? Worth so much to the Crown that she'd be hunted down and returned?

She had to attempt to get away; she owed it to Charlotte to at least try.

Charlotte. The thought energized her as she lunged away from Henry.

He firmly drew her back to his side, tucking her under his arm. "It'll be all right, Matilda."

"H–how can you know that?" She worked to slow her breathing, deliberately avoiding looking in Charlotte's direction.

"Becau—"

His words were cut off as the largest of the soldiers kneed his horse, charging into camp and scattering several of Henry's men out of his way.

"There she is!"

The soldier stopped in front of them, pulling back so sharply on the reins that his horse reared. "There's our little bolter."

"I'm not your little anything," Matilda snapped.

"Hush now," Henry said, squeezing her hand. "You've not been accused of anything."

The soldier pulled a torn paper from the leather pouch that hung at his side. After looking her over with a sneer, he began to read.

"Matilda Brampton. Physical description says you're of short stature, dark hair, green eyes, and a ruddy complexion." He smirked, one lip curling up to reveal yellowed teeth. "Warns of a pugnacious demeanor and penchant for fighting."

It took all of Matilda's meager collection of strength not to cover her cheeks. Ruddy? Suntanned perhaps but not ruddy.

The soldier eyed her over the paper, one eyebrow raised. "Says here you may be in the company of a ch—"

"Aye, that's her," one of the sheepherders called out. "That's the lass's name."

"Bring the irons." The soldier drew out a whip and waved two of the other soldiers closer, a short man with wild black hair and a fair-skinned man whose red nose pronounced him a hearty rum drinker. "I'll need her subdued and secured. I want to be on our way back to Sydney as soon as possible."

"No!" Matilda tore her hand from Henry's grip and ran.

Perhaps she could divert attention from her baby, much like a bird would feign an injury to lead predators away. The tree line that circled their camp loomed only a few yards away.

"Catch her!" the soldier yelled.

She added a burst of speed and prepared to plunge through a small shrub.

Not as long as she had breath to run would she be caught.

Someone grabbed her by the collar and wrenched her backward. Yanked to a halt, she gasped for air, her shirt digging into her throat.

"That'll teach you to run, missy." The man spun her around, revealing himself as the shorter of the soldiers.

He grinned, and her skin crawled with the urge to get away.

"But will you fight me like your little list o' criminal history says?"

"To the death," she said through clenched teeth.

He laughed, and she used the moment of distraction to yank free and dart away. She meant what she said. Death was preferable to returning with soldiers of questionable trustworthiness to the hell the factory represented.

Strong arms caught her around the waist and bore her to the ground.

Gasping for air, she screamed. "Henry!"

The black-haired soldier flipped her over and sat on her. "Where's your fight now, ay?"

With her ear pressed into the dust, Matilda struggled for breath. "Henry," she wheezed. "Save me."

Tears burned fierce at the back of her eyes. How dare they? These soldiers were no better than the ex-convicts roaming the streets of Sydney. What would happen now? What further indignities would they commit?

Henry started toward her, fists balled.

The red-nosed soldier stepped in his path, whip raised. "Do *not* interfere in His Majesty's business."

Henry pressed forward, meeting her eyes over the man's shoulder.

"I'm warning you," the soldier said. "Stay back. She's not worth it."

"Yes. She is," Henry said. His gaze lingered on the whip before meeting hers. "She truly is."

Matilda thrashed, trying to rid herself of the man sitting on her.

He patted her head with a heavy hand, the force pushing her face harder into the ground. "Whoa, there now. You're not going anywhere."

The first soldier laughed. "Anywhere apart from back to the Female Factory." He spun, hands on his hips. "Now, where's that child? I suppose we oughta take that thing back with us, too."

That thing? Charlotte wasn't a *thing* to be taken anywhere. The thought of any of the soldiers picking her up or treating her roughly made her ill.

"You've got what you want, so leave." Henry's voice rang out. He stepped to the side, shielding Charlotte's sleeping place in the pile of blankets.

What was he doing? Matilda stared at him, willing him to look at her.

Briefly, his hard gaze met hers. A look passed between them, almost as if he'd audibly said *trust me*.

A hint of vulnerability swept over him before he jutted his chin as he scowled around the camp. "There is no child."

"That simplifies things." The soldier lifted his rifle, unbarring Henry's way. He gestured toward her. "On your feet."

The weight on her back lifted, allowing air back into her lungs. He grasped her collar and yanked her to her feet, and she stood, gasping for air. The first soldier approached, a set of iron manacles swinging from one finger. After fumbling for her hands, he fastened them around her wrists. He shook her, making her stumble back a step.

"You can be sure you'll face the full extent of your crimes." He tugged her toward his horse.

Matilda dug her boots in, creating deep lines in the dirt behind her. "No. You'll not take me alive."

The soldier continued to drag her. "You're not the first bolter we've hauled back, and I doubt you'll be the last. I takes high pride in me work. Doesn't look good on me record if I'm dragging dead convicts back, now does it? No." He slung her over his saddle and began tying her down before she could kick her way free. "Mark me word, I'll be back in England long before your sentence is up."

"Matilda?"

Henry's face appeared before hers, a frown crinkling his normally smiling face. "I'll come for you. Don't fret. I'll take care of"—he glanced away—"of everything."

Matilda kicked against the ties and found them firm. A sense of calm settled over her, staying her urge to fight her way free. What was the point of fighting or railing against authority? This was going to be her future for the next seven years.

Iron chains.

Barred windows.

Abuse.

No child deserved to grow up in that environment. She'd not asked nor wished to become pregnant. Had no desire to become a mother. Her life in England was at poverty level, no room for suitors or another mouth to feed. Life in Sydney was worse, although there was faint light at the end of her sentence. Her life would be hers to govern once her sentence was completed. But not Charlotte. Her daughter would be torn from her care in three years time. Placed into an orphan school.

But would Henry become a willing cuckoo? Allow another's child to be placed into his care?

"Stay free, Henry." Her voice cracked as a fierceness shook her. "You hear me? Stay free—and don't come after me."

He stepped back and touched his fingers to his hat in a brief salute. " 'Ye shall seek me, and find me, when ye shall search for me with all your heart.' Jeremiah twenty-nine, verse thirteen."

"Mount up," the lead soldier shouted. "And you others—stay back. I'd sure hate for this rifle to go off and scatter all those sheep."

The horse sidestepped, a quiver running through him. Seconds later, the soldier grabbed hold of the saddle, his hand digging into her side as he vaulted up behind her.

Matilda strained for a glimpse of Charlotte, for one final look. If only she could kiss her soft cheeks once more. Stroke her thick black hair. Inhale her milky scent and hold her close as she kicked her legs in excitement.

Twisting, she tried to see behind her, to where Charlotte lay sleeping. The cords tying Matilda down allowed little movement, but still she tried again and again.

"Lie still," the lead soldier said and shoved her shoulders back down. Kicking his horse, the soldier led the way out of camp at a jarring trot.

The tears she'd been holding back escaped and splashed onto her nose.

God, where are You?

Chapter 8

More or Less

Henry listened to the sound of hoofbeats retreat and let out a pent-up breath. Helpless. That's what he was. Useless. Helpless. Faithless. He scrubbed a hand over his stubbled beard. *Less.* That's what he was. He could've, nay, *should've* done more.

Instead, he reverted to the man he'd once been. Cowed, subservient, chained. It had served him well and earned him an early release from his sentence.

"Henry?"

A hand clapped him on the shoulder, and he startled, turning to find John.

John jerked his chin in the direction the soldiers had left. "What's the plan now?"

"Plan?" Henry shook his head. "Did you not see me just then? I was—"

"Biding your time. Yes."

"No. Look, I may have stood up a little to them, but—"

John grasped his shoulders and shook him. "What's done is done. Past." He shook him again. "Finished. Now is what matters. The girl needs you."

"Needs me?" Henry nodded, head bobbing erratically as John shook him. "Yes. Charlotte needs me."

"Not her." John made to grab him again, but Henry blocked him.

"Leave off. I've found my good sense. No need to keep shaking me."

John's face lit up. "Good man."

"They'll be headed to Sydney," Henry said and began to pace. "Correct?"

"Yes. To the Parramatta Female Factory."

"How can I go? I'm responsible for all these sheep. The men. To get us to Bathurst."

"That is a problem," John agreed.

"You know I'm not fond of problems."

"And yet you are fond of this woman?"

"Fond?" Henry pretended to ponder the word. "Nay. One is fond of hot chocolate, of spring rains or a comforting fire. This is simply my sense of duty rearing its head. My need to right a wrong, to"—he broke off with a frown—"Why are you laughing?"

John's laughter rang out again. "Leave the sheep with me, friend. I'm your partner, after all. Go fetch this woman you are more than fond of."

More than fond? Henry paused, turning the notion over and over. *Yes.* He was more than fond of Matilda. What that fondness would lead to he wasn't yet sure. One thing for sure, she warmed him more than any mug of hot chocolate. Refreshed him more than spring rain, and his response to her presence put any fire to shame.

He was not *less*. No, he was made for more. Was no longer a slave, but a joint heir with Christ. Free, in more ways than one.

"Hmm." Henry resumed pacing. "So you'll continue to Bathurst and I'll catch up with you in a few days?"

"Indeed." John stuck out his hand, and Henry clasped it. "You'd best pray for that woman."

"Thank you. We both can." He swung around. "Now, I'll take baby Charlotte with me." He propped hands on his hips as he surveyed the camp. "I'll need my handkerchief, a sling. . .and. . .oh, I'll need a sheep. Not necessarily in that order."

Chapter 9

A Glimpse of Milady

Henry checked the position of the sun as he rode into Sydney. He'd made good time, despite being weighted down with a packhorse, a sheep, and a baby. They'd managed the three-day trek in a little over two days.

No longer needing to keep out of sight or follow the soldiers by tracks alone or to keep out of sight, Henry hurried as he made his way to the group of sandstone buildings that made up the Parramatta Female Factory. The group of soldiers he'd been following parted from their tight formation as they turned a corner, spreading out to reveal Matilda still slung over the saddle of one of the horses.

Henry gasped. Her hair hung down in stringy clumps, clothes brown with dust, and legs flopping with each of the horse's strides.

She looked. . .broken.

Was this why she didn't want him looking for her? To prevent him from seeing her in this state? Or was it to protect Charlotte?

Henry touched a hand to the small child cradled against his chest. In part, he now understood why she didn't want him to follow. This was no place for a woman, let alone a child.

The soldiers stopped in front of a pair of large iron gates. Henry dismounted across the street and hitched his horse to a nearby fence. The men dragged Matilda off the horse, leaving her in a crumpled heap.

Henry broke into a run. "I say! Leave that woman alone."

A cart rolled past, blocking his view. He jumped back to safety and stood on tiptoe, trying to maintain his view of Matilda.

She scrambled to a sitting position and shoved her hair out of her face. A red cut stood out on her cheekbone, and Henry's hands balled into fists. He should help her. Do something. Anything. He started forward, the street now safe to cross.

Before he reached the other side, two soldiers grabbed Matilda under the arms and hauled her upright. She staggered, knees buckling, before elbowing one of the soldiers away from her and standing by herself.

His girl had rallied, come to life again. Unleashed the fiery spirit that he so admired. She raised her head and glanced around. Their gazes locked, and her eyes widened. "Henry."

The word was a whimper but added courage to his heart.

She lifted a hand toward him, fingertips red with crusted blood. Before he could reach her, the gates swung open. The soldiers closed ranks around her, catching her under the arms again and dragging her inside.

He surged forward. "Matilda!"

The gates slammed shut, trapping her in and keeping him out.

"Henry!"

A soldier's hand covered her mouth, silencing her but not the echoing scream.

Henry clutched the iron bars with one hand, the other soothing Charlotte who had begun to whimper. What could he do? He had to do something. Something legal. He loved Matilda, but if he were jailed, he wouldn't be able to help anyone, not her, not Charlotte, and not himself.

He loved Matilda.

He knew that with the same certainty that governed his faith. Squeezing the barred gates in his grip, he bowed his head and prayed. For Matilda. For himself. For their future.

Footsteps from behind drew his attention. The rotund Reverend Samuel Marsden walked briskly toward him. One end of the white cravat blew upward, slapping against his bulbous nose and ruddy cheeks.

The minister stopped, and after shaking hands, he peered into the factory yard and shook his head. "Burden on the government, the poor things."

"The women at the factory?" Henry said.

"Hmm. Yes." The minister eyed him up and down. "What an odd contraption. Looks as if you are carrying your own burden."

"Charlotte? She is a light burden. No, I correct myself. She's a blessing. But what of the others, what can be done for them?" Henry asked.

"I do my part," Reverend Marsden said.

"Part? Oh, you must mean pray," Henry said.

The minister laughed, rippling the folds of his black cloak. "No. I write up the certificates, post the banns, and conduct the ceremonies."

"Certificates?" Henry tracked Matilda's progress as she was hustled into a building and out of sight.

"Yes. Certificates that verify the applicant is the proper person to be a husband to one of these poor wretches."

Wretches?

Matilda's voice continued to sound in memory, pleading, stirring him into action. Wretched situation, for sure. But that didn't make her a wretch.

The minister adjusted his jacket and turned aside. "Like I said. I do my part. Perhaps you'd consider what *you* can do, hmm?"

"Me?" Henry gave the door Matilda had been dragged through one last look. "What can I do?"

"Marry one of the wretches."

"Marriage?" He tapped his chin. "Legal marriage?"

"Humph. Of course." Reverend Marsden brushed a hand over his balding head. "Have a think on that." He nodded his good-bye. "I'll be at the church until four. Your reputation precedes you. Exemplary prisoner behavior. Early ticket of leave. Interest in sheep. I'd be happy to write you a certificate of recommendation."

Henry glanced at the sun's position again. Almost noon. "You said you'll be at the church until four?"

"I did. The front door is always open."

Four. *Excellent.* That gave him time to find lodgings and a place to contain the animals. The minister might retract his recommendation if he turned up to church with "that contraption," two horses, and a sheep in tow.

Chapter 10

The Light of Day

Matilda hugged her knees to her chest, ignoring how the coarse flannel of her dress scratched her cheek, and continued to stare at the solid door, gaze tracing the thin crack of light just visible beneath it.

Footsteps echoed on plank flooring then stopped. Something blocked the light coming under the door. Voices murmured, still too low to make out their words.

Was it time for her daily ration of bread and water? Devoid of all light, except the sliver coming under the door, the cell had melded day and night into one, prolonged night. Matilda reached for her plate, scraping it across the floor as she searched it with groping fingers. Empty. Just as she'd thought.

Keys rattled sharply against the wooden door before it swung open. She blinked against the harsh light that poured in, revealing two men.

"Miss Brampton." The stern face of Francis Oakes hardened as he stood back, allowing sunlight to stream into the cell. "I trust your week has been spent in earnest contemplation of your misdemeanors. Hmm?"

Matilda's gaze swept over the superintendent's neat silver hair, black jacket, and white cravat. At least *he* showed no signs of poor nutrition. Bowing her head, she swallowed hard against the hot words that begged an audience. "Yes."

The second man, a soldier, stepped into her downcast view. "That's no' how you speak to your betters. Address Mr. Oakes properly."

She lifted her chin and met the superintendent's firm gaze. "Yes, *sir*."

He gave a short nod. "Send her to pick oakum for a week."

Matilda rubbed her thumbs over her fingertips, already feeling the rough rope fibers wearing her fingers raw. "But, sir. . ."

Picking oakum was reserved for the worst of the worst prisoners. The mean, rough women who raised their fists as often as their voices. For noisy, angry renegades, intent on slugging through life. She'd not be dragged down to their level.

"Look, Mr. Oakes, she's showin' reform already." The second man grasped her by the elbow. "Second Class?"

"Second Class." The superintendent pocketed his keys. "If her behavior shows improvement, I'll consider allowing her the previous benefits she enjoyed."

Benefits. Ha! Working hard all day to then fall asleep on a smelly pile of wool at night. Suffering vile abuse from other women. Being lined up like cattle at a fair while toothless old stringybarks hemmed and hawed over which woman they'd marry. Mr. Oakes could keep his benefits. They weren't worth the extra calico caps, Sunday clothes, or scant privileges that accompanied them.

The man hurried her along a hallway and outside before tugging her toward the workhouse that contained the oakum pickers. She stumbled several times, her legs unused to moving freely.

Across the yard, she glimpsed the large portcullis. With hands shading his eyes, a man pressed against it, peering through the grating. Her pulse gave a silly little leap. Was it Henry? Did he have Charlotte?

A yank on her arm forced her forward, cutting off her view. *Don't be ridiculous.* Henry would be long gone. She'd told him to do so. Charlotte was gone, just as surely as if the superintendent had pulled the babe from her arms himself. At least this was of her choosing.

But really, what choices did she have?

"Ye shall seek me, and find me. . . ."

The verse Henry had hurriedly spoken came to mind.

Seek who? The Lord?

The soldier came to an abrupt stop and deposited her in a room with several other women. He pointed to a bundle of worn ropes with frizzled ends. "We needs at least a pound a day from each o' ye. Get pickin'."

Numbly, she took a seat beside the other women and began unraveling the rope to then separate each tiny strand.

If Henry wasn't to be found, then who should she look for? The Lord?

She dipped her head, focusing on her fingers already beginning to hurt. "But you aren't lost, Lord. I am."

One of the women near her cackled uncontrollably for several seconds. "Look at her. Talking to herself already. We got ourselves another mad one."

Matilda ignored her. There was no point encouraging interaction from those whose sole purpose was to incite arguments or cause infractions. She separated the rope strands and began briskly rolling the fibers along her thigh to break them apart. If she behaved herself, she could work her way up to First Class and, hopefully, earn a ticket of leave.

Then she could leave and look for Charlotte. See if Henry had made a success of his sheep run.

"Search for me."

Yes. Search. Starting with herself. But how did she find the Lord when she felt so very lost herself? Was there a compass to find her way to heaven?

Briefly closing her eyes, she attempted her first prayer in nearly a year.

"Come find me, Lord. I am waiting."

Chapter 11

All Assemble

This waiting is ridiculous." Henry threw the written permit on the rough slab table, where it fluttered to join his letter to the superintendent and stalked to the door. "That's the third visit in as many days. When are they going to let her out of solitary confinement?"

In her makeshift bed next to the table, Charlotte screwed up her face in preparation to cry.

Henry hurried to scoop her up before she could upset the owner of the small hut, an older woman hard of hearing, but thankfully not hard of heart.

Settling the baby in his arms, he rocked her. "We'll find your mother. Don't you fret. We'll find a way to get her back."

The babe stared up at him, wide eyes trusting and clear. If only she knew how feeble his promises were. How afraid he felt inside.

God hadn't deserted him so far, and he'd not start doubting. Although, it wasn't God he doubted—it was the penal system.

"Lord, please make a way, whatever the cost."

Tomorrow would bring him one step closer to Matilda, but would he leave the Parramatta Female Factory with her?

The permit from the minister and a written notice to the superintendent raised his chances of actually seeing her, but would he have the courage to stand before two hundred women and pledge his heart?

The heat settled over Matilda like a wet wool coat. She blotted sweat from her brow and continued to let the unspun wool slide through her fingers, spinning it onto the spinning wheel's bobbin.

Two weeks back in the Female Factory and time had slowed to a crawl.

"Better'n picking oakum, wouldn't you say?"

Matilda turned at the snide voice. "And who are you?"

"Agnes Galloway." The woman arched her brows before giving Matilda's spinning wheel a soft kick.

"What would you know about picking oakum?" Matilda spat. "You've managed to keep your nose out of trouble. Think you're better than the rest of us, do you?"

The woman gave an exaggerated gasp. "I'll have you know that my grandm—"

"Let me tell *you* something. Nobody cares if you are descended from aristocracy here. You're the same as everybody else here—a big, fat nobody."

The wool fed through her fingers faster and faster as she pumped the treadle, the yarn becoming lumpy and uneven.

Nobody.

Was that who she truly was? Solitary. Alone. Driftwood on life's currents, left to be tossed about without care. Lost.

Agnes continued her tirade on her linage, her voice becoming higher and higher. Matilda continued to spin the wool, the velvety strands catching on her rough fingertips as it slipped through her fingers. *Lost.*

"No," she said softly. She wasn't lost. Not anymore. The Lord had promised to hearken to her. She'd stand on that assurance.

The superintendent bustled in, immediately quieting Agnes and the others in nearby conversations. "All assemble."

Matilda set her wool aside and slowly rose as the other women pushed past her.

"Wait." Mr. Oakes grasped her chin and tilted her head to the side.

She stiffened, fighting the urge to close her eyes and block out his probing stare. Would he deal fairly with her? Good men still remained. Henry had shown her that.

His fingers tightened, pressing the sides of her jaw. "Show your teeth."

"What?" The word came out garbled, muzzled by his hand.

"If I'm to allow you First Class privileges, you'd best have good teeth."

Good teeth? She'd show him *good teeth*—after she'd nipped his fat fingers.

Mr. Oakes snatched his hand back. "Never mind. I see you have enough fortitude to withstand what's ahead of you." He pivoted and strode for the door. "Come along."

"What do you mean, 'what's ahead of me'?"

He glared at her over his shoulder, and she swallowed.

"What's to become of me, *sir*?"

"Matrimony." He swung open a door, revealing a long room packed with bodies. "The sooner you lot are off my hands the better."

Chapter 12

Seek Me and Find Me

The gates of the Parramatta Female Factory squeaked shut, the heavy iron latch falling into place with a bang. Henry's steps faltered. Behind bars—again. The first time for the theft of four geese, now for the woman he loved.

Time would tell if he were the goose.

Chuckling under his breath, he pressed Charlotte close, forcing himself to join several other men and cross the courtyard to the main door of the factory.

He was a free man. The ticket of leave he kept tucked in his saddlebag said so. No one had reason to lock him up...or did they? He *had* harbored a wanted criminal, after all.

Narrowing his eyes, he reviewed his options. He could turn tail and run. Could abandon Matilda. Dank air from the hallway pressed close, making it hard to breathe. *No.* He'd not give in to his cowardly tendencies and think only of himself. But he was no longer a whipped cur. Henry shook the notion away. Had no need to live as a stray dog. God had redeemed him, restored him. Set his feet on a firm foundation. Given him purpose.

Purpose that he desired to share with the woman he loved.

Lengthening his strides, he shouldered through another doorway and into a large, open room, joining a small crowd of curious onlookers on one side of the room. Everywhere he looked, clusters of toothless old men gossiped, thin soldiers in worn uniforms offered faint glares to those unfortunate enough to meet their eyes, and a few men in clean collars and cuffs talked animatedly as they gazed about the room. Most likely they were there for entertainment's sake.

He didn't plan to be there long enough to entertain anyone. Once he'd located Matilda, they could make their escape—their legal escape.

Across from him, a door stood open in the long wall. Women began streaming through, at first in groups of two or three and then in larger bunches. He examined each one, giving the woman's clothing and demeanor a careful once-over. None matched Matilda's description. None made his heart leap.

"After a factory lass to marry, are you?"

"Pardon?" Henry glanced down, catching sight of a young lad who didn't look old enough to shave, let alone seek out a wife.

"One of 'em catch your eye, gov?" The lad scratched at a thatch of scruffy hair in fierce need of soap and a comb. "Best keep away from the old ones. They be already married and returned several times o'er."

"I'll keep that in mind," Henry said, returning his attention to the door and the women who continued to pour into the room.

Had he missed Matilda's entrance? Or was she even eligible to take part in this selection process? More than enough time had elapsed by his reckoning. He'd pray her punishment had been fulfilled.

More men pressed into the room, squeezing around him. The hum of conversation rose, the men's baritone joining the woman's high-pitched conversation. Every now and then, one of the women would cackle or shout out a derogatory comment.

He bracketed his arms around Charlotte, protecting her from any accidental knocks. Thank the good Lord she was too young to understand the ribald conversation he occasionally overheard.

An imposing man bustled through the door and into the room, followed by a small group of women. Henry stood on tiptoe, straining to see over the spectators in front of him. Was one of the women Matilda?

His heart whispered *yes* even as his head urged him to wait.

The man who'd led the last group of women inside marched to the center of the room and began organizing the women into rows.

Sulky or petulant, preening or provocative, the women abandoned their groups to line up into rows that stretched across the room.

As if goaded by an unseen signal, the men surrounding Henry began to trickle past him. They might well have been strolling across the lawns of the Royal Botanic Gardens, so casually did they look the women over. Pausing every few steps, they exclaimed over a woman as one would a native flower, or, ignoring the raucous taunts from the fellow women, leaned in for a closer inspection. Every so often, one of the men would beckon a woman forward. Once she'd complied, they'd talk for several moments before they'd pair off and speak to the man who must be the supervisor.

"See now," the young lad said, "that's how it's done 'ere. The men look 'em over, decide which of 'em has the best behavior and will do as they's told once they're back at his hut."

"Is that so?" Henry stepped closer, his gaze ranging over the lines. Where was Matilda?

"Sure is. Want me to help you pick one out?"

"Pardon?"

"Pick a woman. Then you can ask questions about her. Look at her teeth"—the lad pulled his lips back, exposing his own dubious-looking molars—"and see if she's the lass for you."

"The woman I have in mind is the right one for me. None other will do."

The lad giggled. "Not fussy, then? That'll hurry up the selection."

Henry didn't need a selection. There was only one woman for him. Where was she? *"Search for me with all your heart."*

The words from Jeremiah came to mind.

Lord, I'm searching for her, but I need Your help.

Henry patted his breast pocket as he scanned the last row of women. His mother's handkerchief still safely resided in his pocket. Cradling Charlotte, he adjusted her sling. Any moment he'd find her and—

"Aha," he said as his gaze skipped over a familiar black head of hair and then doubled back. The dark curls stood out from the profusion of brown and blond hair.

Matilda. He'd found her.

He started forward, winding his way through the throng of bodies toward her.

"Ooh. Look at him. Found a girl, have you, gov?" A woman in tattered skirts and a nasally voice stepped into his path. She jutted her chest forward. "I've got just the thing for your babe."

"No, thank you." Henry sidestepped her, trying to keep a clear line of sight with Matilda.

"Thinks he's too good for the likes of us, girls. Ignore him." The woman stuck her nose in the air and turned her back on him.

Several other women heckled him as he made his way down the line of women. The scent of their unwashed bodies made him wish for his lanolin-scented sheep and the clean freshness of a breeze blowing through eucalypts. The bush. Freedom.

The minister said he'd need enough phlegm to endure the teasing and taunts of the women. Oh, he had a slow and stolid temperament, but what he lacked was courage.

"Seek me, and find me, when ye shall search for me with all your heart."

The verse he'd quoted to Matilda. He's searched for her, and now he'd found her. Now to share his heart.

Courage, Father. I need Your courage.

He strode forward. "Milady?"

With a gasp, Matilda's head jerked up. "Henry?"

"Yes?" He guarded his hope as if it were his meat ration.

"Henry, I. . ." She swallowed and bowed her head. "Charlotte?"

"Hale and hearty." Henry waited until Matilda glanced back at him before adding, "And missing her mother."

She stepped back, leaving a gap in the line of women. "I told you not to follow me. Why, Henry?"

"I had to. You forgot something."

Her gaze centered on his chest where Charlotte lay snug in her sling. Pink stained her cheeks. "I'm sorry. I meant n—"

"No, no. You misunderstand. You see, you actually possess something of mine."

"Yours? Whatever do you mean?"

"My heart." Henry placed his hand over his left breast pocket. With two fingers, he pulled his handkerchief free.

It hung between them, a small white flag in a room filled with sordid bodies and unpleasant surroundings. Would she accept the truce?

He lifted his arm, raising the handkerchief to head height.

"Henry, don't—"

"I love you, Matilda." He released the handkerchief, letting it flutter to the floor between them. "Milady, would you do me the honor of—"

Chapter 13

Grace

—marrying me?"

Matilda clapped her hands over her ears, muffling Henry's words. He didn't. He couldn't... Didn't Henry know what she'd done? Was capable of doing? How undeserving of grace she was?

Tears wet her lashes as she backed away. Henry couldn't just propose marriage to her. *Her.*

And love? Was he addled? Choosing her to love.

She stared at the lace-edged square crumpled on the ground between them, her hands falling to her sides. His mother's handkerchief. The one remaining tie he had to England. It didn't belong there any more than he did.

"Won't you come a-waltzing with me?" Henry said, the words dancing to her over the nearby conversation. "Come waltzing with me, m' darling."

"I—I can't." She swallowed against the lump in her throat.

"Why? Is there something about me that's not acceptable?"

"No, Henry."

"About my faith?"

Her head shook, the knot of hair atop her head coming loose. "I—I share your faith."

His eyes widened, the blue shining in the dark room. "Did you find the Lord?"

"I did." She glanced to the narrow window, seeking the warmth of the light. "He found me."

"Then what is the matter?"

Curses on him for his soft tone, for caring, for giving her his heart. And yet...bless him. Bless him for wanting her. Loving her.

"Look at me." She wrapped her arms tight around her waist. "Take a good, hard look at who I am and where I am before deciding to hand off your heart."

"Is that what's bothering you?" Henry grinned, the smile at odds with the serious looks the other men wore.

"Partly troubling me, yes."

"This is the woman I see," Henry said. "I will be found of you, saith the Lord: and I will turn away your captivity, and I will gather you from all the nations, and from all the places whither I have driven you."

"Small words, please," Matilda said.

"I see a woman who is found. Who is loved. Who deserves to be loved."

"Henry, Henry." She shook her head. "What is it with you and being so, so *different*?"

He reached for her hand, cradling it in his own. "Would you have me any other way?"

"No."

This time when he smiled, she joined him. The small cold places within her began to melt. Perhaps he was right. The Lord would turn away her captivity. Would give her the freedom to be loved.

A woman's voice rose above the others. "If you don't want him, then let someone else 'ave him." The large-framed woman swooped down, reaching for the handkerchief.

Before Matilda could react, a young lad pushed past, snatched up the handkerchief and held it aloft.

"I got it for you, gov." He waved it hard, pausing to poke out his tongue at the woman who had pushed in.

"That you did, lad." Henry released her hand to accept the handkerchief. "I owe you my eternal gratitude."

"That your lass? The one you're marrying?" the lad asked.

They both turned to look at her. One small and curious, the other bold and certain. Her Henry. Her incorrigible flirt.

"Yes," she said. "I'm the lass he's marrying."

The lad nodded, nose wrinkled in concentration. "Good choice. I only got one question. Did you check her teeth?"

Chapter 14

The Sensible Flirt

Reverend Marsden's voice rang the church rafters with dour passion. "Thirdly, marriage was ordained for the mutual society, help, and comfort that the one ought to have of the other, both in prosperity and adversity."

Matilda's grip on Henry's hands began to slicken. What could she bring to this marriage? Help and comfort? What did she know about those topics? With her tendency to speak her mind, she was sure to bring more shackles to Henry's life, nothing that could bring about prosperity or blessing.

Henry squeezed her fingers, at first a comfort and then as he squeezed them again, a caress.

She relaxed her shoulders, blowing out a silent breath as she did so. Charlotte slept wrapped in a blanket on one of the pews. Henry chose to stand fast beside her, his menagerie of animals safely tied outside. Adversity was finally behind her. Goodness would surely follow her now.

The minister paused to run a stubby finger down the open page before him. "Into which holy estate these two persons present come now to be joined. Therefore, if any man can show any just cause. . ."

Holy. A tremor ran the length of Matilda's body. Her faith may be fledgling, but she knew well enough that the Lord paid a powerful amount of attention to marriage and to people committing themselves to each other.

She shifted from foot to foot. *Lord, am I making the right decision?*

"I will."

Matilda glanced sharply at Henry and then at the minister. Neither gave any indication that he'd spoken.

Parts of the verse Henry had spoken flooded through her mind.

"I will be found of you. I will turn away your captivity. I will gather you. I will bring you again into the place whence I caused you to be carried away captive. I will."

Peace washed away her remaining doubts. The Lord was not only the great I Am, He was also the great I Will.

". . .why they may not lawfully be joined together, let him now speak, or else hereafter forever hold his peace." Reverend Marsden looked up, one dark eyebrow raised. "Any man?"

A door creaked behind them, and Matilda glanced over her shoulder. Who had reason to interrupt? She'd been an exemplary prisoner since returning to the factory. Marriage was a legal and legitimate reason to earn her freedom.

The door pushed open wider, and a sheep poked its wooly head through. It bleated and hurried its way inside, hooves tapping on the plank floor.

A sheep in the church. She bit down on her lip in an effort to stifle her giggle. A sheep simply enjoying a reprieve from its captivity. An innocent. Not a soldier with orders in hand or government official with the power to return her behind bars. For the first time, she felt an affinity with the lanolin-scented beasts.

"Henry?" Matilda pushed back, releasing herself from his grasp. "Your sheep is interrupting our marriage ceremony."

"Soon to be our sheep, my love." He threw her a grin, before heading for the sheep.

The sheep squeezed between two pews, pausing to nibble the edge of one seat.

"I'm not sure I want to share your sheep if that's how they'll behave," she said out the side of her mouth.

He winked. "Then we'll just have to teach them better manners," he said, motioning her to stand at the end of pew, effectively blocking the sheep's retreat.

"If you are *quite* finished?" Reverend Marsden boomed. "As if marrying convicts wasn't bad enough—an animal defiling the place of God's worship! If only I were among the Maori heathens, as I've so oft asked, I'd not be subject to such as this."

Matilda bit her lip, silencing her quick retort. Really, it wasn't like they were about to sacrifice the animal. It was an honest mistake. A simple misstep. One she could easily forgive and would pray that others would do the same.

The sheep bleated at the minister and trotted forward, its wooly bulk pushing one of the pews back with a scrape.

Henry sprinted to block the other end of the pew. "Sorry, Reverend. I'll catch her and have her tied up outside in the shake of a lamb's—"

"Ahem." Matilda pinned him with a sharp look.

He inched forward toward the sheep, hand outstretched. Matilda held her breath. If he could just catch the rope, they could finish the ceremony. Appease the minister. No longer have her convict sentence hanging over her head.

Henry bent and crept forward another pace. The longer Matilda held her breath, a strange tickle began to itch at the back of her nose.

"Achoo!"

Her sneeze escaped, startling the sheep. It darted forward, slamming into Henry's chest and butting him over, then trotted to the doorway where it stood bleating at them indignantly.

"Enough!" Reverend Marsden stomped toward them. "Be gone with you."

"Who, sir?" Matilda asked. "The sheep or us?"

The minister shook out a linen handkerchief and mopped his brow with exaggerated movements.

"We're not married yet," Henry added, rubbing the place on his chest the sheep butted.

Tucking his handkerchief away, the minister smiled through gritted teeth. "Since the sheep is *still* loose, we'll expedite the proceedings. Henry Powell?"

"Yes?"

"Wilt thou have this woman to thy wedded wife, to live together after God's ordinances in the holy estate of matrimony?"

Henry's gaze centered on her face as he climbed to his feet and moved to take her hands. Gently nudging her back, they rejoined the minister in the center of the aisle. The longer Henry stared, the warmer her face grew. It became harder to breathe, as if he'd taken prisoner all the air in the room.

His grip grew firmer as they stood there. Was he barring her from escaping, or perhaps communicating his affection?

"I will," he said.

"And what of you, Matilda Brampton? Wilt thou have this man to thy wedded husband, to live together after God's ordinances in the holy estate of matrimony?"

A bubble of excitement rose. "I will," she said.

"I will be found of you.

"I will.

"I Am."

In gruff tones, the minister finalized their marriage and joined their hands together. "Those whom God hath joined together let no man put asunder. Go in peace."

Peace. Henry's larger hands wrapped around hers, as if shielding them, protecting her. Exactly the kind of man she'd married. A protector. She tore her gaze from the sight of their hands to glance at the minister.

He frowned at her. "Go!"

She let the happiness in her heart overflow and smiled at him. "God bless you, sir."

Scooping up Charlotte, Matilda followed Henry who caught the now placid sheep, and they exited into the street.

Once free from the confines of the churchyard, she paused, breathing deep the warm afternoon air. Married. She was now Mrs. Matilda Powell. One of a pair. The start of a family. Hers at last.

She hugged Charlotte closer. Father God was doing a wonderful thing. She'd been right to trust him.

"Matilda?"

"Yes?" She reached out and caught his hand, threading her fingers through his. Her smile faded as she caught the seriousness in his eyes.

He gently pulled free from her grip and stepped back toward his horse. "You are free now."

"Pardon?" Some of the exhilaration faded, leaving a hollow feeling. "What do you mean?"

"I'm releasing you." He ducked his head, addressing the cobbled road.

"Releasing me?" His words bounced around her like a basket of spilled oranges. "I don't understand."

His mouth curved up into a sad smile. "You are free to choose your own destiny—both for yourself and the babe."

How kind. Her eyes narrowed. "Henry Powell, let me tell you a thing or two."

A hint of a real smile appeared. "I've no doubt you have something to say."

"Yes!" She stepped closer and jabbed him in the chest. "I'm not some cow you can barter or set free once you're tired of her."

"Tired? I nev—"

"I'm your wife." The word choked her, and she stumbled over the urge to swipe at the wetness gathering on her eyelashes. "Your wife, Henry."

He touched her hand, raising it to his lips in the briefest of kisses. "I know that."

"You said you loved me."

" 'Tis one of the reasons why I must release you."

"But Henry. . ." She stared at him hard. "You can't."

He gathered the reins to his horse, his movement treacle slow. "Why not?"

"Because I love you."

His eyes met hers, the blue sparkle dulled in his eyes, yet sincerity still shone through. "And I you."

"I want to be with you." She adjusted her grip on Charlotte and stepped closer. "I meant every word of my vows. Even the bit about obeying you."

One of his eyebrows rose in question, and she wrinkled her nose.

"Mostly the part about obeying you."

"Really?"

She huffed out a sigh. "All right. Not that part at all. We both know I'll be a terrible wife and will give you nothin' but trouble. But you know what?"

"What?"

"I'll love you something fierce, Henry. I can truly promise you that."

"I can believe that. But I had to give you your freedom. That way you'd know you are truly free. 'Tis your choice to stay by my side." He grinned. "Even if I'm sensible."

"Like feeding my, I mean, *our* daughter sheep's milk and bringing a sheep to feed her while you found a way to free me? Yes. Especially if you're sensible."

He nodded, looking proud of himself. "Well, how else did you think I was able to feed Charlotte?"

Matilda reached him, leaning close as his arms wrapped around her. "You are sensible. And I'm thankful."

"But no longer a flirt?"

"You can be my sensible flirt. Does that suit?"

"Indeed, milady." He tapped her nose. "In fact, I promise to always sensibly flirt with you."

She tilted her head, pretending to consider him. "And what of all the girls in Sydney?"

"None can compare to you." He brushed a kiss across her lips. "I look forward to waltzing my Matilda—wherever that may lead us."

Lucy Thompson is a stay-at-home mum to five precocious children by day and a snoop by night, stalking interesting characters through historical Colorado, and writing about their exploits. She enjoys meeting new people from all over the world and learning about the craft of writing. When she can be separated from her laptop, she is a professional time waster on Facebook, a slave to the towering stack of books on her bedside table, and a bottler, preserving fruit the old-fashioned way so she can swap recipes and tips with her characters. Her home is in central Queensland, Australia, where she does not ride a kangaroo to the shops, mainly because her children won't fit. Represented by Chip MacGregor of MacGregor Literary, she is a member of American Christian Fiction Writers and Romance Writers of America.

A Score to Settle

by Gina Welborn

Dedication:

To Alexis Goring for being my friend.

Acknowledgments

To Rhyinn Welborn for telling me Cyrus's and JoJo's personalities before I started writing. I tried to make JoJo an ENTP like you wanted because they're "the best" (whatever), but JoJo insisted on being an ESTP. I couldn't nurture her out of it. I may not have really tried.

To Jerah Welborn for teaching me that even Shakespeare thought writing was (sexy, but) hard. Time to burst into a spontaneous dance!

To Becca Whitham for patiently reminding me about the need for plot. If not for you, this story would have a whole different ending.

To Cindy Hickey for inviting me to join this anthology.

To Service Master for cleaning what remained after our house fire.

An object at rest will remain at rest unless acted on by an unbalanced force.
An object in motion continues in motion with the same speed and in
the same direction unless acted upon by an unbalanced force.
—Sir Isaac Newton's First Law of Motion

Therefore, as God's chosen people, holy and dearly loved, clothe yourselves with compassion,
kindness, humility, gentleness and patience. Bear with each other and forgive one another
if any of you has a grievance against someone. Forgive as the Lord forgave you.
—Colossians 3:12–13 (niv)

And that's not all. We also celebrate in seasons of suffering because we know that when we
suffer we develop endurance, which shapes our characters. When our characters are refined,
we learn what it means to hope and anticipate God's goodness. And hope will never fail
to satisfy our deepest need because the Holy Spirit that was given
to us has flooded our hearts with God's love.
—Romans 5:3–5 (The Voice)

Chapter 1

Good-humoured, unaffected girls, will not do for a man who has been used
to sensible women. They are two distinct orders of being.
—JANE AUSTEN, *Mansfield Park*

Tuesday, 12:42 p.m.—August 16, 1870
St. Louis, Missouri

Y ou need a wife."

Cyrus Lull ignored his cousin's abrupt pronouncement and continued to observe the workmen who were loading the last of his freight onto the sternwheeler, the *Cleopatra*. He didn't need a wife. Women complicated things. Cyrus liked how his life had been in the last eight months since he'd married off his sister: simple, orderly, and serene.

Not that the levee's loading docks were ever serene.

Or orderly.

Or simple.

St. Louis had become the New York City of the West. The seven blocks of levee north of him, like the three south, bustled with steamships being loaded or unloaded with cargo, logs, and lumber. Some with passengers, grand and plain. Men barked orders. Captains surveyed decks. On the river towboats propelled barges. On the land buildings and warehouses grew wide and high. Somewhere close a brass band played. Near loading docks. Only in St. Louis. The city was as enthralling as she was chaotic. Which was why he loved visiting. But which was also why he yearned to return home to Atchison and to the realistic chaos of managing his mercantile and overseeing his uncle's trading posts.

Chaos brought by women—now this kind he was happy to avoid.

"Stop scowling, Cy. You need a lady who can get you to be spontaneous."

"A woman like that doesn't exist," he muttered before marking a check in his journal next to *twenty-three crates. Supper*, and *last evening in hotel* were the remaining tasks for the day. If he could find a woman who knew how to live according to a schedule, he'd consider marrying her. And because it was true, he added, "I can be spontaneous when I want to be."

"I've never known you to *want to*." Said because Leiden Thomas Baptiste never learned the art of realizing he'd lost the argument. "Everything you do has a purpose or you don't do it."

"Exactly."

"Having a discussion with someone who always believes he's right is frustrating."

"I agree."

Leiden muttered something too low for Cyrus to hear then said, "There's a woman for you. It's a matter of finding her. Newton's law of universal gravitation." Pause. "Even a man of your years—"

"Thirty isn't old," Cyrus groused.

"—can understand the principle of attraction."

Cyrus turned his head a smidgen, enough to see Leiden standing there with a goading smile. This was who'd confiscated *First Principles of Physics* from the crate of old textbooks Cyrus had purchased from the Oberlin College library. He should have known. Besides himself and Leiden, no one in Atchison ever expressed interest in viewing Cyrus's expansive library. Someday someone in their family would earn beyond an eighth-grade education. Someday someone would attend college. At twenty-four, Leiden wasn't too old to be the first one. Having mixed, white-and-savage blood like Cyrus, though, limited his opportunity for intellectual advancements. Not that Leiden ever seemed to mind the prejudice.

Leiden, like Cyrus, was content to learn by reading.

"In the spirit of spontaneity. . ." Cyrus slid his pencil and journal into an outer pocket of his black frock coat. He pointed over his shoulder. "Instead of returning to the hotel, I'm heading on over to the new bookstore next to Burrow's Coffee House."

"Books and coffee? I'm impressed with your sudden foray into because-it-fits-into-my-schedule spontaneity." Leiden started in the direction of Burrow's. "Why are you still standing there?"

Cyrus fell into step next to him. They crossed Wharf Street then headed west on Dock Street, weaving through the numerous pedestrians. They stopped at the intersection and waited as a crowd hurried toward Produce Row.

"Think someone opened a theater down that way?" Cyrus asked, looking in that direction.

Leiden shrugged. "Could explain the music. You want to go check it out? The steamer doesn't leave until morning."

A pair of young men stumbled by, tripping over their own feet, bumping into Cyrus. They laughed, which only intensified the alcohol smell wafting from them. Leiden started to speak, and Cyrus smacked his shoulder.

"Not our business." Spotting a break in the traffic, Cyrus stepped onto the street and—

"Excuse me, sir!"

He stopped and looked over his shoulder. The most breathtaking woman he'd ever seen was walking toward him. Her face shimmered in the noon sun. Why had she called out? They'd never met before. If they had, he would have remembered. She wasn't forgettable.

"Hello! You there!" The statuesque brunette lifted an arm and waved.

He tipped his chin in acknowledgement.

As she approached, he noticed her limp. . .and then the pink tingeing her broad cheekbones. Truly, she looked like an adult version of those German bisque dolls he sold out of a glass case, because of the short-sleeved, white day dress and matching straw hat with white silk ribbons she wore, but that wasn't what mesmerized Cyrus. She smiled. At him. For him. Because she was happy to see him. Him.

Pappan James Cyrus Lull.

She stopped and rested a white-gloved hand on his arm. "Since we are both headed in the same direction"—she tilted her head to the side, and a cocoa-colored curl slipped from her chignon and rested on her bare collarbone—"might I acquire your assistance?"

Cyrus stared at her lips. Were they painted? Had to be. No woman had lips as rosy as hers were.

"Sir?"

He met her guileless gaze. She had the kind of face you wanted to stare at: slanted eyebrows, a snub nose, a rosebud-shaped mouth. Not a wrinkle on her face. She couldn't be much older than Leiden was. Her eyes widened in an expectant look, and Cyrus knew she was waiting on him to speak. For the life of him, he couldn't remember what she'd asked. She was utterly radiant.

And smelled like a freshly cut rose.

Leiden cleared his throat. "My cousin would be honored to help, ma'am."

"It's miss," she said to Leiden, but her vibrant blue-green eyes never looked away from Cyrus. "I'm not married." Her fingers pressed into his arm. "I hope your wife won't mind you being a Good Samaritan to a lady in need."

"He's not married," Leiden put in.

She smiled. "Papa told me I can always trust men with beards," she said, focusing on Cyrus's cheeks that hadn't visited a barber since he and Leiden had left Atchison a week ago. She nodded toward the intersection. "Shall we?"

Cyrus felt his heart pounding against his chest. He checked to ensure there was a lull in the traffic then wrapped her arm around his and escorted her slowly (to be mindful of her injured limb) across the street. Once they reached the sidewalk, he looked around to see Leiden standing on the other side. Leiden shrugged and motioned to a trio of produce carts as if they were what had prevented him from crossing with Cyrus and—

"I don't know your name," he said to the vision still holding his arm.

She just stared at him.

"Miss?" he whispered, feeling like they were the only two people on Dock Street. At an inch over six feet, he was taller than all his Baptiste and Ransome cousins. He'd never stood this close to a woman of her height.

Everything about this one was perfect.

A soft rush of air crossed her plump lips. "I don't know your name, either," she said softly, "but I've never felt like this before." She stepped closer and rested her hands on his chest. "Oh, tell me you feel the same."

He tipped his chin.

She leaned forward and touched her lips to his.

Cyrus felt his eyes widen. "Why did you—" was all he managed to say before she kissed him again. This time with a ferocity every man wanted. At least it was all Cyrus had imagined he wanted. With his wife. Wife? He had to end this. For heaven's sake, they were on a public sidewalk! He had to stop, but she tasted like crumpets and orange marmalade. She was warm, so warm and sweet and demanding. And the way her hands moved along his chest—

"Susan!" a man's voice bellowed.

She jerked back, pushing him away. Face pale. "I'm—uhh, I shouldn't—" Her voice broke, tears welling, chin trembling. "If he finds me—"

"I'll stop him."

"You will?"

Cyrus nodded.

She touched his cheek then tugged the hair on his chin. For a moment, he thought she was going to kiss him again.

"A true knight," she breathed. "Where can I find you?"

"SUSAN!"

"Go," Cyrus ordered, giving her a gentle shove. "Burrow's Coffee House."

After a nod, she hurried away and blended into the crowd.

Cyrus braced himself for an assault by the man chasing her. He waited. Waited. And waited, but no confrontation came. Pedestrians continued to flood toward Produce Row. Surely people had noticed them. They ought to have been arrested for public inde-cency. She'd made him forget his manners, forget his honor.

Something wasn't right. About the abrupt kiss. About her.

Now that he thought about it, her arms had felt boney. Her collarbone looked too prominent. She was thinner than a woman of her class ought to be.

Cyrus dashed up the steps of the nearby town house and surveyed the street, des-perate to see where she'd fled. She couldn't have gone far, not with a limp. Nowhere could he see a lady in a straw hat with white ribbons. Unless she'd made it into Burrow's already. *If* she made it to Burrow's.

Leiden darted across the street. He stood at the bottom step, holding a rolled-up sheet of paper. "Have you lost your mind?"

"She kissed me."

"She bewitched you, and then you kissed her back like a green boy."

Cyrus had no response.

Leiden grimaced. "She could have run off with your coat and you wouldn't have noticed."

Suspicion seeped into Cyrus's consciousness. Reaching into the inner pocket of his frock coat, he found nothing but the realization she had no intention of ever seeing him again. "That miscreant pilfered my wallet."

"I found this on the ground." Leiden offered a paper. "Several people in the crowd were carrying copies."

Cyrus took it.

DOCTOR GRABER'S HOMEOPATHIC MEDICINE COMPANY
Medicines made from the purest Roots, Herbs, Barks, Gums, and Leaves.
Blood-cleansing. Life-sustaining. Health-reviving.

Elixers to diminish ailments from consumption, colic, digestive problems, rheumatism, venereal diseases, stiff joints, sprains, aches, pains, and even "female complaints." Salves *to relieve chapped hands or face, pockmarks, bruises, pimples, blotches, corns, burns, dark spots, freckles, itching piles, and other skin diseases.* Creams *to lift and sculpt skin, smooth wrinkles, and add a youthful glow.*

Manufactured Only By
Graber & Oates
Richmond, Virginia

Cyrus looked at Leiden in surprise. "You think she works for"—he held up the advertisement—"a snake oil salesman?"

"Too spontaneous for you to check out?"

"A girl like her wouldn't—" At Leiden's glare, Cyrus fell silent. What did he know about women like her? To be fair, what did he know about women at all?

JoJo darted up the steps of the showman wagon she shared with Maude. She slammed the door and tossed her straw hat across the small space, almost hitting her dear friend in the process. She then slid to the wood-planked floor. *Breathe.* Her chest rose and fell as she struggled to catch her breath, struggled to make sense of what she'd done. Good heavens, she'd kissed a stranger!

A handsome one.

A well-dressed one.

A gallant one.

One who certainly could afford losing a few dollars to a girl in need. But still. . .he wasn't her husband, and she'd kissed him like he was. She fanned her face frantically with both hands. Her parents had to be rolling in their graves.

"You'd better have a good reason for being late with my hair."

JoJo grimaced. She looked to where Maude stood adjusting the heavy padding under the bodice of her silky crimson gown. Freckles hidden with white face paint and rouge. Pale lashes darkened with oil and coal dust. Ruby necklace and earrings worth nothing more than the paste they were made of. Other than missing the ornate brunette wig to complete her "Lady Lainsfeld" persona, she was ready to perform. The real Maude Ailsworth, aged nineteen, looked nothing like this gaudy character.

"Sorry," JoJo muttered. She carefully removed the wig she wore over the fitted cap hiding her real hair. "You know how Graber is when we don't meet our quotas."

"It's not as if he asks for much." Maude took the proffered wig and then sat at the vanity in their tiny wagon. She adjusted the wig over her muslin cap. "Did you find enough gills to dupe this time?"

"The farther west we travel, the more gills I find."

"True." Maude's voice sounded strangely hollow. "It is a truth universally acknowledged, that men—rich or poor—are suckers for a damsel in distress."

JoJo sighed. "That they are."

"Someday, though, a pair of gentlemen will"—she waved her arm in a circle over her head—"whisk us away from this grand stage."

"They're across the river, waiting for us," JoJo said cheerfully, with a smile as false as her words. Unlike her romantic friend, she had let fail any hope of a man rescuing her from this life. In the five years she had been working for Obadiah Graber, she'd received ninety-eight marriage proposals, yet no one had come along with the bride price Graber required to buy out her contract. She, like Maude, was bound to Graber until death did them part.

Or until they arrived in San Francisco.

At the speed Doctor Graber's Homeopathic Medicine Company was traveling, it'd be a decade before she saw the West Coast. The best years of her life would be spent pretending to be someone she wasn't. Maude's contract was even more hopeless. She didn't have the hope of being freed upon reaching San Francisco. Yet she continued to believe knights in shining armor existed. She believed a man would pay her bride price. She continued to believe a man pretending to be their uncle actually cared about their happiness.

To make Maude happy, JoJo would pretend to believe, too.

Pretend. . .and plan.

JoJo pulled off the stilted shoes she wore to give the appearance of height. She lifted her skirt to reveal the leather wallet she'd wedged inside one of her stockings. She withdrew the wallet and then untied the burlap sack she'd strapped to her calf so the weight would remind her to limp convincingly. She dumped the contents of the bag onto the wooden floor. A gold watch. Eight silver dollars and four pennies. Pocket flask.

Today's reaping.

And the wallet.

"No knife?"

JoJo looked at Maude. "It's the best I could do this morning."

"Uncle Graber had such hope for a knife. He will be disappointed."

JoJo bit back her need to yell, *He's not our uncle!*

Silence stretched through the tiny wagon. They both knew the repercussions for JoJo's failure to procure what Graber wanted. Not that Maude could have done better had she been sent out to find gills to fleece.

"My dear Josephine, I've never met a girl as nimble and clever as you are." Yet for all Graber's praise, JoJo was never spared his wrath when she failed to produce her quota.

"I have until sunset to find a knife," she said more to convince herself than to mollify Maude. "Men always linger after the show."

"You'll succeed." Maude turned back to the vanity mirror and adjusted the pins in the wig. "What's in the wallet?"

JoJo hesitated, her fingers hovering over the worn leather. For some strange reason, her heart beat frantically against her chest. It was only a wallet. Taken from another gullible man. Adding another sin to her already blackened slate. What did it matter? Her soul couldn't feel any more crushed by the weight of her guilt and shame. Besides, he didn't need the money.

Not like she did.

She scooped it up and looked inside. "Greenbacks." Whoa. Over a hundred dollars. Ignoring the bills, she withdrew a worn slip of paper, which she immediately unfolded. In black ink were written five words.

"I was adored once, too," she read. She frowned at Maude. "Why would a man keep a note like this in his wallet?"

"Maybe someone gave it to him. Does the handwriting look like a woman's?"

"It's written in block letters."

"Then I have no idea."

The trumpet blared, signaling the end to the performance of Mr. Deluca's one-man band.

Maude jumped to her feet. "We can wonder later. You need to get dressed."

JoJo moved out of the way for Maude to pass.

Once the door closed, leaving JoJo alone in the wagon, she removed most of the money from the wallet. "I was adored once, too," she read, before tucking the slip of paper inside her bodice. Strange note for an equally strange man. "At least we both had a *once*."

Chapter 2

I was so anxious to do what is right that I forgot to do what is right.
—JANE AUSTEN, *Mansfield Park*

Cyrus maneuvered through the crowd until he found a spot to the left of the stage. . .or what amounted to a stage. Three crates bumped against each other, with a six-panel muslin sheet behind them. Atop the center crate stood a black-clothed Quaker—a lean man with gray, shoulder-length hair. In a deep voice, he spoke slowly, giving the audience his spiel.

". . .and that's why I ask, ladies and gentlemen, how much is thy health worth? A hundred dollars? A thousand?" The man motioned to a woman holding a coughing child in the front row of the crowd. He gave a sad smile to the woman, presumably the child's mother. "Thy own life may be measured in dollars, but that of thy precious children? We will pay all God has given us to bestow upon our children a life abundant and free." He raised a hand in the air. "Praise the Lord, my friends, one half-dollar is all it will take for thee to experience true healing from above."

"Can it help my son?" the mother called out.

"Yes, ma'am." The Quaker knelt on the stage. He withdrew a brown bottle from his coat pocket and offered it to her. "Give thy child a swallow of Graber's True Remedy. Made from nature, from God's own laboratory, with the finest, purest ingredients. For fifty pennies, yes, only fifty pennies, it will cure rheumatism, baldness, bad breath, and, yes. . .a cough."

The mother hurriedly opened the bottle, held it to her child's lips, and coaxed him to drink.

His coughing ceased, and the crowd broke into applause.

Cyrus joined in the clapping.

Leiden leaned against Cyrus's shoulder. "People believe this?"

"People will believe anything if it gives them hope."

"*You* believe this?"

Cyrus gave Leiden a slant-eyed glare to convey his exact belief. "Doesn't mean I can't be polite."

The Quaker stood. "Do not be the only person who does not go home with Graber's True Remedy. While the lovely Lady Matilda Lainsfeld entertains thee in song"—he pointed to a green medicine wagon to the right of the stage—"let us join in one accord and ensure this health-reviving elixir goes home with thee."

As the Quaker left the stage, a young buxom brunette in a shiny red gown more suited for a ballroom than the loading docks approached the crates. A burly man helped her up the steps. "I am honored to sing for you this fine afternoon." A soft British accent tinged her speech. Her gaze shifted until it settled on someone in the center of the crowd. She smiled coyly.

"Whoa," Leiden muttered.

Cyrus ignored him.

The hum of a violin filled the air, and the woman who was no more British than Cyrus began to sing in a soft contralto. "Mine eyes have seen the glory. . ."

This was all a sham dressed in religion to give it authenticity.

Smiling to conceal his disgust, Cyrus turned to the crowd. Those not in line at the wagon craned their necks in hopes of seeing who was playing the violin. Most stared at the singer. Deservedly. She had the finest voice Cyrus had ever heard. He turned his head enough to see his cousin staring, gap-mouthed.

". . .is marching on." She sang the chorus and the next three stanzas. And then the music stopped.

A hush fell over the crowd.

From behind a knife-thrower's wooden wall walked a young Quaker woman with a violin, her gaze focused on the ground, her honey-blond hair in a modest bun and covered with a white prayer cap. She sat on the steps to the stage. Smoothed the apron over her gray skirt. She placed the fiddle under her chin, her cheek caressing it as if it were her most treasured possession. Never once did she look to the crowd.

"Please give a hand for Doctor Graber's beloved niece," the singer called out. "Miss Josephine Score!"

The crowd applauded.

Miss Score rested the bow on the strings and resumed the song at the pace of a funeral march.

"In the beauty of the lilies," sang the faux Lady Lainsfeld, "Christ was born across the sea. . . ."

The moment she reached "marching on," the crowd roared, whistled, and clapped. Their voices joined hers for the final chorus.

The song ended.

Miss Score looked up to where the singer stood.

Cyrus stared in disbelief. "It's her."

Leiden leaned forward, his eyes in a squint. "She's too plain to be your girl."

"It's her," repeated Cyrus, forcing himself not to move, not to run to her and demand she explain her actions. With her face now devoid of paint, she behaved nothing like the vivacious woman who kissed him, but he knew the two were one and the same.

Look at me.

She stood, bowed, and then demurely walked back around the knife-thrower's wooden wall.

"And, because one performance is never enough, Mr. Dulaca!" The singer clapped loudly.

The one-man band walked to the side of the stage, and the applause died. As the duo performed "Oh! Susanna," Cyrus studied the advertisement Leiden had given him.

PERFORMANCES THIS YEAR IN
Cleveland – Cincinnati – Columbus – Indianapolis – Ft. Wayne – Toledo
Detroit – Lansing – Chicago – Milwaukee – Peoria – St. Louis – St. Joseph
Atchison – Kansas City – Topeka – Wichita – Fort Scott – Springfield

Atchison? Cyrus gritted his teeth. His town didn't need a thing from Doctor Graber's Homeopathic Medicine Company. Yet there were enough persuadable residents for the charlatan to sell out his stock. If Cyrus could make it home before Graber and company arrived, one meeting with the mayor and sheriff was all it'd take to convince them to ban Graber from town. Upon his life, he would keep the swindlers out of Atchison.

He looked to Leiden. "They're taking the Lower Missouri up to St. Joseph before moving south. Find out when they are leaving St. Louis and how. Then meet me at Burrow's."

Leiden nodded. He weaved back through the crowd.

Cyrus watched the performance. He joined in the applause and patiently listened between acts to Doctor Graber's taunting promises of showing them something they just wouldn't believe. The young Scottish knife-thrower, Seamus McGregor, and his ginger-haired wife, Marta, were actually impressive. The wife—if she was his wife, since she was also Lady Lainsfeld—never flinched, no matter how close the knife struck.

Miss Score did not return.

"And now," Doctor Graber said, easing to the edge of the stage, "what thou hast been waiting for." From his coat pocket, he withdrew a small black bottle. He held it up for all to see. "Graber's True Cure! Known for its health-giving power, it's made from the finest and rarest oil, procured from one of the deadliest snakes known to man. We would not be able to sell this to thee were it not for the woman gifted by God with the ability to charm the deadly snake." Pause. "Yet not with the butt of her heel, but with the melody of her hands. Cherokee Rose!"

The crowd's applause rose. An Indian maiden, in a beaded leather tunic and matching leggings, stepped up onto the stage with a covered basket. Cyrus's heart pounded against his chest. She wore a feather in the back of the leather headband encircling her long black braids. With soot around her bright blue-green eyes and white-painted lines on her now-tan face, his thief looked like one of those political cartoons he had seen in periodicals—some East Coast man's satirical impression of a native. Yet even dressed like this, she was breathtaking.

She set the basket down.

Holding a pointer finger to her lips, she breathed, "Shhh."

The crowd grew silent.

She removed the lid from the basket then sat cross-legged. From the long sleeve of her tunic, she withdrew a stick with the wood splitting into a V on one end. She tapped the basket. Within seconds a snake lifted its head over the rim, and then another. Finally a third joined in slithering out.

Cyrus reached behind his back for his knife. He paused. Gave a good look.

Bull snakes?

One by one, they curled around her arms.

She stood. Her hips, shoulders, and arms moved in mimicry of the snakes. Their tongues darted in and out as they spun around her. One encircled her neck. Someone gasped. She held a finger again to her pursed lips, quieting the crowd. As she continued to dance, she unwound a snake and returned it to the basket. She repeated the action until all three were safely tucked away.

The roar of the crowd was the largest of the afternoon. People held up greenbacks, demanding to buy a bottle of Graber's True Cure.

All because of a female snake handler.

Look at me, Cyrus silently entreated.

Once again, she quietly slipped away.

Men flocked to the stage, begging Doctor Graber to be introduced to Cherokee Rose, Lady Lainsfeld, and "your niece, Miss Score." Three men and two older women, each with a crate of bottles, moved into the crowd.

Cyrus eased along the edge of the stage. He darted around the knife-thrower's wooden wall, pausing long enough to note the slits from blades actually hitting the boards. A clothesline held the muslin backdrop, which hid two gaudy showman wagons. Guarding the door to the red one that was half the size of the blue one (likely Doctor Graber's) was the knife-thrower, Seamus McGregor in costume: dark shoulder-length hair, muslin shirt, and plaid kilt.

Cyrus strolled over to him. "Could I have a word with"—unsure what to call her, he settled on—"Miss Score?"

"She's busy." His brogue sounded natural.

The wagon shifted, likely from a person (or people) moving inside.

Noticing the shutters on the side window had parted a fraction, Cyrus spoke a little louder. "Could you give her a message?"

The knife-thrower nodded.

Cyrus withdrew the advertisement and his pencil from his coat pocket, jotted down his message, then gave it to him. "Your aim is excellent."

The man scowled at Cyrus's message. "She gonna know what this means?"

"She'll know enough."

Cyrus grinned. And then he walked away.

An hour or so later

JoJo opened the window's shutters, allowing the summer breeze into the stuffy wagon. She returned to the vanity stool. Even stripped down to her chemise, corset, and drawers, and her hair bound under the muslin cap, she was sweating. What she wouldn't give to recline under a canopy on a golden barge while four comely young men dressed as cupids fanned her with palm leaves. And fed her grapes.

While massaging the finest oils into her hair and onto her hands and feet.

If she was going to dream, she wanted it all.

She smoothed the violin case's felt lining one final time to ensure no one could feel the greenbacks she'd hidden. While her partner-for-today's-gleaming, Reuben, hadn't actually seen her pilfer the wallet, he had seen the kiss she had given Mr. Lull. Like every member of the show, Reuben had played his part; as her partner in the performance, a quarter of the day's reaping counted toward his quota. Denying she'd taken anything from Cyrus Lull would be foolish at best. Thus, sixteen dollars stayed in the wallet for JoJo to turn in, along with the coins, flask, and watch.

She wanted to believe Seamus wouldn't tell Graber about the message that Mr. Lull had given him. She'd peeked through the shutter when she'd heard his voice and seen the exchange. She had little hope that Seamus would keep her confidence. Everyone in the medicine show looked out for himself.

Doing so was the only way to survive.

For what had to be the hundredth time in the last hour, she looked at the "message" tacked to the wall of newspaper clippings of the show. So many things Mr. Lull could have shared or even implied, yet in a different handwriting than what was on the slip of paper from his wallet were two words—*CYRUS LULL*. Logic said that was his name. Why did he want her to know it? He'd recognized her, despite the costumes, wigs, and face paint. He could have threatened her. Or demanded her to meet him. He could have contacted a lawman and demanded her arrest, or he could have confronted Graber. Cyrus Lull could have made her life worse. But he hadn't. Why?

What game was the man playing?

Think, think, think.

No logical reason came to mind. . .yet a sordid one did.

JoJo released a slow groan. "Mr. Lull, I'm not what you think I am." At least not *that* kind of girl. Whether he believed her or not, she had standards. There were lines she would not cross.

Except *she*, not he, had initiated the kiss.

JoJo touched her lips.

He was a good kisser. Not that she had anyone to compare him to.

The moment he said, "I'll stop him," she knew he was the kind of man who would run into a burning building and carry a girl out. Not over his shoulder like a sack of grain. He'd cradle her in his arms and ensure she had no wounds. . .and then tend to her if she did.

I was adored once, too.

The words nagged at her. *Someone once loved me* were what the words had to mean, and Mr. Lull clearly hadn't written them, because the penmanship was different than his. Why carry the note in his wallet? Did it refer to someone having once loved him? Or was he the adorer, not the adored? Had he loved and lost? Was that why he wasn't he married? Because of the person who had written the note? Or maybe the note had no meaning. Maybe he was a widower. Maybe the note was a clue to something. Maybe someone else had put the note in his wallet and he didn't even know—

Ugh! Why was she wasting time wondering? She was never going to see him again, if she had any say in the matter.

With a resigned sigh, JoJo secured her violin bow inside the case. She could hide out in the wagon until Graber booked passage on the next available steamboat. Which hopefully would be this afternoon. Steamers departed at sunrise. Until they left St. Louis, Graber would insist upon quotas and performances. There were only so many characters she could play before people began to murmur, *That's the same girl.*

She slammed the case closed. She locked it then placed it in the overhead bin and climbed the steps into the bed she shared with Maude since Annie had—

JoJo rested her head on the pillow. She closed her eyes, banishing all thoughts of her former wagon mate. "Please, God, help me escape. Make a way. Rescue me. I can't do this on my own."

Tap. Pause. *Tap tap tap.*

"Enter," she said, answering Maude's coded question—*I'm alone. Are you?*

Maude entered then shut the door, bolting the lock. Underneath the oversized bonnet, her natural blond hair hung down to the midback in a simple braid. While her face was devoid of paint, her freckled face was pink-tinged. From running? Her nervous gaze shifted to the shutters. Within seconds, the window was sealed shut.

JoJo rolled onto her side. "Why did you do that? I am now seconds away from perishing in this volcanic heat."

"Oh, stop being dramatic." Maude beamed with joy. "I met him."

"Who?"

"My future husband."

As luck would have it, Maude found "future husbands" in every state east of the Mississippi.

JoJo managed what sounded like an excited, "How wonderful!"

"He's beautiful, Josie. Tall, dark, and utterly charming. Our children will be the most handsome in town." Maude reached inside the white apron tied around the drab gray dress that she wore as Miss Amanda Graber, Doctor Graber's other beloved niece. "He gave me his card."

JoJo felt her chest tighten.

She couldn't—she just couldn't look at the white calling card Maude offered, for some reason not wanting to read Cyrus Lull's name. Again. Not that it was his. St. Louis had a plethora of men who were "tall, dark, and utterly charming"...and who had been in this afternoon's audience. For Maude to have met Mr. Lull would be too coincidental.

Unless he was using Maude to get to JoJo. But why? He didn't seem nefarious.

Looks could be deceiving.

He didn't look deceitful.

But he could have—

"It doesn't matter," she muttered.

Of course, Maude had to ask, "What doesn't matter?"

Cyrus Lull.

He was nothing more than another gill JoJo had stolen from.

JoJo grabbed the card...and released the breath JoJo had been holding. It wasn't him. Why that made her happy she didn't want to ponder. "Leiden Thomas Remi Baptiste.

Now that's a mouthful."

Maude stepped to the bed. She crossed her arms, resting them on the feather mattress. "He's from Atchison."

"I saw that on the card." JoJo handed it back. "What is he doing in St. Louis?"

"He works with his cousin buying and selling for their uncle's trading posts."

"Did you tell him who *you* work for?"

Maude nodded. "After I shared how Uncle Graber is struggling to book passage on a steamer, he said he may be able to help." Said with such obvious delight that JoJo knew that to remind Maude about the dangers of trusting a stranger would make herself Scrooge on Christmas Eve.

Thus JoJo kept her mouth shut.

"Oh, he's so gallant," Maude said. Sighed, really.

"Indeed."

Maude stared at her for a long moment, as if trying to decide how to respond to JoJo's jaded view. Sarcasm, mind you, was not a virtue in Obadiah Graber's estimation, and thus he required his underlings to squeal on their fellow show employees when they indulged themselves in it. Contemptuous looks earned a person two lashes—symbolizing Proverbs 30:17: *The eye that mocketh at his father, and despiseth to obey his mother, the ravens of the valley shall pick it out, and the young eagles shall eat it.*

JoJo had lost count of the number of lashes she'd earned over the last five years because of her contemptuous looks and sarcastic tongue.

Maude, being Maude, took the moral high ground. "Mr. Baptiste introduced me to his cousin, and then they took me to meet the captain of the grand steamboat that's taking them back to Atchison. Captain Eads is such a nice man. The steamer won't be able to travel as fast upstream with the added weight of our wagons and livestock, but he was happy to help."

"Amazing what a pretty face—" JoJo bit back her words. She smiled. "Go on."

Maude's blond brows drew close. "Someday you will find a man who will teach you how to assume the best in others instead of the worst."

JoJo shrugged. It didn't matter if she ever met a man like that. Good people were good. Bad people were bad. And sometimes good people stole wallets and bad people pretended to be God-fearing Quakers who mixed beef fat, camphor, and red pepper with mineral oil and called it Graber's True Salve.

"When do we board?" she asked to change the subject. "Do take note how I am presuming your future husband actually helped us."

Maude tucked the calling card into her boot. "Uncle Graber wants us on board before the captain can change his mind."

JoJo slid off the bed. She pulled the gray Quaker dress over her head, assuming the guise of Josephine Score. As JoJo pinned the front of her dress, Maude ripped a paper off the wall. She stared at JoJo in such horror and, even more shockingly, anger, that JoJo took a step back in self-preservation, bumping into the raised bed. And then she chuckled at her silliness. "Good heavens, Maudie, for a moment I thought you were about to rip my spirit from my body."

Maude held up the paper, the words *CYRUS LULL* facing JoJo. "Explain. . .and don't keep any secrets from me or I *will* rip your body and soul asunder."

"He's the gill whose wallet I stole earlier"—JoJo shrugged to convey her apathy— "while I distracted him with a kiss."

"You kissed him!"

"It doesn't matter. He'll never see me again."

"Oh, Josie!" Maude groaned. "Cyrus Lull is Mr. Baptiste's cousin."

Chapter 3

Two days later—6:23 p.m.
Aboard the Cleopatra

M r. Lull, I've been remiss in thanking thee for thy assistance in gaining us passage on this fine vessel."

Cyrus studied the man Captain Eads, at Cyrus's request, had invited to join them for supper, despite being a lower deck passenger. Nothing about Doctor Graber looked or sounded false, but Cyrus didn't trust him. He'd never met nor heard of an honest snake oil salesman. The last four who had conducted business in Atchison had hightailed it out as soon as the allure for their entertainment waned and customers took their complaints to the sheriff.

Cyrus cracked a half smile. "Sir, the Good Book includes the command to be kind one to another."

Leiden nodded. "When your niece, Miss Graber, told me of your need, the least I could do was to speak to my cousin."

"Then thou hast earned my gratitude."

"Seems Miss Graber," Cyrus clarified, "is the one who deserves most of your gratitude. Had she not been at the levee seeking aid, you all would have spent another night in St. Louis. Instead you are heading up the Missouri."

Doctor Graber looked at Cyrus thoughtfully. "How right thou art."

And then he said no more.

Nor did Leiden or Captain Eads, who ate his dinner with the leisure of a man unburdened. Considering the crate of Jamaican molasses and rum he had requested from Cyrus to incentivize his willingness to grant passage for the medicine company, plus the required fare Graber paid, the wily captain was earning a significant profit on this up-river run, even with a heavier load limiting the stern-wheeler's speed.

While servers brought in the dessert plates, a young fashionable couple with unruly children departed the grand saloon. The deck passengers outnumbered cabin passengers three to one. For all the luxurious comfort of this level on the steamer, life for those below was unpleasant. Of the almost two hundred down-deck passengers, based on Cyrus's count, fifteen were members of the medicine company—eight men, four women, two children, and Graber. Since the *Cleopatra* departed St. Louis yesterday morning, Cyrus had not seen either of Graber's nieces. He suspected something more than queasiness kept them hidden.

Cyrus took advantage of the silence at his table to say, "I'm sorry your nieces were unable to join us in a meal."

"This is their first time on a steamboat," Graber said in the same tone of voice Cyrus's father used to convey *this is enough of an answer, so don't ask me any more questions.*

Leiden patted his mouth with his napkin. "Queasiness from nerves, or the thrill?"

The corner of Graber's mouth slowly indented. "I expect both." As the server refilled his goblet, he chewed the last of his prime rib. "Captain Eads, since the war's end, I've noticed the surge to move west. Would it not be more beneficial to divide the lower deck into cabins so thou couldst haul more passengers?"

Eads rested his fork and knife across his empty plate. "Freight takes priority over lower-level passengers who can't pay more than three or four dollars for a ticket west. Trains, while more expensive, travel quicker."

"Ah," Graber said, "the desire to arrive sooner loosens a man's grip on coin."

"That it does." Eads leaned back in his chair. "Freight is what pays the bills."

"How many river runs dost thou make in a month?"

As the two men talked, Cyrus finished his meal and tried to make sense of the Quaker's limited words regarding his nieces. River cruising was a remarkably calm, movement-free journey. Cyrus had never heard of anyone needing "sea legs" on a cruise up or down the river. Even when the river level was high. Though Leiden had offered to give up his stateroom for Graber's nieces, Miss Graber had graciously declined. Thus the two ladies stayed below in their showman wagon, which was packed in tight alongside freight, livestock, bales of hay, the medicine company's four other wagons, hot boilers, and the rest of the almost two hundred deck passengers. Not pleasant smells for anyone with stomach malady.

Why give up a free stateroom? Why sacrifice free comfort?

Graber wasn't a deck-passenger type of person. Cyrus suspected that if the upper deck had had an available private room, Graber would have paid for it. The man seemed completely at ease dining under chandeliers, in rooms with mirrored walls and gilded artwork, while eating cuisine on par with the finest hotels. The real question was— tonight, once the steamer dropped anchor for the night, would he stay in the grand saloon hall once the gambling tables were set up, or lounge on the deck and admire the evening sky?

Truth be told, Cyrus didn't care what Graber did after the meal. . .as long as he stayed on the upper deck. Cyrus was headed below.

"Ugh, that stuff smells worse every time you open the jar." JoJo winced as she lay stomach-down on the bed, Maude sitting next to her. No matter how gentle Maude tried to be, the cold liniment on JoJo's bare backside did nothing to soothe the pain that had lingered since Graber's beating before they boarded the *Cleopatra*. "Does it look better?" she asked before wincing again.

"Worse," Maude said, her voice tight with emotion. "The bruises go from your shoulders down to your calves. I still don't understand how three lashes with the cane produced this much bruising."

Three wouldn't have.

But Graber hadn't limited himself to three this time. The blows had rained down her body and then back up again.

Maude replaced the lid on the liniment tin. "Why would he do this? It's not like him."

How little Maude knew. JoJo lay still, resting the side of her head on her crossed arms. The glow of the oil lamp on the vanity cast a golden, almost heavenly glow, about the wagon. "The first three lashes were for not pilfering a knife." She sucked in her breath as Maude adjusted the drawers and chemise over her tender backside. "The rest were my fault because I refused to thank him for his 'instructions in righteousness.' He went into his usual spiel how he was required by God to correct me."

Maude smoothed JoJo's unbound hair. "Oh, Josie, life is easier if you do what he says and not argue. Why must you provoke him?"

"I never intend to." Tears pooled in her eyes. "I hate him. I'd kill him if I could."

Maude gasped. "You don't mean that."

She didn't. Except—God forgive her—when she did. Like now.

JoJo closed her eyes. Her chest tightened. She clenched her jaw tight until the need to cry abated, because that's what Graber wanted. Her, in tears. Her, broken. Her, believing the words he'd spoken before each lash.

Thou art a worthless and wicked woman. Smack.

Thou art a bitter woman. Smack.

Thou art a contentious woman. Smack.

No man will want thee. No man will ever want thee. . .unless thou repent of thy ungodly ways.

A tear fell. JoJo pinched her eyes tight to keep the rest in. She wasn't worthless. She wasn't. She wasn't wicked. She didn't have to be as beautiful or kindhearted or obliging as Maude for a man to want to marry her. She was smart and clever. She knew how to laugh. What came from Graber's mouth were lies. All lies. If he were hanging on a cliff, gripping the ledge with his bare hands, she wouldn't step on his fingers. She wouldn't aid his fall. But neither would she toss him a rope. That didn't make her wicked, did it?

"Vengeance is mine. . .sayeth the Lord."

Maybe, but she was tired of waiting. How much longer did she have to beg God to rain fire and brimstone down on Obadiah Graber? Or whatever his real name was. His faith in God was no more authentic than the gray wig he removed from his bald head when he wanted to don a different persona, one less of the spirit and more of the flesh.

She wouldn't be surprised if Graber found a way to spend the cruise in first class instead of down here where he belonged. His usual goal was to find a woman to profess his instant and undying love to. . .and then sell her three bottles of True Cure for the price of two.

A soft rap against the wagon door broke the silence.

JoJo followed Maude's gaze to the bolted door.

"Should I answer it?" Maude whispered. "It's probably Uncle with some food."

Doubtful.

"Might as well," JoJo murmured. "If it's not bedbugs, it's fleas."

Cyrus glanced about the lower deck as he waited for the wagon's door to open. From the sound of the verbal sparring inside, the pair sounded in good health. He removed his hat then wiped his brow. With the broiler this close, how could either of them sleep in the wagon? Better to be out on the open deck, enjoying the cool breeze off the river.

The inner bolts unclicked. The door opened partway. Miss Graber's pale, freckled face popped into view. It was a wonder she could hide the myriad freckles with paint and powder.

"Oh, hello, *Mr. Lull*." His name came out louder than the initial greeting. He'd consider it strange, but everything about these women was odd.

"Your health seems to have taken a turn for the better," he answered.

Panic flittered across her lovely features. Then—

She smiled. "Graber's True Remedy settles even the most topsy-turvy stomach. It is a miracle cure. Is Mr. Baptiste with you?"

"He had other business to attend to." Cyrus leaned to the right in hopes of catching a glimpse inside the wagon. Miss Graber blocked any possible view, yet he caught the aroma of liniment wafting from her. The pair were definitely hiding down here for a reason. He wasn't leaving until he discovered how their "chosen" seclusion was connected to Graber. Were they willing accomplices in the man's crimes? Or forced to comply?

Miss Graber peeked farther around the door. "What brings you to see us this fine evening?"

Cyrus tapped his hat against his thigh. "I'd like to know why Miss Score is intentionally hiding from me."

"I'm ill," came Miss Score's hoarse voice. "Terribly ill. Unbelievably ill."

Miss Graber gave him an apologetic look. "My cousin is ill."

Cyrus restrained his grin. He admired Miss Score's spunk. And creativity. Was adapting quickly natural for her, or a consequence of working for a charlatan?

"Contagious as well?" he queried.

"Deathly." From Miss Score.

From Miss Graber came a sigh. "You could come back tomorrow."

Cough.

"A few days might be better," she amended.

Miss Score coughed again.

Miss Graber looked over her shoulder, her long blond braid slipping onto the bodice of her gray dress. "Josie, would you stop—"

Cough. Pause. *Cough.* Pause. *Cough cough cough.*

"No."

Growl.

"He seems perfectly nice to me."

COUGH!

Silence.

Cyrus forced his anxious feet to stay still. Barging into the wagon and demanding Miss Score confess would only make matters worse. Barging in and begging her to confess wasn't a wise tactic, either. She intrigued him all the same.

Something clearly had been conveyed between the two, because when Miss Graber turned back around to face Cyrus, she looked positively delighted. She snatched Cyrus's hat before he realized her intent. "We decided now is the perfect time to talk."

Chapter 4

I think it ought not to be set down as certain, that a man must be
acceptable to every woman he may happen to like himself.
—Jane Austen, *Mansfield Park*

JoJo immediately rolled into a sitting position and, despite the surging pain from sitting on her bruised bottom, frantically grasped at a blanket to cover herself.

Mr. Lull strolled inside the wagon that was not built to host three people, not when one of them was his size. He dipped his neck and shoulders to keep from hitting the ceiling.

"Ahh…stay back," JoJo ordered. She flung the blanket over her bare feet and did her best not to wince from the pain in her backside. "I'm not properly attired to entertain visitors, which is why it's quite ungentlemanly for you to be here. If anyone sees you…" She left the rest of the warning unsaid.

Truth was, no one in the medicine company would care that a man was in the wagon. Graber had never taken issue with any of the men who'd visited Annie, as long as she turned in her weekly quota.

Mr. Lull looked around. His gaze settled on the pair of stilted shoes JoJo had forgotten to put away after she returned from her meeting with (and beating from) Graber.

He frowned then looked at JoJo. "You're about five feet, six inches? Seven at most."

She shrugged.

This—what he saw right now—was the real her. Or real enough. No face paint. No wig. No character clothes.

Just her.

Joia Johanna Byrd.

It was all JoJo could do not to flee. She elected to cough instead.

Maude placed his hat on the vanity, right next to the liniment tin. She motioned to the bench on the side wall. "Please," she said in that perpetually I'm-delighted-to-see-you voice of hers, "have a seat."

He did.

Even in limited light, he looked dashing. And larger than JoJo remembered. This time he wore a gray suit and a blue silk waistcoat. And a grin from ear to ear. Because he was happy to see her? The man was deluded.

Or devious.

She should have never kissed him. But she had. Worst part was, she'd enjoyed it. And he seemed to enjoy it, too. It'd been like nothing she'd ever experienced—desire, certainly. But more. More like the feeling she was free to be different, to be new, to be wild and beautiful and, well, mostly free. Or she was being overly imaginative.

She'd have to kiss him again to know for sure.

Realizing she was staring at his lips, JoJo pulled the blanket up to her neck. *Cough.* "You should hurry with what you have to say." *Cough.* For good measure, she added, "Deathly contagious. When you become ill, do remember you'd been warned. And do not come to me for sympathy, for I will give you none."

"This is true," Maude muttered.

Mr. Lull studied JoJo for a long moment.

"What are you looking at?" she asked.

"You."

"That's obvious. Why?"

"Your hair is red."

Auburn, actually. Like the dying embers of a fire, but now wasn't the time to insist upon clarity in description.

JoJo looked to Maude, who leaned against the vanity as if she had not a care in the world. Of course not. Cyrus Lull hadn't come here to interrogate her. Speaking of the man—

She smiled at him. "And yours is black. Now that we have this settled, you can leave." When he didn't move, she gave him a pointed look and coughed.

He shifted on the bench to face her. "You are a remarkable performer."

"Thank you."

"Let's agree—no more lies."

"In the course of my career I've found that an occasional fib is needed."

Maude snickered. "I don't know about *occasional* with you."

JoJo looked heavenward and sighed.

"Miss Graber," Mr. Lull said without looking away from JoJo, "could you give your cousin and me a moment alone?"

JoJo said, "No," as Maude said, "Certainly." She then dashed outside, closing the door most of the way.

Mr. Lull moved toward JoJo, and she immediately scrambled back against the wall to put as much distance between them as possible. He could grab her legs. But then she'd kick him. First under the chin then his throat. By the time he climbed onto the bed, she'd have the overhead hatch opened. The man weighed at least sixty, maybe seventy pounds more than she did, albeit his added weight was all muscle. Leanness afforded her speed.

He didn't grab her, though.

"You don't have to be afraid of me."

"Keeping my virtue cautions me otherwise."

"I will never lie to you. You have my word." Resting an elbow on the edge of the mattress, he spoke softly, yet with a dangerous edge in his tone. "Does Graber hit you often?"

JoJo raised her chin. "Why would you presume such a thing?"

"You wince after every cough." Said as if it hurt him to see her in pain. He stared at her for an agonizingly long moment. "Graber did this, in St. Louis, after the show, before you boarded the *Cleopatra*. This is why you haven't been seen walking about. The liniment is for the bruises." Before JoJo could think of a convincing lie, he added, "Even the slightest movement hurts, doesn't it?"

She tensed, too startled to speak for a moment. He'd deduced the truth. How? Had someone finally decided to investigate Annie's death? He didn't sound like he was from Wisconsin, but accents could be faked. "Since you are insistent on the truth, then who are you? A marshal? A Pinkerton agent? Bounty hunter?"

"I am nothing more than what you see." He sighed, not as if he was discontent with his life. More like, sad she'd questioned him and doubted his sincerity. "Cyrus Lull, mercantile owner." Said with no sense of shame. The man seemed completely content to be Cyrus Lull, mercantile owner. He would never hide who he was. He would never live under an assumed name.

Not like she was.

"Good heavens, has anyone ever told you how dull that sounds?" she said to cover up how uncomfortable he made her feel.

His face was a perfect picture of surprise. "You have a knack for being a first for me."

That struck her as odd. But to ask him to explain would show she wanted to know more about him, and it was safer not to know. "I don't have your wallet anymore."

"I assume Graber has it. . .*and* everything else you've stolen for him."

She started to say something cheeky, like, "He doesn't have everything I've stolen," but as Mr. Lull watched her, she just sat there, unable to look away from the intensity of his vivid blue eyes, unable to lighten the moment with a flippant remark. It was as if he could see into her soul. But that couldn't be possible because if he could, he would recoil in horror.

She was a liar and a thief.

Men like him didn't care about women like her.

JoJo cleared her throat. "Why are you here, Mr. Lull?"

"I'm going to help you."

"Help me do what?"

"Escape this prison Graber has you in."

She searched his face, looking for any sign of jesting. Nothing. The man truly had no artifice or pretense. He was nothing more than what he said. Strangely enough, she liked that about him.

She swallowed to ease the tightness in her throat. "Why do you want to help me? I'm nobody to you."

"*Were* nobody."

His powerful gaze never flickered from hers. A good three feet separated them. Him standing at the side of the raised bed, her sitting at the back wall. The wagon felt hot, scorching hot, and it wasn't because of the oil lamp, or the boilers on the other end of the deck, or the fact the window shutters and the almost-closed door hindered any evening breeze. Her skin tingled. Her heart raced. And Mr. Lull continued to study her as if he were admiring a beautiful arrangement of oils on canvas.

Men looked at Maude that way. Not JoJo.

As much as she wanted to say "I don't need your help," the words would not form. No more lies. Something about him made her want to be honest, to tell him about her past and why she'd signed the contract to work for Graber. But this would mean trusting him, and some things she trusted with no one, not even Maude.

"Why?" she whispered. "Why do you care about a stranger?"

His gaze fell to where her bare toes peeked out from under the blanket. Then he jerked his gaze upward, his neck reddening. He snatched his hat from off the vanity then walked to the door, leaving her with words that rendered her speechless.

"You kissed me, Miss Score. That changed everything."

The next morning

Cyrus leaned over the deck railing, hands clasped together, as he observed the deck below, more interested in the view than in the smells of coffee, bacon, and biscuits seeping under the grand saloon doors. Miss Graber spoke nearby to a middle-aged man and woman, fellow members of the medicine company, both of a healthy weight. Unlike Graber's nieces. Devoid of padded costumes, their frames were bony. Miss Graber touched her abdomen as she spoke then motioned in the direction of the parked wagon with Miss Score, he presumed, recovering from Graber's beating. The couple shook their heads. Shoulders slumped, Miss Graber walked on.

"She looks hungry," Leiden remarked.

Cyrus nodded. Lower deck passengers had to provide their own food, their own bedding, their own protection from the elements. Last night in the wagon, he hadn't noticed or smelled any food. They could have stored it in the closet, in the under-the-bed cabinet, or in the overhead bins. His gut told him they had little. . .if any.

He looked to Leiden. "I suspect Graber controls their access to food."

"Why?"

"To create dependence on him."

Leiden muttered a pair of foul words. "What do you need me to do to help you steal Miss Score away so you can marry her?"

Cyrus cocked a brow. Not once while he and his cousin talked last night had Cyrus mentioned marriage.

Leiden patted Cyrus's back. "She kissed you. I know how you think."

Cyrus closed his eyes, needing a moment to sort out his thoughts. Of all the women God could have brought into his life for him to help, why this one? Why her? She certainly didn't trust him. She'd made that clear. She was smart, too smart, and too guarded. Depending on how long she'd been working for Graber, she may be past the point of understanding that the beatings weren't her fault. She may believe this was the best life could offer her. What of her friend, the one claiming to be her cousin? He suspected Miss Score and Miss Graber were no more related to each other than they were to Doctor Graber. False names. False connections.

How could Miss Score live with these lies? She should find a sheriff and report Graber. The country had laws about abusing women. Atchison had a whipping post for men who beat their wives.

"Be ye kind one to another."

The kind response would be to forget she ever kissed him. The kind response would be minding his own business. The kind response—

Cyrus released a breath. The kind response meant obeying the words that had echoed in his mind, interfering with his morning prayer and unceasing until he'd answered, "I will." Marry Josephine Score. Marry a woman he barely knew. Why would God ask this of him?

Doing so made no sense.

But so was his absolute certainty that God had spoken.

"I can't help her," he mused, "until she believes I mean her no harm."

Leiden leaned back against the railing. "Women like to be courted."

"Courting takes time. Months."

"If you were on land, you'd be lucky to have three hours a day a few times a week. You are both stuck on a boat. You have twelve to sixteen hours a day to court her. That's—" Leiden's brow furrowed. "That's a week's worth of courting accomplished in one day."

Cyrus looked out at the trees lining the muddy river. At the speed they were traveling, they'd reach Jefferson City tomorrow afternoon and Kansas City in eight or nine days. In Leiden's estimation, that would amount to three mouths of courting. If Cyrus couldn't convince Miss Score to marry him by then, he would disembark in Kansas City and continue on his way to Atchison while the medicine show continued on to St. Joseph. The advertisement had them stopping in Atchison on their way south, but he refused to let Doctor Graber swindle anyone in his hometown. Nor would he permit Graber to lay another hand on Miss Score.

He rose to his full height, confident of his decision. "I never thought I'd marry a redhead."

"Why would you consider it when your heart is set on a particular brunette?"

"*Was* set," Cyrus said gruffly. "She's married now."

Leiden crossed his arms. "If you're no longer in love with her, then why do you continue to refuse to sell goods to her father and husband?"

Cyrus said nothing.

Leiden gripped Cyrus's shoulder. "Helen deserves better than Lou Davies. Everyone in Atchison knows you were the better choice."

"Not everyone."

"You are too good a man to keep holding this grudge."

Cyrus thought about that for a moment then said, "I need you to convince Eads to grant Graber permanent access to the upper deck. Have him invite Miss Graber to join her uncle. Befriend her. Court her. Do whatever needs to be done to keep Graber's attention on her, and not on Miss Score."

"Will do."

"You agreed rather quickly."

"I like to be agreeable."

"When?"

"When a pretty lady is involved." Leiden backed away from Cyrus. "Before you marry Miss Score, you'd better tell her about Helen Davies. The past never stays in the past in a small town."

Chapter 5

Much was said, and much was ate, and all went well.
—JANE AUSTEN, *Mansfield Park*

Saturday—7:42 p.m.—August 27
Kansas City, Kansas

JoJo sat cross-legged atop the stack of hay bales near the steamer's bow. This position gave her a prime view of the *Cleopatra*'s deck passengers disembarking to spend the next two nights in hotels in the port city. She tossed her apple from hand to hand. The baggy tweed suit and Union Army cap she had pilfered in Jefferson City and a little soot on her face enabled her to study the crew's schedule and habits without any unwanted contact. During the last week, the crew had grown used to seeing "Joe Fairfax" scoop animal manure off the deck and do other penny-a-job chores.

She loved being Joe Fairfax. Why had she never worn a male disguise before? Joe Fairfax didn't have a quota. Joe Fairfax had a life. . .all because Obadiah Graber believed he was teaching JoJo a lesson in humility by limiting her to the lower deck while he enjoyed the benefits of Leiden Baptiste's and that railroad baron's competitive courtship of "Miss Amanda Graber."

Poor Maude.

Neither of those men were going to marry her. Graber wouldn't allow any man to steal his prized jewel.

JoJo bit into her apple and smiled as she chewed. Unfortunately for Graber, the person who would steal Maude away from him wasn't a man.

"One step toward redemption, right, Lord?" she said, looking heavenward.

She took another bite of apple. Once today's sun set, except for the handful of men left to stand guard, the crew would disembark and not return until Monday, at 12:01 a.m. God bless Captain Eads for refusing to travel on Sunday. God bless Cyrus Lull for having a cousin in town who insisted he visit. One less person to distract her from her plans.

Although, to be fair, Cyrus *had* suggested she ask the crew for work. Honorable work. . .if one could call cleaning the washroom that. Anything was better than sitting in the wagon and doing nothing. Although, as much as she enjoyed having something to do, what she wouldn't give for a Jane Austen novel to read. If she mentioned it to Cyrus, he'd find her one. Which was why she didn't. For the last ten days, he'd shared his meals. He'd insisted God's great love for her had never waned. Not once pressed her to explain why Graber had hit her. Cyrus brought her flowers, confections, and moments to be herself, not hidden behind a character on the world's stage. He'd been courting her, but why?

He was a saint. And far too good for her.

JoJo looked over her shoulder at the pink, orange, and yellow rays of the setting sun slicing into the turquoise sky. Thirty minutes, give or take a few, before nightfall. No matter how long the night seemed, dawn would come. Never the same burst of colors but always consistent. Always giving her hope that this darkness—what she'd endured these last five years—would not continue forever. Night into day. A new start to be someone better than she was in the darkness. To walk in newness of life.

Turning her back to the sunset, she took another bite of apple.

Next port stop after Kansas City—Leavenworth. And then on to St. Joseph. Not that she would ever make it to St. Joseph. Tonight was the dark moon. Tonight was the night to jump ship.

First, she'd pay a dinghy man to say he ferried them across the river to Kansas City, Missouri. Second, she'd rescue Maude. Third, she'd buy passage on the 10:45 p.m. express train to Atchison. From there they'd head west. Or south. They had enough disguises that no bounty hunter could follow their trail. The plan hinged on one minor detail.

Convincing Maude to run.

How to convince her when she had no motivation to escape? She'd never endured a cane to her backside. She'd never expressed anything but appreciation for the man who had plucked her out of a Chicago factory and taught her how to speak and behave like an educated woman.

JoJo's throat tightened as she swallowed. Graber had limited her time with Maude. And he had banished JoJo to the steamer for the weekend for no logical reason. She'd done nothing to deserve the punishment. She tensed. Was it possible he suspected her plans? He had to know she wouldn't leave without Maude.

JoJo stared at her apple core, unable to shake off the doubts. She should have shared her plan with Cyrus. He would have seen any potential hitches.

"It'll all work out," she muttered.

She slid off the hay bales. She gave the core to the first horse she came across then strolled contently to the wagon, nodding at the two deck men she saw. Time to pack and become "Josephine Score" one last time. With a renewed smile, she hurried up the wagon steps and jerked the door open.

JoJo gasped.

He sat on the bench with his boots propped up on the vanity stool, looking all pleased with himself for being able to surprise her.

"I don't deserve this," she muttered.

"You do, and someday you will thank me." Cyrus grinned. He couldn't help it. Josephine Score was fetching even with soot smeared on her face and in clothes that hid her curves. Looking at her made him feel like it was Christmas morn. "You look lovely tonight," he said, and, as expected, she looked heavenward and sighed.

She stepped inside. "What are you doing here?"

"Following my week's schedule." He withdrew his journal from his coat pocket. Turned to the page he wanted her to see. "Have breakfast with Josie. Have lunch with Josie. Have supper with Josie. Today I've accomplished two of the three." He nodded to the red-gingham-covered bundle sitting on the vanity. "I brought food."

She rested her hands on her hips. "You're supposed to be enjoying a meal with your cousin and her two delightful wards. In town. Five blocks away."

Cyrus nodded. "That I was."

"And?"

"And?"

"Why are you here and not there?" she said in an increasingly snippy voice.

He held up his journal. "I like to be consistent."

"Why are you *really* here?"

What he wanted to say was, "*Because you're the first thing I think of when I wake, and the last when I go to sleep.*" Instead he said, "I am here to supervise your escape plan and ensure it goes off without a hitch." He moved his feet off the vanity stool. "Please. Have a seat."

Annoyed was the nicest emotion he could ascribe to the look she gave him. Yet she sat on the stool. "What makes you think I have an escape plan?"

Cyrus turned to the page in his journal. He gave it to her so she could read the list of her peculiar behaviors over the last ten days: questions she'd asked the crew, her random comments to him that he found suspicious, and his list of possible explanations for her scheming. He'd included four guesses for the latter—jump ship, organize a mutiny, arrange an engagement party, escape Graber—with the most logical one circled.

She opened her mouth. . .then closed it. Not once in the last ten days they spent together had she censured herself. Yet she did now. Why?

Unable to contain his curiosity, he said, "I appreciate frankness and honesty in conversation. I wish to hear your thoughts."

Josie crossed her legs. Rested her clasped hands on her thigh. "You have more sincere faith in God than anyone I have ever met, thus I have no cause to believe your intentions toward me are depraved."

That would've never made his list of ten possible things she was thinking.

"I appreciate the compliment," he answered.

Her mesmerizing blue-green eyes focused on his with a seriousness he rarely saw in her. "Is your objective to marry me?" she asked.

That wasn't an expected thought, either.

"It is."

She jumped to her feet. "Good heavens! Have your lost all sense of reason? You aren't in love with me, and I am certainly not in love with you."

He shifted on the bench. "Love is not a necessity to begin a marriage."

"Cyrus Lull," she bit off, "that is *not* an acceptable answer." She retook her seat, her voice calm. "Although I will concede I agree about love not being a necessity. My parents' marriage was arranged, yet their love grew deep over time." She exhaled loudly. "Why is marrying me your objective?"

"You kissed me," he said flatly.

"Because I kissed you?" She jumped to her feet again, this time slamming her hat to the floor then motioning dramatically with her arms. "It was just a kiss, Cyrus. A kiss!" She wagged her finger at him. "How many times do I have to tell you it was an impulsive action that meant nothing? I do it all the time."

He tensed. "Kiss strangers?"

Her face reddened. "Gracious, no. I meant act impulsively. Kissing you was a first for me, and because of you, I have decided never to kiss another man again."

Cyrus grinned with pleasure. "Good. I wouldn't want my wife to kiss another man."

"That's not what I meant"—she poked his chest—"and you know it."

He burst into laughter.

She let out an unladylike snort. "Your problem is you think you can be all charming and gallant and—oh, please, stop smiling at me."

He didn't. Couldn't.

Life with her was never going to be dull.

Muttering incoherently, she opened the cabinet under the bed and tossed onto the bench next to him a dowdy gray dress, a frayed tapestry bag, and a violin case. She then slammed the cabinet. Her eyes narrowed as she glared at him. "Neither one of us is a Puritan, nor will society demand either of us wear a scarlet *A* if you don't marry me." She drew in a deep breath. "One kiss does not an obligation to marriage make."

"One is an understatement," he pointed out.

She growled.

"Marrying is the right thing to do."

She scowled.

He smiled, confident of his decision. Josephine Score needed a future outside the medicine company. She needed a home that, when she spoke of it, her face would light up with joy—like when she'd spoken of her life in Virginia. She needed a family—a real family who would laugh at her stories. She needed to feel free to hope and to wish and to dream. She needed to be loved.

He already cared for her. From the moment she'd called out to him, he'd sensed a strange, inexplicable bond with her. He may be on the way to falling in love.

She may be, too.

She repeatedly unlocked and relocked the violin case, muttering again. Her face twisted and scrunched as she worked through her thoughts. During the last ten days of courting Josie, for all her drama, Cyrus had learned that once she had time to think, she followed reason and logic. He liked that about her. He loved how resourceful and clever she was. He loved her laugh. He loved how she made him laugh. He even loved how she wore her emotions on her face. Based on the way her lips pursed in resignation—

She abruptly turned to him. "If I had an escape plan—" She held up a hand. "Let me finish. If—and that's a little *if* not a big *if*—if I did, I don't need your—*ugh*," she growled. "Fine. I'm escaping, and I could use your help. I can't even lie to you in good conscience anymore."

"I shall presume now is not the time to compliment your character growth."

She gave him a slant-eyed glare.

Cyrus grinned. He stood and scrunched down to keep from hitting the ceiling. "How about this—you clean up, and then we discuss your plan while we eat. Where's the list?"

Her face drew a blank. "List?"

"The details of your escape plan," he clarified. "I'd like to look it over."

"It's in my head."

"In your head?" he retorted, his voice rising a little. "Whenever I have something important I have to do, I write down all the details to ensure I don't miss something. You should have written this down."

"And risk Graber finding it?" Her gaze fell to the violin case. She gripped the locks. . .and then nothing. No click. No lock and unlock and repeat. She held tight, immobilized by something in her thoughts.

"Please, talk to me," he begged, needing words to understand the distress ebbing from her.

"You don't understand what that man is capable of."

Cyrus wanted nothing more than to wrap his arms around her and say, "I will protect you," over and over until she believed him. Until she knew in her heart she could trust him. He couldn't. Not yet. He needed the answer to the question that had plagued his sleep since he first spoke to her in the wagon.

"Why did Graber beat you?" he asked softly.

Silence lingered until he thought she wouldn't answer.

And then—

"I failed to bring him a knife." Her words were clipped and cold.

"A knife?" If she had shared her need the day she kissed him, he would've given her the blade he carried behind his back, despite it being a gift from his grandfather. "Why did he want one?"

"It wasn't about want. The man has dozens."

"Then why ask for one?"

She exhaled in obvious frustration. "It's the game he plays. If I bring back what he asks for—could be a knife, an arrowhead, red stockings, something with a pearl, or whatever strikes his mood—he's delighted. If I don't, he's still delighted because he now has an excuse to provide me an 'instruction in righteousness.'" Before Cyrus could ask for clarification, she said, "Graber derives pleasure from another's pain. When the beating is over, he requires that I thank him for teaching me to be submissive. He's a sick, vile man."

Cyrus sat back on the bench, nauseated. He'd never anticipated the depth of Graber's depravation. He had to ask, and braced himself for the worst. "Has he ever done more than beat you?"

"No."

"Has he hurt anyone else?"

She nipped her bottom lip and looked to the wagon door, open for anyone to see inside.

"The remaining crew has enough tasks to occupy their interest," he assured her. "No one is around to hear. What was her name? The girl he hurt."

She turned to him. Gone was the fear he'd seen in her lovely blue-green eyes, replaced by a fierce determination. "Doesn't matter. I'm escaping tonight. Do you truly want to help?"

Cyrus stood, more resolved than ever. "I do."

She studied him for a long moment. "Why are you doing this?"

"I have a score to settle."

"With me?"

With her. With Graber. With himself.

Before he could further explain, she sighed. "I should never have kissed you."

"But you did." Invariably his gaze fell to her lips and the memory resurfaced. The way her lips had brushed against his, the way she'd branded herself on him. The memory was ever present, haunting his dreams, distracting his thoughts. He stepped forward. "Josie, if you would just marry—"

"Oh, no, you don't." She braced her arms on his chest. "Whatever this is between us—"

"Friendship?" he offered. It was the best foundation for wedded bliss.

Her gaze fell to where she touched him. She jerked back, face reddening, he presumed, in remembrance of the last time they stood this close. "Please go. I need to change."

"And then we eat and plan."

"Yes, but this doesn't mean I will entertain any more talk of marriage."

"And I won't give any. . .if you agree to consider alternative escape ideas I may have."

"Fine." Pause. "But this doesn't mean I like you."

"I expected as much."

She looked heavenward and sighed. Yet the corner of her mouth indented as she pointed to the door.

Cyrus was at the bottom of the wagon steps when the door closed behind him. He sat, leaned back, his elbows on a tread. And then he smiled. Everything was going his way. By this time tomorrow, Miss Graber would be protected by his mother and Josie would be protected by his name. Graber wouldn't be able to touch either one of them ever again.

Chapter 6

Every moment has its pleasures and its hope.
—Jane Austen, *Mansfield Park*

JoJo gripped the violin case handle with her left hand and Cyrus's bicep with her right one as they stood under a glowing lamppost outside the entrance of the wooden, two-story building. Not the most (nor the least) prestigious hotel she'd ever been in. The front windows afforded her a view of the empty lobby. Graber and Maude must be in their rooms. The rest of the medicine company had to be out scouting the town. Where they slept never mattered to Graber. Everyone always returned to the fold. Except Annie. Her mistake was a lesson to all—*If you run, don't get caught. If you do, you die.*

JoJo took a step forward then stopped. Putting her life in danger was one thing. Putting Cyrus's. . . What had she been thinking when she agreed to him traveling with them on the express to Atchison? She shouldn't have agreed to hide among his mother's people.

Cyrus leaned close. "What's wrong?"

"This is a bad idea." She tightened her grip on his arm. "If Graber sees—"

"I won't let him hurt you again." He kept staring at her as if desperate for her to believe him.

"I know," she whispered. She couldn't lie to herself anymore—this was the kind of man she wanted to marry. The kind she would have married had the war not destroyed all that she loved. "Cyrus, it's not me I'm afraid of him hurting."

"He can't hurt me."

JoJo shook her head at his overconfidence. He was underestimating Graber. She opened her mouth to tell Cyrus she needed to do this on her own and not involve his family, but then she noticed his eyes were closed. In prayer? In frustration? What she wouldn't give to be able to lean against him. To rest in his embrace. To listen to the rumble in his chest as he prayed for her, for them, for their future, just as her father had when she was a little girl. She'd crawled onto his lap and rested because she knew he'd keep her safe.

She wanted Cyrus to be her Rock of Gibraltar. She wanted his still, soft strength.

How easy it would be to love him.

JoJo blinked at the warm tears blurring her vision.

"Ready?"

Gaze straight ahead, she nodded and walked with him to the hotel door. By this time tomorrow, she and Maude would be hidden among the Shawnee. Graber couldn't touch them while they stayed on the reservation. As much as she wanted to believe Cyrus would marry her if she'd agree, she knew it was only his conscience driving his actions. Once they had distance, his need to play the rescuer would fade. He would be thankful he hadn't done something so hasty as to marry a stranger. Not so much a stranger, really. He said he was her friend. She wanted to be his friend, his wife, his love.

The man was a saint.

He deserved someone better.

The moment they stepped inside the hotel, JoJo assumed the demure demeanor of Miss Josephine Score. One last performance and then she would be free. They stopped at the front desk. She softly inquired about the room number for her cousin, Miss Amanda Graber.

"Graber? She the blond with all the"—the clerk wove his hand in a circle around his face—"freckles?"

"An older Quaker, her uncle, took a room also," Cyrus put in.

The clerk nodded. "They haven't returned from dining with Mr. Tankersly."

JoJo didn't know anyone by that name. She looked at Cyrus in confusion.

"The railroad man."

Oh, the one on the steamer who'd been competing with Captain Eads and Leiden Baptiste for Maude's attention. Graber was sure to be pitting them against each other, too.

She thanked the clerk then pulled Cyrus to a secluded spot near the staircase, next to a potted palm. "I can pick the door lock," she said in a low voice, "and then we can wait in her room. Well, I can try picking it. It's not one of my better skills."

Cyrus looked down at her with an amused expression. "Someday your first solution to a problem will not be one of a criminal bent. You, my dear, are fortunate Graber agreed to Leiden's recommendation that they stay in this particular hotel." He wove his fingers through hers and led her to a side stairway and then down to the housekeeper's basement office.

He knocked on the door frame.

A light-skinned colored woman with bits of silver in her close-cropped dark hair exited a connecting side room to the office. Her face brightened with a smile. "Cyrus Lull, where are my coffee beans?"

"And here I thought you missed me." He released JoJo's hand, set her bag on the floor, then enveloped the woman in an exuberant hug. "Your beans are packed in a crate on the steamer. Mother wants to deliver them."

She stepped out of his embrace, her hazel eyes narrowed. "Then why are you here? I know you don't miss my cooking."

Cyrus drew JoJo into the office. "I brought a friend. This is Miss Josephine Score. Josie, meet Miss Bettine Baptiste. She's Leiden's aunt." Then he added, "Bettine was born in New Orleans to a colored composer and a white Frenchwoman."

JoJo looked back and forth between the two, unsure how to respond. Who other people married was none of her business.

"Josie plays the violin," Cyrus announced.

Miss Baptiste looked in expectation at JoJo.

"My grandmother taught me." When neither responded, JoJo added, "She fled Paris when the Revolution began, escaping with this"—she waved the violin case—"from Louis XVI's palace. Grandmère claimed she stole it from under the king's nose. Mama said it was a gift from a suitor and that Grandmère liked to embellish her stories."

"Who do you believe?" Miss Baptiste asked.

JoJo cocked her head and stared at Miss Baptiste thoughtfully. "When faced with the option of believing your grandmother was either a liar or a thief, would you not choose to believe her actions, whatever they were, were motivated for a good reason?"

Miss Baptiste's lips curved. "I believe I would." She looked to Cyrus. "When are you going to marry this one?"

"He's not," JoJo rushed to say. "Mr. Lull and I met on the steamer, and he offered to help me rescue my friend."

"Mother will hide her on the reservation until the danger has passed."

The lovely housekeeper studied them with undisguised interest. She slid her hands in her apron pockets then sat on the edge of her desk. "I suspect you two intend on conscripting me into service. Start explaining."

Minutes later, the three of them were standing outside Maude's room on the second floor. Cyrus held JoJo's bag and violin as Miss Baptiste unlocked the door. JoJo dashed inside. She snatched Maude's tapestry bag off the carpet. After she set it on the bed, she noticed Cyrus and Miss Baptiste still standing outside the room.

"What are you two doing?"

"Guarding the door," Cyrus answered, his gaze on the hall leading to the public staircase.

"Why?" JoJo tossed Maude's nightgown into the bag. "The plan is to wait in here until Maude arrives. We don't want Graber to see us."

Miss Baptiste's hazel-eyed gaze shifted from JoJo to Cyrus. "Choose in or out," she ordered in a hushed voice. "I need to lock this door before I'm caught helping you."

He looked decidedly uncomfortable.

"Stop being such a prude." She shoved him inside. "Step out onto the balcony if your honor can't handle being alone in a room with a female." Her voice softened. "If you miss the ten forty-five express, come back here. I know people."

She closed the door. The key rattled in the lock.

Click.

Cyrus set JoJo's bag and violin on the dresser. He glanced nervously about the room, his gaze shifting from the bed to the balcony door and then to everything but her. Poor man.

The kindest thing she could do was confront his fear and make him laugh about it. And then they could go back to being Cyrus Lull, mercantile owner, and Josephine Score, violinist. Two friends keeping each other company while they waited for one of them to die. Figuratively speaking.

Thus, JoJo plopped onto the squeaky bed. "Isn't this exciting?"

Cyrus didn't know what to make of her comment. They were alone. In a room. In a *locked* room, and he wanted to kiss her more than he wanted to breathe. Every day he'd watched the sunset with her, he wanted to kiss her. The moment she'd confessed the details of her plan, he wanted to kiss her. Riding to the hotel in the hackney, he'd wanted to kiss her. It was an ever-present desire. She wasn't that much of an innocent not to recognize the signs.

He needed to leave. He needed out of this tiny room.

Cyrus used his hat to fan his face.

Josie smiled at him from her spot on the bed. "Oh, Cyrus, the look on your face is a riot. Should I holler for a preacher man?" She pitched her voice another octave higher. "Help me, sir, help me! This man compromised my virtue even though he was standing ten feet away."

"You're being ridiculous."

She laughed. "Me?" Her smile died. "A woman's freedom to choose whom she marries, for centuries, has been stripped from her by unscrupulous men who know how to manipulate society's strict code of conduct. Dance three times—oh, no, you have to marry. Use each other's Christian names—quick, ring the wedding bells. Travel together unchaperoned—cue Mendelssohn's 'Wedding March.'"

"Men have also been ensnared against their will."

"Exactly!" She slapped her palms against the bed. "Two people forced into marriage because someone decided a woman's reputation was damaged if her bare hand touched a man's bare hand. It's not fair."

"It's not fair to either party." Cyrus strode to the door leading to the balcony that wrapped around the wooden building, fully intending to step outside. He paused. Doing so would risk Graber seeing him, but maybe not if he kept his back to the street. "Josie," he said, staring at the door handle, unsure of what to do, "as a gentleman, I must protect any slight to your reputation." To be fair, he needed to protect both of them from what he wanted at this moment.

He expected another laugh.

As the silence stretched, he turned around.

She stared absently at the bed. A tear slid down her cheek—from laughter or heartbreak, he wasn't sure.

"You think too highly of me." She moistened her lips. "No one will insist you marry me to redeem my assumed soiled reputation. No one, not even Graber. He's received ninety-eight requests to marry Josephine Score. . .or Cherokee Rose. . .or any one of my other personas. Every man balks when Graber asks for a bride price. Sometimes it's a couple hundred dollars. Once it was a thousand." She fell back against the bed and chuckled bitterly. "He puts too great a value on my worth."

Cyrus wanted to insist that Graber put *too little* value, but she was too wounded to believe him. In time he would convince her otherwise.

"My father had two wives," he said softly.

She sat up, eyes wide. "No jest?"

He nodded.

"Whoa," she breathed.

Cyrus rested against the wall, one leg bent backward for support. "It's a common practice among frontiersmen to have a squaw consort and a white wife back East. My father bought my mother for six hundred dollars' worth of guns, tobacco, alcohol, and beads. He insisted a priest marry them. The summer after I took my first step, his father demanded that he return home and marry the daughter of his business partner, or else they would sell the company to pay debts and Father would inherit nothing."

As the words left Cyrus's mouth, somehow the stories Mrs. Lull had told him about owing Father a "great debt" because of his "sacrifice" became clear. Father had committed polygamy to salvage *her* inheritance, not his. It didn't make what Father did right. It didn't justify his sin. It did explain why he considered King David his favorite character in the Bible. Father had empathized with the man who'd considered himself a friend of God and yet who'd disobeyed and dishonored God by taking multiple wives.

Cyrus looked to Josie.

She stared at him, her blue-green eyes filled with curiosity and a touch of disbelief, which wasn't surprising. After all the amusing tales he'd shared of his childhood and youth, she insisted he had a blessed life. He did. He had wealth, family, laughter. . .and no scars from the war. His mother was alive. His father had been until twenty months ago. He was loved. He was free to make any choice he wanted.

That's what Josie believed.

She was partially right.

He cleared his throat. "My father spent part of the year in Kansas, part in Cleveland, Ohio. Three years ago he invited me to return with him to his family home. He was dying and *needed*—his word, not mine—me to manage his estate."

"How did his other family respond to your arrival?" She gasped. "Did they even know?"

"About me?"

She nodded.

"Mrs. Lull knew before they married. Despite his sin of polygamy, Father was honest with both women. Being educated and lighter skinned made my reception"—*welcomed* was too generous a word to describe what he'd endured from Cleveland society, so he settled on—"less awkward. I cared for and honored Mrs. Lull as if she were my mother. I was chaperone to my sister, protecting her from unscrupulous men and ensuring she married the man she loved."

"You called her your sister, instead of half sister."

"That I did."

Cyrus smiled inwardly, thinking of how Clara had asked him to escort her down the aisle. She could have hated him. She could have mocked him like a few of her friends had. Were it not for those friends—those prominent society members—who'd remain in Cleveland long after he returned to Kansas, he would have escorted her. He could have taken his rightful place as the head of the family. Instead he'd insisted Mrs. Lull's cousin escort Clara.

"After Clara's wedding this past Christmas," he said, "I returned home with nothing from my father except his name."

Josie's mouth gaped open. "He left you out of his will?"

"I insisted he provide for his wives and his daughter so that finances would never be their motivation to marry." Cyrus felt something warm, something tight and odd in the vicinity of his heart. "My father respected me, he trusted me to care for the three women he loved most, and he treated me as his equal. Those gifts are more valuable to me than land and riches."

"You're a better person than I would be in your place." She shifted, drawing her knees up to her chest, covering her boots with her skirt. "It only took me a few days to realize you do nothing on a whim. You always have a reason. Why are you telling me about your father?"

"You are a white woman. I am a half-breed," he said grimly. "We could stay in this room all night and not even the most pious church lady would force you to marry me." Josie had regaled him with enough tales of the medicine company that he knew she'd not lived a sheltered, whites-only life in the last five years. Yet she understood social hierarchies. He was low rung.

But being low rung didn't excuse him from being a gentleman.

Her brow slowly furrowed. "I'm confused. Then why do you feel obligated to marry me because I kissed you?"

"Not obligated," he clarified. "I have no moral or legal or spiritual duty to marry you."

"So it's a matter of your honor requiring it?"

His honor did. His character did. Even so did his belief that he didn't have to live according to society's low standards for a man's morality. He refused to live with ramifications of wild oats. He refused to subjugate his future wife to living with the knowledge he'd been with other women. It was possible for a man to stay pure before marriage. Not easy. But possible. Certainly more possible when the man wasn't in a locked hotel room with the woman he desired mightily.

Josie moistened her lips again.

Cyrus raked a hand through his hair. Miss Graber had better arrive soon. "The first girl I ever loved married the man her father had chosen for her. She had no choice but to comply." He paused to give Josie a moment for his words to sink in. "Two days before her rushed wedding, I'd asked Mr. Davies for permission to marry Helen, but he refused to grant it. Said my blood made me unworthy. As silly and prudish as it sounds, when I left his house, I vowed that the next woman I kissed would be my wife."

She gave him a strange—he'd say admiring, but this was the woman who said their kiss meant nothing—look. "I don't think that sounds silly or prudish."

Her response, those eight simple words, caused his chest to warm. If people could fall in love in an instant, this was what it had to feel like. Two people understanding each other. No pretense. No lies. No flattery.

Two people in perfect accord.

He smiled.

Her lips curved just so—a bit mysterious, a bit oh-Cyrus-you-are-such-a-romantic—and his heart verily skipped a beat. Josephine Score was unlike any woman he'd ever met. And somehow it became clear. She was a gift from God. To him to love and cherish. For him to protect. All because he'd been patient and restrained and had honored his father and his God. He just needed to be patient a little longer, until Josie's heart and mind caught up with his. It would happen. Someday.

The two of them. . .in perfect accord.

"Did she marry well?"

Cyrus sought to remember what they'd been talking about. "His family owns an orchard in northeastern Kansas."

"Are they happy?"

"I heard she's with child. Their first."

"Do you ever see her?"

"She left Atchison after the wedding and hasn't been back since." Cyrus checked his pocket watch. "It's nine twenty-three. Is it possible they went to a show?" When she didn't respond, he looked up and forgot what else he was going to say.

She'd unpinned the top button on her modest gray dress and was working on the second button. Now the third, exposing her porcelain neck and the top of her chemise. He was red-blooded like any other man. He had wants and desires, none of which needed to be forefront in his mind while they were in a hotel room.

Alone.

"Stop!" he croaked.

She gave him a mild look of annoyance then withdrew a slip of paper from inside her chemise. "Oh, Cyrus. I'm not going to seduce you. I just want to give this back while I'm thinking of it."

Chapter 7

JoJo offered him the note. "I presume it's from her, the girl you loved," she said, ignoring the odd ache in her chest. "I'm sorry her father couldn't see what a good man you are."

A wrinkle deepened between Cyrus's brows.

He paused for what seemed an hour but was probably only a few seconds. He walked to her then sat on the bed's edge. Took the note. "We had to write our favorite lines from a work of fiction. This is from William Shakespeare's *Twelfth Night*."

"Her favorite?"

He nodded. The sound of paper tearing rent through the silence. He ripped and ripped and ripped until the note was in bits. The pieces fluttered to the wooden floor.

JoJo looked from the bits to him. "That's one way to let go of the past."

He grinned. "Indeed it is."

The doorknob rattled. *Click.*

JoJo turned to see the door slowly creak open and—

A hand grabbed the edge, holding it firm. "Thou must remember a man's word is worth only as much as his actions."

Whatever Maude said in response was too muffled to be understood.

JoJo looked to Cyrus in panic. *Graber*, she mouthed.

"I would prefer thee wait." Pause. "However, thy happiness is more important to me. You have my blessing."

Maude squealed. "Oh, Uncle! Thank you!"

The door swung open.

Instantly Cyrus grabbed JoJo's hand and knelt on the floor. "That's your final answer?"

Final answer?

Maude gasped.

Realizing her own mouth was gaping, JoJo closed it and looked to where Maude stood, Graber next to her, tapping his walking stick on the floor. "Uhhh..." Not a single explanation came to JoJo's confused mind. *That's your final answer?* What was Cyrus about?

Graber's eyes narrowed. "Mr. Lull, thou seems to have misplaced thyself in my niece's private quarters."

"I'm exactly where I wish to be." Still holding JoJo's hand, he stood and faced Graber. "Sir, after ten days of courting Miss Score, I'm at my wit's end at how to convince her my affections are true. I am here in desperation."

Graber's gaze shifted to JoJo's unbuttoned bodice. "And hast thou proven to her thy devotion?"

"I'd like to hope so," Cyrus answered. He didn't look the least bit fazed by Graber's indirect insinuation. "Unfortunately, Miss Score has repeatedly turned down my marriage requests. Clearly I erred in not speaking to you first."

Graber's head slowly bobbed back and forth as he looked from Cyrus to JoJo then back to Cyrus. "Thou hast erred, Mr. Lull, in that we can agree. Far be it from me that I not give thee an opportunity for repentance or give my dear niece a chance for redemption. Return in the morning and we shall discuss a bride price."

"No. We will discuss it *now*."

JoJo could not take her eyes off Cyrus. The power emanating from him was a sight to behold. No one spoke to Graber in this manner.

"Now," Cyrus repeated.

Graber stood still, unmoving, unflinching, his gaze hard and suspicious. Of Cyrus's marriage request? Of her being in Maude's room? JoJo tensed. He couldn't know her plan to escape. She'd written nothing down. She hadn't even told Maude. He couldn't know. . .could he? She'd been banished to the steamer for the weekend. She shouldn't be here. He had to have seen her bag and violin case on the dresser, and Maude's half-filled bag still sat on the bed. Graber was too shrewd not to consider the possibility of an escape.

Graber's grip tightened on the handle of his walking stick.

Maude touched his arm. "Please, Uncle. Josie deserves the happiness you've given me."

His chin tipped. "How right thou art." He brushed his knuckles down Maude's cheek. "Thy loyalty brings me joy, as it will thy husband." He then looked to JoJo. "Wait here, dear niece. After I have spoken to thy gentleman suitor, I shall bring thee his offer."

JoJo nodded.

Cyrus knelt again, cradling her hands in his. "Josie, those dreams of yours—I will do whatever is necessary, no matter how long it takes tonight, to make them a reality. . .even if it means sacrificing my plans, my desires." His blue eyes studied hers. "Do you understand what I am saying?"

"I think so," she whispered. He was doing this because he thought he loved her. But he knew she wasn't going to marry him. He knew Graber wouldn't agree to a reasonable bride price. He certainly had to know that if she was here when Graber returned, she'd endure a beating. If she survived—

Oh.

She looked down to where his hands held hers, to where they touched. He was doing this to distract Graber so she and Maude had time to catch the ten forty-five express. Without him. And from there she would head west. Without him.

JoJo blinked but couldn't stop the tears from falling. "Why are you doing this?"

"Because I love you."

"You can't."

"Trust me."

Trust that he loved her? That he would protect her from Graber? That he would ensure she had the time she needed to escape? She finally trusted him. . .and he now was expecting her to leave his life as quickly as she entered.

Throat too tight to speak, she nodded.

He lifted her hands to his lips and kissed both. "Thank you," he whispered. And then he joined Graber in walking to the door.

"Cyrus?"

He stopped and looked over his shoulder, his brows raised.

JoJo gave him a grateful smile, one hopefully conveying her appreciation for all he'd done to help her. "No matter how much we want something—*I* want something—sometimes the price is too high to pay." She shifted her gaze for a second to Maude. "I can't leave what matters to me here."

Something flickered in his eyes.

He turned away.

The moment he and Graber were gone, the door clicking closed, JoJo scrambled off the bed. "Maude, we're running away tonight."

"What do you mean?"

"While Cyrus is distracting Graber with a bride price negotiation," she said, grabbing Maude's bag, "you and I are going to catch the ten forty-five express train to Atchison. In the morning we will take the first train heading out west. In my bag are wigs and dresses. With the disguises, we can disappear and not leave a trail. Graber won't be able to find us."

Maude shook her head. "Mr. Tankersly paid my bride price. We're getting married in the morning." She snatched her bag from JoJo. "I'm sorry, Josie. I'm not leaving with you. Mr. Tankersly is waiting for me downstairs."

"Where are you going?"

"He desires to introduce me to his family before the wedding."

JoJo blinked. Had she been this gullible at nineteen? At twenty, she'd been naive when she trusted Graber would agree to honor the contract, when she believed it'd only take two years to travel from Richmond to San Francisco, and when she signed her life in exchange for her mother's debt to Doctor Oates, Graber's business partner.

"You're going to his home?"

Maude nodded. "He has daguerreotypes of his parents, sisters, and their families that he wishes to show me."

JoJo stared at her. "To see pictures, not living people?"

"Yes, but they will be returning home in the morning. Meeting dozens of people at one time can be daunting. He said this way I can be prepared."

Gullible she had been. But not this!

She kept her voice calm. "He is taking you to his home where you will be alone all night. No one to chaperone you. Doesn't that seem suspicious at all?"

Maude stared at her.

Then she stared at the bag she clenched to her chest.

And JoJo waited and waited and waited for Maude to answer. They didn't have time for Maude to take her usual minutes to mull over things.

Yet Maude looked to the door.

Then looked back at JoJo.

Then sighed.

Then worried her bottom lip.

Finally—"A little, but Uncle had Mr. Tankersly sign a contract. I saw the money. A man wouldn't pay that much if he wasn't sincere about marriage."

JoJo gripped the handle on Maude's bag, holding tight yet not tearing it away. When Maude left this room, it'd be with her, not to spend the evening with a paying customer. She tugged until Maude followed her to the bed. They sat on the edge. JoJo tried to keep her exasperation with Maude and disgust with Graber and Tankersly out of her expression. While Maude wasn't the quickest of wits, she had grown up in a Catholic orphanage. She'd been taught to be wary. But that was before she'd lived under Graber's twisted influence.

That was before Graber had fed her romantic dreams with lies.

"Whatever money Tankersly gave Graber," JoJo gently explained, "it isn't for marriage. You—your voice, your beauty—are too valuable to Graber to lose. I know this is hard to hear. In the last seventeen months, he's taught you to how to be a lady. He's treated you kindly."

"He says I am precious to him."

"And you have no reason to not believe this. He's never taken a cane to your backside. He doesn't have to. That's the role he's assigned to me." JoJo paused. "But it wasn't that way when I first joined the medicine company."

Maude's brow furrowed.

JoJo glanced about the room in futile hope of seeing a clock. This was taking too long. Ten minutes? Fifteen? They had to hurry. They couldn't be here when Graber returned.

She looked at Maude. "Before *you* joined the company, I was Graber's beloved niece and Annie was the one who endured his wrath. Before me, Annie was beloved and a woman named Prudence took the beatings."

She gave Maude time to think about the names carved in the wagon's ceiling. Annie had never shared what her real name was, or about her life prior to joining the medicine show, but she'd been open about Prudence.

She'd repeatedly warned JoJo about Graber.

If only she'd believed Annie.

By the time she had, Annie was dead, and JoJo was too frightened to run.

Maude exhaled. "Why didn't you tell me this when I first asked about their names on the ceiling?"

"I feared what Graber would do to me if he found out I told you."

"I asked him who they were," Maude said defiantly. "Prudence was his wife and Annie his daughter. They died from cholera during the war."

JoJo said nothing. Truth was too rich a food to consume quickly.

Their eyes met, and JoJo smiled just a bit.

Please, Lord, help her see through Graber's lies.

"If you don't leave with me," JoJo said softly, "you will become me, and Graber will find a replacement for you."

Tears pooled in Maude's eyes. "Tankersly proposed."

JoJo's chest tightened. She knew Maude's fears. She knew Maude's yearning for a husband and a family. She knew Maude's desperation for the lies to be true. Worst of all, she knew—lived with—the shame of having been played the fool.

The cycle didn't have to continue.

They could break it.

JoJo held her hand out to Maude. Her eyes burned with tears. "I'm Joia Johanna Byrd," she said, her voice choking over speaking the name she'd not uttered aloud in five years. "I'm starting a new life out West. Miss Ailsworth, would you like to join me?"

Tears fell from Maude's eyes. "Yes," she whispered.

They quickly gathered the remainder of Maude's things.

JoJo collected her bag and violin case. As she reached for the door handle, the door opened. Graber stood there with a familiar smile on his face.

"Where art thou going?"

And then his cane struck her jaw.

10:42 p.m.
Kansas Pacific Railway

Cyrus paced the loading platform, too wound up from running three blocks down James Street to the depot. Where were they? He'd checked the passenger train. According to the conductor, everyone who'd purchased tickets was on board. Neither Josie nor Miss Graber were there in any of their disguises.

The train's whistle blew. Smoke billowed around the engine.

Cyrus continued to pace. Continued to watch the minute hand move on the depot clock.

He could send his mother a telegraph, asking her to check the station. But if Josie and Miss Graber weren't on this train, what good would that do? They could have taken the stage. That one departed this late on a Saturday night was doubtful. They could have hired a ferry to take them across the river to Missouri, but why? Josie specifically said she wanted to head west, not east.

She also said Graber's bride prices were always high.

Two hundred dollars seemed too low, and Graber's agreement to Cyrus's counter-offer of one hundred fifty too swift. Had he wanted to end the conversation quickly?

Graber insisted on giving Josie the news himself.

Cyrus hadn't thought anything of it. He needed all the time he could get to make it to the station to see the ladies safely on board.

But they weren't on board.

The clock's hand shifted.

Ten forty-five.

The train's whistle blew, and the engine rolled forward.

Bettine's words popped into Cyrus's mind—*"If you miss the ten forty-five express, come back here. I know people."*

Josie may have realized they couldn't make it to the express in time and elected to go to Bettine for help. A reasonable adjustment to her escape plan.

Cyrus dashed through the depot and hailed a cab. He climbed in. Breathing deeply, he reasoned away his worries. Josie was industrious and clever. Josie would be with Bettine. Once he verified she was safe, he'd find Leiden. His cousin should be in his room at the hotel.

Minutes later the cab rolled to a stop in front of the Hotel Normandy.

Cyrus paid the driver then jumped out. He hurried into the hotel lobby, glancing around. No Graber. No Josie, either, not that he expected to see her. Other than the desk clerk, the only person in the foyer was a blond man in a black suit, leaning against the spiral volute at the bottom of the staircase, his expression curious. His gaze narrowed on Cyrus. He pushed off the volute, strolling forward with great purpose. At that moment Cyrus noticed the badge on the man's lapel—Wyandotte County Deputy Sheriff. He tensed. The panic in the pit of his stomach spread throughout his body. Something had happened to Josie. He should never have left the hotel. He should have kept Graber in the lobby longer to give the ladies more time to leave. He should have—

"Cyrus Lull?" the man asked.

Cyrus nodded. "What's going on?"

The man withdrew a pair of handcuffs. "Mr. Lull, you are under arrest for aggravated assault and attempted rape."

Chapter 8

Every moment has its pleasures and its hope.
—JANE AUSTEN, *Mansfield Park*

Monday morning—6:16 a.m.
County Jail

Cyrus focused on the man leaning against the jail cell door, tapping a spoon against a tin mug and spearing him with a dubious stare. Or possibly a convinced one. The scar on his left cheek left the interpretation indistinguishable.

"That's everything?" Sheriff Rule said.

"Captain Eads, my cousin, and Miss Bettine Baptiste will all confirm what I've shared." Cyrus glanced to the barred window, where orange and gold brightened the horizon. "You have to stop the *Cleopatra* from departing."

"You sure Miss Score will be on board?"

Cyrus shook his head. "I'm not sure of anything anymore. I do know that Graber's medicine company is heading north to St. Joseph. Their flyer is in my stateroom. Cabin four."

Sheriff Rule nodded. "I read the testimonies that Graber and his nieces gave to my deputy on Saturday night. After the alleged incident. They were pretty convincing."

"Graber forced them." Cyrus walked to the cell door. "Don't take my word for it. Interview them yourself."

"Seems I have no choice."

Sunrise

JoJo marched behind Maude and Graber, Captain Eads leading them and the Kansas City sheriff into the grand saloon aboard the *Cleopatra*, a deputy bringing up the rear. Pity she could walk. Had it not been for Maude promising Graber she would never leave, the beating JoJo endured on Saturday night would have been worse. If only it had been. Neither lawman had shown any emotional response upon seeing her swollen lip and bruised mouth after they arrived at the steamer and stopped her from leaving port. Graber hadn't seemed fazed by the sheriff's explanation that he'd spoken with the accused and felt it necessary to confirm their testimonies.

"Ladies, have a seat." Sheriff Rule motioned to a table in an alcove. He nodded to Graber. "Sir, come with me."

"Certainly." Graber's walking stick tapped on the carpet as they strolled farther into the saloon. Far enough away to not be overheard. Yet within view.

Deputy Pierce sat at the table with JoJo and Maude. He opened his journal. "Names, ages, location of birth, and marital status."

The moment Maude said, "Amanda Graber," JoJo looked from her to where Graber sat. He smiled as he spoke to the sheriff. As he wove enough truth in his lies to make everything sound believable. To make himself the innocent one. His game would have worked if Cyrus hadn't convinced the sheriff to doubt the sworn testimonies they'd given.

"The truth shall make you free."

It didn't always, not in her experience. Maybe today it would.

"Maude Ailsworth," she said, interrupting Maude. "That's her real name. She grew up in an orphanage in Chicago. I don't know the name of it, but it was run by a Catholic charity."

Maude kicked Josie's ankle and gave her a pointed, warning stare. After Graber knocked on their wagon's door and explained that the sheriff wanted a second interview, he warned them to stick with the story. Stick with the lies. Play their parts as his beloved nieces. Just two more gills to dupe.

"We don't have to play his game anymore." JoJo grabbed Maude's hand. "This may be your last chance to escape Graber. Tell the truth."

Maude jerked her hand free. "Deputy Pierce, everything I've told you is true. When my cousin misses her medicine, she. . .she makes up stories. She sees things that aren't real. Uncle says we may have to put her in an asylum."

JoJo saw red.

She stood abruptly, knocking her chair over. She wanted freedom. She'd worked for it but never gone to battle for it. Until now.

She raised her voice to ensure Graber, Captain Eads, and the sheriff heard her. "Mr. Lull never hurt me. He never attempted to rape me. He did nothing more than try to help me escape"—she pointed at Graber—"that man."

To her shock, Graber looked uncomfortable. Worried.

At least to her he seemed that way. Anyone who didn't know him may not recognize the difference in his stiff smile.

Could Sheriff Rule tell?

"Five years ago," she said, "I signed a contract with Obadiah Graber. I would play my violin during his shows for two years in exchange for paying off the debt my mother owed his partner, Doctor Owens, who was no more a trained medical professional than Graber is. Sheriff Rule?"

He stood. "Yes, ma'am?"

JoJo never looked away from Graber. "I have lied for Obadiah Graber. I have stolen for him. I should go to jail for my crimes. If you leave me in that man's custody, he will beat me to death, but I would rather die in truth than keep living a lie. And I won't be the first girl he murdered. Eighteen months ago the medicine company was in Milwaukee, Wisconsin. Graber broke Annie's neck during one of his 'instructions in righteousness.'"

The movement was slight, but Graber flinched.

"Don't be fooled by his speech or his dress," she insisted. "His faith is no more real than that wig he wears."

Sheriff Rule leaned to the side to get a better look at Graber.

JoJo continued with: "He and a medicine company man named Reuben tossed her body out in the red-light district because they knew a dead girl found there would not raise suspicions against them. I knew her as Annie DeMott. She had long black hair and a birthmark on the back of her left thigh."

Graber stood. "Josie, this has gone on long enough." He looked at the sheriff. "She needs her medicine."

JoJo laughed. "Really? That's the best lie you can come up with? Sheriff Rule, I recant every word of the testimony I gave your deputy two nights ago. It was made under duress. He did this to me. He threatened to hurt Maude if I didn't repeat his story."

Graber gave a sad shake to his head. Whatever he said to the sheriff wasn't loud enough for her to hear.

Deputy Pierce spoke to Maude. "Is what she says true?"

Cyrus jumped off the cot the moment he heard voices in the sheriff's office.

The door to the jail cells opened.

Sheriff Rule gripped Josie's arm as they walked to Cyrus's cell. He unlocked the door, opened it, and, without a word, left the two of them alone.

Cyrus stared at Josie's swollen lip and the bruises around her mouth. He couldn't speak, could barely move out of fear he'd bring more pain if he touched her bruised body. What he'd give to hold her close.

She motioned to the cot. "Mind if I sit?"

"Are you sure it won't hurt?"

She stared at him in confusion, and then she gasped. "Oh. Graber restrained himself this time to my face."

Cyrus immediately brushed off the canvas cot. He waited until she was seated before he sat next to her.

"Even after I confessed to all Graber had done, I wasn't sure the sheriff believed me. Maude could have continued Graber's lie. Because she didn't, the rest of the company followed suit. Graber should spend the rest of his life in jail." She glanced about the cell, sized to accommodate two people. "If you hadn't convinced the sheriff to investigate, the *Cleopatra* would be halfway to Atchison by now." She reached over and rested her hand atop his. She gave it a gentle squeeze. "I owe you my life."

Cyrus couldn't help but smile.

She let out a little snort. "I will take that as a 'you're welcome.'"

It was that and so much more.

They sat in silence for several minutes. Josie holding his hand, and Cyrus letting her. He had spent the morning praying the sheriff would reach the *Cleopatra* in time, begging God to shine the truth on Graber's lies, and hoping Josie wouldn't leave Kansas City without him. She could have caught the next train. She came here. She found him.

He wanted to believe that meant what he wanted it to mean.

She let out a little sigh. "Before Maude joined the medicine show, I shared the wagon with a girl who called herself Annie DeMott." Starting absently at the floor, she mused, "I don't know if that was her real name. I wish I did, because someone out there may be looking for her. Or maybe she had no one, like me, like Maude. Graber favored orphans."

"You have someone." He waited until her blue-green eyes settled on him. "I would look for you."

She shifted on the cot to face him. "I know you would."

"Am I that predicable?"

"You are."

He hesitated. "Would you prefer me to be more spontaneous?"

"I like that you are a constant. It's an admirable trait." Her smile paused halfway. "Do you know this is the second time in two days that we've been locked together in a room?"

"I wouldn't count this as a room."

She shrugged.

Cyrus dipped his head in the direction of the open door. "We aren't locked in."

"Good point." Josie dashed to the door, closed it, and reclaimed her place next to him. She looked utterly pleased with herself. "Almost locked in. Practically locked in. That's close enough."

He grinned. "Why do I have a feeling you have no intention of letting either of us leave this jail cell any time soon?"

"I've been thinking for a while about how I ought to settle down."

"In a jail cell?"

"I'm looking for something a little more stable."

"Some*thing*?" Cyrus's heart leaped in his chest. "Or some*one*?"

"Someone," she answered in a soft, almost nervous voice, unlike anything he'd heard from her. "I think I might be. . .or maybe I am in love with him, but I would need forty or fifty years of marriage to be sure. He proposed"—she grimaced—"well, I *think* he asked me to marry him. The moment was rather chaotic and not the most proper, and others were watching. I want to think he was sincere, but—"

"He was," Cyrus blurted out.

She was watching him, studying him, and her expression was hopeful. . .and a bit wary, a bit unconvinced. He didn't fault her. Graber had taught Josie not to trust anyone.

"Josie, I meant every word."

"It was only a ten-day courtship."

"Ten days of courting on a steamboat is the land-equivalent of three months," he insisted. "Trust me. I've done the calculations."

"Cyrus, be serious." A wrinkle deepened between her brows. "How can you know for sure that you want to marry me? You don't really know me. Everything I've told you about my past could be a lie."

She was giving him an opportunity to cry off.

Cyrus knelt before her, cradling her hands in his. "Sir Isaac Newton's first law of motion states that an object at rest will remain at rest unless acted on by an unbalanced force. I was a man at rest until the day we met. You are the most beautiful, unbalanced force I could ever want."

Her smile grew. At least he thought it did. With how swollen and bruised her mouth was, she could be smirking. Certainly not a frown, though.

"Miss Jospehine Sc—" He stopped. Like Cherokee Rose, Josephine Score was a small part of her, but neither were the real her. Cyrus leaned close. "I know enough of you to know I want to spend my future getting to know the rest of you. I just don't know you name."

Her eyes grew teary.

Yet she looked to him as if he'd given her the world.

"Joia Johanna Byrd." She winked. "You can call me JoJo."

Cyrus smiled, studying the woman he'd have the pleasure of waking up next to for the next forty or fifty years. "Miss Joia Johanna Byrd, my mother's people have a saying. 'When someone saves your life, you give him yours.' Considering I owe you my life, will you marry me?"

"Marriage would make things more convenient."

"It would."

She thought for a moment. Her expression grew serious. "Cyrus, I didn't rescue you from anything."

He slid back onto the cot. "You kissed me."

"And?"

"That's close enough."

Cyrus touched her jaw, tipping her face toward his, moving his lips toward the unbruised corner of her mouth. He paused to give her a moment to understand his intention, to understand the significance. She dipped her chin, barely a nod.

He grinned. "I will take that as a 'yes, I'll marry you.'"

She looked heavenward, but before she could sigh, he kissed her.

ECPA-bestselling author **Gina Welborn** worked for a news radio station until she fell in love with writing romances. She serves on the American Christian Fiction Writers Foundation Board. Sharing her husband's love for the premier American sports car, she is a founding member of the Southwest Oklahoma Corvette Club and a lifetime member of the National Corvette Museum. Gina lives with her husband, three of their five Okie-Hokie children, two rabbits, two guinea pigs, and a dog that doesn't realize rabbits and pigs are edible. Find her online at www.ginawelborn.com!